SELINA R. GONZALEZ

THE MERCENARY
AND THE MAGE

THE COMPLETE SERIES

Table of Contents

WORLD MAP

Segledus
Geirah
Craigailte
Khastalland
Carasom
Monparth
Vanelt
Ismuire Sea
Motu
Hedengal
Bhitra
N

MAP OF MONPARTH

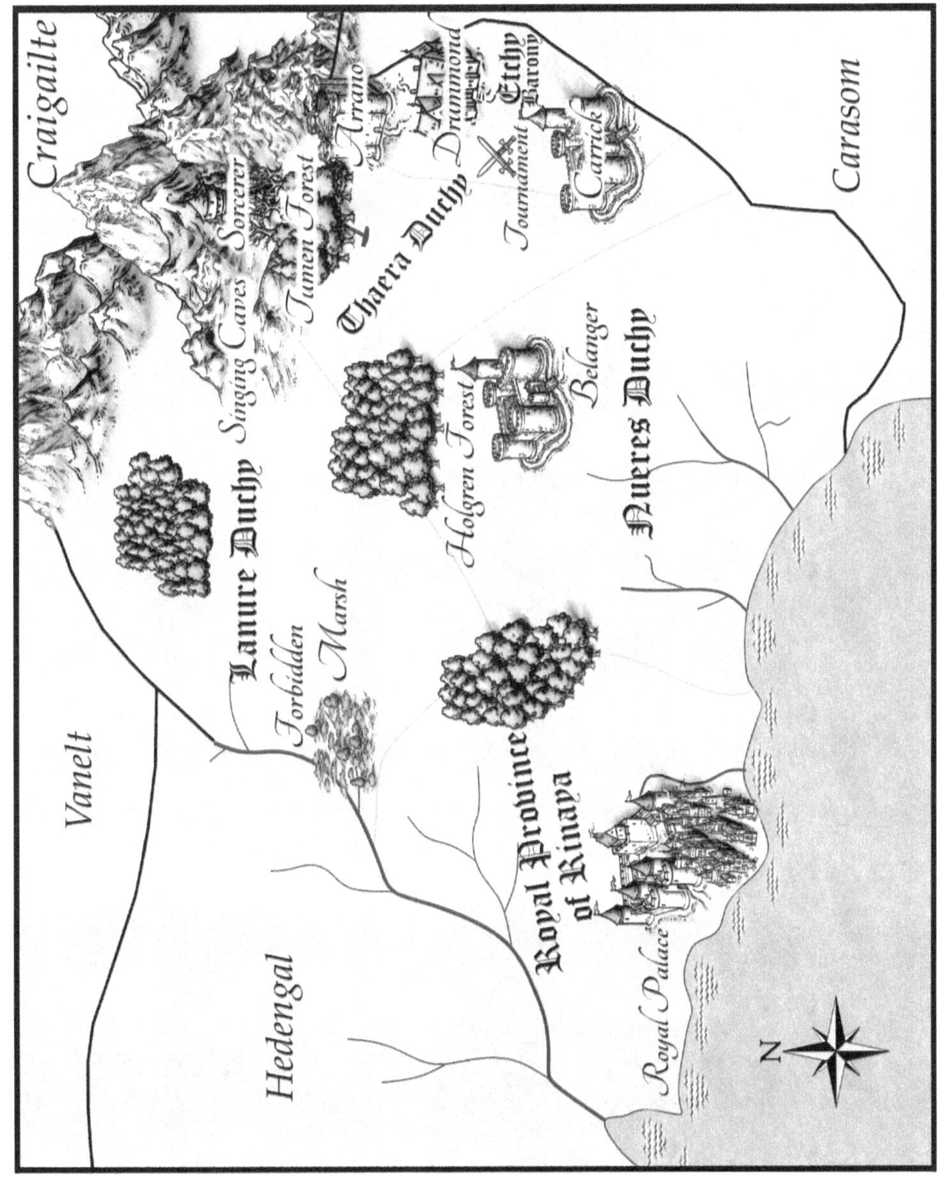

PRINCE OF SHADOW AND ASH

THE MERCENARY AND THE MAGE

BOOK ONE

CHAPTER 1

THIS QUEST for a marsh flower would be easier without the hulking black armor and oversized black sword.

Regulus tried to stretch his neck, but his helm and the bulky pauldrons impeded the movement. Curse the sorcerer and his driving, inexplicable need for theatricality. At least Regulus had the more practical hunting knife across his lower back.

Not as if he needed the heavy armor, anyway. The sorcery inside him kept him alive, and without the armor, his progress would have been faster. With an agitated groan, he gripped his helm by its decorative metal horns and removed it. Instead of the usual relief of fresh air on his face, humidity clung to his skin.

The marsh stank like rotting carcasses. His damp hair stuck to his forehead and neck and the sweat made the old scar that traced across his right cheek through the corner of his mouth to his chin itch. He turned his head, working out the tension in his neck and scanning for potential enemies. Muddy water— or maybe it was watery mud—stretched in every direction, broken up with patches of marsh grass, green-tipped cattails, and tangled briars. Fog drifted over everything, diluting the sunlight into a drab gray and providing cover for any lurking beasts.

Regulus had grown up near the Forbidden Marsh, and he'd heard all the stories. Stories of people who entered and never came out. Tales of screams carried on the wind that rustled the cattails. Rumors claimed monsters lurked in the Marsh. Human-hating centaurs, devious fairies, even the last of the red-claws—gaunt, tall, pale creatures with strange long limbs and six-inch-long claws stained permanently red by the blood of their victims.

He had dismissed them as tall tales, designed to frighten children into compliance. That was, after all, how his cruel childhood guardian had used the Marsh and its monsters. As a threat. But now, with the marsh grasses and cattails rasping around him and the unnatural gray mist, his nerves were on edge.

And yet, after over an hour of wandering wild, untamed growth and solid-looking moss that gave way beneath his boots, he had found nothing. Not a single monster, and no sign of the magical flower he hunted. He pulled the drawing of the starshade plant out of his belt and studied it. A short black plant with thick stalks and small black flowers that the sorcerer said should glow blue.

He refolded the parchment, pulled the helm back on, and trudged onward. The black helm had wide slanted rectangles for eye openings and fine holes to allow airflow over the mouth. Two long, thick horns curved from the top like the horns of a bull. His master got some twisted pleasure out of scaring anyone Regulus might encounter on his missions. He would have left it off, but he needed his hands free to draw his sword.

As he continued his search, the desolation of the marsh seemed ominous. As if something out there watched him, unseen in the gray haze. The muck of the marsh squelched under his boots. Each footstep sounded like a blade being pulled from a wound.

He shook his head. Maybe monsters prowled the Marsh, maybe they didn't. He had no reason to fear monsters. He was one of them. All that mattered was finding the flower as commanded and getting back home.

Home. Regulus smiled. Poor Harold would faint when he saw the state of the armor. The boy had adjusted well from the life of mercenary baggage boy to squire. Better than Regulus had adjusted to the life of a lord. His smile faded. *Harold is a far more loyal and dedicated squire than a slave like me deserves.*

The sharp snap of a breaking twig interrupted his thoughts. He drew his sword, turning slowly. The ebony-black blade glinted. The four-foot-long blade was nearly as wide as his palm at the cross-guard and narrowed down to a sharp point. He surveyed the marsh grasses and brush. Nothing. To his right, he heard what sounded like…muttering?

Regulus spun to face a dense stand of marsh grass. The grass mumbled in a quiet, scratchy voice, "Smells like venison. Venison is tasty, yes."

"Who's there?"

With a squeal like an injured piglet, a pale green hobgoblin with a long pointy chin and nose, wearing what looked like dead vines as clothes, leapt up at him. Cursing, Regulus swung his sword, but the hobgoblin was too small, maybe as long as Regulus' forearm from its webbed toes to the mossy-looking hair on its head. The creature grabbed onto his breastplate and scrambled around.

"Get off!" He swatted at the hobgoblin with his right hand, still awkwardly holding his sword in the other. The menace scurried down to Regulus' right hip, toward the satchel looped onto his belt, muttering about venison.

"Don't you dare!" He seized the vines around its torso. The hobgoblin screamed and flailed. Regulus tried to throw it away, but it grabbed onto his gauntlet with unexpected strength. The vines in his hand broke, and the creature jumped onto his side again.

With an irritated growl, Regulus drew his hunting knife. The hobgoblin yanked on his satchel and gnawed on the loops, trying to free it. Regulus stabbed at the creature, but it moved as if it sensed the knife coming. The blade glanced across Regulus' armor and sliced through part of his satchel.

The hobgoblin grunted as it tugged, and the fabric ripped. Dried venison and an apple went flying. The hobgoblin hooted in victory, catching most of the meat midair. Desperate, Regulus swung his arms, trying to catch the green-skinned menace. To his surprise, it worked. But now he had an angry hobgoblin pinned between his chest and forearms and a weapon in each hand. *Idiot.* At least his men weren't there to witness his humiliation.

The hobgoblin screamed and wiggled, and Regulus realized he didn't have any other options. He dropped his arms, and the little beast scampered off with a gleeful squeal. Regulus sheathed his dagger and his sword and checked his torn satchel. Empty. He groaned and looked around his feet, but the mud had swallowed any food the hobgoblin hadn't stolen.

He kicked at the muck, then grabbed for the parchment at his belt. Gone. He cursed. Well, he had looked at it a dozen times, he didn't need it. Besides, there couldn't be that many glowing flowers. He checked the water horn on his left side—at least that was still there. Nothing to do but press on.

The thick clouds made judging the passing time difficult. Why did the sorcerer send him, anyway? He could probably use some spell to lead him right to the stupid plants. *And I* know *he could hover over this filth.*

A faint blue shine on the other side of a tangled mass of briars caught his eye. Hope sparked as he cut his way into a small clearing. A ring of sludge surrounded a raised patch of grass-covered ground, no more than two paces wide. And interspersed over the miniature island—starshade plants. Relieved, Regulus drew his knife and knelt next to the nearest plant.

After digging up ten of the plants to collect their roots, he tied them together using strips of fabric from his ripped satchel. He tied the roots to his belt and stood. Now to find his way back out of the marsh.

An hour later, he trudged on, lost and starving. *Is anything in this Etiros-forsaken marsh edible?* A bramble bush covered in juicy-looking red berries drew his attention. He scrambled for them, then stopped. They could be poisonous. *Can poison kill me?* He shrugged. What did it matter? Dresden would scold him for such thoughts—but Dresden wouldn't know.

He picked a berry and tossed it in his mouth. It tasted tart yet sweet, and not bad. He ate berries as quickly as his gloved hands allowed. Once he had eaten several handfuls, he took a long drink of water from his horn and looked around.

The marsh stretched on forever. The large standing stones that marked the entrance and where he had left his horse were nowhere to be seen. He squinted at the sun, trying to judge the time and the direction he needed to go. Finally, he decided it must be around two in the afternoon. *Based on that, I need to go…* He turned to his left and pointed at nothing. *That way.*

Before long, he felt a painful twinge in his stomach. Then another. His gut twisted violently, and his vision blacked out. He blinked and stumbled forward as his eyes cleared, wrestling his helm off and dropping it into the muck. Pain wracked his body and heat radiated from his stomach. He fell onto all fours and vomited.

Red marsh berries: poisonous.

Sorcery: expels poison.

The muscles in his abdomen contracted, and he groaned as bile burned his throat. He reached up to wipe sweat off his forehead, but mud coated his gloved hand. The foamy vomit had a stench different from the stench of the marsh. He moaned and clutched at his stomach as he vomited a third time, his whole body shaking and achy. *Times like this, I wish I could die.*

He heard a new sound among the quiet rustling of the marsh. Clomp, squelch, clomp, squelch from every side. He blinked back the sweat running into his eyes and looked up through the mud and hair sticking around his face. Tall marsh grass blocked his view. His hand shook as he drew his sword and used it to push himself to his feet. His vision blacked out again, and his head spun. He closed his eyes, steadying himself.

He opened his eyes to a towering centaur staring down at him. The horse half was the size of a destrier, with a dark brown coat the same shade as the human half's skin. A large broadsword gleamed in the centaur's hands, held in front of a leather breastplate. The centaur stomped a hoof, and the muscles in his bare arms bulged as he pointed his sword at Regulus.

Great. Regulus had only had the misfortune of crossing a band of centaurs once, and he and his men had barely escaped alive. On the bright side, his stomach was unclenching, the burning in his throat subsiding, and the lightheaded feeling receding.

"You have stolen from the Forbidden Marsh." The centaur's voice was commanding and deep. "You cannot leave the marsh with the starshade roots. Surrender them or die."

Regulus counted six other centaurs surrounding him. Three men with swords, two women with drawn bows, and a smaller male centaur whose human half looked to be maybe fourteen. The young centaur gripped a spear and swayed, his eyes wide. *Not a child. Etiros, why?* Regulus swallowed, his anguished heart crying out in the hope that somehow, after all he had done, the creator-god still heard his prayers. *Not a child.*

Regulus looked back at the centaur who had spoken. "I don't want trouble," he said slowly. He raised his sword and assumed a defensive position. "But I'm afraid I can't give up the roots."

"Starshade roots are only good for poison and sorcery!" A female centaur to his right eyed Regulus down the shaft of an arrow.

Of course they were. Why else would the sorcerer want them?

"We are the protectors of the Forbidden Marsh," the first centaur said. "You will leave the roots or die."

If only. Regulus rolled his shoulders, his strength returning. He took a step back. "Please. Don't attack me. I *really* don't want to hurt anyone."

The centaur frowned. "You are a very good liar."

"It's the truth." Regulus eyed his helm lying in the mud. "I wish you no harm. But I have no choice. I have to take the starshade roots. And you won't kill me. You can't."

"Jaresha." The centaur stomped a hoof.

He heard the twang of a bowstring and dove for his helm. An arrow flew over him as he replaced his mud-covered helm on his head. Another arrow pinged off his armor. He bolted for the space to the brown centaur's right. These centaurs weren't evil. They didn't deserve to die. He wouldn't kill them unnecessarily. The power of the sorcerer's mark lent speed to his legs, giving him a slim chance of outrunning the centaurs.

Pain burned from the mark hidden under the gauntlet on his right arm. He groaned and skidded to a stop, remembering the sorcerer's directions. *"Kill anyone or anything that tries to stop you."* He turned, and the pain faded. The brown centaur charged.

The centaur slammed his broadsword into Regulus' chest, knocking him onto his back. Regulus swung at the centaur's forelegs and the centaur screamed as the massive blade cleaved through bone. Regulus winced at the sound. One of the female centaurs shrieked while the wounded centaur collapsed.

Regulus scrambled to his feet and turned to go. The pain in his arm redoubled. *No. I don't want to do this.*

"Don't try to stop me!" Some part of his mind whispered it wouldn't matter, they had already tried, the mark wouldn't let him leave until they were all dead, but he had to hope. He had to try.

An arrow found the gap under the side of Regulus' helm and buried in his neck. He choked and swayed as his vision spotted from the pain. He ripped the arrow out. As he fell forward, he jammed his sword into the ground and used it to remain standing. An agonizing prickling sensation pulled at the hole in his neck until it closed. He took a deep breath and straightened.

A female centaur with a white coat and golden hair gaped, her face pale. Her bow trembled in her hands. The lead male centaur had fallen on his side and was hyperventilating between shrieks. Both human and equine lungs heaved. Regulus looked at the hacked-off end of the centaurs' leg. *At this point, it's a mercy.* The mark on his arm burned and ached, goading him on. He raised the sword and swung. The other centaurs screamed. He looked away from the headless body.

"I'm leaving. You're not stopping me," Regulus said. He turned away and bit back a cry as pain sliced up his right arm from the mark to his shoulder.

"He must have a bond," a male voice said behind him. Disturbed wonder laced the centaur's strained voice. "He can't die."

Regulus took another step. *They're letting me go,* he told himself. As if maybe he could convince the mark. Pain spread over his shoulder and reached into his chest, clawing across his skin and grinding through his bones. His heart ached, but he turned back around. *Maybe if they say it…*

"Say you're not stopping me. You're letting me go."

The centaurs shuffled and glanced at each other. Muck flew up from the boy's frantically tapping hooves. The boy glanced at the dead centaur and whimpered. His spear shook in his hands.

The pain stopped. Regulus felt a tickle at the back of his head, like something wiggling into his brain. He barely had time to think *no, not again* before he lost all control of his body. He could still sense everything. His hands gripping the sword. The sharp tang of centaur blood. He still stared at the group of frightened and uncertain-looking centaurs. But he couldn't so much as blink. The sorcerer's presence in his mind felt like a tiny piece of sharp, cold iron lodged in his head.

His mouth moved at the sorcerer's command. Regulus' voice came out, but the words were not his. "What is going on?" He looked down at the dead centaur as the sorcerer controlled his body, looking through his eyes.

No, stop. He tried to close his eyes, to look away, anything. But he couldn't. The sorcerer gazed at Regulus' bloody handiwork, meaning Regulus did, too. He looked at the centaurs who were still alive. Regulus' consciousness felt trapped in someone else's body. His mind screamed. His body didn't care.

Regulus sighed, but the sigh wasn't his. "First, I feel my power draining away to heal you twice in rapid succession, then I sense you defying me. I'm trying to decipher this ridiculous code. I don't need distractions."

Regulus' arms raised his sword, and his legs moved him forward. The centaurs backed up, their faces contorted in horror. Regulus mentally begged them to run.

"What is so difficult about following instructions, boy?" his mouth said. "Kill them and get back here, or we'll have a conversation about your friends." Regulus' mind shuddered and protested, but his body didn't respond. "And be quick about it!"

The feeling of cold iron slipped out of his brain. Regulus teetered forward as control of his body reverted to his own mind. The mark burned faintly. The centaurs stood frozen. One of them muttered something in a language he didn't understand and drew a strange symbol in the air.

Regulus steeled himself. *At least they're not human. Most centaurs don't even like humans.* The thought didn't bring comfort. *At least they're not my friends.*

He let his instincts and training take over and lunged. Years of sword fighting experience and every ounce of magically enhanced strength, agility, and speed powered his blade. He aimed a thrust at the golden-haired female's equine ribcage. She gasped and reared back, but that just allowed him to bury the sword straight up through horse and human. She was dead before he pulled his blade free.

Regulus turned and slashed across the hind legs of the second female as she turned to flee, then drove his sword through her back. He turned and found himself staring at the young centaur. The boy stood shaking, rooted to the ground, like a sapling shuddering in a strong wind.

"Run," Regulus rumbled. He turned from the boy and blocked the sword of a male centaur with a white-and-brown coat. Within moments, the centaur was dead. Regulus spun, looking for the remaining two adult males. Hooves pounded into his chest and Regulus fell backward, gasping for air.

The centaur raised his sword and aimed for Regulus' neck. Regulus rolled and scrambled to his feet. The centaur turned, his face red. "Sorcerous abomination!"

The centaur swung wildly in his rage. Regulus easily parried the attack and drove his sword up under the bottom edge of the centaur's leather breastplate. The centaur screamed and toppled over as Regulus pulled out his sword. He looked around. He stood surrounded by centaur corpses, watery mud stained with red swirls, and cattails that rasped against each other, making a sound like mourning. The boy and the last male centaur were gone.

He waited for the mark to burn, to tell him to hunt them down. But it didn't. He sobbed with relief and left the centaur bodies before his stomach tried to force up nothing. He cleaned some of the blood off his blade with marsh grass. It took him a couple tries to sheath the oversized sword; his hands shook so badly.

Better them than Dresden or Harold or any of the others. Better centaurs in a marsh than my friends in my castle. Still, the screams of the centaurs echoed in his ears. Killing wasn't difficult—in fact, he was good at it. But he had always followed a strict no-killing-innocents policy. Until the sorcerer.

He double-checked the roots tied to his belt. After re-determining his direction, he trudged on. Guilt dragged him down more than the mud and water clogging his boots as the day wore on.

The sun had dipped low to the horizon when he spotted the standing stones. He picked up his pace, eager to be out of that dreadful marsh. His black stallion, Sieger, was waiting where he had left him, munching grass. He mounted Sieger with ease despite his heavy armor and the exhaustion and blood loss. His blood-soaked tunic had dried into stiff, uncomfortable folds beneath his neck.

Regulus made camp after midnight. Increased abilities and healing or no, he still needed rest. Time to recover. Not that he slept well. By himself, he couldn't remove most of his armor. He slept for a few hours before waking to a pain in his back. Moonlight shone through the trees. With a groan, he stretched as best he could and staggered to his feet. *Can't die, but can still feel like death.* He put his greaves, gloves, and helm back on.

"I'm sorry, Sieger." He rubbed the stallion's neck, coaxing him awake. "It's time to go again."

Sieger nickered and shook his mane.

"I know, I know." Regulus rubbed Sieger's muzzle. He would have given almost anything to be asleep in his own bed. But such was not his lot. He removed his helm to take a drink of water and was disappointed to find only one gulp left in his horn. Now he was out of food and water, and with little time to spare to get more. The sorcerer expected him back soon. Begrudgingly, he turned back to Sieger and gripped the pommel of the saddle.

He froze as a branch snapped behind him.

Chapter 2

REGULUS INCHED his hand toward his sword. Rustling and the crunch of last autumn's leaves sounded some five paces behind him. Someone or something lurked in the bushes. He focused his hearing as he wrapped his fingers around the sword's grip, his mind racing to rule out possibilities. No heavy breathing, and the intruder had gotten quite close before he heard them. Ruled out anything as big as a bear or troll. No creak of leather or clink or scrape of metal, so it wasn't armored. No clomp of hooves, so neither centaur nor minotaur.

He tried to think of where he was, what sort of creatures lived here. Goblins? Unlikely this far from any caves. Monparth had driven most monsters into uninhabited areas, but there were periodic incursions. Could be something as harmless as a satyr or dangerous as a thike, a medium-sized lithe feline with poisonous barbs on its long tail. Or a human, which were best not underestimated. He turned, bringing his sword into a guard position.

Nothing.

His eyes strained to peer into the shadows. Only moments had passed; whatever or whoever had been there must still be there. He moved toward the bushes. There, in a small clearing. A humanoid shape, hidden in a dark robe. The person or creature appeared to be facing away from him. Maybe they weren't even aware of his presence.

Regulus leapt through the bushes at the figure. It started to turn at the sudden noise, but he pressed the point of the sword against the figure's back. "Who are you?"

"Wh-what?" a normal-sounding man stuttered.

"What are you doing out here in the middle of the night?"

The man quivered. "I—I'm just—"

"Spit it out!"

A woman's scream ripped through the night. Regulus whipped his head up. A woman in a dark cloak stood in the clearing, her hands covering her mouth. Moonlight glinted off the whites of her wide eyes.

"Carolyn, run!" the man shouted. But Carolyn stood as if frozen in place.

Regulus looked down at the man, then back at the woman. Back and forth. Heat rushed to his cheeks. "You're just...meeting..." He moved his sword away from the man's back. "Sorry."

The man staggered forward. He looked over his shoulder at Regulus. "You mad…" His jaw slackened. "What…who are you?"

Oh, you had to ask. A burning sensation emanated from the mark on Regulus' forearm, and he gritted his teeth. "I am the Black Knight. And I serve the Prince of Shadow and Ash." He sheathed his sword as the pain in his arm vanished. "Go. Now."

The lovers hurried away, their faces drawn and pale. This was why he preferred traveling at night and avoided roads. Every disputed sighting of the now legendary Black Knight made him more nervous he would get caught.

Monparth's laws forbade the use of dark, corrupted magic. And after over twenty years without mages, wielders of pure magic, people were extra wary of any hint of sorcery. The authorities would consider Regulus the sorcerer's accomplice, and his men guilty by association. He couldn't die, but his men could. At least the loathsome horned helm protected his identity.

Regulus rode all day, keeping Sieger at a trot as much as possible and stopping only to steal a couple apples as he passed an orchard. Despite the days growing longer as summer approached, the sun set too soon. He stopped and managed to sleep for a few hours until a pinch from the mark on his arm woke him.

"I can only cross the kingdom so fast," Regulus growled under his breath as he slammed the helm back on and rode into the night.

Around midday, he neared the sorcerer's tower in the Tumen Forest. He always knew when he was close.

The bark on trees turned black. Dead, midnight-colored leaves clung to lifeless ebony-shaded branches and covered the forest floor. Brittle tangles of dead wood vine made a pale contrast where the vines wrapped around branches. As the tower came into view, the trees became white, skeletal. All their bark had fallen away, revealing wood drained of all color and life. Barren fir branches stuck out like spikes, while naked deciduous boughs reached out like bony fingers.

Not even grass grew this close to the tower. The only thing that did grow were mushrooms. Velvety purple mushrooms shaped like thimbles, bright red domed mushrooms, flat round mushrooms as yellow as a daisy's center. A faint glow emanated from underneath some. Regulus assumed all of them were poisonous.

Two years ago, when he was first bound to the sorcerer, there had been only a small circle of blackened trees. Sometimes obviously, sometimes imperceptibly, the decay had spread. Now the deathly forest stretched a ten-minute ride in every direction around the sorcerer's tower.

Built of reddish brick darkened by time and sorcery, the tower itself stood around four stories tall, topped with narrow crenellations and covered in layers of dead wood vine. Yellow light filtered through the rough grayish glass of the single gothic window in the top level. Regulus used to wonder why someone who called himself a prince would live in such a drab old tower. He didn't care anymore. Although, he suspected the Prince of Shadow and Ash simply liked dead, creepy things as much as he liked torturing Regulus.

Sore, hungry, and exhausted, Regulus dismounted with difficulty. He stuffed the helm in his saddlebag. The iron-latticed oak door opened, and the sorcerer stepped out.

A man of below-average height, the sorcerer's physique belied his power. A wide, dark leather belt set with polished obsidian secured a long black tunic over his stomach paunch. Crimson accents edged the tunic. The hood of a gold-stitched sable robe shadowed his face, hiding his eyes above a pinched-looking nose. A graying brown beard fell in waves down to his chest. But he walked and spoke with the authority of the prince he pretended to be.

"You're late." The sorcerer's dark tone chilled Regulus' blood.

He untied the roots from his belt. "I got here as quickly as I could, my lord."

"After trying to disobey." The sorcerer strode forward and snatched the roots from Regulus with pale, knobby fingers. "Do we have a problem, mercenary?"

Regulus swallowed and bowed his head. *Don't take the bait.* "No, my lord." *I'm not a mercenary anymore. And yes, we have many problems.*

"Kill all the centaurs?"

"Yes." *No.* He kept his expression calm and neutral.

"Good." The sorcerer counted the roots under his breath. "Ten," he muttered. "Good thing, too. Room for error. Tricky business, breaking an enchantment." He looked at Regulus. "I need one more thing."

Regulus stopped himself from protesting. He needed to rest and eat. He wanted to go home, even if only for a couple days. The sorcerer never sent him out again immediately after returning. But it was no use arguing. The sorcerer got what he wanted. Always. "Yes, my lord?"

"Wait here." The sorcerer took the roots inside the tower and returned with a tin goblet and a small carving knife. "Take off your glove and give me your arm. I need your blood."

"What?" Regulus gaped. "Why?"

The corners of the sorcerer's mouth turned down. Tendrils of pain, like red-hot vines growing under his skin, shot up Regulus' right arm. He grunted and used his teeth to pull his glove off his right hand.

"Yes, my lord." The pain faded as he held his arm toward the sorcerer.

"Better." A momentary flicker of a smile made the sorcerer's beard twitch. "You should be thanking me. I thought about making you bring me the blood of one of your friends. Maybe the one with the beard. Or the boy."

Regulus flinched. "I've been obeying you, my lord," he said, choosing his words carefully as the sorcerer grabbed his hand. "I only hesitated today, and I did as you commanded and slaughtered the centaurs. There's no need to harm my men." *Please, Etiros. Let him be forgiving.*

The sorcerer pulled down on Regulus' hand so he could see the underside of his wrist beneath his gauntlet. "Mm, yes. You've become such an obedient pet. Almost a pity. I did so enjoy making you hurt them." The sorcerer sliced the knife across Regulus' wrist. Regulus drew in a sharp breath that hissed between his teeth. "But hesitate again, and I'm going to lose my temper."

Regulus stared at the dead wood vine and hoped his master wouldn't notice his rage. Any defiance always ended in pain. If he was lucky, only his own. The sorcerer let his blood drain into the goblet until the bond linking his life to the sorcerer's closed the wound, preventing him from bleeding out.

The sorcerer waved Regulus away as he walked back inside. "Run on home. I have important matters to attend to." The door slammed shut, leaving Regulus and Sieger alone with the dead forest.

Shoulders sagging, Regulus remounted. "Let's go home, Sieger."

The stars had been out for hours when he arrived at Arrano castle. It was an old castle, long out of style, but it was his. The square central tower and surrounding four-story wall stood atop a hill. A flag bearing the Arrano crest—a red rose over crossed white swords on a field of black—flew from the north wall turret. The barren hill rose in a gradual incline to the front of the castle.

Regulus didn't follow the road up the hill. Instead, he struck out around the castle. Far downhill, with enough space around the hill to ensure a clear line of sight in case of attack, the woods began again. A massive willow tree grew at the edge of the woods. Regulus scanned the surrounding area, ensuring no one was near, then led Sieger under the swaying curtain of the willow's hanging branches. The stallion whinnied, protesting what came next.

"I know." He patted Sieger's neck. "I know."

Near the tree's trunk rested a large boulder. Regulus picked it up, the strength the sorcerer's mark granted him making the task easy. A large chunk of grassy ground pulled away with the stone—a dirt and grass-covered wooden panel cemented to the boulder's base. A hole appeared where the panel and boulder had been, with dirt steps leading into the earth.

He set the boulder down so the edge of the panel jutted out over the opening. He descended halfway, turned to his right, and felt for the hole in the dirt wall. His fingers found the torch, flint, and an apple where he had left them, and he set about lighting the torch. With the apple and lit torch in hand, he went back for Sieger.

The stallion shook his head, pawed the ground, and snorted. Regulus sighed. "Come on, boy." He held out the apple, and Sieger reached for it. Regulus pulled it back a little and backed down the stairs. With a snort of frustration, Sieger followed. Once down the steps, Regulus gave Sieger the apple. While Sieger crunched the apple, Regulus stuck the torch in an iron rung in the dirt wall. He returned to the steps and pulled the panel and boulder back over the tunnel entrance. Maneuvering it into place over his head by holding onto the handles on the bottom was awkward, but he'd done it enough times it didn't take long.

The tunnel, which was just tall enough and wide enough for Sieger, sloped upward. He led Sieger until they reached another set of packed dirt steps. Another wooden panel blocked the exit, this one covered with stones to make it blend in with the floor of the stables and to give it extra weight. He deposited the torch in an iron ring in the wall and heaved the trapdoor aside. He extinguished the torch and led Sieger out of the tunnel.

It took a moment for his eyes to adjust. Stalls abutted the outer castle wall to his right, and to his left stretched a wooden wall with shuttered windows. Narrow bands of moonlight streaked across the hay-strewn dirt floor. The smell of horses and manure filled his nostrils, and the quiet, steady breathing of horses provided a backdrop to the muffled stomp of Sieger's hooves. He led Sieger to his stall and returned the cover to the tunnel entrance. He left Sieger, still wearing all his tack, and headed through his private hedge-protected lane from the stables to a side door in the castle. All part of preventing his few servants from knowing about the Black Knight. He pulled off his helm, closing his eyes as welcome night air cooled his skin.

A lamp and flint stood on a pedestal near the castle door, waiting for him. With the lamp in one hand and helm in the other, he crept up the stairs, his armor echoing. He knocked on a plain wooden door near the top of the stairs and waited. Nothing. He couldn't blame the boy, but he also couldn't get out of his armor unaided. He knocked again, harder, and opened the door.

"Harold."

The young man sat up in his bed. "Wha…my lord?" Harold rubbed his eyes. A lad of sixteen years, Harold was lanky and a touch fidgety. His dark blond hair was a mess, and he had drool in the scraggly beard he was so proud of.

"Yes. Get up, I need help with my armor."

"Of course, my lord." Harold teetered out of bed and toward the door, blinking. Regulus suppressed a smile. "I'll carry the lamp, my lord."

They continued up the winding staircase, went through a door into a hallway, and walked down to Regulus' room. Harold unlocked and opened the door.

A giant mass of dark fur bolted through the door and jumped on Regulus, knocking him back. Despite his exhaustion, Regulus grinned.

"Hey, Magnus." Regulus scratched the dog behind a floppy ear as its giant pink tongue licked his face. Standing on his hind legs, the massive dog was almost as tall as Regulus. "All right, down boy."

Magnus trotted back into Regulus' room, wagging his fluffy, light brown tail, and jumped on the bed. His fur—of which he had a copious amount—was black on his face, chest, and haunches, and the rest was brown, getting lighter to the pale fur on the underside of his tail.

The curtains on the wall-length window were open, and dim moonlight illuminated the room. A large four-poster bed, currently occupied by Magnus, took up most of the room. Next to the bed, a nightstand just big enough for a food tray stood empty. A massive fireplace filled most of the wall opposite his bed, with a small armchair and footstool placed in front of it. Other than his large oak dresser and a small desk and chair, the only other furnishing was a couple of large trunks, one padlocked shut, and a large rug. Harold set the lamp on the nightstand and headed for the fireplace.

"Armor first, Harold," Regulus said, unwilling to stay in the heavy, stinking armor any longer.

"Of course, my lord."

Regulus stared out the window at the stars while Harold removed his armor piece by piece, tutting at the muck covering it. "Did you go for a swim in a giant mud puddle?"

Regulus chuckled half-heartedly. "More or less."

"I think you'll be needing a bath, my lord."

No argument there. "Tomorrow, Harold." Regulus peeled off his blood-encrusted tunic. "For now, I need sleep. No, leave that," he added as Harold moved to collect the armor for cleaning. "Go back to bed."

Harold nodded. "Thank you, my lord."

The young man slipped out and Regulus went to his bed. Magnus shifted over just enough to allow Regulus to crawl under the covers, then burrowed against his side.

The sun had passed its zenith when Regulus awoke to Harold hauling his armor out of the room. Magnus placed his head on Regulus' chest, panting happily. Harold offered to draw a bath and bring food, which Regulus gratefully accepted.

As he waited, Regulus rubbed his thumb over the mark on the underside of his right forearm. Although the mark itself was smooth, the skin around and under it was rough from repeated scarring. The product of too many failed attempts to remove it. The black mark looked like two hollow diamonds connected to a V, with the open side toward his wrist. Despite the scarring, the mark remained, clear as when it first appeared. He stood and walked to the window.

Best not to dwell on what you can't change. His father's cousin had said that when Regulus went to live with him at six. *"Make the most of your lot in life,"* Lord Kimberly would say, usually after punishing Regulus for some minor infraction. *"It could be worse."*

No, he chided himself. Dresden's voice replaced Kimberly's in his mind. *"You're my brother."* He could be alone. *All* his friends could be dead. Or they could have abandoned him any time in the two years he had borne the sorcerer's mark. They probably should have. Things could be worse. But that knowledge did nothing for his aching soul.

After food and a bath, Regulus strapped on his sword and headed out to the courtyard. Not the oversized black sword. He hated it, and the armor. Both given to him by the sorcerer. No, this was one of his own standard steel broadswords. He didn't need it within his own castle, but after years as a mercenary, he felt exposed without it. Magnus loped beside him. Even down on all fours, the dog's head came up nearly to his waist.

A couple servants nodded at him deferentially as he walked to the stables. Something after two years, he was still getting used to. He only had eight servants running the entire castle, plus a handful of guards. The gardens were overgrown and the extra rooms dusty and generally everything was shabby, but he couldn't risk more watching eyes. He found Sieger groomed and chomping on hay in the stable. The stallion nickered at Regulus.

"Good boy, Sieger." He scratched Sieger's neck.

"Glad to see you're up, Reg," a voice said from behind him.

Regulus smiled and turned around. "Hey, Drez."

A little shorter than Regulus and a year younger, Dresden Jakobs was muscular with a constant low-level energy. Thick black brows shadowed his dark eyes, and he kept his thick black hair and beard short and well-groomed. He had a long, angular nose and a dark olive complexion, like most Carasians. Twin scimitars crisscrossed his back as usual.

Dresden was silent for a moment as his piercing gaze bored into Regulus. "Maybe you wouldn't come back so tired if you let me help."

"No. If one of you died, what would be the point?" Regulus stroked Sieger's neck. "I'm not discussing it again." By the hurt look Dresden gave him, Regulus must have slipped into his captain voice again. "We agreed," he added quietly.

Agreed I need your support here more than out there.

"I know." Dresden's brow furrowed as he scratched behind Magnus' ears. "What was it this time?"

"Roots of some glowing plant in the Forbidden Marsh guarded by hobgoblins and centaurs."

"I *hate* hobgoblins." Dresden spat.

"I'm aware, old friend." He didn't bother to hide his amusement.

"Nasty, troublesome creatures."

"Apparently they like venison, not just your collection of lucky rabbit feet."

"I maintain their theft is linked to our getting trapped for two days in that ravine."

Regulus laughed. "I maintain that link is completely circumstantial."

"Whatever you say." Dresden stopped petting Magnus. "Oh, almost forgot." He pulled a crumpled letter out of his belt and handed it to Regulus.

Regulus glanced at the broken red wax seal on the parchment. A raven's head over an axe. *Drummond.* "Reading my missives again, Drez?"

"Only the interesting-looking ones." Dresden leaned back on his elbows on the door of an empty stall across from Sieger's. "Plus, we never know how long you'll be gone. What if it's pressing?"

"I suppose that's fair." Regulus read over the letter.

Lord and Lady Drummond cordially invite you to join them on Springtide the 26th, at 6 in the evening, for a supper party to honor the visit of Lady Tamina Belanger and her daughter, Lady Adelaide Belanger.

He frowned. He hated these parties. Dresden loved them, but Drez flirted with every unmarried woman who would talk to him from the serving girls to the guests.

"Are you going?" Drez asked. "If Adelaide is as pretty as her sister, might be worth it for once."

Regulus folded the invite and looked at Dresden. "And when have you met her sister?"

"Lady Minerva, Sir Drummond's wife." Dresden shrugged. "That's why they're visiting, because Minerva Drummond is pregnant."

He raised a brow. "You know as much gossip as a barmaid."

"How else am I supposed to amuse myself while you're off fighting centaurs? So," Dresden pressed. "You going? It'll be good for you. Drink some wine, talk to a pretty girl."

"Assuming I'm not called away," he said grimly. "And only because it's the polite thing to do. But I doubt I'll be talking to any pretty girls." He elbowed Drez. "You coming along?"

"Obviously. If you're too stoic and frowny-faced to engage Lady Belanger, you can bet your immortality I will."

"Frowny-faced? Really."

Dresden pointed at Regulus' face. "Exactly! Just like that."

Regulus realized he was right and rolled his eyes. "Okay, okay. But I'm not looking for a wife—"

"Yes, you are. You're nearly thirty, a lord with enough land and income to live comfortably, and no family. Your bachelorhood is an affront to common decency."

"What?" Regulus blinked. Sure, Drez had hinted in the past he wanted Regulus to marry. Even as mercenaries, Dresden had sometimes tried to play matchmaker, despite Regulus' protests. A wife was impractical for a mercenary, and he'd had no interest in casual romance.

"You need somebody other than Magnus, Reg."

Regulus bent down and covered Magnus' soft, floppy ears. "Hey, you'll hurt his feelings. Besides, I have you."

Even as he said it, he knew Drez had a point. He scratched Magnus' head. Okay, yes, sometimes he envied his married knights. Sometimes he not only wondered what it would be like to have someone look at him the way Sarah looked at Jerrick, or to hold someone the way Perceval held Leonora, but wanted that. Sure, he wouldn't mind having someone waiting for him at home. But he couldn't have that. Not right now. He sighed and straightened.

"Look, maybe if things were different. But with the sorcerer—"

"To hell with the sorcerer."

Regulus flinched. Even though the sorcerer couldn't have overheard, Regulus almost expected the mark on his arm to start burning. Nothing happened.

Dresden cursed and shook his head. "See, this is my point! You need a distraction. You need something to get your confidence back."

"A wife isn't a distraction, that's a commitment." A commitment Etiros knew he couldn't make while the sorcerer's slave.

"I'm not asking you to carry the next eligible noblewoman you meet straight to a chapel." Drez looked down and kicked at the dirt. "I'm asking you to live your life. I'm asking you to find some joy." He looked up, his brows pinched. "You might not be free yet, but that doesn't mean you have to live like a slave. I'm asking you to live like you're going to be free. Because you will be. Has…he given any indication of how close you are?"

"No." *Sometimes I'm not sure he actually plans to let me go.* But he couldn't think like that. The sorcerer had given his word he would release him when his debt was paid. He had to believe that was true, or he'd lose his mind.

"Well, he will, eventually." Dresden smirked. "And then you're going to have no idea what to do with yourself after spending all your time moping. Besides, the moping is insufferable. And this lone wolf act doesn't suit you. So go meet a pretty girl. Fall in love. Be happy."

Regulus stared across the courtyard, watching a sparrow flitting through the flower-covered apple trees. All he wanted, all he had ever wanted, was a normal life. But he didn't want to play pretend. "Not yet. Maybe when—"

"No!" Drez clenched his fists. Magnus whined and licked Dresden's hand. Dresden relaxed, but he fixed Regulus with an intent glare. "No excuses. We agreed. What's our mantra?"

Regulus rubbed his forehead. "My circumstances don't define me. I choose who I am. Not the sorcerer." The words had helped once. A reminder that his worth, his identity, were not dictated by the sorcerer, or anyone else. That even when his options were limited, his choices still mattered. After two years, the words felt hollow. But to tell Dresden that would feel like letting him down.

"Don't let him take your life," Dresden said. Magnus tried to weave between Dresden's legs, and he pushed the dog aside with an affectionate smile. "So you're going to be friendly and at least consider getting to know the lovely, eligible Lady Belanger. Do it for me."

Regulus rubbed the side of his neck. "Drez, she won't look at me twice."

"Why?"

"This, for one." He pointed at the scar stretching down his right cheek to his chin. "Second, even I have heard of Lord Alfred Belanger. He's wealthy and knows the king. I'm a—"

"Lord," Dresden cut in.

"Bastard."

They glared at each other. It shouldn't matter. He *was* a lord. But it did, and they both knew it.

"And a mercenary."

"Former." Drez scratched his beard. "And a good, honorable, kind man. You're talking to her." He nodded once, as if that settled it.

Regulus frowned. "Last I checked, I give the orders around here." Dresden's jaw tightened, and he wished he could take it back. Guilt twisted his gut. He hung his head. "Okay."

Dresden grinned, his anger and concern vanishing. "You have to at least try to engage her in conversation. Promise me."

"Fine." Regulus gave a terse nod. "But give me a chance. She sees you and your beard first and she won't want anything to do with my scarred face."

Dresden stroked his beard. "Ha! I knew you were jealous of my beard."

Chapter 3

THE KNIFE spun through the air, the sharp edges reflecting the cloudy after-noon sunlight as it arced up and back down. Adelaide caught the blade between her fingertips and absent-mindedly flipped it back up. It cartwheeled up and back down, the hilt landing in her palm. She leaned on the pommel of her saddle, holding the knife out to her side, and stared at the back of Sir Ruddard's helm, glinting silver above his maroon cloak, as if he weren't there. She heard the clomp of hooves on the packed, uneven dirt road as if from a distance. Two long days of riding, from before the sun cast its warm glow until the moon cooled the land, had driven her past boredom until her mind—and her legs and rear—felt numb.

Ahead, a large, half-dead walnut tree stretched barren branches over the road. Adelaide moved her fingers down to the smooth, rounded end of the knife's flat hilt. She raised her arm, and with a fluid motion, straightened her elbow and released the knife. The blade made a soft thunk as it stuck into a low branch, just as Sir Ruddard rode under the bough.

"Adelaide!"

Adelaide jumped at her mother's voice. She looked back over her shoulder at Mother. The breeze teased fly-away hairs from Mother's crown of dark brown braids. Her skin, a burnt umber a few shades darker than Adelaide's, had a warm glow from riding all day.

Mother frowned. "What if you had hit Sir Ruddard?" Her Khastallander accent made her vowels sound exaggerated.

"Me?" Adelaide chuckled. "Miss? Not in ages."

"*Garhaa soondir haninai,*" Mother said, slipping into Khast as she often did when rebuking her children or when her emotions ran high. *Haughtiness is unbecoming.*

"Yes, Mother," Adelaide replied in Khast. She turned as she approached the branch. As she rode beneath the dead limb, she reached up and pulled the knife free. "But even if I *had* missed, he's wearing armor," she said, subconsciously switching back to Monparthian. "He would have been fine."

"And your blade might have been dulled or chipped," Mother chided, also switching back to Monparthian. "A *hamila* takes care of her blade." *A lady.*

Adelaide leaned over and slipped the knife back into her boot and adjusted her skirt. "It's just that the time is going so slowly!" A raindrop fell on her nose, and she glowered at the gray sky. Thunder rumbled in the distance. "Beautiful weather for two days, and in late Springtide, no less. So naturally it would rain the last day."

Mother laughed. "That should be reason for gratitude, not grumbling."

She shifted in her saddle. "It seems worse, somehow. Like nature is laughing at us. 'You thought you could make it all the way to Etchy without getting wet? Let me send a rainstorm your way.'" A big raindrop fell on her forehead, and she wiped it away.

"We could make camp until the rain passes, my ladies," Sir Ruddard called over his shoulder. Ruddard had taken up the vanguard today. Sir Charing and Sir Hayes rode behind Adelaide, her mother, their two handmaids, and two pack horses. Like knight bookends, Adelaide thought.

"Nonsense," Mother said. "If it gets too bad, we can stop. But Adelaide has a point. I am tired of traveling. We press on."

"Yes, my lady."

Nothing sounded better than finishing this journey, even if Adelaide was unsure about staying with her sister's new family. Getting off of horseback would be welcome, as would sleeping in a real bed again. More importantly, the sooner they arrived at the Drummond's, the sooner she saw Minerva. Two years felt like an eternity, and the occasional letter did little to ease her loneliness.

Adelaide pulled the hood of her cloak over her head as the rain fell faster. Why did they have to be riding across pastureland instead of through a forest when it rained? Some trees between her and the sky would be wonderful. She prodded her blue roan gelding, Zephyr, into a trot and moved next to Ruddard.

The rain formed little rivulets down Ruddard's helm. Droplets clung to his scraggly gray beard. Even though his horse was taller than Zephyr, he was still shorter than her.

"If we don't stop, when do you think we will arrive?"

Ruddard pulled his cloak tighter around his shoulders to protect his chain-mail tunic from the rain. "Mid-evening, optimistically."

That left at least four more hours of riding. She let Zephyr fall back into line. *Don't get me wrong, Zephyr; I love you. But I'm tired. I'm sure you are, too.*

About an hour later, hail drove them to a small stand of trees a short distance out of their way. The trees, their leaves still small, provided little protection.

Worse, they had to share the space with three cows that refused to move.

While they waited, they ate the last of their food. They started out again as soon as the rain subsided to a light shower. Darkness fell, and a waning crescent moon glinted between clouds. Ruddard slowed his horse and signaled for them to stop as they approached a pass between a couple small wooded hills. The knights behind them pressed in, forcing their caravan into a tighter group. Adelaide eyed the trees. Had he seen something? She leaned forward, pulled her dagger from her right boot, and two throwing knives from her left. Steel scraped against leather as Ruddard drew his sword. Her heart rate increased as her gaze darted from shadow to shadow.

"Is someone there?" Mother murmured.

"Not sure." Ruddard prodded his horse forward. "Best to be cautious."

Behind them, Sir Charing drew his sword. Adelaide glanced back as Sir Hayes nocked an arrow. Moonlight glinted on the blade of Mother's dagger. The maids' eyes were wide in their pale faces. If anyone attacked them, the handmaids would be useless. Not for the first time, and doubtless not for the last, Adelaide mentally chided the entire kingdom of Monparth for teaching its daughters to rely on men to defend them. As if there would always be a good man available. All the same, she would rather not have today be the day she had to put her training to the test.

They were halfway through the pass when torches lit on either side of them. A dozen or so men dressed in dark, ragged clothing stepped out of the trees. Handkerchiefs hid the lower half of their faces, and they carried an array of battered swords and spears. A large, muscular man bearing a longsword stepped closer.

"My, my. What have we here?" His deep voice carried a note of amusement. "Don't you know robbers roam these roads after dark?"

"You are bold"—Ruddard adjusted his grip on his sword—"attacking travelers so close to the Drummond Estate."

"Drummond?" The man laughed. "Nearly an hour away. And we haven't attacked nobody." He ran his hand along the flat of his blade, admiring the weapon. Even in the faint light, Adelaide could tell it needed sharpening. "Yet."

Adelaide prepped the throwing knives, keeping one in her palm while she gripped the other between her thumb and the side of her forefinger. Still, she prayed to Etiros that she wouldn't need to use them. As her pulse rose, the magic inside her stirred, a constrained energy coursing through her veins. But she had years of practice keeping it hidden.

"Look, this is simple," the man continued. "You hand over your valuables, no attacking necessary."

Adelaide snorted before she could stop herself. She didn't have any driving desire to fight them, but she wasn't about to hand over their bags like a beat dog abandoning its bone.

The man looked at her. "You think your big, strong knights will protect you, pretty lady?" He gestured to his companions. "They're outnumbered. Three to twelve."

The bandit stepped closer to her horse, and Ruddard held out his sword. "Stay back," Ruddard warned.

The man ignored him. "See, lady, just give us your jewelry, and you don't have to watch us kill your brave knights."

"Three to twelve, you say?" Mother mused.

"That's right." The leader shifted his attention to Mother. "It'd be a shame if something happened to you lasses while your knights were engaged."

"A foreigner," another bandit said. "To come this far, they must have something valuable."

Adelaide gripped her dagger tighter, ignoring the sweat making the hilt slick.

"I question your math." Mother urged her horse closer to Adelaide and the bandit. "I count five on our side. I like our chances; don't you, Sir Ruddard?"

"Aye, my lady," Sir Ruddard said.

Adelaide's breathing became faster, shallower. She glanced from bandit to bandit, wondering if she would have to fight them. Would she have to kill one? A chill ran down her arms, followed by a rush of energy. She focused on keeping the thrumming magic inside. The last thing she needed was for bandits to spread word of a brown-skinned female mage to every corner of the kingdom. All her years of hiding would be for nothing.

The large man guffawed. "Oh, are the lovely ladies armed? How adorable." He sauntered up to Zephyr and held his sword a few inches from Adelaide's neck. She stiffened. He was within her reach. "We'll be takin' our payment for your travel through our pass now. In gold or blood. Your choice."

Adelaide batted the man's sword aside with the flat of her dagger's blade. Just as she had drilled, she stabbed into the base of his neck, driving deep above his clavicle and the neckline of his loose chainmail. The bandit screamed and staggered back as she ripped the blade away. Blood erupted after it, and her stomach twisted, but she didn't have time to be repulsed. Another bandit charged her, brandishing a spear.

She arced her left hand forward and threw a knife. It buried deep in his throat, and he fell. She vaguely noted the *whoosh, thump, whoosh, thump* of Sir Hayes shooting arrows and the clang of swords, but she focused on the bandit coming toward her from behind. She threw the other knife. He dodged—not fast enough. It struck his right shoulder, burying into his arm to the side of his leather chest-plate. He yelped, and his sword fell from his hand. He yanked the knife free as Adelaide pulled her last throwing knife from her boot. Before she even had finished drawing it, another knife slammed into the bandit's forehead. His eyes glassed over, and he collapsed forward.

Adelaide looked over at Mother, but she had turned to a bandit on her other side. The man tried to pull Mother off her horse. Mother stabbed without hesitation. The man clutched his neck, stumbling back as Mother withdrew her blade.

It was over. The bandits all lay dead or dying. Adelaide's heart raced as she scanned the dark trees. *Never let your guard down until you are certain the fight is won.* Nothing but the gentle creak of trees and the panting of horses reached her ears.

Years. Years of practice. Of training. Of preparing but being told to hope killing was never necessary. Thousands of times stabbing mannequins of straw and dirt. But stabbing a real person felt different.

Killing felt different.

She didn't care for it.

Not that death was foreign. In her twenty-one years, Adelaide had heard about and seen her share of the violence in Monparth. She had seen Father's knights return from run-ins with brigands, blood staining their clothes. Years ago, she had traveled through the remains of a village destroyed by a horde of goblins driven from their caves by a mining operation. The blood had dried all over the cracked bricks and collapsed wood walls. She'd witnessed a hanging. Seen a murderer's head on a pike. But death at your own hand… She looked down at the dagger in her hand. Blood dripped from the tip, staining her skirt. Her hand shook. She took a deep breath and dismounted.

Mother walked up next to her and placed a hand on her shoulder. *"Kiah tuhn theack hi?" Are you all right?*

"Yes." Her voice cracked, betraying her.

To her surprise, Mother pulled her into an embrace. "Oh, Adelaide." Her tone was soothing. "They were murderers, robbers, and villains." Adelaide nodded into her mother's shoulder, breathing in the smell of cinnamon.

"I'm sorry, Ad. I was younger than you are when I first took a life. But I remember." She stroked Adelaide's hair.

The shaking eased. Adelaide's breathing leveled out. Mother broke the embrace.

"Come, *Tha Shiraa*," Mother said. *Little Tigress*. For once, the nickname made Adelaide wince. Mother lifted her chin with her forefinger, forcing her to make eye contact. "A lady cares for her blade. Clean your dagger. If you can, collect your knives."

Adelaide nodded. She couldn't seem to get her tongue working again. Numbly, she used her already blood-stained dress to clean her dagger then returned it to her right boot. The maids still sat on their horses, the whites of their eyes shining in the starlight. Sir Hayes walked from bandit to bandit, confirming they were all dead.

She walked toward the first man she had thrown a knife at. He lay sprawled on his belly, his neck twisted with his head looking to the side at an odd angle. The flat handle of her throwing knife protruded from just beneath his collarbone in a pool of blood. Her stomach roiling, she retrieved the knife. *Etiros, forgive me*. She moved to the next bandit. Sir Charing rolled the dead man onto his back while Mother stood by. Mother pulled her knife from his head and walked away. Adelaide bent down, averting her gaze from the wide eyes in his blood-stained face as she pulled her knife from the dead man's arm. Sir Charing watched her stand back up.

"You did well," he said, his voice quiet, respectful. "Although I shouldn't have allowed him to get so close in the first place."

"What? No." Adelaide shook her head.

Despite the heaviness in her limbs, the clenching in her stomach, and the headache forming behind her eyes, she had to disagree with Monparthian culture. She may have been born to a Monparthian father and raised in Monparth, but Mother had taught her the same beliefs she had learned from her mother. Men should protect, yes, but women had every right to defend themselves.

"You were waiting for a command. I would have asked for your help if I needed it."

Sir Charing knit his brow. "I have watched you train, my lady. I am not sorry I did not protect you. I am sorry I did not save you from taking a life."

Adelaide busied herself cleaning her knives. But as she remembered the scream…the glassy, vacant eyes of the last bandit…her hands shook again. She knew what would happen when she chose to act. Mother had told her often enough. *"Blades are for hurting and killing. Using them is a grave responsibility."* Adelaide had thought she understood that before. Now she actually did. She exhaled, trying to get her muscles under control. Her hand slipped, and the blade nicked the fleshy part of her hand beneath her thumb. She winced and turned away.

"The first battle, the first kill…if a knight tells you it was not difficult, that it did not take time for them to…forgive themselves," Sir Charing said, his tone somber, "they are either lying or monsters."

She nodded and released a little of the magic pent up inside her into her palm. Warmth radiated across the cut, numbing and healing. A soft blue light shone between her fingers in her clenched fist, but she kept her hand close to her stomach and cupped her other hand over it to hide the glow. Mother would have a fit if she saw Adelaide breaking their no-magic rule.

There had once been mages in Monparth. Now, so far as Adelaide knew, she was the only one. A couple years before her birth, every mage in Monparth was massacred. Then the killer vanished, just like shadows. So that's what people called the unknown murderer, when they spoke of the massacre at all: The Shadow. And Adelaide hid her magic so a decades-old threat wouldn't re-emerge to ensure her magic-infused blood soaked the ground.

But the cut was small; healing it wouldn't take long. No one would see. The light faded. She opened her fist. All healed. She returned her knives to the straps sewn into her boot and turned back to Sir Charing. "Does it get better?"

Charing frowned. "This feeling will fade, yes. You will feel better, in the sun of another day, when this is in the past, yes. Does killing get better? No. Easier? Regretfully…yes."

Adelaide returned to Zephyr as Mother and Sir Charing also remounted. As they continued toward the Drummonds, Adelaide's thoughts wandered.

She appreciated Sir Charing's honesty. Of all her father's knights, only Sir Charing and Sir Ruddard had never disparaged her or Minerva for learning to use knives and daggers. Only Sir Charing had ever helped. The others, Adelaide knew, spoke disapprovingly behind their backs of Mother continuing the Khastallander tradition of mothers teaching their daughters to defend themselves. Father hadn't minded. He adored Mother and usually agreed with her. Her half-siblings, however, were as disdainful about Adelaide keeping blades in her boots as they were about…pretty much everything else about her and Minerva and their mother. Never in front of Father, of course. At least since four of her five half-siblings had moved away, she no longer had to deal with them. Father's eldest son was more dismissive than outright antagonistic, but she was still glad to leave him and his snobbish wife behind.

Finally, they arrived at the Drummond estate. Firelight flickered from various windows in the three-story stone mansion. A guard paced the crenellated roof. Adelaide thought the combination of villa and castle looked strange and boxy. The Drummonds had no personal chapel, like the small, plain stone structure within Father's castle walls. But Minerva had said in her letters they attended the parish chapel a half days' ride away if they needed the council of a priest or to pay the gratitude tax to Etiros after the harvest. The party dismounted in the courtyard as servants rushed to take care of their horses and trunks.

Minerva and her husband, Sir Gaius Drummond, met them at the entrance. Minerva was shorter than Adelaide, making Min just above average height for a woman in Monparth. She had a slender build Adelaide envied. Her stomach had an almost imperceptible bump, but she was just over four months pregnant. Wisps of her dark hair, piled in braids on her head with silver pins, framed her soft features and round cheeks. Like Adelaide, she had a deep tan complexion and brown eyes, although Minerva's eyes and skin were lighter. Of the two of them, Minerva had gotten more of their father's Monparthian looks.

Sir Gaius was barely taller than Adelaide, with an athletic build. Strong, but lean. Neatly combed reddish hair and a short red beard framed his ruddy face. His blue eyes sparkled as he greeted them with a warm yet nervous smile.

Minerva ran up to their mother and hugged her, planting a kiss on her cheek. "Mother! I'm so glad you could come!"

"As am I." Tears glistened in the corners of Mother's eyes. "Your father regrets he couldn't join us, but he felt he couldn't leave in the middle of the renovations."

Minerva turned to Adelaide, her smile wrinkling around her eyes. "Ad!" Her expression changed from delight to horror. "Is that…blood?"

"I'm fine," she said in a rush. "It's not mine."

"What happened?" Minerva demanded.

"Bandits." Sir Ruddard spoke up from behind them. "Everyone is safe and unharmed."

Gaius looked alarmed. "Where? Do we need to send men?"

"No, no. There were only twelve, and they are all dead."

Gaius ushered Minerva deeper inside. "Perhaps we should finish discussing this alone, sir." He smiled at Minerva. "You ladies go upstairs."

Minerva cocked an eyebrow. "If you are concerned about us *ladies* hearing about fighting, you should take another look at my sister's dress."

The muscles on the back of Adelaide's neck knotted. She chased away the tension with an uncomfortable laugh. "Come, Sir Gaius, you've been married to my sister long enough to know we have claws."

"I only…" Gaius flushed. "You shouldn't need to fight. It is our duty to protect as far as we are able. And it is my honor to protect you." He kissed Minerva's forehead. "But mostly I think your mother and sister look ready to sleep."

Part of Adelaide wanted to argue, but she couldn't disagree with him on the ready for sleep part. She wanted nothing more than to lie down on a nice, comfy bed. Two days on the hard ground was not her idea of a good time.

"Of course!" Minerva grabbed Adelaide's hand and led them into the manor. She linked one arm with Adelaide's and the other with Mother's arm. "I'll take you to your rooms."

Gaius bowed as they passed, the stiffness in his smile making him look uncomfortable. Adelaide and Mother's handmaids followed a short distance behind them, while the knights helped the servants with the horses and their belongings. As they walked up the stairs, Adelaide admired the intricate knots carved on the wood paneling lining the walls.

"How are you feeling?" Mother asked.

"Oh, better now," Minerva said. "I was ill most mornings for a while, but lately I've felt much better and less exhausted. Gaius' mother has been very kind and helpful." She leaned her head on Mother's shoulder. Her voice softened, a warm whisper. "But she's not you."

Minerva led them to a wooden door carved with peacocks and led them inside. "This is your room, Addie."

Adelaide half smirked, half scowled. "You know I don't answer to that."

Minerva winked. "As your *older* sister, I can call you whatever I choose."

"Be nice, *Tha Lonri*," Mother said with a smile. *Little Fox.* Mother always said Minerva was playful like a fox, and Adelaide was bold like a tigress.

Minerva kissed Adelaide's cheek. "See you in the morning, *Adelaide*."

CHAPTER 4

THE NEXT few days were heavenly. Adelaide had missed her sister even more than she'd realized, especially laughing together. The Drummonds were amicable. Minerva convinced Adelaide and Gaius to play checkers, and her victory in the first game sparked a competition. They played a few rounds each night. By the end of the fourth day, she was up by three, and Gaius had relaxed into the friendly, if serious, man she remembered from his visits during Minerva's courtship.

Lady Drummond recruited Adelaide and her mother into helping with a tapestry depicting Saint Melvius' taming of jaguars. Adelaide was a fair embroiderer, but it wasn't her favorite hobby. She preferred sewing clothes to embroidery. Far more exciting, Lord Drummond granted her unrestricted access to his library.

One cloudy afternoon, Adelaide ran her fingertips over the book spines. The scents of old parchment, worn leather, dusty tapestries, cold stone, and old ash in the fireplace combined into a comforting musty smell. She sank into the large leather chair in front of the fireplace and looked around at the four large bookshelves, all lined with books. So much knowledge. So many stories. She grinned to herself. What would she find? What did she want to read? Where to start?

She turned and surveyed the three floor-to-ceiling walls of books, enjoying the silence as motes drifted in the muted sunlight slanting through the window. Finally, she began perusing the books. Some were stiff and old. Some new. A prayer book sported a gold-overlaid cover. She took a bestiary featuring color paintings. A book of heraldry caught her eye, and she flipped through the colorful illustrations before returning it to the shelf. She found a collection of romance poetry and added it to the bestiary. Only the crinkle of parchment and muted protest of leather and the shuffle of her bare feet on the carpet broke the silence. She bent down to a bottom shelf and pulled out a book with an iron-bound cover. Something shifted behind it.

Down on her knees, she peered into the empty space on the shelf. She could just see a worn leather cover. She moved some other books out of the way and freed the trapped book. The plain leather back had been facing her. She flipped it over and ran her fingertips over the embossed metal image of a man enwreathed in swirling flames. He held his hands out to his sides, his expression calm.

She opened the book and read the blue ink of the title page. *A Compendium of Known Magical Abilities and Tales of Mages of Legend.* She gasped. A book on magic? She clutched the book to her chest, looking around furtively. No one watched her. She was as alone as she had been when she first entered. Still, her ears burned, and her spine tingled with anticipation at the discovery of her new treasure.

After all these years…finally. Mother would return home in a week, leaving Adelaide unsupervised. She could read this book and learn how to *use* her magic. To be a real mage. She did feel a little guilty. Mother and Father just wanted to protect her, and she used to agree with their reasons for keeping her abilities secret and inactive. She didn't *want* to be murdered. Even if she often wished she hadn't spent three years of her childhood alone with Mother in a cottage learning to hide her magic, she never blamed her parents for their protectiveness. But over twenty years had passed since mages were eradicated from Monparth. If The Shadow still hunted mages, wouldn't it have found her by now?

A few years ago, Adelaide had tried to argue the threat was in the past. She had never seen Mother so angry, ranting in Khast about murder and foolish risks. Even if The Shadow didn't find her, did she have any idea how many people would want to use the only mage in Monparth for their own ends? Did she want people to view her as a commodity, a weapon? Adelaide had learned several new Khast curse words that day and didn't use her magic for months. But the energy inside her begged for release. So she practiced in her room, with the curtains drawn and the door locked. And she tried not to think about getting murdered by an unknown threat.

If she could learn to control her power, she could protect herself. Right? Unwanted images of bloody, glassy-eyed bandits popped into her mind. She pushed them away. Maybe she could defend herself without killing. It might be easier with magic. And she might not always have her dagger and knives. Now she had a way to learn. So far, she had managed to create blue-tinted light, fire, and on a few occasions, a solid blast of light capable of knocking over a heavy object, like a full trunk. But she had no idea what else she was even *capable* of doing and finding time to test herself when no one would catch her was difficult.

Mother wouldn't approve. But…it was part of her, wasn't it? Mother taught her to use daggers and throwing knives, just like every other Khastallander mother, all the way in Monparth, because Mother was Khastallander. Mother would not deny her culture, her identity, even after marrying Father and moving to Monparth. *And I am a mage. Whether or not my parents like it. Whether I am the last mage alive in Monparth or not.* Etiros had seen fit to make her a mage. How could she deny a part of herself?

She looked at the book in her hands. Just parchment, leather, metal and ink. Like any book on the shelves. But so much more. Knowledge and power and more control of her life. She smiled and added it to her small pile.

The fourth day after their arrival, the Drummonds hosted a supper party in their honor. Adelaide tended to dislike these social gatherings. People hid behind carved smiles and pleasant lies. Plus, Lady Drummond had requested she recite. A common enough request. Adelaide had been to many feasts where a member of the nobility would recite a poem or ballade—usually a legend of Monparth, sometimes a romance. It was an accepted way of thanking your host. But she had never volunteered.

What would people truly think as they watched her? Would they see her as any other noble performing a recitation? Or would they focus on the warm brown of her skin? The occasional Khastallander roundness of a vowel that always seemed to appear when she got nervous? Minerva said she was too self-conscious, but then, Minerva wasn't as tall as most men, and blended in better with the Monparthians than Adelaide. But it would be rude to refuse. And if being Khastallander didn't bother Mother, it wouldn't bother her, either.

The day of the party, Adelaide wandered into the sitting room where Minerva and Mother were discussing pregnancy and babies. She joined them on the sunlit couch and hugged a pillow edged in aqua tassels to her chest. "Anyone interesting coming tonight?"

"Don't be in too big a rush to find a suitor," Mother said without looking up from stitching a baby blanket.

Adelaide blushed. "That's not what I meant!" *Although, I'm not uninterested…*

There were many reasons Adelaide wasn't married, why she had never had a proper suitor. Several older siblings, for one. For another, noble Monparthian men showed less interest in a half-Khastallander with brown skin. She knew her half-noble blood made some see her as an inferior choice. Other times she suspected the men who flirted with her simply found her foreign appearance intriguing. Minerva had experienced the same issues, although her marriage to Gaius had given Adelaide hope again. But there were other reasons.

One main one.

Courting was difficult when she had a secret to keep. She couldn't court someone she didn't trust, but how could she know if she trusted someone enough to tell him the truth about her magic until she courted him?

"Let's see…" Minerva said. "Baron and Baroness Carrick. Maybe their eldest son, Lord Carrick and his wife? I'm not sure if they could make it. I believe the baron's youngest son is coming, Sir Nolan." Minerva gave her a saucy grin. "That reminds me, Lady Drummond says to tell you he's twenty-seven and very eligible."

"Oh, really?" Adelaide smirked back.

"Yes, but also a flirt and a scoundrel, I've heard. So…be careful, I suppose." Minerva thought for a moment. "Lord and Lady Russelthorn. Several other knights and ladies. Lord and Lady Drummond took care of the invites and all the planning." Her fingertips traced circles on her stomach. "I am immensely grateful. Having to deal with these social niceties and remember everyone when some mornings I couldn't stand up straight would have been a nightmare."

"I wish we didn't have to meet everyone." Adelaide rested her chin on the pillow. "We're here to see *you*, not strangers."

Mother frowned. "And I thought I taught you better manners."

"Oh, don't worry, I'll be perfectly polite." Adelaide fiddled with the tassels on the pillow. "I just hope the conversation is more interesting than"—she went into an affected falsetto—"yes, the weather *has* been lovely. I understand the tournament in Red Falls is spectacular, I may go this year."

Minerva chuckled, and Mother shook her head, smiling.

"Well, the tournament in Red Falls *is* spectacular."

Adelaide jumped at the sound of Gaius' voice behind her. She looked back and spotted him standing in the doorway. "Ah…how long have you been standing there?"

Gaius laughed as he walked over to Minerva. "Long enough to know you have low expectations for the conversation this evening." He kissed the top of Minerva's head. "Mother sent me to let you all know the guests will start arriving in about two hours, and to recommend you get dressed."

"All right." Minerva stood. "I'll see you in a couple hours." She winked at Adelaide. "And I promise I'll bring my best conversational skills."

Adelaide fidgeted with the azure silk scarf. Nothing she did with it felt right. Draped in front? No. In back? No. Over her head…? Definitely not. Wrapped around her shoulders? Too slippery. In the crook of her elbows? Too awkward. What was she supposed to *do* with it? But Lady Drummond had given it to her as a gift, so she couldn't go without it.

"You look fine, dear." Mother whispered as they stood in the foyer, waiting for the guests to enter. "Stop fidgeting."

Various knights and ladies whose names she would never remember greeted her and Mother in the entrance hall. Adelaide smiled and curtsied and fussed with her scarf. She had moved it down to her elbows when one end slid out and fell behind her. She curtsied to a Sir Mowbray and Dame Mowbray, ignoring the trailing scarf. After they passed by, she looked down and behind her, searching for the end of the scarf and losing the other end. *Darn slippery thing.* She stepped to the side, trying to spot the scarf on the ground.

There. All right. I need to find a way to retrieve it quickly when no one is looking—

A man's boots appeared on the other side of the scarf, and Adelaide's eyes widened. The man crouched down and picked up the scarf. *Oh, the embarrassment.* Her cheeks burned as the man held the scarf out to her. She reached for it, looking up at the man who had retrieved it.

He was tall. *So* tall. For the first time, she felt almost…diminutive. She guessed he must be nearing thirty years old. He wore a black jerkin over a dark green long-sleeved tunic with sleeves that pulled across his muscles. Thick black hair hung in loose curls around his ears and neck. He was clean-shaven, with a sharp jaw and high, angular cheekbones. A rough pinkish scar ran diagonally across his right cheek, from under the outside corner of his eye to the corner of his lips before it curved down his chin to his jawline. His brows furrowed together. But her gaze fixed on the way his light gray irises caught the fading sunlight, almost seeming to have a light of their own. Dark lashes framed his eyes, drawing attention to the piercing ferocity behind them.

"I believe this is yours?" His voice was clear, deep, and warm.

She gingerly took the scarf, her stomach twisting. "Thank you." The words came out in a horrifying squeak, and the heat in her face spread to her ears.

"Pardon *me*," a man's voice said behind him, brimming with condescension. "But you and your man here are blocking the way."

Adelaide hadn't even registered the man standing to the scarred man's left. He had a deep olive complexion, aquiline nose, and thick, dark beard trimmed close to his face. The bearded man frowned at the impatient guest behind them.

The handsome man with the scar looked over his shoulder. "Apologies." He looked back to Adelaide and nodded. "My lady." He turned into the great hall, followed by the bearded man.

"Wait!" Adelaide's chest tightened as she realized in a panic how loudly she had spoken. The men paused and looked back. "I…" *Now is not the time to get all tongue-tied!* "Um, that is… I apologize, I didn't hear your name."

The man's scarred lips turned up in a slight smile. "Oh. Lord Regulus Hargreaves of Arrano, my lady." He inclined his head to her. "And my lieuten—um, one of my knights, Sir Dresden Jakobs." He gestured to the man with the beard, who bowed.

"Pardon me, my lady," interrupted the same male voice, but in a much warmer tone. "Sir Nolan Carrick, at your service."

Adelaide looked over in surprise as Sir Carrick snatched up her hand and kissed her fingers. She curtsied, trying to mask her confusion. She glanced toward Lord Hargreaves, but he and his knight had disappeared into the main hall. "Adelaide Belanger."

Sir Carrick gave her a crooked smile. "I know. I am honored and most pleased to make your acquaintance, Lady Belanger."

Nolan Carrick looked younger than the man with the scar, and far less battle-worn. He wasn't much taller than her. A crimson doublet with ostentatious silver stitching covered a black shirt that clung to strong arms. He had a square face, with a clean-shaven, defined jaw. With his blue eyes and well-combed, light brown hair, he was fairly attractive. But Adelaide was so distracted thinking about the gray-eyed Lord Hargreaves of Arrano, she didn't care.

Nolan moved on, and Baron and Baroness Carrick entered next. A few more nobles of varying status arrived, and they all entered the dining hall. To Adelaide's disappointment, Lord Hargreaves sat at a distant table. She wanted to ask Minerva about him but could hardly do so at supper.

Finally, the fish, fowl, bread, and pudding courses were all finished. Lady

Drummond invited her to recite. Nerves knotted her full stomach, but she curtsied and stood on the dais at the end of the table with Lord and Lady Drummond and Baron and Baroness Carrick. Adelaide recited the Ballad of Elwynn and Leander, star-crossed lovers who died trying to bring peace to a kingdom torn asunder by war. The assembled nobility applauded daintily when she finished. Now the difficult part of the evening: mingling.

CHAPTER 5

Regulus kept looking over at Adelaide during supper. His distraction prevented him from engaging in conversation, but no one at the table seemed interested in talking with him, anyway. Dresden elbowed him in the side.

"She's going to catch you staring," he whispered. "Ease up a little. You don't want to scare her."

As if that mattered. He glanced across the hall at Sir Mowbray. A little over two years ago, Mowbray had hired Regulus as a mercenary. Now Regulus was a lord—Mowbray's superior. The pointed way Mowbray ignored Regulus at social events made Mowbray's feelings on the matter clear.

Everyone seems to either fear or hate me. Certainly no one trusts me. I'm just the bastard mercenary to them. These people will tell Adelaide what they think of me, and then she won't so much as look my way. Like everyone else. Not to mention that while the sorcerer's mark marred his arm, he shouldn't want her to look his way. But he did.

He couldn't help himself—she was lovely. He hadn't expected to find her so attractive. Her height surprised him. Fine, it was superficial, but he liked a tall woman. Most women looked small and fragile; like he could accidently crush them even without his enhanced strength. He didn't get that feeling from her. She felt solid and…magnetic. Her thick black hair escaped from her hairpins, wavy strands brushing against her round face and cheeks. Her complexion was darker than Dresden's, and even if he hadn't met her mother, he saw the Khastallander in her. He'd enjoyed his time in Khastalland. By and large, he had found Khastallanders to be a sincere and passionate people.

After supper, Adelaide stood to do a recitation. Her gray-blue dress had a wide, scooping neckline that showed off her shoulders and collarbones without being showy, but still hugged her figure. A wide, V-shaped brass belt accentuated her waist. She kept fiddling with the bright blue scarf she had dropped earlier as she recited a poem whose words Regulus barely comprehended. He was too busy telling himself *stop thinking about how beautiful she is. Stop. The sorcerer won't care if she's angelic or a hag, he'd just care if hurting her would hurt me.* But as Adelaide spoke, saying something about lovers and sacrifice, her gaze momentarily met his. *What was I thinking about again?*

Her clear, low voice washed over him, releasing tension in his muscles. He had never been so relaxed when surrounded by other nobles. He could have sat there and listened to her all night. *No.* He was doing this to please Drez, nothing more. When she finished and people rose to move around and socialize, Dresden punched him on the shoulder.

"So, are you going to sit here frowning, or are you going to go talk to her?"

Regulus forced his face to relax. He felt uncomfortably warm. "I'm not frowning."

"You're always frowning." Drez gestured in Adelaide's direction. "Go. You gave your word."

"Hmph." But he stood and walked toward where Adelaide stood near the dais. He kept his word. And he owed Dresden.

Regulus was acutely aware of the nobles watching him and whispering as he passed. He swallowed back the urge to leave. If only she weren't standing at the head of the room. To his relief, she stepped over toward the corner after ending her conversation with an older couple.

Adelaide stared up at a stained-glass window with a floral vine design. With the sun set, the details of the design were difficult to see. Flickering orange light from a nearby tall iron candelabra reflected in the glasswork, but that didn't seem worthy of her undivided attention. Perhaps she didn't want to talk to anyone. He glanced at Dresden, who held up his hands as if asking *what are you waiting for?*

"Lady Belanger?"

She turned toward him and smiled. At *him.* Like she was *pleased.* "Oh. Lord Arrano. Or is it Lord Hargreaves? I…um…thank you. For saving my scarf." She blushed and waved the end of the scarf in his direction, looking about as awkward as he felt. He smiled in amusement.

A little flirting *would* please Drez…

"Of course. And it's Hargreaves. I'm just lord of Arrano estate." Regulus cleared his throat. "Your recite…reciting…you have a lovely voice for recitation." *Oh, this is going smoothly.* He clasped his hands behind his back. Sweat tickled his neck. "One of the loveliest things I've ever heard."

She blinked. "One of? I've already had four people tell me it was the most beautiful thing they've had the pleasure of hearing."

Regulus glanced away. For once, he wished he knew how to talk like the nobles.

Adelaide laughed. "Of course, every one of them was lying."

He looked back at her and furrowed his brow, surprised both by her relaxed laughter and her bluntness.

"I mean, really. The way some people go on, you would suppose I was an angel, which is ridiculous. So. What was it, then?" She pulled her scarf up over her shoulders.

"What was what?" His mind raced to catch up, still stuck on the possibility of Adelaide being an angel.

"The most beautiful sound you've ever heard?"

He paused. He didn't need to consider the answer, but whether or not to share. "It's a long story, but laughing while crying. Joy overpowering sorrow." He stared into the distance. "I'll never forget that sound. The relief, the happiness. That's what I think freedom sounds like."

"That's…beautiful." She looked thoughtful, her lips turned up in a slight smile. For a moment, they just looked at each other.

"So…" He laughed nervously. *So what, Regulus! Where were you going with this?* Why couldn't he think straight? *This is your fault, Drez.*

"My father and mother laughing."

He blinked. "What?"

"The most beautiful sound I've ever heard. My parents giggling like newly-weds when they don't know anyone is around. Because it's the sound of how much they love each other. It sounds like freedom—not caring what anyone else thinks." She glanced away, then studied the scarf in her hands.

"My father met my mother when he was away, fighting in the Trade War. His first wife had died a couple years prior. I'm glad they found each other." Adelaide looked up at him, a stray curl of hair falling over her eye. She watched him as if weighing his reaction. "Whenever my stepsiblings or snobbish nobles look down on my mother because she's the daughter of a traveling merchant from Khastalland, that sound gives me hope. None of that matters to my parents."

Regulus' heart lurched in sympathy. "The nobles, they can be…" He trailed off before he said something he would regret. "People matter more than lineages. What's the point in judging someone for something they can't control?"

"You sound like you mean that." She tilted her head, her brows knit in contemplation and a slight smile on her pink lips.

"Of course…" *Ah. She doesn't know what I am.* How to tell her? Perhaps, of all people, she wouldn't judge him for his bastardy. But a rich merchant's daughter was a far cry from an unwed serving girl.

Adelaide pulled her scarf tighter around her shoulders. "Earlier today I was complaining no one ever says anything interesting, and certainly never anything true, at these parties. I'm glad to be wrong."

He smiled, searching for something to say to keep the conversation going—and interesting, even though part of his brain warned him not to go getting attached. He couldn't court her, regardless of what Dresden said. *Right?* But he was actually enjoying himself for once. "Your mother is Khastallander?"

"Yes." Adelaide's face clouded.

Idiot, she thinks you're judging her. He rushed on. "I visited Khastalland once. I loved it. So vibrant. Hot as—" He coughed, narrowly saving himself from slipping into the vulgarity he had picked up as a mercenary. "Very hot. Even the food."

"Oh, I love Khastallander spices," Adelaide exclaimed. "My mother brought a cook with her. She does what she can with what she can get here, but I love when she makes Khastalland recipes. My favorite is this flaky dessert pastry with chocolate that's a little bit spicy, they call it—"

"Nalotavi," Regulus said at the same time as Adelaide. They laughed.

"You know it?"

"Know it, it's my favorite!" He grinned. "Sarah—that is, the wife of one of my knights—she's a baker, and she makes excellent nalotavi for someone who has never been to Khastalland."

"Hmm, I may have to borrow this Sarah's services. I'd love to surprise Minerva. I'm certain she hasn't had nalotavi since she moved here."

"I'll have to send you some." *Was that too forward?* He shifted uncomfortably as the conversation stalled. *It was too forward. Pull it together, Regulus!*

"Is Sarah married to the knight who came with you? Sir—what was his name again? Sorry, I met so many people tonight."

"Dresden Jakobs." He chuckled. "And no, Dresden's unmarried."

Adelaide nodded. "Did you knight him?"

"Yes?" He hadn't meant it to sound like a question, but he didn't understand why she was asking.

"How long has his family been in Monparth? He's not Monparthian by blood, is he?"

Wait, what? "No, he's Carasian." Why the sudden interest in Dresden's family history? "Just his parents. Moved here from Carasom before he was born."

"Nobles?"

"No…" Suddenly, he understood. She found Dresden attractive. Girls always found Dresden attractive. He was probably right about the beard. Regulus had to fight the impulse to touch his scar. Worse, she wanted to know if Dresden was suitable marriage material. *I guess I misjudged her. Lineage matters to her.*

Adelaide tilted her head to the side. "And the one who married the baker. Noble?"

His mood soured. *Oh.* "Most of my knights were not noble-born, Lady Belanger."

Regulus braced himself for the inevitable look of distaste, the questions about why or casual judgment. He should just admit his bastardy and mercenary past now. Maybe she would walk away, and he wouldn't have to see her lovely face twist into disgust.

"So it's not empty talk." She beamed, sounding delighted. "You don't just say things, you do them."

He rubbed the back of his neck, off kilter and unsure what to make of the direction of this conversation. "I'm not sure—"

"People matter more than lineages." Adelaide nodded, like a judge making a ruling. "You believe that."

"Of course I do." He dropped his hand to his side, relief and surprise flooding him. "I don't say things I don't mean."

Her eyes glinted, teasing and slightly dangerous. "And what do you think of me, Lord Hargreaves?" Her bronze skin took on extra color as she blushed.

"Ah…" His throat seemed to close up and heat flared over his face. *I think I'd like to get to know you better.* He wished he had a glass of water. *What?* his mind screamed. *Get to know her better?* His heart screamed back, *yes,* silencing thoughts of the sorcerer. What was the question again? What he thought of her? How was a gentleman supposed to answer a question like that?

Before he could answer, a man with perfectly combed dark blond hair stepped partly between them. Baron Carrick's youngest, Nolan Carrick, again.

"Begging your pardon, my lady," Carrick said, his back to Regulus. "I *must* congratulate you. I have never heard anything so beautiful in my life."

Adelaide raised an eyebrow and glanced at Regulus. Regulus stifled a snicker, despite his irritation at the interruption.

"Please," Carrick offered her his arm. "My parents would *love* to speak with you."

"Oh." Adelaide nodded, but didn't take his arm. "I was in the middle of a conversation with Lord Hargreaves, but I will be sure to speak with them after."

Regulus suppressed a grin. She would rather talk to him than a baronial family? Maybe she didn't realize Carrick was a wealthy bachelor. Or maybe— and his heart leapt at the thought—she just didn't care.

"I'm sure Hargreaves can wait, and I did tell my parents I'd bring you over." Carrick moved his arm, inviting her to take it. "Barons do hate to be kept waiting."

Adelaide glanced at Regulus apologetically, but took Carrick's arm. "Of course."

Regulus' spirits fell as they walked away. He turned and scanned the crowd for Dresden. He spotted him talking to a young noblewoman standing against a wall. Drez leaned toward her with a teasing smile as he spoke, and the girl blushed and laughed and rolled her eyes. Regulus shook his head. Did all his knights have to be ladies' men, while he couldn't manage one full conversation without a blunder? He spotted Adelaide conversing with the baron and baroness. Carrick stepped closer and placed his hand on Adelaide's lower back, and she didn't move away.

Who am I joking? If Dresden saw him, he would doubtless point out he was frowning again. *She's perfect, and I'm…* He swallowed down his self-loathing. *No woman would want me over a Carrick. And they'd be right, too.* He hated he'd let Dresden's nonsense get into his head. To think he could be just a man who liked a girl, not a scarred slave who shouldn't even be here. Stupidity. The worst kind, too. Felt amazing in the moment, but left you aching.

Dresden now leaned against the wall next to the young lady and had a strand of her hair curled around his finger. With a sigh, Regulus made his way to the door. He wouldn't pull Drez away when he was enjoying himself. He retrieved his cloak from the page at the front entrance, and headed home.

CHAPTER 6

As Sir Nolan Carrick led her toward his parents, Adelaide glanced back over her shoulder. Lord Hargreaves was already looking away. *I thought our conversation was engaging. Perhaps I was wrong.* She looked forward again. *Maybe I don't want to know what he would have said.* She didn't know why she'd asked. He'd handed her an opportunity to ask someone's honest opinion. The way he'd turned red and looked like a cornered rabbit left only two choices. In the moment, she had thought he intended to say something complimentary and was embarrassed. But maybe he was trying to figure out how to avoid telling her a harsher truth.

Sir Nolan leaned toward her, his voice low. "I apologize if that came across as rude, but the code of chivalry leaves me honor-bound not to leave a maiden in distress."

"Distress?" Adelaide frowned and shifted her hand on his arm so they weren't walking so close. "I wasn't in distress."

"Oh?" Nolan raised his brows. "I couldn't imagine you were talking to that bastard mercenary willingly."

Her mouth fell open in shock. "I *beg* your pardon?"

"I mean, sure, he's not a mercenary anymore." He shrugged. "Supposedly."

She didn't try to mask her shock and disgust. "That is hardly a civilized way to discuss a nobleman."

"You clearly haven't heard about Hargreaves." He smiled slyly. "I'll tell you the abridged version—he's not to be trusted. Ah, here we are." He leaned close and whispered, "They didn't actually ask to speak to you, but it was the best excuse I could think of."

Adelaide swallowed back her disdain and plastered on a smile as they stopped in front of the baron and baroness. She used the opportunity to curtsy as a pretense to release Nolan's arm.

"A splendid recitation, my dear." The baroness smiled. A few short, wispy white-gray strands of hair peeked out from her wimple. *How old fashioned.* She was short and had a full face etched with smile lines.

"Thank you, my lady." Back to boring niceties.

"Indeed," Baron Carrick raised his glass of wine toward her, as if offering a toast.

"Tell me," the baroness said, "what are your interests? Hobbies?"

"Oh." Adelaide moved the scarf to her neck. "Calligraphy, sewing. I love reading." *Probably best not to mention the ancient dagger technique of Khastalland. Obviously can't mention the magic.*

"Do you enjoy dancing?" Nolan inquired.

"Of course."

"Brilliant." Nolan stepped closer to her and placed his hand on her lower back.

A knot formed in Adelaide's throat and her whole body tensed. But stepping away would appear insulting.

"I was thinking, Father, that it has been far too long since a proper dance has been held in Etchy Barony." Nolan's tone was too sweet, taking on a pleading, manipulative edge. He smiled at Adelaide. "You *would* join us, wouldn't you?"

She mustered her politest tone. "Certainly, Sir Carrick."

"Please." Nolan rubbed his thumb against her back, and she straightened uncomfortably. "I do hope you will call me Nolan."

"Oh, we hardly know each other, Sir Carrick." She looked to his parents. "That hardly seems appropriate at this time."

The baron chuckled. "You could learn something from her, Nolan."

"Well, I'll certainly do my best to remedy that and get to know you as soon as possible, Lady Belanger." Nolan smiled coyly and moved his hand to her hip. Heat rushed to her face. Worse, heat was building in the palm of her right hand. She clenched her fists. *Control it.*

Adelaide cleared her throat, every fiber of her body on alert. "Forgive me, Baron Carrick, Baroness." Her words came out in a rushed gasp. "But I…" She couldn't come up with a reasonable excuse to leave. "I…need a moment. To freshen up." She bobbed a half curtsy. "Thank you for coming," she added breathlessly before hurrying off.

She darted into a parlor off the main hall and leaned on the back of a couch, her right hand still clenched. Faint rays of moonlight crisscrossed the floor following the lattice-work on the window. Her chest heaved as she realized she'd been holding her breath. *"He's a scoundrel."* That's what Minerva had said. *"Be careful."* She stared at the logs stacked in the cold fireplace. *The nerve…* Never had a man dared be so forward with her. She exhaled slowly, trying to steady her breathing. *It was nothing. He just put his hand on my back.*

Unexpectedly.

For no reason.

She groaned and opened her clenched fist, letting the warmth grow as magic flowed into her palm. Her skin glowed sky blue. She thrust her hand toward the fireplace, directing her energy into a stream of yellow-orange fire that hit the logs with a crackling roar. She let the energy wane, the magic recede. The extra warmth and the light in her palm faded away. With a sigh, she sank down onto the couch. Nolan hadn't done anything terribly wrong. But she'd still felt trapped. *I've never liked being trapped.*

The door opened and she darted to her feet. "Oh—Minerva." She sat back down. "I know; I should be out there. I just…needed a moment."

Minerva eased the door closed. She looked at Adelaide, at the lively fire and back again. "Some servant is going to take the fall for that, you know."

Adelaide blushed. "I'll put it out before I leave."

Minerva sat next to her. "Is everything all right? I saw you walking away from the baron and baroness in a hurry." She paused. "Did they say something…unkind?"

"Oh, no. Nolan Carrick is—friendly. I wasn't sure how to react." They sat in silence for a moment. "Do you know anything about Lord Hargreaves? Sir Nolan said some odd things."

Minerva leaned back against the couch. "I know he's illegitimate and because of that was sent away when he was very young. It's why he's Lord of Arrano, not Lord Arrano."

No wonder he doesn't care about lineages. Adelaide's heart wrenched. *But being treated differently for something that's not your fault…sent away from the people you love. The life you know.* She clutched the pillow tighter. *I understand how that feels. Even if not that extreme.*

Minerva must have known what she was thinking, because she put her arm around Adelaide's shoulders. "He worked as a mercenary until he inherited Arrano when the legitimate heir died childless. Other than that, only rumors."

So he was a mercenary. Adelaide tucked an escaped strand of hair behind her ear and turned so she could see Minerva's face. This hairstyle was *not* cooperating tonight. "What sort of rumors?"

Minerva shifted, her hand resting on her stomach. "When he arrived to claim Arrano, his step-mother was still alive, as was his half-brother's wife. They put forth a champion to challenge him. People say he won the duel too easily. No one has heard from the Arrano ladies since. Rational minds say they went to family in Craigailte. But between that and the fact he often disappears alone and has never once invited anyone into Arrano castle, it's led to some wild speculation." She chuckled. "My personal favorite is he's a vampire."

Adelaide laughed in disbelief. "He's hardly pale enough for that."

"There are other stories. He's a sorcerer. He made a deal with a demon to get his father's estate and title. He's hiding something terrible in his castle. Some say he's still a mercenary."

Adelaide frowned. None of this lined up with the sweet, slightly awkward man she had talked to. "If people think he's so horrible, why did Lord and Lady Drummond invite him?"

"Oh, it would be terribly impolite not to," Minerva said matter-of-factly. "So most people invite him, although he doesn't always come. I suspect some nobles do so out of fear. If he is a supernatural being or demonic servant, they fear offending him." She shrugged. "But mostly people are curious. They hope one day he will observe proper social protocol and return the invite, and they can see inside Arrano."

Adelaide stared at the dancing flames. "Do you think he's dangerous?"

Minerva thought for a moment. "Possibly. He doesn't look particularly friendly. But I have never seen him be anything but polite and reserved. Maybe if he smiled more people would be willing to give him a chance."

"He smiled tonight." *He smiled for me.*

"Well, he left, so you don't have to worry about him. Your blades can stay stowed in your boots." Minerva stood and held out her hand. "Come on. Our guests are waiting."

"Humph." Despite how much she wanted to continue avoiding said guests, Adelaide took Minerva's hand and they headed toward the door. "Oh—wait. Nearly forgot." She turned toward the fireplace and held out both hands, concentrating. Her palms glowed as she slammed her hands into fists. The fire collapsed on itself, going out with a *whoosh*.

"Adelaide!" Minerva's eyes widened. She peered around, as if afraid someone could have seen. "Did Father and Mother change their minds?"

Adelaide's heart beat faster. "Please don't tell—"

"I see." Minerva sighed. "I won't. But you have to stop."

"It's not that easy." Adelaide fiddled with her scarf. "It's part of me."

The deep shadows on Minerva's face in the moonlight made her look extra afraid and disapproving. "I don't want to lose you."

"I'm being careful. No one knows. Besides, I have my daggers." She smiled, but Min's frown deepened.

"The Shadow killed warrior mages, too." Min took a deep breath through her nose and exhaled. "I've always admired your courage, Ad. But you know it's safest to hide." Minerva turned toward the door. "Just…don't do anything stupid, all right?"

"I won't," she said as Minerva opened the door. *But I still hate hiding.*

Adelaide managed to avoid Sir Nolan for the rest of the party, although he seemed to keep appearing nearby. To her disappointment, Lord Hargreaves had disappeared. Guests flowed out, with gracious but empty well-wishes for her and Mother and gratitude to the Drummonds for hosting. Lord Hargreaves' knight, Sir Dresden, lingered in front of her.

"Lord Hargreaves asked me to tell you he enjoyed your conversation and regrets he had to leave early to attend to other business. He hopes your paths cross again soon." Sir Dresden smiled, more of a charming, playful smirk. "Might I bring him a message from you, my lady?"

"Oh." *So he was interested?* She glanced at Mother, but she was busy talking to a woman with silver-streaked blond hair. Dresden waited expectantly. What on earth was she supposed to say? She didn't want to be too forward, but she also didn't want to appear uninterested. "I wish Lord Hargreaves hadn't left so soon. I would have liked to continue our conversation. It was the only real conversation I had all night."

Dresden bowed, his eyes dancing. "Excellent. I wish you the best, Lady Belanger."

"Wait!" She pushed a strand of hair away from her eye as Dresden's brows pinched. "Can…can you tell him I know? And I don't care about lineages, either?"

The corner of Dresden's mouth quirked upward. "I will, my lady."

Adelaide felt flustered for the next several farewells and hoped it didn't show. Eventually the line of guests ended, and Lord Drummond closed the door, but she was certain the Carricks hadn't passed her. How did she completely miss them?

Looking more relaxed with the guests gone, Gaius leaned over to kiss Minerva's cheek, but she turned her head and kissed him. Adelaide grinned. Lady Drummond breezed past with a broad smile.

"Thank you for waiting, Baron."

Adelaide turned and her eyes widened. The Carricks stood at the back of the small foyer, near the staircase leading up to the residential floors. Nolan leaned against an oak table bearing a marble bust of one of the previous Lord Drummonds, looking right at her. He smiled when he caught her gaze.

"Your trunks were already brought up. If you will follow me." Lady Drummond turned and headed up the stairs. The baron and baroness followed. Nolan languidly pushed off the table, his gaze never leaving her. He winked before following his parents.

Adelaide whirled back toward Minerva and Gaius, who were laughing with Mother. "The Carricks are staying the night?"

Gaius nodded. "It's a day's ride from here to the Carrick's castle. Offering them accommodation to thank them for making the trip is proper. They'll breakfast with us in the morning, and return home."

"Breakfast?" Adelaide started pulling half-fallen hairpins out of her hair. "Min, you didn't warn me?"

"I didn't know." Minerva looked apologetic. "As I said, Lady Drummond took care of all the arrangements."

"Oh, right." *Great.*

That night, Adelaide lay awake in bed. Sir Nolan's playful wink had left her unsettled, and his rude interruptions irked her. Lord Hargreaves, however, had been so pleasant and friendly and…genuine. That might have been the only honest conversation she'd ever had at a party. He had opened up to her. *How could he possibly be as horrible as people think?* But then why did he keep to himself in his castle? He was a mystery, and her brain couldn't leave the puzzle alone, even though she had no way to discover the answer. She wished he had stayed longer. Maybe she'd see him again while she stayed with Minerva during the pregnancy. She hoped so. Even after she fell asleep, Regulus Hargreaves' pale gray eyes haunted her dreams.

THE NEXT morning Adelaide skipped down the stairs to breakfast, wishing she could have asked Regulus Hargreaves about his time in Khastalland. Did he know any Khast? She'd have to ask him the next time she saw him. As she careened around the corner into the landing to the second floor, she nearly collided with Baroness Carrick. Baron Carrick and Sir Nolan stood just behind the baroness, Nolan with an amused expression.

"Oh, pardon me, my lady!" Adelaide curtsied as her pulse spiked and a string of Khast curses went through her head. *I forgot.* She smoothed her lavender-gray skirt and took another step back, hoping she hadn't offended them. If she'd remembered, she wouldn't have worn a sleeveless dress with a low neckline and would have done something with her hair beyond brushing it. She'd been thinking of going riding in the summer sun, not looking proper in front of a baronial family. "I apologize; I should have been paying more attention."

Baroness Carrick's eyebrows lifted. "Ah, well." Her face relaxed into a small smile. "No harm done."

The baron looked at her appraisingly. "It's good to see a young lady with both beauty and energy. You must have many suitors."

Her cheeks burned. "N-no." She fiddled with her hands. *Why couldn't Minerva be here? She's so much smoother with the nobles.*

"Shall we continue to breakfast?" Baroness Carrick took her husband's arm and headed downstairs.

Nolan's gaze swept over Adelaide, and she combed her fingers through her hair. "You have a unique sense of style, Lady Adelaide."

"Khastallander based—that is, its pattern…my mother." *Stop stammering.* "My mother taught me to sew using Khastallander patterns."

"Well, you look lovely." Nolan chuckled. The grin on his face suggested he thought her stammering indicated his attentions pleasantly flustered her. If anything, she felt the opposite. He offered her his arm. She didn't want to accept, but she wouldn't be impolite to her hosts' guest and a baron's son.

They followed his parents. A servant directed them to the smaller dining hall, used for the Drummond family's private meals. Lord and Lady Drummond and Mother were already in the hall, but not yet seated. Gaius and Minerva entered after them. Once the baron and baroness had taken their seats, Lord and Lady Drummond sat down. Nolan pulled out a chair for Adelaide and sat next to her. *Grand.*

Lord Drummond, Baron Carrick, and Gaius jumped into a discussion about rumors of goblins spotted at the distant Vanelt-Monparth border. Lady Drummond pulled Mother, Minerva, and the baroness into discussing newborns while servants carried in trays of place settings and delicious-smelling food.

"I had hoped to speak more with you last night, but you always seemed to be otherwise engaged," Nolan said quietly. "I must have seemed a cad for interrupting your conversation with Lord Hargreaves and didn't want to repeat my offense. But I assure you, I acted out of concern."

Adelaide watched a maid pour water into her goblet. "Sir Carrick—"

"Nolan, please. I much prefer it." He gave her a saccharine smile.

"Sir Nolan," she amended, hoping this compromise would keep him distant but placated, "has Lord Hargreaves done something to offend you?"

"Other than claiming a title he doesn't deserve and running innocent, noble ladies out of Monparth—assuming they are even still alive—no, I suppose not." He turned toward her as he piled eggs and roast duck on his plate. His knee bumped hers under the table and she twisted her legs away. "But I wish to talk about you, Adelaide." His voice dipped as he spoke her name, becoming low and husky.

She gulped down water. "There isn't much to me." *Not much I can or want to tell you, anyway.* She spread jam over a piece of toast, wishing Minerva wasn't focused on Baroness Carrick.

"Oh, that seems unlikely." A touch at her shoulder startled her. Nolan trailed his fingertips down her arm with a sly grin.

"Don't," Adelaide whispered, her thoughts snapping to the blades hidden in her boots. *My bare skin is not an invitation.*

"Sorry." He pulled his hand away, looking sheepish. "I got carried away. You're hard to resist."

She took an unladylike, large bite of toast she hoped would discourage further conversation, at least until the uncomfortable feeling in her stomach faded. She turned her attention to the other conversations at the table.

"The Black Knight has been spotted again," Gaius said. "Near the eastern marshes, according to Sir Tobias."

Adelaide swallowed her toast. "Who's the Black Knight?"

All four men looked at her.

"Who's the Black Knight?" Gaius lowered his fork, his raised eyebrows pinched together. "What do you mean, who's the Black Knight?"

Lady Drummond clicked her tongue, looking uncomfortable. "Gaius, dear, this is hardly a topic of conversation for gentle young ladies."

Baroness Carrick chuckled. "Young ladies love stories of terrifying monsters. It gives them a reason to seek comfort from a strong young knight." Her eyes danced as she glanced between Adelaide and Nolan.

Adelaide ignored her insinuation. "So is the Black Knight a monster or a man?"

Lord Drummond tapped his fingers on the table. "The Black Knight is a legend. Nothing more."

Gaius rolled his eyes. "He's real, I'm sure of it. Sure, no one can prove he exists, but enough people claim to have seen him he must be real. It's this knight dressed in all-black armor, from his helm to his greaves. Hulking armor with horns on his helm." His voice was eager. "He's tall as an ogre, strong as a troll, quick as a nymph and deadly as a viper. He shows up in different places, slaying monsters and killing anyone who gets in his way. It's said he can't be defeated."

"Gaius thinks he's a hero of old legend, come back to life," Minerva said with a laugh. "Here to rid the world of monsters."

"That's ridiculous." Nolan reached for his goblet. "If a hero of legend came back to life, they wouldn't parade about looking like demon spawn."

Gaius raised a brow. "I have a bet with Flynn Greensburg. I think the Black Knight's a hero. Flynn thinks he's a malicious spirit that kills for fun. Hunts down magical creatures for the thrill of the fight."

"What of the rumors he's told people he serves a Prince of Shadow and Ash?" the baron asked. "That hardly sounds heroic."

"Peasants," Gaius said with a dismissive wave. "Probably made it up."

Adelaide placed a piece of fish on her plate. "And how will either of you win this bet?"

"If the Black Knight is real, eventually someone will see something or talk to him even." Gaius shrugged. "Or he'll go berserk and start killing everything and then Flynn will be right."

Adelaide shuddered, but Baron Carrick laughed. "I think your friend has the better odds," the baron said, "although I certainly hope he's wrong."

Adelaide tried to picture this hulking knight in black armor wearing a helm with horns. "Has anyone seen him in Thaera?" She shouldn't want someone or something so menacing to be in the duchy she herself was in, but she couldn't help her curiosity.

"Not just in Thaera Duchy, but in Etchy Barony." The baron's countenance darkened. "I don't like these rumors. They make my people uneasy."

The Drummonds lived within the Carrick's barony. That was uncomfortably close. Nolan patted her thigh under the table. "Don't worry. You're perfectly safe."

She shifted farther away from him and focused on her breakfast. *Safe from the Black Knight? Or safe from you?*

Thankfully, the Carricks left after breakfast. Adelaide forgot all about Nolan Carrick until a messenger arrived with a letter addressed to her two days later. She worked a knife under the gryphon-stamped wax seal and eased the letter open, considering tossing it without reading. Mother and Minerva watched from across the drawing room while a small fire popped in the fireplace and cloudy afternoon sunlight angled across the wood paneled floor. A pressed navy-blue flower fell out of the letter onto her lap.

> *Dear Lady Adelaide Belanger,*
>
> *I greatly enjoyed spending even such a brief time in your presence. I hope soon to have the opportunity to get to know you more intimately. Until then, accept this flower as a token of my regard—a dark and lovely bloom that, I fear, cannot come close to equaling your beauty.*
>
> *Affectionately,*
> *Sir Nolan Carrick*

"Etiros spare me." Adelaide rolled her eyes.

"What does it say?" Minerva asked.

Adelaide scowled at the letter, resisting the urge to ignite it in her hand. "I am a dark and lovely flower, and Sir Nolan Carrick wishes to know me more"—her upper lip curled in distaste—"intimately."

Mother huffed and muttered something under her breath in Khast about daggers and pretentious boys' faces. Minerva chided Mother while Adelaide laughed and tossed the letter and flower into the fireplace. Later that afternoon, another letter arrived, this one addressed to both Mother and Adelaide. Mother showed the wax seal, imprinted with a rose over crossed swords, to Minerva.

"Do you recognize this?"

Minerva frowned. "It's vaguely familiar. I'm not sure."

Adelaide snatched away the letter, opened it, and read it aloud—which she immediately regretted.

Dear Ladies Tamina and Adelaide Belanger,

I was honored to make your acquaintance. I wish to apologize for abandoning the festivities early and assure you I meant no disrespect. I hope our paths will cross again—preferably when other duties do not draw me away prematurely from the pleasure of your company.

Sincerely yours,

Lord Regulus Hargreaves of Arrano

Adelaide blushed when Mother frowned and said, "Who is Lord Hargreaves?" The letter was addressed to both of them, but it was obvious its message was for Adelaide. She wanted to respond, but Mother wouldn't hear of it.

"It's acceptable for him to apologize for an impolite exit," Mother said. "But you are a lady and will not write a man letters unless he is formally courting you."

That only made Adelaide more embarrassed. As if she could think about courting him after one conversation. But that night, as she thought about Regulus Hargreaves' note and the look in his gray eyes as he talked about his favorite sound…she wondered what it would be like to court him.

Over the next days, Adelaide perfected the art of avoiding Lady Drummond and her tapestry. Gaius got ahead of her in checkers, but she had her revenge and regained the lead. Mother thought their rivalry had grown out of control and wasn't very lady-like, and Lady Drummond agreed. Adelaide didn't care. Gaius felt like the brother she had never had, and she *did* have two half-brothers. But neither of them had ever had much interest in her.

When it came time for Mother to leave, Adelaide couldn't believe they had already been at the Drummonds for nearly three weeks. Minerva tried to talk her into staying longer, but Mother said she missed Father, and needed to get back so she could resume overseeing the household. As previously agreed, Adelaide would stay to support Minerva through the pregnancy.

The day after Mother left, the Drummonds and Adelaide received invitations to a dance to be hosted in a week's time by Baron and Baroness Carrick. It would be quite the affair—supper, entertainment, dancing, and a grand breakfast for all attendees who stayed the night. Lady Drummond declared they would most certainly stay the night.

Adelaide didn't share Lord and Lady Drummond's enthusiasm over the invitation. Something about Nolan Carrick made her uncomfortable. Beyond his rude attitude toward Lord Hargreaves, even beyond his uninvited touches. *Trust your woman's intuition*, Mother always said. Well, her intuition said not to trust Nolan Carrick. She put the invitation on her vanity and stared at it, wishing she could decline. But it would be unthinkable to refuse a higher-ranking noble's invitation without the excuse of another engagement.

Hmmm. Adelaide smiled to herself. *Which means Lord Hargreaves will likely be there.* Her mood lightened. If she could talk to Lord Hargreaves, maybe get a chance to satisfy her curiosity and learn some of the truth about him… She could endure an evening with a smug, spoiled show-off like Nolan Carrick. She stared at the quill and ink pot on the back of the vanity. Her fingers twitched. *Mother will never know.* She smiled to herself as she penned a quick note.

She sealed the letter and set it aside. Her gaze moved to the stack of books she had borrowed from Lord Drummond's library. Right now, she had more important things to occupy her thoughts than men. Mother had left. Adelaide had locked the door to her room. Her maid Giselle was out doing laundry and wouldn't be back for a while. Adelaide sorted through the books. *A History of Monparth, Part III. Saint Kardeman's Bestiary and Herbal. The Life of King Saewyne the Magnificent.* All interesting titles, but not what she wanted just now.

She pulled out a volume whose dark leather binding displayed cracks from getting dried out and leaned forward in her seat in front of the vanity. The pages crinkled as she opened it. *Careful. Don't break it!* She ran her index finger over the title on the first page. *A Compendium of Known Magical Abilities and Tales of Mages of Legend.* No author was listed.

She could imagine Mother's disapproving voice as she began reading. *"You don't want to make yourself a target."* Well, if simple farmers and even children weren't spared, her level of knowledge wasn't the issue. And if whatever dark force was behind The Shadow came after her, she would need more than knives to defend herself. She took a deep breath and turned the page to a list of subjects, broken down by category: light, fire, horticulture, healing, combat, bindings, and storing magic in objects.

"In the beginning, Etiros imbued all living things with magic." Adelaide skimmed the preface. Generalities on magic being a pure form of energy that Etiros used to give life, but that an excess of this energy in a person resulted in a mage. It said magic could be *"corrupted into sorcery by malicious intent or when used to take instead of give."*

It also gave a sobering warning; one her parents had never given. *"Because magic is inextricably tied to a living thing's life energy, use of magic wearies the mage. Over-exertion of magical ability can cause long periods of slumber, fainting, and on occasion, death."* Adelaide couldn't imagine the desperation a mage would have to feel to push their abilities so far they killed themselves. She hurried on.

Each category in the *Compendium* started with basic, boring abilities. Although, stories of mages forming a free-floating source of light, erecting a solid barrier, and maintaining a constant heat of flame in a furnace were interesting.

Mages supposedly could force plants to grow faster and fruit to ripen, and calm animals. She marveled at descriptions of mages healing broken bones, curing illnesses, and a rumor a mage had reattached a severed limb. Adelaide had figured out basic healing early, as receiving your first dagger at age five resulted in many cuts. If only the *Compendium* explained *how* to do all these things. She fanned through the pages.

An illustration caught her eye, and she flipped back. A man held a gigantic white sword that appeared to be emitting flames. She looked at the facing page and read under her breath.

"Substantive magic. Subset: Conjure weapons of light and flame.

"Mages can shape the light they produce to form a weapon which, while composed entirely of light and sometimes of flame, is none-the-less material…"

Adelaide looked up and stared at her reflection in the vanity mirror. "Form a weapon of solid light. I can do that?"

The rest of the entry detailed the history of the technique and variations on weapon types. No instructions, other than "shape the light they produce." She slumped back in her chair.

"Maybe if I just concentrate…" She stood and moved away from the vanity. The curtains were drawn, no one would see. She raised her hand, palm up, and let the tingle of energy flow to her hand. A soft sphere of periwinkle-tinted light ignited above her outstretched palm. It had taken months of secret practice to form that sphere, instead of releasing a burst of flame. She stared at the sphere, willing it to become a sword. Nothing.

Okay…start smaller. A dagger?

Her mind ached from the concentration. The sphere elongated, became rectangular, then narrowed. "Yes!" She grinned, and the rectangle of pale blue light vanished like water from a burst skin. "No." She rubbed her forehead and rolled her shoulders back. *Come on. You can do it.*

Once again, she conjured the light and focused on shaping it. She practiced for over an hour. Finally, the light took the shape of a crude dagger. A plain, round hilt as long as her palm was wide, attached to a long, thin blade. It looked soft around the edges, but the center appeared solid.

Her pulse racing, she reached for the handle. *The moment of truth.* Her fingers closed around the hilt—

Knocking echoed from the door, and Adelaide jumped. The dagger vanished. She threw her head back and groaned. *No! I was so close!* She placed the *Compendium* back under the other books and unlocked the door.

Giselle walked in carrying a basket of clean clothes. "Everything all right, m'lady?"

"Of course. Just doing some reading."

THE DAY was cloudy but warm, and the smell of earth and new leaves and grass filled the air. Regulus adjusted his back against the tree trunk. Above him, the oak leaves stood out bright green against the pale gray clouds.

"If I were you, I'd call on her." Jerrick slouched against the rail fence encircling the archery range behind the castle and bit into another bread roll. A dull thunk sounded as Dresden threw another knife at the archery target.

Originally from Bhitra, Jerrick Faras' accent made his vowels sound long and his consonants hard. He was about average height and muscular and could wield a battle-axe with deadly precision. His short black hair clung to his head in tight curls. He favored brightly dyed fabrics because of how well they contrasted with his dark skin. Today he wore a yellow tunic Regulus would never dream of attempting to wear.

"Call on her?"

"Yes," Jerrick said around a mouthful of bread. "Go visit her at the Drummonds' like a man."

"That's what I've been telling him!" Dresden threw his hands up in exasperation. He stood on the other side of the fence, inside the archery range. He didn't have his bow today, though, just the knives stuck in the top rail of the fence. "I told you, she wants to talk to you!"

"Because you lied to her. I didn't ask you to say anything. I didn't even speak to you before I left!"

"Ah, but was I wrong?" Dresden pulled another throwing knife out of the top rail of the fence. "You enjoyed your conversation and regretted leaving early. That's not a lie. And she *likes* you. I'm sure of it. So do something."

"I sent her that letter you forced me to write." Regulus pulled at a handful of grass.

Dresden rolled his eyes. "Which you also addressed to her mother like a dunce."

Regulus threw the grass over the fence at Drez, his irritation rising. What did it matter? Romance wasn't his lot in life. Servitude was.

"Drez knows what he's talking about," Jerrick said. "I'd know. *I* have a wife."

"See?" Dresden slapped Jerrick's shoulder and turned back toward the canvas-covered wooden target. He threw the knife in a swift motion, and it buried at the edge of the red center of the target near three other knives.

Regulus nodded at Dresden's target. "I see Estevan's lessons are paying off."

"Yes, just don't tell him that. He already walks with enough of a swagger." Drez pulled out another knife and shook it at Regulus. "But you're trying to change the subject. Do what Jerrick would do."

"If I recall, Jerrick, your courtship, for lack of a better term, consisted of you claiming you visited the same baker every day because he had the best bread you'd ever tasted when you were actually trying to seduce his daughter." Regulus grinned, propped his hands behind his head, and leaned back against the oak trunk.

"Hey." Jerrick pointed at Regulus, still holding a half-eaten roll. "He did have the best bread. He also had the most beautiful daughter. Now I have the best wife *and* the best bread." He bit into the roll and wagged his finger at Regulus. "Don't underestimate the power of freshly baked bread."

"There you go." Dresden spread out his hands. "Send her Sarah's rolls. You'll win her heart in no time."

"Let's not get ahead of ourselves." *Although, sending Adelaide some nalotavi might not be the worst idea.* He swatted a beetle off his pant leg. *No, sending her anything is a bad idea.* "We barely spoke."

"And yet you can't stop thinking about her," Drez teased.

Regulus closed his eyes, picturing Adelaide's brown eyes, her soft-looking dark hair. The way she smiled at him. He remembered Nolan Carrick, standing close to her, his hand on her back... He opened his eyes. "So? I'm sure she's forgotten all about me."

"Well, you haven't done much to keep yourself in her thoughts," Jerrick said. "It's been two weeks since the letter. At this point, sending her rolls *would* be an improvement."

Footsteps from the opposite side of the garden drew Regulus' attention away from Jerrick. Perceval Williamson clomped toward them, scowling. He was older than Regulus by a few years, and his repeatedly broken nose had odd bumps. Perceval must have been working the fields around his and Leonora's cottage again, because his face sported a light sunburn under his short, stiff brown hair.

Regulus stood. "What's happened?"

"You've been snubbed, Captain." Despite no longer being mercenaries, and despite the fact he'd asked his friends to call him Regulus, Perceval still insisted on calling him Captain. Perceval waved a folded letter. "The Carricks are hosting a party next week, and it doesn't seem you're invited."

"Etiros above, I thought we might have a problem on our borders or something serious." Regulus shrugged. "So? The Carricks never invite me. Carrick's a baron, he can choose not to invite a lesser noble. Besides, I hate parties."

"True." Perceval grinned, his eyebrows lifting like he had a secret. "But those parties usually don't have a certain dark-haired lady in attendance."

"Adelaide will be there?" Regulus regretted how eager he sounded as Drez smirked. He reached over the fence and smacked the back of Dresden's head.

"Indeed." Perceval handed Regulus the letter. *Lord Regulus Hargreaves of Arrano* was written across the front in curling script.

"I thought you said I *wasn't* invited?" Regulus flipped it over and sighed when he saw the broken seal. "Is it so hard for you all not to read my personal correspondence?"

"Didn't recognize the seal," Perceval grunted. "Precautionary measure."

"What can a letter do to me, Perce?" Regulus eyed the rearing unicorn impressed on the torn red wax. He didn't recognize it, either. He unfolded the parchment.

> *Dear Lord Regulus Hargreaves,*
>
> *I apologize I did not write sooner. I hope you don't think I bear you any ill-will for needing to leave early, although I wish you'd said goodbye. I hope to continue our conversation at Baron Carrick's party. I do hope you'll stay longer. Perhaps I can discover if you are as good a dancer as you are a conversationalist.*
>
> *Signed,*
>
> *Lady Adelaide Belanger*

Regulus' heart about stopped. As he reread the letter, his emotions jumped from elated to defeated. Adelaide wanted to see him again. She wanted to talk to him. She wanted to *dance* with him. But he had received no invite. He stared at the gentle curves of her signature. *Wait.* He jerked his head up and glared at Perceval. "You read this?"

Perceval held up his hands. "How was I supposed to know it was from Lady Belanger?"

"Wait, what?" Dresden leaned over the fence, trying to read the note. Regulus shoved the letter into his belt.

"Lady Belanger wants to dance with the Captain," Perceval said with a chuckle.

Regulus' face heated. "It doesn't matter. I can't show up uninvited." *And she'll realize what a poor choice I am when she knows I wasn't invited.*

"Can't you though?" Perceval grinned, a manic light behind his eyes. "It's so fun to rile the nobles. You should have seen the look on my father's face when I showed up to a supper party drunk."

"And to think you didn't do well at university," Jerrick said with mock amazement.

"No," Dresden said, turning the throwing knife over in his hand thoughtfully. "But, when the Carricks host a party, the other nobles feel they have to reciprocate. You should get invited to at least a couple of those parties. This is excellent. Oh, you'll get another chance to woo the lovely Adelaide."

"I'm not going to woo her, Drez."

"Then by Hallilek"—Jerrick invoked the Bhitran deity with a perplexed expression—"why are we having this conversation?"

Dresden leaned his hip against the fence. "And why not?"

"You know why not." *Because I'm a monster.*

Jerrick and Perceval shifted and glanced at each other.

"We talked about this, Reg," Drez said quietly. "Perce, Jerrick, back me up. He can't hide here forever."

Perceval grunted. "You need a wife."

"Might give you something to look forward to," Jerrick said. "Make life more bearable."

"Or someone else to hurt." Regulus shook his head. "I shouldn't have written that letter."

"Then why'd you do it?" Dresden snapped.

Regulus poked his finger in a knot in the fence and avoided Dresden's intense regard. *Because I like her; because I wanted to. Because she said she didn't care about my bastardy. Because, for a moment, I pretended I was normal, and it felt good.* "Moment of weakness."

"Doing something because it brings you joy isn't weakness." Drez sighed and scratched his beard. "It was one time. The sorcerer controlled you once in two years. And you know how to avoid it happening again."

Regulus snorted. *If only you knew.* "One time, but I still almost—" He stopped as the mark on his right arm tingled, like the gentlest touch of the points of a thousand needles. He grabbed his arm and grimaced.

"The mark?" Dresden murmured.

Regulus nodded. His men watched him leave in silence. There was nothing to say; nothing they could do. Nothing that wouldn't make things worse, anyway. Up in his room, Regulus unlocked the chest that housed the black suit of armor and a bronze mirror. The rectangular mirror was just larger than Regulus' head, with a plain frame. He hesitated before he picked it up and placed it on a nail on the wall.

"I'm here, my lord."

The mirror shimmered and an image of the sorcerer replaced the burnished surface. "Excellent." Deep shadows hid the sorcerer's eyes beneath his ever-present hood. "I need you to go to the Singing Caves. There's a cave marked by a white elm with golden leaves. Enter it and retrieve a relic from the dragon's horde."

"The what?" Regulus gaped at the sorcerer.

"The dragon, the dragon!" The sorcerer waved his hands. "Kill the dragon if necessary, find the relic it is guarding, and bring it to me."

Regulus massaged his temples. An actual dragon? "But—"

Pain sliced up his arm from the mark.

"Question," he gasped. "Not—defiance." The pain vanished. "Don't dragons usually have piles of treasure, my lord? How will I recognize the relic?"

The sorcerer harrumphed. "It will be separate from the other treasures, perhaps even displayed in a difficult-to-reach area. And, it looks like this." He held a parchment in front of the mirror. A drawing of what looked like a hollow oval composed of thick wire swirling into a rounded point at each end filled the mirror. The sorcerer waited a moment, then pulled the drawing away. "It shouldn't be hard to find, if you have half a brain."

Regulus' shoulders tensed as he tried to hide his indignation. He could not afford to anger the sorcerer with his men so close. "Anything else I should know?"

"Just that it's powerful, so if you let that dragon destroy it, I'll destroy you. And I want it quickly. It will take you a couple days to ride to the Caves. Best leave now." The image shimmered and reverted to a dull mirror. Regulus' hazy reflection stared back. Judging him.

A powerful relic guarded by a dragon sounded ominous. Evil. Giving the sorcerer more power seemed a mistake. But what else could he do? *I can't resist him.* Regulus rubbed the mark through his sleeve. *I've tried.*

He sank onto his bed and pulled out Adelaide's letter. He touched her signature and let himself imagine dancing with her, holding her. It was flattering she thought he would be invited. Would she mind that he wasn't? He looked up at the mirror. It didn't matter. No woman deserved a sorcerer's slave. Regulus' heart clenched as he ripped the letter in half.

CHAPTER 9

ADELAIDE LEANED out of the carriage window as they approached the Carrick's massive castle. Fading daylight cast an orange glow over the long, wide drive lined with chestnut trees and filled with other carriages and riders. The deep, crenelated wall encompassing the castle, extensive gardens, and courtyards stood three stories tall. Towers emerged above the wall about every fifty paces. The bottom of a portcullis peeked out of the archway above the towering iron-covered front gates. A water fountain depicting a mermaid holding a giant shell over her head dominated the courtyard.

The castle itself was four stories tall and square, with large, round five-story-tall towers at each corner. Crenellations wrapped around the entirety of the castle. Pale limestone formed the edifice, including the gargoyles and grotesques depicting mythical creatures spaced along the top of the castle. Not for nothing were the Carricks known as the wealthiest baronial family in Monparth. Rumor had it their wealth approached that of the ducal families.

Carriages, horses, and servants filled the courtyard. The sound of creaking carriages, hoof-beats, neighs, bubbling water, and chatter echoed against the walls of the castle. Smoke from the myriad of torches arranged around the courtyard wafted in the air. A servant greeted their party, directing others to see to their mounts and baggage. Adelaide turned around, wide-eyed, taking in everything. And she thought Father's castle was impressive. Minerva shook Adelaide's shoulder, diverting her attention from the displays of power. They were being escorted inside.

Inside was just as grand. The foyer sported vaulted ceilings and brightly colored tapestries covered stone walls. Coats of armor and bronze statues stood guard in the halls. A marble statue of an embracing woman and man on the brink of sharing a kiss stood on a large limestone pedestal in the center of the foyer. Adelaide slowed to a stop, marveling at the intricate detail on their simple, draping clothes. They even had fingernails.

"It's a beautiful piece," a male voice said near her shoulder. Adelaide jumped and turned toward the speaker. Nolan simpered. "Apologies. I didn't mean to startle you, Lady Adelaide."

"Sir Carrick." She smiled and curtsied, but her pulse hammered behind her temple.

"I thought we had agreed on Nolan?" He looked up at the statue. "My father acquired this when he was fighting in the Trade War. I understand your father won a good deal of his fortune in that conflict."

"Yes." Adelaide fixed her gaze on the marble curls of the woman's hair. "King Olfan was generous in rewarding his bravery." She hated when people made it sound like her father was a mere robber warrior, even if war spoils had added to his wealth.

"He met your mother while in Carasom, is that correct?"

"Yes. She was traveling with her father." Adelaide braced herself for the inevitable casual judgment of her mother's non-noble lineage.

"She must have made quite an impression. You take after her—impossible to ignore."

Wait…what? She glanced sideways at Nolan. His mouth curved up in a slight smile and his eyes glinted as his gaze wandered over her. Her cheeks flushed, and she looked back to the statue.

Nolan laughed. "Don't be shy." He gestured to the statue. "Beautiful things are meant to be admired."

"Pardon me, Sir Carrick." Adelaide was relieved to hear Lady Drummond's voice. "But I'm afraid I must steal Lady Belanger. We were just on our way to our quarters."

"Ah, forgive me." Nolan bowed and swept up Adelaide's hand, brushing a kiss against her fingers. He smiled as he released her hand. "I look forward to seeing you at supper."

As they followed a maid down the hall, Lady Drummond smiled conspiratorially. "I believe Sir Nolan has it in mind to court you, dear girl. Lucky you!"

"Yes," Adelaide murmured. "Lucky me."

They had just enough time to get dressed and freshen their hair before heading down for the banquet. Adelaide wore a light blue dress with fitted sleeves under a sleeveless silk overdress of dark blue, comprised of two long pieces of fabric sewn together at her shoulders and laced together at her sides with a thick crimson satin cord. A braided crimson and gold belt tied in front, the long tails hanging down almost to the bottom of the dress. A single teardrop-shaped sapphire hung on the end of her thin gold necklace. The outfit had been a gift from Lady Drummond, made for Adelaide expressly for the Carrick's party.

She could only guess Lady Drummond worried she would choose something too Khastallander and embarrass the Drummonds.

As the guests entered the great hall, servants showed them to their seats. To Adelaide's confusion, a page beckoned her in a different direction than her sister and Lady Drummond. "Pardon me, are we headed the right direction?"

The boy looked over his shoulder. "Yes, my lady. This way, my lady." They walked toward the head of the hall.

"I think you may have me confused with someone else. Lady Adelaide Belanger. I'm here with my sister, Lady Minerva Drummond, and the Drummonds?" She looked around for them, spotting them moving to their seats at a long table on the side of the hall. "I think a mistake has been made—"

"No mistake, Lady Adelaide." Nolan flashed a cavalier smile as he walked up beside her. "You are seated next to me."

Adelaide blinked, trying to hide her surprise. Nolan had changed as well. He now wore a royal blue knee-length tunic lined with crimson and pale blue stockings. A sword hung at his hip from an intricately engraved leather belt with a gold buckle. A gold brooch of a gryphon, the symbol of the Carrick family, secured a blue half cape to his right shoulder. He offered her his arm.

"Wonderful," she managed. Gingerly, she tucked her hand in the crook of his elbow. Only when she glanced down did the truth hit her. They were dressed to match. Too much so to be a coincidence. Heat rushed to her ears. *I could slap Lady Drummond! When did she tell him what I was wearing?* If Adelaide had known, she would have worn tomorrow's traveling dress. Now she stood in a room full of nobles, her clothing screaming *I am courting Nolan Carrick* against her will.

"You are breathtaking." Nolan's voice was low, personal.

Somehow, she managed to respond. "Thank you, Sir Nolan." *Be polite. Return the compliment.* "You look handsome yourself." It wasn't untrue. He did look fetching. But she couldn't seem to relax around him. *It's just nerves. I've never had a proper suitor.*

"Well, Sir Nolan is an improvement over Sir Carrick, so I'll take it." He winked.

Nolan led her to a seat at the table below the dais. Food already covered the table on the dais like all the others, but the four chairs behind it were empty. Nolan pulled out a chair at the lower table for her, and Adelaide sat down, aware of the many eyes around the room watching her. She wondered how much of the low hum of conversation was about her. She searched the crowd for Minerva. Even a quick smile from her sister would calm her nerves. Unfortunately, Min sat with her back toward Adelaide, and she was deep in conversation with Lady Drummond.

"I knew blue and crimson would suit you." Nolan sat next to her. "I hope finding the fabric wasn't too much trouble."

"What? You requested this?"

He frowned. "Yes… And you…accepted?"

"No. I had no idea."

They stared at each other. Nolan cleared his throat. "I sent a messenger to the Drummonds, asking you to wear these colors. The messenger said you'd accepted."

"Lady Drummond must have accepted on my behalf," Adelaide said flatly. She fiddled with her silver utensils as anger heated her skin. "And didn't tell me."

"I'm sorry." He sounded genuine. "Do you…mind, though?"

She stared at the ceramic plate and silver goblet in front of her. "I was unprepared," she said carefully. She didn't want to make this evening too miserable. *Please let supper start soon.*

Adelaide surveyed the room. Nobles were still entering and being seated. So far, no sign of Lord Regulus Hargreaves. *He's quite tall, you'd think he would be easy to spot.* The influx of guests slowed, but even as her disappointment grew, she felt relieved he wasn't there. She didn't want him to see her with Nolan like…this.

A servant showed a man to the empty seat on her other side. The woman next to him must have recognized him, because they struck up a conversation.

Nolan's warm hand covered hers. "Will you attend the tournament next month?"

"Tournament?" She smoothed her skirts as an excuse to remove her hand from under his.

Disappointment flickered over Nolan's face, but his usual self-assured smile returned. "Yes, the Etchy Tournament? My father hosts it every year."

She forced herself to look at him, to be polite. "Will you be competing?"

"Oh, of course!" He reached over and brushed a strand of hair behind her ear. She managed not to grimace. "I was rather hoping I could compete in your honor."

Her cheeks flushed as panic crippled her mind. "I…um…" A trumpet flare mercifully interrupted, and silence fell over the room.

Baron and Baroness Carrick entered, followed by a man who was clearly Carrick's eldest son and a woman who seemed to be his wife. They moved to their seats, and the baron welcomed the guests and sat down.

Cupbearers moved among the tables bearing large containers of wine. A group of minstrels entered and played in a corner. A juggler and two acrobats leapt into the open area in the middle of the hall. Adelaide had never been so thankful for the distraction of entertainment and the excuse of food to avoid conversation. The nobleman to her right, Sir Morris MacCombe, son of Baron MacCombe, was friendly. Their conversation, while comprised of standard supper party small talk, was amiable. MacCombe, in fact, seemed eager to engage her. Nolan and MacCombe never acknowledged each other, at times outright ignoring each other when the conversation could have included both. It made her even more uncomfortable, but at least MacCombe was kind and didn't flirt with or touch her.

Part of her felt foolish and guilty. Nolan was handsome, with his silky chestnut hair, merry blue eyes, and square jaw. He came from a wealthy, powerful, and respected family. A small part of her relished the flattering attention, the knowledge that many young noblewomen would swoon for Nolan. However, he had done nothing so far to impress her, to set him apart from any other young nobleman with too much time and money. Besides, she had always fancied taller men, like Regulus Hargreaves. The ease of the thought surprised her, and she choked on a sip of wine.

"Are you all right?" Nolan asked.

"Oh, yes." She dabbed her mouth with a cloth napkin. Her tongue seemed to get ahead of her brain. "I notice Lord Hargreaves is not in attendance."

"The mercenary?" Nolan rolled his eyes. "Of course not."

Adelaide looked at him, her brow furrowed. "I understand he used to be a mercenary, but he is a nobleman now, isn't he?"

"He's a petty lord of little account. And the only reason he's a noble at all is because his philandering father was so taken with his peasant mother he added their mongrel son to his will. Arrano even buried her under a statue of an angel. Disgraceful." He plopped a grape in his mouth.

"You're saying Lord Hargreaves wasn't invited?" Her heart twisted. *Oh, no. My letter…* She felt horrible she'd assumed and hoped Regulus hadn't taken it as an insult.

Nolan cocked an eyebrow. "Why should the Baron and Baroness Carrick invite the son of a washing wench into their home?"

She stared at him as she clenched her fork in a white-knuckled fist. "That's unfair and uncalled for."

He shifted and glanced about. "I'm sorry. Some people are best avoided, and Hargreaves is the worst of them. He may hold the title of lord, but it's not who he is. He could have been knighted, but he took off and became a mercenary. Mercenaries are not men of honor. Hargreaves only left the life because he inherited Arrano's land and title. He likely killed Lady Arrano and her daughter-in-law. Then he had the audacity to knight his mercenaries. Three of them aren't even Monparthian."

"Have something against non-Monparthians?" A hard edge crept into her voice.

Nolan reddened. "No, of course not." He cleared his throat. "Hargreaves keeps mostly to himself and often disappears alone for unknown reasons. But I have a theory: once a mercenary, always a mercenary. I suspect he misses the life and runs off to satiate his blood-lust." He rested his hand on her arm and looked into her eyes. "Hargreaves is not to be trusted. I advise you keep your distance, for your own safety."

"I can take care of myself." She looked away. "Can you prove all this?"

"Unfortunately, no. But a knight's intuition is never wrong."

Adelaide stifled a snicker. It hardly seemed chivalrous to be hasty in judgment. But perhaps she was doing the same with Nolan. *No. He has proven himself to be prejudiced, condescending, and a flirt.*

"But enough of such talk." Nolan grabbed his goblet. "It's a party, after all."

Adelaide stared past the acrobats, wishing Minerva would turn around. This party couldn't end soon enough.

ADELAIDE DID her best to try at least a bite of each course, but her appetite had vanished. She couldn't decide which bothered her more: the idea of Regulus Hargreaves being a blood-thirsty, self-serving villain, or Nolan Carrick's crass haughtiness. She had difficulty reconciling the kind laughter, easy conversation, and apparent humility she had seen in Regulus with the murderer Nolan described. And yet... What did a person truly know about another after one brief conversation?

Nothing.

She would have given anything to retire after supper, but her parents had raised her to be decorous and respectful, and leaving before dancing would be insulting to the Carricks.

Nolan wasted no time asking her to dance. As the lute players and pipers began to play, they joined other couples in a stately dance. The way Nolan's piercing gaze did not leave her face made her far more uncomfortable than his warm fingertips underneath hers. Every time the steps of the dance dictated that they part or turn away from each other was a short reprieve from his intense and undesired attentions. The dance ended, and she curtsied as best she could with Nolan's fingers still curled under her own. He bowed, bringing her fingers to his lips, his eyes fixed on hers.

The air in the room was far too hot. Adelaide forced a smile and inclined her head. "Thank you for the dance, Sir Nolan. I fear I need to sit down for a while."

"You're not feeling unwell, I hope? The night has scarcely begun." He rubbed his thumb over her knuckles.

Perhaps she was projecting her own urgent desire to escape, but she thought she detected a hint of panic in his words. She shifted and pulled her hand away. "Just...a little lightheaded."

"I'm sorry to hear that." Nolan moved to her side, wrapping an arm around her shoulders.

This is the opposite of what I wanted!

"Here." He guided her to some chairs near the wall. "Wait right here. I'd like to introduce you to my brother."

"Oh—" But Nolan darted away before she could protest. He returned a couple minutes later with his brother. The elder Carrick was just shorter than Nolan, with similar light brown hair and blue eyes. He sported a neatly trimmed mustache.

"Lady Adelaide, this is my eldest brother, William. Will, this is Adelaide."

William bowed and Adelaide moved to stand and curtsy, but William held up his hand. "Please, sit. I understand you're not feeling well."

She shifted. "I needed a moment to breathe and cool down."

The corner of William's mouth twitched. "Yes, Nolan can have that effect."

She rubbed the side of her neck, unsure what to say, since *I'm not all warm and breathless over your brother's charms* seemed a bit…antagonistic and forward. "Don't you have another brother?" she asked, desperate to change the subject.

"Yes, Michael," Nolan said. His eyes narrowed.

William clasped his hands behind his back. "Michael married Baron MacCombe's daughter, Elaine, a few years ago. They live in a castle along the Monparth-Carasom border that Baron MacCombe gave them."

"How generous." Adelaide slipped into the small talk expected at these gatherings. "I spoke with Sir Morris MacCombe over supper. He was friendly."

Nolan's jaw tightened. "Yes, well, he's likely to announce an engagement to Duke Randall's daughter Elizabeth soon." The irritation in his voice was unmistakable, but the cause baffled Adelaide. *Is he irritated MacCombe was friendly to me, or irritated he's marrying Elizabeth Randall?*

William cast a sidelong glance at his brother, but his expression remained serene. "Elizabeth is my wife's sister. But Sir Morris and Nolan had a bit of a…quarrel last year."

"Bygones." Nolan glared at his brother as Adelaide fidgeted with her skirt so she wouldn't have to look at the brothers.

"Yes, well." William slapped Nolan's back. "Nolan has matured in the last year. He's a bright, talented young man. We expect him to do well at the Etchy Tournament. He marginally lost the joust last year. But I'm not competing this year, so his chances are good." She looked up in surprise at William's teasing tone. Nolan looked like he'd tasted something sour.

"Joking aside," William continued, "I wouldn't place any bets against him. Not that you would gamble, of course. But I fear I have other guests to see." He bowed. "It was an honor and a pleasure to make your acquaintance, Lady Belanger. I expect I'll be seeing you again. Soon and often."

"The honor was mine, Lord Carrick."

William nodded, then turned and ambled away. *Soon and often.* The Carrick family *expected* her to court Nolan. *Perfect.*

Nolan recovered his composure and looked unbothered by his brother's teasing. "Feeling any better?"

"Actually, I'm developing a headache," she lied.

Nolan sat next to her, his forehead wrinkled. "Shall I send for the physician?"

"Oh, no, I think I need to sleep." She stood. "I'll just go to my room—"

"Then I will accompany you," he declared as he stood. "It's a large castle, I'd hate for you to get lost."

She stiffened. "Thank you, but I can find my way on my own. I won't tear you away from your party—"

"Adelaide, please." Nolan placed his hand on her shoulder and stepped in closer. "There is no party with you gone."

She willed herself not to laugh or gag. *Etiros, spare me.*

"*You* are the reason for hosting this event; the only reason I care about this party at all. Please." He looked like a puppy begging for scraps from the table. His hand slid down her arm and he took her hand. "I don't need to dance. Just…sit with me. Stay with me."

How in Monparth was she supposed to respond to *that?* Especially when all she could think about was getting some space to herself?

Nolan took another step closer and placed his free hand on the side of Adelaide's neck. Her heart leapt into her throat. "Don't leave," he breathed. His gaze fell to her lips as his thumb caressed her cheek.

"I…I'm sorry." Adelaide yanked her hand free and made as hasty a departure as possible without sacrificing all decorum.

Once in her room and dressed in her nightgown, she found sleep evaded her, so she paced. Too many thoughts swirled in her mind—most related to the fact every noble at the party would suspect an impending courtship.

She despised Nolan's cockiness and disregard for her personal space. And his vehemence toward Lord Regulus. It didn't seem Nolan had ever even *tried* to get to know Regulus or hear his side of the story. He just hated Regulus because his mother was a peasant. Didn't Regulus deserve a chance to defend himself and his own honor?

As Adelaide paced, her irritation mounted. Her palms warmed as magical energy coursed through her. She needed a distraction. Something to do, something else to focus on. She held her hand out and her palm filled with eggshell-blue light. She focused on the light, drawing it out of her palm and into a tight, dense orb. She expanded the orb, letting it grow until it was as large as her head, but still hovering above her palm.

"Now the real test," she murmured. She raised her palm and concentrated on sending the orb up. A grin spread over her face as the orb floated above her, illuminating the entire room.

But could she do something else now? Walk away? Do other magic, even? She conjured a dagger—a trick she had been practicing every chance she got ever since she first tried it. The solid light dagger now materialized as desired about eighty percent of the time. She gripped the simple dagger in her hand and laughed in delight when the orb stayed in place.

Oh, yes! Her spirits fell as she looked around the empty room. *If only I could share this with someone.*

The first time she hit the bullseye on a target with a throwing knife, she was seven. "That's my little tigress," Mother had said in Khast. Father had kissed her forehead and said he was proud. Minerva and Adelaide then spent the afternoon competing to land more bullseyes. Minerva was only a little disappointed when Adelaide won. But practicing magic? That earned her the opposite reaction. Dread and reprimands instead of pride. Like when she quenched the fire in front of Minerva.

The dagger faded, and the orb flickered out. Adelaide flopped onto the bed and stared at the dark green canopy above her. Keeping secrets made her feel so alone. But did she have a choice?

"It's too dangerous, *Tha Shiraa*," Mother's warning to her at age five had been seared into her mind. "No one knows who or what was behind The Shadow. We don't want them to come for you, too."

The Shadow. Most people didn't talk about the massacre of the mages, but when they did, it was with terrified reverence. Mages had never been abundant in Monparth, but Father said mages once did everything from farming to working as healers to leading warriors in battle.

Then mages started turning up dead. Murdered. Killed in their sleep. An arrow through their neck as they went about their daily tasks. Poisoned in their own homes. Some were found dead with no visible cause. Within weeks, every single mage within Monparth, from infants to the elderly, was dead.

Initially, some had thought the killings ordered by King Olfan, the current king's father, to prevent sorcerers. Olfan's eldest son had been a mage, but Monparthian law forbade mages from inheriting the throne. Too much power for one individual, too much risk of a mage becoming a sorcerer—and the history of sorcerer-kings was written in blood. The prince had disappeared for several years only to reemerge as a sorcerer and attempt regicide—or patricide. The court mages drove him out, hunted him down, and killed him. A year later, mages started being murdered. Then the court mages were slaughtered, and people stopped blaming the king. No one was ever caught.

A few years later, Adelaide's magic escaped for the first time. She was three. And she'd been hiding ever since. If the worry The Shadow would kill her wasn't enough, the only living mage in Monparth would be valuable—for healing, for protection, for war. And as Father said, above all else, men with power crave more power. Her parents insisted she not practice magic and tell no one. Not even her half-siblings knew.

That was the real reason she wouldn't court Nolan, beyond his prejudice against Regulus. Something deep in her gut warned her she couldn't trust Nolan with her secret. And if she couldn't tell him the truth, she couldn't marry him. Again she wished Regulus had come. She wanted to talk to him, find out if he seemed trustworthy, or if Nolan was right. She made a face at the canopy. *Why, so you can court him? Stop being ridiculous.*

Someone knocked on the door and Adelaide jumped.

"Adelaide?" Minerva's voice.

Adelaide answered the door, and Minerva entered, a deep furrow between her brows. "Are you all right? Sir Carrick said you weren't feeling well."

Adelaide slumped against the door as she closed it. "I'm fine. I just…needed some space." She looked at Minerva accusingly. "Did you see his clothes? Did you know—"

"Heavens, no!" Minerva's eyes widened. "Lady Drummond is very proud of herself. She thinks you'll thank her later. I was horrified and told her as much. I'm so sorry, Ad."

"Well, good." Adelaide forced herself to keep a straight face. "Because I had sworn to never speak to you again if you had anything to do with it." She smiled, and Minerva laughed.

"I take it you don't care for him?"

Adelaide twirled a ribbon on her dressing gown around her finger.

"He's…haughty. Self-absorbed. I think he hates Lord Hargreaves simply because he's illegitimate, which is ridiculous." She let the ribbon unravel and fall off her finger. "Maybe it's unfair of me, but I don't trust him."

"Thank Etiros." Minerva's relieved tone surprised Adelaide. Min sat on the edge of her bed. "I honestly don't like him, either. I overheard some ladies claiming Nolan Carrick's charm has…undone a few women. I hate unsubstantiated rumors, but it makes me uncomfortable."

"You're uncomfortable? I don't want to know what rumors they'll spread about me now." She slouched on the bed next to Minerva.

"Are you sure you're fine?" Minerva stroked Adelaide's hair. "You know you can tell me anything, right?"

"I know." *Do I?* They sat in silence until Adelaide couldn't take it anymore. "I found a book on magic in Lord Drummond's library."

Minerva's hand froze on Adelaide's back. "Ad…"

"I know, I know. But…it's been twenty-three years. Surely it's safe by now."

"You don't know that. You can't know that."

"If someone was still hunting mages, why didn't they find me as a child?" Adelaide stood. "Do you have any idea how difficult it is to keep this power inside me? It's this constant pressure, begging for release."

Minerva dropped her gaze. "Ad—"

"Just…look." Adelaide formed a dagger. The blue light of the blade cast odd shadows on Minerva's face as she held the magic weapon out to her sister.

"Oh," Minerva whispered, her eyes wide and jaw slack. She reached out and brushed her fingers against the hilt. "It's…solid. That's…" She shook her head. "You *have* daggers, Adelaide."

"But what if sometime I don't? And what else could I do? I can help people!"

"With a dagger?"

Adelaide groaned. "All right, look. Mother panicked when she caught me doing this, so I've never told you I can. But watch. And don't panic." She drew the blade of her magic dagger across her palm and winced from the sharp pain.

"Adelaide!" Minerva gasped.

"It's all right!" Adelaide vanished the blade and healed her hand. A comforting numb sensation spread over the cut, and the skin pulled back together. The blue glow of her palm illuminated Minerva's horrified expression. The light dimmed, and Adelaide rinsed her hand in the water bowl on the dresser. She turned back to Minerva. "See?"

Minerva grabbed her hand and ran her fingers over the smooth skin. "It's…like it never happened," she breathed.

"Exactly!" Adelaide smiled broadly, excitement making her heart race. "Mother and Father want to keep me safe; I *know* that. But…isn't magic a gift? It's a natural part of the world. The priests say Etiros imbued all living things with magic. Isn't it a source of goodness Etiros gave me access to for a reason?"

Minerva's sad eyes filled with pity. "And what about all those mages who died? What good did their gift do them?"

"Just because they died doesn't mean they had done nothing good with their magic before that," Adelaide countered.

"Ad…" Minerva massaged her forehead. "I can't stop you. And I won't try. But I don't want to lose you, either. And what if it's not only your own life you put in danger?" She rubbed her growing belly protectively.

Adelaide's posture fell. Maybe her sister was right. But maybe she wasn't. "I'll be careful."

"Thank you." Minerva held out her hand, and Adelaide helped her stand. "Get some rest. I'll see you tomorrow."

In the morning, Adelaide faked illness as an excuse to avoid breakfast. Gaius and Minerva stole a few indulgently sweet fruit-filled pastries, which Adelaide devoured as she waited for their carriage in the bustling courtyard. She spied Nolan wandering the chaos of departing guests as if searching for someone. Their carriage pulled around, and she rushed inside. Relief filled her when Carrick castle faded from sight.

REGULUS REINED in Sieger at the crest of a hill covered in tall grass. A wide valley that deepened and narrowed into a ravine stretched out ahead of them. Beyond, the spur of the Pelandian Mountains known as the Barren Range rose behind a blue-gray haze. Oaks, maples, and juniper bushes grew scattered near the valley entrance, and the mouths of caves yawned dark in the ravine walls. A strong breeze tugged on his cloak and carried the scent of apple trees. The gust moved across the cave mouths, creating a faint sound somewhere between a whistle and a soft cry.

The famous Singing Caves.

He clicked his tongue and Sieger started forward again at a gentle trot. At the entrance to the valley, he tied Sieger to a low branch of a young maple, tight enough the horse wouldn't wander off, but loose enough if something came at Sieger and he tried to run, he could pull free. He removed his cloak and hung it over another branch. A cloak was a liability in battle, and anyone who happened by would assume the owner was nearby and likely leave Sieger alone. Before setting out, he double-checked his gear and supplies. He had the massive black sword from the sorcerer, a hunting knife across his lower back, and a dagger and water horn on his right hip. Blackened iron covered the front of a kite-shaped shield, its wooden back wrapped in hardened leather. He slung a bag of miscellaneous supplies over his shoulder and started out.

Regulus chewed on dried venison as he walked, savoring the salty, smoky flavor. Only the rustle of grass, leaves, and the sighing of wind in the caves reached his ears. He hadn't seen a living thing since before the last hill. He peered into each cave as he passed, listening and watching the shadows. Nothing moved in the valley or the caves. The valley deepened, the hills on either side rising the closer he got to the Barren Mountains. Gradually, the ravine narrowed. The sides became more uneven, with more caves and craggy spurs of rock. More places for things to hide.

At last, he spied the white elm with golden leaves. It grew so close to the mouth of the cave the trunk had melded with the stone. The branches spread over the entrance, deepening the shadows within. The mouth of the cave stretched over twice as tall as Regulus, and nearly as wide. *Okay. The dragon's no bigger than the entrance, right? Big, but not as big as I feared.* The golden leaves of the white elm rustled in the breeze while the caves moaned and whistled. Wind snuck between his helm and the back of his breastplate, chilling his neck. His instincts told him not to enter that cave. He ate a last bite of venison, pulled a torch from his bag, and lit it. He held it at arm's length and peered into the darkness filling the cave. With a deep breath to steady his nerves, he headed in.

As his eyes adjusted to the gloom of the cave and the torchlight, Regulus scanned the shadows. He kept his right hand on the hilt of his sheathed sword. Breezes swirled past, occasionally whistling in the caves. His footsteps echoed, every clank of his armor magnified as the sound bounced. After a while, he heard the trickle of water. Rivulets ran down the sides of the cave. The cave widened and curved as he progressed, making it difficult to see into the dark shadows. All sunlight had long since disappeared. The air grew dank, heavy, and stale as the wind stopped. A rotten and burnt smell became more apparent. After walking for around half an hour, he heard a new sound. Like the sighing, whistling wind, but different.

Several minutes later, the cave forked. To his right, the roof of the cave sloped down, and the cave narrowed. To his left, the cave widened. The noise, which sounded uncomfortably like breathing, came from the left.

Why are you hesitating? You know the dragon's to the left. He took a deep breath. *Well, yes, that's why I'm hesitating. I've never faced an actual dragon before.*

He stretched as much as his armor and the shield strapped to his left arm would allow and double-checked his weapons. "Here goes," he said aloud. His voice sounded hollow in his helm. Head held high and every muscle straining with nervous energy, he strode into the left passage.

After a couple minutes, he had no doubt the sound was breathing. He passed a pile of bones. A deer, maybe. More unsettling was what looked like massive troll bones. A slight, warm, fetid breeze rushed toward him in time with the breathing. The stench worsened, and the cool dampness of the cave transitioned into warm humidity. Sweat rolled down his forehead under his helm. He rounded yet another curve. *Where is that infernal—*

Dragon.

The beast slept on a mound of gold, silver, jewels, and bones, curled into a ball like a gargantuan cat. It looked like an oversized lizard, covered in dull scales the color of dried sage. The dragon's head, longer than Regulus' height, rested on a front foot the size of Regulus' torso and legs, with five claws the length of his forearm. Dull black horns curled back from the crown of its head. Its nostrils flared as it breathed out, its breath sulfuric and hot. The tip of its tail, shaped like a barbed arrow as wide as Regulus' chest, twitched in front of its snout. It had no wings, just four legs like oak trees.

Regulus swallowed and looked around for the relic in the dim light. His torch sputtered in the dragon's breath, making the shadows in the cave flicker. As quietly as possible, he walked around the dragon. He saw nothing that looked like the drawing in the pile under the dragon, but that didn't mean it wasn't there. Hopefully the sorcerer was right, and it was somewhere else in the cave.

Technically, the sorcerer had told him to kill the dragon *if necessary* and take the relic. If he could skip the fighting the dragon part, he would do so. True, the dragon couldn't kill him. But it could burn him, cut him, scar him. Dying was still painful. The feeling of death without the release of dying was a hellish experience, one he tried to avoid.

He proceeded cautiously, holding up his torch to illuminate as much of the cave as possible. The dragon's breath vibrated the floor. Behind the dragon, near the back of the cave, a white stone caught the torchlight. The square pedestal stood about as tall as Regulus' waist. A faded, repulsive gray-brown rotting pillow rested on top. Cradled on the pillow lay an object made of thick gold wire twisted into the shape of a hollow egg and coated in dust.

The relic was about half a foot long and slightly narrower, with a short rod in the hollow center that looked like a mount for something that was missing. He picked it up and shook off some of the dust, but with the humidity of the room, most of it stuck. He shrugged and deposited it in his bag, then froze.

The rhythm of the dragon's breathing had changed. *Clink. Clink.* Metallic rustling and clattering echoed in the cave. Regulus pressed his eyes closed. *You couldn't stay asleep, could you?* He adjusted his grip on his shield, set the torch down on the pillow, which caught fire, and drew his sword. A low growl reverberated around the room and resonated in his chest. He turned, praying dragons didn't really breathe fire.

The dragon, now towering over him, its red serpentine eyes flashing, snarled. Its mouth glowed orange. Regulus yanked his shield up, hiding as much of his body behind it as possible. Fire pummeled the shield. The heat was terrible, the roar of the flames loud, the force of the blast startling. He leaned into the shield, pushing hard against the rock floor to brace himself. Without his enhanced strength, he wouldn't have withstood the onslaught. The stream of fire ended, and Regulus blinked sweat out of his eyes.

The dragon roared, the sound deafening in the cave. Regulus straightened and ran forward, keeping the shield between him and the dragon. He swung at the dragon's neck. The blade met scales with an echoing clang as a shock ran up his arm. He yanked the sword down, leaving only a scratch. Regulus gulped. *This is not good.* The dragon snarled again, baring sharp, yellowed teeth.

Regulus blocked a swipe of its huge front foot with his shield, but the force knocked him sideways. Its claws dragged against the front of the shield with a piercing grating noise. The weight pulled his arm down. He dropped his sword, drew his dagger, and reached over the shield, stabbing into the dragon's foot right between two black-clawed toes. The blade slipped between scales and Regulus pushed it in to its hilt. The dragon roared. It yanked its foot back, tearing the dagger out of Regulus' hand. As the dragon howled, Regulus spotted a small, lighter area unprotected by thick scales at the top of its neck, under its chin. He snatched the sword back up and lunged toward the dragon's neck, breathing hard.

The dragon recovered, and Regulus narrowly dodged another swipe of its foot. But now the dragon had tucked down its head, and rows of pointed teeth were between him and his target. He spun to the side, trying to disorient the creature. The dragon dove, and he ducked. Teeth as big as his hands clamped onto the shield. Frantic, he pulled his arm out of the shield. His gauntlet caught on the first strap. *Too tight!* His heart raced as he fought against the dragon's pull and the strap.

He had barely freed his arm when the dragon forced its jaws closed. The shield bent, the metal making a piercing grinding sound as wood splinters flew everywhere. The dragon spit the shield away, flames curling around the crushed metal and remaining fragments of wood. Regulus scrambled back. *Focus.* He had found a potential striking point. He just needed to get close enough. Curse the sorcerer's showy armor. What he needed was maneuverability, not a dramatic appearance.

Something slammed into his stomach, throwing him back against the cave wall. His sword fell from his hand with a clatter. Whatever had hit him tore through his armor with a metallic rending that tormented his ears. Regulus screamed as pain flared. He grabbed for whatever had lodged itself in his torso and found the barbed arrowhead tip of the dragon's tail buried in his abdomen.

His blood flowed between dark scales. He choked as blood forced its way up his throat. He couldn't. Breathe.

His chest tightened and his neck stiffened as he attempted to cough up the blood gagging him, but the dragon's tail had destroyed his abdominal muscles. The dragon yanked its tail away, and Regulus collapsed to his knees. Pain turned the world white. His own rumbling pulse filled his ears.

He could breathe again. Pulling and pinching added to his already immeasurable pain as dark magic coursed through his body. He rolled onto his side, screaming, unable to even think about the dragon. He felt the gash mending back together; like millions of white-hot needles stitching him together from the inside out with thread laced with poison ivy. He looked up and saw the dragon's wide-open mouth careening toward him.

On instinct, he rolled to the side. The dragon slammed its snout into the cave floor as Regulus struggled to his knees. *There.* His sword lay only a few feet away. The dragon growled and shook its head. It raised a massive forefoot to step on him. Regulus waited as long as he dared before darting forward, his gut wrenching.

The claws hit the cave floor with a sharp clack. Dust and pebbles flew. Regulus crawled forward and grasped the hilt of his sword. He rolled onto his back as the dragon lunged again, its tongue flicking between its teeth. From his back, Regulus thrust his sword up as the dragon's open mouth descended. He looked away, clenching his eyes shut and grimacing. Some part of him wondered whether he would finally die if the dragon bit him in half.

Sword met flesh. The dragon's growl vibrated his arms. The force of the dragon's attack drove the sword down, but Regulus pushed up, his eyes still pressed closed as the dragon's breath scorched his skin. His sword pulled to the side, and he lost his grip. He opened his eyes to the dragon staggering and pawing at the sword buried deep in the roof of its mouth. Smoke curled from its flaring nostrils and its eyes rolled, turning white. He staggered to his feet while drawing his hunting knife. The dragon roared and flailed, sending gold and jewels flying.

Regulus jumped forward and skirted a blindly thrown foot. He stumbled over the whipping tail. Coins pinged off his armor. His wound had closed. It still throbbed, but it was healed. The dragon, still holding its mouth wide open, looked up at the cave ceiling. Regulus jumped onto the monster's leg, clutching the knife with both hands. He pushed off the leg with a shout and leapt toward the dragon's throat, his gaze fixed on the paler, less scaled patch.

With every ounce of his strength, he thrust up into the dragon's throat. The knife dug into the center of the spot. The dragon screeched. Regulus pushed the blade in deep. The momentum of his jump spent, he fell. With a grunt, he yanked the knife back out and bubbling deep green blood flowed out, splattering over his armor.

He landed hard on the ground as the dragon stumbled. Regulus scurried back. With a crash, the cacophony of treasure being scattered, and the scrape of scales on stone, the dragon fell. The cave shook and Regulus stumbled. Its eyes rolled around in its head, then went still. A great sigh rushed through the cave like wind, and the dragon stopped breathing.

Regulus watched, unmoving. His nerves buzzed and his muscles twitched. He crept forward and nudged the dragon's muzzle with the tip of his boot. *Dead.* He exhaled heavily, wrenched off his helm, and tossed it away with a clatter. His hands on his knees, he gulped in putrid air as if he had been drowning. Which, he supposed, he probably *had* nearly drowned, choking on his own blood. With a shudder, he vomited. Bloody bile splashed onto his dragon-blood flecked greaves.

All this pain. All this suffering. Being dragged back from the brink of death. For *what?* What was so Etiros-forsaken important to the sorcerer about these artifacts and relics? Why did the sorcerer make him do all this? And why wouldn't it just end?

Some part of him whispered he could have let the dragon eat him. Couldn't be brought back from digestion, right? Then again, sometimes the power of the sorcerer frightened him.

But no. He wouldn't give up, not now. Not this close to being free, not after he'd fought for so long. Not after everything his friends had done for him; after he'd promised to keep going. He thought of Dresden. *"You'll get through this. I'll help."* They stayed for him; he could stay around for them.

As the burning in his throat and mouth subsided, leaving behind a sour taste, Regulus straightened. He eyed the dragon. He'd killed countless dozens of violent beasts over his years as a mercenary. Gryphons, ice serpents, manticores, therarns—creatures of the deserts like great cats but covered in scales, and more. He'd never felt remorse for any of them. They had terrorized innocent people. But this dragon's only offense was being in the sorcerer's way. He shook the twinge of pity for the beautifully fearsome creature away. It had attacked him. Still, part of him whispered it hadn't needed to die.

He reached for the bag and realized it had fallen off. *Wonderful.* His boots clacked on the cave floor as he circled the dragon's head. Its mouth was open, and Regulus struggled to force it open further. His muscles strained as he pressed on its lower lip, the dragon's body already hardening. He had to crawl on its massive, serpentine tongue to reach his sword. It took a bit of effort to dislodge it from the back of the monster's mouth. Then he moved the dragon's jaw again to retrieve his hunting knife.

Wonder if my dagger's still in its foot. Sure enough, it was. He pulled it out, and hands full of green dragon blood-soaked blades, he began looking for his bag. Gold and silver coins, goblets, jewel-encrusted necklaces, and even a couple crowns were strewn about the cave. He searched in the fading light of the dying torch, which had been knocked to the ground during the brawl. He spotted the bag and reached in, holding his breath. His fingers closed around thick metal wire. He closed his eyes and released his breath.

He pulled out a handkerchief and wiped off his blades before he returned them to their respective sheaths. Riches glittered in the torchlight. He paused, then added a few jewel-covered gold trinkets to the bag. If he was going to play mercenary for the sorcerer, he might as well get paid. His weary steps dragged as he picked up the torch, fetched his helm, and left the dragon behind.

The torch didn't last long, and he had to make his way based on where the air smelled freshest. After running into a couple walls, he walked with his hands held out in front of him. *Etiros, please. Get me out of here.* Eventually, he spied a faint light, and made for it. The light grew blinding. As fresh air blew into his face and he glimpsed green, he sighed in relief.

Thank you. If Etiros still heard him after all he had done, Regulus didn't know. But he needed to believe he wasn't alone.

Chapter 12

THE CORRUPTION around the sorcerer's tower had spread again. The dead trees started sooner. Charcoal leaves, as if they had been scorched, littered the forest floor and maintained a fragile grip on blackened branches. The white branches closer to the tower swayed, dead fingers clawing the sky. Sieger whinnied and snorted, tensing beneath Regulus.

"I know, boy." He rubbed Sieger's neck. "I don't like it, either."

Could air smell…lifeless? Not musty with the stench of decay. Just…empty, lacking vibrancy. Leaves made a dull rustle beneath Sieger's hooves. Sieger stepped on a twig, and a sharp snap interrupted the eerie silence.

The sorcerer waited in front of his tower, arms crossed, mouth pressed into a tight line. "I told you to *kill the dragon,* not *get killed* by the dragon!" His beard twitched in rhythm with his rapid, sharp speech. "It's exhausting keeping you alive!"

Then why bother? And try dying, that's not a leisure activity! But Regulus kept his tongue in check as he dismounted and removed his helm. He pulled the relic out of his bag. "I did kill it, my lord. And here's…whatever this is."

The sorcerer snatched the hollow gold egg out of his hand. "Doesn't matter." He looked it over, inspecting it. Apparently satisfied, he tucked it under his arm. His lips curled downward as he looked at Regulus. "This won't do."

The sorcerer held out his hand. Ivy-colored light emanated from his palm toward Regulus' abdomen. The first time Regulus saw the sorcerer flashed through his mind. Shards of green light. His men dying. Irrational dread coiled in his chest, but he shoved aside the painful memory. *He isn't attacking.* The torn armor screeched and groaned as the sorcerer mended the jagged hole left by the dragon's tail. Once done, the sorcerer turned toward the tower.

Regulus stared at the relic in the crook of the sorcerer's arm. Two years of service, and he still had the same questions. *Why do all this? What is so important? What's he doing?*

"Why are you still standing there?" The sorcerer looked over his shoulder, pausing at the door. "What do you want? A biscuit? Go away!"

"I fought a dragon." Regulus rubbed the back of his neck. Asking was a bad idea. But… "A *dragon.* Nearly died, again. And I wondered—"

The sorcerer laughed; deep, coarse, and mocking. "No. You still have plenty of debt to pay off." He smiled, a patronizing flash of white teeth. "I'm keeping track. But this piece is a good step. You're getting close. I'll release you as soon as we're even."

"Actually, my lord"—Regulus took a deep breath—"I just wondered why."

The sorcerer's amused smile vanished. "Slaves don't know their master's business. You don't need to know what it's for to retrieve it, any more than a dog needs to know anatomy to chew on a bone."

Regulus' jaw tightened. He turned back to Sieger.

"Hargreaves."

He closed his eyes, then faced the sorcerer again. "Yes, my lord?"

"I don't like intrusive questions."

Anger and trepidation squeezed his chest. It wasn't fair. A question didn't demand an answer. A question wasn't dangerous. But he knew better. He bowed his head and braced for the pain. "I apologize, my lord."

The sorcerer tapped his forefinger against the relic. "Are you forgetting your place?"

"No, my lord. I apologize. I had no right to ask." He stared at the ground, outrage battling against fear the sorcerer's anger wouldn't be satisfied with hurting him. "Forgive me."

"I think your title has gone to your head. I was planning on a mercenary, not a lord."

Regulus gulped, unsure how to respond. Safest to say nothing. The pain would come. The sorcerer would let him go. He just needed to avoid angering the sorcerer into taking control of his body. *I can't hurt my friends again.*

"Do you need reminded how powerless you are?"

"No, my lord." Desperate, he knelt and bowed his head. He would suffer any humiliation to spare his men. "You are the Prince of Shadow and Ash. I am…nothing." Silently, he prayed to Etiros for mercy. Mercy for his friends. "I won't question you again, my lord."

The sorcerer was quiet. Regulus tapped his toes inside his boot, panic rising as he cursed his own stupidity. He bowed until his hot forehead touched cool earth. *Please. Please.*

"You've irritated me, Hargreaves. Between taking all my energy to keep you from dying, asking impertinent questions, and wasting my time, I'm feeling the need to hurt someone. Choose."

Regulus raised his head, the blood draining from his face. "My lord?"

"You, or one of your friends. Choose."

He didn't hesitate as relief flooded him. "Me."

"Predictable and boring. Suit yourself."

Searing heat and the sensation of thousands of tiny cuts raced up Regulus' right arm from the mark and spread over his chest before covering his whole body. He bit back a cry. The pain intensified, and a strangled scream caught in his throat. He fell forward on his hands, his arms shaking. He dug his fingers into the blackened dirt as darkness pressed in on the edges of his vision. The pain pushed deeper, through his bones and organs, beyond bearing. His scream scraped his throat raw. The pain faded back toward his mark and stopped. Sweat rolled down his face, and he hung his head, his body still trembling.

"Next time," the sorcerer said as he headed into the tower, "you won't get to choose."

Regulus slept for a day and a half after arriving back at his estate. When he emerged from his room, he headed to Arrano's overgrown garden. Dresden appeared out of nowhere, waving a piece of parchment in the bright sunlight.

"I come bearing good news!"

Regulus eyed the parchment and grunted. He turned down another grass-infested path, his sword bumping a stone bench. As ever, Magnus followed close behind, his shaggy tan tail wagging leisurely, large pink tongue hanging out of his black muzzle.

"Oh, cheer up." Drez propped his arm on Regulus' shoulder and leaned on him, holding up the parchment. "'To Lord Regulus Hargreaves of Arrano,'" he read aloud. "'Sir Thomas Glower and Dame Isabelle Glower cordially invite you to join them for a feast to be held on their estate a week hence on the eleventh of Verdanmunth at six o'clock in the evening.' I told their messenger you would attend."

"Great. This is meant to cheer me?" Regulus shrugged Dresden off his shoulder.

"That's only half of the good news." Drez pulled another letter from the back of his belt and held it out, the unbroken seal toward Regulus. "I even had the courtesy not to read this one, despite my curiosity."

The wax bore an impression of a rearing unicorn. Regulus' breath caught, but he wouldn't give Dresden the satisfaction of admitting it. Unfortunately, he grabbed the parchment too eagerly, and Drez laughed.

Regulus turned away and opened the letter. The words indented the parchment and globs of ink marred the letters, as if she had been pressing too hard.

Dear Lord Regulus Hargreaves,

I apologize for any offense I caused. Please forgive my impertinence. I had no idea the Carricks were so prejudiced as to not invite you. If it helps, it was a miserable party. I hope I'll see you at some other party. I've had my fill of shallow nobles, and your honesty and acceptance are refreshing.

Sincerely,

Lady Adelaide Belanger

Regulus leaned against a tree, willing his heart to stop dancing. He should put the letter down. He should burn it. Instead, he read it again. And again. And again.

"Well, is it good news? Because you're clutching it like you're afraid it will turn to ash in your hands, and your expression keeps flickering between pleased and confused."

Regulus hesitated, then handed the letter to Dresden. Dresden read it and grinned as he handed it back. "I'm so glad I told the Glowers you're going. She'll likely be there."

"You're incorrigible." *And irritating. I can't see her again.* Because he knew, deep down, he wouldn't be able to stay away from her.

"Pick a good outfit—"

"Drez." Regulus rubbed Magnus' head. "The sorcerer says I'm getting close, but… I killed a dragon, and even that's not enough."

"You killed a dragon?"

"Did you say *dragon*?" a voice asked from Regulus' right.

Two of his knights, Caleb and Estevan, walked toward them. Both men wore swords at their sides. As usual, Estevan was playing with a knife. This one had a round hole in the end of the hilt, and he was spinning it around his forefinger and catching the grip. Spin, catch. Spin the opposite direction, catch.

Regulus didn't know where Estevan was from, because Estevan himself wasn't sure. His family were nomads, and his accent was a strange amalgam of places he'd lived. A liberal sprinkling of freckles covered his tan face. His thick, curly brown hair refused to be tamed. The wing of a tattoo of a gryphon on his back peeked out from under his shirt collar at his shoulder. At twenty-two, Estevan was the youngest of Regulus' knights, and accordingly, the cockiest.

"Dragon," Regulus confirmed.

"Like, big, scaly, horned, fire-breathing, winged dragon?" Estevan pressed.

"Yes to everything but the wings."

Estevan whistled. "You kill it?"

"Barely."

"It kill you?" Estevan grinned.

"Hey!" Caleb smacked Estevan's shoulder. "Show a little respect."

Caleb was in his mid-thirties but liked to act much younger. He had a lanky yet strong build, as light and deadly as the long bows he favored. His unkempt dark blond hair hung around his pale face, and a scruffy short beard covered his cheeks and chin.

Estevan nodded. "Of course. We must always show proper respect for the dead." Both men put on melodramatically somber expressions and bowed their heads in mock respect.

Regulus rolled his eyes but chuckled. "Yes, it probably killed me." He grimaced at the memory of the dragon's sharp tail sliding out of his abdomen.

Estevan flipped the knife again. "Not an experience I envy. Still. Would've been something to see a real, live dragon."

"Something terrifying," Dresden said. "What would you do, throw a knife at it?"

"Of course." Estevan sighted down the blade. "Right at its eye. Blind it. Then when it tries to spit fire, throw one down its gullet."

"Hm." Regulus nodded. "Not a terrible plan. I'll keep that in mind. Maybe I'll use a bow, though."

"Yes, your knife-throwing skills are…non-existent." Estevan threw the knife past Regulus' head. It whirred past his ear, and Regulus turned as the knife stuck into a tree a few paces behind him. He turned back toward Estevan, who bowed with a flourish.

"Show-off."

"The words of the dead can't hurt me." Estevan strode past him, his posture self-assured. "We're headed to town and the tavern, if anyone is interested. Grabbing Perce and Jerrick, too."

Dresden snorted. "It's barely past three."

"By the time we arrive, it will be quarter to five," Caleb said.

Estevan retrieved the knife and stuck it in his boot. "Gives time to get a nice steak pie, down a few pints, flirt with a few barmaids, smoke a pipe, and get back at a decent hour."

"Well"—Caleb grinned as he followed Estevan—"the hour we get back depends on how well the flirting goes."

A smile betrayed Regulus' amusement. He looked at Drez. "If nothing else, I better go to keep an eye on them."

"On one condition." Drez crossed his arms. "You promise to go the Glower's banquet and talk to Lady Belanger."

"I thought you'd be pleased I'm going with them, the way you go on about leaving the castle." Regulus headed toward the stables. "You going to stop me if I say no?"

He *did* want to go to the party. He wanted to see Adelaide. But he couldn't. The abomination who didn't die when a dragon ripped open his gut didn't deserve her. And when a misstep with the sorcerer endangered his loved ones, he couldn't put her in danger. *Not that the sorcerer would know about her. I could keep the relationship secret. I could be free soon.*

"Stop you? No." Dresden strolled next to him. "I'll get Caleb to sing and play his lute at the tavern, which will make Perceval drink more. Which will make it easy to trick Perceval into starting a brawl that Jerrick will join. Then I'll tell Leonora and Sarah you started the fight. Or at least didn't stop them."

"You wouldn't."

"Would. They'll let loose on you, then on their husbands, and then Perce and Jerrick will complain to you…it'll be a nightmare."

"Drez." Regulus ran his hand through his hair and rested it on the pommel of his sword. "I don't deserve Adel—"

"No." Drez shook his head, his eyes flashing. "I won't have it. You're more than good enough, and you deserve to be happy."

Arguing would only make Dresden more stubborn. Besides, he would like to believe Dresden. Regulus switched tactics. "It's too danger—"

"No. No excuses. Look at us." Drez spread his arms out. "We're all fine. You'll be free before long. You've managed not to anger the sorcerer in over a year and a half."

That I've told you. Still, Regulus' resolve was crumbling. He never would have guessed she would write him again, and it only heightened his curiosity and interest. Would she consider him as a suitor? It was a foolish thought, but he stubbornly wanted to know.

"I'm not kidding about Sarah and Leonora." Drez winked.

"Aw, fine." Regulus pushed Dresden away, frowning to keep from smiling. "I'll go! Barring any sorcerous intervention, I'll go."

Drez rubbed his shoulder, even though Regulus hadn't shoved him hard enough to warrant such drama. "Excellent." Dresden stuck his thumbs in his belt and whistled as he headed to the stables. Magnus bounded after Drez. Regulus followed, wondering if Adelaide liked dogs.

THE DOOR clicked shut and the Prince of Shadow and Ash leaned against it, allowing himself to catch his breath. Curse it all. He would never let on to Hargreaves that torturing him wasn't effortless. It wasn't terrible—already most of the expended magical energy had returned—but how often he needed to divert power into controlling Hargreaves made him irritable. At least it had some benefits.

He smiled, cherishing the agony on Hargreaves' face, the scream his slave had tried to suppress. A welcome diversion from the monotony of planning his vengeance.

He had known Hargreaves would choose pain for himself before he allowed any of his men to be harmed. However, torturing Hargreaves through the bond was far less draining than taking control of his body—especially with the fight Hargreaves put up. The man's mental thrashing whenever the Prince took over gave him a headache for hours afterward. He would rather not spend the requisite energy to force Hargreaves to hurt his own friends. But Hargreaves needn't know that. The threat was enough.

Fear was a powerful motivator.

The Prince ascended the stairs that wound around the interior of his tower, the top piece of the staff tucked under his arm. Willing slaves were considerably easier to control. He had required someone with a good heart to get past the magical enchantments around one of the other pieces, but he hadn't expected a mercenary to be so stubbornly moral. The ones he had sent to slaughter Monparth's mages had been bloodthirsty and grateful for the bond that let them dole out violence without risk to themselves. They had begged him not to release them, but he'd had no reason to let them leech from his sorcery after the mages were obliterated. Meanwhile, Hargreaves was desperate to lose his bond.

The Prince snorted. *Idiot.*

He set the gold oval topper next to the three rods that formed the rest of the staff. Only one piece left. He was close to deciphering its location. Some of what he'd discovered made him nervous, though. Potential complications to retrieving the final piece. Ah, well. He would solve that riddle when he heard it. Nothing would stop him from achieving his goal. Not this time.

The Prince sat at his desk and opened a faded leather-bound journal, marked with water stains and discolored with age. The brittle pages crackled. He laid his new journal open next to it, dipped his quill in ink, and returned to the arduous task of translating the old Monparthian.

He had work to do before he could unleash his vengeance on Monparth.

SWEAT TICKLED the back of Regulus' neck as he entered the Glower's banquet hall. Two rows of tables ran the length of the long hall, decked with candles and tin place settings on navy blue tablecloths. Tall candelabras lined the stone walls, positioned between large vases stuffed with fragrant flowers in bright colors. Some nobles sat at the long tables; others were being shown to their seats. He scanned the room for Adelaide but didn't see her. He couldn't decide if that made him more anxious or less. *This is stupid. It's just supper.*

"Good evening, Lord Hargreaves, Sir Jakobs." A servant stepped toward them and bowed. "This way."

"Pardon me," Dresden said, surprising Regulus. "Have the Drummonds arrived yet?"

"No, sir."

"Might it be possible for my lord to be seated next to Lady Belanger?"

The servant looked over his shoulder, forehead creased. "I fear the seating has already been arranged—"

Dresden pulled a pouch of coins off his belt. "I would gladly compensate you for any inconvenience."

Regulus stiffened. *A bribe?* What was Dresden thinking? But sitting next to Adelaide *would* make supper more interesting. The idea both excited and terrified him.

The servant's eyes darted around in mild alarm, but he discreetly took the pouch. "I've just remembered, you're seated over here, my lord." He made an adjustment in his course and indicated a couple seats. "I would take the seat on the left, my lord," he added.

Regulus nodded and he and Drez took their seats. "The hell, Drez?" he muttered.

"Breathe," Dresden whispered.

"I *am* breathing."

"You look like you're holding your breath."

He forced himself to relax. "This is a bad idea." His stomach roiled.

Dresden turned toward him, leaning his forearm on the table in front of the delicate tin plate. "What have we talked about?"

Surely Drez wasn't going to do this right here, right now.

"You need to *live* your life and stop moping over things you can't control. Choices, Regulus. Choose some joy." Dresden smiled. "Get to know her."

Regulus fiddled with his spoon, watching the flickering candlelight reflect in its dull surface. Fine, he wanted to get to know her. Didn't mean he should. Sometimes he wanted alcohol before noon. Didn't mean that was a good idea.

"Lord Hargreaves?"

Regulus snapped his head up and found himself looking into Adelaide's rich brown eyes outlined by dark lashes. His mind seemed to break. *Etiros, she's beautiful.* For a moment, he couldn't find his voice. "Lady Belanger." *How articulate.*

"It appears we are seated next to each other."

"Are we?" Regulus bolted to his feet and pulled out her chair. Next to her, Sir Gaius was helping his wife, with her now visible stomach bump, into her chair. Lord and Lady Drummond sat on Lady Minerva's other side. Adelaide sat and Regulus pushed her seat forward before retaking his own.

She smirked. "What a fortunate coincidence."

Regulus' jaw went slack, and Dresden stifled a chuckle. "I…"

"I'm sure our hosts won't notice." She laughed, and he calmed.

"Allow me to explain, my lady." Drez leaned forward, looking around Regulus at Adelaide. "Regulus mentioned wishing he could get to know you better, so I persuaded a servant to seat you together. Please forgive my minor transgression of protocol. I hope you don't find me impertinent."

Adelaide raised a brow, looking positively regal. "Sir Dresden Jakobs, right?"

"Yes, my lady."

"It sounds to me like Lord Hargreaves is fortunate to have you as a friend." Her eyes shone playfully.

A friend. As if two words could sum up their complicated relationship. All the times Regulus hadn't been a worthy friend to Dresden threatened to overwhelm him.

"Drez is a better friend than I deserve," he admitted. "He's had my back for years. We've been through everything together. There's no one I trust more or owe as much to."

Dresden laughed, but it sounded uncomfortable. "He owes me nothing. I'm far more fortunate to have Regulus as a friend."

As if that's true. He knew Drez meant it. He just didn't agree.

Adelaide didn't respond. Was she judging him for being too familiar with one of his knights? Or wondering about his past? She watched him, her head tilted, gaze intense. Heat crept up his neck and he looked away.

Across the room, a man stared at him. He looked closer. Nolan Carrick stood rigid, glaring. Without breaking eye contact, Carrick moved his hand to the dagger at his belt and gave the smallest shake of his head. Carrick smiled, as if nothing had happened, and followed a squire to a seat next to Sir Glower.

Regulus shifted and looked back at Adelaide. She watched Carrick take his seat, and his chest constricted with disappointment. But her eyes narrowed, and her jaw tightened. She shook her head and her features relaxed. He recalled her letter. *"It was a miserable party."*

"Does this mean I didn't offend you?" Adelaide's quiet voice interrupted his confused thoughts. "You never wrote back."

His face burned. "No. I'm sorry I didn't respond. I've been traveling on business"—he faltered—"for a friend." And he hadn't known what to say.

She traced a slender finger over the edge of her plate. "I'm truly sorry."

He grasped for a proper response. "I'm sorry you suffered a miserable party. Although, I assumed the Carricks would host extraordinary parties."

"Oh, the party was spectacular." Her hand curled into a fist, her voice dark. "The company was miserable." She darted a glance at Regulus, then fixated on her plate. "Have you…heard anything? About the Carrick's dance?"

"Should I have?"

"No." Her posture relaxed as she exhaled.

The gentle clanking of a fork against a goblet drew their attention to the head of the room. Sir Glower welcomed everyone and thanked them for coming and Etiros for providing for their safety and health.

As servants filled their goblets with wine, Adelaide spoke. "According to Sir Jakobs, you wanted to get to know me. What do you want to know?"

"Oh." His mind blanked. "I…well, I don't know much about you. What would you want me to know?"

"Hm. No one's ever asked me that." She smiled at a servant as he set a basket of bread in front of them.

Regulus studied Adelaide while she buttered a roll and thought. Her round cheeks and slender nose. The dark brown of her eyes. Her soft pink lips. Her hair, tumbling about her shoulders in black waves. Like a calm sea on a dark night. The wide collar of her crimson dress hugged her upper arms, leaving the top of her shoulders exposed. Her black hair against the rich brown of her skin and the vibrant contrast of the red nearly took his breath away. He forced himself to stop staring. A servant set down a roast duck and began carving it in front of them.

"I speak Khast," Adelaide said between bites of roll. "My mother taught Minerva and me, although I'm more fluent than Min. Mother always says, 'I may have left Khastalland, but I am and always will be a Khastallander. It is part of me, and it is part of you, even though you have never seen it, *Tha Shiraa.*'"

Regulus inclined his head, trying to remember the few Khast words he had picked up, but he hadn't had reason to think of them in years. "Thah Sheer-ah?"

She blushed and tucked a strand of hair behind her ear. "My mother's nickname for me, in Khast. *Tha Shiraa.* Little Tigress." She pulled a comb from the other side of her head and showed it to him. An ivory carving of a sleeping tiger curled into a ball, delicately painted in striking orange and black. "It's why she gave me this." She returned the comb to her hair.

"*Tha Shiraa,*" he repeated. "Why tigress?"

"Too many times testing the limits, pushing the bounds of safety. And a penchant for speaking out of turn. Father said I was bold, and Mother agreed."

"Bold like a tigress." Regulus chuckled as he cut into the roast duck the servant set on his plate. "That's wonderful."

"Really?" Adelaide looked at him.

"Of course," he murmured, transfixed by the intensity of her eyes.

"Many find boldness…unfeminine," she said, not breaking eye contact.

He couldn't suppress a snort. "Many people are fools."

"Indeed." She finally looked away.

After a moment, she continued. "I have five half-siblings, my father's children with his first wife. The youngest, twins, were two when their mother died. The oldest was only eight." She poked the roast duck with her fork. "My father went to war shortly after and met my mother. He returned with a new wife who soon was pregnant. It was hard on them. Not as much when they were younger, but the older we got… We were different." She shrugged. "It didn't help I spent several years away as a child because I was—sickly." She cleared her throat. "Thank Etiros for Minerva, or I might have lost my mind."

Even as he empathized with her lack of connection with her half-siblings, he latched onto her mention of Etiros. Until that moment, he hadn't considered that most Khastallanders venerated the pantheistic god Prakasroht, not the creator-god worshiped in Carasom and Monparth. At least religious disagreements wouldn't be an issue, especially if they had children—*wait, what? Slow down.*

She gave him a weak smile. "So that's Adelaide Belanger. Half-noble daughter of a lord's second wife who speaks Khast and barely knows her half-siblings."

The loneliness and rejection in her words cut his heart. He had the sudden and strong urge to take her hand or caress her face. That would be wildly improper. A voice in the back of his mind urged caution, reminding him of the dangers of getting too involved, but he wasn't listening.

"What a strange way to describe yourself."

"What?" Adelaide glanced at him askance.

"If I were you"—Regulus smiled—"I would say, 'Adelaide Belanger, daughter of a war hero, woman of intellect who speaks Khast and Monparthian, paragon of honesty and grace with the heart of a tigress.'"

She stared, and his palms grew slick. He sounded like an idiot boy, writing atrocious love poetry. Adelaide grinned, and the embarrassment faded. "I like your version better, too."

"Wait until I tell the men about this…" Drez whispered, so low Regulus barely heard him. Regulus stomped on his foot, and Drez jammed his knee into the table. A servant came by with a wine jug, and Regulus held up his goblet, ignoring Drez's glare.

"And how would you describe yourself, Lord Hargreaves?"

He swirled the wine in his goblet. *Bastard son of a lord of little account who became a mercenary, swore an oath that made him an evil sorcerer's slave, and has too many deaths on his conscience.*

"I'm afraid Regulus has never been good at self-praise." Dresden leaned around him. "Allow me. Regulus Hargreaves, a strong leader, a good man, and a selfless friend who needs to take better care of himself."

Regulus took a long drink and swallowed hard. *And a fool.* A fool who wished he hadn't come and wished the night would never end all at once.

Adelaide leaned on the table. "Tell me, Sir Jakobs—"

"My friends call me Dresden, my lady," Drez interrupted. "Or even Drez."

"All right, Dresden." Her smile looked full of mischief. "Be honest with me."

"On my honor."

She squinted and dropped her voice in a fake whisper. "Is Lord Hargreaves a vampire?"

Regulus' eyes widened. "Wh—"

"Oh, no," Dresden said, his tone serious. "He's a shape-shifting spirit."

Adelaide and Dresden both laughed, and Regulus realized how tense his shoulders were. He took a deep breath. "Hilarious."

She turned back to her food. "Tell me, Lord Hargreaves, what do you want me to know about you?"

What *did* he want her to know? What did he dare tell her?

Dresden elbowed his side. "Speak up, man, or I'll tell her every dirty prank you've ever pulled." Regulus suppressed his scowl.

"I wouldn't have thought you the prankster type." Confusion and amusement mixed in Adelaide's expression.

He wasn't sure what to make of that. "To be honest, Dresden is the prankster. I just sometimes helped. What type *do* you think me?"

She studied him, lips pursed. "Strong. Serious. Observant. Diligent." She paused. "Kind." She returned to her food. "But you still haven't answered."

He laughed nervously. "Right." He poked at the peas on his plate. So many things he could tell her. So many he couldn't. He recalled her teasing question, *is Lord Hargreaves a vampire?* Which rumor to address? "I didn't send my father's wife and my sister-in-law away. Or kill them."

Adelaide paused and lowered her fork, watching him.

"I offered to let them stay at Arrano, even after they challenged me, and I won against their champion." He couldn't take her unwavering regard any longer and traced his forefinger over the vine pattern in the tablecloth. "I hoped my father's wife might forgive me, but..." He shrugged. "She always hated me." *She wanted me dead.* "So they left. Wouldn't accept any help from me. I don't even know if they made it to Craigailte as they had planned."

Adelaide's fork rested on her plate with the same bite of food as she listened.

"I was a mercenary, but I believe in honor." He met her eyes. "I may be a killer, but I'm not a murderer." *Not by choice, at least.* "That's what I'd want you to know. To believe."

"Oh, Lord Hargreaves." Her sad smile made him feel uncomfortably vulnerable. "I'm sorry about the vampire comment. I didn't mean...I never believed you killed them." They looked at each other for a long moment. She picked her fork back up.

"Well," Dresden said. "The prize for terrible supper conversation goes to Regulus bringing up murder."

Adelaide laughed, and Regulus' stomach unknotted enough for him to continue eating.

"Don't think you get out of sharing, Dresden," Adelaide said as she picked up her goblet. "What should I know about you?"

"Oh." Dresden shifted. "I fight with scimitars. I'm Carasian, although I grew up in Monparth, so I consider myself Monparthian. And… I am drawing a blank on things that are both interesting and appropriate to say."

Regulus snorted. "I wish I was surprised."

"All right, then…" Adelaide chuckled. "So you moved here with your family? I'd love to hear about them."

A burning coal settled in Regulus' stomach. He opened his mouth to shift the conversation, but Dresden answered, his tone casual.

"My parents moved before I was born, but I left my family to join a nobles' household when I was very young. Not far—a day's travel. Apparently, that was still too far to visit. I didn't really blame them, but I couldn't leave." Drez shrugged.

Regulus hoped his guilt wasn't written all over his face. His childhood guardian didn't let him or Dresden wander that far, but it still felt like Dresden's estrangement from his family was Regulus' fault. And the careful way Dresden chose his words, telling the truth while hiding he had left his impoverished family to be Regulus' servant, just reminded Regulus how much he was hiding from Adelaide.

"You don't talk to someone for years, they become strangers." Drez prodded the carrots on his plate. "By the time rejoining them was an option, I doubt they would have recognized me. It was easier not to go back. So Regulus got stuck with me." He clapped his hand on Regulus' shoulder and grinned. "We were a couple hot-headed boys without close family, so we became mercenaries and traveled the world."

Adelaide's soft eyes looked between Regulus and Dresden, compassionate, but also curious. "I'm glad you two found each other."

"Wait." Dresden sat up straighter. "I've got it. I dislike rules."

"Really?" Sarcasm dripped from Adelaide's voice. "I never would have guessed, sir bribed-the-servant." Regulus flushed.

Dresden choked. "I never said—"

"*Persuaded?* Mm-hm." She lifted a brow, a poorly suppressed smile twisting her lips. "Was it worth it?"

"You tell me," Drez said. If Regulus didn't know better, he would have called his tone flirtatious.

Adelaide cocked her head, her gaze flicking from Dresden to Regulus. Regulus' heart about stopped. He swore her cheeks pinkened. "I'm glad you dislike rules."

The conversation turned to less personal matters—hobbies and interests and likes and dislikes. As they ate and chatted, Regulus' nervousness abated. For the first time in his life, he didn't feel out of place among the nobles, didn't feel like an unwanted intruder. He felt like he belonged.

ADELAIDE COULDN'T remember a better banquet. Not that the food itself was special. The Carricks, with their great wealth, had provided better. But the company… Regulus Hargreaves was a tantalizing mystery. A little awkward, but she found it authentic and endearing. He clearly didn't judge her for her bloodline, nor did he seem superficially attracted to her Khastallander features. And he hadn't tried to touch her once. She still knew precious little about Regulus, but what she knew, she liked.

As he described places he'd visited in Khastalland, sights and sounds and tastes, she studied him. He had a smile that crinkled his eyes. A deep, hearty laugh. He radiated an acceptance and understanding she found rare. Dresden grabbed Regulus' arm, laughing as he reminded Regulus of a humorous anecdote from their travels. A simple gesture, one between friends, not lord and vassal. Their easy rapport spoke volumes about Regulus' character and humility.

The rough, shiny scar that ran from the outside of Regulus' right eye through the corner of his mouth to his chin gave him a roguish quality. His eyes were sharp, his movements controlled but energetic. He seemed on alert, taut, like a drawn bowstring. He felt dangerous yet not threatening, like a friendly wolf.

Perhaps his frank admission to being a mercenary, a killer, should have bothered her. But Father had found Mother while fighting a war, and bandits' blood had stained her own weapons, so she couldn't fault him. Everything about his earnest and quiet demeanor indicated he wasn't a blood-thirsty savage without honor any more than her own father was.

Supper ended; servants cleared the tables. Minstrels played, the notes of the flute and lyre drifting over the sound of multiplying conversations. Minerva and Gaius wandered away. Even Dresden left with a remark about a pretty girl that made Regulus sigh and roll his eyes. But neither of them made any move to leave their chairs.

"Have you heard of this Black Knight?" Adelaide asked. "Sir Gaius told me some strange rumors."

"Yes." Regulus cleared his throat and worked his jaw as if the question irritated him. "I've heard of him. Often."

"Do you think he's real?"

"Yes. I'm afraid I do."

She turned and wrapped her arm around the back of her chair. "You haven't seen him, have you?"

"No." He shifted in his seat. "Drez did. From a distance. Not recently."

"Really?" Adelaide made a mental note to ask Dresden about his sighting later. "It's said someone killed a dragon in the Singing Caves. Some are claiming the Black Knight was seen in the area. Lord Drummond says dragons don't exist in Monparth anymore, and neither does the Black Knight. But people are selling dragon scales." She rested her chin on the back of the chair. "What do you think?"

He went pale and closed his eyes as sweat gleamed on his forehead.

"Lord Hargreaves?" Adelaide reached for his arm, alarmed. "Are you all right?" He looked at her hand on his arm. She snatched it back. *Too forward, Adelaide!*

"I'm sorry." He sighed. "I've fought a dragon before. It brought back some…painful memories."

She gasped. "You…you've fought a dragon?" Words tumbled out of her mouth. "When? Where? How? Did you kill it? Did it breathe fire? What did it look like?"

Regulus massaged his forehead, his expression pinched.

"I'm sorry," she blurted. "I didn't mean to pry."

"No, no." He smiled, but it didn't reach his eyes. "I can't blame you." He chuckled. "Even if I wasn't prepared for so many questions on the subject from a lady."

"Oh." She snapped her mouth closed and angled away.

"No, I didn't mean that negatively!" Regulus said quickly. "I appreciate that you're interested. I just wasn't expecting it—I have little experience talking to ladies."

Her heart softened and she turned back toward him. "It must have been horrible. You don't need to tell me."

"And disappoint you?" He shook his head. "Let's see… Yes, a real, live dragon. Not terribly long—"

"You have some nerve, Hargreaves," Nolan's voice interrupted at Adelaide's shoulder. She looked up to see him glowering as if Regulus had insulted the entire Carrick line. His casual stance and crossed arms relayed a haughty and careless belief in himself, likely in his own superiority. His short, light brown hair had been perfectly combed.

"Pardon?" She looked back at Regulus, who glared at Nolan.

"Should you even be here?" Nolan asked, ignoring her. "Let alone talking with someone of Lady Belanger's quality."

"I was invited," Regulus said evenly. "Same as you."

"Same as me?" Disdain rang in every word Nolan spoke. "Not even close. *I* didn't need to bribe a servant to avoid sitting at the end of the hall." He stepped past Adelaide's shoulder, closer to Regulus. "It's not safe to let a mongrel wolf into the house with the dogs. The Glowers should know better."

Adelaide gasped and stood. "Sir Nolan!"

Nolan put an arm around her shoulders protectively—no, possessively. "Don't worry. He won't bother you any longer."

She shoved his arm off. "Bother me? Lord Hargreaves isn't the one bothering me. He has been nothing but a gentleman all evening. The only wolf here is you and your insolent pride. You owe Lord Hargreaves an apology."

"I—what?" Nolan lowered his voice as he grabbed her arm. She stared at his hand, dumbfounded. "Hargreaves is no gentleman, I don't—"

She yanked her arm away. "Touch me again without my consent and I will stab you."

"*Stab* me?"

In a swift, fluid motion, Adelaide bent down and drew the dagger out of her boot. She pointed the dagger at Nolan. "Regulus is no threat. And if he were, I can take care of myself."

"I meant no offense to you, Adelaide—"

"But you caused offense. And you certainly meant offense to Regulus." Warmth spread through her body as her magic kindled. She took a deep breath, forcing herself to be calm and keep her power in check. "You should leave before you make things worse."

A vein in Nolan's forehead bulged. He looked at her, then behind her, eyes flashing. He bowed curtly. "Forgive me, my lady, for having your best interests at heart." He opened and closed his mouth a few times before giving the most forced smile Adelaide had ever seen. "I spoke out of concern for a lady's well-being, safety, and reputation. I beg your pardon, Lord Hargreaves." He strode away.

In the wake of his departure, she realized several nearby nobles were staring and whispering. She dropped her hand, hiding her dagger in the folds of her skirt. At least the interaction might end any rumors she was courting Nolan.

She turned back to Regulus and almost bumped into his chest; he stood so close behind her. The skin around his long scar pulled tight and puckered around his deep frown. His features softened as he lowered his gaze to her face.

"Bold like a tigress," he murmured, smiling.

Adelaide hid her smile by sheathing her dagger and retaking her seat. "I apologize. He—"

"I've heard worse." Regulus rubbed the back of his neck. He sat without looking at her. "What he said…about your reputation." His throat bobbed. "He's likely right."

"What?"

"My blood is…tainted. My past—"

"I told you, I don't care."

"They do." He motioned around them.

She hesitated, then spoke quietly. "I only know from accidental eavesdropping, but my half-siblings resent our mother for…sullying Father. And for replacing their mother." She bit her cheek. "They said Minerva and I would make better servants than nobility."

Regulus winced.

She indicated the room. "So, I don't particularly care what *they* might think, Lord Hargreaves."

"A minute ago…" His posture relaxed as he glanced at her. "You called me Regulus."

Heat rushed up her neck to the tips of her ears. "I…did I?"

"You don't have to stop. If you like." Regulus reddened. "May I call you Adelaide?"

"I'd like that." Her voice came out soft. His piercing gray eyes glittered as the corner of his mouth quirked upward. Her stomach fluttered.

Oh. Oh, no.

I like him.

Chapter 16

THE BARRIER of blue light stretched from floor to ceiling down the length of one side of her bed. Adelaide smiled to herself. She had lost count of how many times she had attempted conjuring a barrier. Only two days prior—the day after the banquet, in fact—had she managed to get a barrier about the size of a small shield to stay up after she broke the link between the barrier and her hands. She walked around the edge of her bed, examining the thin barrier of shimmering, near-transparent azure light.

Now for the real test. She picked a throwing knife up off her desk and threw it at the barrier. It hit the barrier, and a ripple of energy pulsed out from the point of impact as the knife bounced back and fell onto her bed.

"Yes!" She clapped her hands over her mouth. Her heart hammered as she listened.

No one came knocking.

The barrier held.

Adelaide giggled and tried throwing the knife again. Same result. "I wonder…"

She walked around to the other side and raised her glowing palm. A point of light appeared over her outstretched hand and exploded into a small ball of flame. She launched the small fireball at the barrier.

The barrier absorbed the fire with a sound like distant wind.

Adelaide gave a little jump. She rubbed her hands together, pondering what to try next.

Someone knocked on the door of her room and she nearly jumped out of her skin. "Just a moment!" She waved her hand, and the barrier wavered then disappeared.

After taking a moment to collect herself and slow her panicked breathing, she unlocked and opened the door. One of the Drummonds' maids stood at the door, holding a short, square wooden box.

"A messenger just delivered these for you, my lady." The maid offered the box and a letter with a slight bow of her head. "From Sir Nolan Carrick."

Adelaide rolled her eyes. "Thank you." She closed the door and sat on her bed. The letter bore her name in a neat, flowing script. She broke the crimson wax seal of a gryphon on the back and read quickly.

Dear Lady Adelaide,

I pray you will forgive me for my inexcusable behavior at the Glower banquet. I admit I had drunk too much wine, and I am not ashamed to admit that I acted partly out of jealousy for your attentions. You are a rare and incomparable lady of good name and angelic beauty, and you deserve the affection of a man of similarly good name and appearance. I acted rashly, not as a gentleman, I fear, but as a man blinded by his admiration for you and a desire to see you unsullied by the dark forces of this world. I urge you, as a man of chivalry and honor, and as one who cares for you, not to trust Regulus Hargreaves. Please accept this humble token of my sincere apology and my admiration for your strong spirit, kind heart, and indescribable beauty.

Yours in heart and soul,
Nolan Carrick

Adelaide made a disgusted sound and tossed the letter aside. More out of curiosity than anything else, she lifted the lid off the box. Inside, on a blue velvet cloth, lay a necklace. It was a collar, really, formed of solid, flat silver wire, shaped to fit around the neck, with an elegant swirling design framing either side of a large, oval moonstone she guessed would rest between her collarbones if she put it on. She had no intention of ever doing so.

"Forgive me, and love me, because I'm rich!" she muttered. She replaced the lid and stuck the box and letter in a drawer in the vanity desk. She rolled her neck, pushing thoughts of Nolan's stubborn pride and selfish behavior away. Back to practicing magic.

Another knock on the door, and Adelaide stifled a groan. The same servant held a basket covered with a rough brown cloth with another letter resting on top. The maid giggled and smiled. "Just delivered for you, from—"

"Nolan Carrick, yes, yes." She halfheartedly reached for the basket.

"No, my lady." The maid winked. "From Lord Regulus Hargreaves of Arrano."

An unexpected catch in her breath. Adelaide grabbed the basket with a little more intensity than necessary or proper. "Thank you." She slammed the door shut as she hurried to her bed. The letter had her name on the front, although not in as precise and elegant of a script. A red seal on the back was imprinted with a rose over a pair of crossed swords. She broke the seal and fell back on the bed, holding the letter above her as she read.

Dear Lady Adelaide Belanger,

I greatly enjoyed your company at the Glowers' feast. Your conversation turned an evening that would have been long and trying into an enjoyable night that passed far too quickly. I am impressed by your wit, your honesty, your thoughtfulness, and your bold heart. I hope I am not being too forward in sending a small token of my admiration. I hope my little gift reminds you of home—and keeps me in your thoughts, as you are in mine. I look forward to when our paths cross again. Until then, I shall have to settle for fond memories of your gentle face framed by silky black hair and the deep warmth of your dark brown eyes.

Sincerely yours,

Regulus

In a different, more curving script at the bottom, was a postscript.

P.S. Regulus threw this note away because he feared it was too sentimental and forward, but I switched out the letters because this one is a more accurate representation of his heart. Perhaps it can be our secret? I should very much like to live. —Dresden Jakobs

Adelaide chuckled and reread the note. It was sappy, yes. But it felt honest. Real. She rolled over and pulled the cloth off the top of the basket and gasped.

Nalotavi. Four large, perfectly flaky, chocolatey and spicy smelling nalotavi rolls. She tossed the cloth back over the basket and raced down the hall to Minerva's study. She didn't even bother knocking, just walked in, basket in hand.

Minerva looked up in surprise from her needlework. "You startled me. Is everything—"

"Min, look!" She held the basket in front of her sister and yanked off the cloth.

Min's mouth fell open. "Is that…"

"Nalotavi, yes!" Adelaide grabbed one out of the basket and took a bite. "Mmm." She let the flaky, buttery, chocolate-laced pastry dissolve in her mouth and savored the gentle kick of the ginger and cinnamon at the end. Minerva didn't wait for an invitation; she took one of the other rolls and bit into it.

Contented ecstasy spread over Minerva's face. "Where did you get this?" she asked after several bites.

Adelaide finished chewing and swallowed. "A gift. From Lord Regulus."

"Mm-hmmm." Minerva winked.

"Stop it." She took a large bite to signal she wouldn't answer any more questions.

"Oh!" Minerva gasped and waved Adelaide over. "Come here, hurry!"

"What's wrong?" Adelaide set the basket and her roll on an empty armchair and rushed to kneel next to her sister, her insides knotting.

"Nothing, here!" Min grabbed her hand and pressed it to her round stomach. "Right…" She shifted Adelaide's hand over the soft fabric of her dress. "Hm…"

Something jabbed against Adelaide's palm. "Min! Was that—" The baby moved again.

"Mm-hm!" Minerva laughed, still holding Adelaide's hand on her belly.

"Oh, Min." Adelaide beamed, her throat tight and eyes moist.

"I've been waiting for the little one to move when you're in the room." Minerva chuckled. "Gaius is going to be jealous. He keeps falling asleep with his hand on my stomach; he loves feeling the baby move. I think he's more impatient for him or her to arrive than I am."

"Well, over halfway there." Adelaide pulled her hand away, as the baby seemed to have gotten comfortable.

Minerva pointed to the basket. "Might I steal another nalotavi roll? I think the baby likes them." She winked and Adelaide laughed.

"Fine. For the baby." She handed Minerva another roll and picked her own back up.

"I have to admit," Min said between bites, "this is working well in Lord Hargreaves' favor."

Adelaide didn't respond, but she had to agree.

REGULUS SAT in a large armchair in his room across from the small fire crackling in the fireplace, feet propped up on a cushioned stool. The orange light of the fire provided the only illumination now that the sun had set. He rubbed his thumb over the mark on his arm. Nearly three weeks had passed since he had returned from killing the dragon, and he hadn't heard from the sorcerer. In the two years since receiving the mark, there had been times he had gone three months without the sorcerer contacting him. Still, if the sorcerer was too busy to bother him, what was he busy with?

The sudden appearance of Magnus' large head in his lap pulled him out of his gloomy thoughts. "Hey, boy." He scratched under Magnus' chin. Magnus licked the rough, scarred mark on Regulus arm. "I'm afraid you can't clean that off, buddy." He pulled his sleeve back down and massaged Magnus' big, floppy ears. Magnus stood with his head resting on Regulus' thigh. As Regulus massaged his ears and the side of his head, Magnus closed his eyes and panted. Someone knocked on the door.

"Come in."

Dresden walked in, his face like stone. "Care to explain this?" He held up a piece of parchment. Magnus left to rub against Dresden's legs.

"Explain what?" Regulus knit his brows. "Is that a letter?"

Drez strode over and shoved the parchment in his face. "You left this in the dining hall."

As Regulus' eyes focused on the writing in the dim light, he recognized it as the letter confirming his entry into the Etchy Tournament. "Oh. That. I was going to tell you about that."

"When? It's in four days! We'll have to leave the day after next!" Dresden dropped the letter in Regulus' lap as Magnus curled up on the rug in front of the fireplace. "'Oh, Drez, get ready for a trip. Where? The Etchy Tournament, time to go, no time to talk.'"

Regulus ducked his head. "Something of the sort did cross my mind."

"Reg, there's a reason you don't do tournaments!" With a groan, Drez sat on the end of Regulus' bed.

"I know—"

"Then explain! Did the sorcerer tell you he won't need you for the next week?"

"Well, no—"

"So you could have to up and leave with no explanation?"

"That wouldn't be so strange—"

"And has your superhuman strength disappeared recently?"

"No—"

"Are you still healing supernaturally quickly?"

"Drez—"

"Is sorcery still a capital offense? What changed, Regulus? What?" Dresden looked uncharacteristically tired as he drew his hand down his face. "You're going to get caught."

Regulus stared at the fire. Every objection Dresden raised and more had already occurred to him. He knew he was being foolish; he just didn't care. Because for once, something was going right.

"I can be careful. I can hold myself back. I've practiced, you've seen it."

"When have you ever cared about tournaments?" Drez walked over to the fireplace. He knelt and scratched Magnus' head. "You told me you didn't want to take part in the nobles' games of vanity and posturing, regardless of the danger of doing so with your… Condition."

"Things change."

"What changed?" Dresden leaned against the wood-paneled wall next to the fireplace and crossed his arms. "Based on the checklist I went down, nothing…has…" A stricken expression came over his face. "Don't say it. Don't you say it."

Regulus offered a guilty half smile. "You wanted this."

"Oh, for the love of…" Drez rubbed his forehead. "Do you even know if she will be there?"

"She asked if I'd be there. I couldn't tell her no." *The yes was out of my mouth before I could stop myself.* He couldn't disappoint Adelaide now. And even though it was dangerous—for himself and Adelaide—he wanted to go. After she pulled a dagger on Carrick, Regulus knew he was a lost cause. He would do anything she asked. The way her eyes lit up when he said he'd be there… *She's making me reckless.*

"You're an idiot."

Yes, probably. "I'll be careful. I won't be found out." He looked down at his hands. "But if something goes wrong…well, same plan. None of you knew anything."

"I'm not abandoning you, Reg." Dresden's voice was tight with anger. "The others won't, either. Don't you get that yet?"

It's the only reason I keep coming back. "I'm not letting any of you die because of me."

"You're only in this mess because of me and the others," Dresden said quietly.

He took his feet off the stool and sat forward in his chair. "No. This was my choice. Something goes wrong; you swear on everything you can think of you didn't know. Or what is the point of what I've done?"

Dresden glowered at the floor in silence. "Well…don't get caught and it won't be an issue." He straightened. "So, you really like her?"

No. I think I might love her. "I know I shouldn't—"

Drez cursed. "Stop. You don't have to be afraid of being happy."

"I'm not afraid of being happy. I'm afraid of hurting her." Regulus rubbed the tension building in his shoulder. "When I'm here, it's easier to tell myself it's dangerous. But when I'm around her…" He shrugged, his face heating. *I believe in a better life.*

"You're more yourself." The corner of Drez's mouth pulled up in a bitter-sweet smile. "You better win. Make this ridiculous risk worth it."

Regulus smiled wryly. "Obviously."

THE TOURNAMENT grounds were already buzzing with activity as Adelaide dismounted. She held her hand up to shade her eyes from the bright afternoon sun as Gaius helped Minerva out of their carriage. Lord and Lady Drummond had decided not to attend the tournament as Lord Drummond had sprained his ankle. All the better for Adelaide, who could get away with riding Zephyr instead of being trapped in the carriage. Since Lady Drummond wasn't around to purse her lips at Adelaide's fashion choices, Adelaide wore a comfortable riding dress.

The close-fitting bodice of the gray-blue dress had long, fitted sleeves. The skirt, split beneath a wide black belt, parted when she walked to reveal a dark blue, smaller skirt that came to her mid-thigh. While still Monparthian and conservative in style, the split skirt would have scandalized Gaius' prim-and-proper mother.

Adelaide wandered toward whatever caught her attention. She admired a fine bay stallion here, looked at the archery field being assembled there. Gaius and Minerva followed as she wove between tents and rushing servants and squires leading enormous destriers. Dust coated everything, and the air smelled of manure, cooking food, and sweat.

As they walked, Adelaide spotted a large group of men. They wore clean but plain clothes, and most had a sword on their belt, but none wore armor. Probably knights there serving their lords and not competing; a few of the younger ones might be squires. A glint of sunlight on flying metal caught her eye, and she looked closer, slowing. Another glint of metal. Knives. They were throwing knives. A thrill went through her, and she sped toward the group.

Several knives with red handles were embedded in a large, sprawling beech tree a few paces away from the group. A few of the red-handled knives had blue-handled knives near them. Sometimes the red and blue were right next to each other, sometimes they had a good bit of space. Plenty of holes showed where knives had been thrown and removed.

A stocky man with a balding head and bushy black beard threw another blue-handled knife. It scraped across a branch, just below a red-handled knife, but fell to the ground. Several men groaned. The thrower stood next to a post with three more blue-handled knives stuck in it. Adelaide watched with interest as the man threw the remaining knives with no better luck.

"Not bad," a thin man with salt-and-pepper hair said. "But Estevan wins another round." Several men grumbled while others gloated as money exchanged hands. A boy of about ten ran out to the tree and pulled all the knives free.

"Any other takers?" Salt-and-Pepper asked.

"What exactly is going on?" Adelaide asked a lean man with a weathered face and blond hair.

He looked at her in surprise. "Oh, just a bit of fun, m'lady. That there is Estevan." He pointed at a young man of average height and a thin but muscular build with tan skin and thick, curly brown hair. The dark edge of a tattoo showed just above his collar. "He's about one of the best knife-throwers there is. He gets the first throw. His opponent throws second. If he can get all of his knives within four fingers' breadth of Estevan's, he wins. If not, Estevan wins."

Adelaide nodded, as Salt-and-Pepper kept asking for volunteers. "I take it Estevan hasn't lost yet."

"No, m'lady."

"Come on," the older man crooned. "Is no one bold and skilled enough to knock this upstart down a peg or two? Someone must want to try their hand at it."

"I'll throw." Adelaide said it before she even realized she was speaking. Minerva sighed behind her and Gaius choked.

Amusement, shock, and confusion showed on the men's faces. Adelaide cleared her throat. "I'll throw," she repeated. No way would she back down now.

"With all due respect my lady," Salt-and-Pepper said, looking uncomfortable, "this is a gambling game—"

Adelaide reached into the purse at her belt and pulled out a few silver coins. "Is this enough?"

"Um…" The man looked lost and confused, so Adelaide smiled sweetly at Estevan.

"Won't you let a lady have a little fun?"

Estevan chuckled. "I'm not going to make it easy for you."

Adelaide grinned. "I should hope not. Fair's fair."

"All right… I guess the lady throws." Salt-and-Pepper shrugged.

Estevan stepped forward, and the boy stuck the red-handled knives into the post. Estevan threw in rapid succession, each knife burying deep into the oak in different places and angles. Adelaide studied him, noting his ease, balanced stance, and excellent follow-through. Once he'd thrown all eight knives, he stepped back. "My lady."

The men whispered to each other and a few sniggered, but she ignored them and handed the man in charge her silver. As she walked to the post, she studied the position of the knives in the tree. All right. A few tricky angles and a couple thinner branches. But not terrible. The boy stuck the blue-handled knives into the post and stepped away.

Adelaide pulled the first one free and held it for a moment, judging its weight and balance. She tossed it in the air and caught it a couple times. She took a deep breath, stood as near as she could to where Estevan had stood, and threw the knife.

"Okay, but do you *need* to do three events?" Dresden asked as they walked across the dusty tournament grounds.

People were everywhere. Noblewomen cast furtive glances their way and noblemen poorly hid their surprise at seeing Regulus. Young men caroused and winked at giggling young women. Servants hurried to do their masters' bidding and freemen shouted to each other as they finished constructing rough arenas and stands with benches for the audience. The air was rank with the smell of horses. A lord whose name he'd forgotten cast a suspicious glance his way, but Regulus squared his shoulders. He had every right to compete.

Regulus stepped around a pile of horse manure. "Define *need*."

Dresden rolled his eyes. "I get the joust. What's the point if you enter a tournament and don't joust, right? Sword makes sense, even if it's a touch risky. Archery, though?"

"I've been practicing so much, I'd like to see how I do," Regulus said, a little defensively.

"Archery has never been your strongest point."

"Then there's room for improvement. If nothing else, watching the others will give me some ideas."

"You are a strange man."

"I suppose you would know, wouldn't you?"

Dresden snorted. He pointed at a group of men. "Looks like Estevan is getting up to mischief already."

"Oh?" Regulus looked as Estevan threw a knife at an oak tree and stepped back. "Should have known we'd find him throwing knives. Likely gambling, too." They ambled toward the group to see how his opponent would fare. Regulus stumbled.

"Is that—"

"Adelaide," Regulus breathed. Adelaide strode to the post were Estevan had stood moments before. Her blue dress parted as she walked, revealing black boots and fitted breeches. A boy stuck several knives in the post.

"She's not…throwing knives…is she?" Dresden asked.

Adelaide pulled out one of the knives, hefting it in her hand.

Regulus waved his hand. "Khastallanders teach women to use daggers and throwing knives. So…"

"So she thought she'd compete against Estevan?" Dresden shook his head as they stopped at the edge of the group of bystanders.

Adelaide adjusted her stance, raised her arm. She threw the knife. With a flash of reflected sunlight, it arced through the air and buried in the tree with a soft thud, less than a palm's breadth from one of Estevan's knives. She tilted her head to the side, then grabbed another knife. The onlookers, most of whom had been talking and several laughing, had fallen silent. She threw the next knife, then threw the rest as quickly as she could pull them from the post, which was impressively fast. When she finished, she leaned back on her heels, crossed her arms, and grinned at Estevan.

All her knives had landed close to Estevan's. Three of her knives were practically touching his. Estevan stared at the tree, jaw slack. Silence. Regulus looked back and forth between the knives and Adelaide's jubilant expression. Her eyes sparkled over her confident smile. Regulus' heart squeezed strangely. *Etiros, I'm in love.*

"Let's hear it for the lady," one man shouted. The rest of the congregated men cheered, and Adelaide blushed and gave a small curtsy. A few of the men looked downcast as they handed over coins to jubilant friends.

"We have a new winner," said a man with gray-flecked black hair. He handed Adelaide a handful of coins. "Most impressive, m'lady."

Adelaide pocketed her winnings and crossed over to Estevan with a smile. "Excellent throwing."

"You too," Estevan said slowly, jaw still slack. He shook his head and smiled. "I'm sorry. That was…spectacular. Congratulations, Lady…?"

"Belanger."

"Lady Belanger." Estevan's eyes went wide. "B-Belanger?" Regulus watched in amusement as terrified realization dawned on Estevan's face.

"Yes…?" Adelaide chuckled awkwardly.

Regulus walked up to them. "Lady Adelaide."

She looked up and beamed. "Lord Regulus!"

He smiled. "I see you've met another of my knights, Sir Estevan Wolgemuth."

Estevan bowed, although his face was red. "It's an honor to meet you, my lady, even an honor to lose to you. Reg—Lord Hargreaves speaks highly of you."

"Does he?" She pushed some of her hair back behind her ear, momentarily hiding her face.

"Never letting you live this down," Dresden whispered to Estevan. Estevan scowled and went to retrieve the knives from the tree.

Sir Gaius and Lady Minerva came up next to Adelaide. Sir Gaius chuckled and shook his head. "I knew you threw knives, but by my sword, that was something to watch." Minerva elbowed him. "What? Swearing? Your sister just gambled and threw knives against a man she didn't even know, I think I can be forgiven for an innocent oath."

Regulus bowed. "Sir Gaius. Lady Minerva."

"Lord Hargreaves," they said in unison as they bowed and curtsied.

"Dresden and I were on our way to see the jousting arena." He looked at Adelaide. "Perhaps you all would walk with us?"

"We would love to," Adelaide said.

Regulus smiled. "Excellent." For a moment, he hesitated. He offered her his arm. She placed her hand in the crook of his elbow and stepped closer to him. Close enough her skirt brushed his leg. He cleared his throat and started toward the jousting arena.

Dresden and Sir Gaius and Minerva fell behind them. Regulus suspected this to be on purpose, probably a design of Dresden's. But he couldn't think of anything other than Adelaide's hand on his arm.

"I thought Estevan was the best knife-thrower I'd ever met." He chuckled. "I may have to re-evaluate."

"That wasn't exactly ladylike, I suppose."

He looked down at her in surprise. "What? Why not?"

She looked up, brow creased. "Gaius is right. I gambled *and* threw knives in competition against someone I didn't even know. Not things ladies are supposed to do."

"Why?"

Adelaide wrinkled her nose. "I don't know why. I've been asking for years and no one will tell me!"

They laughed and Regulus felt warmth spread through his chest.

"It truly doesn't bother you?"

Regulus shrugged. "Can I be honest?"

"All right…"

"It was beautiful."

Adelaide tripped forward and he caught her shoulders. She leaned into his side for the briefest moment, and his lungs squeezed. She steadied herself, returning her hand to the crook of his elbow. He swallowed hard. Forced himself to breathe.

"There was a rock," she muttered.

After a moment, Regulus continued. "I saw beauty. Confident dignity in your posture. Sophistication in your movements, grace in the arc of the blades. I saw nothing unladylike. Just elegant, mesmerizing strength. You know your own capabilities, and that confidence is attractive."

Adelaide looked at him sideways, a smile dancing at the corner of her lips. "Attractive?"

His face heated. "I…um…" Panic rose in his chest. Had it been too forward to say that?

"I suppose you called my *confidence* attractive," Adelaide said, her voice thoughtful. "So, there's room for debate on whether *I* am attractive."

Their eyes met. In unison, they just…stopped walking. Stood there. So close together. Her lips parted slightly, and he felt the sudden, strong urge to lean down and kiss her.

"No," he whispered, his voice hoarse. "No debate. Not from me."

"If we're being honest," she murmured, "you're pretty good-looking yourself."

His heart thudded. "Better without the scar, I'd imagine," he said without thinking.

She cocked her head to the side and grinned. "I like it."

He ran his free hand through his hair, then rubbed the pommel of his sword. His scar? She…liked it?

A woman cleared her throat in an obvious attempt at getting their attention. Adelaide reddened as they stepped back from each other and her hand slipped off his arm.

"Having a good conversation, are we?" Minerva said as she walked up to them with Dresden and Gaius. Dresden winked at Regulus. Hopefully Adelaide hadn't noticed.

"Yes, *actually*," Adelaide replied. "*Ahpak, bes bahda dahlen ped, hei neah?*" Regulus recognized the Khast but didn't have any idea what she had said.

Minerva giggled and responded in Khast.

Whatever Minerva had said made Adelaide's cheeks darken. *"Kop reho!"*

That he thought he understood. Best guess? *Shut up.*

Minerva held her pregnant stomach as she laughed again.

Gaius looked at Regulus with sympathy. "They do this sometimes. It's most unfair."

"Maybe you should learn Khast," Dresden said.

"Minerva tried to teach me, but I fear I'm a poor student." Gaius wrapped his arm around Minerva's shoulders, and Regulus envied how comfortable and at ease they looked, with her shoulder tucked between his chest and arm.

"Shall we continue?" Adelaide asked, looking as if she had recovered her composure.

"Right." Regulus nodded. "Nearly there."

ADELAIDE FOCUSED on maintaining a composed exterior as they continued on their way. She left a little extra space between her and Regulus and didn't take his arm again. She still felt a little…dizzy? Winded? For a moment, she'd wondered if he was going to kiss her. If she was honest, she had wished he would, although the thought made her legs feel weak. Adelaide had never been kissed, and the idea of kissing Regulus was both nerve-wracking and tantalizing. Hence, the extra space between them now. Plus, something Minerva had said, even in teasing, troubled her.

Maybe he should talk to Father.

Father was cautious with all his daughters, but with Adelaide most of all. She was the youngest, and more importantly, she was a mage. What if Father—or Mother, who could be even more fiercely protective—didn't think Regulus could be trusted with her secret? Adelaide glanced over. She had a gut feeling she could trust Regulus. *He's a good man. I'm sure of it.* If she wanted to marry him, would Father forbid her?

Oh. A realization hit her with the force of one of her throwing knives, right in her heart. *I'm thinking about marrying him.* A whirlwind of emotions. Excitement. Fear. Confusion. Giddiness.

True, Father would do anything to protect her. But Father loved her, and he trusted her. If Adelaide trusted Regulus, Father would, too. She looked over at Regulus again and caught him looking at her. She blushed and glanced away, smiling to herself.

Might as well admit it. You're falling hard.

"Lady Adelaide!"

Adelaide groaned internally as she recognized the voice. She forced a pleasant smile and turned toward Nolan.

Nolan approached flanked by a couple knights. He had paired an ostentatious aquamarine doublet with a white shirt and navy trousers. A sword hung from a leather belt embroidered with silver thread, as if he feared someone might forget his parents were wealthy. His light brown hair, as usual, was perfect. What a marked contrast to Regulus' loose, open-necked black shirt, plain sword belt, and longer, tousled wavy black hair.

"It is a pleasure to see you, Lady Adelaide." Nolan bowed, predictably snatching up her hand to kiss her fingers. She hated the flamboyant gesture. He bowed toward the rest of the party. "And you as well, Sir Gaius, Lady Minerva. Lord Hargreaves." He sounded terse as he addressed Regulus, but his expression stayed agreeable. "I'm surprised to see you here. I didn't think you competed."

"I haven't had the desire in the past," Regulus said, to Adelaide's surprise. "But I will compete in archery, sword, and joust this time."

"Interesting." Nolan looked at Dresden. "And…tell me your name again?"

"Sir Jakobs." Dresden sounded unamused.

"Right. I don't expect *you'll* be competing? Not allowed, I'd wager."

Shock rushed through her at Nolan's flaunting of Dresden's non-noble blood.

"No," Dresden said, his tone cool. "Only because the officials feared I'd kill some poor noble."

"Mm." Nolan directed his attention back to Adelaide. Sorrow shadowed his face. "My lady, you wound me."

"Pardon?"

He gestured toward her neck. "I had hoped to see my gift around that beautiful neck."

"Oh." Adelaide's fingers drifted to her bare neck. "The necklace was very…um, thoughtful." She floundered. "But—"

"Not your style?" Nolan sighed. "My mother warned me against jewelry, but I wanted something that at least approached your beauty."

How do you politely say, "Thank you, not interested?"

"Perhaps over supper you can tell me more about yourself, and I can send better tokens of my affection in the future."

Supper? Future! Adelaide took a step backward, her words caught in her throat.

"I'm sorry?" Regulus choked out.

Adelaide's palms grew slick. This conversation had careened out of control.

"Good luck with that." Minerva snorted. "Perhaps you should ask Lord Hargreaves what kinds of gifts Adelaide enjoys."

Nolan opened and closed his mouth as he shot a glare Regulus' direction. "I suppose," he said with a pleasant smile, "until I can offer gifts more suited to your tastes, Adelaide, I'll have to win this tournament in your honor."

Adelaide shook her head. "Oh—"

"Has someone else already dedicated their victory to you?" Nolan raised a brow.

"Well, no, but—"

"Good. I wouldn't expect too much from Hargreaves' first tournament, to be blunt."

"I'll enjoy proving you wrong," Regulus said evenly.

Adelaide huffed. Annoying male egos. "Sir Nolan—"

"Please, just Nolan."

"*Sir Carrick.*" She took a deep breath. "I think there may have been a misunderstanding."

"Then what is there to misunderstand?" Nolan looked into her eyes. "Every blow with my sword, every hit with my lance. Every win, and my ultimate victory, will be for you. When I am weak, I will look to you and your smiling face will give me strength."

Adelaide raised her brows, jaw agape. *Is he for real?* "Sir Carrick—"

"Nolan," he said, an edge to his voice. She took a deep breath as her irritation grew.

"Sir Carrick," Gaius said. "The lady is trying to let you down gently."

Nolan looked to Gaius, then back at her. "Is this true?"

"I'm sorry. I don't return your feelings."

"Obviously," Dresden muttered.

Nolan glared at Regulus. "Because of him?"

She couldn't contain her irritation any longer. "Because of you! You're insufferable! You're vain and rude and presumptuous!" She clenched her hands into fists as she shoved down the urge to knock him backwards with a magic blast. "Just…go!"

Nolan hung his head. "I apologize profusely, my lady. I meant no offense. My heart ran away with me, and if in my zeal to show you my affection, I appeared vain and presumptuous, I am most ashamed."

His sudden show of humility caught her by surprise. He certainly knew how to speak well when he so desired.

"I would give anything for a chance to redeem myself." Nolan stepped closer. Regulus moved around her, his hand on his sword. She didn't need him to, but she appreciated the protective instinct.

"Lady Belanger asked you to leave," Regulus said, his voice deep and emphatic. Gracious, that was attractive.

Nolan backed up. "As for rude, I blame my sincere desire to protect you from a man I do not believe to be worthy of your trust or your affections." He bowed, then sauntered past, followed by his knights. As he passed Regulus, he said in a voice so low she almost didn't hear him, "I'll see you in the lists, mongrel."

Regulus watched him go, his expression stony.

"I do not like that man," Dresden said. "The villain." He spat.

"Drez!" Regulus snapped.

"That seems harsh," Gaius said. He stood behind Minerva with his arms wrapped around her stomach.

"I've heard things," Dresden said. "Scandalous rumors. About why his engagement was called off."

"Nolan was engaged?" Adelaide asked, the information like a slap to her face. Regulus' expression shuttered at her use of Nolan's first name, and she felt an immediate twinge of guilt.

"It wasn't very public," Dresden explained. "But rumor has it his parents had arranged a marriage for him a couple years back. Some say to Baron Gaveston's daughter, but who knows. He offended the bride's father, who called it off. If that weren't enough to call him a villain, one of the Carricks' servants will swear up and down that Baron Esmil's oldest daughter was forced to join a convent after she was caught…" He cleared his throat. "*With* Nolan Carrick."

Adelaide's face heated as she recalled Nolan's offer to walk her to her room at Carrick castle.

"That's a terrible thing to say based on rumor," Gaius said.

"I've heard something similar." Minerva nodded. "And I know a few young ladies who've admitted to pushing the boundaries of propriety for Nolan Carrick's charm."

Adelaide shrugged. "Hopefully that means he'll easily find someone else to bother with his bravado."

"Or he's run out of other viable options," Dresden said. Adelaide did *not* care for that possibility. She must have looked upset, because Dresden added, "But that seems unlikely. He'll probably have moved on by this time tomorrow."

"Enough about Nolan Carrick." She waved her hand. "He's wasted enough of our time."

Regulus ducked out of his tent and stretched. The sun just peeked above the horizon and the chill air bit through his worn, loose linen shirt and trousers. His bare toes curled into the grass. The clatter of pots, sound of footsteps, rustle of tents, and snatches of quiet conversation drifted through the air. He breathed in deeply as he stretched, and immediately regretted it. The air stank of dust, smoke, horses, and body odor. It smelled like camp and took him back to his days as a mercenary. He had many fond memories of those days, but he wouldn't go back. He didn't miss camping with dozens of sweaty men who hadn't bathed in weeks.

"Good morning, my lord!" Harold beamed as he rounded a tent, arms full of firewood.

"You're particularly cheery today," Regulus noted.

Harold bent down to arrange the logs in the ash from last night's fire. "Never been to a tournament," he said. "It's exciting."

"Never?"

"Never, my lord."

"Huh." Regulus supposed that made sense. Since becoming a lord two years ago, he had avoided tournaments. People were already suspicious of him, with his checkered background and the ease with which he defeated Lady Arrano's champion. Best to keep a low profile and avoid any accidental displays of the supernatural side effects of the sorcerer's mark.

Thinking of the mark made him uncomfortable. Was he endangering Adelaide by courting her? Could he risk marrying her? *Oh, Etiros, do I want to marry her.* He had assumed he would never marry. Too much darkness. Too much shame. But then Adelaide. She gave him hope. She liked his scar. His past and his scar, two things he thought made him undesirable, and she accepted them. But could she accept his mark? Could she love him if she knew the truth? Knew the oath he had made? The evil he served?

Not forever. Until his debt was paid.

If the sorcerer kept his word.

"Are you all right, my lord?" Harold's brow puckered.

"Oh, yes." He smiled. "Just thinking."

"You should do less of that," Dresden said, emerging from the tent opposite Regulus'. "Makes your face all frowny."

"According to you I'm always frowning."

Drez yawned. "Yes, but less so yesterday. I'd like to keep this new trend of smiling Regulus going."

Regulus shook his head and rolled his eyes.

"I agree with Dresden." Regulus nearly jumped out of his skin at the sound of Adelaide's voice. He spun to see her standing with her hands held behind her back on the other side of Harold, who was busy cracking eggs into a pan over the fire. Another woman stood a little behind her to her left, dressed in the simple clothing of a maidservant.

Adelaide wore a dress of deep purplish-red with white, fitted sleeves. The wide collar was embroidered in gold with flowers that matched the color of the dress. A belt of engraved bronze squares rested on her hips. She wore her black hair loose in waves over her shoulders.

Regulus tried to stop staring. "You've made an early start of the day."

She shrugged. "I like mornings. Helps clear the mind."

Adelaide walked around Harold and the fire. Regulus caught her gaze flitting down to his torso. Part of him wished he had put on proper clothes before coming out of his tent, rather than standing there in a thin shirt and frayed trousers. A vainer part of him felt more than a little pleased and wanted her to look. *So long as she can't see the scars through the shirt.*

"I…" Adelaide hesitated, then pulled her hands in front of her. She held a piece of fabric around a foot long and about as wide as his hand that matched the purplish-red of her dress. She blushed as she held it out to him. "I thought…that is, I wondered…" She muttered something in Khast. "Would you wear this?"

Regulus smiled. He hadn't smiled like this in years. His scar pulled on his lips and cheek, the skin so tight it was almost painful. He didn't care. "I would be honored." He reached out, wrapped his fingers around the cloth—and over her fingers.

She smiled back. Lingered for a moment with her fingers against his. She eased her hold on the cloth and pulled her hand away. "I'll watch for you on the field." Adelaide bit her lower lip, turned, and walked away, trailed by her handmaid.

Regulus wished she'd stayed. He was glad she didn't. If she had, he might have kissed her. He watched her until she disappeared between the tents. The soft cloth in his hands still held her warmth. He looked up and saw Dresden smirking.

He pointed at Dresden. "Not. A. Word."

A SQUIRE squeezed past Regulus with a muttered "pardon me." The space around the archery arena buzzed with conversation and hurried footsteps. Regulus moved closer to the low fence surrounding the arena and checked the fabric tied to his upper right arm again. Still there.

He strung his bow and looked for Adelaide. He glimpsed the purple-red of her dress, but then lost her in the crowd. *You're being a fool, Regulus. Focus on the competition.*

"You know," Carrick's cool voice cut through his thoughts, "I may have to review the entry guidelines with the heralds. I'm not sure you carry the necessary lineage to legally compete, Lord Half-Breed."

Carrick stood next to him but looked straight ahead as he adjusted his gloves. He wore armor with engraved edges and lines and points that provided more style than function.

"The law requires proof of nobility on one side only, and proof of legal title." Regulus shoved down his anger. "I am well within my rights."

"Sounds like the law needs adjusted if we're to keep the rabble out."

"Do we have a problem, Sir Carrick?" Regulus turned toward Carrick, reveling in the fact that he towered over him.

Carrick continued looking straight ahead, as unfazed and sure of himself as ever. "Yes, actually. Stay away from Adelaide."

"Excuse me?"

Carrick finally faced him. "I won't tell you again. She's above your station." He shrugged. "A little beneath mine, but that's beside the point. I don't know what she finds so fascinating about your scarred face, peasant blood, and murderer-for-hire past, but sooner or later she'll realize you're not a good match."

Regulus clenched his fist, every muscle taunt. *Save it for the field.* He gritted his teeth. "You should go."

"I'm going. I'm needed in the polearm arena." Carrick's gaze fell to Adelaide's token. "Pity you're competing in archery instead. I suppose I must wait until the sword competition this afternoon to cut that off your arm." He turned and strode away.

Regulus shook his head and tried to focus on archery.

The archery competition went both worse and better than Regulus had expected. He hadn't expected to win, but he had wanted to. He felt Adelaide's token put a little extra pressure on him to do well. To show he deserved to wear it. To not put her to shame.

Adelaide would probably find that ridiculous. He couldn't find her in the chaos of the dispersing crowd, but she hadn't said a word that morning about winning. Still, he wondered if she found his underperformance embarrassing. Not that he did poorly. He placed sixth out of seventeen, which wasn't terrible, all things considered. Although Caleb would be disappointed his lessons hadn't had more of an impact.

Caleb should be competing. Caleb would have won. But that couldn't happen. His knights had come to support him and enjoy the spectacle of the tournament, but not to compete. Caleb's father had been a minor lord, but after his father died and left everything to his three older brothers, Caleb left his old life behind, and he no longer had anything to prove his nobility. Perceval could have competed if he wanted, since he *could* prove his ancestry of nobility. But, in his own words, he "fought too dirty and had too many hard feelings toward nobles to get in a sparring ring with those prissy pretty boys." Dresden, Jerrick, and Estevan couldn't claim a drop of noble blood. And, unfortunately, lineage mattered at tournaments in Monparthian law, not the knighthood Regulus had bestowed.

Regulus strolled across the massive tournament grounds back toward the tents, Dresden, Caleb, and Perceval beside him.

"Well, I won't say you haven't improved," Caleb said.

Regulus raised an eyebrow. "That sounds like you *want* to say I haven't."

"Oh, no, no!" Caleb held his hands out and shook his head. "I mean you *have.*"

"It's the double negatives," Perceval said. "Sounds like you're sayin' opposite of what you said."

Regulus looked at him in confusion.

"What? I went to university, remember?"

"For two and a half weeks." Drez snorted.

"Still longer than any of you, makin' me the most educated member of this band." Perceval inclined his head. "All due respect, Captain."

"And the least genteel." Caleb shook his head with exaggerated sadness.

"I suppose you think you're the most genteel?" Dresden asked.

Caleb bowed with a flourish of his hand. "Obviously."

"I don't know." Regulus scratched his chin. "Drez should get some gentility points for his well-kept beard alone."

Caleb made a sound of protest, his mouth agape. "Now that's just cruel." He rubbed the stubble on his jawline with the back of his fingers. "It's not my fault my beard grows out all scraggly. Besides, the ladies love a little five o'clock shadow."

"Ladies love a full, soft, closely trimmed beard," Dresden said.

"Says the two single men." Perceval harrumphed. "You think I'm clean shaven because I enjoy shaving? Hm? I prefer kisses from my wife, thank you."

"You have a beard like a porcupine, it doesn't count." Dresden stroked his beard.

Regulus shook his head as they arrived at the tents. "All right, enough!"

After lunch, Harold helped Regulus into his armor, and Drez tied Adelaide's token to his arm, tucking the knot under the pauldron to ensure it wouldn't come off. The plain armor emphasized strength and maneuverability over looks. Lots of curves to help blows glance off.

Compared to the bulk of the Black Knight armor, this felt like heavy clothes, so he had to be extra careful to control his strength. Plus, he carried his own sword. A standard broadsword, it was considerably lighter than the massive black sword hidden with the chest of armor in his tent. Although he prayed the sorcerer would not call on him during the tournament, he had no way of knowing when he would next feel his mark burn.

But he couldn't think about that, not now. He intended, for the first time in over two years, to act like his own man. For the tournament, he would forget about the sorcerer's threats looming over him, ignore his recklessness, and be present in the moment and enjoy it. Fight for sport instead of for his life. Love a spectacular woman. Today, he would ignore the darkness. Today, nothing would bring him down. Because today, he wore his heart on his sleeve as literally as possible.

His men accompanied him to the sword-fighting arena. Perceval and Caleb were still bickering about something, while Estevan occasionally interjected, stoking the flames. Harold and Jerrick seemed to be placing bets on whether Perceval would punch Caleb.

"I need to concentrate!" Regulus snapped as they approached the fence surrounding the arena. Waiting competitors and their attendants crowded about. "What in creation are you two fighting about now?"

"Perce thinks he's high and mighty because he got kicked out of university," Caleb said.

"Captain, you think they'll let me and Cal borrow the sword-fighting arena for a minute?" Perceval crossed his arms. The man had about the most intimidating scowl Regulus had ever seen, but Caleb just snickered.

Dresden smacked the back of Perceval's head. "Hey, you're distracting Reg."

"My, my, your men have the decorum of peasant children." Carrick leaned back against the fence, looking at Regulus and his men with clear disdain. "But then, that's presumably what they are. Just like their false lord."

Perceval moved forward. Regulus blocked him with his arm. His blood boiled, but he wouldn't give Carrick the satisfaction of a reaction.

Carrick looked across the arena at the crowds filing into the wood stadium seating. He jutted his chin toward the spectators. "Oh, excellent. Adelaide is here."

Regulus looked where Carrick had indicated as Adelaide took a seat in a box near the center of the arena with the Drummonds.

"She will have an excellent view when you're flat on your back with me standing over you." Carrick smiled viciously.

Keep calm. Regulus took a deep breath and smiled back. "Or perhaps the other way around." He held out his hand. *Never let them see they're getting to you.* "Good luck, Sir Carrick."

Carrick's top lip curled. But then he took Regulus' hand and squeezed harder than necessary as he smiled again. Regulus summoned every ounce of self-control to not just break his hand.

"May the best man win, mercenary." Carrick dropped Regulus' hand and sauntered over to the herald overseeing the event.

"See?" Perceval jabbed his finger in the air. "This. This is why I don't compete. I'd cut that"—he said a few choice words describing Carrick—"head clean off."

"And this is why you're the least genteel," Caleb said.

"Contestants to the field!" the herald called. "All contestants competing in the sword, please enter the arena!"

"I'd recommend not cutting his head off," Dresden said solemnly.

"I'll try to keep that in mind." Regulus kept his tone light and jocular, but he knew Dresden was right. The way Carrick got under his skin… He would have to be careful.

The herald welcomed the contestants and spectators and explained the event. Pairs had been pre-chosen for the first round. Winners would compete in new pairs in the next round, and so on until only two knights remained. One loser picked by Baron Carrick, who sat in a large box centered in the middle of the arena, would compete in the second round to ensure an even number of competitors. There would be five rounds total. Five rounds, five opponents between him and victory.

The herald announced the pairs. Regulus would go eleventh, fighting against Sir Morris MacCombe. Regulus had met Baron MacComb's eldest before. A polite man in his early thirties with a reputation for chivalry and some skill with a sword. The combatants bowed to the spectators and filed out of the arena, except the first two combatants—Lord Thorne, one of Baron MacComb's vassals, and Carrick. Regulus found it suspicious that Carrick dueled first, but it provided a good opportunity to study him, should they end up facing each other. He hoped they would.

Lord Thorne was a short, stocky man with a steely gaze, muscles that protruded from his thick neck, a stubbly gray beard, and long gray hair tied back at the nape of his neck. He had fought in the Trade Wars and had a reputation for smashing in skulls with a war-hammer. It would be interesting to see how he fared with a sword.

The men shook hands then put on their helms. Flaxen horsehair formed a plume on Carrick's. *Let's see if your skill matches your flair, Carrick.* The men drew their swords and circled each other. Regulus leaned on the fence, eyes narrowed.

Thorne attacked with the force of a charging wild boar—all strength and speed, but little finesse. Rather than attempt to block the blow, Carrick sidestepped and parried Thorne's sword from the side. Begrudgingly, Regulus nodded. The force of a blow like that could shatter an arm if taken directly. Despite the force of his swing, Thorne adjusted, attacking from the side before Carrick had a chance to counter. Carrick blocked, moving back to absorb the impact of the blow. Thorne stepped forward, pressing his advantage.

Carrick gave way, backing up here, sidestepping there. Parrying rather than blocking whenever possible. He was letting Thorne wear himself down.

Thorne had a distinct advantage over Carrick in mass and muscle. But Carrick made the smallest movements possible, conserving his energy. Thorne brought a weaker strike from the left, and Regulus had seen enough fights to know Carrick was about to make his move. Carrick stepped into the strike, holding the flat of his blade up to block. With a resounding clang, Thorne's sword pushed Carrick's to the side. Carrick stumbled, and several people gasped. But Regulus noted the careful placement of Carrick's feet as he stumbled, how he adjusted his grip on his sword. A feint. Emboldened, Thorne raised his sword, preparing for a mighty downward swing. Carrick prepared to block the blow. Thorne swung.

Carrick spun to the side and Thorne's sword tore through empty air and slammed into the ground, sending up chunks of dirt. Carrick moved to the offensive, driving Thorne back. Caught unprepared, Thorne had difficulty getting his stance corrected. He moved backward off-balance, his energy lagging. Carrick, on the other hand, unleashed his speed and strength.

The crowd cheered as Carrick landed repeat blows on Thorne's breastplate. Thorne tried to counter, to turn back to the offensive. Carrick let him, just for a moment, then parried, knocking Thorne's sword aside. He kicked the back of Thorne's knee, and the older man stumbled forward. A blow to his back, and Thorne fell to his knees. Carrick swung, bringing his sword to a stop just before Thorne's neck. Thorne dropped his sword. The crowd applauded and hollered. Carrick would continue to the second round.

ADELAIDE SIGHED as Carrick jabbed his sword into the air, celebrating his victory. Part of her had expected him to be all style and no substance, despite William Carrick's advice not to bet against him. When Lord Thorne appeared to have the upper hand, she felt smug. But once Nolan moved to the offensive, she realized he had always been in control. He had a plan from the beginning, and it worked. Reluctantly, she applauded as he removed his helm. Nolan had his faults, but he *had* apologized. He had not approached her since the afternoon prior. And based on his congenial handshake with Regulus before the contestants entered the field, they must have worked out their differences. It made her dislike him a little less.

Carrick looked directly at her as he bowed. He flashed a charming smile and mouthed something that looked like *"for you."* She clenched her jaw as he turned and swaggered out of the arena. *Never mind.* Some might find his determined pursuit attractive, but she found it annoying. What was his goal, wear her down until she was so tired of saying no, she said yes? How unromantic.

Regulus leaned against the fence, a deep, thoughtful frown on his face. He looked toward her, and Adelaide smiled. His expression softened, and his hand strayed to the strip of fabric fastened to his arm. Minerva poked her side.

"The next competitors have entered the field, in case you missed it while making love eyes at Lord Hargreaves."

Adelaide scowled. "You're ridiculous. What even *are* love eyes?"

"The look you were just giving Regulus Hargreaves." Min laughed as Adelaide rolled her eyes.

"How convenient and vague a definition." She looked back at Regulus, but he had turned his attention to the new combatants.

Nobles from as young as seventeen to as old as fifty took their turns in the arena. Most fights ended quickly. Others had her on the edge of her seat as evenly matched opponents went back and forth, gaining and losing the upperhand at staggering speed. Between each match she looked to Regulus, and he always met her gaze before turning his attention back to the combat.

Finally, Regulus entered the field. Her pulse quickened. Regulus nodded at Adelaide before he turned to his opponent. Regulus was taller Sir Morris

MacCombe, but they had similar muscular builds and the same air of resolve as they shook hands. She remembered liking Sir MacCombe at the Carrick's dance, but she hoped Regulus beat him. A loss wouldn't change her feelings, but she wanted Carrick to see Regulus win. And she didn't care to see the disappointed expression Regulus had after he lost the archery contest again.

Regulus pulled on his helm and took up his stance. Feet planted, knees bent. Chin tucked in as he looked through his visor. Adelaide leaned forward and wrapped her fingers around the edge of the wooden bench.

MacCombe shifted to his right, and Regulus did the same, moving his feet in a fluid movement close to the ground. The men circled for a moment, sizing each other up. Both moved at the same time. Their swords met with a ringing clang. Their blades parted as they both carried through their momentum and stepped back. MacCombe swung. Adelaide gripped the bench harder.

Regulus parried, pushing MacCombe's blade aside. As MacCombe adjusted, Regulus attacked, but MacCombe blocked then pushed back. Regulus retreated but kept his guard up and his stance forward. They ranged back and forth, a flurry of attacks, parries, and blocks. Adelaide scarcely blinked.

"Lord Hargreaves is good, isn't he?" Minerva murmured.

"Indeed," Gaius said. "I'd heard he was, but…my word. He's impressive. Did you see how—"

"Shush!" Adelaide released her iron grip on the bench to wave in Gaius' direction.

Minerva giggled. "Are we not allowed to talk about your suitor?"

Adelaide pursed her lips but didn't take her eyes off the duel. "You're distracting me from the sparring."

Gaius chuckled and whispered something to Minerva that made her laugh and hold her belly. Adelaide ignored them, focused on Regulus' every movement.

Regulus moved with ease and controlled awareness. She knew what control looked like. It took control to throw knives quickly with accuracy. A subconscious awareness of your body, of each miniscule movement of your arm from your shoulder to the tips of your fingers. Honed control of the rotation of your shoulder, the straightening of your elbow, even your breathing. Practice until control and awareness became second nature, the movement reflexive, the knives an extension of your hand. That was how Regulus moved. With precision. But there was something else.

He was holding back.

She couldn't pinpoint how she knew. Something about the ease with which he swung his sword. The way he pressed into an attack, but not as far as he could. A forceful parry where he seemed to stop short. It was miniscule. But there was an energy there she knew all too well. A pent-up power that tried to push itself out of every limb. The constrained feeling of keeping her magic caged when it coursed through her and she wanted to let it out, to release the power trapped inside. Something in her gut told her Regulus had strength he wasn't letting out. She just couldn't understand why.

She pushed her confusion away, taking in every strike, every swing. Every crash of metal-on-metal vibrated in her chest. MacCombe landed a glancing blow on Regulus' shoulder. Her fingers hurt from clenching the bench, so she grabbed fistfuls of her skirt instead. Regulus fell back, on the defensive. MacCombe swung. Regulus thrust his sword forward. MacCombe quickly countered, batting away Regulus' blade, but now he was off balance. Regulus let the force of MacCombe's counter do most of the work as he swung his sword up and around. MacCombe's sword was too far to his right as Regulus brought his blade around on the side of MacCombe's head.

Regulus didn't pause, landing blow after blow. MacCombe's sword slipped out of his fingers and fell on the dirt as he raised his hands. Regulus pulled back. Adelaide leapt to her feet, cheering with the rest of the crowd. Regulus sheathed his sword and offered his hand to MacCombe. MacCombe accepted the handshake, then retrieved his sword. Regulus turned toward the spectators and removed his helm, bowing toward Baron Carrick. As he straightened, he looked at her and the scarred corner of his mouth turned up in a slight smile. He did not swagger as he walked off the field, as Nolan had, but he held his head up and his shoulders back.

The last four pairs of swordsmen fought, and Baron Carrick called a break while he decided pairs for the next round—and which loser would get a chance at redemption. Adelaide left her sister and the Drummonds and made her way to the waiting competitors.

Regulus grinned as she approached, his silver-gray eyes sparkling. Despite the rivulets of sweat on his skin, making his slicked-down hair stick to his face, he still looked good. Her heart leapt. Behind Regulus, Dresden stood with four other knights.

Estevan, the knife-thrower. A muscular knight with a crooked nose and short brown hair. One knight had longer, dark blond hair and a stubbly beard that made quite a contrast with Dresden's thick, short beard. The fourth had dark skin and black, short hair in tight curls. They all looked at her as she curtsied.

Regulus smiled. "Do we need such formality?"

"Do we ever *need* formality?" Adelaide grinned. "Formality is demanded by societal ideas of politeness, not necessity."

Crooked Nose chuckled. "Oh, I like her, Captain."

"Captain?" She hadn't meant to voice her confusion aloud, but she couldn't help it.

Regulus shrugged. "I've told him repeatedly we're not mercenaries anymore. I'm not his captain. But he's stubborn and foolhardy and will never change."

"See?" Stubble said. "Regulus agrees with me. You're an idiot."

"Charming." Dresden rolled his eyes. "I thought you were the genteel one. This is why you don't have a woman."

"I'd contradict you but there's a lady present."

Regulus rubbed the side of his head then gestured to Stubble. "Adelaide, this is Sir Caleb Rathburn."

Rathburn bowed with a flourish of his hand and a toothy grin. "A pleasure to finally meet you, my lady."

"You know Estevan," Regulus said. Estevan bowed. "This is Sir Jerrick Faras." The dark-skinned man bowed with a smile. "And this charming individual"—Regulus gestured to Crooked Nose—"is Sir Perceval Williamson."

Williamson gave a stiff half bow but smiled warmly. "Be gentle with the Captain, my lady."

Adelaide cocked an eyebrow. "You're worried I'll hurt him?"

"No. But he's been hurt enough."

Regulus cleared his throat. "Have you been enjoying the tournament so far?"

"Oh, yes. I—"

A trumpet sounded, indicating that the competition would recommence. Adelaide adjusted her token on his arm. Not that it needed adjusting. She just needed the excuse to be close to him.

"Good luck," she whispered. She headed back for her seat.

As Adelaide picked her way between spectators, she caught some of them staring. Others glanced her way furtively. She listened closer to the muddled cacophony of voices and latched onto snippets that seemed to be about her or Regulus.

"…matches Belanger's dress."

"Wasn't he a mercenary?"

"…heard her mother's a Khastallander freewoman. Not even noble." Adelaide clenched her jaw.

"…no-good bastard."

"I can't imagine Lord Belanger approves."

"I thought she was courting Nolan Carrick?"

"She's a flirt."

Adelaide ducked her head and made her way to her seat as quickly as she could.

Minerva looked up, but her smile faded. "Is everything all right? You look…upset."

"I'm fine."

The mockery wasn't new. *I don't care. Their opinion doesn't matter.* But it still hurt. However, the fact that some people thought she and Nolan were courting… It both embarrassed her and made her furious. People talked too much. Angry tears threatened to well up, so she shook her head and focused on the competition.

REGULUS SIGHED as Adelaide wove away through the crowd. A man's voice intruded on his bliss. "Lord Hargreaves?"

He looked over as Sir MacCombe approached. "Yes, Sir MacCombe?"

MacCombe nodded toward Adelaide. "That was Lady Adelaide Belanger, wasn't it?" Regulus nodded. MacCombe looked thoughtful. "That's her token?"

"Yes."

Something dark and dangerous sparked behind MacCombe's eyes. "I was under the impression Nolan Carrick was courting her. There were rumors of a pending engagement."

Dresden snorted but said nothing.

Regulus tried not to sound too riled. "No."

MacCombe stepped closer, his voice low. "I'm pleased to hear it. I've had the pleasure of speaking with Lady Adelaide. She's a lovely woman. Too good for Nolan Carrick. You fight with honor, Lord Hargreaves of Arrano, and were gracious in victory, so I will offer a word of warning. Nolan Carrick is not lightly trifled with, and there are many who blindly trust the Carrick name. If you have stolen his object of desire, you should watch your back." MacCombe grimaced. "And your love. Especially your love."

Regulus nodded, wanting to ask for clarification but not daring to be rude. "Thank you."

"And one more thing." MacCombe's eyes flashed. "Since you defeated me, I cannot do what I came here to do. If you get the chance—give Nolan Carrick a sound beating. He deserves it more than you know." He walked away.

If Dresden was right about Carrick offending Baron Gaveston and the reason Baron Esmil's daughter joined a convent, that made three baronial families with a grudge against Nolan Carrick. Regulus relished the information. A man made that many enemies, eventually, he'd be ruined.

The herald called the winners and runner-up back onto the field, then announced the eight pairs for the second round. Regulus would go second against Sir Luke Arthur. Arthur had done well in the first round, but he leaned into his right side, making his strikes unbalanced. A small flaw that would be easily exploited.

He had to admit, he was enjoying the tournament. The competition provided more excitement than practicing with his knights. Winning felt more satisfying in a competition, even if he had an unfair advantage. But he held back and tried to keep the playing field as level as he could. He also much preferred this to fighting for the sorcerer.

After watching the first pair of contestants, Regulus reentered the arena. He shook hands with Sir Arthur, a bald man in his early forties built of lean muscle, before putting on his helm. Regulus attacked first, and Arthur parried with expert ease. Regulus half-smiled under his helm. This would be a good duel.

They moved back and forth across the arena, attacking and parrying, thrusting and blocking, swinging and dodging. Regulus kept positioning himself on Arthur's right, causing him to lean more and more onto his dominant side. As Regulus dodged a thrust of Arthur's sword, he moved toward the left and let Arthur continue to attack. The swing from left to right finally came. Regulus stepped back, not blocking or parrying. He had to lean away to avoid the tip of Arthur's blade. Right as Arthur's center of balance shifted a little too far to the right, Regulus swung his sword.

Arthur was too far off center to block the attack, and Regulus' blade slammed into Arthur's back. Arthur stumbled and Regulus landed hits on Arthur's chest and back. As Arthur blocked, Regulus pushed toward Arthur's right. Arthur tripped. Regulus slammed his shoulder into Arthur's left side, and his opponent fell onto his right knee. With a mighty swing of his sword, Regulus knocked Arthur's sword out of his hands. The sword hit the ground a couple feet away. Arthur held up his hands.

The crowd of spectators cheered. The sound filled Regulus to his core. He could imagine a different life, a version of himself that the nobles didn't mistrust or resent. He offered Arthur his hand. Arthur ignored him as he stood and fetched his sword. The rejection tore the illusion away. Regulus sighed, removed his helm, and bowed to the spectators. Adelaide beamed, but her smile seemed dimmed.

Maybe she noticed Sir Arthur's snub. Does she wonder now about giving her token to the son of a servant? Or maybe I'm so convinced this is too good to be true I'm looking for negatives. He smiled and clapped his hand over her token on his arm. She blushed. *I'm overthinking it.* He walked out of the arena.

Carrick won his match, which on the one hand irritated Regulus. He showed no grace in victory, only smug conceit. He entered the arena with the laidback carriage and playful, crowd-winning smile of a man entering a party and left with a kiss for the spectators, a swagger in his step, and a smirk on his face. On the other hand, Regulus now had a one in four chance of facing Carrick in the next round. Never had Regulus so strongly wished to cross steel with a particular person. He forced aside the mental image of knocking Carrick to the ground and focused on the next contestants. He had a one in four chance of dueling Carrick but had equal chances of fighting the other winners. So he studied his potential opponents.

A fifteen-minute recess was called to give the winners time to catch their breath and adjust their armor. Perceval leaned back, his elbows resting on top of the fence.

"Got some decent competition there, Captain." Perceval nodded thoughtfully. "A few of 'em might even make good mercenaries."

Regulus laughed. "Don't let them hear you. Pretty sure you'll offend them."

"Eh, I can take any of 'em." Perceval shrugged. None of them argued. Perce was the best swordsman Regulus knew. He'd even beaten Regulus once.

After the break, the herald announced the last four pairs. Carrick would face Sir Bartley. Regulus would face Lord Barden. Based on their fighting styles, Regulus predicted a win for Carrick. Lord Barden wouldn't be difficult. His aggressive style counted on beating down his opponent so he couldn't strike back. Accordingly, Barden left himself open for counterattack. All Regulus had to do was accept a couple blows rather than blocking them.

Adelaide winced as Lord Barden landed two powerful blows in quick succession on Regulus' chest. Was he even *trying* to block them? Barden swung again, and Adelaide flinched as the blow landed on Regulus' shoulder. Regulus slammed his sword across Barden's abdomen. Barden stumbled back. The crowd gasped. Regulus attacked without pause. Barden tried to block and parry, but his defense was weak. Regulus swung and Barden's sword flew out of his grasp. Adelaide held her breath. Barden raised his hands, yielding the fight. Adelaide applauded, feeling an inordinate amount of pride.

Still, nerves made her twitchy. Nolan had won his match, with a good show of skill, at that. Regulus had a fifty-fifty chance of facing Nolan in the semifinal round. She had confidence Regulus would best Nolan. And yet… She knew Nolan's type. If Regulus lost, Nolan would interpret that as a clear sign of his superiority and Regulus' unworthiness. That was how chivalry worked in romances, wasn't it? Disputes were decided by arms. Suffering defeat while wearing a lady's token dishonored the lady. To the victor go the spoils.

Nonsense. *Love isn't won on the battlefield. A heart is not a trophy.* But Nolan would see a victory in the field as proof Regulus wasn't worthy of her. Before and after each duel, Nolan made eye contact with her. He winked as he bowed. Mouthed *for you* as he held up his sword in celebration. He blew a kiss to the crowd after each victory, but the look in his eyes said the kiss was for her.

I don't want your victories and I don't want your kisses! If Regulus won, perhaps Nolan would be too ashamed to approach her again. *Please win, Regulus.*

The herald announced the round. First up, Regulus and Sir Morrigan, not Nolan. Then Nolan and Lord Thealane. Regulus won his round with ease. He seemed to have found his rhythm.

A nobleman nearby said, "That mercenary is unstoppable." Adelaide found the speaker and watched him out of the corner of her eye. He was pudgy and balding.

"Seems unfair," said a man with a thick silvery blond beard. "Over half these men haven't seen real battle. We've been playing war at tournaments for over twenty-five years. The mercenary, though…"

"True," Balding said. "He's probably killed more men than some of these competitors have sparred with. But can't refuse him entry because he has more experience."

"Probably should have based on his bastardy, though," said a third man she couldn't see around the other two.

Minerva put a hand on hers and whispered, "Ignore them."

"He has a name," she muttered. "A title. He's not *the mercenary.*"

"People are selfish and cruel, Ad." Minerva leaned forward, forcing Adelaide to look into her eyes.

"Why can't they get over themselves?" Adelaide gripped her skirt in her hands.

"You know why. The nobles think what is different taints their carefully constructed superiority. Lord Hargreaves is very different. They aren't likely to accept him easily." Minerva pushed Adelaide's hair over her shoulder. "Adelaide, if talk like that is going to bother you, you can't court him."

Adelaide stiffened.

"If you marry him, that won't stop the whispers. It may make them worse." Minerva bit her lip. "We have both heard the things people have said about Mother and Father. I know some nobles are less than thrilled about me and Gaius. If you can't have thick skin, your relationship with Regulus will fall apart." She squeezed Adelaide's hand. "You will have to be certain you love him more than you need acceptance."

Adelaide shifted on the bench. "You don't have to be right all the time, you know."

"That's why I'm here, don't you know." They laughed.

Adelaide looked across the field. Nolan and Lord Thealane had started their match. Regulus watched, his brow furrowed, eyes narrowed. His mouth cocked to the right, making the skin pucker around his scar. As he observed, his arm would twitch or he would duck slightly, or he would move a foot forward or back. As if doing in miniature what he would do if he were one of the combatants. She chuckled to herself. Why was that so…endearing?

She wouldn't say she loved him. Not yet. But like? *Oh, heavens yes.* Find attractive? She recalled Regulus standing in front of his tent in loose linen trousers and a thin linen shirt that hung asymmetrically on his shoulders. Her entire body grew hot. *Double-yes.* Even with the scar low on the side of his neck she hadn't seen before and the faint scars on his shoulders.

No, she didn't know if she could claim her affection toward Regulus Hargreaves of Arrano as love yet. But she could handle gossip and condescension at least long enough to find out if she loved him.

Cheers pulled her out of her thoughts and back to the field. She tore her gaze away from Regulus. Lord Thealane staggered off the field. Nolan thrust his sword into the air, looking right at her. *For you,* he mouthed. He bowed deeply, winking as he straightened. He sheathed his sword, put his right fist over his heart, and made another bow toward her with a simper. Before leaving the field, he blew the crowd a kiss.

Regulus and Nolan would face each other for the final victory.

Adelaide wiped sweat off her palms on her skirt. *Please, Regulus. For the love of Etiros, please win.*

SO, HE would fight Carrick after all. Regulus checked Adelaide's token on his arm. He shouldn't be so happy about it. But it would feel good to knock Carrick down. He had hardly kept himself from drawing his sword yesterday, when Carrick kept talking over Adelaide. The egotistical lowlife. But Adelaide had a fire in her and had proven she could and would defend herself. He wouldn't assume she wanted or needed his help. He only stepped in because Carrick started acting aggressive, and he would not abide such behavior.

Anticipation and tension hung in the air as they walked into the arena. A low monotone of whispered conversations buzzed in his ears, too far away and too quiet for him to hear specifics. Did any support him? He saw a couple noblemen shake hands, both with smug expressions. Well, people were betting on him at least. But people bet on horses, hounds, and dice, so that didn't say much. Maybe he had changed some of their minds. Or perhaps some of them would be more open to him. Probably not. He pushed thoughts of the nobles' acceptance away. They had never accepted him. Why would it matter now?

He found Adelaide in the crowd. Maybe it did matter now. What if the other nobles turned her against him? She smiled and winked. *"I don't much care what they think,"* her voice repeated in his mind. The tension in his shoulders dissipated. In the middle of the arena he bowed to the spectators, then turned toward his opponent.

Carrick gave him a haughty smile as they shook hands. "This should be fun, mercenary. Try to last long enough you don't completely embarrass her. I want to win, but I don't want to make her angry. I want her to see which of us is the real man, and which is, well…whatever kind of mongrel you are."

Regulus clenched his jaw until his teeth hurt. He smiled. "You know what, Carrick? You're right."

"What?"

"This *is* going to be fun." With that, Regulus pulled on his helm and drew his sword.

Carrick scoffed and put on his plumed helm. He drew his sword and attacked, moving blade from scabbard to slicing toward Regulus' chest in one fluid movement. Regulus blocked, the impact of their swords meeting jarring his bones. He shoved back on Carrick's blade, pushing it aside. He reversed directions and aimed for Carrick's side.

Carrick recovered and parried with no difficulty. Regulus moved for another attack from above, adjusting his stance as he watched Carrick through the slit in his visor. Carrick inched his left foot back and drew back his right shoulder. Regulus adjusted, stepping to the right and pulling his sword around to swing from the left. Carrick couldn't change course fast enough, and he blocked just as Regulus' sword made contact with Carrick's shoulder. Carrick parried with surprising force, then counter-attacked. Regulus blocked or dodged each blow. He countered with a flurry of combination cuts, thrusts, and swings. Carrick fell back but blocked or parried each attack.

Sweat dripped into Regulus' eyes and trickled down his neck. Every muscle in his body strained with energy. Sunlight glinted off of Carrick's polished armor, making Regulus squint. Carrick blocked another cut, and Regulus grit his teeth. Some part of his brain whispered *you could end this right now. Stop holding back. You could stop his blade with your hand and pull it right out of his grasp.* He licked his dry lips, tasting salty sweat. No. He would win this fight as Regulus Hargreaves, not as the magically enhanced Black Knight.

Move. Keep moving. He stepped into another stance reflexively as Carrick parried and swung for his head. *Look for weaknesses.* He leaned back as Carrick's sword rushed past within a feather's breadth of his visor. He aimed a blow at Carrick's arm. Carrick's grip faltered as Regulus' sword bounced off Carrick's bracer. Regulus pressed his advantage, landing several blows on Carrick's chest and shoulders.

Holding back got harder by the second. His concentration threatened to break as he tired. The rush of the combat seemed like fuel on the fire burning in his veins and muscles, demanding to be unleashed. *Focus! No foolish risks.* Carrick swung for his torso, and Regulus moved to block. At the last moment, Carrick adjusted, lunging around Regulus' side. The edge of his sword sliced into the back of Regulus' knee.

A string of curse words rushed through Regulus' mind as his knee smarted and blood seeped into his trouser leg. He would heal. This fight needed to end before anyone noticed. He spun and swung toward Carrick, who, as he expected, blocked the blow. Regulus pushed their swords to the side and slammed his shoulder into Carrick. Carrick stumbled back and Regulus thrust toward the gap in Carrick's armor under his pauldron. Carrick parried, but Regulus kept moving closer, forcing him to retreat backward.

As they moved across the field, Regulus making attacks for speed, not accuracy, Carrick's stance got weaker and less grounded. Regulus kept an eye on the terrain, and just before Carrick stepped onto an uneven patch of ground, he drew his sword back over his head, leaving himself open. Carrick did what he expected—he swung at Regulus' shoulder. But as Carrick put his foot down and attempted to move forward into his attack, his boot caught. He faltered for the briefest moment as he regained his balance.

With every ounce of control, Regulus brought his sword down. Carrick realized too late he needed to move or block and made an attempt, but Regulus' blade hit the side of Carrick's helm and continued down to his shoulder. Carrick reeled, his grip on his sword slipping. Regulus pulled back his sword and thrust toward Carrick's neck. Carrick parried, but Regulus flicked his blade in a circular binding motion and pulled against Carrick's blade. His grip already weakened, the sword ripped out of Carrick's hands.

Before Regulus raised his sword to Carrick's chest, Carrick dove around him. Regulus turned as Carrick kicked the cut in the back of his knee and Regulus' leg buckled. Pain shot up and down his leg. The cut had started to close, and the impact reopened the wound, making it feel like his flesh was sliced through all over again. He gasped and spun on Carrick, who snatched his sword off the ground. Regulus adjusted his grip on his sword and blocked a hastily thrown attack. Their swords clanged together, and Regulus moved forward, guiding his sword down Carrick's blade. He slammed his head into Carrick's helm.

The impact rang in his ears, made his helm vibrate against his skull. Carrick teetered and lowered his sword. Regulus slammed the pommel of his sword into the side of Carrick's helm. A blow across Carrick's back, and Carrick fell to his knees. Regulus put the tip of his blade against Carrick's neck below his helm. Carrick froze. He let go of his sword and raised his hands.

Regulus swallowed against the dryness in his mouth and throat. His pulse pounded in his ears as he lowered then sheathed his sword and stepped away from Carrick. He offered his hand, but Carrick shoved it away.

"You'll pay for this, Hargreaves." Carrick's voice sounded tinny and muted through his visor. "I'm not done with you." He stomped away without removing his helm.

Regulus turned toward the spectators, his focus shifting from Carrick to the cacophony of applause, cheers…and booing. He removed his helm. Baron Carrick stood, clapping leisurely, but his expression was hard as stone. Regulus' gaze wandered over the crowd. Many stood, some smiling and cheering. Some yelling. He looked to Adelaide. She beamed, her broad smile making her cheeks round and her eyes crinkle as she stood and applauded. Baron Carrick held out a hand and the crowd's excitement dropped off to silence.

"The winner of this year's Etchy Tournament's sword competition," Baron Carrick said, his rich baritone ringing out over the arena, "is Lord Regulus Hargreaves of Arrano."

Most of the crowd cheered, although some jeered. The herald walked onto the field, carrying a miniature model of a knight with gold armor and a silver sword. He presented the little figure to Regulus, who accepted it with a deep bow.

Off the field, his knights greeted him with whoops and slaps on the back and shoulders. His pulse raced. He grinned and couldn't stop. Their exuberance heightened his own soaring emotions. But Regulus locked eyes on the woman moving through the crowd toward him. He shoved his helm and the tiny knight into the hands of one of his men, he wasn't even sure which. He pushed past them, only aware of her.

Adelaide's smile and shining eyes made his breath come faster. He strode toward her, ignoring the congratulations of the men he walked past. He knew what he wanted to do. Grab her by the waist, spin around as he lifted her into the air, and when he put her back down, kiss her. But that would be crazy. They weren't there. Not yet. But as they stopped, a little too close together, ideas of proper and crazy and logical and irrational blurred and then vanished. His chest tightened as he drifted toward her upturned face. His gaze drifted to her lips.

Searing pain prickled his right arm, and he winced. Her smile faded. His heart felt heavy. *Not now. Why now, Etiros? Why at all?* Anger rushed through him, followed by despair.

"Are you all right?" Adelaide placed her fingertips on his breastplate.

"Yes." He forced a smile. "Just the cut on my leg."

Her forehead wrinkled, concern in her eyes. "Is it deep? You should see the tournament physician at once."

"It's fine." He took her hand off his chest and held it. "I've had much worse."

Adelaide glanced at the scar on his cheek then met his eyes. "Still. Better get it stitched." She looked like she wanted to say something else, but she pulled her hand out of his and smiled coyly. "The sooner you get that mended, the more likely you will be able to dance after supper tonight."

She went up on her toes and planted a kiss on his unscarred cheek before he could react. His jaw went slack. He could still feel the soft, warm brush of her lips on his skin after she pulled away.

"See you tonight." She darted away.

"Right," he responded in a breathy whisper. "Yes." *Idiot.* The mark on his arm continued to tingle. A dull pain like a minor burn. He turned and headed for his tent.

"Now *that* looked promising," Dresden said, walking beside him. "So where are you headed in such a hurry?"

"I need to look to my leg." His words sounded blunter and harsher than intended.

"Oh. Right. Yes, good." Dresden dropped his voice to a whisper as they left the crowd behind. "Got to cover that before anyone notices." He nudged Regulus with his elbow. "And then did I hear something about dancing?"

"I don't think I'll be dancing." His throat pulled taut as he spoke in a low, sharp tone. *I'll have other business to attend to.*

"Reg, what's wrong?"

He wanted to scream. To punch something, or someone. To grab the sorcerer by the neck and shove him into a brick wall. He wanted to collapse to his knees and sob. Because he had known better. Now he knew more clearly than ever. His mark had burned right as he stood on the brink of careless joy. At the edge of love. It cut through his euphoria, pulling him back, reminding him what he was.

"Reg, slow down."

He couldn't risk hurting her.

"Is it the mark?"

He couldn't tell her the truth.

"Regulus!" Dresden grabbed his shoulders, forcing him to stop.

He had fallen for a daydream. Tried to live in one of the happily-ever-after romance ballads Caleb sang. But his life wasn't a romance.

"Reg?"

The truth crushed him, like his heart was being squeezed. His lungs compressed. His life wasn't a romance. It was a tragedy. Even if she accepted him, he might hurt her. *Not if you obey,* a selfish voice whispered. *"Such an obedient pet,"* the sorcerer's voice taunted. *"Next time, you won't get to choose."* He pushed Dresden aside.

"Regulus!"

Until he had paid his debt, he had no business loving Adelaide Belanger. Or anyone.

Because he wasn't his own man.

And slaves don't get the girl.

CHAPTER 25

AFTER REMOVING his armor, Regulus double-checked each knot holding the tent flap closed. Dresden sat lounging on a stool in front of the entrance as an extra precaution. Caleb had pulled out his lute and was playing it as loudly as possible. All the surrounding tents were his knights', but Regulus couldn't chance a passerby hearing anything suspicious.

He pulled a chain out from under his armor and over his head. The key hanging on the chain glinted in the lamplight. His hand hovered in front of the lock as he crouched in front of the chest. The mark burned hotter, the pain sharpening as he hesitated. A reminder the sorcerer would not be denied or ignored. He unlocked the chest and pulled out the mirror, then hooked it on a nail he had hammered into the tent post next to his cot for this exact eventuality.

With a deep breath he focused on keeping the anger and bitterness out of his face and voice. He wouldn't risk incurring the sorcerer's wrath in the middle of the tournament campground. "I'm here, my lord."

The mirror shimmered, and the sorcerer appeared. His hood was thrown back, revealing graying brown hair pulled away from his face. Regulus stifled a gasp. He had never seen the sorcerer's eyes before. The whites were bloodshot around coal-black irises rimmed with a thin line of green.

"Good! I—" The sorcerer squinted. "What are you doing? Where are you? This isn't familiar." He moved closer to the mirror, craning his head as if to look around Regulus' tent. "Where are you?"

What good would lying do him? "I'm competing in a tournament."

"A tournament? Interesting. Winning, I'd imagine."

"Yes, my lord," he kept his voice level, "but on my own strength." *I don't owe you anything.*

"Hmph. Ungrateful idiot. But that's not relevant right now." The sorcerer tugged on his beard, his movements frantic. "I've hit a wall. It's infuriating. You get so close to everything you've planned, you think you've thought of every-thing, that vengeance is finally assured, and just like that…a wall. A wall of my own creating! Isn't that darkly poetic." He glowered at Regulus, as if whatever wall he was talking about was Regulus' fault.

Regulus didn't respond. The sorcerer would get to the point eventually.

"Fix one problem, create another. Just have to do it all over again!" The sorcerer shook his head. "If those thrice-cursed mages weren't already long dead, I'd kill them. Such a hassle. Should have seen it coming, though."

Regulus tried to look uninterested and keep his confusion hidden. *What mages? Should have seen* what *coming?*

"No matter. Always work-arounds. See you, for example." The sorcerer chuckled to himself. "Just time-consuming. And requires *precision*. And it's exhausting."

Regulus clenched his jaw. *Don't ask. Obey. Pay your debt.* If he earned his release, he could court Adelaide. The thought made him much more willing to play the obedient servant.

"I need several very specific things from you," the sorcerer continued. "So pay attention. One thing out of place, and this won't work. And if this doesn't work, I swear by every dark curse I know I will kill you and everyone you care about. Understand?"

Regulus swallowed and nodded. "Yes, my lord." He was grateful the sorcerer didn't know about Adelaide. *Just follow his instructions, and no one will be hurt.*

"Good." The sorcerer crossed his arms. "First, I need a circlet of silver. It must be pure silver, no other metals. Second, I need a bushel of white flowers. Doesn't matter what kind, but they must be white. Third, I need clamshells. Eight large shells should do it. Fourth, and this is where things get difficult, I need the blood of an innocent person. Doesn't have to be a lot, just a few drops. And finally, I need a foot-long piece of a root of a neumenet tree."

"What?" Regulus gaped. "Blood?"

"Of an innocent person, that's important." The sorcerer waved his hand. "Yours won't do."

Regulus winced, guilt pricking his conscience, but moved on to another problem. "What's a neumenet tree?"

The sorcerer groaned. "Don't you know anything?"

Regulus stayed silent.

"Useless. Neumenet trees were considered sacred for thousands of years. They're very rare, and strong vessels of magic energy. People used to try to conceive their children in their shade, hoping to have a baby born with magic abilities. Sometimes worked, too. They have bark like obsidian and leaves that look like shards of glass but feel like feathers."

"And where do I find one?"

"There's one in Holgren Forest."

"But that's a royal forest!"

The sorcerer thrashed his teeth. "And I'm the Prince of Shadow and Ash! That forest belongs to me!"

Regulus recoiled. He had claimed that title the first time Regulus met him. Had bound him to tell any who asked the Black Knight who he was that he served the Prince of Shadow and Ash. Regulus had assumed the sorcerer was being grandiose. But now he realized—the sorcerer seemed to think himself *actually* royal.

"With all due respect, my lord," Regulus said, trying to sound as humble as possible, "I don't think any sheriffs or forest rangers will care."

"Well"—the sorcerer grinned coldly—"then kill them. Better yet, don't get caught."

"Yes, my lord."

"Now, tell me what you're bringing me."

Regulus sighed. "A circlet of pure silver. A bushel of white flowers. Eight clamshells. The..." He swallowed, his mouth dry. "The blood of an innocent person. The root of a neumenet tree." Whatever such specific and odd ingredients were for, he suspected he would regret being a part of it. As if the sorcerer interrupting a wonderful moment wasn't bad enough, that made his mood worse.

"Good. Make your plans. I *must* have everything *before* the next full moon, do you understand?"

Regulus shook his head, trying not to let his irritation with the sorcerer's tone show on his face. "When is the next full moon?"

"You are such an idiot." The sorcerer rolled his eyes. "A useful idiot, luckily for you."

Regulus clenched his teeth.

"Eleven days. You have eleven days. That should be enough time to gather everything. If I don't have all the ingredients on the eleventh day, or if you bring me the wrong ingredients—I will consider your debt unfulfilled. And I will collect in full."

He bit his tongue to stop his panicked protests as a shudder raced down his spine. "And...if I succeed, my lord?"

"Then we'll be much closer to being even." The image shimmered and reverted to a mirror.

Regulus stared at his scarred reflection. Eleven days. The mark had stopped burning. So long as he intended to obey, the mark should leave him alone. He could finish the tournament and still make it on time. He bit his cheek. *"I will collect,"* the sorcerer's voice echoed in his mind. No. He wouldn't be that selfish. He needed to leave Adelaide alone until he was free.

He locked the mirror back in the trunk and opened the flap of his tent. Dresden raised an eyebrow in a silent question. Regulus motioned him inside. Caleb continued to play his lute.

"What did he want?" Dresden sat on the small stool next to Regulus' bed.

"Flowers. Clamshells. A pure silver circlet. The root of a magical tree in a royal forest. Oh, and the blood of an innocent person."

Dresden gawked. "What?"

"I know." Regulus sat down on his cot and put his head in his hands. "He's doing something, working to accomplish some plan. He needs all of that before the next full moon, in eleven days." He dug his fingers into his skull. "If I don't get him the right ingredients on time, he will consider my debt unfulfilled and collect."

"But…that would mean…"

"Yes." Regulus laid back on the cot, his hands clammy and stomach churning. *You'll all be killed.* Acid burned at his throat. "But if I do this, he said we'd be close to being even."

"So the end is in sight."

"But at what cost, Drez?" He sat back up and wiped his forehead with his sleeve. "I have no idea what I'm helping him do! I think…he might have designs on the throne."

"Two years you've done his bidding. He's holed up in that infernal tower. Maybe you're wrong and he's not dangerous."

"Maybe." *I doubt it.* He hung his head. "But I can't refuse him. We know how that ends."

They sat in silence for a couple minutes until Dresden suddenly sat up straighter. "Wait, eleven days?"

"Yes."

Dresden grinned. "Then I propose you go dancing."

"Drez—"

"Come on. It'll cheer you right up. Get you to see some positives."

"I can't." Regulus shook his head. "I was a fool. I can't do this."

"Do what?"

"Court Adelaide!" He yanked his sleeve up, revealing the mark. His face burned with humiliation and guilt. "I'm not the hero in a romance. I let myself forget it, but I received a cruel reminder today."

"You said yourself, you're getting close." The gentleness and pity in Dresden's eyes made Regulus more irritated. "You *will* be free one day. Live like it. You choose who—"

"I am, yes. Right." He shook his head. "What if he orders me to do something I can't? What if…" His throat tightened, and he closed his eyes.

"You won't hurt her."

He met Dresden's eyes. "But what if—"

"You'll do what he wants, and he'll set you free." Dresden spoke slowly, his palms pressed together.

"Free or not, after everything I've done…" Regulus slumped. "I'm not worthy."

"Worthy? Etiros above, Regulus. You're a respected swordsman, a lord who can live comfortably, the best commander I've ever met, and the kindest, most selfless man I know."

Regulus flinched under the praise. "But I—"

"You are on the verge of having everything you never thought you could have. You're a lord with loyal knights. You won a contest of swords, and people cheered. For *you*. They might not all accept you, but some of them are coming around. You've found a chance at love."

Regulus rubbed the mark on his arm, his thumb pressing against the irregular scars. He wanted to believe Dresden. But he was a slave with blood-stained hands. He'd taken lives long before he met the sorcerer, but it wasn't the same. Guilt weighed on his shoulders while frustration mounted. Anger at what the sorcerer had forced him to become. Anger at the guilt that wouldn't die. Anger at Dresden for not understanding his despair.

"You can have a normal life," Drez said. "You can stop hiding in your castle. Stop living behind this wall you've put up around yourself and I've only seen you lower around her. You don't have to live the rest of your life shutting people out. Don't throw that all away."

"I don't shut you out," Regulus said weakly.

"Yes, you do!" Dresden stood and paced away. He turned around and Regulus recoiled from the anger in his friend's eyes. "We know your secret, but you don't let us help. You rarely tell us where you go or what you do. You push us all away! And don't say to protect us. You do it because you're too proud to admit you're afraid." Dresden shook his head. "After two years, I don't know if I can keep having the same conversations with you, Reg. How can I hold you up when you're so determined to drown!"

Regulus' heart twisted as Dresden's frustration stoked his own anger. He yanked his sleeve down. "If that's how you feel, why don't you go? I never asked you to stay!"

"You idiot!" Dresden cursed. "You didn't have to!"

Regulus turned away. "Just leave."

"No." Dresden sat on the ground and folded his arms. "Not until you stop being a fool, believe that you'll get through this, and agree to dance with Adelaide tonight and joust tomorrow. You didn't come all the way here—"

"You don't get it! You don't understand what it's like!" Regulus stood and pointed at the tent door, fury and hopelessness burning under his skin. He hadn't asked for a lecture. "Get out!"

Dresden scowled. "I'm here as your friend. You can't give me orders."

"I can and I am. Leave, or I'll throw you out." Regulus pointed again, more emphatically, but Dresden didn't budge. "Now, Jakobs! Go!"

Dresden turned crimson. "I see." His neck muscles bulged as he swallowed hard and stood. "Anything you want me to do once I leave, *Captain*? Or is it my lord?" He gave a messy, low, mocking bow, his voice bitter. "Command me, master. I live to serve."

Blood rushed to Regulus' face. He dropped his hand to his side. Dresden turned toward the tent entrance.

"Drez, wait—"

"That's a bit familiar for your servant, isn't it, *master*?"

"I didn't—" But Drez walked out of his tent. "…mean it." Shame twisted Regulus' stomach. He groaned and kicked the leg of the cot.

Regulus had never viewed Dresden as inferior, despite their often unequal and complicated relationship. Dresden calling Regulus master had only been to appease Regulus' strict childhood guardian. One of many things Regulus had done over the years to protect his friend. But nothing could erase that Dresden had been little more than a slave for seven years. Nothing negated that there had been times as a captain when Regulus couldn't make an exception, not even for his lieutenant. He shouldn't have snapped. But it was Dresden's own fault for pushing him. And Dresden shouldn't have thrown such a low blow in return.

It took Regulus an hour to cool off and swallow his pride enough to leave his tent, but he couldn't leave things like that. Caleb lounged in front of his own tent, strumming on his lute. Harold and Jerrick were talking while Harold polished a pair of boots. They all went silent and looked up at Regulus.

"He's in his tent." Jerrick looked at Regulus through narrowed eyes. "But enter at your own risk."

Caleb plucked at a string on his lute, pointedly not making eye contact with Regulus. "Haven't seen him that riled in a while."

Thankfully, Dresden hadn't fastened his tent door closed. Regulus ducked inside. Dresden had his double scimitars in both hands, moving through his drills between his cot and a small leather trunk. He spun around just as Regulus entered, and Regulus jumped back. Dresden lowered the blades and bowed his head.

"Yes, my lord?"

"Drez, don't. I told you never to call me that." Regulus chewed on his cheek. "I'm sorry, okay?" *No, it's not okay.* "I crossed a line. I didn't mean anything by it. And I'm sorry."

Dresden's scimitars twitched, but he raised his head.

"You're right. I don't talk to you." Regulus rubbed the back of his neck. "Yes, I'm afraid. Afraid I'll hurt one of you. Afraid you'd lose all respect for me if you knew the things I've done."

"Reg." Drez sighed, hurt in his pinched expression. "Don't you know me better than that? We're brothers. We need each other. Being a lone wolf doesn't make you stronger, just lonely and vulnerable. You used to tell the mercenaries wolves were strongest when they worked together. When did you stop believing that?"

When my presence became a threat. Drez didn't give him time to reply.

"And we're mercenaries. We're not squeamish. Besides, it's not you. It's not who you are. You're doing what you have to; it's not like you enjoy it."

"But I'm still doing it." He stared at the trampled grass beneath his boots. Dresden shuffled his feet. "If it was me…would you leave?"

Of course not. "I don't know. You've never attacked me in cold blood."

"I've felt like attacking you in hot blood." A hint of mirth crept into Dresden's voice. He placed the weapons on the trunk. "I'm still not abandoning you. Even if I have to tell you a hundred times a day: it's going to be okay, you'll make it through this, you're still worthy, still my brother. And Regulus…it wasn't you. If Harold and I can accept that, why can't you?"

Because it was still my fault. The words stuck in his throat, too raw, too shameful and excruciating to let out of the darkness of his mind. *Because I saw the light in your eyes fading, felt you dying as I squeezed your throat. Because your tear-stained face as you begged me to remember you—when I did, when I knew you, but I couldn't control my own body—still haunts my dreams.*

The cot squeaked as Dresden sat on it. "He hasn't controlled you—"

"He has." Regulus didn't look at Dresden.

"…what?"

Regulus closed his eyes and spoke quietly. "Four times since then. Just not at the castle. A momentary hesitation, a brief refusal, temporary uncertainty. Usually just long enough to remind me he can. And I've been tortured so many times I've lost count." The silence that followed his admission threatened to swallow him alive.

"Etiros above, Regulus. Why?"

Regulus opened his eyes. "He's easily angered. And I'm…stubborn and resentful."

"No. Why haven't you told me?" Hurt reflected in Dresden's eyes.

"Telling you doesn't change it."

"You're a damned fool."

"You're right," he murmured. "That's why I don't deserve Adelaide."

Dresden was silent for a moment. "So? You haven't endangered us; you won't endanger her. Maybe having someone else to protect will help you be smarter. You're better around her, Reg. More hopeful. You should tell her the truth."

"What?" Regulus jerked his head up. "Are you out of your mind?"

"You're so afraid she won't accept you, you're about to push her away. Why not give her that choice? You will lose her by walking away, anyway. Doesn't she deserve a chance to decide for herself if she wants to take the risk? Just like the rest of us did?"

Regulus worked his jaw. Dresden had a point. If Regulus and Adelaide's roles were reversed, wouldn't he want the truth? Wouldn't he want a chance to choose acceptance or not? But if he walked away now…yes, he might lose her. But he wouldn't have to live with the pain of seeing the way she looked at him change. But if she could understand, if she could love him anyway… He longed for her acceptance as much as he longed for freedom.

"Do you even like her, Reg?"

"Excuse me?"

Drez threw his hands in the air. "You're giving up so easily, she must not be that special."

Heat flared in his chest. "Of course she's special!"

"Then tell me why!"

"She's…" Regulus looked away and took a deep breath as he pictured her smile. The thought of her calmed his jittery nerves. "She's smart and capable and confident. She's humorous and kind. She's honest. And…she *sees* me. Not a servant's son, or a mercenary, or a captain. Not someone she owes anything to. More than a walking testament to my father's infidelity. Not an imposter or just a title. Not a slave. I haven't met someone who sees me apart from all of that since we were children. And it took you months to see me as your friend."

As he spoke, he understood. He might never find someone like Adelaide again. And if she could see him now, maybe she could see him in spite of his link to the sorcerer. Drez was right. He wasn't protecting her. He was hiding.

"If you mean all that, how can you walk away?"

"Fine." Regulus nodded. "I'll consider telling her."

"And you'll go to the dance?" Dresden crossed his arms, his gaze sharp, the hard slant of his mouth allowing no argument. "You owe me after that ordering stunt."

Regulus winced. *An opportunity to hold Adelaide in my arms?* He sighed, losing the battle with both himself and Drez. "Yes."

"YOU KNOW what Mother would say?" Minerva sat on Adelaide's cot. Early evening light still filtered through the heavy green fabric of the tent. A few candles illuminated the interior—her cot on a small wooden frame, Giselle's straw mattress in the corner, and a trunk with a cloak on it. A large rug covered most of the ground.

Adelaide sat on a stool, looking at her reflection in a small mirror hung on the tent wall. She stuck another pin in her hair to hold the ribbon-accented braid in place atop her head. "Probably something cautionary I don't want to hear."

"She'd probably say you can't go getting swept off your feet by any good swordsman."

"I'm not in love with him because he's a good swordsman." She stuck in another pin.

"Ah, but you admit you're in love with him."

"What? I—" She jabbed herself in the head with a pin and winced. "*In love* is a little much. Besides, I thought you were supporting this…whatever it is?"

"Courtship?"

She glared at Minerva. "We're not courting."

"Not officially." Minerva smirked. "But you might as well be. Gracious, after his victory I thought you two were going to kiss. And not the little peck I saw you give him."

"Hmph." Adelaide turned back to the mirror, trying to act nonchalant. There was a moment there…he had been so close. She had felt a fluttering in her stomach. The look in his eyes, intense as a bonfire yet clear as an undisturbed lake on a cool morning. She had *wanted* him to kiss her. To put his hand behind her head and pull her in. For a moment, she had considered kissing him herself. But then that look of pain. That… Sadness in his eyes.

She tried to ignore the nagging impression something was wrong. Maybe she saw in him what she felt in herself. That feeling of lying. Of hiding the truth. When he reminded her of the cut on his leg, she had wanted to heal it. She could have insisted she go with him to the physician's tent, pulled him aside on the way and healed him. Good as new.

As soon as the idea had occurred to her, she decided against it. Not yet. But if she couldn't trust him now, could she ever trust him? Was her hesitance only the echoes of warnings from her parents? Or something more? What should she do when her heart screamed to trust him and her mind urged caution?

Minerva laid a hand on her shoulder. "What are you thinking?"

"About why—or if—I trust Regulus." Adelaide chewed on her lower lip. "I'm too used to *not* trusting. How do I know if I should? Father always says to never let emotions make your decisions. But when your emotions are so involved, how can you tell if you're being rational or not? Am I paranoid not to trust him? Am I foolish *to* trust him?"

Minerva squeezed her shoulder. "These are things you can determine with time, Ad. You don't need to decide if you're marrying him today. Sooner or later, you'll know. Like I knew with Gaius."

"Yes, but you didn't have a secret."

"I knew yours. I still keep that one."

Adelaide paused, her hands poised above her head as she checked the braid. "I'm sorry. It can't be easy."

Minerva shrugged and stroked her growing belly. "Sometimes, I'd like to talk to him. It's not that I don't trust him; I know if I told him he wouldn't tell a soul. But it's not my secret to share."

"But it is mine." Adelaide dropped her hands to her lap. "What if…" She fiddled with the belt of her dress. "What if I tell him, and it's not that he wants to use my power, or he tells someone he shouldn't? What if…"

"What if it scares him?"

Adelaide looked at Minerva. Anxiety gnawed at her stomach.

Minerva chuckled and shook her head. "Based on what I've heard, how he acts, and how he fought today, I'm not sure anything scares that man."

"But what if it's too…strange?"

"Regulus hasn't lived his whole life in Monparth. For all you know, he's met a mage before."

She hadn't considered that.

"All right." Adelaide nodded. "I'll get to know him more. Focus on that, not whether or when to tell him."

"Good." Minerva held out her hand, and Adelaide helped her to her feet. "Ready for supper and dancing?"

Adelaide smiled as her gaze went to Min's belly. "Only if little Adelaide is."

"Oh ho, really?" Minerva laughed. "Gaius' mother is determined it's a boy."

Adelaide laughed and hunched over to talk to Min's stomach. "You're a girl, aren't you? We shall throw knives and climb trees and speak Khast and I'll tell you stories about your mother's childhood shenanigans."

"I think not on that last one." Minerva rolled her eyes as she grinned. "And just because you're the better knife thrower doesn't mean you can steal my job. *If* the little one's a girl, I'll teach her like Mother taught me." Her grin turned mischievous and her eyes glinted. "You can teach future little girl Hargreaves to throw knives."

Adelaide choked on a gasp as her face flushed. "That's it, I'm not speaking to you for the rest of the night, *Tha Lonri.*" She took one final glance in the mirror and headed out, Minerva's laughter following her.

Regulus walked into the gate at the end of the jousting arena and looked around, impressed. Benches and tables filled the arena. Lanterns hung from posts positioned around the low walls and in the stands. Candelabras glowed on each table. Commoners crowded stands, taking full advantage of the hospitality of the tournament. They would eat the same food as the nobles, but they weren't allowed to eat with them. Nobles were already finding seats at the tables in the arena. No one told them where to sit in the spirit of the tournament. All hereditary nobles could compete, and thus all were equal at the tournament. Except they weren't.

The nobles sorted themselves. Knighted freemen, like Regulus' knights, sat with the commoners. They could get into the arena if they wanted, no one checked letters of nobility here. A title would suffice. But the legacy nobles made their disdain clear. Even most poor knights felt more comfortable with the other freemen. Within the arena, the wealthier and more famous nobles claimed the seats closest to Baron Carrick's table, positioned below his viewing box in the center of the arena.

Regulus headed for that table. As one of the day's champions, he had been invited to sit with the tournament's host. Baron and Baroness Carrick's high-backed chairs sat in the middle, flanked by two chairs on either side. A page stood to the table's left. A couple other winners were also arriving. Regulus recognized the sturdy man with silver hair as Sir Gerald Malone, champion of the archery competition. He hadn't watched or paid attention to any of the other competitions that day, so he didn't recognize the tall, lithe man with the red hair and beard.

The page directed Sir Malone to the chair on the far right and directed Red to the next seat. He pointed Regulus to the chair on the far left. Regulus leaned on the arm of the empty chair next to him and extended his hand across three seats to Red. "Lord Regulus Hargreaves."

The man shook his hand with a grip like a vise. "I know." He had a deep, commanding voice. "Everyone is talking about you, Lord Hargreaves. I only caught your last fight, but it was impressive."

"And you are?" Regulus felt a little swell of pride, but kept his posture relaxed.

"Lord Frederick Ganlar, son of Duke Ganlar. Long staff champion."

Regulus nearly gasped. As one of three ducal families in Monparth, the Ganlars were practically royalty. Three barons and several lords, including Adelaide's father, owed Duke Ganlar their fealty. What was he doing competing in a tournament held by a lesser noble?

Ganlar laughed. "I know what you're thinking, Lord Hargreaves. I'm here for the same reason as everyone else. Sport, my friend."

"Pardon my confusion, but you came all the way from Nueres Duchy to compete in the long staff?"

"And why not? As you can see, I'm good at it." He held up his hands and lifted one shoulder. "But mostly, I can't compete in Nueres. Men get nervous about fighting their liege's heir. They make mistakes they otherwise wouldn't. Takes all the fun out of it."

"But…why not the sword?" Sir Malone asked the question Regulus hadn't dared.

"Because that's what everyone would expect." Ganlar stroked his big red beard. "I enjoy surprising people. But mostly I enjoy the long staff. It has its own unique cadence. And the added challenge of not being able to rely on any sharp edges."

"Speaking of which, that looked to be a nasty cut Sir Carrick landed on your leg," Sir Malone said. "I'd rather expected you to have a limp."

"Oh." Dread circled Regulus' throat. "It wasn't as bad as it looked. And the physician did a good job."

"Not to be crass," Ganlar said, leaning back in his chair, "but you look like you're not a stranger to pain."

Regulus clenched his fist under the table. "I suppose that's accurate."

"Oh, brilliant." Carrick's voice behind Regulus was cold as ice. "Whose idea was *this* seating arrangement?"

"Mine." Baron Carrick approached the table, his wife at his side. "I'm giving you a second chance to demonstrate honor in defeat. You have one victory and one loss today, but if you continue to act like a child, you will have lost your dignity." His mouth turned down. "So far you're not doing well." Baron and Baroness Carrick took their seats, the Baron sitting beside Lord Ganlar.

Carrick hesitated for a moment, then took the seat between the baroness and Regulus. Regulus ignored him. He sensed Carrick's animosity, and it sparked a reciprocal loathing.

The baron welcomed and thanked the attendees and praised the competitors. Carrick had won the polearm competition. Once the baron gave the word, servants began dispersing food and the cacophony of hundreds of voices in competing conversations filled the arena.

"My mistake," Carrick said, his voice a low whisper, his head angled toward Regulus, "was doing polearm and sword. If I had skipped polearm, I would have had more energy. I would have beaten you."

Regulus bit into a turkey leg. He wanted to ignore Carrick. Pretend he hadn't heard. But what was the saying? Kindness burns like hot coals? Something like that. "You fought admirably, Sir Carrick. Particularly after winning in the polearm. Perhaps you are correct. But regardless, you should not be ashamed of how you fared."

Carrick gripped his flagon so hard his knuckles turned white. "I'm the son of a baron. Shame isn't an emotion I feel. But you will. I promise you."

"Did you say something, Nolan?" The baroness looked at them with a smile, but her eyes were cold beneath her blue wimple. Such an old-fashioned woman.

"Just congratulating Lord Hargreaves on his win, Mother." Carrick's smile looked painfully forced. "And looking forward to tomorrow's joust."

Baroness Carrick sighed. "Perhaps if you had an ounce of humility and a touch more civility, you'd have a wife by now." Her voice reminded Regulus of the time Caleb tightened the strings on his lute too far and one snapped.

Carrick aggressively bit into a piece of roast quail and didn't respond.

Regulus looked over the crowd as he ate, seeking Adelaide. Wherever she was, he couldn't find her among the crowded tables.

"Lord Hargreaves," Baron Carrick's voice cut through his thoughts.

He cleared his throat. "Yes, my lord?" Being so close to the baron felt odd. Regulus hadn't spoken to him in the two years since he'd sworn his fealty and Baron Carrick had confirmed the transference of his title and land.

"I'm curious why I haven't seen you compete before."

The whole table looked at Regulus. The back of his neck itched. "I spent twenty-seven years of my life without a title, unable to compete in tournaments. Once titled, I hadn't changed, only my legal status. I was in no rush to risk my neck seeking glory among those who hadn't yet accepted me when I could finally rest and stop risking my neck for those too rich to risk their own."

The row of faces stared at Regulus in mute shock.

He hadn't intended to be so blunt or accusatory. The words just...spilled out. His mind seemed to relish the chance to lash out instead of suffering judgmental looks and whispered conversations in silence. *Well done, Regulus.*

"Then you're not still a mercenary?" Carrick's haughty tone made Regulus' fingers ache to grip a sword.

"No."

"And why would he be?" Baron Carrick pulled a grape off a bunch on the table in front of him. "Such pursuits are for men cut off, with no inheritance or title."

Carrick shot his father a scalding glance before returning to eating and drinking.

"You think very little of the men who hired you as a mercenary?" Lord Ganlar asked, his expression solemn.

"By and large they seemed to think very little of me," Regulus said, on edge. "When you fight another man's battles and he treats you like a hunting hound, it's difficult to maintain a high regard for that man." He thought of the sorcerer with delusions of royalty. His fingers dug into his leg, and he willed himself to relax.

Ganlar looked thoughtful, if guarded. "I suppose that's fair."

"At least hounds are loyal to their lord. Mercenaries can't even claim that dignity." Carrick sipped from his tankard, the look in his eyes daring Regulus to retaliate.

Regulus kept his tone even. "I never took conflicting contracts, I chose my benefactors carefully, and I refused to work with unscrupulous mercenaries. I only helped innocents, never harmed them. So don't think me without honor because I served no lord. I was loyal to my men, and my men to me." He inclined his head, realizing he should cover his bases. "As Lord of Arrano, I am loyal to Baron Carrick and to the king." *Although I hope they never collect on my fealty.*

"I am pleased to have men with skills such as yours I can count on." Baron Carrick's voice was steady and pleasant, but he didn't look at Regulus. Eventually, the others fell to talking amongst themselves. Regulus ate in silence, and no one asked him any more questions.

After supper, Regulus wove between guests and dodged servants carrying tables and benches, seeking Adelaide. He found her as the musicians started playing. She grinned and his stress evaporated. *Don't get carried away,* he reminded himself.

"May I have this dance?" Regulus bowed and held out his hand.

"I think you've earned it." Adelaide took his hand with a teasing laugh.

Her skin on his sent a thrill up his arm. She wore a scarlet dress with a low square neckline. Swirling gold embroidery covered the bodice and cuffed the sleeves at her elbows. Below her elbows, sheer red fabric hung down to her wrists. A gold pendant set with a small ruby hung from the gold chain around her neck, the gold contrasting well with her soft brown skin. She looked like a dream.

As they danced, everything else seemed to fade. To become less important. More manageable. The awkwardness of supper seemed trivial. Even the mark on his arm seemed inconvenient rather than life-ending. *The sorcerer said I'm getting close.* Adelaide spun, the lantern light reflecting off the red ribbon and gold pins in her black braid. Her arm brushed his, and reckless hope burned anew in his chest. *I can do this. I can love her and earn my freedom.*

They moved through the steps. Closer together, her nearness an ache in his heart. Further apart, her distance suffocating. She spun as the song ended, and Regulus stepped forward. Adelaide bumped into him, her hands resting on his chest. A pleasurable tremor skittered down his spine as his hands found her waist.

His eyes darted down to her lips. The warmth of her body so close to his was intoxicating. He leaned forward. She didn't pull back, but he thought of the sorcerer and hesitated. She deserved to know the truth first. To have a choice. He wanted to kiss her—Etiros above did he want to kiss her—but he wanted her to kiss him with full knowledge of everything he was. She bit her lower lip and his heart raced like a startled deer.

"Come to Arrano for supper," he whispered, breathless. He forced himself to look back at her eyes.

Her gaze dropped momentarily, as if she were disappointed. "When?"

"As soon as you can." Suddenly, he realized she couldn't just come over. Not alone, anyway. "You, your sister. Sir Gaius. I want you to come to my estate for supper."

She cocked her head to the side. "There's the tournament. Then getting back. Five days from now?"

Regulus shook his head, remembering the sorcerer. "I forgot. I have an…engagement. I promised I would help someone and will be away for a few days. In twelve days?"

Adelaide's shoulders slumped. "That's the day before Lord Drummond is hosting Lord Thealane and his family for three days. We won't be able to get away."

"What about in eleven days?" The sorcerer needed his ingredients *before* the full moon, not *on* that day. He could get the ingredients and be back by then.

"All right. I'll check with Gaius and Minerva." She pulled away from him, and he let her go with reluctance. He moved further away from the couples trying to dance around him, some looking at him with pursed lips. Within a couple minutes, Adelaide found him again. She beamed. "We'll be there."

"Six in the evening?"

"Sounds perfect."

Regulus took her hand and danced with her until the musicians stopped playing. They talked and laughed. As the last note faded, he cupped her face in his hands. He swallowed against the lump in his throat. *Not yet.* He wouldn't try to kiss her in front of all these strangers—several of whom cast disapproving frowns their way. No, he wouldn't take advantage of the rush of dancing so close to each other. He still needed to tell her the truth. *Patience.* He brushed a soft kiss against her forehead and stepped away before he lost his resolve.

"I'll see you tomorrow."

Adelaide nodded, a bashful smile on her face. "Tomorrow."

He watched her find her sister and Sir Gaius and disappear among the crowd leaving the arena. He sighed. Deep. Contented. For the first time in years, he knew exactly what to do.

Joust. Win. Take care of the sorcerer's shopping list. Have supper with Adelaide, Gaius, and Minerva. Get Adelaide alone. Tell her everything. And if things went how he hoped, once free, he'd ask her to marry him.

Regulus felt too exhilarated and nervous at once to sleep, so he exited the opposite end of the jousting arena. The waxing moon and glittering stars shone in the cloudless sky. The cool summer night air comfortable after so much dancing.

He wasn't a good dancer, never had been. Adequate, sure. But Adelaide didn't seem to mind. No one had bothered them. Even Carrick hadn't shown his face. And Regulus had been too busy looking at Adelaide to bother noticing anyone else.

Footsteps. A rustling, behind him and to his right. He spun around.

Carrick stepped out from behind a large bush, sword hanging from his belt. "Hello, mercenary." He sneered. "Where are your peasant friends? The Carasian who's always trailing you like a shadow?" Four more men stepped around Carrick, although none of them carried swords.

Regulus reached for his sword. His fingers grasped at empty air. *Feast. Dancing. No swords.* A string of curses went through his mind.

"Missing something?" Carrick drawled. "You look better without the sword. More like what you really are—the son of a servant."

Regulus' hands clenched. "What do you want?"

"I'd like your head." Carrick rested his hand on his sword hilt. "But it would be suspicious if you turned up dead. So, I'm not going to kill you. But I'll settle for your humiliation. Kneel."

"Excuse me?"

"You said you're loyal to my father. Prove it. Kneel."

Regulus worked his jaw and eyed the other men, weighing his options. If he walked away, Carrick could attack from behind. "I do not need to kneel before a spare son with a title beneath my own." Carrick grimaced, and Regulus knew he'd struck a nerve. "But out of deference for your father…" He bowed at the waist. "Have a good evening, my lord."

Carrick glowered. "Break the bastard's arms."

The four men moved forward. Regulus stepped back, trying to decide if he should fight or run. "You would assault a lord?"

Carrick shrugged. "My father and I are not on the best of terms, as you probably noticed. But who will he believe? You? Or me and the sons of some of the most respected knights in Thaera Duchy?"

"All this over a lost contest?" Regulus shook his head, watching the other four men. "Why is it so important to you?"

Carrick's expression darkened. "You think this is about one contest?" He jutted his chin at Regulus. "Take him down."

The other knights lunged forward. Regulus hesitated only a moment. He couldn't risk them discovering his secret. He turned to run.

"Coward!" He ignored Nolan's taunt.

An arrow whistled and Regulus scanned the darkness. An archer stood half-hidden in the shadow of a small tree ten paces ahead of him. He didn't find the arrow fast enough to dodge it. The head bit into his left arm, the shaft sinking deep into his flesh. He gritted his teeth as he changed course away from the archer. The tip of his boot caught on the ground and he tripped. Not enough to make him fall, but enough to slow him. One of the knights threw himself against his back. Regulus fell to the ground.

MINERVA HELD Adelaide's hand, squeezing it in her excitement as they walked back to their tents. Gaius chuckled and shook his head as Minerva rattled off questions.

"Is he a good dancer? Did you kiss him? He invited just us? How do we dress for that? Did he say anything about courtship? Marriage? Do—"

"Slow down, Min." Adelaide giggled. "One at a time."

"All right, all right. Is he a good dancer?"

"I'll be honest; I've danced with better." She squeezed Minerva's hand. "But that was the most fun I've ever had dancing."

"So?" Minerva elbowed her. "Did he kiss you?"

"Min!"

"Is that a yes?" Minerva winked.

"No." Adelaide bit her lip. "He seemed hesitant. I nearly kissed him myself, but then, I thought…maybe he should know first."

"Know what?" Gaius asked. Her eyes widened in alarm.

"That Father's picky about suitors," Min said. Adelaide relaxed.

"Truth." Gaius laughed. "Curious, though. Hargreaves hasn't invited anyone to Arrano castle since he arrived."

Adelaide shrugged. "I guess you'll see Arrano in eleven days. The third of next month."

"What do we wear?" Minerva rubbed her stomach. "It's not a party, but he is a lord…"

"I'm pretty sure he doesn't care."

"Mm, true, we *are* only invited because he couldn't invite only you."

Adelaide rolled her eyes to hide her embarrassment.

"Did he say anything about courtship or marriage?" Minerva prodded.

"Well, no." She pinched the sheer fabric of one of her sleeves between her fingers. "We were a little preoccupied with dancing. And talking about…everything and nothing. Sword fighting. Daggers. Food. Stories from when we were children."

"Maybe that's something you should talk about before the tournament ends," Minerva said. "Might be a good idea to make sure you're on the same page about where this is going before we go to his estate."

Blood rushed to her face. "Are you doubting his intentions?"

"No, just…" Minerva's expression communicated more than words. Understanding. Sympathy. Love. Protectiveness. "Regulus seems like a good man. I like him. And I won't lie, I like the idea of you living closer." She winked. "But anyone can put on a good act, and I don't want you to get hurt."

"I *can* take care of myself you know."

"I'm not talking about physical pain." Minerva rubbed her thumb on Adelaide's hand as they stopped in front of Adelaide's tent. "I don't want him to break your heart. I want to make sure you're staying grounded."

"Don't worry." Adelaide pulled her hand away and smiled. "I'm using my heart *and* my head."

"All right." Minerva rubbed Adelaide's arm. A comforting gesture she had picked up from Mother. "I'll see you in the morning." She and Gaius headed toward their tent.

Giselle held open the entrance to the tent. "Shall I help you change, my lady?"

Adelaide peered into the dark tent. How could she sleep right now? The rush she had felt when Regulus cupped her face in his hands hadn't quite worn off. She still felt the touch of his lips on her forehead. The strength of his hands on her waist as they danced. Still saw the longing in his eyes. She'd felt pulled to him, like he was magnetic.

No, she couldn't sleep yet. Too much energy still thrummed through her. "Actually"—she ducked inside to grab her riding cloak—"let's go for a walk."

As they wandered away from the tents and the accompanying fires and lanterns, Adelaide realized they should have brought a torch. But her eyes adjusted to the moonlight well enough. Giselle followed a short distance behind her, more a consideration of propriety than any kind of safety.

Away from the crowded tents, the noises of the night took over. The whisper of leaves brushing against each other. The chirping of crickets. An occasional croak of a frog or hoot of an owl. Adelaide breathed in the cool air, letting it calm her. Distant shouting jarred her out of her reverie. On instinct, she turned toward the noise. Grunts, shouts, and gasps carried through the night. Pulse rising, she drew her dagger from her boot.

"Wait right here! Understand?"

Giselle nodded, her face pale in the moonlight.

Adelaide hurried toward the sound. The voices came into focus. "…strong!"

"Kick him harder!" A man yelped, others shouted. "Stay down!" Gasps. The sound of flesh hitting flesh.

"Get off me!"

Adelaide's breath came out in a rush. *Regulus?* Magic flared in her veins, a wild inferno of desperate energy under her skin. She ran past a couple trees. Several feet ahead, a group of four men leaned over a man on the ground, hitting and kicking him, while another man looked on. The man on the ground grabbed the shirt of one of the attackers and pushed him away. The assailant stumbled back, and moonlight fell on the downed man's face.

"Regulus!" Adelaide screamed as she ran toward the group.

They all looked up, surprise on their faces, even as one of the men sent his boot into the side of Regulus' head.

Anger rushed through her like fire. "Leave him *alone*!" She swung her dagger, although she wasn't yet close enough to hit any of them. Fire erupted from her hand, traveling down the dagger and throwing an arc of flame toward Regulus' attackers. They yelled and jumped back. Her dagger burned in her hand, and she tossed it aside. She grabbed a throwing knife out of her other boot. "Get back!"

"What was that?" one of the men demanded.

Panic clawed at her insides. "My torch. It went out." She held up her knife as she advanced. "But I still have this knife, and I'll throw it into the head of the next man that harms him!"

The men looked at each other. "Let's go," the onlooker said.

Her hand dropped as she recognized his voice. She looked over, shock replaced by fury. "Nolan?"

Nolan's hard expression was unreadable. "We're done here. I'll leave you with your strong hero." He turned and strode away, followed by the other men. Another man she hadn't noticed walked past her and Regulus, following the others, a bow in his hands. *Fool. You rushed in without checking your surroundings!* Father would be ashamed.

Adelaide dropped to her knees next to Regulus and let the knife slip out of her hand. He pushed himself up.

"Stop! Wait! How badly are you hurt?" She put her hands on his shoulders, forcing him to lie on his back. That's when she noticed the arrow in his left arm.

He grasped her hand with his right hand and sat up. Blood ran down the side of his face. "I'm fine. Honestly."

"You're hurt!"

Regulus lifted his right shoulder but kept his left arm still. "I've been worse."

Her chest heaved as she looked him up and down. Regulus' clothes were torn. Moonlight reflected off the blood on his face and on his arm around the arrow, and he might have additional wounds she couldn't see. "Is anything broken?"

He winced as he shifted. "I don't think so." He still held her hand in his. "What are you doing out here?"

"I was going for a walk." She pulled her right hand free and reached for his head. He gasped and jerked away when she touched his hairline. She clenched her jaw. "What happened?"

"It doesn't matter."

"You're hurt! And Nolan…it matters!"

"I'll be fine." He rubbed a circle on her hand with his thumb. "Thank you."

"We have to tell Baron Carrick."

"Adelaide, no."

"What?" She looked into his eyes. "What do you mean, no?"

"It's not worth it. I'm fine. Dresden has stitched me up plenty of times. He'll make short work of my arm. Okay?"

She looked at the arrow embedded in his arm. How he was acting so unbothered, she didn't know. She was about to ask if she should go find Dresden when he spoke.

"Adelaide." Her pulse quickened. Her mind screamed an alarm at his odd tone. "I didn't see a torch."

Her breathing turned shaky. Blood drained from her face. Her hands felt clammy, so she pulled her hand free of his. "I…tossed it aside when it went out." She looked toward where she had thrown her dagger. Why was she lying? Because she wasn't used to telling the truth. Because her parents had been so afraid of the truth. *I want to trust him. I should tell him…*

Regulus gently pulled on her chin, turning her face back toward him. "I've seen something like that before. In Vanelt. A mage gifted in manipulating fire working for a circus." There was no accusation in his voice. Just an observation. Only kindness, and a touch of sadness, showed in his eyes. The warmth in his tone calmed some of her panic.

"I…" She licked her lips, unsure how to proceed.

"It's okay." He cupped the side of her face in his large hand. "I won't tell anyone. And you don't have to talk about it. I shouldn't have said anything."

"My parents…" She swallowed. "They worry it's dangerous. After…"

"After The Shadow."

She nodded, her breathing normalizing. "You don't…" She put her hand over his on her cheek. "You aren't afraid? Or angry I didn't tell you?"

"What? No!" Regulus scooted closer and grimaced. "You just saved me. How could I be afraid of you? And I can't imagine what it's like to be, possibly, the only mage in all Monparth. You must feel so alone." His voice held sympathy. Like he knew the burden of carrying a secret.

"I wanted to tell you," Adelaide whispered, "but I'm so used to hiding. My parents don't want me to use my power at all. They're afraid." Her words rushed out, fed by relief at no longer hiding and the need to explain herself. "Afraid The Shadow will find me if I use my magic. Or that people might try to kill me before I could hurt them. Or that others would try to use me."

He nodded. "I can see the wisdom in hiding a truth that dangerous."

"I'm sorry—"

"No, don't apologize." He rubbed his thumb over her cheekbone. "Wait." He looked around. "Are you out here all alone?"

She gestured vaguely behind her. "I left my maid back there when I heard shouting."

"You heard shouting, so you ran toward it?"

"It sounded like someone needed help."

Regulus chuckled. "Brave like a tigress indeed."

She bit her lip. "Do you think Nolan or any of his friends noticed?"

"None of them seem particularly bright. I'm sure you're fine." He smiled. "But you might want to try not conjuring fire if you want to keep being a mage a secret."

"I didn't do it on purpose!" Adelaide groaned. "It's…sometimes difficult to control. Although I'm getting better." *Which means I can help.* She straightened and scanned the shadows. "Hello? Anyone there?"

Regulus lowered his hand from her cheek. "What—"

"Shh." She listened and watched the darkness. "Just checking. All right. I don't think anyone is around."

"Why—"

Adelaide held out her hand and summoned a ball of azure-tinged light. It hung in the air, illuminating Regulus' wounds. "I can't believe Nolan would attack you." Literally. Her mind refused to believe what she had seen. As if there had to be another explanation. She clenched her teeth as she inspected the arrow buried in his upper arm. "Why would he do this?"

Regulus gazed at the orb, lips parted. "To send a message. To humiliate me. To prevent me from competing tomorrow. Take your pick."

She gently parted his hair and found the cut on his head. It wasn't as bad as expected. "You'll compete tomorrow," she declared. "And you'll knock Nolan Carrick off his horse." She held her hand over the cut. Warmth spread across her glowing palm as the blue light made the blood look purplish.

"What are you... Oh." He relaxed, and she focused on the cut until it closed.

"That felt like..." Regulus blinked a few times. "Comforting. It eased the pain and then... The pain just left. I felt nothing." He touched his head. "There's not even a scar?" His voice held wonder.

"I can do more." Adelaide blushed. "Or I'm trying, anyway. I'm teaching myself."

"I thought you said your parents didn't want you using your powers?"

"They don't know." She wrapped her hand around the protruding shaft of the arrow. "I'm sorry." She met his eyes. "This will hurt, but only for a second."

He nodded. "Nothing I haven't felt before."

Adelaide ripped the arrow out of Regulus' arm. He groaned through clenched teeth as blood poured from the gaping hole. His muscles bulged against the sleeve. She held her hand over the wound, energy coursing through her arm and out of her hand as light shimmered from her palm. Regulus relaxed. The wound pulled together and closed. She lowered her hand and let the sphere of light go out before anyone could wander by.

"Is there pain anywhere else?"

He shook his head. "They weren't able to do much before you scared them off."

"Are you sure?" It felt good to use her powers. To help someone, like she had wanted to do for so long. *And nothing terrible has happened.*

"I'm sure." His gaze held hers, his gray irises silvery in the moonlight.

She smiled sheepishly. "You don't mind?"

"Mind? I think it's wonderful. You're wonderful." He brushed a curl of hair behind her ear. "Mage or not."

Her heart danced. *Kiss me, damn you.*

"Thank you." Regulus' voice lowered, becoming husky. He leaned forward. "You're spectacular. Breathtaking. Adelaide... I..." He trailed off as his fingers tangled in her hair.

Adelaide couldn't stand the tension anymore. She closed the space between them and kissed him. As her mouth met his, her breath seemed stolen away. Her eyes closed; her mind emptied. She started to pull away, afraid she'd been too forward, or done it wrong. But Regulus grabbed her waist and kissed her. She sank into him, breathed him in as she wrapped her arms around his neck. A spark of reckless joy ignited in her chest and she trembled. He gripped her waist firmer, pulled her closer against his muscled chest. Slowly, his mouth left hers, his quick breaths hot on her lips. She opened her eyes.

It took her a couple tries to speak. "I should go. Before Giselle panics." *And before I forget which way is back.* She stood.

"Wait." He grabbed her hand and gently pulled her back down. Her breathing hitched as he leaned forward. Regulus kissed her again, and Adelaide felt weightless and invincible all at once. He pulled away too soon, and she sighed. He chuckled.

Adelaide's eyes flew open. "What?"

"It's just..." He ran his thumb over the back of her hand. "You've bested me. You've won my heart." He looked into her eyes with gentle longing, bordering on adoration. Like she was the only thing that mattered, the only person he ever wanted to look at. It was so close to the way Father looked at Mother, Adelaide's throat caught.

She touched his face, her fingers caressing his scar. She didn't need to think anymore. Her heart had taken over. She kissed his lips, then his scar. His hand released hers and pressed against her lower back as he kissed her, pulling her close while his other hand buried in her hair.

"Adelaide? Oh, thank Et—*Hargreaves!*"

She jumped at Gaius' uncharacteristically enraged voice and broke away from Regulus' kiss. Regulus' hands tightened on her as his eyes snapped open, alert and battle-ready.

Adelaide looked back and saw Gaius and two of his knights running toward them, swords drawn. Shuddering light from a torch one of the knights carried spilled over her and Regulus as the men slowed. Regulus released her.

"Gaius?" She flushed as Gaius grabbed her arm and pulled her to her feet.

"Are you hurt?" He held her hand up in the torchlight. "You're bleeding!"

"No, I'm fine—"

Gaius turned and pointed his sword at Regulus, still holding her arm. "I might just run you through if you don't have a good explain, Lord—wait, are *you* bleeding, too?"

"Gaius!" She yanked her arm free. "I'm fine, it's Regulus' blood!"

Regulus touched the blood on the side of his face. "It's only a scratch."

"And your arm, too." Gaius lowered his sword, the anger on his face softening. "What happened?"

"Nolan Carrick and his friends attacked him." Adelaide's anger returned full force.

"It was just some ruffians. Probably had too much to drink," Regulus said, holding up a hand. "I didn't see any of their faces. And I'm fine. A couple minor scratches."

She clenched her jaw. Nolan shouldn't get away with it simply because his father was a baron. Anger stirred her magic, but she forced it down.

"I see." Gaius sheathed his sword and rounded on Adelaide. "So you're not hurt?" He looked her up and down.

"I'm fine, Gaius."

"Actually," Regulus said as he stood, "she saved me. Threw a torch at the miscreants and threatened to put a throwing knife through their skulls. Speaking of," he bent down and picked up her dropped throwing knife, the light from the torch glinting on the blade. "This is yours."

"What are you doing here?" Adelaide asked Gaius as she returned the knife to her boot.

"Giselle came and got me. She said you went running off toward what sounded like shouting and ordered her to stay behind, but she was worried for your safety. Min's in a panic." He looked at Regulus, lips pursed. "And then when we arrived there was only you two, alone, in the dark, on the ground, a bit…tangled…" Adelaide's face heated.

Regulus inclined his head. "I understand your concern. But I assure you, I would never hurt Adelaide. Or intentionally impugn her honor."

"*And* I can take care of myself, Gaius."

"Clearly. But even champions can be taken by surprise." He gestured to Regulus. "You're Minerva's sister, so you're my sister, too. That is both a privilege and a duty, and one that I take as seriously as protecting my wife."

He was right, and just being kind. Even if his protectiveness grated on her nerves. "Thank you." Adelaide smiled. "Minerva is lucky to have you."

Gaius grinned. "I assure you it's the other way around, but I try." His smile vanished. "As for all…this. I think it would be best if all parties returned to their own tents immediately."

"Yes, of course." She looked at Regulus. "I'll find you before the joust tomorrow?"

"I'll be looking for you."

Adelaide walked over to the knight with the torch. "Could I borrow that? I dropped something." He handed her the torch, and she scanned the ground for her dagger. After a moment, she found it. It looked normal and was cool in her hand. She slid it into her boot and handed back the torch. "Shall we?"

BLOOD TURNED the water in the bowl pink as Regulus wrung out the cloth. He turned back toward Dresden.

"I mean, I thought about telling her." Regulus scrubbed at the blood on his ear, looking at his reflection in the small square mirror propped against the side of the tent, its bottom edge resting on his cot. "But then she kissed me…" He sighed, remembering the taste of her lips, the feel of her body pressed against his. Nothing in his life had ever felt as *right* as holding Adelaide, kissing her. "It didn't seem like the right time."

"How is that not the right time?" Dresden threw out his hands in annoyance. "You were sharing secrets!"

"And what was I supposed to say?" Regulus plunged the rag back into the bowl of water. "'Oh, you're a mage? I owe a life-debt to a sorcerer. You know, the corrupted, evil version of you? He completely owns me and runs my life and people I care about will die if I don't do his bidding.' In what world is that a good response to being healed or kissed by a beautiful woman?"

"That's…okay, that's a valid point. But this could be good. You said it yourself. The sorcerer is a corrupted mage. Maybe a mage can undo what a sorcerer did."

Regulus rubbed the wet rag through his hair. "I wondered the same thing, that's the only reason I told you. I promised her I wouldn't tell anyone she's a mage." He smiled wryly. "But I know you can keep a secret."

"I suppose I am something of an expert." Dresden stroked his beard.

"But not even the others. No one."

"I get it. But…you don't look like you took a beating. Won't Carrick notice?"

Regulus tossed the cloth back into the bowl. "I'll be wearing armor. It was dark, so not as if he could have seen my injuries to even know what to look for." He pulled off his shirt and threw it on the ground. "Well, that's a perfectly good shirt ruined."

Dresden crossed his arms and leaned back on the stool, using a tent pole as a backrest. "Don't go too easy on Carrick tomorrow. The world would probably be better off if his neck snapped when he gets knocked off his horse."

"I'm not a murderer." He wiped dried blood off his arm. "Besides, we might not even face each other."

"If he's as good with a lance as he is with a polearm and a sword, you probably will."

"I don't think it's about the tournament for him." Regulus pulled on a linen undershirt. "It's about Adelaide. He thinks he can win her over if he defeats me. He's fixated. Maybe I should let him win. If he wins and realizes Adelaide *still* doesn't want him, maybe he'll find a new obsession."

Dresden frowned. "Didn't you say she *told* you to beat him? To 'throw him off his horse?'"

"She was angry."

"And you're not?"

"Of course I'm angry!" Regulus sat on his cot. "But it drew Adelaide and I closer together, so it worked out. Carrick is just a spoiled noble brat. I've dealt with his ilk all my life."

"Sure, but the last time someone tried to murder you, we became mercenaries."

"That was different. And he didn't try to murder me." Regulus kicked off his boots. "I probably should let him win. But you know as well as I do, I can't. It's not who I am."

"Thank Etiros." Dresden stood and stretched. "I was worried falling in love had addled your brain." He exited the tent.

Regulus laid back. Yes, he had a growing hatred for Carrick. But right now, all he could think about was Adelaide. How beautiful and brave and kind she was. Her kiss. Why dwell on hate when he had so much to love?

"PARDON ME." Adelaide darted between a page leading an enormous gray destrier and a knight decked in full heavy jousting armor. Dresden waved to her across the chaos of knights, attendants, and horses. A squire ran past with a panicked expression, his shouted "sorry, my lady!" muffled in the rattle of armor and stomp of hooves. A white horse lowered its head, and she spotted the back of Regulus' head, his black locks curling near his neck. She dodged the end of a lance as a page walked by.

Regulus turned as she approached, his face wrinkling into a wide smile. "Good morning, Adelaide."

"Good morning." She held out a strip of dark green cloth that matched her sleeveless dress. The sleeveless style wasn't fashionable, but her skin welcomed the warm sunlight and the cooling gentle breeze. Honestly, as pale as some of these Monparthian women were, they could stand to ditch sleeves on occasion.

Regulus took the cloth, letting his fingers slip over her hand and down to the fabric. "You look beautiful."

Adelaide took in his armor, bulkier and thicker than yesterday's swordfighting armor. "You look handsome and heroic."

His face contorted in a grimace but returned to a pleased smile before she could even blink. "I'll look for you in the stands."

"You better. Try not to break anything other than your lance."

"Here I thought the lady visited her knight before a joust to wish him luck."

"Please." She smirked. "I have a feeling you don't need luck."

"A little extra luck never hurt anyone," he said with a shrug, his tone teasing.

Her heart fluttered. "All right." She reached up and grabbed the back of Regulus' neck, pulling his head down to hers. Her fingers wove through his hair as they kissed. She stepped back, her heart beating fast, her emotions a whirlwind of light and song and beautiful, perfect things. Her fingers slipped off his neck. He opened his eyes, a dazed look on his face. She bit back a chuckle. "Good luck."

"I think you broke him." Dresden held a fist over his mouth. From the twinkling in his eyes, he appeared to be trying not to laugh.

Regulus blinked. "Don't you have something better to do?"

"The only thing I have to do is tell you to get to the lists before you're late."

"I thought that was my job." A thin young man walked closer. He had a mess of dark blond hair and a short, patchy beard. He held a helm in one hand and clutched the reins of one of the tallest destriers Adelaide had ever seen in the other. The muscles across the black stallion's broad chest rippled as he stomped his foreleg.

Adelaide gasped in admiration. "Is this your horse?"

"This is Sieger." Regulus moved to the horse's shoulder and patted its thick neck. He pointed to the youth. "And that's my squire, Harold."

Adelaide held her palm out to Sieger. "He's gorgeous!" Sieger rubbed her hand with his soft muzzle.

"Bad news, Reg," Dresden said. "Your horse has stolen your lady. You're only handsome, but he's gorgeous."

She shook her head at Dresden, then looked back at the horse. Sieger's wavy black forelock tickled the back of her hand as she rubbed between his eyes.

"He likes you," Regulus said. "He's picky about who he lets touch his face."

"I'd best let you get to the arena." She scratched under Sieger's chin. "Take care of him, Sieger." The horse whinnied, as if agreeing.

Regulus tensed. His hand moved to his belt, but he wasn't wearing a sword for the joust. Adelaide followed his icy gaze as she turned around. Nolan stared at Regulus with obvious rage and a little confusion.

"Competing, Hargreaves?"

Her stomach twisted at the venom in his words.

"Why wouldn't I be?" Regulus said flatly.

Nolan shrugged, his armor creaking. A vein in his temple pulsed. "Sure you're in good enough shape to hold your own with a lance?"

"I'll manage fine."

"Hm." Nolan shifted his gaze from Regulus to Adelaide. His eyes narrowed, and he tilted his head to the side, considering her. "You look…enchanting, my lady."

A feeling like a ball of hot lead settled behind her sternum. *He knows. Oh, Etiros, he knows.* She swallowed against the tightness in her throat.

Nolan eyed her token in Regulus' hand. "Hopefully you don't regret that." He offered a curt bow and continued on, followed by a squire leading a large white horse with a braided mane and tail.

"Hey." Regulus put a hand on her shoulder. "Ignore him."

She forced a smile and laughed nervously. "Yes. I'll see you soon." She rushed away, weaving between knights and mounts and servants.

Minerva frowned as Adelaide approached. "What happened? You look frightened."

Adelaide gulped. Her fear was that obvious? "Nothing. Everything's fine."

"You don't sound fine." Gaius shook his head. "Shouldn't have let you go alone."

"Nothing happened. I just…" What could she say? Gaius didn't know her secret. And there were so many people around.

Gaius' expression softened. "He'll be fine. He seemed all right last night, and he's strong. If he has anywhere near the skill on a horse that he demonstrated yesterday on foot, I'm sure he's in no danger."

"Thank you, Gaius."

As they walked toward the stands, she pulled Minerva back. With their arms linked, she leaned in close. "I need to tell you something about last night."

Minerva glanced at her but said nothing.

"I messed up. It was an accident. I saw Regulus on the ground, getting pummeled. I didn't mean to. It just happened." She glanced around, making sure no one appeared to be trying to overhear her whispered conversation.

"What happened, Adelaide?" Minerva's hushed words came out in a rush.

"Fire. I threw fire at them. I said I had a torch that went out," Adelaide added in response to Minerva's horrified squeak. "But, I think they bought it. Most of them."

"Adelaide…"

"Regulus knows." Adelaide lowered her head, keeping her voice as quiet as possible. The sounds of the chattering crowd also headed to the joust helped hide their conversation. "You were right. He'd seen magic before. He didn't care, and he promised not to tell. And I trust him."

"Then why do you look so worried?"

"Nolan." Her lower lip trembled. "I saw him just now. The look he gave me…something he said… I think he knows." Her breath came out shaky.

"Are you certain?" Minerva clutched Adelaide's arm, her fingers digging into her skin.

"He's at least suspicious. Curious." She adjusted her arm, and Minerva's grip lessened. "What do I do, Min?"

Her sister shook her head. "I don't know. I'm not sure there is anything you *can* do, other than be cautious and alert. This is why Mother and Father didn't want you using your abilities."

"It's not as if something like this hasn't happened before," Adelaide reminded her. "It's part of why I wanted to learn. To control it."

"That's working splendidly."

Adelaide looked at the ground.

"I'm sorry. That was cruel. It's going to be all right. Worrying won't fix it. So let's enjoy the joust, and figure out what to do if, and only if, this becomes a problem."

"All right." She nodded as the tightness in her chest eased. "Good."

They found some seats close to Baron Carrick's box. All the signs of the feast from last night were gone, replaced by a tilt, the wooden fence running down the middle of the length of the rectangular arena. Once nearly everyone was seated, a herald sounded a trumpet, and the competitors rode into the lists. People applauded, loud cheers going up now and then as favorites rode past. The competitors, twenty-six in all, rode once around the arena. They sported a variety of decorative pieces, from plumes on helms to full body caparisons on horses. Some knights, such as Regulus, had little to no decoration, and wore simple armor. While all the horses wore criniere armor pieces over their chests, they had a wide range of barding, from full armor to only the criniere.

Regulus received a few cheers from people who had been impressed with his performance in the sword competition. He nodded at Adelaide as he passed, a crooked smile beneath his raised visor. She heard the name "Belanger" from someone seated lower down in the stands and strained to hear, even though her gut told her she shouldn't.

"Well," a man said, "he traveled all over as a mercenary. Probably developed a taste for foreign women."

"Not to be crude," a woman said, "but it seems fitting, doesn't it? They're both mongrels of sorts."

A loud cheer as another jouster rode past drowned out the conversation. Other conversations filled her ears, and she couldn't hear any more. Adelaide's eyes stung. She gritted her teeth. But the woman was right, in a way.

They *were* both mongrels of sorts, although she hated that derisive term. Both looked down on because of their parentage. Maybe it was fitting, but not in the judgmental way the snobby noblewoman thought. Perhaps that was why they were so comfortable. Why they understood each other so well.

She watched Regulus ride out of the arena, a pleasant warmth settling in her chest. Let them talk. Their talk had never determined her worth, and it wouldn't define her now. Talk didn't determine Regulus' worth, either. And if they couldn't see him for the good man he was—a man who wouldn't press charges against his attackers, a man who accepted her secret without question, fear, or selfishness, a lord who treated his knights as equals—their loss.

The first competitors took their lances, and Adelaide got caught up in the excitement of the joust. Baron Carrick had opted to choose combatants at random, rather than using a tree of shields. Apparently last year the right to choose your own opponent had been abused to further personal feuds, and Carrick wanted to keep things civil.

To her right, a knight with a small metal eagle with spread wings on his helm rode a dappled gray destrier with hooves the size of supper plates. On the other side of the arena, a knight rode a blue roan with a spiked chanfron over its face. Hooves pounded the ground as they charged, sending up little clouds of dust. Lances shattered with a resounding crack. The first pass ended in a tie, with both men landing solid hits on the other's ecranche, the small shield affixed to the left shoulder. Both lances broke. Three points out of a possible four—one for broken lance, two for hitting the ecranche. They had two more passes to secure victory in the round. Unless, of course, one unhorsed his opponent in the second pass.

Adelaide shifted forward in her seat as the knights re-queued. The horses nickered and pawed at the ground, waiting for the squires to release them to charge again. The knights picked up their lances and the squires dropped the reins. A roar went up from the crowd as the horses surged forward, power in the thunder of their hoof falls. The knight on the blue roan struggled to couch his lance, and the tip bounced off his opponent's breastplate. Eagle knight's lance crashed into the other knight's solid visor. The lance exploded from the impact, sending shards flying high into the air. Adelaide gasped, as did most of the rest of the crowd, as the second knight's head whipped back. His left hand grabbed desperately at the pommel of his saddle as he leaned backward until his back hovered over the blue roan's flanks. But he kept his seat.

One point for the knight on the blue roan. Four for eagle-helm knight. Adelaide enjoyed the joust for the tension, the uncertainty of it all. The eagle knight's chances looked good. He just needed to get another good hit. But if their luck reversed in the third tilt and they tied, they would have to take an extra pass. If the blue roan knight could unhorse eagle knight, he would win. She tapped her hands on her lap in anticipation.

The knights charged forward again. Their horses leaned away from each other as they met in the center of the arena. The snap of breaking lances echoed as pieces of wood scattered. Blue roan knight had managed a clean hit on eagle knight's chest but had missed the ecranche. Eagle knight hit the ecranche and won by four points.

Adelaide applauded. The knights exited the arena and the next competitors entered while servants cleared wood shards from the ground. The matches flew by, not least because of how easy it was to get caught up in the crowd's fervor. Nolan won his match. She didn't applaud him. He didn't acknowledge her.

At last, Regulus entered the lists. Green fabric fluttered around his right bicep, tied around his armor. He smiled at her before closing his visor over his face. Only two thin slits indicated where his eyes were under his helm. His opponent, a knight who looked more mountain than man, rode a brown destrier as large as Sieger. *How in creation is anyone supposed to unhorse him!* A caparison of red chevrons on a field of dark blue covered the horse to its knees. She recognized the heraldry. *Must be Sir Edgar Druadan.*

Her heart pounded as Regulus and Sir Druadan charged each other. As hooves threw up clots of dirt and horse nostrils flared, they leveled their lances. Adelaide leaned forward, clenching her fists. The impact of their lances on each other's ecranches and the simultaneous burst of lances into tinder sounded like a clap of thunder. Both men swayed in their seats, but kept their balance. The crowd roared in delight. Adelaide released a shaky breath.

They rode to the end of the arena and wheeled around. Pages handed them fresh lances. Minerva reached over and squeezed her fist.

"Relax!"

"I remember you being similarly tense last time Gaius tilted," she scolded.

Minerva laughed. "All right, that's true."

Her gaze remained trained on Regulus as the horses leapt forward. The pounding of their hooves seemed to vibrate in her chest. Both men's heads snapped backward as lances met helms. Her eyes widened and her nails bit into her palms. Splintered wood rained onto the ground. Regulus swayed but made it to the end of the arena. Harold turned Sieger around. Regulus shook his head and adjusted his helm before taking a new lance. She looked to the opposite end of the lists. Druadan had also maintained his seat. They were tied.

Her jaw hurt from clenching her teeth. She released a long exhale and tried to shake some of the tension from her shoulders. Both men raised their lances, signaling they were ready. Their squires released the reins. The horses charged. Adelaide pressed her palms together and raised her hands to her mouth, her thumbs tucked under her chin. Hooves thudded. The crowd cheered.

Druadan's lance pummeled into Regulus' visor, pushing his head back as the lance snapped in half. Regulus' lance slammed into the left side of Druadan's chest, just shy of his ecranche. The lance bowed. Regulus leaned forward, even as his head whipped backward. Adelaide gasped.

Druadan leaned back in his saddle. The broken lance slipped from his grasp, clattering to the ground. Regulus' lance burst, sending out shards like dozens of forcefully thrown wooden knives. Druadan flailed as he twisted backward and sideways over his horse's flank. He hit the ground with a clang. Regulus had won.

Adelaide leapt to her feet, applauding as a cacophony of cheers, gasps, and boos erupted from the crowd. Regulus leaned forward on Sieger, his head swaying from side to side. She froze. *Oh, Etiros, please. Let him be all right.*

Harold seized the reins and stopped Sieger. Adelaide looked over the heads of other standing spectators, watching with bated breath. Regulus removed his helm and looked back over his shoulder. He caught her gaze and smiled. Relief rushed over her as she smiled back.

REGULUS STRETCHED his neck. The pain was fading, but that was cutting it close. Sure, he had seen knights take similar blows and walk away. But not exactly fine; a hit like that often sent knights home. Hopefully, everyone was too caught up with his opponent's unhorsing to notice him take a blow that could have snapped his neck in half. In fact, he suspected something *had* cracked. The sorcerer's dark magic was at work, making his neck tingle and ache.

Once free, he would have to relearn how to fight without the ability to take risks he knew might kill him. Learn how to fight to live again, instead of accepting he couldn't die.

One thing he knew, he wouldn't miss how it felt. The pinching, the burning, the prickling. So different from Adelaide's healing. That had been soothing. Cool and warm all at once. Numbing and mending without pain and leaving no scars. If it wasn't already clear that the sorcerer's healing came from a place of corrupted magic, Adelaide's magic proved it.

As Regulus stretched and waited for his next joust, his thoughts wandered. What a pair they made. Adelaide also carried a weighty secret that she lived in fear of someone discovering. But her secret, while dangerous, at least was not *bad*. Not like his. He worried that the pure magic in her would sense the corrupt magic in him. But if she hadn't detected it yet, she couldn't, right?

He had to tell her the truth.

He rubbed Sieger's neck as he checked him over, looking for any cuts or protruding bits of lance. The simple criniere protected Sieger's shoulders and chest, the areas most susceptible to damage from broken lances. He had a couple small nicks on his lower legs, but nothing concerning.

The roar of the crowd provided a buzzing backdrop to his thoughts. He had to tell her, but the thought of losing her made his heart physically ache. Was that ridiculous? He hadn't even known Adelaide long, yet… He felt like he had known her forever. Or like he had been waiting forever to know her.

Dresden sauntered over and stood on the opposite side of Sieger. He leaned across the saddle. "It should please you to know that Adelaide looked absolutely terrified for you."

Regulus' brow furrowed. "Why would that please me? I don't want her terrified."

"When you're jousting? Yes, you do, numbskull." Drez rolled his eyes. "She's scared you'll get hurt. It means she cares about you and what happens to you. The more terrified, the more she cares."

"I, on the other hand," said a smug voice behind him that he quickly recognized as Carrick's, "sincerely hope you fall and break your neck."

Regulus turned as Carrick's page led his horse past, but Carrick paused.

"I'd rather hoped your neck would snap with that last hit, but I guess it wasn't as hard a hit as I wanted it to be."

"What exactly is your problem?" Dresden rounded Sieger's flank.

Carrick looked down his nose at Dresden. "Your master and I are talking, Carasian."

Regulus put himself between Drez and Carrick before Drez did anything stupid. "I hold no malice for you, Sir Carrick. I see no reason for this continued hostility."

"*You* hold no malice for *me*?" Carrick laughed. "Ah, but I have more than enough for *you*. You've taken something I want, something I need. I won't rest until she's mine."

Regulus' hand curled into a fist. His jaw tensed. "Adelaide is not *something* to be taken or owned. She's a person who makes her own choices."

"Then she's made a profoundly stupid choice." Carrick stepped closer. "She should be honored I want her. Flattered that someone of my quality would desire her, common Khastallander mother and all. And yet she settles for a nobody." He sneered. "An illegitimate mutt turned mercenary who doesn't deserve the title he shouldn't even have."

Regulus exhaled. If he could keep his temper when taunted by the sorcerer, he could do so when facing Carrick. Several nearby lords, knights and squires watched them out of the corner of their eyes. Not one said anything. Suddenly, Regulus latched onto something Carrick had said. "What do you mean, you *need* her?"

"Doesn't matter. I just want you to know the stakes. I have no intention of playing fair. If I were you, I'd bow out before anyone gets hurt."

Regulus stepped forward, capitalizing on his height to look as menacing as possible. "Are you threatening Adelaide?"

"Don't worry, I won't hurt *her*." He glanced at Dresden, then looked back at Regulus and sneered. "I'm saying you should consider what you're willing to lose to keep her." He walked after his horse toward the arena.

"Did…did he just threaten me?" Dresden sputtered.

"I think it was a pretty generalized threat against me and anyone in my circle," Regulus said grimly. "He's insane." All the same, he sent up a quick prayer to Etiros that Carrick wouldn't act on his threats.

Drez gestured at the men in the area and muttered, "And no one cares."

Regulus unseated his next opponent in the first pass, which the crowd greeted with exuberant cheers and some disgruntled boos. The next joust he won by five points. Then he faced Carrick.

His anger flared as he stared at Carrick down the list. Carrick gave him a smug smile before closing his visor. *"I'd bow out before anyone gets hurt." Should have heeded your own advice, Carrick.* Sieger shifted beneath him, eager to charge. Regulus adjusted his grip on his lance and raised it above his head. Carrick did the same. Harold released the reins.

Wind whistled in the gaps in his armor. Sieger's chest heaved as he raced down the list. Regulus brought the lance down, couching it in the crook of his arm. He aimed for Carrick's heart. The lance slammed into Carrick's chest, sending a shudder down his arm. Carrick's lance hit Regulus' helm but bounced off. Regulus' lance bent and shattered, making the bones in his arm vibrate. Carrick flipped backward off his horse.

Under his helm, Regulus smiled.

He reached the end of the arena and wheeled around. Pages rushed to help Carrick to his feet, but he pushed them away and strode off the field—albeit with a slight limp. Regulus pulled off his helm and looked at Adelaide. Her wide smile accentuated her round cheeks. He would do anything for that dazzling smile. She nodded at him while she applauded. He looked at Carrick, exiting the gate at the end of the arena. Carrick looked back and held up a fist.

The message was clear. This meant war. Carrick's feud was only getting started. Regulus' spirits fell. What had he done?

Regulus' last couple matches were close—he won by only one point in the semi-final and was losing the final joust by three points until he unhorsed his opponent. But he won. He had to admit, he enjoyed the cheers. Between the thrill of the joust and the applause and Adelaide's smiles meant for him alone, he felt like he could fly. The exhilaration of winning buried even worries about Carrick's plans for revenge.

He rode Sieger to the middle of the arena and dismounted in front of Baron

Carrick's box. Servants carried in a narrow, tall wooden podium and a set of steep wooden steps. They placed the podium in front of Carrick's box with the stairs behind it. Once atop the podium, Regulus removed his helm to cheering from the spectators.

Baron Carrick moved to the barrier at the end of his box, standing a couple arm's lengths away. He raised his hands. The noise of the crowd hushed.

"Lord Regulus Hargreaves of Arrano," the baron said, his voice ringing out over the arena. "Today you have demonstrated your horsemanship, your skill with a lance, and your prowess on the battlefield." Cheers. A smile tugged at the corner of Regulus' mouth, but he focused on looking dignified.

"You have thrilled and entertained with your expertise and strength and impressed with your precision," the Baron continued. "You have earned our respect and admiration and honored the lady whose token you wear."

Regulus' gaze darted toward Adelaide, a small smile breaking his serious deference.

"You have tilted and emerged victorious. It is my honor as host of the Etchy Tournament to name you champion of the joust!" Baron Carrick applauded and the crowd joined in. As the cheering quieted, the Baron turned. A servant handed him a bulging leather pouch and a dagger with a handle inlaid with swirling ivory and sheath inset with small circles of mother-of-pearl. "In recognition of your triumph, I award you the prizes of the joust."

The Baron held out the pouch of coins and dagger. Regulus tucked his helm under his arm and retrieved the prizes of coins with a bow.

"Ladies and gentlemen," the Baron gestured for him to turn around, and Regulus turned and faced the other side of the arena. "I present to you your jousting champion, Lord Regulus Hargreaves of Arrano!"

Regulus bowed as the crowd hollered and whistled and applauded. Large groups stood, honoring the champion of the joust. Honoring *him*. Some ladies waved handkerchiefs and scarves at him. A few even blew him a kiss. His face heated, and he looked to Adelaide. She was looking right at him and grinning, apparently not noticing the other ladies. He breathed a sigh of relief, even as part of him enjoyed the unusual attention. Harold had walked into the arena during the prize ceremony and held Sieger's reins. Regulus handed him the pouch of coins and dagger. He took the reins and remounted. Sounds of praise followed him out of the arena.

After changing out of his armor and a quick, cold bath, he set out to find

Adelaide. He held the prize dagger in his hand. He had to ask a few servants and a couple knights for directions, but soon enough he found the Drummond's and Adelaide's tents. Adelaide sat on a stool in front of her tent, combing her glossy dark hair. Regulus held his hands and the dagger behind him as he approached. She spotted him and smiled.

"Congratulations, champion of the joust." Adelaide stood and set the comb down on the stool. "What brings you to our humble tents?"

He laughed. "I heard a rumor there's a beautiful lady here who fancies me. You wouldn't happen to know anything about that, would you?"

Adelaide feigned shock. "That's a scandalous rumor. You should be ashamed."

"If loving her should make me ashamed, then I am the most ashamed man in Monparth."

She snorted and shook her head.

"Okay, that sounded better in my head," he admitted. "But I do have a reason for being here, other than seeing your smile again."

She blushed. "Oh?"

"Three things, actually." He brought his hands in front and presented the dagger on his palms. "I haven't been able to think of anything other than giving you this since Baron Carrick handed it to me. It is beautiful yet strong. Elegant yet dangerous. Like you."

"Regulus…" Adelaide ran her fingertips over the sheathed dagger. "But this is yours."

"And I want you to have it. I can't think of a better owner."

Her fingers brushed his palm as she picked the dagger up. She pulled the dagger out of the sheath and admired the blade, assessed its weight and tested its balance. Rubbed her thumb crossway over the edge to check its sharpness. He grinned as she evaluated the dagger in much the same way knights considered a new sword.

"Are you certain?" She slipped the dagger back into the sheath. "This is exquisite. The craftsmanship is superb."

"An exquisite dagger for an exquisite woman. I can't think of a better gift to start our courtship."

Adelaide's gaze snapped up to his eyes. "Our…" Her lips parted in what looked to be pleasant surprise.

He took her hand, his heart stuttering with nerves far worse than those before a battle. "I was hoping you would be favorable to me asking your father for his permission to court you? I won't be able to yet. My business for my friend will take me in the opposite direction, and I'd rather ask him in person than by letter."

"Yes," she murmured. Then louder, "Yes!"

"Smart decision to ask in person," Minerva said from the side. "Father turned down several potential suitors for his daughters over the years because he said asking by messenger demonstrated either laziness and lack of resolve or cowardice. Caused quite a fight with our half-sister Dulcina on one occasion."

Goosebumps prickled his arms, and he looked to Adelaide. "Is your father likely to turn me down?" *He could do better for his daughter than a bastard.*

"Father can be…protective." Adelaide sighed. "But if you ask him bearing letters from myself and Minerva, that should help."

"I'll write a letter of recommendation, if that will help," Gaius said, walking around a tent and putting his arms around his wife. His eyes narrowed. "Assuming there's no more nonsense like last night."

"No, of course." Regulus nodded, a lump in his throat. "Definitely. Thank you."

"You said there were three things," Adelaide reminded him.

"Right." He cleared his throat. "Baron Carrick said the lady whose token I wore during the joust may dine with me at his table tonight. Would you do me the honor of accompanying me to tonight's feast?"

"I would love to!" She looked at Gaius and Minerva. "If…that's all right."

Minerva rolled her eyes. "As if anyone could stop you, anyway."

Supper passed pleasantly. Carrick sat with his parents, but he sat on the opposite side and didn't address Regulus or Adelaide the entire meal. After supper, he occasionally caught sight of Carrick laughing with other knights or dancing and flirting with various ladies.

He and Adelaide danced and laughed and talked. She told him about her mother taking her away to a cottage in the woods from age four to seven, until she no longer caused fires or made her hands emit light by accident. All to keep her abilities secret. How it took years for her and Minerva to get close after that, and how her half-siblings treated her with suspicion or indifference. They talked around her magic, never using the word and keeping their voices low.

He talked a little about his childhood. How he lived at Arrano with his mother, calling Lord Arrano Father despite Lady Arrano's protestations—until the birth of a legitimate son when Regulus was six. Then his father sent him away to live with a distant cousin halfway across Monparth. He mentioned training as a knight but never being treated as an equal. But instead of recounting sob stories about his cousin's cruelty, he focused on humorous tales, such as the time Drez got boxed on the ears by a cook at fourteen after he tried to flirt his way into stealing food.

Adelaide laughed. "So the noble household Dresden joined, that was your cousin's? Was he already there when you arrived, or did you meet him later?"

Regulus glanced away. He didn't want to lie to her, but Drez was sensitive about that. "You can't tell him I told you."

She chuckled, her confusion evident. "All right..."

"And don't think worse of him." He hesitated. "Or me."

Her forehead wrinkled.

"When I was eleven," he said quietly, thankful for the music and party conversation to cover his voice, "my father decided I needed a servant. He sent money to his cousin, who found Dresden's family. They needed the money."

"He..." Adelaide tripped, and they stopped dancing. "He was your servant?"

"I held his indenture for seven years. I should have released him sooner." Regulus forced himself to meet her eyes. "He was my only friend. I asked him to become a mercenary with me, and he did. And when I became a lord, I knighted him. He's my brother, not that I deserve him."

As Adelaide stared, he tried to interpret her expression. It wasn't judgement or distaste, she looked...pleased. She dropped his hands and embraced him, laying her head against his shoulder. He wrapped his arms around her, despite the glares from couples trying to dance around them, and kissed the top of her head.

The night ended too soon. But before everyone headed back to their tents, Adelaide kissed him again. Her kiss both set all his senses on edge and dulled them at once. The crowd around them faded like dying embers while his all-encompassing awareness of her lit his heart on fire. But then her sister was there, and he had to say goodbye. His chest ached as he watched her leave.

His knights walked back with him. After Carrick's attack, they had no intention of letting him wander unprotected. Perceval carried a torch, illuminating their way as clouds obscured the moon. The men laughed and discussed the ladies they had danced with and the amounts of mead they had drank. Their jocular mood vanished as they arrived at the tents to find chaos. One tent had collapsed, as if something had fallen on it. No fire or torches burned as they should. Scattered ashes and scuff marks in the dirt indicated a scuffle.

"Harold?" No response. Regulus' pulse quickened. "Harold!"

"Over here." Coughing. "My…lord."

Regulus snatched the torch from Perceval and darted toward Harold's muffled voice coming from the other side of a tent. The others followed, murmuring their surprise and concern.

Harold sat on the ground next to Sieger, who was lying on his side, his nostrils flaring and chest heaving with labored breathing.

"Sieger?"

"I…I tried to stop them, my lord." Harold looked up. Dust covered his face, except where streams of tears had washed the dirt away. Dried blood covered his mouth and chin, and his nose had a new crooked bump. A green and purple bruise blossomed around his right eye. "There were too many." Harold coughed and winced, putting a hand to his chest. "Four of them. Their faces were covered. I'm sorry…" He choked back a sob.

Regulus fell to his knees and laid a hand on Harold's shoulder, his gut twisting. "Harold…" He looked over his squire, noting his disheveled clothing and the blood covering his hands. Rage burned under his skin. "How badly are you hurt?"

"Mostly bruised." Harold coughed and groaned. "Maybe a cracked rib." He looked at Sieger, his lower lip trembling. "The blood is…it's Sieger's."

Regulus' breath caught. He moved around Harold and held out the torch. Sieger whinnied painfully and raised his head. The torchlight reflected in his eye, open so wide white showed around the edges. Regulus' gaze fixed on Sieger's legs. They had sliced his legs.

The low-life cowards had beaten his squire and cut his horse's legs.

Rage burned down his throat and lit an inferno in his chest. Blood-soaked cloths wrapped around the lower part of all four of Sieger's legs. Regulus clenched his jaw. The torch in his hand snapped in half as he squeezed it. Without a word, he strode away.

"Regulus." Dresden ran after him. "Regulus!" Dresden grabbed his arm. "Where are you going? You can't attack the son of a baron without proof."

"I'm not," he said through gritted teeth. "Tell the men to tidy up the camp and get a fire going. Get Harold to a cot. And put a tent over Sieger. I'll be back soon."

Dresden stopped as Regulus broke into a jog. "Where are you going?"

"To get Adelaide."

CHAPTER 31

"ADELAIDE!" THE panic in Regulus' voice chilled Adelaide to her core.

She pushed Giselle aside and ran out of her tent, not caring that Giselle had eased the lacing on the back of her dress and that it sagged a little around her shoulders.

Light from a nearby torch reflected in Regulus' wide eyes. His scar pulled at his skin, wrinkling against his grimace. "I need your help," he panted. "Please."

"What's going on?" Gaius walked out of his tent, followed by Minerva. "Lord Hargreaves?"

"Please," Regulus begged. "I need your…I need your help."

"Help for *what?*" Gaius demanded.

"Regulus, what's wrong?" Adelaide placed a hand on Regulus' forearm and his shoulders sank further.

His throat bobbed as he swallowed. His chest heaved. "Harold and Sieger. They've been attacked. They're hurt."

"What?" she gasped.

"Harold says he's all right, but…I…he—I'm not sure he is." Regulus hung his head. "And Sieger…" His voice broke. "I—I might have to… Please." He took a shaky breath as his shoulders quivered, and her heart cracked. "I… I understand if you can't help. But…I had to ask." He met her eyes. "I'm sorry. I had to ask."

Fear slid like ice down her spine. *Someone could find out.* But he looked so broken. *Nolan might already know, anyway…*

"This is my fault," he whispered, looking away.

"Nolan," she guessed, anger melting away her fear.

Regulus shook his head. "He was mingling with other nobles all night. But he has to be behind it."

If Nolan was behind the attack, and if Nolan suspected her magic, healing Regulus' horse would confirm her power. But if Nolan was behind the attack, it was likely because he hated she had chosen Regulus. It wasn't Regulus' fault, or hers. But she understood his guilt.

Regulus lifted his head, hope dying in his pain-filled eyes. "It was selfish to ask. I'm sorry." He turned to leave, but she slipped her hand down to grip his shaking hand. Her gut wrenched.

"Take me to them."

He paused and gave her a relieved smile. "Thank you." He started forward, but Minerva stepped into his path.

"Adelaide—"

"I can help." She met her sister's glare with determination. "Mother always encouraged kindness. If I can help, I will."

"Adelaide," Minerva repeated, her tone harsh. "You—"

"This is my decision, Minerva. Mine." Adelaide led Regulus around Minerva, their hands still clasped.

"What is going *on*?" Gaius' voice crept toward a shout.

Adelaide looked back at him. "You might as well know. Come on." She looked to Regulus, and he led the way, his footsteps rushed. Gaius followed.

After several minutes of hurried walking, Regulus slowed. They rounded a tent and Dresden looked up from a fire in surprise. "She came?"

Adelaide raised a brow at Regulus. He turned red. "Dresden has kept more secrets for me than I can count. I know I promised—"

"It's all right." She understood. She never could keep things from Minerva for long.

"Where's Harold?" Regulus asked.

Dresden pointed at one of the tents, and Regulus led her inside. Estevan and the blond knight—Caleb, if she remembered correctly—stood as they entered. Caleb held a soiled, wet cloth in his hand. Harold laid on a cot in the middle of the tent.

"I gave him my bed," Estevan said. He looked at her. "Why's—"

"Wait outside," Regulus said. Caleb and Estevan glanced at each other uncertainly but left the tent.

Gaius crossed his arms. "I'm not waiting outside."

"That's fine." Adelaide knelt next to the cot. Harold's eye was bruised, his nose broken. His breath came short and sharp, his face pinched. Her hands felt clammy. What if she *couldn't* help him?

Regulus knelt on the other side of the cot, his eyebrows knit. "Can you help?"

Harold watched Adelaide with wide, confused eyes. She wet her lips. "I'll try. Where does it hurt most, Harold?"

"My—" Harold groaned. "Ribs." He placed a trembling hand over the left side of his rib cage. "It's a dull pain, but sometimes, it"—he winced—"it feels like I'm being stabbed."

She pushed his shirt up. Blue bruises covered his left side. Regulus cursed under his breath.

"Are you a physician?" Harold sounded bewildered.

"No." Gingerly, Adelaide prodded Harold's ribs. He grimaced. Her fingertips brushed a sharp edge. Harold yelped, and she drew her hand back and bit her lip. Self-doubt chilled her. Regulus grabbed Harold's hand and put his other hand on Harold's shoulder, steadying him.

"Sorry. I needed to know where to focus." She looked to Regulus. "I've never healed a bone before."

Regulus nodded, a vein on his temple standing out. "I understand."

She held her palm over Harold's broken ribs. *Help me, Etiros.*

Gaius moved closer. "What is—" Her palm shone. "—going…" Gaius's words died on his lips.

Warmth spread across her hand. Harold sighed and his breathing normalized. Energy drained from her, like a cloth soaking up water. Somehow, she could sense the bone. As if she could feel it moving and coming back together. The bruising faded. She lowered her hand as it stopped glowing. She pressed on his ribs, and relaxed when they felt whole and Harold didn't cry out. She'd done it. Pride and joy surged along with gratitude to Etiros for her gift. She pulled her hand away.

"You can sit up now."

Harold sat up and pulled his shirt down. "How did you *do* that?"

"You're…you're…" Gaius sputtered.

"A mage, yes." She tilted her head, studying Harold's face. "Close your eyes."

He did, and she placed her palm over his nose. She heard the bone snap into place as his nose straightened. Harold jumped, but didn't whimper or open his eyes. The bruise over his eye turned yellow then disappeared, and she dropped her hand. "You can open them now."

Harold opened his eyes and touched his nose. "Thank you, my lady. I…I can never repay you."

"A good start is keeping her secret," Regulus said. Harold nodded.

Adelaide stood. "Sieger?"

Regulus clapped Harold on the shoulder and met his eyes. Something unspoken passed between them, and Regulus wrapped one arm around the squire's shoulders in a quick embrace. Regulus' eyes glistened as he stood. "Sieger's this way."

"Um," Gaius said. "I have questions—"

She nodded. "Later."

Regulus led her outside, and Gaius followed. The knights, standing around the fire, watched them duck inside another tent with curious expressions. The sharp scent of sweat and blood mixed with dirt stung Adelaide's nostrils. A lantern hung from the tent poles. The tent was otherwise empty, except for Sieger.

Sieger laid on his side, foam around his mouth as he panted. Blood seeped through the bandages around his lower legs and into the ground. He tried to get up as Regulus entered. The stallion released a neigh that sounded like a scream and flopped back onto his side. Regulus paled to the same whiteness as his scar.

"Oh, Sieger." Adelaide sat on the ground as her throat constricted. "He's lost a lot of blood," she murmured.

"I know." She barely heard Regulus' response.

"I think I can heal the cuts, but I don't know if that will be enough." She didn't look up as he sat next to her.

"I won't blame you if…" He trailed off, and from the tension in his voice, she knew he couldn't bring himself to say it.

She unwrapped a bandage and gasped. The cut exposed bone. She closed her eyes and reached for Regulus with her left hand. He took her hand. She held her right hand over the uncovered wound. The flesh pulled, moving back together, covering the blood and bone. Even after she sensed that the wound was closed, she kept going, praying it would help counteract the blood loss. She did the same for the other three cuts. When she had finished, she felt drained, as tired as if she had run a great distance. She leaned back into Regulus' shoulder. A wave of dizziness made her sway.

Regulus wrapped an arm around her. "Hey, easy. Are you okay?"

"Just tired." She wiped sweat from her brow. "I've never used that much magic before."

Sieger raised his head. He pulled his legs under himself and nuzzled Regulus' head, playing with his hair with his lips. Regulus laughed. Sieger lowered his head, lying on his stomach with his legs tucked under him.

"He must be tired from the stress and loss of blood," Adelaide mused.

"But he seems better." Regulus sounded considerably calmer. "I feel like he's going to be okay."

"I hope you're right."

They sat there for a moment in silence, the fingers of her left hand entwined with his and his arm wrapped around her shoulders. She liked it. The press of his muscular body, the gentle movement of his chest, the way he held her shoulders like he couldn't bear to let her go. She laid her head on his shoulder.

Gaius cleared his throat and Adelaide blushed. He still stood behind them. She'd forgotten he was there. "Can I ask my questions *now*?"

GAIUS ASKED a string of questions about when, how, what she could do, and who knew. Adelaide answered every question, even though she looked exhausted. Regulus didn't mind all the questions, though. He would have sat there all night with her tucked against him, their fingers laced together. But her eyelids drooped, and weariness tugged at him. Once Gaius was satisfied, Regulus helped her to her feet.

"I can't thank you enough." Regulus placed his hand on the side of Adelaide's neck and caressed her jawline with his thumb. "I am forever in your debt. And I promise, my men won't tell anyone. I trust all of them."

She leaned into his hand, her skin warm on his palm. "I'm glad to finally help. I hate hiding." She looked down. "But I'm also not sure I'm ready for everyone to know. So I appreciate the promise."

"You have a beautiful heart," he murmured.

"What are we going to do about Carrick?" She looked up, anger burning in her tired eyes. "He can't get away with this. I don't care if he was at the feast all evening. He *had* to have sent the men who did this."

"I can't prove that. And as relieved and thrilled as I am that you were able to heal them…there's no evidence an attack happened at all."

She worked her jaw. "And what if he tries again?"

"My men are exceptional fighters. And in the morning, we're heading back to my castle. He won't be able to do something like this again." *Let him try. I'll kill him.*

"It's not right."

"I know." He pulled her into an embrace.

Adelaide wrapped her arms around him and leaned her cheek on his shoulder. It amazed and bewildered him how comfortable they felt together. "What did you mean when you said it was your fault?"

"What? Oh." He took a deep breath. "Something Carrick said. A vague threat I didn't heed." He glanced at Gaius, who stood near the tent entrance, looking anywhere but at them. "I should have let him win the joust."

Gaius shook his head. "No. There's something else at play here. Something far more personal than a lost joust. And I suspect you know what it is."

Regulus clenched his jaw. He wouldn't say it. Not in front of Adelaide. He wouldn't put that pressure on her. He met Gaius' eyes, then looked down at Adelaide's head resting on his shoulder. Gaius squinted. His jaw slackened as he understood. He opened his mouth to say something, but Regulus shook his head.

He pulled away from Adelaide, even though he hated to do so. "You should return to your tent. You look exhausted."

"Can I see you in the morning?"

"I'm afraid not." His shoulders fell, thinking about all he had to do. About the truth he hid from her. It made him nauseous after what she had done for him. But he could hardly tell her in front of Gaius. "We'll be leaving before daybreak. And you need to rest. But I'll see you for supper on the third." He kissed her forehead. *And I'll tell you everything.*

Everything.

ADELAIDE FELL asleep as soon as she pulled on her blanket. She hadn't slept so soundly in ages. But when Giselle woke her, she felt refreshed. The festival grounds echoed with the sounds of tents being collapsed, horses and carriages prepared, and the chatter of everyone from nobles to servants. While servants loaded their belongings onto palfreys and mules, she took Zephyr and found a small grove of trees a short ride away. A quiet place where she could feed him oats and a few sugar cubes in peace and not worry about being in the way.

After a short while, hoof beats approached. She turned to look, expecting Sir Gaius or one of the Drummonds' servants. Zephyr's lips tickled her outstretched palm, and she smiled. But then she saw the intruder's face. Her smile vanished as she clenched her jaw. "You're not welcome here, Sir Carrick."

Nolan chuckled, as if she were teasing. He dismounted and sauntered closer as her whole body tensed. "That's hardly polite of you."

"I know what you did," she said, her voice low and accusing.

"And what's that?" His playful tone and crooked smile taunted her as he moved closer.

"Regulus' squire and horse were attacked last night. I know you're behind it." She raised her chin. "So you are not. Welcome. Here."

"Interesting." Nolan stepped closer and rubbed Zephyr's neck, looking at the gelding in admiration. Her heart pounded against her ribs. "Because I know something, too." He met her eyes. "*I* know what *you* are."

She stopped breathing. Icy tendrils wormed through her chest. "What are you talking about?" She had meant to speak with confidence, but her words came out breathy.

"I wasn't certain what I saw when you showed up and played the knight to Half-Breed's damsel. An amusing moment, that. But then the mercenary didn't sustain injuries. I heard you visited the mongrel's camp last night. And this morning, he apparently rode his horse away before dawn, despite whispers the horse was maimed. I also heard a rumor someone broke his squire's nose, but he looked fine. The look on your face confirms my theory."

The last sugar cube in her hand slipped from her fingers and fell to the ground. She felt light-headed. Goosebumps pricked her arms.

Nolan laughed and looked back at Zephyr, still stroking her horse's neck. "Don't worry. I won't tell." He shrugged. "Not yet, anyway."

"What do you want?" Her voice sounded hoarse.

"I would have thought it was obvious, my dear." He gave her a wicked grin and stepped toward her, his hand falling from Zephyr's neck. "I want *you*."

Indignation crackled under her skin. She clenched her fists. "You're out of your mind."

"No. I just know what I want. And I get what I want. Marry me, Adelaide."

She fixed him with a death glare. "What in creation makes you think I would ever marry *you*? After everything you've done?"

"Oh, I realized a while ago I wasn't going to win you over by charm alone." He gave a dismissive frown. "I'm not used to that, to be honest. I thought to scare you away from Hargreaves, but that failed too. When I left you with him after the attack, I hoped you'd see him as weak and move on, but no. I thought I would threaten the mercenary into leaving you. But that seems to have failed as well."

"So what?" Her thoughts turned to the weapons stowed in her boots. "You're here to threaten me now?"

"Not threaten yet, no. Blackmail. I know your secret, Adelaide."

Nervousness made her shiver, but she squared her shoulders. "Fine. Tell who you will. I'm done hiding who I am."

One side of Nolan's mouth curved up in a condescending smile. "You say that, but I don't see you broadcasting your"—he lowered his voice conspiratorially—"abilities." He crossed his arms. "I can't say I blame you. If everyone like me had been brutally hunted down and murdered, I also would want to keep my identity secret."

She narrowed her eyes. "Listen closely. I would rather the entire *world* knew my secret than *ever* marry you. Why are you so desperate, anyway? If ladies usually find you so charming, why am I so important? What makes you want to marry *me* so badly?"

Irritation clouded his eyes, but then his usual careless smile returned. "I know your secret; you might as well know mine. I'm out of viable marriage options. Either my brothers already married into the best families, the families of my station don't have eligible daughters of a decent age, or…" He shrugged. "I've burned one too many bridges, it seems. My *gracious* parents," he spat the words, "have threatened to disinherit me. They gave me a deadline, and if I don't marry, they'll disown me and throw me out of Carrick Barony with no inheritance. I'm down to a month."

"How tragic for you." *Serves you right.* "Go bother another young lady."

"Ah, but why would I do that? I had resigned myself to marrying some moderately attractive woman who would have a smaller dowry than a nobleman of my standing deserves—"

Adelaide snorted. "What a shining example of chivalry you are."

He ignored her and continued. "And then I met you. The daughter of the renowned, wealthy war hero Lord Alfred Belanger. You would come with respectability, in spite of your mother. Prestige. And, I'm certain, a generous dowry." His smile took on a wolfish, hungry quality. "And to top it all off, you're beautiful. Even with your Khastallander complexion."

"Is this supposed to improve my opinion of you? Because it's having the opposite effect."

"No." Nolan's voice became low, menacing. "It's so you understand what is at stake. My entire life hinges on marrying. And you're the best option, sweetheart. At this point, likely my only option. And the only thing that stands between me and the lifestyle I want, I *deserve*, is that thrice-accursed mercenary."

"And me." She folded her arms. "I won't be bullied any more than Regulus."

"You don't want to go to war with me, love." He stepped forward and she stepped back, pulling her dagger out of her boot with practiced speed. She had picked too secluded of a spot. No one could see his aggressive behavior.

"Take another step and I'll cut your heart out."

Nolan looked at the dagger in her hand, the one Regulus had given her. He grunted. "Very well, my lady." He turned toward his horse. Some of the tension drained from her body and she lowered her dagger.

Nolan spun around and lunged forward. She cursed herself for lowering her guard as she stepped back and slashed at his face. He dodged, but the tip of her dagger still nicked his cheek. Blood beaded from the cut and Nolan hissed and grabbed her wrist with both hands. She reached for his face with her free hand, but he wrenched her hand down, twisting her wrist. Adelaide yelled and dropped the dagger. He caught her other hand right before her fingernails scratched his eye.

"That. Stung."

"You dare assault a lady?"

He released her and Adelaide stepped back. Tears stung her eyes. She cradled her throbbing wrist with her other hand.

"Just showing you I'm not to be trifled with." Nolan nodded at her wrist. "I'd apologize, but I imagine it'll be whole in no time." He bent down and picked up the dagger. "This is nice." He stuck it in his belt.

"Give that back!" She reached for him and whimpered as the movement sent a stab of pain through her wrist.

He wiped blood off his cheek, but lines of blood continued to flow from the shallow cut. "So demanding."

There was still no one in sight. She raised her left hand as a ball of fire grew in front of it.

He clicked his tongue and shook his head. "I wouldn't do that. Do you think no one knows I'm here? You kill me and you'll be hanged for murder."

"Maybe I don't kill you," she bit out. He could be lying. But she wasn't confident enough to risk being accused of murder. And if his body was found scorched to death, she would have a lot of explaining to do.

All humor fled Nolan's face. "*Now* I'm threatening you. All I have to do is say a word, and I have men who can discretely sabotage your sister's carriage. I can't imagine a carriage wreck being healthy for her or the baby."

Adelaide gasped. *Etiros, no.* She wanted to believe he wouldn't. But after Harold and Sieger… Nolan looked at her with cold, indifferent resolve. She dropped her hand to her side, the flames extinguished.

"Good girl."

"You still can't take that," she said, but her voice held no confidence. "Your father gave it to Regulus."

"Who gave it to you, and you kindly gave it to me."

Adelaide felt helpless. She had never felt helpless. Her mother hadn't raised her to be helpless. *Etiros, what do I do?* She could roast Nolan alive, or throw a knife at his back as he walked away, even though she was far less accurate with her left hand.

But she couldn't. She couldn't put her family at risk. And she didn't want to hang for murder—or even really want to kill again. He tapped his foot on the ground, waiting.

"Please." Adelaide lowered her head, staring at the ground. Her wrist ached and her eyes watered. Her heart felt made of lead. "Please."

"All right." She looked up, surprised. "I'll give it back." He leered. "For a kiss."

"Troll take you!"

Nolan shrugged. "Have it your way." He turned and walked away, Regulus'—her—dagger still in his belt. He mounted his horse. "See you soon, love. And if I were you"—he smiled cruelly—"I'd think very carefully about how you will answer next time I ask for your hand."

After Nolan left, Adelaide healed her wrist. Tears of despair stung her eyes as she sent anguished, rage-filled prayers to Etiros. She waited until she had stopped crying to ride back to camp. She couldn't tell Minerva. Minerva would tell Gaius; Gaius would challenge Nolan. Adelaide had seen them both fight. Nolan would win.

Minerva would be a widow with a baby due in three months.

No. She wouldn't put Minerva and Gaius in the middle of this. She wouldn't risk their safety and their lives. A month didn't give her much time, but at least Nolan wasn't trying to force her into marrying him next week. She would tell Regulus after their supper. They would come up with a plan together. She combed her fingers through Zephyr's mane.

Maybe Regulus would ask her to marry him. She couldn't marry Nolan if she was betrothed to Regulus.

Right?

C H A P T E R   3 4

REGULUS DUG through his closet, tossing aside shirts and trousers and boots. Where had he put it? He glimpsed a corner of the small wooden box and seized it. The silver inlay of an *A* on the lid gleamed in the sunlight streaming through his window. The oak box was about the same size as both his hands, and heavy. He undid the latch and opened the box.

Inside, a large silver medallion stamped with a rose over crossed swords rested on red satin. The Arrano crest. The pure silver medallion had been left to Regulus, along with everything else, when his half-brother died and his father's title transferred to him. Lady Arrano had thrown it at his head after he defeated her champion.

Regulus had tried to give it back to her. She could have sold it. But she resented his kindness. So it sat in its box, buried deep in his closet. Now his blacksmith would fashion it into a circlet for the thrice-accursed sorcerer. He snapped the lid closed.

One ingredient out of five.

He had already instructed his bewildered steward to find and purchase fifteen clams. They didn't even have to be in good condition, he only needed their shells. But he decided to play it safe and get more than necessary. Just in case. Steward Preston didn't question the uncharacteristic request.

Regulus had talked to Jerrick and to Perceval's wife Leonora about flowers. They both did some recreational gardening and knew a good amount about plants. Between the two of them, they assured him they could secure a bushel of assorted white flowers. That left the neumenet root and the blood of an innocent. Regulus dropped off the medallion with his blacksmith before heading out. Holgren Forest was over a day's ride away. It had already taken a day and a half to get back to his estate. He had spent the prior afternoon and evening making arrangements. Best not to delay.

Sieger had made a full recovery. Even after the long trek back to Arrano, his stallion was eager to leave again. As Regulus had decided he wanted to draw as little attention to himself as possible, he left the Black Knight armor behind. Dresden accompanied him. Regulus had tried to talk him out of coming, but between the risk of getting caught entering a royal forest without a permit, concerns about a chance encounter with Carrick, and anger over hiding how bad things had been with the sorcerer, Dresden would not be dissuaded. Regulus decided to be thankful no one else tried to tag along.

Dresden's concerns proved unfounded. They arrived at Holgren Forest the following morning without incident but searched all day without finding the neumenet tree. Holgren Forest was large, so they had a discouraging amount of ground to cover. When darkness fell, they were deep in the forest. They had no choice but to make camp and hope no forest rangers, or worse, a royal sheriff, happened upon them.

They spent the next day searching. Every snap of a branch or sudden rustling put Regulus on edge. Several deer startled him, and Dresden teased him relentlessly about being more skittish than a doe. Despair crept in as the shadows deepened in the forest.

"Reg." Dresden pointed. "Did you see that?"

"What?" He turned Sieger, scanning the branches where Dresden pointed. Then he saw it. A flash of light. Like sunlight on water, but high in the trees.

Like sunlight on glass.

Bark like obsidian and leaves like shards of glass but soft as feathers.

They rode toward the flashes of light. They rounded a large willow and Regulus held up his hand to shade his eyes, squinting.

Some twenty paces ahead stood a tree several stories tall. Wide branches spread out, stretching over a meadow and nearby trees. He couldn't look directly at the branches. Sunlight reflected off tens of thousands of silvery-white leaves, illuminating the surrounding forest. No trees stood within ten paces of its massive, shiny black trunk. Light bounced off leaves and gave the obsidian bark a dull glow. After a moment of gawking, he rode forward. Dresden followed.

The closer they got to the tree, the more leaves from the neumenet tree covered the ground. As long as his hand and no wider than two finger's breadth and opaque, they looked like shards of glass after a heavy frost. He dismounted and retrieved a spade from his saddlebag. The leaves made a quiet rustling beneath his feet as he walked closer to the trunk. Like walking on straw. Curious, he knelt down. He touched one, half expecting it to cut him. Instead, it gave way beneath his fingers. He picked the leaf up. It was solid, yet light and soft to the touch. He dropped it, and it drifted to the ground.

He had the strangest sensation. Like the earth and forest around him were extra alive. The bizarre whisper of a breeze in the leaves of the neumenet tree above him sounded at once welcoming and foreboding. As if the tree itself invited him to rest in its shade, but with an undercurrent of doubt and warning. He shook his head and scanned the ground. Paranoia.

He saw a hint of black root breaking the surface of the ground and knelt next to it. Dresden joined him, also bearing a spade. Together, they dug around the root until a little over a foot was exposed. Regulus' hunting knife made a high-pitched rasp as he sawed through the black wood. Dresden started on the other end, and the sound made Regulus' ears ache.

Unlike the trunk, the root had no shine. But it was hard, sweat-inducing work. Every so often, a low, rumbling creak sounded from the trunk. Almost a groan. As if the tree felt pain. *Ridiculous. Trees don't feel pain. Right?* He wiped away some sweat from his forehead before it dripped into his eyes. *This is wrong.* He felt in his soul there was something special, sacred even, about this place. About this tree.

But his freedom depended on getting this root.

His future. His ability to marry Adelaide.

Etiros, forgive me. I know I ask often. But forgive me.

Finally, he cut through the root. He could have sworn the tree shuddered. Glittering leaves drifted to the ground all around. He shifted and took over for Dresden, who sat back, panting. It took another couple minutes to cut through again. He picked up the root and strapped it to his saddlebags. A woody groaning followed them away from the tree. Regulus' heart and conscience felt heavy.

They made it back to Arrano without being stopped, but Regulus didn't relax until they arrived. They had been gone nearly five days. Eight days had passed since the sorcerer contacted him. Adelaide would arrive for supper in three days. It would take two to get to the sorcerer's tower and back.

To his relief, everything else was ready. The circlet complete. Fifteen whole clamshells were in a bag, cleaned and ready. A guest bedroom was crowded with white flowers in vases, bowls, and jars. He only needed one more thing. One more thing to ask Etiros to forgive him for.

He knocked on Harold's door. The small tin vial and knife in his hands seemed heavy as a boulder. Harold opened the door and smiled.

"What can I…" Harold's brows knit. "What's wrong, my lord?"

Regulus exhaled and his shoulders dipped down. He hated himself for doing this. His hands grew slick. His head ached.

Harold looked down at the vial and dagger in Regulus' hands. "My lord?" The confusion and anxiety in his voice made Regulus' stomach turn.

He looked away from Harold's face, unable to meet his eyes as he held out the knife and vial. "I…" He swallowed. "I have to ask something of you."

"I don't understand."

"I need…" Another gulp. "The sorcerer needs your blood. The blood of an innocent person. You have a good heart, a kind soul, and have never killed." He tasted bile at the back of his throat. "He said he only needs a few drops. I'm not asking as your lord." He forced himself to look at his squire. "I'm asking as your friend. I won't force you—"

"This will help free you?"

"I hope so."

Harold nodded, then took the dagger. "My life is yours, my lord. I can spare a few drops of blood. That's a small favor." He made a small cut on the side of his hand. He held the blade against the wound and blood pooled on it.

Feeling wretched, Regulus pulled the stopper out of the vial. Harold placed the tip of the dagger in the top, and a small rivulet of blood dripped in. Regulus replaced the stopper. Harold handed back the dagger and held his other hand over the cut.

"Thank you," Regulus said quietly. "You're a good man."

Harold shrugged. "I have a good example to follow."

Regulus trudged up the stairs, the vial of Harold's blood clutched in his hand. *I don't deserve your admiration.*

Regulus didn't wear the Black Knight armor on the way to the sorcerer's tower, either. *Let him be angry.* Regulus needed speed, not theatrics. His saddlebags bulged. One end of the black neumenet root stuck out from under the flap. Leaves from the flowers poked out everywhere. If anyone stopped him, they would have plenty of questions.

He kept off the main roads, cutting across fields and through woods to take the most direct route. Stars appeared as he reached the dead forest surrounding the sorcerer's tower. Moonlight made the barren white trees look ghostly. He dismounted and knocked on the door. After a couple minutes, a deadbolt clanged on the other side of the door. The door opened, and the sorcerer stepped onto the threshold. Firelight flickered inside the tower. Even standing a step below him, Regulus stood taller than him. But the dark power emanating from the sorcerer made Regulus feel weak.

"Ah. You're early." The shadow cast by the sorcerer's black hood hid his expression. The black stones set in his red and black belt seemed to absorb all light, while the silver hairs in his brown beard glowed white in the moonlight. "Come on. Bring it all in." He turned and went back inside, his tunics and robe rustling.

The sorcerer had never invited Regulus inside. He recovered from his momentary shock and removed the bulging saddlebags, then followed the sorcerer.

The ground floor consisted of one large circular room. A modest fire burned in a huge stone fireplace across from the door. An ornamental rug covered the entire floor beneath a leather armchair. Two floor-to-ceiling bookshelves stood on either side of the fireplace, filled with leather-bound tomes and stark white human skulls. The sorcerer headed up a spiral staircase to the right of the door.

"Close the door," he called as he disappeared around a curve. Regulus nudged the door closed with his boot and followed.

They passed two more open circular rooms as the staircase spiraled around the outside of the tower. Regulus peeked through the open doorways as they passed. One had several desks, some covered with open books, others with large pieces of parchment. Another fire crackled in the fireplace behind a desk covered in rocks and gemstones of various sizes and colors. The next room contained a massive four-poster bed, a small writing desk, and a closet. Were any clothes in the closet? He'd never seen the sorcerer wear anything other than the layered black and red tunics and robes he wore now. None of the rooms had windows.

The staircase opened into the final room at the top of the tower. A long table with a workbench sat in the middle of the room. Four gold rods were laid end-to-end on the table. He recognized the one that widened at the top as the first thing the sorcerer had made him retrieve. The sight of it gave him flashbacks to the first time he had discovered he couldn't die. A minotaur had impaled him on a spear. Right through his chest. He recognized two of the other three pieces as well with a sickening twist of his stomach. He'd killed a monk who wouldn't get out of way for one of them. Not on purpose. He'd tossed him aside, still adjusting to his new strength, and the man's head had cracked open on the stone wall of the monastery. The man's vacant eyes still haunted him.

Positioned just above the rods lay the strange hollow gold egg he had taken from the dragon's lair. As he looked at the five pieces positioned in a line, he realized they belonged together. They formed a staff. But the sorcerer hadn't forged them back together.

Regulus looked around as the sorcerer motioned him inside. A bronze mirror identical to the one locked in his chest hung on the wall near the fireplace. Light flickered from the fire and from numerous candelabras on the walls around the room. Smaller desks were placed around the edges of the room, covered in various flora in glass jars. A large, shallow bronze bowl sat on one of the tables. The sorcerer pushed aside some books piled on another table.

"Unpack it all here so I can examine it," the sorcerer commanded.

Regulus complied. The flowers came out first and the sorcerer grunted approval. The sorcerer snatched up the neumenet root, inspecting it and muttering to himself while Regulus emptied the bag of shells onto the table. Apparently satisfied, the sorcerer set the root next to the flowers. He checked the shells while Regulus set the silver circlet on the table.

"Hm." The sorcerer picked up the circlet. His hands glowed with green light and the circlet made a quiet thrumming sound. "Pure. Good." He put the circlet down and Regulus exhaled in relief. "And the blood?"

Regulus handed him the vial. "From my squire. A good young man who has never taken a life. An innocent if I ever met one."

"Excellent." The sorcerer removed the stopper and peered inside. "Should be enough."

"Will that be all, my lord?" Regulus stepped back from the table.

"For now." The sorcerer replaced the stopper and set it next to the other ingredients.

Regulus clutched the saddlebag. Nothing but dried venison, a bit of rope, and a spare dagger left in it now. "And…my debt?"

"You annoy me with your constant nagging." The sorcerer pursed his lips. "I'd think you would be more grateful. I made you the strongest, fastest man in Monparth, possibly in the world. And immortal. Yet you can't wait to give it up."

I want to be free. "You mentioned this"—he indicated the ingredients—"would get me close."

"Fine." The sorcerer waved his hand. "One or two more tasks, and your debt will be paid in full. I'm close now." He looked away, and Regulus followed his gaze to the separated staff on the table in the center of the room. "So close I can taste it. This time, I won't fail."

The sorcerer looked back to Regulus. "I'll be needing you soon. You must be prepared to act quickly when the time comes. Now go." He waved his hands like he was shooing away a small child. "Your presence irritates me."

Then why trick me into being your slave in the first place! But Regulus turned and left.

THE PRINCE of Shadow and Ash spent the next two days preparing for the full moon. Thanks to that gratingly honorable mercenary-turned-lord, he could take his time. Make sure everything was exact. The roots and shells ground into powder. The flower petals plucked and dried. It was time consuming, but life had taught him patience and the value of doing things properly. He rubbed his scarred shoulder. It would be different this time. If he could find what he needed. Ironically, the same thing that had stopped him last time.

The full moon rose into a clear sky. He moved a table into the moonlight spilling through his window and placed the wide, shallow bronze bowl on top and filled it with water. He mixed in the ground root. Once the water was black, he used his sorcery to heat the black water to boiling. Next, he stirred in two handfuls of powdered shells. After the shells had dissolved, he forced the water to cool, making the bowl glow a dim green, then covered the surface of the water with the dried petals. He enchanted the silver circlet so it would float and positioned it in the center of the bowl. All part of activating the magic inherent in the items, or imbuing them with his own magic.

Last, he opened the vial. The enchantment he had placed on it as soon as Hargreaves had given it to him kept the blood as fresh as possible. He tilted the vial and three drops of blood dripped into the center of the bowl, staining the petals red. He held his hands over the bowl. Emerald light radiated from his palms. Steam and smoke rose from the bowl. The petals inside the silver circlet melted and silver bled into the water. He mentally reached out, drawing more energy to replenish his magic from the forest outside as green light swirled around him. He had to reach farther and farther each time he needed extra power.

The water inside the circlet shimmered silver with a greenish tint, then became clear as glass. An image shifted into focus and the sorcerer dropped his hands to his side and scrutinized the image.

An infant. He snorted in disgust. Useless. He waved over the bowl, and the image shifted. A scrawny young man stumbled out of a tavern, obviously drunk. As if this pathetic creature could possibly have enough control to do what he needed. Would not even be worth the effort to have him killed. He waved his hand again. A young girl no older than four with tight blond curls bounced on a middle-aged man's knee.

"Curse my thoroughness!" The prince waved his hand again, rage boiling his blood.

A young woman. Probably noble, based on her fine clothing. Certainly wealthy. Her skin was dark for a Monparthian. Maybe Carasian or Khastallander. But she had to be in Monparth, since he had only searched within the kingdom. She smiled and laughed between sips of wine, looking confident and at ease. He held his hand over the water and pulled up, forcing the image to move in on her face. Bright, intelligent brown eyes. He pushed back down toward the water, and the image pulled back, showing more of her surroundings. A smile curled his lips. He stroked his beard and leaned back from the bowl.

"Interesting."

CHAPTER 36

"HOW DO I look?" Regulus ran his fingers through his hair.

Dresden rolled his eyes. "Like you always do."

"This is a bad idea." Regulus paced back and forth in the foyer, the clack of his boots echoing in the vaulted ceiling. Magnus padded along after him, tongue hanging out of his mouth and tail wagging. Two curving staircases rose on either side of the room, meeting at the top and leading into the great hall. The only decorations were a couple suits of armor on either side of the door centered between the two staircases that led to the wine cellar. He had never cared for ostentation, so when he moved in, he had cleared away the oversized vases and faded blue carpets that reminded him too much of his father's wife. Besides, he had never had guests before.

"What if I can't get her alone to explain? What if she doesn't understand?"

Dresden leaned against one of the stone bannisters. "Relax."

"What if supper is awkward?" Regulus stopped short and Magnus pushed his head under his hand. He scratched behind the big dog's floppy ears. "I think Sir Gaius has mixed opinions of me. What if I do something he dislikes? Or worse, I do something that offends Lady Minerva?"

"You're offending me with your incessant worrying."

The doors to the foyer swung inward and Regulus turned. Magnus stepped in front of him with a low growl. Steward Preston led Adelaide, Gaius, and Minerva into the castle. His anxiety melted away as she smiled. "They're friends, Magnus."

Magnus looked back at him, his tongue hanging out of what looked like a grin.

Adelaide knelt in front of Magnus. "Hello, Magnus." He panted as she scratched beneath his chin. "Aren't you a handsome big boy. Regulus told me all about you." Magnus licked her bare forearm—she wore a sleeveless dress today. She laughed.

"First your horse, now your dog," Dresden said. "Maybe she wants to steal your animals, not your heart."

Adelaide stood and crossed her arms, but he caught the slight blush in her cheeks. She cocked an eyebrow. "Really, Dresden," her tone was teasing. "If you put as much effort into your manners as you did into maintaining your beard, you'd have a wife by now."

"All right, all right." Dresden laughed. "The lady knows how to spar. I humbly fold."

Regulus held out his arm. "Shall we head in?"

Adelaide took his arm and they entered the hall. Magnus pushed between them, rubbing against their legs. He looked from one to the other, whimpering for attention. They moved to their seats as the rest of his knights arrived to join them for supper. Perceval's wife Sarah and Jerrick's wife Leonora joined as well. Adelaide sat in the chair to the right of the head of the table, Gaius in the chair to the left. Regulus pushed in her seat and sat down. Magnus laid between his and Adelaide's feet.

Contrary to his fears, supper progressed wonderfully. Gaius seemed relaxed and Minerva was as sassy as she was sweet. Adelaide's laugh made his heart soar. The warm chatter that echoed down the long table filled his soul. This was all he ever wanted. To be surrounded by people he cared about and who cared for him in return. To see the joy on their faces.

Halfway through supper, Estevan regaled them with a story about the time Perceval stepped in a hunter's snare and refused help for an entire hour while he kept trying to cut himself down, all while hanging upside down. Regulus reached for his goblet, watching Adelaide's eyes sparkle with mirth. Searing pain sliced up his arm. His hand jerked, and he knocked over his goblet with a clatter. Wine spilled over the table. He clenched his teeth against the stabbing, burning sensation covering his right forearm. The mark had never hurt like this when the sorcerer summoned him before.

Estevan stopped mid-sentence. All eyes turned toward him.

"Regulus? What's wrong?" Alarm rang in Adelaide's tone.

"Nothing." Another stab of pain. He gripped the edge of the table. "An old injury acting up. Excuse me for a moment." He left the table, their stares clinging to him.

Magnus followed, but he shook his head. "You stay here, boy." Magnus cocked his head, and Regulus pointed back toward the table. The dog padded back and laid down at Adelaide's feet. It pleased him Magnus liked her, but the searing pain commanded his attention.

Dresden cleared his throat. "You haven't gotten to the best part yet, man! Keep going."

Good old Drez.

The pain kept increasing, spreading from his arm to his shoulder to his chest. Regulus raced up the stairs, stumbling as his ribs ached. He threw open his door and slammed it behind him. He fumbled with the key, his hand shaking from the pain that wasn't abating despite his obedience. It seemed to take forever to lock the door. *I'm coming!* He cursed.

He struggled again with the lock on the chest. What in creation was the sorcerer's problem? He yanked out the mirror and the pain eased. "I'm here." He hung the mirror on the wall and stepped back.

The mirror shimmered and the sorcerer appeared, an ecstatic grin on his face. The pain vanished.

"Yes, my lord?" Regulus said, not hiding the irritation in his voice. "What's with the…urgency? What if I had been out?"

"I knew you weren't," he said, as if this were obvious. "I've found what I'm looking for."

Regulus sighed. "Which is?"

"You see," the sorcerer said, bobbing up and down as if rocking back and forth onto his toes, "some twenty or so years ago, I lose count, I tracked down and killed—or rather, had killed, mostly—every mage in Monparth. Every sniveling idiot with pure magic in their veins."

"You…" Regulus' jaw dropped. *Of course. Idiot.* Of course the self-proclaimed Prince of Shadow and Ash *was* The Shadow that had caused the extinction of mages in Monparth. His thoughts turned to Adelaide downstairs. *Almost extinction.* Panic surged, but he snapped his jaw closed.

"Yes, that was me. Who else could have that much power?" The sorcerer paused, but Regulus didn't know how to respond, so the sorcerer continued. "The trouble is, the final relic I need is hidden behind an enchanted wall. It's like a gigantic lock. And only a *mage*"—he snarled—"can open it. It repels sorcery."

"So you used those ingredients to find mages again," Regulus guessed, his spirit sinking.

"What do you know. You're not a complete idiot."

Regulus tried to keep his voice from shaking. To look indifferent and uninterested. "Did you find any, my lord?"

"Oh, yes." A sickening grin spread over the sorcerer's face. "Would you believe a mage is downstairs, in your home, this very moment?"

No. No, no, no. "Downstairs?" The word came out choked. *Etiros, please, no!*

"Yes, pretty young woman." The mirror turned watery and shifted to an image of Adelaide in Arrano's hall. She rested her chin on her palm, her elbow propped on the table as she spoke. The image shifted back to the sorcerer.

Regulus swallowed back the bile rising in his throat. "You…you're certain?"

The sorcerer's smile turned into a frown. "I don't make mistakes! She's a mage as certainly as I'm a sorcerer. Hopefully she has the power to do what I need. What's her name, anyway?"

Regulus grit his teeth. His hands balled into fists.

"I asked you a question, boy."

Pain burned his arm, and he grunted.

"Her name?"

He stared at the ground, clutching his forearm. "Adelaide Belanger." The pain subsided.

"You told the truth. Very good. At least bringing her to me should be easy. You know right where to find her."

Regulus hung his head. "Please. Don't kill her."

"I won't kill her, weren't you listening? I just need her magic."

And after you've used her magic? He swallowed hard. "Surely there is someone else—"

Agony exploded up his arm. He clutched his chest and doubled over as the pain spread from his sternum. A moan stuck in his throat.

"I. Want. Her. As soon as possible."

Shouts sounded from the hallway. Cries of "Lord Hargreaves!" echoed up the stairs.

Confused and gasping for breath, Regulus looked toward the door. He panted out, "My lord, I should go check—" before he fell to his knees as the pain redoubled, spreading over his entire body.

"You will bring her to me."

Regulus' eyes watered as his breathing grew more labored. The shouts continued, muffled and unintelligible.

"I…can't…" He swallowed back a scream as it felt like fire filled his veins. His vision blacked out, and he curled into a ball on the floor.

"You're my slave. You do what I tell you."

His heart felt like it would burst. Dying. He was dying. *Etiros…save me.*

"Do this, and your debt will be paid."

The pain ceased. Regulus took several deep breaths to steady himself. The darkness shrouding his vision receded. He stood, his knees shaking.

"I expect to see you tomorrow with Belanger. I don't want to harm her. But you must bring her." The sorcerer's voice became dark and menacing. "If I have to force you, every pain I have inflicted on you will seem as nothing compared to the pain *you* will inflict on everyone you care about, including the girl. And then you will die in more pain than you can imagine."

Regulus looked up. The mirror was blank—just a bronze mirror. He stuffed it in the trunk as someone pounded on his door. The muffled shouting from downstairs continued.

"My lord!" Harold sounded panicked. "I am sorry, but you *must* come downstairs."

Regulus opened the door. "What is it? What's going on?"

"We couldn't stop them," Harold panted. "The sheriff has a warrant—"

"Sheriff?" Regulus cursed. They had been spotted in Holgren. Someone must have recognized him or his description. Regulus grabbed his sheathed sword from next to his door and pushed past Harold, fastening the belt around his hips as he hurried down the stairs. If he was going to be accused of hunting in the royal forest—a theft against the crown—he needed to look like a lord.

Because a lord might get away with a heavy fine. But a commoner could be hanged. If they tried to hang him, he would live. He would be exposed for the monster he was.

Adelaide watched Regulus go with an unsettled feeling in her gut. He was hiding something. Dresden urged Estevan to continue his story. She would have to ask Regulus for the truth later—when she told him about Nolan's threats.

Regulus' abrupt exit distracted her from the end of Estevan's story. Something about Perceval injuring himself trying to escape from a hunter's trap. The other knights laughed like this was the funniest thing in the world. Their laughter was infectious, even though Adelaide scarcely understood the cause.

"That's why he's the blockhead and I'm the smart one," Caleb said, his tone serious but mirth in the wrinkles around his eyes.

Perceval pointed at him. "No, you're the one askin' for a beating."

Caleb gasped and put a hand over his heart. "To say such things in front of ladies! Including your own wife!"

Leonora giggled. The curvy brunette wrapped her hands around Perceval's muscular upper arm and leaned against her husband's shoulder. "He has a point, Cal. You'll push him too far one day." She winked.

Adelaide laughed and propped her elbow on the table, resting her chin in her hand. "What is it between you two?"

"Ah, see that's all on account of—"

"Caleb Rathburn you shut your obnoxious mouth!" Perceval threw a bread crust at Caleb's head, which he ducked.

"Don't interrupt me when I'm talking to a lady." Caleb clicked his tongue. "What *would* your instructors at university say?"

Adelaide looked at Perceval than back at Caleb. "Perceval went to university?"

"Perceval got kicked *out* of university," Caleb said.

"I quit!" Perceval snatched up his goblet.

Dresden leaned toward her. "This is a common argument," he whispered.

"Why were you kicked out or…quit? Whichever it was," Gaius said as he cut into the roast quail on his plate.

"Well, see—" A loud banging from the foyer interrupted Caleb.

Dresden frowned. "That's odd." He rose from his seat and headed out of the hall. "Pardon me a moment."

"You cannot barge—" Adelaide recognized the voice of the steward who had greeted them in the courtyard.

"I am the Sheriff of Relton, and I serve the king!" another man's voice interrupted. "These men are my deputies. The others are here in case of trouble."

"Trouble? What business has a sheriff here?" Dresden's voice. "Why—Carrick."

A tremor ran down Adelaide's spine. Surely Nolan wasn't here? Now?

"*Sir* Carrick. I'm here as a witness, as are my knights."

Her stomach churned, her appetite gone.

"I am here to arrest Regulus Hargreaves for treason," the sheriff said. Her head spun.

"Treason?" Dresden's voice echoed as he shouted. "You're out of your mind!"

"Where is your master, Carasian?" Nolan asked. She could hear the sneer in his voice.

"My *lord* is not. Present."

"Check the hall," the sheriff ordered. A moment later three men she didn't recognize strode into the hall, followed by a red-faced Dresden.

"This is an outrage!" Dresden shouted. "Lord Hargreaves isn't even home! And you have no proof! How can you possibly—"

"He was heard conspiring to kill the king," the sheriff said as he walked into the hall. He was of average height, with a drawn countenance and a balding head.

"That's ridiculous," Adelaide blurted.

The sheriff looked down his nose at her. "You are hosting guests without your lord present?" He eyed the empty chair at the head of the table. "Or perhaps you mean the treasonous coward has already fled." He raised his voice. "Hargreaves, show yourself!"

Three more men walked in. Nolan and two other knights. He stopped in his tracks and stared. "Adelaide? What are you doing here?"

She stood, glaring. "*I* was invited! What are *you* doing here?"

Nolan shrugged. "I'm here to positively identify the man whom my knights and I heard discussing plans to murder the king."

All of Regulus' knights stood, shouting over each other, protesting Regulus' innocence and accusing Nolan and his knights of lying. Magnus stood, too. He stalked around the table and growled at the intruders. Gaius stood and turned toward the men.

"Gentlemen," he said, his voice calm and level, "perhaps there has been a misunderstanding. I hardly think Regulus Hargreaves capable of plotting treason. What reason could he possibly have?" Regulus' knights shouted their assent.

"The courts will determine the truth!" the sheriff bellowed.

"There's no proof!" Adelaide shot back. "Just his word against theirs!" She pointed at Nolan. "Nolan Carrick has a personal feud with Lord Hargreaves. He is lying!"

Regulus' knights talked over each other again, confirming what she said and calling Nolan all kinds of unsavory names. Nolan and his knights put their hands on their swords, as did the deputies. Perceval was the only one of Regulus' knights wearing a sword, and he put his hand on his sword as well, pushing his wife toward the door at the far end of the hall with the other. Leonora grabbed Sarah's hand, and they left the hall. Estevan pulled a strange dagger from the back of his belt. It was long, curved and sharp along one edge, with no handle. Opposite from the sharpened edge was a grip with four holes. Estevan put his fingers through and held the grip in his fist. Jerrick and Caleb grabbed carving knives off the table. Dresden eyed a sword hanging on the wall on the other side of the intruders.

Gaius held out his hands. His face was pale as he moved to shield Minerva. "Now, gentlemen. Let's not be hasty." Magnus barked between low, rumbling growls.

"Magnus!"

Adelaide spun toward Regulus' voice. Magnus ran to Regulus in the stairway but continued to snarl. Regulus now wore a sword. He stroked Magnus' head. "Upstairs." The dog whined, but obeyed, and Regulus shut the door behind him. "I demand to know what is going on!"

"That's him." Nolan pointed at Regulus.

"Regulus Hargreaves," the sheriff said, "you are under arrest for conspiracy to commit treason against the crown."

Regulus looked confused, then angry. "Carrick." He said it like a curse word. "You dare come into my home and spread lies?"

"My men and I overheard you talking to some other men," Nolan said, motioning to the knights on either side of him, "plotting to murder the king."

Perceval drew his sword. Nolan, his knights, and the bailiffs did the same. Regulus followed suit.

"In here!" Nolan called.

A dozen more men poured into the hall, all wearing swords. Adelaide's lips parted in shock. Gaius grabbed Minerva and pulled her away, toward the far end of the hall.

"Adelaide!" Minerva called, her voice desperate.

"Go," she said. Gaius hurried Minerva out of the hall.

Nolan nodded at Adelaide. "You should go, too."

"I'm not leaving until you take back your accusations."

"Hargreaves will stand trial. The courts will determine if the accusations are true," the sheriff repeated.

"And who will the courts believe?" Regulus shouted. He strode away from the closed stairwell door until he stood near her at the head of the table. "How am I to prove what I did or did not say? When was this supposed to be? I've been away on business. Does that even matter to you? To the courts? Or only the word of a baron's son? I'll take my chances with my sword, thank you." He spun the sword around like it weighed no more than a stick.

Nolan rolled his eyes. "An honest lord would come willingly, Half-Breed." Adelaide could have punched his perfect face.

"As an agent of the crown, I am authorized to use any force necessary to take you into custody so you can stand trial." The sheriff ignored Regulus' questions. Doubtless because he knew that the judge would favor the testimony of a baron's son over the word of a lesser lord and former mercenary. The sheriff nodded to the three bailiffs, and they moved toward Regulus. "If you resist, you will be killed."

"So my choices are death or death?" Regulus said, his voice hot with rage. He leaned toward her and whispered, "You need to leave. Now. I'm sorry."

"If you are innocent, you have nothing to fear." Nolan sneered.

Sure, right. Adelaide stepped in front of Regulus. "This is nonsense!"

Nolan scowled. "Get her out of here."

Four more men stepped toward her and Regulus. Her first instinct was to pull her dagger from her boot, but what good would that do? There were close to twenty men in the hall, including Nolan and the sheriff. Regulus gently grabbed her arm and moved her aside.

"No one touches her." Regulus looked at Nolan. "You have a problem with me? Fine. Be a man and challenge me to a duel."

Panic rose in Adelaide's chest. *Etiros, how do we stop Nolan?*

"Mm, no."

"Then I challenge you!" Regulus pointed his sword at Nolan.

"Ha." Nolan shook his head. "I don't have to accept a challenge from a man accused of treason."

"You think these men are enough to take me and my men?" A menacing smile spread over Regulus' face and for the first time, Adelaide understood the mercenary that was all some people saw when they looked at him.

"Confident, aren't we?" Nolan shrugged. "I'd wager they could, but if they can't, there's another ten in the foyer and fifteen more on standby in the court-yard. You can't escape."

"I don't run," Regulus said in a low voice. He raised his sword and adjusted his footing.

Adelaide clenched her fists. *No, no. This can't be happening!*

"If you fight back, what happens?" Nolan asked with a wicked smile. He pointed to Regulus' men. Perceval still held his drawn sword, his eyes fixed on Regulus like he was waiting for a signal to attack. Caleb and Jerrick held the carving knives at the ready, their eyes roving over the men in the hall. Estevan paced back and forth, a cat ready to pounce. Dresden's fingers twitched, his gaze fixed on the knight nearest him. "If they fight with you, they'll die with you."

"That's what we do," Perceval said, his tone icy. "I know loyalty must be a difficult concept for a snake like you."

"You want to be the first to die?" Nolan's lip curled up in a sneer.

Perceval took a step toward Nolan, and Nolan's knights moved to intercept him. Adelaide felt rooted to the floor, her voice trapped in her throat.

"Stand down, men," Regulus said, his voice heavy. Perceval froze, as did the knights. They all looked at Regulus.

Adelaide's breath caught. Regulus' sword clattered to the stone floor, and the sound made her jump as it reverberated through the hall. Regulus raised his hands.

"I surrender."

Adelaide froze. The men who had been moving toward her jumped forward and surrounded Regulus. Two of them grabbed Regulus' arms. Perceval and the others stared at Regulus, their disbelief clear.

"I said, stand down," Regulus repeated as the knights pinned his arms behind his back and pushed him toward the doors. Perceval sheathed his sword, his face red.

"What? No!" Adelaide grabbed at one of the men and tried to pull him off Regulus. "Let him go!" Another man pushed her away as they hurried Regulus out of the hall. Her boot caught on the hem of her skirt, and she started to fall.

Hands grasped her arms and steadied her. Nolan smiled, a picture of carefree calm. "Easy there."

She pulled away. Regulus had already disappeared through the doorway out of the hall, trailed by his fuming men. "What is wrong with you! What are you *doing?*"

"I would have thought it was obvious. Getting rid of an obstacle." He looked at her patronizingly. "I warned you. You don't want to go to war with me."

"Treason? They'll *hang* him!"

"I certainly hope so."

"You…" That's when she saw the dagger in his belt. Regulus' dagger. Her dagger. He must have caught her gaze, because he rested his hand on the hilt and smirked.

Maybe she should just kill him. Then there would be no witnesses to Regulus' supposed crime. Just several witnesses for her, murdering a baron's son in front of a sheriff.

"You can put a stop to this, you know." Nolan stepped closer. "Say you'll marry me, and I promise, the bastard will live. I'll leave him and his alone."

The breath seemed sucked from her lungs. She couldn't even push her *never* past her stuck tongue. She looked toward the door. Regulus' men stood on the other side, at the top of the stairs leading down in the foyer, their backs to her. The sheriff stood in the hall, watching her and Nolan with disinterest.

"I guess he dies, then."

She looked back as Nolan crossed his arms and stared into her eyes. Waiting for her to break.

"You know, others were with him, when he was plotting treason." He looked at his fingernails. "One of whom, now that I saw him here, looked suspiciously like your brother-in-law."

Adelaide covered her mouth with her fist and gasped. Her gut clenched. *Etiros, please.* Her face burned. So did her hands, and she clenched her fists tighter to keep her magic under control. "You're a monster."

"I'm just a man willing to do whatever it takes to get what I want." The icy look in his eyes made her shiver.

"You think I could ever love you?"

"Eventually, yes, I think you will." He shrugged. "But I don't need you to love me. I need you to marry me and act happy about it."

No. This was all wrong. This wasn't supposed to happen. She had to…had to… Her shoulders drooped. She had to protect her family. And she couldn't let Regulus die because of her. "Fine," she whispered.

Nolan stepped so close her skirt brushed his boots. "What was that?"

"I'll marry you." The words tasted like vinegar. "So long as they *all* live. You can't let them hurt or kill Regulus."

Nolan grinned. "Sheriff!" He stepped around her. "I've just realized—we've got the wrong man. Turns out he's innocent." Nolan held up a hand, as if saying *oh well*.

"You want him arrested, or don't you?" the sheriff huffed.

Nolan took Adelaide's hand and strode toward the sheriff, pulling her along. "Not anymore." He lowered his voice. "Don't worry, you'll still get paid."

Adelaide's mouth hung open, but both men ignored her as they walked out into the foyer full of armed men, with Regulus in the center. Gaius and Minerva stood off to the side. Minerva's eyes were wide in her ashen face. Gaius's forehead wrinkled and his lips pinched, eyes narrowed. Nolan, Adelaide, and the sheriff passed Dresden and the others at the top of the staircase as they walked down toward Regulus. The sheriff approached Regulus, and Nolan followed with Adelaide in tow.

"You say this *isn't* the man?" the sheriff asked Nolan.

Regulus looked at the sheriff in surprise, then at Nolan. His eyes flashed when his gaze landed on her hand in Nolan's.

"I realized it when I was talking to Adelaide," Nolan said flippantly. "The man looked almost exactly like Hargreaves, but now that I look at him, he's far too tall. The man I overheard was about Adelaide's height, so it couldn't be Hargreaves."

Regulus stared at Nolan like he was seeing a specter.

"It seems you are innocent after all," the sheriff said to Regulus. "Forgive us the intrusion." He bowed stiffly. "Release him." The men holding Regulus stepped back and his arms fell to his sides.

"A simple mistake, I'm afraid," Nolan said with a wave of his free hand. "My apologies. However, threatening to attack bailiffs, agents of the law, and all this fighting to the death bravado…" He clicked his tongue and put his arm around Adelaide's waist and pulled her against his side. She wanted to recoil from his touch, but she bit her tongue and forced herself to stand still. "I don't want my betrothed around such violent men."

"Your..." Hurt and confusion flickered over Regulus' face before the fire in his eyes returned even brighter. "What happened?"

"Didn't she tell you, Hargreaves?" Nolan gloated. "We're engaged to be married." He pulled the dagger from his belt and held it out on his palm. "She gave me this as a token of her affection and a symbol of our betrothal."

Regulus' face pinched as he looked at the dagger. The dagger he had given her. She clenched her jaw, her stomach roiling. He looked at her. "No," Regulus said. Then again, his voice stronger. "No."

"I'm sorry, Regulus." Her voice sounded strained, and she swallowed. What lie to tell to get him to stand down? If Nolan had paid off the sheriff, he would only have to say the word and these men would run Regulus through on the spot and claim he had resisted arrest. "This isn't how I wanted to tell you."

"You...but..." Regulus reached toward her. Nolan pulled her back and pointed the dagger at Regulus. Several men around them drew their swords. Regulus held up his hands and stepped back as Nolan returned the dagger to his belt.

"What is this?" Minerva's voice. Adelaide looked over her shoulder as Minerva and Gaius wove between armed men toward them. "You two are not betrothed!"

"Well, we have to speak to your father to make it official, but she has accepted my proposal." Nolan squeezed her waist. "Isn't that right, love?" He sounded so cavalier.

"Yes." She couldn't meet Minerva's eyes.

Gaius's cheeks reddened. "You're lying."

No, Gaius. Please don't.

"If I know anything about my sister," Minerva spoke with the sharpness of the daggers they had trained with, "I know she wants nothing to do with you." She looked at Adelaide. "Did he hurt you?"

"No." Adelaide forced herself to look at Minerva, begging her with her eyes to stop. To accept it. "I..." Her tongue stuck in her mouth. She thought of Regulus, being forced to his knees in front of an executioner. Of Gaius beside him. With all sincerity, but not about Nolan, she said, "I love him." *I love him.* The realization cracked through her heart. *I love Regulus more than I hate Nolan.*

"Horse manure," Dresden spat as he walked down the stairs. "What did he do?"

"You think I, a man of chivalry, would harm or threaten a lady?" Nolan sounded hurt and disappointed. He turned and brushed her hair behind her ear. "How could I hurt you, love?" His voice was soft, his eyes tender. He played the part maddeningly well, but his false gentleness filled her with disgust.

"She looks uncomfortable," Gaius ventured.

Nolan frowned at Gaius. "I had expected joy for our announcement; not to be attacked like this." His fingers dug into Adelaide's side, pinching her.

"I was wrong about Nolan." She forced a smile and laid a hand on his chest. "I was confused about my feelings." It felt like swallowing sawdust. "He's a…worthy man."

"Like hell." Regulus pointed at Nolan. "After what he did—"

"Regulus," Adelaide said. This was not going well. *What did Nolan think would happen?* "Lord Hargreaves." Regulus blinked like she had slapped him. "You have to let me go. Please. It's for the best."

"Best for who?" Gaius demanded.

"Adelaide, obviously." Nolan gestured around the foyer. "Look around. This place looks like a mausoleum. Tight on funds, Hargreaves? Based on the state of this place, I'm shocked you could afford the tournament entry fee. What can you offer the daughter of Lord Alfred Belanger? Or were you hoping to seduce your way into a dowry? You have nothing a woman of Lady Belanger's pedigree desires or needs."

Regulus opened and closed his mouth like he was trying to formulate a response but couldn't. He looked to Adelaide, his eyes full of doubt and questions. Adelaide's heart twisted. *No, Regulus. Don't believe that.* She couldn't help but note the bitter irony of Nolan accusing Regulus of using her for riches.

"But…" Regulus' throat bobbed. "He… Harold and—"

"Nolan wasn't behind the attack." Adelaide stared at the floor.

"I was appalled when I heard," Nolan said. "Attacking a boy and a defenseless animal? That's unforgivable. I hope you find out who did it."

Regulus stepped forward and drew back his fist. Several knights drew their swords and pointed them at Regulus. Adelaide sucked in a breath and held it as a knight placed the edge of his blade across Regulus' neck.

Nolan chuckled darkly. "I wouldn't try anything, mercenary."

Regulus' shoulders heaved, but he lowered his fist. A vein in his temple pulsed as he stepped back. Adelaide's chest shuddered as she released her breath.

Nolan brushed his lips against Adelaide's cheek and she barely suppressed a grimace. "Frankly, we don't owe any of you an explanation." He looked at Regulus. "We shouldn't linger in the house of murderers. Don't you agree, love?" His thumb pressed into her side.

"Agreed." She licked her lips. "My love."

Regulus took a tiny step back, his lips parted, eyes pinched, posture sagging as if he could scarcely stay standing. She looked away from his anguish. *Better heartbroken than dead.*

Nolan guided her toward the front entrance. "Don't bother following us, mercenary."

Night had fallen. The full moon cast long shadows across the courtyard and highlighted the group of armed men bearing torches standing at the ready.

"You there," Nolan called to a servant walking through the courtyard, "Lady Belanger and Sir and Lady Drummond require their horses at once." The man nodded, then changed course.

Several saddled horses stood grazing in the courtyard. The sheriff and bailiffs headed to their horses and mounted. Nolan left her side and retrieved a bulging pouch from a brown riding horse's saddlebag and handed it to the sheriff. Nausea grew in the pit of Adelaide's stomach. She moved next to Minerva and Gaius.

"What happened?" Minerva whispered. "Did he threaten you?"

Nolan turned away from the sheriff and looked at Adelaide. She shook her head. The sheriff and the bailiffs rode out of the courtyard, and all but the two knights who had entered the hall with Nolan left with them.

Nolan sauntered over, confident, cocky, and at-ease as always. Hatred burned her skin and coiled in her chest, making her fingers itch for a blade and magic tingle along her skin. Servants led Zephyr and the horses drawing Minerva and Gaius' carriage into the courtyard as Nolan stopped in front of her.

"I imagine this has been a frightening and exhausting evening." Nolan brushed her hair over her shoulder. "It's best you get home as soon as possible." He looked to Gaius. "My knights and I will gladly accompany you, for safety and peace of mind." He ran his hand down her bare arm and clasped her hand.

Adelaide stared at the backs of the men leaving the courtyard. He had no intention of affording her an opportunity to tell Gaius and Minerva the truth. Her heart sank.

"Oh." Gaius cleared his throat, sounding ill at ease. "That's not necessary."

"Please, I insist," Nolan said.

"Are you going to have a sword held to my throat if I refuse?" Gaius snapped. Adelaide tensed, squeezing Nolan's hand in her panic.

"Why would you refuse?" Nolan sneered. "Don't you want me along, Adelaide?"

She forced as much pleasantness into her voice as she could. "Of course I would like my betrothed to accompany us."

As they rode away, she cast one last look back at Arrano castle. *I'm sorry, Regulus.*

REGULUS STARED at the closed front door. All his anger—at the sorcerer, at magic, at Carrick, at the sheriff—had melted away, leaving him hollow and numb. What had just happened?

"Did you see anything?" he demanded of Dresden. "Did he hurt her?"

"I was too focused on you." Dresden's look of pity grated on his nerves. "But she looked unharmed."

Nolan must have threatened her. There was no way she *wanted* to marry that villain. She couldn't.

Regulus stepped toward the door, his heart fracturing while Adelaide calling Nolan *my love* replayed in his mind. "Something's going on."

Dresden blocked his path. "They have a small army. Carrick will have you killed if you try to stop them from leaving."

Regulus groaned and turned away. But then…there might be one blessing here. He had asked Etiros for aid, and now he had a valid barrier to bringing Adelaide to the sorcerer. Carrick would see to it he never went near her again. As much as it hurt, Regulus could let her marry that rogue if it kept her safe from the sorcerer. He ran back to his room, ignoring his men's shouted questions. Once he had locked the door to his room, he pulled the mirror back out. He had never tried this, but why shouldn't it work?

"I need to talk to you."

Nothing.

"It's about the mage."

After a moment, the mirror shimmered, and the sorcerer appeared. "What? What is it?"

"I can't bring you Adelaide Belanger. She is beyond my reach."

"Likely story."

"She's engaged to a personal enemy of mine." He closed his eyes for a moment, the words bitter. He worked his jaw, forced himself to continue. To see the blessing in this waking nightmare. "He's taken her, and he won't let me near her. Who else is there?"

"There is no one else!" the sorcerer shrieked. He took a deep breath, then spoke calmly. "She's in no danger from me. I need her to open a door. That's all."

"But there is no way for me—" He gasped as his mark burned. He wanted to claw it off, but he knew that didn't work, so he gritted his teeth against the pain.

"You've killed a dragon! You can handle some nobleman!" The pain in his arm subsided. "It's simple. Once she helps me, I'll remove the mark and let you both go. I'll be gracious and give you two days to bring her to me. But if in two days I don't have her, you will carve your friend's heart from his chest. And I'll kill the mage when I'm done with her." The sorcerer disappeared.

Regulus stared at his reflection, his mind blank. Someone knocked on his door. More by habit than by conscious decision, he crossed to the door and opened it. Dresden walked in, followed by Magnus.

Regulus moved back, his footsteps heavy. "He wants Adelaide."

"Carrick? Obviously."

"The sorcerer." Regulus sank onto his bed, exhausted. Magnus jumped up and laid his head on his lap. He couldn't even muster the energy to stroke Magnus' head.

"What? Why?"

"He needs her magic. He says he doesn't want to hurt her." Regulus stared at the cold fireplace. "Bringing her will repay my debt. And if I don't…" His gaze darted to Dresden as he shuddered. "You're all in danger."

"Then what's the problem? You know what you have to do, so let's make a plan."

"I can't!"

"Because of Carrick?"

"Because I love her!" Traitorous tears ran hot down Regulus' cheeks. He wiped them away and looked down at Magnus' large furry head in his lap. "What if the sorcerer takes her captive? What if he makes *her* his slave? Or—"

"What if you don't do it?" Dresden asked roughly. He stood across from Regulus with a forbidding expression, his arms crossed. "Best-case scenario, he sends someone else. Someone who might hurt her. Worst case—you kill us all, kill the Drummonds' guards to get her, and take her while not yourself and covered in the blood of her family and friends. You don't have a choice, Reg."

He opened and closed his mouth several times, trying to think of a response. He had considered having Dresden chain him in the cellar, where the sorcerer couldn't make him hurt anyone. But that was assuming the sorcerer couldn't use sorcery to lose his bonds. And didn't account for the sorcerer sending someone else. He had killed every mage in Monparth without Regulus, he could capture one inexperienced mage without him.

"There is the chance Adelaide can heal it," Dresden said.

"And if she can't?"

"Then nothing has changed." They looked at each other for a long moment.

"There is another option," Regulus said slowly. "It wouldn't kill me."

Drez paled. "No. He said he won't hurt or kill her, and then you'll be free. You're so *close*, and it might not even work."

The thought turned his stomach, but it was better than hurting Adelaide. "But it—"

"Damn it, Regulus!" Dresden punched the back of the armchair. "I'm not cutting your arm off! I'm not letting you do it, either! We discussed this! The mark came back when you cut it out; what if it just moves? You'll have accomplished *nothing* but losing your arm. She'll be okay. He'll keep his word, just like he has so far. You'll both be fine, you'll be free, and you'll be glad to have both arms."

Regulus opened his mouth, but Dresden pointed at him, his hand shaking.

"You promised me. You *promised.*"

Regulus nodded. Relief and guilt warred within him. Relief at solid reasons for not cutting off his arm, or worse. Guilt that he wasn't strong enough to do whatever it took to protect Adelaide. Guilt that he had nearly broken his promise to Dresden to endure and not hurt himself again.

"All right. I'll start figuring out how to…" He hung his head. "How to kidnap her."

CHAPTER 39

ADELAIDE POSITIONED herself close by the side of Minerva and Gaius' carriage, but it didn't take long for Nolan to move from behind the carriage and ride up next to her. He snatched the reins from her and pulled them over Zephyr's head and out of her reach.

"Hey—"

"We need to talk, love." He kicked his horse forward, leading Zephyr after him, much to Adelaide's displeasure. Once they were well ahead of the carriage, he let the horses slow.

"What?" She threw all her rage behind the word.

Nolan glanced over, the moonlight casting shadows over his disapproving frown. "Now, now, let's try to be civil—"

"Civil!" She grabbed for the reins, but he moved them out of her reach, causing Zephyr to drift closer to his horse. She leaned back and crossed her arms as Nolan tied her reins to the pommel of his saddle. "Civil would be giving me my reins back. And civil isn't blackmailing and threatening me into marrying you. Civil isn't bringing false accusations against an innocent man—"

Nolan's snort cut her off. "Innocent? He's a mercenary and a bastard who drove his father's wife out of her home. Even if he didn't plot treason, *innocent* is a stretch."

"She left because she wanted to. He's not a mercenary anymore, and you can't be guilty for your blood or the circumstances of your birth."

"Once a mercenary, always a mercenary." He shook his head. "But I don't want to talk about the mongrel. I want to talk about you. About us."

Adelaide ground her teeth. If she found a way around Nolan's threats, there would be no *us*. Instead, she latched onto her irritation at his constant and unfair commenting on Regulus' birth. "Oh, so you want to talk about the *other* mongrel?"

"What?" He twisted toward her. "Oh. The half-Khastallander thing? It doesn't bother me. You are your father's daughter, that's what matters."

"*Meim apaneh mahn keh bateh hohm,*" she snapped, then translated for him. "I'm my mother's daughter. I'm Khastallander, too."

"Well, obviously." He gestured at her. "But you're still attractive, regardless."

Her face heated. "Regardless? Thank you, that's so flattering."

Nolan reined in his horse and they stopped. "I'm trying to compliment you." His warm, husky voice didn't match the way his brows pulled together in annoyance. He leaned toward her and placed his hand on her hip as he moved in for a kiss. *Not likely.* Adelaide kicked Zephyr's sides, and the horse bolted forward, as did Nolan's horse.

"Charming," Nolan said once he'd recovered from the unexpected movement. "You'll have to kiss me eventually, you know."

Heat spread to her scalp. "Insulting my appearance and heritage is a good way to make me want to avoid that."

"I didn't…" He sighed heavily. "Look, I'm sorry, all right? I didn't mean to offend you. That's the last thing I want. You're beautiful, end of story."

She glanced at him out of the corner of her eye. "Anything else you would like to apologize for while you're at it?"

"Mmm, no?"

"You *hurt* me," Adelaide hissed, trying not to let her voice carry back to the carriage. "You threatened my family. And you tried to get Regulus killed!"

"I was making a point." He spoke airily, as if none of this mattered. "You healed, as I knew you would. I don't want to hurt your family, and since you've agreed to marry me, that shouldn't be a problem. As for Hargreaves, I'm sorry you were there. I'm sorry if I frightened you. And frankly, I'm sorry I let him go."

Adelaide opened and closed her mouth, at a loss for words. She wove her fingers into Zephyr's mane to keep her anger—and her magic—at bay. She stared straight ahead, unwilling to so much as look at Nolan. "You didn't frighten me, you infuriated me. And, just to make it clear, the last thing I want is to kiss someone who threatened the life of the man I *actually* love."

In a blink, his hand circled her wrist and squeezed. She tried to pull away, but he dug his fingers into the underside of her wrist. "Listen closely." His voice was low and threatening. "You're betrothed to *me*. You are going to forget about Hargreaves, or I'm going to forget about sparing his life."

"You're hurting me."

"Good." He pushed her arm back toward her and released his painful grip. "Now you know how I feel when you talk about *him*. So we're even."

She massaged her wrist. *If Father finds out how he treats me, he'll cut Nolan's head clean off. If Nolan doesn't orchestrate an accident or something first.*

Nolan rubbed his forehead. "I'm sorry. That was uncalled for. I don't want to have to hurt you. I love you. Just…accept me. Don't fight me. And I'll be kind in return."

Right. Because love looked like veiled threats? *Love isn't meeting a sharp tongue with a hard fist. It's not earning kindness. That's control and fear, not love.* But she couldn't risk his threats shifting from her to Minerva and Gaius, so she kept silent.

"I don't lose," Nolan said, his voice low. "I'm a spare son. I'm used to fighting for what I want, even if it takes time. I had to work harder, be stronger, smarter, more charming, just…more, to get the same recognition as my brothers. If I'm not given respect, I take it. Fighting me won't end well."

Adelaide slumped in her saddle. Best to appear compliant until she figured something else out. She stayed quiet the rest of the ride back to the Drummond estate. When Nolan tried to discuss wedding dates, how long it would take her to make a dress, or where they would live, she responded with single-syllable words.

Nolan insisted on helping her dismount in the courtyard. He had returned her reins shortly before they arrived, so nothing looked amiss when Gaius and Minerva stepped out of their carriage. They watched as Nolan took her hand and guided her to the ground, but Minerva looked halfway between confused and concerned. Nolan took Adelaide's arm and led her to the door, giving her no opportunity to speak to her sister.

Lady Drummond opened the door just before they reached the entryway. "So, was Arrano—Sir Carrick!" Her eyebrows shot up, and she curtsied. "Why…it is a pleasure to see you. What brings you to our home?" Her gaze fell on Adelaide's arm hooked through Nolan's, and a smile cracked her face. Adelaide wanted to pull her arm free but didn't dare. She needed to play the part if she didn't want to raise Nolan's ire.

"Lady Drummond." Nolan simpered. "There was a bit of confusion and a case of mistaken identity. My men and I thought we overheard Lord Hargreaves plotting against the king and accompanied the sheriff to arrest him for treason."

Lady Drummond gasped. "Wouldn't surprise me in the least. I hope the scoundrel didn't give you trouble!" She looked past them at Gaius and Minerva, worry creasing her forehead. Adelaide winced at *scoundrel.* Lady Drummond would believe Nolan, after all her conspiring to get them together.

"Fortunately, we realized it was a mistake," Nolan said, "and Hargreaves was not the man we overheard." Adelaide clenched her jaw tighter. "Unfortunately, I didn't realize that until after Hargreaves tried to fight fifty men and did a great deal of yelling." Nolan patted Adelaide's arm in a sickening gesture of comfort. "The whole ordeal was understandably upsetting to the ladies, so instead of heading straight home, I accompanied my betrothed. To help put her at ease."

Lady Drummond clasped her hands together and giggled. Adelaide's stomach turned. "Betrothed? Oh, Adelaide, that's wonderful! Congratulations!" Lady Drummond covered her heart with her hand. "I'm so glad you realized what a catch Sir Carrick is before things went any further with that strange Hargreaves. I honestly don't know what you saw in him, with his past and the…" She traced her finger over her cheek where Regulus had his scar.

Adelaide's shoulders shook as she exhaled and tried to keep calm. Nolan seemed to be waiting for her to say something, and when she didn't, he cleared his throat.

"Yes, well. I made the offer at the tournament, but she wanted to think about it. When she saw the violent and foolhardy way Hargreaves reacted to being lawfully placed under arrest, she made her choice." He smiled. "Right, love?"

"Right." She forced a smile.

"Well, come in, come in!" Lady Drummond stepped out of the doorway and Nolan led Adelaide inside. "I hope you will stay the night, Sir Carrick. And join us for breakfast in the morning?"

Oh, no.

Nolan smiled. "Thank you, Lady Drummond, that would be perfect." His gentle squeeze on her arm told her he had been counting on that invitation.

Minerva entered after them, followed by Gaius. She regarded Nolan with narrowed eyes. "Ad, I don't recall you mentioning Sir Carrick proposing. Surely you would have told me."

Nolan's fingers dug into her arm. She swallowed and gave a noncommittal shrug. "I didn't want someone else's opinion to cloud my judgment. I needed time alone with my thoughts." She met Min's eyes and hoped she saw the apology written there—and the plea that she not continue this line of questioning.

"It is odd." Gaius' hand tapped his leg as he pushed the door closed. "With all due respect, before the tournament, Adelaide was clear she wasn't interested."

"And I changed her mind." Nolan slipped his arm out of hers, looped it around her waist and drew her against his side. She desperately wanted to push him away. "I helped her understand what a smart match we make." He ran his fingers down her cheek, making her skin crawl, and turned her face toward him. "We had our misunderstandings, but we're on the same page now, aren't we, love?"

"Yes," she whispered, stiff as a frozen tree. "Dear."

She realized what he was doing just before his lips met hers. Her hands curled into fists. It was a quick peck, a brief brush of his lips that didn't even give her enough time to pull away, but enough to make her feel used and her skin itch.

Lady Drummond tittered. "Oh, look at you blush!"

It doesn't mean what you think it does. "I'm quite tired after this…ordeal." Adelaide slipped out of Nolan's arm and headed for the stairs. "Goodnight."

"That was…brusque," Gaius said as she turned up the stairs.

"Ad, wait." Minerva hurried after her. Adelaide paused and turned back. Nolan looked at her with warning in his eyes. For one terrifying moment as Minerva passed Nolan, Adelaide's heart seemed to stop. *Don't you touch her.* But Minerva passed Nolan without a problem and was by her side as they headed up the stairs.

Minerva waited until they were close to Adelaide's room before she spoke. "What's going on? You love Regulus, don't deny it. And I saw your fists when he kissed you. What happened?"

Adelaide looked over her shoulder. They were alone in the hallway. Nolan wouldn't overhear. All the same, she didn't answer. Instead, she grabbed Min's hand and hurried into her room. Once inside, she locked the door, then sat on her bed. Minerva sat next to her.

"If I tell you, you have to promise not to tell another soul. Not Gaius, not Mother or Father. No one."

Minerva's frown deepened. "Adelaide, what—"

"Promise me."

"How can I promise that when I don't know what's going on?"

Adelaide's shoulders slumped. "Just promise, Min. Please. Or I won't tell you."

"Fine." Minerva didn't sound happy, or convincing. But Adelaide couldn't keep this in any longer.

"He didn't exactly ask me at the tournament. After I helped Regulus…" Adelaide buried her face in her hands. "Nolan figured it out. He threatened to reveal my secret if I didn't marry him and told me to think about that. And tonight…his plan was to kill Regulus to remove him as—as a rival." She drew in a ragged breath.

"He said he would drop the charges against Regulus if I agreed to marry him. If I don't marry him, he'll have Regulus killed." Adelaide lifted her eyes to Minerva's horrified expression. "You can't tell anyone! He'll hurt…everyone. If he duels Gaius, he'll win. He threatened to hurt you, to orchestrate a carriage accident. He threatened to have Gaius arrested, too."

Minerva's hands covered the lower half of her face.

"You can't tell anyone. Not until I figure out a way to make sure he can't make good on any of his threats."

Minerva stood, her arms wrapped over her pregnant stomach. "I…Adelaide. This is insane. How are you supposed to keep him from making good on his word? We can't wait until you're married to him!"

"Keep your voice down." She held her hands up and glanced toward the door. It would be crazy for Nolan to be on this floor. Lady Drummond wouldn't stand for the impropriety. But Nolan was a snake. "I couldn't let him take Regulus. He wouldn't have lasted the night. And I couldn't let him arrest Gaius."

Minerva chewed on her thumbnail. "We have to tell Father."

"And then what? Gaius gets attacked like Regulus' squire, Harold? Something happens to you? I couldn't live with myself, Min."

"And I can't live with you married to someone capable of doing any of that!" Minerva sat back down and placed a hand on her arm. "Gaius is already suspicious that Nolan threatened you or something. He…" She hesitated. "Hasn't hurt you?"

Adelaide shrugged. "Not really." *Nothing permanent. For me.* She patted Minerva's shoulder. "Get some sleep. And tell Gaius everything is fine. Tell him I want this." She tried to smile, but her lip quivered. "Act like everything is fine at breakfast."

"I don't like it." Minerva embraced her tightly and the tears Adelaide didn't realize she'd been holding back threatened to spill. "I'll play along for now. But I'm not letting you marry a man you hate."

"He's handsome, at least." Her attempt to lighten the mood didn't help the sickened feeling in her gut. "I mean; it could be worse." A tremor ran through her body and Minerva hugged her tighter. "I'll be all right."

Nolan and his knights joined them for breakfast. Adelaide suffered through Nolan talking about how enamored he was with her and Lord and Lady Drummond's warm congratulations. Minerva watched with fire in her eyes as Nolan's hand traced up and down Adelaide's rigid back and tangled in her hair. Adelaide spoke little. Gaius didn't make eye contact with her or Nolan.

After breakfast, Adelaide headed to the stables. She needed some time alone to clear her head. She didn't even ask for help, but prepared Zephyr herself. The stable gate creaked.

"Don't you have servants for that?" Nolan strolled in, looking as debonair as ever.

She stiffened. "What do you want?"

"Just checking on my lovely bride-to-be." He flashed a toothy smile that made him look beastly. "Making sure you're not having any…foolish ideas. I'd hate for anyone to get hurt."

She pulled the bridle over Zephyr's head. "Murderer."

"My dear, I would never."

"Right, you'd have someone else do it for you." Anger made her hands shake as she struggled to buckle the bridle in place.

"Maybe I'll hire one of Hargreaves' so-called knights." He leaned back against the stall on the other side of Zephyr. "They kill for money, don't they? I wonder if they'd off their master for the right price."

Adelaide stilled. "We agreed. I'll only do this if he's not harmed."

"Mm, fine. But honestly, I'd be doing the world a favor."

"You're a fiend." Her face burned as she double-checked the cinching on the saddle.

"Get your face out of mine or I'll cut it."

Nolan slapped her, and she blinked, stumbling back from Zephyr's side. She covered her stinging cheek with her hand. He moved around Zephyr, gaze fixed on her. "You're awfully rude for someone who has lives depending on her good behavior. Including your own. I know your secret, remember?"

"And I told you I don't care who knows, remember?" Her cheek still stung, but she set her jaw and lowered her hand. She wouldn't give him the satisfaction of seeing her pain. "I'll marry you to keep you from having Regulus or anyone else killed. But I won't fawn over you."

"What I'm hearing is you're only agreeing to marry me so long as you can't think of another way to keep me from having the mercenary's head chopped off."

Danger echoed in Nolan's words, so Adelaide didn't answer. But the look on her face must have confirmed his suspicion, because his lips curled into a scowl. He stalked toward her and she backed into the wall, her palms flush against the rough wood. He darted forward and grabbed her face. His body pressed into hers, and the frantic beat of her heart reverberated into his chest.

Nolan leaned forward, his mouth by her ear. Adelaide shook as his fingernails dug into her cheek. "I don't know what you see in that scarred mongrel that you don't see in me. But you're pushing your luck, *sweetheart*." He released her face and leaned back. His gaze fixed on her lips. "Why fight me? I've been told I'm an excellent kisser."

Fury and revulsion drove back her fear. She put her hands on his chest. A blast of blue light pulsed from her palms and sent him flying backward. Zephyr whinnied as Nolan shot behind the horse, hit the opposite wall of the stable, and fell to the ground. He sat in the straw and dirt and glared up at her. She could kill him now. Throw a magical spear through his heart. And probably hang for his murder.

"I'm going for a ride, *sweetheart*." She drew herself up to her full height and raised her chin. "I'll be back when I'm back. Please, follow me. If you do, I'll put a knife through your throat and claim you surprised me, and I thought you were a bandit. I'll shed many tears."

Nolan bared his teeth in a silent snarl. "You'll be back in an hour or I'll take Gaius and my men and come looking for you. You won't kill me in front of witnesses."

"Fine." Adelaide led Zephyr out of the stables. She didn't know where she was going. She didn't care. But as the events of last night ran over and over again through her mind, she found herself on the road leading to Arrano. Let Nolan go looking for her. She urged Zephyr into a trot. She had some explaining to do.

CHAPTER 40

REGULUS SAT in the hall long after a servant cleared away his breakfast. The silence in the room pressed around him. Sunlight from the windows set high in the hall walls streamed across the table. He scratched Magnus' head and stared at nothing. He had tossed and turned most of the night, trying to think of a way to protect both Adelaide and his men. Every idea had holes. Dresden was right. Obeying was the best option.

The question was how to get her. The simplest way would be to take her unseen, but he didn't have time to stalk the Drummonds' estate until she wandered away on her own. He could go as the Black Knight and demand her. There would be a fight, people would get hurt. Or he could hope Carrick wasn't around, ask her to walk with him—

The door to the foyer groaned open and his steward walked in. "My lord." He bowed. "Lady Belanger is here to see you."

"What?" Regulus stood, knocking his knees on the table. "Just Lady Belanger?"

Adelaide walked in, wearing a long-sleeved gray riding dress with an asymmetrical skirt that ended above her knees in the front, revealing black fitted trousers and boots.

"Just me." She smiled, but it was weak and forced. The steward left, closing the door behind him. Magnus bounded over to Adelaide, and she rubbed his head.

"Adelaide." Regulus rushed to her, reached for her—but stopped shy of grabbing her shoulders. The momentary joy of seeing her fled behind his confusion over last night and his heartache at what he had to do. His hands fell to his sides. "Why are you here?"

"I…" She looked defeated. "I wanted to explain. No, I *need* to explain. I don't want you to think…"

"I knew it." He tensed as his pulse pounded. "Carrick threatened you."

"He threatened you. And your knights. And Gaius and Minerva." Adelaide placed her hand on his chest. "I couldn't let you or anyone else die. The whole arrest—he was trying to get you killed! He told the sheriff he was mistaken after—"

"After you promised to marry him," he finished. He'd suspected as much. It didn't make him any less angry.

"He's a coward without honor." Her hand balled into a fist against his chest. "You can't challenge him. He'll have you killed or arrested before he would fight you. You can't tell anyone. I'm only telling you because you deserve to know. I can't stand by while he hurts or kills people I love." She looked into his eyes, and he saw her anguish. "Please. I can't let him—"

"Shhh." Regulus grabbed her shoulders and pulled her to his chest. As he held her, a thousand emotions battled within him. Relief that Adelaide didn't want to marry Carrick. Anger that Carrick was forcing her into a marriage she didn't want. Fury that she didn't want him to fight for her, even if he understood the reasoning. Resentment that she was right. Carrick would never duel him. Happiness that she cared enough that she didn't want him to die. Sympathy, because he understood doing things you hated to protect the people you loved.

But mostly panic and sorrow. Because she was here. Alone. Already the mark burned as he ignored his opportunity.

"Adelaide…" He stepped away, his guilt drowning him. "I need to tell you something. We should sit." Regulus returned to his seat and Magnus loped after him. After a moment, Adelaide sat in the seat to his left. He hesitated. He had never told anyone this story. Before Adelaide, anyone who mattered already knew. They had been there.

"Regulus?"

"This isn't how I wanted to tell you. This isn't the circumstances I wanted. But you deserve the truth." He looked at her, shame heavy on his soul. "You've been honest with me, and I've lied in return. Pretended I'm not what I am."

"I don't understand." He winced at the undertone of alarm in her voice.

He traced a knot in the tabletop with his finger. "A little over two years ago, I was leading a small company of fifteen mercenaries. We were near the Tumen Forest for a contract dealing with a couple territorial gryphons. We came across this boy." He took a breath to steady himself, the memory still fresh. "He begged us for help. Said his village was being attacked by goblins. He was destitute. Not even shoes on his feet. There would be no money in helping. But I couldn't turn my back on him. So we followed."

She watched him, clearly trying to understand why he was telling her this now.

"He didn't lead us to a village; it was just a forester's hut. He ran in, and I followed. His parents were bound and gagged inside. The boy went to help them, and I turned around as this…flash of green light nearly blinded me."

"Green light…" Adelaide looked down at her hands and her eyes widened. "A sorcerer?"

"Yes." He swallowed. "I couldn't tell at first. There was a man in dark robes throwing fire and sharp projectiles that glowed green. My men were falling. Dying. I rushed him with my sword, but…" He looked at his palm, remembering. "The hilt burned in my hand and I dropped it. The sorcerer held enchanted ropes, binding my men who were still standing. They couldn't fight or get free. The ropes curled around their throats. I went for the man with my bare hands."

His hand trembled. Adelaide covered it with hers. Steadied him. He took a deep breath and continued.

"A blast of light knocked me back. I looked up to see my men choking to death. Dresden. Perceval." Regulus dug his fingernails into the wood. "Estevan. Jerrick. Caleb. Even Harold, a baggage boy who barely knew how to hold a sword. So many were already dead—" His voice broke, and it took him a moment to continue. "The sorcerer gave me a choice. Watch the rest of my men die and the forester and his wife and son burn alive—or swear to serve him."

Her mouth hung open, but she didn't speak.

"I didn't think, I just agreed." His breath escaped in a shaky exhale. "He made me take an oath. I would serve him until I had repaid the life-debt for every person he didn't kill that day. I've done his will ever since. He has me retrieve things. Magical plants. Ancient relics. I've stolen for him… Killed for him."

Her hand slipped off his. Silence pressed against him. His chest burned. He couldn't bring himself to look at her, to see the horror and disgust. He hid his face in his hands. *I knew she wouldn't want me if she knew the truth.*

To his surprise, her fingers clasped his hands. She pulled them away from his face.

"You did what you had to in order to save the people you love." He met her eyes and saw kindness, understanding, and sorrow. "That sounds familiar."

If it wasn't for what he had to say next, her understanding and acceptance would have soothed him. Comforted him. Healed him. Instead, it destroyed him.

"There's more." Regulus freed his hands from Adelaide's grasp. "The sorcerer wants something different this time." He closed his eyes. "A mage." He wouldn't take the coward's path. He looked at Adelaide. Her kind, beautiful deep brown eyes narrowed. "He wants you."

"WHAT?" IT sounded more like a gasp than an actual word. Adelaide's pulse quickened, and she pulled her hands back as the betrayal seared straight through her. Her magic awakened in response, warming her palms. "You told a sorcerer about me? I trusted—"

"No!" Regulus held up his hands, his face pale as he shook his head. "I swear I didn't tell him, not a word. He did something to find mages, and he found you. He needs a mage to open some kind of door."

At least he had kept his promise to guard her secret. And it didn't even matter. But now…would he hand her over to this sorcerer? "You're not…you won't…you can't want to—"

"I don't want to," Regulus said, agony in his words. "But I have to."

"You can refuse!" Fear and anger gave an edge to her voice. She tried to rein it in, but her hysteria rose. "You don't have to—"

"No." She jumped at Dresden's voice and looked toward the dark stairway in the corner. Dresden emerged from the shadows and strode over, his eyes furious. "You didn't tell her everything. Show her."

Regulus' gaze dropped.

"Show her!" Dresden grabbed Regulus' right arm and pushed up his sleeve. "Tell her the full truth!"

Rough scars marred the underside of Regulus' forearm. Against the scars, a black mark stood out in sharp contrast—two hollow diamonds laid end-to-end with another half diamond open towards his wrist.

She eyed the tattoo, confused. "What is it?"

"It appeared when I took the oath," Regulus said quietly as Dresden dropped his arm. "It's a link, from the sorcerer to me. So he can control me."

Her mind struggled to keep up. "How?"

"Like this." Dresden reached across the table and grabbed her hand. He yanked it over to Regulus' arm and forced her palm against the mark. She yelped as heat burned her skin. She tried to pull away, but Dresden held her hand in place a moment longer before releasing her. Her hand still burned.

"He tortures Regulus," Dresden said, venom in his voice. "Because he's not obeying. He knows what his orders are, and he's not fulfilling them. Somehow, the sorcerer knows, and uses the mark to punish him into compliance."

"You're in pain?" Guilt and pity replaced the betrayal, even as fear put a vise around her chest.

"It's not bad right now." Regulus pulled his sleeve down, hiding the mark.

"The sorcerer can manipulate it, make the pain spread." Dresden sat in the chair to Regulus' right. "Cause him to writhe on the floor, screaming in pain. But maybe there's something you can do."

"You think I…" Adelaide gulped.

"Maybe you can remove it," Regulus whispered, but his voice rose with intensity. "Corrupted magic put it there; maybe pure magic can remove it."

"I…" She hesitated, full of self-doubt. Could trying make things any worse? And if she succeeded, Regulus wouldn't be in pain. And he wouldn't have to bring her to this sorcerer. Yesterday, she would have said he would never betray her. But today, faced with sorcery she didn't understand and knowing he would be tortured if he didn't… She couldn't rely on his strength of will to resist a force like that. "I can try."

Regulus rolled his sleeve back and held his arm forward. Nervous, she reached out, summoning her power. Her palm warmed and glowed with soft blue light as she stretched her hand out over the mark. The light grew in intensity, bathing his skin. Some of the scars around and under the mark faded, but the mark seemed just as dark and defined. She summoned more power, trying to will the mark off his arm.

Regulus screamed. Adelaide yanked her hand back, terror stealing her breath. He pulled away from her, clutching his arm to his chest and knocking over his chair with a clatter as his screams pierced her ears. Magnus jumped to his feet with a growl. The dog barked at her then whined at Regulus. Regulus continued to scream and fell to his knees, his eyes rolling up into his head. Her light died as she clenched her fist, her heart pounding. *What did I do? What do I do?*

She pushed away her chair as she stood, trembling. "Regulus!" She reached toward him and Magnus snarled. Dresden grabbed the huge dog.

Magnus snapped at him, but Dresden said in a firm voice, "Magnus, up-stairs. Obey!" The dog tucked its tail and whined. "Magnus, go upstairs," Dresden commanded over Regulus' howls. The dog headed up the stairs, and Dresden closed the stairwell door behind him. He went to Regulus and grabbed his shoulders. "Regulus!"

Regulus stopped screaming, and Adelaide leaned against the table, relieved. His arm fell to his side. He looked at her, his expression unreadable. Dresden released Regulus' shoulders and took a step back, caution radiating from him. "Reg?"

"Oh, dear me." Regulus shook his head and stood. "Tried to remove our bond again, did you, Hargreaves?" He clicked his tongue. "Naughty boy. And you." He looked Adelaide dead in the eyes, his gaze filled with loathing that hurt far worse than when she thought he'd shared her secret. "Stupid little she-mage. That. *Hurt*. I don't appreciate it. You're giving me second thoughts about the whole not-harming-you thing."

She recoiled, bumping into a chair. Did Regulus just…talk to himself? Stupid she-mage? Nothing he said made sense. "Regulus?"

"No." Dresden placed himself between her and Regulus. "It's the sorcerer." His voice wavered, and the hand he held out to shield her shook.

"He can do that?" Her tongue stuck, threatening to choke her.

"That's Prince of Shadow and Ash to you." Regulus glanced at Dresden with distaste. "Yes, I can do that. Not for long. But long enough to make him kill one or both of you. The bearded one and that squire barely escaped last time." He smiled, cruelty in his usually kind eyes.

"Run!" Dresden looked over his shoulder. "Just avoid him long enough—"

Regulus bolted forward with unbelievable speed and grabbed Dresden by the neck. Dresden clawed at his hands as Regulus lifted him into the air. Like he was tossing aside a dirty shirt, Regulus threw Dresden. Dresden flew several feet and landed with a horrible thud and a sickening crack as his head hit stone. Adelaide's heart lodged in her throat. Dresden moaned, and she gasped. *He's alive*. But now Regulus' icy gaze fixed on her.

She drew her dagger from her boot as she stumbled away, tripping over a chair. *This can't be happening. This* can't *be happening*. That wasn't Regulus. But it was. Did she dare use her dagger against him?

"I need your pure magic, girl." Regulus advanced toward her. "There's at least a couple others, but they'd hardly be useful. Drunks and children. So, you see, Hargreaves has a choice."

It was surreal to see Regulus with cruelty in his eyes. To hear him talk about himself as someone else. Her heel caught on an uneven bit of stone, and she fell backward.

"He can bring you to me, you help me, everybody lives and is happy. Or he can kill you." Regulus lunged.

She half-heartedly stabbed toward his right shoulder, but he grabbed the blade with his left hand. Blood seeped between his fingers.

"You can't kill him to save yourself," Regulus' voice said. "His life is tied to mine. So long as I live, he lives." Regulus' right hand closed around her neck.

His large hand encircled her throat and squeezed, his skin hot against her throat. She released the dagger and pulled at his fingers, coughing and choking. He pulled her to her knees. Her throat and lungs burned from the effort to breathe. Her thoughts turned fuzzy. He dropped her dagger, and it clattered to the ground.

"Please," she croaked, "stop…"

The edges of her sight turned black. Bright spots swam in her vision as Regulus' sneering face went in and out of focus. She scratched at his hand but felt herself weakening. *Etiros, he's going to kill me! I'm. Going. To. Die.*

He released her and stepped back. She fell on her hands and knees, gasping for air and coughing. Her throat felt raw, like she had been screaming. Her neck ached and throbbed. She looked up in fear as she struggled to catch her breath. But Regulus had withdrawn a couple feet and collapsed to his knees on the ground. He rested his arms on his legs, palms up, his left hand dripping blood, and stared at the floor.

Dresden, one hand clutching his head, staggered over. He hesitantly put a hand on Regulus' shoulder. Regulus flinched, but otherwise didn't move.

Adelaide healed her neck and dropped her hands to the cool stone. As her breathing evened out, she eyed Regulus, trying to determine if he had regained control. His cheeks glistened in the sunlight, and she realized he was crying.

She moved closer, swallowing back her fear. That wasn't him. Regulus wouldn't hurt her. Not as himself. Slowly, she reached for him. "Regulus…"

He drew back from her touch. "Don't," he whispered. "Don't come close."

She looked at her hand and pulled it back. "Oh. Right. I'm sorry. I didn't mean to—"

"What?" Regulus looked up, his brow furrowed above watery eyes. "Why are you apologizing?"

She swallowed, her mouth still dry. "For hurting you."

Bewilderment showed in his expression. "You…think I blame you?" He laughed, but it was a bitter, angry sound. "You tried to help. Then I…" He choked and looked away. "I hurt *you*. I'm sorry. I feared something like this would happen." He hung his head, his chin resting on his chest. "I should have stayed far away from you. I should have ended this before it began."

She wrapped her arms around her torso as his words slashed into her heart. Her gaze dropped to the stone floor. "You wish we didn't know each other?"

"Maybe the sorcerer would have picked someone else if you hadn't been with me when he searched for a mage. Now you're part of my mess. Now you're in danger." His voice seemed small in the vast hall.

She moved closer to him. Blood pooled on his left hand. If she attempted to heal it, would her magic clash with the sorcery within him again? It hadn't last time she healed him. But the fury in his eyes as he had strangled her made her hesitate. *Coward.*

"I've tried everything to break the bond." Regulus clenched his fists. The muscles in his neck bulged with tension. Understanding of the scars on his arm dragged her heart down to her gut. "I can't even die." The whispered words hung in the air between them.

Dresden paced back and forth behind Regulus' bent form, his hands clasped behind his back. "You have to help him. The sorcerer said if Regulus brings you to him, his debt will be repaid. He will be free."

Regulus shook his head. "He could be lying."

"Here." Adelaide took his left hand, pulled back the fingers. "Let me…" Blood still covered his hand, but she didn't see a cut. "You…healed."

"Hm?" He looked down. "Oh. Yes."

"I thought sorcery couldn't heal."

"Not the way pure magic does," Regulus said. "This is evil. Corrupted. It hurts as it heals…and sometimes after. It leaves scars. And it doesn't heal minor injuries. Just ones that affect my ability to be a useful slave. I could have bled out. My bond to the sorcerer won't allow that. So it healed." His tone was flat, emotionless.

"Reg." Dresden sat at the table. "You can't avoid this."

"I know," Regulus murmured. He looked at Adelaide, sorrow and apology in his eyes. "I can't let him… *I* can't kill you. Or Dresden. Or Harold. Innocent people, people I care about, will die at my hand." His gaze fell to her throat, his face twisting with horror. "I can't control myself when he takes over, but I can see and feel everything. It's as if I'm a puppet that has gained consciousness and sensation, but I can only do what the puppet master wishes. I could—" His voice cracked, and he looked away again.

She shuddered, remembering his hand crushing her throat. *He was suffering as much as I was.* She pressed his blood-stained hand between hers, but he pulled away. She wiped his blood off on her dress. "Regulus—"

"I could feel your skin." His jaw pulsed as he clenched and unclenched his teeth. "I felt your throat as you tried to breathe, your hands trying to pull mine away. I saw the fear and panic in your eyes. And I couldn't stop it. I tried. Etiros, I tried. I only stopped when he let me go. When he had gotten his point across."

She gazed at the broken man before her, at the hopelessness on his face. The man who had sacrificed his freedom to save the lives of his friends. The man who fought against the desires of this sorcerer, despite the pain he brought on himself. The man who won tournaments but recoiled from her touch in fear of himself. He didn't deserve this. No one deserved this.

Adelaide pulled Regulus' sleeve up past the mark. She thought the diamonds looked like chains as she placed her hand on it and winced. He was in pain. Because of her. Was facing a sorcerer any worse than facing Nolan? She slid her hand down and entwined her fingers in his. His gaze drifted up to her eyes, surprised.

"I see you. Your heart. Your strength. Your courage." She cradled his face in her other hand. "And I love you."

Regulus' mouth trembled as his eyes searched hers, hope and fear, joy and dread warring in their silvery depths. "You…"

"I love you, Regulus." She blinked to hold back the tears that threatened to fall as Regulus' eyes watered.

He crumpled toward her and drew her into his arms, his forehead pressing against her shoulder. "I love you." His arms tightened around her. "I tried not to, for your safety, but… I love you, Adelaide. Completely and utterly. I can't begin to express how much I love you." His shoulders shook. "I wish… I'm so sorry."

"It's not your fault." She stroked his back, her throat thick with emotion. "We should go, before he hurts you again, or worse."

Regulus pulled away, relief mixed with defeat in his expression. "You'll come willingly?"

"Yes." She had wanted to sound braver than that. If Regulus could be brave when a sorcerer could take control of his body at any moment and force him to hurt his friends, she could be brave, too. "I'll do what the sorcerer wants."

Surety returned to her voice as she spoke. "We will free you. If he refuses to honor his word, we will find another way. There must be a way. And then figure out how to stop Nolan. Together."

A smile pulled at Regulus' mouth as his gaze filled with devotion and warmth. But then his expression fell. "There's something else."

What else can there be?

"The sorcerer…" His throat bobbed. "He's The Shadow. He promised not to kill you. But you should know."

The Shadow. Her lips parted. The threat she had hid from her entire life, the reason she was alone and didn't understand her magic. The Shadow that hated mages enough to murder children. Her breathing went shallow. What if he didn't keep his word?

But Regulus was in pain. He was enslaved to the evil she feared. And they didn't have another choice. She could go willingly…or she could watch the love leave his eyes as the sorcerer took over again.

"Thank you for telling me." Her voice barely made it past her lips. She cleared her throat. "But it doesn't change anything. It only makes me want you free more."

Regulus released a breath. "I don't deserve you." He reached for her face with his free hand, then grimaced at his bloody palm and drew it back.

"I hate to say it," Dresden said, "but you two need to go."

Regulus nodded glumly. "Can you wait here? I need to change."

She nodded, and Regulus trudged upstairs. She felt drained. Too many complicated emotions. Dresden still sat at the table, watching her. She stood, and he did the same, steely gaze never leaving her.

"I'm not going to run, if that's what you're thinking."

Dresden's fingers drifted to his own bruising throat. "I wouldn't blame you if you did." He clasped his hands behind his back. "I like you. Truly. But I would do anything for Regulus. Including things he might not appreciate—like knocking you unconscious if you try to run."

"I understand." She stepped forward. "Here. I can heal those bruises."

Dresden blinked. "I…okay. Thank you."

She healed his bruises, mulling over the sorcerer's words through Regulus. *"The bearded one and that squire barely escaped last time."* "He attacked you. Before today."

"Yes." Dresden rubbed his healed neck, his eyes sad. "Me and Harold. Terrified Harold. But it broke Regulus. It's…taken him a long time to heal."

Adelaide looked at the shadowy stairwell, her heart aching.

"I think you're good for him," Dresden said quietly, drawing her attention back. "He felt he had to distance himself from us. He's a wolf who tried to protect his own pack by leaving it, but Regulus is at his best with others, when he feels like he has a place to belong. And you bring out the best in him."

She blushed and lowered her gaze. "He's a good man. A better and braver man than most."

"A good man?" Dresden's mouth curved into a half smile. "He's the best man I've ever known."

REGULUS WAS silent as Harold helped him into the Black Knight armor. Magnus sat next to him, incessantly licking his hand. Harold moved around the big shaggy dog, cinching and straightening the layered pieces of armor. He respected Regulus' unspoken need for silence. He didn't ask about the blood Regulus washed off his hand in the water basin. Didn't question the scratches on the back of Regulus' hands as he buckled each oversized piece into place. Regulus gazed out the window, staring at nothing. Hoping against hope this was the last time he would don this armor.

He didn't want to wear it. But he didn't know where this door Adelaide was supposed to unlock was—or what might be on the other side. More importantly, he wanted to keep the sorcerer as happy as possible. Besides, if anyone spotted them, they would see Adelaide captured by the legendary Black Knight, not running away with Regulus Hargreaves.

Regulus sheathed the sword and took the helm from Harold, his heart heavy. Why couldn't he be stronger? Why was he too weak to fight the sorcerer's will? He wished he had found another way to save his men two years ago. And why couldn't he have saved them *all*? But such thoughts changed nothing. He laid a black-gloved hand on Harold's shoulder, the metal plating on the brace and gloves clinking. "Thank you, Harold."

"Of course, my lord." Concern wrinkled Harold's forehead.

"Can you pack some food and bring it out to the stables? Enough for…for two."

"Yes, my lord."

Regulus bit the inside of his lip. "If things go right, when I return, I'll be free. But if they don't—I might not come back." He held Harold's gaze and squeezed his shoulder. "You and Drez look out for each other, okay?"

Harold nodded slowly, his eyes wide, then shook his head, fast and hard. "No." He threw his arms around Regulus' armored chest. "We all need you to come back."

Regulus returned the embrace, his breath catching. "I'll try."

"Good." Harold pulled away and took a deep breath. "Be safe, my lord."

Regulus smiled weakly and headed downstairs. The heavy fall of his boots and metallic rubbing of his armor reverberated in the winding staircase. He emerged into the hall and felt surprised yet relieved to see Adelaide and Dresden sitting peaceably.

"You didn't leave," he said before he could stop himself.

Adelaide looked up, lips pursed. As she took in his appearance, he noted the slight widening of her eyes, the inaudible gasp. "You're…" Her jaw hung open. "The Black Knight. *You're* the Black Knight?"

"Oh." His face heated. "Yes."

"Several things just made a lot of sense." She shook her head, her expression softening. "As for not running away, you don't have sole ownership over the role of self-sacrificial hero." Her tone was confident and teasing but kind.

"I love you." The words tumbled out as a mix of emotions from adoration to guilt twisted his gut.

Adelaide smiled and walked to him, her hips swaying. She took the helm from his hands and examined it, then glanced at Dresden. "You're blessed not to have borne this alone." Regulus felt a stab of guilt over how often he had shunned Dresden's help.

"Please." Drez scoffed. "We do what we can, but the fool always goes it alone."

"Not this time." Adelaide handed the helm back, then brushed her fingertips over the scar on his face. "We do this together." He still felt the lingering touch after she dropped her hand. "Shall we?"

Regulus nodded. "Together."

He led her through the hedged lane to the stables. Adelaide went to mount her horse, but he stopped her. "This way." She shrugged and followed him to the trap door. As he stepped down onto the dirt steps, Harold ran into the stables.

"You have to hurry!" Harold panted. "Nolan Carrick is here with Sir Gaius, Lord Drummond, and several knights. The gate was open for deliveries, and they just rode in, didn't even slow for the guard. Carrick says Lady Belanger is missing and he's accusing you of kidnapping her. Dresden said you're not at home, but Carrick wants to search the castle, and I don't think Drez can stop him. You need to go *now*. I'll put a barrel over the trap door. Go!"

Anger surged, but Regulus couldn't do anything about Carrick. He led Sieger down into the tunnel, not bothering with stopping to light the torch. Adelaide followed close behind, but her horse whinnied and pulled back.

"Easy, boy." She stroked his face. "Come on." The horse backed away from the tunnel, yanking on the reins.

"You have to go!" Harold's voice sounded muffled from above the tunnel.

"Let's try this." Adelaide placed her hand on the horse's forehead. A faint blue shone between her skin and the horse's forelock. The gelding calmed, and she led it down into the tunnel. Harold closed the trap door and the tunnel became pitch black. A scraping sound indicated Harold moving a barrel over the door.

"There's a torch in a nook over the steps if you can get to it," Regulus said.

"No need." A soft blue glow illuminated her face and grew to a pale blue shining orb hovering over her palm. As Adelaide lifted her hand, the orb drifted just below the top of the tunnel, above Sieger's rump.

"Right." He smiled sheepishly.

The blue-white light illuminated the tunnel. They walked in silence, the orb floating with them. At the end of the tunnel, Regulus moved aside the door and boulder and put on his helm before emerging into the space beneath the tree. No one around. Good. He went back down for Sieger, and Adelaide followed, her orb of light vanishing without a sound.

Regulus replaced the door and boulder over the tunnel entrance and turned to find Adelaide watching him, her forehead wrinkled and head tilted.

"I was right." She looked at the boulder and back at him. "You were holding back at the tournament."

He blinked. "Yes. The mark enhances my strength. You…could tell?"

"I'm used to holding back power."

"Oh." He went to Sieger's saddlebags and paused, biting his cheek. "I don't want you to take this the wrong way. And you can say no. But I think it might be a good idea if…" *There's no good way of saying this.* "If we tied your reins to my pommel and bound your hands."

"Why?" Adelaide stepped back, uncertainty flashing over her features.

"I'm not doubting you!" he said quickly. "But there's a chance someone could see us. I try not to be seen, but it happens. You know, you've heard the stories. It might be better for your reputation and safety if someone sees us if they think you're a captive." He held up a hand as she frowned. "Just a thought. You don't—"

Adelaide sighed. "You have rope?"

He pointed at his saddlebag with his thumb. "Yes."

"All right." She mounted Zephyr. "Do it."

He tied the ropes as loose as possible without them falling off. She could get free easily, but at a glance, the binding was convincing. He pulled the reins over Zephyr's head and tied them to his own saddle before mounting.

Regulus kept off the roads as much as possible and listened and watched for signs of people so he could avoid them. They narrowly evaded a hunting party. A few minutes later, a solitary man in bright clothes, riding a gray horse and brandishing a bow, broke through the brush.

"Gerard, I swear if you leave—" He stopped short as he realized they were *not* his hunting party. His wide eyes looked to Adelaide. "My lady…" He knocked an arrow and trained the bow on Regulus, but his hands quivered, making the arrow bounce against the side of the bow. "Release the lady, foul villain!"

"Stand down." Regulus lowered his voice, letting it rumble in his helm. The man released the arrow. Frightened as the hunter was, it would have flown right past Regulus. He reached out and caught it anyway. Both the man and Adelaide gasped.

"Run!" Adelaide screamed. Regulus looked back at her, startled by her high-pitched outburst. "Flee!" She gave him the slightest nod. Oh, she was clever. "Find the Drummonds and Nolan Carrick! Find Regulus Hargreaves of Arrano!"

He pulled the reins to her horse, drawing Zephyr closer. "Silence!"

"Tell Lord Hargreaves the Black Knight has taken Adelaide!" The hysteria in her voice made the man turn pale. He backed his horse up, jaw trembling.

"I said *silence!*" Regulus covered her mouth with his hand but didn't touch her.

She pulled his hand down. "Tell Nolan Carrick!"

Regulus yanked his hand free and covered her mouth for real this time. "You will be silent!" He cringed under the helm. The man turned his horse and fled. Regulus dropped his hand. "I'm sorry. Are you all right?"

She nodded. "If he does as I asked, you should be in the clear. Hopefully."

"You nearly had me convinced." He looked around and prodded Sieger forward. "We better get out of here. The rest of the hunting party might have heard you."

Other than a couple peasants out gathering firewood, who saw them, dropped their bundles of wood, and ran, they didn't see anyone else. Regulus wondered what Carrick had made of his absence from Arrano; if Dresden had convinced Carrick that he and Adelaide hadn't seen each other since the previous night when Carrick took her away. Would that coward of a hunter go to

Arrano or the Drummond estate? What would Carrick make of the news Adelaide had been captured? And what about Gaius? Minerva?

He looked over at Adelaide through his helm. "What about Minerva?"

"What about—" She paled. "She doesn't know I'm safe." She said a string of what he was pretty sure were Khast curse words. Her shoulders slumped, and his heart ached. "What have I done? If that hunter goes to the Drummonds, she'll think…" She straightened. "She will think it's peculiar I told him to find you and Nolan." A hopeful look came over her face. "She's smart. She'll realize I wouldn't ask him for help. Hopefully."

"Maybe." He tried to sound optimistic, but his voice sounded harsh in the helm.

Night had fallen when they arrived at the tower. Adelaide gawked at the dead trees as they rode in the moonlight and shadow. His heart grew heavier as each hoof beat brought them closer to the sorcerer. The most dangerous man he had ever met. And he was leading the woman he loved right to him. They stopped in front of the tower and he dismounted. He stuffed his helm in his saddlebag then crossed to Zephyr's side. Adelaide looked at the bone-white trees as he removed the rope from her hands.

"What happened to them?"

"I don't know. It's like his sorcery infects them, and they just die."

He helped her down. The door to the tower creaked open as her feet hit the ground. They both looked toward the door as the sorcerer emerged, cloaked in black and red and gold, his face half-hidden under his hood as usual.

The sorcerer smiled and stroked his beard. "I knew you'd find a way, boy."

"I brought her, as you commanded." Regulus ground his teeth. "You said you would release me."

The sorcerer laughed, dark and menacing. "I said I would release you *after* she helped me." He walked toward them, and Regulus covered Adelaide with his own body. "Oh, move out of the way." The sorcerer flicked his hand, a hint of green light shooting from his fingers and forming a blast that knocked Regulus aside.

"Don't hurt—" Regulus gasped and fell to one knee as pain erupted on his arm.

"Stop!" Adelaide moved toward him, but the sorcerer raised a shimmering transparent wall that gleamed faintly with green light between them, from the base of the tower far into the trees. She looked back at the sorcerer and squared her shoulders, her chin lifted. Regulus smiled despite the pain. The sorcerer looked her up and down.

"Hm." The sorcerer turned and walked back toward the tower, leaving the wall separating Regulus and Adelaide standing. "Let's see what, if anything, you can do." He whirled around and thrust out his hand, sending several large, pointed shards that glowed green toward Adelaide.

"No!" Regulus leapt to his feet, but a shock of pain sent him back down.

Adelaide gasped and held out her hands. A shield of cobalt-tinged light flashed into existence in front of her, just before the shards slammed into it with a crackling sound. The shards disintegrated, but Adelaide staggered back, and the shield blinked out of existence. At least she knew how to defend herself. But why was the sorcerer doing this?

"You said you wouldn't hurt her!"

"And I won't, if she stops me." The sorcerer held out his hands and ropes glowing a sickly green snaked out of his wide sleeves.

Panic crushed Regulus' chest. *Not again. Etiros, please, not again.* He fought through the pain and tried to get to Adelaide through the sorcerer's barrier, but it knocked him back as the ropes swayed toward her.

Adelaide held out her hands and jets of fire enveloped the ropes. Regulus could feel the heat even through the transparent wall. The sorcerer hissed and clenched his fists, then pulled his hands back. She stumbled forward, and the flames withered. The ropes lengthened and shot toward her.

"ADELAIDE!" Regulus punched the wall, which rippled but remained intact.

She summoned another shield of blue light. The ropes bounced around the shield and wrapped around her arms, pinning them to her sides. Regulus franticly shoved his shoulder against the barrier, but it wouldn't give. Adelaide curled her hands into fists and screamed. Not a high-pitched scream of fear. A low scream that started in her chest and built. A scream of anger. A scream of strength. Not a scream at all.

A war cry.

Regulus had been in enough fights to recognize that desperate anger. Pale blue light flashed, and she pulled her arms away from her sides in a quick motion. The ropes snapped and disintegrated. Her chest heaved. A nearly imperceptible blue aura shone off her skin.

Regulus gaped at Adelaide. At the power she had kept hidden. She raised her hand and a spear of blue light materialized in her fist. She threw it at the sorcerer with fury. The sorcerer erected his own shield, which absorbed her spear.

The sorcerer applauded slowly. "Well—"

Adelaide made a sound like a growl and three sharp, shining magic throwing knives appeared between her fingers.

The sorcerer scowled. "That's quite enough." He clenched his right hand into a fist. Regulus collapsed and screamed as his blood boiled within him, burning from the inside out.

"No, stop!" Adelaide cried over his screams.

The pain subsided. Regulus looked up, his vision swimming. The magical barrier vanished, and Adelaide knelt next to him. She put her arms around him.

"Please," she said. "Stop. I'll help you. Just don't hurt him. I'll do whatever you want; don't hurt him."

Regulus wanted to tell her not to make promises like that on his behalf, but he was having difficulty getting his mouth to work, still recovering from the sorcerer's torture.

"Isn't that touching." The sorcerer smirked. "I'm impressed he's won such loyalty, even after delivering you to me. Even after you know what he is." Regulus winced.

"I'll help you, and you'll free him and let us go." She spoke with confidence, but Regulus caught the slight tremor in her voice.

"Yes, yes." The sorcerer turned toward the tower. "Follow me."

CHAPTER 43

ADELAIDE TOOK Regulus' gloved hand as she followed the sorcerer up the winding staircase to the top of the tower. Once there, the sorcerer indicated a table in the center of the room. Three gold rods laid end-to-end but not quite touching, topped with a half-foot-long oval formed of spiraling gold. A small mount was attached to the inside of the bottom of the oval, as if something was missing.

"I only need one piece to complete this staff," the sorcerer said, moving to the opposite side of the table. "An opal. I've searched for decades and finally have found its location." He glanced to Regulus. "Thanks to Hargreaves for bringing me three of the other four pieces. I spent years figuring out how to retrieve this one." He tapped the top rod. "I didn't even bother trying to find the rest until I secured it. Went through dozens of men before he walked into my trap."

"Why couldn't you get it?" she asked. Regulus squeezed her hand, quick and hard, as if warning her not to ask questions.

"Because the dolt mages who hid it hundreds of years ago put a spell on the cave it was hidden in." Irritation rang in the sorcerer's voice. "Only a good man with a selfless heart could find and retrieve the piece. When your man here traded his life to save others, I hoped I had finally found someone good enough to get it. I was right. Lucky for him."

Regulus stiffened next to her. She looked up at the hard lines on his strained face. His eyes widened. This must be the first he had heard of the sorcerer's reasons for doing what he did.

"They've done a similar rotten trick with the opal." The sorcerer tapped the mount inside the top piece of the staff. "There's a rock wall that acts like a door to where they hid the opal. But it can only be opened by"—he sneered—"*uncorrupted* magic. By a *mage*." He practically spat the word. "I've read everything I can get my hands on and gone myself. There's no other way in, and no way to trick the door. It won't open for me." He looked at her. "But it will open for you."

"And if I can't open it?"

"Do you actually need me to answer that?" He gestured toward Regulus.

The muscles in Adelaide's back tightened. She wouldn't listen to Regulus scream like that again. The sorcerer pulled a map out of his robes and spread it over the table. "You have to go here." He tapped the map, pointing at a spot high in the Pelandian Mountains, on the other side of the Tumen Forest where they currently were. Almost within Craigailte's borders. "You'll find a path up the mountain marked by cairns. At the top, the path will appear to dead-end at a wall of rock. That's the door."

"So, she opens the door," Regulus said, "and we just…go inside?"

"There may or may not be a guardian of some kind. The sources are in conflict."

"Great." Regulus' deadpan echoed the dread that made the hair on her neck stand on end.

"Why do you need it?" she asked.

"My business with the Staff of Nightfall is my own." The sorcerer's mouth turned down. "All that should matter to you is what will happen to you and your friends and family if you fail me."

The sorcerer folded the map and held it out. His movements cautious, Regulus stepped forward and took the map. He tucked it into his belt and turned to leave. She did the same, but the sorcerer's voice stopped them.

"Mage."

Adelaide turned back as the sorcerer slunk toward her. Regulus held his arm in front of her. Shielding her. As if that would make a difference. The intensity with which the sorcerer watched her made her feel exposed.

"I don't like needing you. And I don't trust you." His eyes glowed green in the shadow of his hood.

Regulus went rigid. He spun toward her and clamped his hand around her throat.

"Reg…" She choked as Regulus squeezed hard enough to hurt, but not enough to strangle her. She grabbed his hand as he looked down at her, his gray eyes cold as stone, his mouth set in a hard line.

"I'm not taking any chances, mage." The sorcerer grabbed her right wrist with surprising strength and wrenched her arm down. He shoved her sleeve up and put his hand on the underside of her forearm above her wrist.

White-hot pain seared into her arm. A scream rasped up her strangled throat, scraping and burning. Her vision blacked out and her stomach twisted. Right when she thought she would pass out, the sorcerer drew his hand away.

The burning cooled and disappeared. Regulus released her throat, and she fell to her knees.

Harsh black lines stood out against the brown of her arm. Two touching hollow diamonds and a half diamond open toward her wrist. The same as the mark on Regulus' arm.

REGULUS BLINKED as the sorcerer relinquished control. Fury and shock slid like ice through his veins. "What did you do?"

He knelt next to Adelaide. She held her right arm, underside up, in her lap. Staring at the mark on her skin. The mark that matched his own. He glared at the sorcerer. "You said you wouldn't hurt her!" His throat constricted, making his voice hoarse and scratchy. His hands hovered above Adelaide's shoulders, unsure what to do. Unsure if he dared touch her.

Her fingers trembled as she brushed them over the black lines.

"She didn't agree to this! You had no right!" Tears stung at Regulus' eyes. Her scream still rang in his ears.

"Oh, please. She agreed outside, remember? She said she'd help me, do whatever I want. Not my fault she didn't understand the weight of her words." The sorcerer turned away with a shrug, but his posture sagged, and he moved slowly. "This is temporary. When the opal is mine, I'll remove both marks."

"You say that, but you said you wouldn't harm her! You said she wouldn't be in danger!"

"I said I didn't *want* to harm her. An unavoidable side effect, I'm afraid. And now she can't die, just like you. So she's not in *mortal* danger."

If Regulus could have gotten in more than a step before the sorcerer crippled him with pain or took over, he would have lunged at him. Cut his head clean off; thrown him out the window. His tongue stuck as he looked back down at Adelaide. She sat motionless, her back curved and shoulders hunched. He swallowed back his rage and guilt, but his hands still trembled as he grabbed her shoulders and helped her to her feet.

"Let's go," he whispered.

She didn't respond. Didn't look up from the ground as she blinked against tears. *I shouldn't have brought her. I shouldn't have obeyed the last two years. This is my fault.*

Regulus guided Adelaide out of the tower, across the dead ground to where their horses waited, pawing the ground and glancing around.

"I'm sorry." The words came out strained. He closed his eyes, the fright on her face too much to bear. Shame blazed across his skin.

"Regulus." The gentleness in her voice cut deeper than any wound he had ever received. "Look at me."

He forced his eyes open. Trapped breath pushed against his ribs. She looked into his eyes.

"This isn't your doing."

The breath wrenched out of him in a pathetic sob. He drew her to his chest, and she wrapped her arms around his bulky armor. "I'm sorry. I should have protected you. I'm sorry. Adelaide, I'm sorry." She quivered while his tears soaked into her dress. Her tears splashed onto his neck. "I'm so sorry." His throat was raw from trying to swallow back his sobs.

"Stop," she said. "Please."

He held her and hoped that somehow, she was finding comfort in his iron embrace. He took several deep breaths, his lungs burning. Slowly, he straightened.

"I'm—"

"If you apologize one more time, I will punch you." She smiled, although it didn't reach her eyes. "You didn't do this."

"I brought you here."

"I *came* here. I chose to come. Because I believed you were a good man. Because I loved you." Adelaide brushed her fingers over his wet cheek. "I still believe that. And I still love you."

Joy warred with overwhelming guilt. He pulled her hand down and turned over her arm to see the mark. How could she forgive him? How could he forgive himself?

"Regulus?" Doubt crept into her voice.

He leaned down, lifted her arm, and kissed the mark with the salt of his tears still on his lips. "I love you." He pulled her sleeve down. "I. Love. You."

"Great!" The sorcerer's shout drifted down from the opened window above them. "Now go before I lose my temper!"

They rode for a few hours before he stopped Sieger in the dark forest. "We'll camp here."

Adelaide's eyelids drooped. "But the sorcerer—"

"Can wait." He dismounted and tied Sieger to a low-hanging branch of a tree. "We're still on our way. We're still planning on getting what he wants. But we have to rest." She yawned. "*You* have to rest."

"Mm, fine." She dismounted and tied Zephyr next to Sieger. Regulus pulled his cloak from his saddlebag and held it out to her. Even in midsummer, the nights were chilly this close to the mountains. And winter was already on the peaks. He should have asked Harold to pack extra gear. *Idiot.* She took it, and he sat down with his back against a nearby tree. She still stood, watching him with the cloak in her hands. "You're not sleeping like that?"

"Like what?"

"In that armor."

He shrugged, the armor rasping and clinking. "I always do. Can't get it off."

"Hmph." She created an orb of light. "Stand up."

"Ad—"

"Now." The authority in her voice brought him to his feet like a scolded schoolboy. In the bluish light, she looked for the straps securing his pauldrons.

"We should sl—"

"Hush." She sounded exhausted. "I'm concentrating." The pauldron on his left shoulder loosened. She slipped it off and placed it on the ground next to him. It didn't take her long to remove it all and place it in a neat pile.

"I'm impressed." He turned to face her. "Harold does that all the time and isn't much faster."

"There was an old set of my father's armor in the cottage my mother and I stayed in." She rubbed her arm, her face downcast. "I tried to see how fast I could take it all off the display mannequin and put it back on. To pass time."

He didn't know how to respond to the loneliness in her admission, so he did the only thing he could. He pulled her into an embrace. She tucked her arms under his and hooked them over his shoulders. Her breathing deepened as she rested her head on his shoulder. Regulus wasn't sure if he was holding Adelaide together or if she was keeping him from falling apart. Maybe they both needed the other to hold them, to keep them standing. A surreal, detached calm settled over him. But as much as he didn't want to let go, they couldn't stay like that.

"We need to sleep," he whispered into her hair.

"Mm." She stepped back. Sleep pulled at her eyes as she laid down on a grassy area under a maple tree, pulling his cloak over her. He laid down a short distance away, his sword close at hand. She propped herself up on her elbow. "Where's your cloak?"

"I forgot to grab an extra. Don't worry, I'm fine." Regulus closed his eyes, then opened them as he heard grass rustle. Adelaide laid down next to him and threw the cloak over them both. She rolled onto her side, her back pressed against him. He didn't move; his breath caught. The gentle beat of her heart pulsed against his side. He relaxed as the steady rhythm of her breathing lulled him to sleep.

Light woke Regulus. He felt Adelaide next to him before he opened his eyes. He had rolled onto his side in the night, and lay pressed against her, her back curled against his chest. His right arm wrapped around her over his cloak. He blinked away the sleepiness and eased himself up on his left elbow. Mist swirled in the ethereal pale glow of early morning, and dew clung to every surface—including her dark hair. Sunlight caught in the droplets, making her hair sparkle.

The first night Regulus saw Adelaide, he had thought she looked angelic. Now, with dew drops glittering in her hair like diamonds, the peaceful, untroubled look on her face as she slept, and the sunlight highlighting her brown skin, she took his breath away.

He moved to stand, but she wrapped her hands around his arm. She grunted in her sleep and pulled his arm closer to her chest. So Regulus did the only thing that made sense. He settled back down in the grass next to her until Adelaide finally stirred. She shifted, rolling over onto her back with a stifled groan. He propped up his elbow and rested his cheek on his fist.

"What are you smiling at?"

"Has anyone ever told you," he said as he stroked her damp hair, "that you're pretty?"

"That's the best you've got?"

"No." He gazed into her eyes. "You're spectacular. Kind. Strong. Brave. Unrelenting. You're a tigress. My tigress. My *shiraa*."

"And you're my *ekaleh hadya*." Her eyes shone with playfulness. "My lone wolf."

A pang stabbed at his chest. "I don't want to be alone anymore."

Regulus leaned over her and planted his right hand on the damp grass near her head. Adelaide gazed up at him, her chest rising and falling with each breath. Her hand drifted up to his chest and her fingers spread across his sternum. Her touch felt like the warmth of a fire on a cold night, igniting him from the inside out. He shouldn't be this close. He wanted to be closer. Her breath brushed across his face. A sudden stinging attacked his forearm. She winced, and he knew she felt it, too. He hung his head, his hair brushing the grass next to her face.

"You're not alone." Adelaide turned his face toward her. "And if we make it out of this, I'm never leaving you again." A grin broke over her face. "Marry me, Regulus."

He laughed, his elation and surprise erupting out of him. "I'd be a fool not to." He leaned down and kissed her, the pinch from the mark forgotten in the ferocity of her kiss. But the mark sent a shock up his arm, and he pulled away with an agitated sigh. He stood and offered her his hand. Her stomach growled as he helped her to her feet.

"How much food did you bring?"

"Harold packed enough for a couple days for us both." He crossed to Sieger and pulled a leather pouch of venison jerky out of the saddlebag. He took a large piece and tossed the bag to Adelaide.

"We'd better get going." Regulus grinned. "Help me with my armor?"

CHAPTER 45

THE HIGHER they rode up into the mountains, the denser the forest became. Pines and firs overtook deciduous trees. Adelaide scanned the forest while Regulus consulted the map and the scribbled directions written on the back. She listened to the rustling of pine needles and creak of branches. The irregular chitter of squirrels and chirping of birds.

Regulus looked at the map, at the trees, back at the map. "All I see are trees. I *think* we're still headed in the right direction, but…these notes aren't particularly helpful."

"I say we keep going straight."

"You sound awfully confident." He cocked a brow. "How do you know?"

She shrugged. "The mark. It doesn't hurt. That means we're going the right way, right?"

"Not necessarily." He dragged his hand over his face. "It just means we're trying to obey."

"Hm." She looked around again. "You have a better idea?"

"Fair point."

They rode until her stomach twisted with hunger. Regulus pulled some jerky from his saddlebag, but they didn't stop. The dry, chewy jerky mostly tasted like salt, but it quelled the rumbling in her stomach. They rode out of the trees into a wide path, overgrown with grass. It stretched out to the right and curved up further into the mountains to their left.

"I think this is it," he said, consulting the map.

The winding trail upward narrowed the higher it progressed into the mountains until the encroaching brush forced them to ride single file. It was midafternoon and long shadows stretched across the path when they reached a fork. A dilapidated wooden sign pointed to the left branch and said only "Craigailte." The branch to the right was little more than a steep footpath over tangled roots and exposed bedrock.

"Well." She looked at the path to the right. "We're not going to Craigailte."

"No." Regulus dismounted. He pulled up the sprawling branches of a juniper bush, revealing a cairn covered in blue-green juniper berries. "We'll have to leave the horses. We'll tie them off the path, out of sight."

He made her wear his cloak. She didn't argue. The air already held a chill. She was glad she'd worn one of her riding dresses with sleeves. Regulus pulled his helm out of the saddlebag and put it on. He tied the saddlebag over his shoulder, and they set out up the footpath.

Trees and bushes caught on her dress and cloak and gravel shifted under her feet. The scent of pine and falling leaves filled the air. Regulus walked ahead of her, scanning the trees and warning her of loose and slippery rocks.

"I don't know what we'll find at the top," Regulus said as he picked his way around a sapling growing out of the middle of the path. "There are many dangerous creatures in these mountains, and the sorcerer mentioned there might be something guarding the opal. If we're attacked, I want you to run. Get to safety."

Adelaide stopped short, offended that he would expect her to leave him behind—or that she couldn't help. "You're joking, right?"

"About your safety? Never." He glanced over his bulky pauldron, but she couldn't see his eyes under the black, horned helm. "I can't die. I'll catch up."

"I can't either, remember?" She held up her right arm, even though her sleeve covered the sorcerer's mark.

Regulus turned around and took off his helm. His gaze dragged across the ground before meeting her eyes. "I've been brought back from the brink of death more times than I care to count." His voice strained. "It *hurts*, Adelaide. It still feels like dying. And the sorcerer's magic isn't like yours. There's no comfort or relief. Just pain that slowly fades."

That sounded horrible, but she wouldn't back down. "I won't abandon you." She met his gaze, challenging him. "I have my dagger and my knives. I have my magic. You know I can help."

"I don't want you to suffer if you don't have to. I don't want you to get hurt."

"And I don't want *you* to get hurt!" Emotion she hadn't even realized she had been holding in rushed out and tears gathered in the corner of her eyes. "I don't want to be here! I don't want to help this sorcerer, I don't want to have this mark on my arm, I don't want to think about my sister not knowing if I'm all right, I don't want to wonder if Nolan is threatening my family trying to find me! We don't always get what we want!" She wrapped her arms around herself and closed her eyes.

"But I *want* to help you." She looked up and whispered, "Let me help you."

"Okay," he murmured.

The tenderness and guilt written all over Regulus' face nearly broke her. She wiped her face with her sleeve as he put his helm on and started back up the path.

Regulus froze, his hand out to the side. Adelaide listened intently and leaned sideways, trying to see around him. She heard it first. A rumbling low breath that sounded more like a growl. A loud snort. Its head reared up, appearing high above Regulus. Bear. Its black nose twitched as it sniffed the air; beady eyes gleaming in the dim sunlight. Thick brown fur rippled in the slight breeze. Its front paws, held in front of its chest as it stretched up on its hind legs, were as big as Regulus' helm.

Her breath hitched as her heart thudded. Regulus eased the saddlebag from his shoulder to the ground. His hand crept toward his sword. The blade scraped against the scabbard and the bear's round ears twitched. He drew the sword faster. The bear roared. The sound vibrated through her, from her skull down into the ground, and shook the trees. Her eyes widened as she stared at the bits of bloodied fur stuck between its huge yellowed teeth. Regulus drew back his massive sword and swung. The bear swiped a paw at him, hitting him in the shoulder and knocking him to the side before he could land his swing. He fell on top of a tangle of mountain sage and juniper. The bear fell onto all fours, landing on top of Regulus. One paw landed on his chest, the other on his sword arm. He grunted and struggled against the bear's weight. She swallowed and snapped out of her momentary paralysis.

"Hey!" Adelaide pulled out her throwing knives as the bear turned its head toward her. Regulus pushed on the paw on his chest with his left arm. She threw the first knife, aiming for its shoulder. If she killed it and it collapsed on Regulus, she'd never be able to move it off him. The knife disappeared deep in the bear's fur. The beast roared and stepped off Regulus' sword arm, but that put more pressure on the paw on his chest and he groaned. The paw came down on the other side of Regulus' head as the bear turned toward her. She stepped back and threw her next knife at the bear's chest. It sank in, glinting in the mass of fur. The bear charged.

Adelaide gasped and stepped back, throwing the last knife at its head. It moved as if it saw the knife, and the blade sunk into the bear's neck where it met its shoulders. She threw up a magic shield and crouched down just before the bear slammed headfirst into the shield. She struggled to keep the shield in place as she slid on the gravelly path.

Regulus shouted from behind the bear, loud, low and guttural. The bear ignored the sound, clawing at her shield of transparent blue light. She looked up at its snarling lips, only a barrier of light between her face and its teeth. She saw the dull sheen of light on black armor as Regulus jumped on the bear's back. He brought his sword straight down, the hilt clasped in both hands above his head. The sword sunk behind the bear's head and emerged from its neck in a fountain of blood that sizzled against her shield. She dropped the shield and scrambled back as the bear fell. Its weight shook the ground as it hit the earth. She held her hands out, steadying herself and breathing hard.

Regulus stood on the bear's back as he pulled on his sword. The blade freed with the scrape of metal on bone and a sucking sound. He looked terrifying, the waning sunlight glinting off the hulking black armor and curving horns rising above his helm. Blood soaked the oversized sword in his hands and ran off the tip in a glittering stream of crimson. Now she understood why he hadn't wanted to tell her the truth.

Because in that moment he didn't look like the man she loved. The man before her was the Black Knight of whispered terrors. He didn't look kind or good. He looked dangerous. Cruel.

He looked like a monster.

CHAPTER 46

REGULUS DROPPED the sword and yanked his helm off, but it was too late. He saw the look in Adelaide's eyes. The fear. Not fear of the sorcerer. Fear of *him*. The helm slipped from his hands and clattered to the ground. *Please, no.* Her right foot inched back and his soul crumbled. He slid down the bear's side and reached toward her. "Adelaide…"

She blinked, and the fear vanished. He breathed a sigh of relief. "Why do you wear that?" Her gaze ran over his armor and her mouth twisted down. "It's not you."

"Requirement of the sorcerer's."

"When this is over, I want to burn it. Melt it down and destroy it."

Regulus laughed as the energy of the fight and tension of seeing her afraid of him wore off. "Agreed." He held out his hand and Adelaide took it. "We need to keep moving. Every creature on the mountain will have heard that. And it's getting dark."

He led her around the bear's corpse and retrieved his sword. He left the helm lying next to the body. Adelaide left her knives buried under the bear's bulk, the time required to retrieve them not worth the trouble.

Dusk plunged into night. Adelaide conjured a light to hover along the ground ahead of them, and another that hovered above their heads. Gnarled roots twisted over the rocky, narrow trail as it curved ever up the mountain. The higher they went, the steeper the trail became, but at least their exertion helped combat the increasing cold.

They walked for hours, snacking on the dwindling supply of jerky to keep their energy up. They would have to hunt on their way back.

The trees creaked and rustled and sounds of animals whispered from the forbidding darkness between trees. A few times he caught sight of a pair of reflective yellow eyes, but nothing attacked them. He kept alert, even as his attention split between the surrounding forest and listening to Adelaide's footsteps and breathing behind him. A small part of him took comfort in the mark on her arm. If something attacked—wolves, chimera, goblins, dragon for all he knew—at least she would live.

Regulus walked out of the trees onto a ledge overlooking a steep precipice.

A narrow ledge curved around a sheer rock face. Had they taken a wrong turn in the dark? He scanned the ground in the illumination from Adelaide's orbs. There. A cairn sat by the rock face at the beginning of the ledge, a rock on the top shaped like a rough arrow pointing along the exposed rock. He stepped to the side. "You go first."

She peered at the ledge and her jaw slackened. "Why?"

"So I can catch you if you fall."

Adelaide swallowed, then headed out onto the ledge. The rock face seemed to stretch on forever. To their left were the shadowy tops of pines. Freezing wind blew into their faces, making his cheeks burn and his nose sting. Rock crumbled beneath Adelaide's foot and she stumbled. He wrapped his arm around her waist, pinned her to the rock face.

Her chest heaved as she caught her breath. "Thank you."

He nodded, and they continued.

Finally, the ledge widened, and the rock face curved away. They walked into an open meadow. Patches of half-melted snow littered the grass. A cairn pointed across the meadow. Tall grasses rustled around them, accompanied by the crunch of icy snow beneath their feet.

He heard a snap of branches. Heavy foot falls. He drew his sword. Adelaide froze, watching him. He scanned the trees, desperate to see whatever stalked them. A crack of snapping wood echoed as thudding moved closer. Whatever it was, it was big. Pines to their right parted and something emerged from the shadows. Cold moonlight illuminated leathery skin and reflected in huge white eyes.

Adelaide gasped. "Is that a…"

"Mountain troll."

The troll looked at them, foggy breaths puffing from its flat, wide nostrils. Regulus heard Adelaide mutter a prayer under her breath. The troll's legs were short under its colossal torso and massive shoulders. It leaned forward, black-clawed hands dragging on the ground at the end of long, hulking arms. It grunted and ran toward them, using its fisted hands to make up for its short legs. Regulus raised his sword and moved into a defensive stance, his feet planted under his shoulders as his pulse quickened in anticipation of the fight.

Adelaide gave a defiant yell and threw her hands forward. A dozen blue shards of light flew from her hands. A few whipped past the lumbering troll, but most hit. They lodged in the monster's thick hide. Regulus readied himself, waiting for the perfect moment to charge. Next to him, Adelaide punched her right hand forward. An arc of aqua light exploded from her fist and slammed into the troll. It roared and stumbled. Regulus ran forward and sliced at the troll's short, fat neck. It lurched back and blocked with its arm. His sword bit through thick hide into flesh and cracked against bone. He yanked back, slicing through more flesh as he freed his blade.

The troll screeched and lurched. Its hand hung from a strip of throbbing, blood-covered muscle and leathery skin. A spear of blue light slammed into its left shoulder and it reeled to the side. Regulus darted forward and slid under the troll, dragging his sword deep across its torso. He stood, but the troll didn't fall. It stumbled toward him, roaring. He stabbed his sword into its chest, and it leaned into the sword, clawing at him with its good hand. Its weight pressed him back, and he fell to his knees as the troll reached for him. The blade sunk deeper into the troll's chest. Its claws raked over his breastplate with a jarring screech of rending metal.

Then Adelaide was there, a sword of light wreathed in flames in her hands. Her teeth showed as her lips curled back in a yell. The flames reflected in her ferocious eyes. She swung at the troll's throat. The smell of burning leather and flesh joined the stench of blood and troll as the blade of light sliced through the trolls' neck. The head rolled over its shoulder and fell. Blood splattered over Regulus. Its body fell to the side, wrenching his sword out of his grasp.

For a second, Adelaide stood over him, his cloak and her skirt swaying around her. Shoulders squared, spine straight and tall, outlined from behind by the moon and bathed in the flickering light of orange flames and the soft blue-white glow of the sword in her hands. Her eyes shone with golden light. Fierce. Powerful. Intimidating. Beautiful.

The sword vanished from her hands and the meadow fell into darkness. She created a new orb of light and knelt next to him. "Are you all right?"

"Yes... How did you do that?"

She blushed. "Honestly, I don't know. I just...did. I saw you fall and I... I stopped thinking so hard about it and did it."

"You're amazing." Regulus leaned toward Adelaide, reaching for her waist. She grimaced and leaned away from him.

"You're covered in troll blood." Her mouth curved down. "And the troll smells. I'll throw up if I kiss you right now."

He grinned. "You've got troll blood on you too, you know."

She looked at her blood-splattered dress. "Still not kissing you."

"Later, then." He winked and stood, then retrieved his sword. "We'd best keep going."

On the other side of the meadow, the path turned into winding stone steps that climbed almost straight up into the darkness. They climbed for an hour before reaching the top. Adelaide kept pace behind him the whole way, and when they stepped into the wide clearing at the top of the steps, they were scarcely winded. At least their bond to the sorcerer gave them extra strength and stamina, not just pain and servitude. If only it would protect them against the cold. Regulus' ears felt numb and his joints ached under the freezing armor.

The moonlight illuminated the rock wall some twenty feet ahead of them. Smooth, undisturbed snow glistened and crunched beneath their feet. Wind whistled in his ears and rustled in the pines. No other sounds filled the night. They stopped in the shadow at the base of the wall and stared up as it stretched toward the stars.

"I guess this is it." Regulus looked at Adelaide. Her nose was red, and she clutched his cloak tighter about her. "This part is all you."

"So I…" She looked at him and back at the wall. "What?"

He shrugged. "I don't know how you do what you do."

"Hm." She placed her hand on the icy rock. Pale blue light shone under her palm. Nothing happened. He tucked his hands under his arms and shifted his weight from one foot to the other, trying to keep warm. She added her other hand. Still nothing. "All right." She stepped back, and he moved back farther. She shone a bright beam of light from her hands to the wall. Still nothing. "Are we *sure* this is the right wall?"

"It lines up with his notes and description."

Adelaide blasted the wall with fire. It warmed him for a moment, but had no impact on the stone. She threw daggers of light at it. Still nothing. "Why." Another blast of fire. "Won't." Her voice rose as a glowing spear pinged off the wall. "It!" A torrent of flames. "OPEN!" She shoved her hands forward, throwing a blast of light at the wall.

A sharp crack like a lightning strike rent the air and rattled his bones. A fissure opened in the bottom of the wall and raced up some ten feet before spreading right and left. The rock in front of them crumbled and crashed to the ground. He covered his face as dust billowed. When he lowered his arm, a gaping hole in the wall opened into inky blackness. They looked at each other, then headed inside, an orb of blue light leading their way.

They stood inside a round stone room no more than six paces in diameter. In the center of the room stood a marble statue. They moved closer, and the light fell on the statue—a woman in flowing robes. The marble woman's eyes were closed, and her head lowered. She held one hand over her face, hiding one eye. The stone beneath her visible eye was stained, making her look like she had been crying. Her other hand was cupped, palm up, in front of her stomach. In her palm glittered a huge opal of black and purple with flecks of orange and red. It was polished into an oval and about as long as a little finger. Adelaide reached out and curled her fingers around the opal. Regulus held his breath as she pulled her hand back.

The statue moved.

The marble woman blinked, her lids grating over pupil-less eyes with a rasping sound. She raised her head with a creak of stone. Adelaide stepped closer to Regulus, clutching the opal to her chest. The statue's white lips parted.

"Do not seek to re-forge the Staff of Nightfall." The statue's cold voice filled the room. "The Staff brings only death and destruction. The sorceress who created it is dead, along with all her victims." She reached out her hand, the marble groaning. "You are pure of heart to enter here. The Staff's power cannot be used for good. Its desire is tainted. Return the opal and seal the door, or the Staff will bring endless night."

His heart sank. Whatever the sorcerer wanted with a staff that brought death and destruction, it wasn't good. Regardless of whether *endless night* was a metaphor, he didn't like the sound of it. *Etiros…forgive me.*

"Who are you?" Adelaide's voice sounded small in the stone chamber.

"I am the spirit of those who died by the power of the Staff of Nightfall." The statue blinked again and tears—real tears—ran from her marble eyes. Regulus recoiled.

Adelaide's fist moved from her chest. She cried out. In the same moment, a burning sensation spread from the mark on his own arm. She was considering leaving the opal. And the sorcerer knew.

"Return the opal." Tears dripped over the polished marble of the statue's face and splashed on the stone floor.

Adelaide screamed and Regulus groaned as they both fell to their knees. Regulus knew what she was feeling, because the same slicing, burning pain cut up his arm and across his chest. But he had experienced it before. Adelaide shook beside him, sobbing. He wrapped his arm around her as the pain made his head pound. She whimpered and rocked back and forth. His eyes watered—not from his own pain as much as for hers.

"Adelaide." He placed a trembling hand against her cheek.

She shook her head. "We can't, we—" She arched backward and screamed. A stifled scream ground up his own throat as it felt like his heart was being wound round and round with hot wire. The opal slipped from Adelaide's fingers and clattered across the stone.

"We don't have a choice," Regulus whispered, holding her shoulders. "He controls us."

She nodded, tears running down her cheeks and neck. "All right. All right."

The pain rushed out of his chest, down his arm, and disappeared. Adelaide leaned against him, breathing hard. After a moment, Regulus scooped the opal off the ground and put it in his saddlebag before helping her to her feet. The marble statue creaked as they walked toward the entrance, and he looked over his shoulder.

Both her stone hands covered her face.

THE WALL closed with a rumble behind them. Adelaide's feet dragged as they stepped into the moonlight. She was too physically and emotionally exhausted to climb back down tonight. She still believed bringing the sorcerer the opal was wrong, but what could she do? He would either torture them into submission or take control of one of them. She just wanted this nightmare to be over. And she had promised Regulus she would do what the sorcerer wanted so he could be free.

They walked over to a small spruce tree several yards away from the path. The branches had kept the ground around the trunk free of snow. Adelaide used her magic to push snow off the lower boughs. They made a little pile of dead branches and needles near the edge of the dry ground so the smoke wouldn't get trapped, and she lit them on fire. She helped Regulus out of his armor, and they held each other for warmth and comfort, his cloak wrapped around them. Even the troll blood in his hair couldn't stop her from pressing as close to him as possible.

She slept fitfully, dreaming of crying statues, screaming men, women, and children, and glassy-eyed corpses. Regulus still had his arms around her when she awoke in the morning. Soft grayish light glittered on the icy surface of the snow and her breath fogged in the air. Somewhere a jay trilled a song. She buried her icy face in his shoulder, not wanting to move. Too cold.

"As much as I enjoy this," Regulus said, his voice scratchy, "how about a fire? I can barely feel my face."

Adelaide groaned as they separated and sat up. She held her hands between them and conjured a flame. It was more draining to maintain the flame than to start a fire, but she was too stiff to get up and look for kindling. Feeling crept back to her feet and nose. Regulus scooted over until his shoulder pressed against hers.

"You know what might help chase the cold away?" he whispered, his voice husky and his breath warm on her ear.

She smirked at the small fire hovering above her hands. "What's that?" He kissed her cheek, then brushed gentle kisses along her jawline. Warmth tingled over her skin and spread through her torso. "You still stink like troll," she said.

But she turned her head and kissed him. The fire faded away, and she clenched the front of his shirt. He held her close, his arms strong against her back as he gripped the back of her neck. They separated, their mouths still close.

"Warmer now?" she murmured.

"Mm, almost." He kissed her again and flames seemed to dance over her skin. She wrapped her hands around the back of his head. Tremors of joy ran down her back as she relaxed, relishing him. "Better."

She laughed at the smile in his voice. They held each other a moment longer, ignoring the rest of the world. Savoring this moment of quiet. Of being together. A slight tingle pricked the mark, making Adelaide wince. She pulled back, her hands slipping down his arms.

"Don't." He held her arms, his eyes pleading. "Not yet."

"We have to go."

His shoulders fell. "I know." He pushed her sleeve back and ran his thumb over the mark on her arm. "Let's go get rid of this."

Regulus left the armor behind, to Adelaide's relief. If the sorcerer kept his word, he wouldn't need it anymore. He kept the sword, just in case. Nothing bothered them on the way down the mountain, although she thought she saw shadows moving in the trees. She finally mentioned them to Regulus.

"Yes, I noticed. Whatever is out there probably smells the troll blood and are keeping their distance. We're either trolls, which are difficult to kill, or we killed a troll, making us more dangerous."

Once they returned to their horses, they rode straight to the sorcerer's tower, late into the night. They crossed from vibrant, living trees to blackened, lifeless trees, then naked, bark-barren trees with wood like bone. Had the decay spread further?

As they dismounted, she looked at Regulus. "The decay…was it this bad two years ago?"

He shook his head. "No. Only the vines on the tower and the trees closest to the tower were dead then."

The tower door creaked open. "Yes, well." The sorcerer strode toward them, a torch in hand. "It takes a lot of energy, keeping you alive. I have to get that energy from somewhere." He held out his hand. "Where is it?"

Regulus reached into the saddlebag and pulled out the opal. The light of the torch made the stone sparkle black, blue, purple, red, and orange. Regulus clutched the stone. "You'll release us? Both of us? And let us leave alive?"

"Yes, yes. Hand it over!"

"Now?" Adelaide confirmed.

"Yes. I'm a man of my word. Now give it here!" The sorcerer snatched the opal. He turned it over in his hand and held it up, inspecting it. Nerves and anticipation knotted Adelaide's stomach as the sorcerer rubbed his fingers across the stone. Apparently satisfied, he slipped it into his belt. "Give me your arm."

She watched as Regulus pushed up his sleeve and held out his right arm. The sorcerer pressed his hand over the mark. "I release you."

Regulus winced. When the sorcerer pulled his hand away, the mark was gone. Regulus stared at his arm, now marred only by faded scars. Adelaide pushed her sleeve up as the sorcerer approached her.

"I know you considered betraying me," the sorcerer said as he put his hand over the mark on her arm. "But you didn't. So I release you." A burning, ripping sensation coursed over her skin. She bit her tongue to keep from crying out. The feeling faded and she relaxed. "But I need a little more from you." His hand encircled her wrist.

"Wh—" Her vision went white. All the air was sucked from her lungs. She collapsed to her knees, but still the sorcerer held her wrist. Her energy drained, like when she used a lot of magic, but this felt different. Like it was being drawn out; like she was a rapidly emptying well. Regulus screamed her name, but he sounded distant.

The sorcerer's muffled voice said, "Touch me or her and I'll kill her."

Her mouth hung open, but she couldn't draw in a breath. His grip released and her hand dropped. She gasped as if she had been drowning and crumpled to the side. Muscular arms caught her before she hit the ground. She saw shadows and then smudged colors.

"Adelaide? Adelaide!" Regulus' voice sounded strange and muted. "What did you do?"

"She'll be fine in a moment. Now leave. If I see either of you here again, I'll kill you."

"Adelaide?" Regulus shook her shoulders. "Adelaide, please." His voice cut through the fog in her mind, and she blinked. With every blink, her vision cleared until she saw Regulus' deathly pale face hovering above her.

She clutched his sleeves and curled into his chest. He pulled her closer, his heart hammering against her ear. The tower door was closed, the sorcerer gone.

Regulus rubbed her back.

"You're okay," he said, almost as if trying to assure himself. "It's over, we're safe. You're all right."

But she wasn't all right.

She couldn't get her thick tongue to work. She tried to speak, but only a broken sob emerged. Above them, green and yellow light flashed from the tower window. Regulus guided her arm over his shoulders, picked her up, and stumbled to his feet. He put her on Sieger, then tied Zephyr's reins to the pommel of his saddle. Regulus mounted behind her, his arms around her waist, and they rode away from the tower and the ominous flashes of light.

It took several more tries to speak past her taut vocal cords. "Regulus."

"You're safe," he repeated, his voice wavering. "It's over. We did it. I'm free. We're both free. Praise Etiros, we're free." He kissed her temple. "He won't hurt you again." His arms tightened around her middle. "I won't let him near you again."

Even with the jostling of Sieger's gallop, Regulus' racing heartbeat and deep, shaky breaths vibrated against her back. She didn't want to ruin his joy at being freed. But she couldn't keep any more secrets from him.

"He took it." Her voice cracked. "My magic. It's gone."

STAFF
OF
NIGHTFALL

Map of Monparth

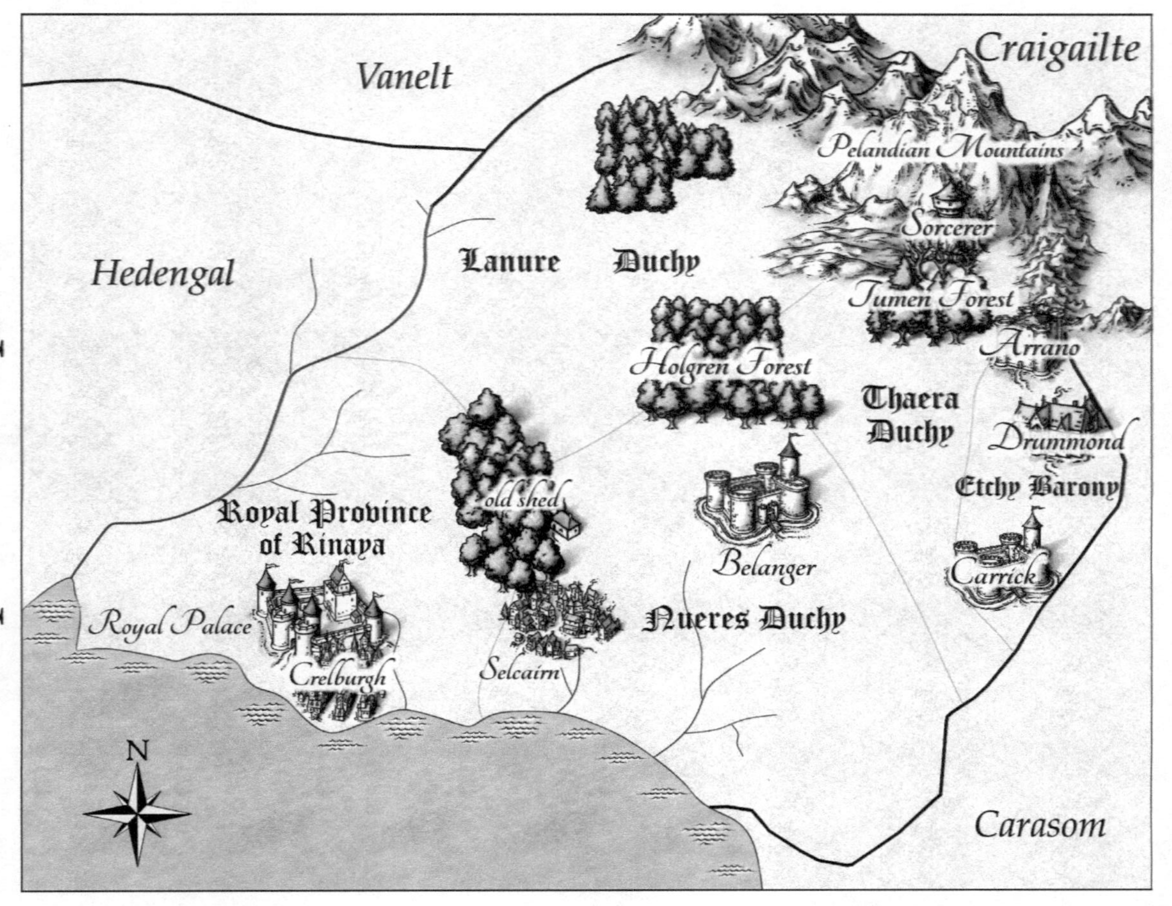

Chapter 1

REGULUS CLUTCHED Adelaide tighter. His heart thudded against his ribs. Every hoof beat as Sieger galloped through the woods sent a jolt through his body. Adelaide's gelding Zephyr raced behind them. The light from the window in the top of the sorcerer's accursed tower flashed through the forest, growing fainter as the trees transitioned from dead and blackened to healthy pines and birches.

His tongue stuck to the roof of his mouth as Adelaide's words echoed in his mind. *"He took it. My magic. It's gone."* Her hair flew in his eyes, his mouth. He pulled the hair away and placed his cheek next to her head, wrapping his hand back over hers. *"Gone. He took it."*

As the scene flashed through his mind again, he closed his eyes and tried to will it away but couldn't. Couldn't stop the scene replaying. Adelaide falling to her knees before the sorcerer, her head thrown back in a silent scream. Her eyes glazed over, rolling back in her head until almost all that was visible were the whites.

Regulus opened his eyes. *My fault. My fault. My fault.* The words hammered through his head in time with the pounding of his heart. He should have been right next to her; should have pushed the sorcerer away before he wound his hand around her wrist. He shouldn't have taken her in the first place. Two years ago he shouldn't have agreed to serve the sorcerer.

But that was foolishness, and he knew it. Even had he been closer, he might not have been able to stop the sorcerer. And he hated to admit it, but he would make the same choices all over again. Because Dresden and Harold and the others were still alive. Because, even with her magic stolen, Adelaide was still alive. But would she ever forgive him?

They rode until the horses panted, their chests heaving, and necks drenched with sweat. Sieger snorted as he slowed, tired by the fast pace and the weight of two riders. Regulus pulled back on the reins, bringing the stallion to a halt. Zephyr snorted, following Sieger's lead and stopping as well. Regulus shifted Adelaide forward and dismounted, then picked her up and carried her off the saddle.

"I'm fine." But her voice sounded weak, and she didn't fight him.

He set her on a mossy patch of ground under a beech tree. She slumped against the trunk as he knelt in front of her and tossed aside the oversized black sword—the last piece of the Black Knight ensemble the sorcerer had given him. He was free, he didn't need it now. He pushed her hair out of her face. In the pale moonlight, tears glistened on Adelaide's cheeks. What could he say? *I'm sorry* felt hollow. Crass.

She turned away and pressed against the tree trunk, curled in on herself, staring at the ground. Regulus ducked his head, trying to catch her eyes. *Etiros, help me.* "I'm—"

"Don't." She lunged forward and wrapped her arms around him, her fists clenching his shirt and her breath hot on his neck. "Don't you dare apologize."

"I don't know what to do," he whispered. He pulled her onto his lap and stroked her hair, his fingers brushing against her back.

"Just…" She turned and rested her head on his shoulder. "Don't let go. Please. Don't let go."

"I—"

Zephyr snorted and pawed the ground, startling Regulus. Sieger sniffed the air, then whinnied. Regulus looked around, still stroking Adelaide's hair. Shadows moved in the trees. He couldn't tell if it was just the light, a trick of his tired eyes. Or if something actually—a glint of yellow. He stiffened and watched the same spot. There. Two eyes, a dull, reflective yellow-green in the moonlight. They vanished. A growl reverberated nearby. Adelaide jumped away. Sieger reared; Zephyr kicked his back legs. The horses took off. Regulus leapt to his feet and grabbed the oversized sword.

"What is it?" Adelaide whispered as she stood, her dagger glinting in her hand.

Regulus scanned the shadows. His newly non-enhanced muscles strained against the unwieldy sword's weight. "Not sure."

More growling and snarling sounded from the darkness on all sides. Adelaide only had a dagger. She hadn't retrieved her throwing knives from the bear. Why would she need to? She had magic. *Had.* Regulus gulped back the rising panic. They stood beneath the beech tree, surrounded by unknown creatures. An average woman and an average man. No immortality. No magically enhanced strength or speed. No magic.

Adelaide crouched, her feet spread and planted, her hands raised in front of her face, her dagger in her right hand. A good defensive stance. Protecting her torso and keeping a strong center of balance. Some measure of calm settled over his nerves.

No. Not an average man and woman. Adelaide was anything but average. And there were those who said the name Regulus Hargreaves with equal parts admiration and fear long before he met the sorcerer. He'd killed plenty of men and monsters. And Adelaide had killed a troll. He squared his shoulders and adjusted his own stance, confidence growing. *Grant us mercy, Etiros. Give us victory.* The same prayer he'd prayed as a mercenary.

The beasts still hadn't moved from the shadows. As if they were sizing them up, trying to decide if they were worth the trouble. Maybe they would give up—movement to the right drew his attention. Yellow-green eyes flashed low in the darkness. Something shifted forward.

The canine was thin, built like a racing hound, but as tall as Regulus' middle. Shaggy gray fur hung from its lithe frame, except along its neck and underbelly, which were covered with segmented bone plating. Its black lips pulled back in a snarl over long, yellowed fangs.

"What…" Adelaide breathed.

"Kanadosus," he murmured. "Pack hunters. Armored underbelly, except for just under its jaw." He didn't mention he'd seen three men ripped limb from limb by kanadosi back in his early days as a mercenary, but he recalled their screams.

Two more kanadosi crept out of the brush. Rustling and growling sounded behind them. Adelaide turned. He'd have to trust her to deal with the ones behind him.

The kanadosi growled and surged forward together. One jumped at his chest. He raised his sword and swung at the kanadosus' neck. The swing was awkward, but the beast fell, its neck half severed. Another kanadosus sunk its teeth into his right arm and he groaned. He hit the pommel on the beast's head, and it released his arm and fell back with a yelp. He swung but aimed poorly. The blade cut into its shoulder at the base of its neck and lodged fast in the armor plating on its chest. The kanadosus thrashed, and the sword ripped out of Regulus' grip. Adelaide cried out, and Regulus spun toward her. A kanadosus lay dead between them, another limped away with blood flowing down its shoulder.

But his eyes snapped up to Adelaide, pinned against the tree, a snarling kanadosus clawing and snapping at her. She held the beast at arm's length, gripping its shoulders. He ran, his heart plummeting as her elbows buckled. She jerked her head away from its bite, her scream chilling. He grabbed the kanadosus and threw it aside as another beast jumped on his back. Its claws dug into him, slicing through his shirt. He staggered and tried to reach up to grab the writhing creature. It bit his left shoulder, and he yelled.

Adelaide ran forward, bending to snatch up her dagger as she went. Regulus ducked as she stabbed at the kanadosus on his back. It collapsed with a strangled whimper. He threw it off his back and looked about wildly. Adelaide stood at the ready, her hands empty. She must not have been able to pull her dagger free. He saw one of the kanadosi disappear into the shadows. The rustling quieted as the remaining kanadosi fled. His pulse hammered in his ears as he scanned the darkness for any sign of movement, any shadow out of place.

Nothing. They were alone with the corpses of kanadosi and no horses. As the adrenaline wore off, he winced, light-headed. He stumbled toward Adelaide, frowning as he pointed at her right arm. Her sleeve hung in tatters, and blood dripped from her hand.

"You're hurt." He tripped, and she steadied him. His right arm and left shoulder burned and ached. She frowned.

"Not as badly as you are." She guided him to the ground. "Hang on." She fetched her dagger from the jaw of the last kanadosus, limping as she walked.

"Your leg…?"

"My foot." She sat next to him, cutting strips from her dress. "Just got twisted." She kept wincing as she worked with her left foot out to the side. The leather of her boot was mangled, but he didn't see any blood on her foot. Only on her arm. She moved to wrap his arm, but he stopped her.

"You first."

"It's just some scratches. You're bleeding more. I…" Her voice cracked. "Let me do what I still can."

Guilt pricked him as she tightly bound his forearm. "Thank you."

She nodded and wrapped wide strips of cloth over his shoulder, across his chest, and under his arm. The pressure made the wounds ache but would help stem the bleeding. When she finished, Regulus wrapped the last strip around her forearm. His tired hands struggled. A cloud drifted over the moon, making it difficult to tell where the cuts began and ended, so he wrapped as much of her arm as he could. The memory of the lights Adelaide had conjured before brought another stab of guilt.

"I'm sorry I didn't stop him," he said in a strained whisper. He cleared his throat. "I should have—"

"What, Reg?"

He blinked at her use of his nickname. His hands hovered over the knot he had tied on her wrist as he met her eyes.

"Should have, could have." She pulled her arm to her torso and looked away. "It doesn't change anything."

The bitterness in her voice made him wince. He wanted to ask how to fix this, how to fix them, what she wanted from him. Wanted to beg her for forgiveness. But the words stuck in his throat. Too painful to speak aloud. Too afraid to find out the answer.

"We should look for the horses. And find a place to rest, away from the…" He gestured toward the dead kanadosi.

His heart fell further as she stood without looking at him. He followed her in the direction the horses had bolted, leaving the now difficult-to-wield sword of the Black Knight behind. The horses' rapid pace had left an obvious trail in the moss, pine needles, and dirt, even in the dim moonlight. They followed the tracks, calling to their horses.

The space Adelaide maintained between them stung more than the bites on his arm and shoulder. Her limp worsened as they walked, but with the way she wouldn't meet his eyes, he didn't dare offer to let her lean on him. He was about to suggest they halt their search until morning when a whinny caught his attention. He scanned the woods to his right.

"Sieger?"

"Zephyr?" Adelaide called.

Hoof beats, then Sieger trotted around a tree toward them. Zephyr trailed behind, still tied to Sieger's saddle. Regulus sighed with relief and caught Sieger's bridle.

"Hey. There's my boy." He patted Sieger's neck, and his hand came away sticky with sweat. "Sorry you had such a fright."

He glanced around Sieger's neck at Adelaide rubbing Zephyr's forehead. She murmured something he couldn't hear. He gave her a moment before finding a nearby pine suitable for both tying up the horses and taking shelter. He fetched his knife from the saddlebag, then ducked under the branches where Adelaide had already curled onto her side. With a suppressed sigh, he laid down a couple feet away from her, his knife close at hand. The soft sounds of the horses and the background noise of insects filled the air as he drifted to sleep.

Regulus awoke to find Adelaide curled against him, her injured arm crossed in front of her chest between them, her other arm thrown over his torso. His bandaged right arm wrapped up and around her shoulders. The sun had already risen high into the sky, but in the shade of the pine, the air felt cool. The heat of her body against his, the way she fit against his side, her face tucked into his shoulder, healed him and broke him all at once. His shoulder felt stiff and sore around the bite, and his right arm ached. The longer he lay there, the more aware he became of the stinging in his back from where the wolf's claws had scratched him. He needed to move. He *should* move. She probably had drifted next to him in her sleep. But he kept still, treasuring the moment.

Afraid when she woke, she would resent him for what had happened to her.

Afraid to lose her.

ADELAIDE SHIFTED and woke up. Her right forearm stung. Worse was the dead emptiness, deep in her soul, a hollow carved out when the sorcerer ripped away her magic. Instead of a gentle thrum of energy in her veins, she felt only silence. Months of practice, honing her ability in secret, and just when she was getting a strong grasp on her gift, it was stolen. *Etiros, why?* She shifted, squeezing her eyes against tears, and pushed against something soft and warm. She forced her eyes open to shaded daylight. Regulus lay on his back, his right arm curved around her. He moved away and sat up, stretching. The sudden departure of his body felt like a blanket being ripped away.

"Sorry." His voice, gravelly and deep, reverberated down her spine. "I didn't want to wake you. I wasn't…I didn't mean to…" He glanced away, prodding the bite on his shoulder.

"Oh." Her heart twisted. She stood and turned away, hiding the heat that rose to her cheeks and the tears that pricked at her eyes. After his odd behavior last night, the way he wouldn't meet her eyes now…

Was that really all it took? Having her magic taken? Was it that she was weak? Or broken? She touched the gray cloth strip dotted with dried blood wrapped around her forearm. Regulus hadn't always known she had magic. But it wasn't just going back to how things were before. She had been drained. Damaged. She swallowed a sob. The ache of her missing magic made her feel incomplete. Losing Regulus, too…

Regulus cleared his throat. "Adelaide?"

"Hm?" She didn't trust herself to face him.

"I don't know how to convince you I'm sorry. I failed you. I'm sorry I couldn't protect you. I don't know how to make it up to you. I probably can't."

She turned around in surprise. Regulus stood with his hands clasped behind his back, staring at his feet.

"I know this is my fault. I won't pretend I don't deserve your blame—"

"What?" she gasped. "Blame?"

"I only wanted to protect the people I love." He looked up, the desperation in his eyes wringing out her emotions. "If I could put this right, I would. I understand if you're…if we're…" He swallowed and dropped his head. "Done.

I want you to know—"

"You think I'm angry with you?" Adelaide bit her lip and wrapped her arms over her stomach. "I thought—you were acting like I was broken. Different. I thought you didn't want me anymore."

For an awful moment, Regulus was silent. Then he laughed. Her face heated.

"I blamed myself and thought you did, too. I thought you didn't want *me*." Regulus strode over in the space of a heartbeat and placed one hand on her hip, the other on her cheek. Her breath caught. "There is nothing, no magic, no sorcery, no pain or pleasure, nothing on this earth that can make me stop loving you. I want you and will love none other."

His warm palm pressed against her cheek. She stared into his eyes. Those eyes, intense like molten silver yet gentle. Her lips parted, but she couldn't piece together a coherent thought.

"I am yours, Adelaide." The huskiness in his voice made her heart tremble. "You have all of me, now and forever. If you want me."

She reached up, touching the stubble growing along his jaw. She ran her thumb over his lips. "And I am yours. Heart and soul."

A smirking half-smile warned her just before he pulled her in and kissed her. She leaned into his kiss, melting against him. Regulus' fingers curled against her back and she quivered with joy, not even caring about the scratchiness of his coarse stubble.

"Marry me," he whispered.

She chuckled, breathless. "I already asked you, remember?"

"I'll take that as a yes." He kissed the hollow between her collarbones, then her neck, moving agonizingly slowly up to her mouth. She sighed as his lips found hers and wrapped her arms around his neck. He flinched with a grunt as her arm bumped his wounded shoulder.

"Sorry." She leaned back, concern conquering her desire to kiss him until she could no longer stand. "We should get going. Those bites need tended."

Regulus nodded, although he sighed with obvious disappointment as he looked around. Deciduous trees surrounded them, spaced far apart. The tallest peaks of the Pelandian Mountains glinted white between the trees behind Regulus.

"If we're about where I think we are," he said, "there should be a path nearby. If I'm right, we should reach the Drummonds' by the end of the day."

"No!" She clutched his shirt and forced herself to sound less panicked. "We can't go there."

"What? Why—"

"Nolan might be waiting there. I can't…" She rested her head against his shoulder. "We need a plan before we face him. And even if he's not there, Lord and Lady Drummond believe we're engaged." And Lady Drummond didn't like Regulus, but she wasn't about to say that.

"Oh. So, Arrano, then?"

"Also no good." She sighed, a headache forming in the middle of her forehead. "If Nolan found out I was there, he would accuse you of kidnapping me or something. I was thinking…" She chewed on her lip. The idea had occurred to her as she fell asleep last night, but she wasn't sure what Regulus would think. "We need help. I think we need to talk to my father."

"Your…oh." She could practically hear his mind churning as he spoke. "And tell him…?"

"Everything."

He pulled away and looked into her face, holding her shoulders. "Everything… Everything?"

Adelaide knew it wouldn't be easy for him. He'd barely been able to tell her the truth. She didn't relish telling her parents what had happened to her or what she had done, either. But she was out of ideas. Maybe it was childish, but she trusted Father to protect them from Nolan.

"My father is wise. And has powerful connections. He'll know what to do. But…he's astute. He won't trust you if he suspects any dishonesty or omission." She sighed. "We'll have to tell him the full truth. Is that…all right?"

After a moment, Regulus nodded. "If that's what you want to do, that's what I'll do. You won't let him kill me, right?"

She smiled. "That's what we're trying to avoid, remember?"

After a brief detour to catch and cook a rabbit, they set out. They kept up a trot as long as possible, giving their horses walking breaks before hurrying onward. The sun dipped low and Adelaide's stomach rumbled, but still they rode on. They followed the roads, but cut across fields for speed's sake. Their ragged, bloodied appearance drew plenty of stares. She was beyond caring. They made do with a meager meal of berries and a very chewy squirrel for supper, then spent the night hidden in a copse of trees and bushes, curled against each other.

The next morning, they crossed a stream and caught a couple fish. Cooking them on a stick wasn't ideal, but it tasted infinitely better than squirrel. Shortly after noon they spied a group approaching, so they moved into the tall grass alongside the rough dirt road. Sunlight glinted on helms and chainmail. There looked to be ten mounted knights and several servants on palfreys weighed down with baggage. She watched the unusual group move at a surprising pace.

"What do you make of that?"

"Nothing good results in a group like that." Regulus furrowed his brow, looking over his shoulder at the knights. "Certainly trouble somewhere."

"Hm." She halted Zephyr and raised her hand to shield her eyes from the sun. It was a curious sight. She squinted at the lead knight. The bright blue of the caparison on that lead horse… Decorated with something white…

"It can't be." She wheeled Zephyr around and took off toward the road.

She heard Regulus calling her name and following her, but the heraldry on the leader's horse consumed her focus. A rearing white unicorn was embroidered on the blue caparison over the horse's flank—the Belanger crest. The knight wore a helm, and the raised visor cast his face in shadow, but the horse she recognized. A large dappled gray destrier with a dark mane and tail.

"Father?" She urged Zephyr into a gallop, her heart leaping. "Father!"

The man slowed his horse and turned toward her. She grinned as his features came into focus. The shadow of a beard. The deep laugh lines around his mouth. His defined nose. His wide, deep-set green eyes.

"Father!"

Father reined in his horse and held up his hand, halting his knights behind him. "Adelaide?"

She jumped off Zephyr's back at the edge of the road and regretted it as her ankle smarted, but she ignored the pain and ran toward her father as fast as her throbbing foot allowed. Father dismounted and tossed his helm down as he ran to her. She registered that he was crying moments before he enveloped her in a crushing embrace.

"You're here," Father said into her hair. "How are you here? Are you all right?" He held her at arm's length, looking her over. Tears rolled down his smiling face. He grabbed her hand to look at her wrapped forearm. "What happened? How bad is it?" Without waiting for an answer, he hugged her again, his hand clutching the back of her head.

She relaxed against him, all her stress and worry melting away as she rested her forehead on his shoulder. *Everything's all right now.* She didn't even mind the chainmail under his tunic pushing into her skin.

"I was afraid I'd lost you," Father whispered.

"What?" She leaned back to look up into his eyes.

"How did you escape?" Worry lined Father's usually joyful face. He pushed her tangled hair over her shoulder. "No, no, actually, we have to get you home. Your mother is worried sick. You can tell us everything after you've gotten cleaned up and rested."

"I don't understand." She smiled despite her confusion. "Where are you going? How did you know I was in trouble? Did Minerva send word?"

"We were going to look for you." Father rubbed her shoulder, his laugh lines crinkling into a familiar smile that warmed her very soul. "And Minerva did send word, but her messenger was followed very shortly by someone else." His smile wavered as his brows knit together. "I must admit…I am confused you agreed to a marriage before I'd even met the young man in question."

Her stomach fell like a rock. *No. Etiros, please. No, no, no…*

"Hello, love." The world swayed as she turned from her father toward Nolan's voice. Nolan smiled broadly, looking relieved as he swept her into an embrace. Her whole body went stiff as one of her throwing knives, her arms plastered to her sides.

"Get the hell *away* from her!" Boots pounded dirt as Regulus ran up behind Adelaide. He grabbed her shoulder and pulled her back, shoving Nolan's shoulder with his free hand as he drew her in close. "You don't touch her."

"Hargreaves." Nolan's eyes narrowed. "I'm very interested to hear how you ended up wandering around *alone* with *my* betrothed. Seize him."

Panic turned her limbs to stone. Had Nolan already turned Father against Regulus? But Father's knights made no move to dismount.

"I give the orders here, Sir Carrick." Father held his left hand out to her, his right grasping his sheathed sword. "Adelaide, what's going on?"

She reached for his hand, like a little girl who wanted her father to keep her safe. *No. Wait.* Father needed to know she trusted Regulus, not Nolan. She shook her head and pressed against Regulus' chest.

"This is my betrothed, Lord Regulus Hargreaves."

Regulus gave her shoulder a gentle squeeze.

"Ha!" Nolan drew his sword. "I had my suspicions. The Black Knight rode a large, black horse. That's what that witless Sir Hostland said." He pointed the sword at Sieger. "You have a large, black horse. You were missing when Adelaide went missing. And you tried to challenge me to a duel when you learned of our engagement. *You're* the Black Knight who kidnapped *my* betrothed."

"You and I are not engaged, Nolan!" Adelaide glared as she wound her fingers between Regulus'. She glanced at the knights, waiting in the road a little behind Father. She recognized all of them, although Sir Ruddard and others were absent. Sir Charing looked relieved and happy to see her. Most watched impassively.

She couldn't admit Nolan had forced her into agreeing to his marriage proposal, not in front of knights who knew she always had a blade on her. So many had mocked the Khastallander tradition behind her back, but her training had earned begrudging respect from most of them. She wouldn't appear weak and afraid, or give them reason to think they were right to doubt her.

"Adelaide, love." Nolan's look of pity and tenderness made bile rise in her throat. "Whatever this mercenary did, whatever threats he made, you're safe now. I don't care what happened. I still love you." He pointed his sword at Regulus. "But if you kidnapped and despoiled her to try to force her into marrying you, I'll have your head."

"Enough!" Father's authoritative bellow rang out like a command on a battlefield. Nolan actually shrank back. Father's iron grip latched onto Adelaide's arm, and he led her away. With reluctance, she let her hand slip out of Regulus'. She felt the tension in Father's body as he put his arm around her and led her several paces from Regulus, Nolan, and the knights. His eyes flashed as he turned toward her. Crimson flooded his strained face.

"Did this man…harm you?" Fury laced Father's clipped whisper.

"No! He saved me."

"Is that the truth?" Father cradled the side of her face in his hand. "It wouldn't be your fault. You should know that. No one will ever know. Sir Nolan seems sincere, and I would hold him to his word. But if this…Hargreaves hurt you, if he touched you—"

"Father, no." She pulled his hand down and held it between hers. She shuffled her feet and glanced toward Nolan and Regulus. They glared at each other, Nolan in chainmail and still holding his sword at the ready while Regulus stood unarmed and without armor. She gulped. The knights looked down at them from their horses. Would they be able to stop Nolan in time if he attacked? She couldn't risk provoking him. "I promise we will explain everything. But for now, trust that Regulus isn't a threat. He would never hurt me."

Father sighed, then looked over her shoulder. "I don't know what's going on here, but I agree that you have a lot to explain, Lord Hargreaves." He looked at Nolan. "You all do."

After sending a knight to the Drummonds to inform them of Adelaide's safe return, they headed home. Father insisted he ride next to her as they returned to his castle. She didn't mind. She'd missed him more than she had realized. To her relief, Father also insisted Regulus and Nolan ride on opposite sides of the group where neither could harm the other.

It was almost midnight when they arrived at the castle. Even in the dark, with hardly any moonlight thanks to the clouds, she recognized every angle and curve of the immense crenellated walls and towers. The northern part of the wall to the left of the main gate was whole again after being knocked down to accommodate adding a one-level expansion of five rooms and a second hall for Father's eldest, Landon, and his wife and infant. In the dim light, she made out the shadowy outline of scaffolding and piles of unfinished stone.

Father left the men with instructions to keep Regulus and Nolan separate and to tell the steward to put them in guest rooms. He led her to his own suite, but Mother greeted them in the hall before they even neared the door. Her black hair hung over her shoulder in a loose braid. The light of Father's candle reflected off Mother's tears, making her brown skin glisten. Her silk robes swished as she ran to Adelaide, sobbing.

"I couldn't sleep. Then when I saw your father had returned, I thought…" She cried into Adelaide's shoulder and squeezed so tight, Adelaide could hardly breathe. "*Meana sohka keh ton ner suche oh, mareh piahry ledekah.*" *I thought you were dead, my darling girl.*

"I'm all right." It was only half true, and her voice broke on a sob. "I'm alive."

Mother finally pulled back and looked her over. She wiped away Adelaide's tears and then her own. "What's this?" She brushed her fingertips against Adelaide's bandaged arm. "Are you hurt?"

"Just some scratches." She shrugged. "We were attacked by kanadosi."

Mother looked around, then lowered her voice. "You didn't heal it? I don't want you using your abilities, but this doesn't look good."

"I can't." Adelaide looked at her feet sinking into the plush red carpet in the hallway and held her arm against her chest. She took a deep breath to steady herself. The words lodged in her throat. Father placed a comforting hand on her back. "I don't have my magic anymore."

Mother gasped and Father's fingers tightened against her back.

"It's a long story. I'm too tired to tell it now."

"Right." Mother took her hand. "Come, I'll have a servant draw a bath—"

"I just want to sleep."

"Of course. Sleep well, Adelaide." Father kissed the top of her head. "We'll talk tomorrow."

CHAPTER 3

BEFORE COLLAPSING onto the plush bed in a cozy guest room, Regulus locked the door and wedged a wood chair under the handle. He wasn't about to risk Carrick sneaking in to cut his throat in the middle of the night. He wished he knew for certain Adelaide was safe, but he would have to trust the castle was secure enough to keep Carrick from getting to her. Dreams of prowling through the castle to relieve Carrick of his head wove through his sleep.

The next morning, a short, portly servant with a balding head knocked on his door and brought in a tub, followed by several servants bearing buckets of heated water. As they filled the tub, another servant brought in a silver tray piled with eggs, ham, and potatoes. Regulus devoured the food. The balding man left and then reappeared with clothes, which he laid on the chair. He told Regulus he would wait outside to escort him to Lord Belanger after his bath.

The bath water turned repulsive, filling with dirt and blood. His bites and scratches burned. The wound on his upper arm wasn't bad, but the one on his shoulder started bleeding afresh. He had to hold his soiled shirt on it for several minutes before the bite stopped bleeding, covered by a thin layer of clotted blood. He scrubbed himself clean then put on the clothes, a pair of brown trousers, and a dark blue shirt. They fit him well enough, if a little tight across the shoulders.

Once he'd pulled on his boots, he met the balding servant in the hallway. The man led him down several hallways and two staircases. Regulus marveled at the decorative weapons, massive tapestries, and oil paintings on the walls. He knew Lord Belanger was wealthy, but…this was impressive. The man had to be nearly as wealthy as Baron Carrick himself. Not that Regulus had ever been inside the baron's castle. Still, Carrick hadn't been wrong. Arrano needed some beautifying to deserve Adelaide.

The servant opened a door and motioned for Regulus to enter. He walked into a spacious room with tall, open windows, bookshelf-lined walls, a few cushioned armchairs, and a couch. Lord Alfred Belanger stood looking out a window, his hands clasped behind his back. He turned as the servant closed the door.

Lord Belanger wasn't as tall as Regulus, but taller than average. Short, gray hair framed his square face and broad forehead. He had to be in his late fifties. Wrinkles around his eyes and mouth hinted at a playful personality, but he wasn't smiling now. In fact, he looked murderous. He stood tall, his spine straight as a lance. His shoulders back, feet planted. A stance that conveyed authority and anticipated respect. The stance of a warrior. Of a commander.

"Lord Hargreaves." His rich baritone was icy.

"Lord Belanger." Regulus bowed. "Thank you for your hosp—"

"I have neither time nor patience for niceties, Hargreaves." Belanger rubbed his temple. "I want to know your story. I've heard Nolan Carrick's. I know his father, and he seems a sincere young man. He made some serious accusations against you." Belanger's right hand twitched like he longed to grasp a sword. "But there are many things that do not add up and he cannot explain. My daughter is…" He worked his jaw and clasped his hands behind his back again. "Hurt. I want to know how and why. So tell me your story."

Regulus shifted. "First, Lord Belanger, I want you to know I love your daughter. I only want to protect her."

"Sir Carrick said the same thing."

"Carrick is a liar and villain!" He bit his tongue and tried to rein in his temper. To display proper decorum. He was starting behind, and he needed to give a favorable impression.

"Again," Belanger said dryly, "Carrick said the same of you."

"Of course he did." Regulus rubbed the back of his neck, his shoulders drawing together. "My lord, where *is* Adelaide?"

"That's not your concern at this moment."

"With all due respect, it's my *only* concern at this moment." Regulus glanced behind him at the door. "I need to know she's safe. Where's Carrick?"

"Are you implying Sir Carrick is a threat to my daughter's safety?"

"No, my lord. I'm telling you plainly that he is." Regulus crossed his arms. "I swear I will tell you the full truth. I promised Adelaide I would. But not until I know she is safe."

Belanger frowned, his gaze cold as steel. "You dare insult me by suggesting my daughter is not safe in my own home?" Before Regulus could answer, the door banged open.

"Oh, thank Etiros!" Adelaide ran in, still limping, followed by her mother. She hugged Regulus, her damp hair smelling of lavender. "I couldn't sit still for fear of Carrick and you running across each other alone. And I wanted—"

"Adelaide!" Lady Belanger's voice held both warning and disapproval, and her accent thickened. "I told you, your father wishes to speak to Lord Hargreaves alone."

Adelaide laced her fingers between Regulus' and turned to face her father. Her shoulder pressed against his. "I'm not leaving him to face Father alone." She smiled up at Regulus and some of the tension in his shoulders eased. He smiled back. She looked at her father. "And I'm not being apart from him while Nolan Carrick is here. Where is he?"

"If he's where I sent him, waiting in his guest room." Belanger tapped his foot, his frown deepening. "Why?" He gestured toward them. "Why do you throw yourself at this man you claim is your betrothed, then ask about another man who tells me *he* is your betrothed? Why do you both seem to think Carrick a threat?" Belanger's voice rose to a shout. "And why does everyone think you can be betrothed when I haven't agreed to anything?"

Regulus squeezed Adelaide's hand, hoping she sensed his support for whatever she chose to say. He wanted to defend her. But honestly, he had no idea where to start. And Belanger seemed distrustful of him already.

"I'm not throwing myself at anyone," Adelaide said, her tone irritated. "And I love Regulus." She squeezed his hand in return. His spirit gave a little leap of joy, and he couldn't stop his grin. Belanger squinted at him, lips pursed.

"Nolan was trying to court me," Adelaide continued. "He needs to marry or his parents will disown him." Regulus raised his brows. She had left out that detail, but things suddenly made more sense. "Technically, I *did* agree to marry him—"

"You shouldn't be agreeing to marry anyone without consulting your mother and me, and you've promised yourself to two men?" Belanger sounded equal parts bewildered and furious. "I would never have expected such dishonorable—"

"Nolan was threatening to have Regulus arrested and hanged for treason against the king!" Adelaide's shoulder rubbed against his as she took a deep breath. "Among other threats. He threatened and blackmailed me into an engagement."

Belanger's jaw went slack. He took a few steps to a nearby armchair and leaned against its back as his face turned ashen. "Did he hurt you?"

"No—well…I'm fine."

Sensing her hesitation, Regulus looked down at her with a frown. She shuffled her feet, a look of indecision reflected in her brown eyes. Hot rage flamed over his skin.

"You didn't tell me he hurt you."

She fiddled with her hair. "It was nothing."

"Did he hurt you or not?" Belanger asked softly.

"I…" She licked her lips. "Fine, yes."

"What? When?" Regulus shifted to see her face better. "That night at Arrano?"

"No." She didn't meet his eyes. "After the tournament. The morning after Harold and Sieger. I shouldn't have wandered so far off; been so secluded."

Regulus clenched his free hand. "As if being alone excuses him?"

"Well, no—"

"What. Did. He. Do." His chest heaved with each word. *When I see Carrick next…*

Adelaide kept her gaze on the floor. "He threatened to reveal I was a mage if I didn't marry him. I told him to tell whoever he wanted. He got too close and I drew my dagger. I nicked his cheek, but he was too quick. Too strong. He broke my wrist and took my"—she glanced up at him apologetically— "your dagger."

Regulus worked his jaw. So that was the real reason Carrick had the dagger Regulus had won in the joust and given to Adelaide as a courtship gift. Carrick had realized she could heal her wrist so he could get away with hurting her. And that monster was somewhere in this castle. Worse than Regulus' anger was his guilt. She had agreed to marry Nolan, knowing if he had hurt her once, he might again. All to save his pathetic life.

"I was going to tell you. After dinner. But then he was there, and after he agreed to leave you alone if I married him, I couldn't…" Adelaide gripped her skirt and stared at the floor. "He told me there would be consequences for not agreeing to marry him. I didn't think he would move so quickly. If I hadn't been there…"

"He'd have killed me," Regulus finished. "Or tried, anyway."

Adelaide looked up with watery eyes. "This is why I didn't tell you. I didn't want to see the look in your eyes that you have now."

Regulus unclenched his fist and tried to relax. He knew what she must be seeing. The fury and violent intent. The stony determination he wore into battle like a second set of armor. All the darkest parts of himself. The parts that didn't deserve her.

"Nolan Carrick will pay for his crimes," Lord Belanger said, drawing their attention. A vein in Belanger's temple throbbed and his white-knuckled hands gripped the back of the armchair. "But that doesn't clarify what has happened since Adelaide disappeared. So…what?" He massaged his forehead with the palm of his hand. "You two ran away? Were you captured by a Black Knight and Hargreaves saved you, or was Carrick correct in his assessment that Hargreaves *is* the Black Knight and he kidnapped you?"

"No!" Adelaide exclaimed. "I mean, that is—well…sort of. It wasn't…uh…"

All right, Regulus. The truth. However painful. He breathed in, his shoulders rising and falling as he gathered his resolve. "Carrick wasn't lying about everything. I did take Adelaide. And his guess wasn't wrong. I am—was—the Black Knight."

Behind them, Lady Belanger gasped. Lord Belanger stepped around the chair toward him, rage in his eyes. Adelaide stepped in front of him, blocking her father from attacking.

"Wait! He didn't exactly *take* me." Adelaide cast a chastising glare at Regulus that made his cheeks burn. All right, perhaps he might have been more tactful. She looked back at her father. "I agreed to help him." She turned around and placed a hand on his chest. Looked into his eyes. "Tell him. Tell him exactly what you told me." His gut clenched, but he took courage from the love in her gaze.

"It all started two years ago."

He told the entire story. The forest. The sorcerer's demand that Regulus serve him or watch his men die. They moved to the seats. Lord and Lady Belanger took a couple of the armchairs. Regulus and Adelaide sat with their thighs touching and held each other's hands on the couch. He didn't have the mark anymore, but he showed them the scars from his attempts to remove it.

He told them about the sorcerer admitting he was the Shadow that had hunted down all the mages in Monparth twenty-two years ago. About the sorcerer demanding he deliver Adelaide. Together they told the rest. Nolan showing up at Arrano. Adelaide visiting him the next day and agreeing to go to the sorcerer. The mark the sorcerer put on her arm. Their trek up the mountains, the crying statue predicting death and destruction, everything. Whenever his throat tightened with shame over what he had done, Adelaide filled in the details, somehow making him seem less at fault than he felt. Sometimes they had to go back and clarify something out of chronological order. A few times Lord Belanger looked on the verge of leaping across the room and strangling him.

"I could scarcely believe my eyes when the mark was gone," Regulus said. "And then he removed Adelaide's. I was finally free. *We* were free. But then…" He bit his cheek. "It happened too fast. I didn't know what was happening, but he was hurting her. He said if I intervened, he'd kill her."

"It's not your fault," Adelaide murmured.

"What's not his fault?" Lord Belanger demanded.

Lady Belanger said something in Khast, her eyes wide and tone breathless.

"Yes. The sorcerer took my magic." Adelaide shuddered, and Regulus squeezed her hand. "But look. This is why I was looking for you." She beamed at Regulus, then held her free hand in front of her. After a moment, her palm glowed faintly blue, then brighter.

Regulus gasped. "It's…back?"

The light died out and she sighed, her shoulders sagging. "A little. I can feel a tiny spark of energy for the first time since he took it, but…it's weak, and more exhausting to summon."

Relief and hope surged through Regulus. "Maybe you just need time."

"Maybe." She shrugged, but he saw the fear in her eyes.

"What happened next?" Belanger coaxed. "Your injuries?"

"We left while the sorcerer repaired the staff," Regulus said. "The injuries were from kanadosi."

"Then we came here." Adelaide looked to her parents. "To ask for help with Nolan."

There was one other reason why Regulus had both supported and dreaded going to the Belanger's. He wanted her father's blessing. But perhaps they should allow her parents to process everything else, first, before he added marriage to the list.

"We thought we would be safe here," Regulus added. "Thought we could avoid Carrick until we had a plan."

Lord Belanger steepled his fingers, his elbows resting on the arms of his chair. But when he spoke, it wasn't what Regulus was expecting. "This…sorcerer. What did you say he called himself again?"

"The Prince of Shadow and Ash." Regulus hated saying the ridiculous title after two years of only saying it under compulsion. "He fancies himself royalty."

"And he *is* the Shadow? He killed the mages?" Regulus nodded, and Belanger rested his chin on his fingers. "And ash…" Belanger shook his head, deep wrinkles lining his forehead. "What does he look like?"

Regulus and Adelaide exchanged a confused glance. "Short," he said. "Built like a baker, or a scholar, I suppose. A bit tubby."

"Graying brown beard," Adelaide added. "Maybe in his early fifties. Very pale. Narrow nose. Deep-set eyes."

"Usually his face is partly hidden under a hood. But he has long graying brown hair and wiry eyebrows. Black eyes." He looked at Lord Belanger, suspicious. "Is this a test? Do you think we're lying?"

"I wish you were." Belanger stood, his eyebrows knitting together. He left without another word. Regulus looked to Adelaide, but she shook her head. So he looked to Lady Belanger, but she was staring at the open doorway, looking equally bewildered. She must have felt him looking, because her gaze cut to him. Regulus' chest tightened. That look was not promising. She muttered something under her breath in Khast.

"Mother!" Adelaide's eyes widened. She responded in Khast, her words rushed and offended. He looked desperately between them, trying to determine what they had said. Based on the ruddy tone in Adelaide's cheeks and the shock in her eyes, plus the judgmental scowl Lady Belanger was giving him, something unfavorable toward him.

Lord Belanger returned carrying a framed canvas as big as his torso with the back toward them. He set it on an armchair and stepped aside. Regulus' blood froze and his mouth fell open. Adelaide's grip on his hand tightened. He blinked at the painting.

A man who at first glance might have been the sorcerer, except he wore a black doublet, a red cape, and a gold crown. And on closer inspection, he didn't look that much like him. This man was kinder and younger, with a wider nose and blue eyes. But the man in the painting and the sorcerer could be…no.

"Please tell me that's not what I think it is," Adelaide said. Her fingers dug into his palm.

"It's the portrait I had commissioned of His Royal Majesty King Gawain a few months ago." Belanger sighed. "And your faces answer my question. He bears a resemblance to this sorcerer."

Regulus' mind spun. The sorcerer prince. The king's elder brother, born a mage. As per Monparth's laws in agreement with an ancient treaty with the surrounding kingdoms, his magic prohibited him from inheriting the throne. The prince who, as the story went, disappeared before returning as a sorcerer and trying to murder his own parents. What was his name?

"The sorcerer prince was killed," Adelaide breathed. "King Olfan said he died."

"And King Gawain told me in confidence that the mages sent after his brother wounded him, but he escaped. He doesn't know if his brother is dead. King Olfan often wondered if his son was behind the Shadow. But he couldn't very well admit that." Belanger looked at the painting and tapped his hand against his leg.

Regulus wanted to look away from the portrait, but his horror left him frozen, staring at this kinder version of the monster he had served.

"I assured the king it seemed unlikely. Years without so much as a whisper, surely he was dead," Belanger continued. "But a sorcerer of the correct age, claiming to be a prince, who you both clearly think bears at least a passing resemblance to the king…" He sighed and shook his head. "And there's more."

Regulus glanced at Adelaide, his nervousness and discomfort rising. Her eyes mirrored his panic.

"When Kirven tried to kill King Olfan and Queen Gwyneth, may they rest in peace, he told them he would take Monparth if he had to burn it to the ground. Even if it meant he would be a king of nothing but ash." He drew his lips into a hard, thin line.

His words hung in the air like smoke trapped in a room without a chimney. *Shadow and Ash. Death and destruction.* Regulus pushed off the couch as the world swayed. He leaned on the arm of the couch as his stomach seized and his hands shook.

"No. No, it can't be." Regulus shook his head. He pushed his sleeves up over his elbows, trying to cool down. The fireplace still stood empty, but he could have sworn he was standing near a raging inferno. "He can't be…that would mean…"

Treason. He'd aided a man who had tried to kill the king. And if he had tried once, now that he had a weapon designed to destroy… Words failed him, and he dropped to his knees with a strangled cry of anguish and rested his feverish face against the side of the couch.

"Oh, Etiros. What have I done?"

"The Staff…" Adelaide's voice resounded in his head like a gong as he fought the panic strangling him. "He said he searched for the pieces for decades. That's all he was waiting for. He wants to kill the king. He is going to take Monparth by force."

"We have to warn the king." Regulus stood, even though his legs shook. "I have to. He gathered all the pieces because of me."

"Hm." The new voice startled him, and Regulus spun toward the sound. Carrick stood in the doorway, arms crossed, leaning his shoulder against the frame. "Aren't you all—"

Regulus didn't wait for him to finish his thought. His anger from earlier returned full force, shocking him out of his stupor.

"You!" He charged at Carrick, angling his shoulder to slam into Carrick's chest. Carrick straightened and braced his hands against Regulus' shoulders. Regulus squinted in confusion as Carrick pushed back like Regulus was a weak, unruly child. With force that threatened to snap his clavicles, Carrick shoved. Regulus' heel caught on the rug and he teetered. Had he really lost this much strength and stamina when the sorcerer removed the mark? He straightened as Carrick kicked him in the ribs. The impact felt more like a battering ram than a boot.

Pain exploded across his ribs and he fell onto his back. The back of his head slammed onto the floor, the rug doing little to cushion the blow. Adelaide shouted his name. He couldn't suck in a breath. His right lung ached behind his injured ribs. The tightness and pain likely meant one thing. They were cracked.

"As I was *saying*." Carrick closed the door and pulled down the bookshelf next to it to barricade the door. "Aren't you all clever. Well done, Lord Belanger." He applauded sarcastically as Regulus finally drew in a full breath. "But I can't let you warn His Majesty."

CHAPTER 4

ADELAIDE GASPED, snapping out of the shock that rooted her in place. She rounded the couch. "Nolan, what are you doing?"

Something wasn't right. Nolan shouldn't have been able to get Regulus down that effortlessly.

"Really. This could have been simple." Nolan rolled his eyes. "I'd stay there if I were you, Lord Belanger."

Father strode past, his face pinched with fury. Before his hand found Nolan's throat, Nolan stepped forward and grabbed Father's shirt with both hands. Her heart stopped as Nolan picked Father up and threw him across the room. Father hit the stone next to the fireplace and crashed to the ground. Adelaide screamed. Mother ran to him, crying out for the guards. Adelaide's throat constricted as Mother knelt beside Father, his body looking like a discarded rag doll. He raised his head, then moaned and let his head fall back to the carpet.

Regulus stood, bent over and clearly in pain. As Nolan turned back, Regulus threw a wild punch. His fist made contact with Nolan's jaw with a crack. He drew back for another punch, but Nolan shoved against Regulus' chest while moving his foot behind Regulus' leg. Regulus stumbled backward and fell to the ground with a groan.

"Regulus!" She darted forward as Nolan grabbed Regulus' right arm and yanked it backward against his leg. The snap of bone nearly made her vomit. Regulus yelled in agony.

Adelaide pulled her dagger out of her boot and sliced at Nolan's chest, but he evaded her blade. She stood next to Regulus, dagger held in front of her and at the ready. Nolan took another step back, and she risked a glance down. Below Regulus' rolled-up sleeve, the sharp edge of a bone pushed against the skin in his forearm, like the bone wanted to break through but couldn't. She gagged. His face looked deathly pale, and huge drops of sweat beaded on his forehead.

Nolan adjusted his belt and smoothed his shirt. "I must admit, I didn't expect the mercenary to tell the truth. I hoped if he did, the good lord and lady wouldn't believe it. A sorcerer living in the woods, forcing your obedience? How unrealistic compared to a tale of kidnapping and seduction and dishonorable behavior. I didn't think he would, but I'd hoped Belanger would kill you, Hargreaves. He looked ready to after I spun my tale this morning. Alas, no. But I *really* wasn't prepared for you to figure out the sorcerer is Prince Kirven. Well done."

She stared, her hands going cold. Her heart raced. None of this made sense. "How do *you* know about the sorcerer?"

"Oh, Adelaide. If you had paid more attention to me instead of Lord Half-Breed, you'd know I'm an expert hunter." Nolan flashed her a smile with all the warmth of knives. "That was clever, making it look like the Black Knight kidnapped you and telling that knight to tell both Hargreaves and me in order to turn suspicion away from Hargreaves. He rode straight to Arrano, where I was tearing the place apart looking for you. I had my suspicions about the authenticity of your supposed kidnapping, so I went after you with only my men. I tracked you. Right to the prince's tower. What an interesting conversation we had."

Her lungs felt leaden, like she had forgotten how to breathe. Dread grew in the pit of her stomach. "About what?"

"Oh, you know. Power, politics, revenge, mutual goals and annoyances." Nolan looked pointedly at Regulus. "Plans for overthrowing the king. Normal treason things."

No. Please, no. She gulped, horrified at her rising suspicion.

"I made a nice deal with the prince." Nolan rolled up his sleeve, and the sight of the mark on the interior of his right forearm—two hollow black diamonds and a half diamond open toward his wrist—made her shudder. "I serve him when he calls, and I get strength, speed, and agility beyond belief…and immortality." He pulled his sleeve back down. "I don't understand why you were in such a hurry to get rid of it, mercenary. If you didn't have a martyr complex, you wouldn't have had to deal with the pain. But don't worry." He reached behind him and drew a dagger.

He tossed the dagger in the air and caught it, and Adelaide's grip on her own dagger tightened as she recognized the flash of swirling ivory. Regulus' dagger from the tournament.

"You can't feel pain when you're dead." Nolan moved forward, eyes fixed on Regulus.

"No!" She lunged toward Nolan and aimed a cut at his stomach. He dodged, as she knew he would, but she was already coming around with a stab aimed at his heart. Nolan hit her arm away with his forearm, and her blade sliced across the side of his arm. He hissed and grabbed her neck. Before she could react, he threw her backward. She coughed as she hit the ground beside Regulus. Her dagger slipped out of her hand and spun across the floor.

Panting, she turned and threw herself over Regulus. She wrapped her arms around his head, shielding his torso and head, but careful not to lie on his broken arm. Her entire body shook as she looked up at Nolan. She needed to distract him.

"Why would the sorcerer want you? Why would he need you?"

Nolan paused and shrugged. "Because he gave his word he would free Hargreaves. And, for whatever reason, his word is important to him. He wanted a new assistant to help him put his plans of conquering and domination into effect."

"He told you his plans?" Regulus asked, his voice weak and tight. He coughed and groaned. She wished he would shut up instead of drawing attention to himself.

"See, if you had been thankful for the gifts he gave you for one moment instead of fighting him all the time, he might have let you in, too. But, no. I'm certainly not going to tell you all his secrets." Nolan knelt near Regulus' head and met Adelaide's eyes. She leaned lower over Regulus and held Nolan's gaze, silently daring him to go through her to get to him.

Nolan balanced Regulus' dagger on the tips of his fingers. "But I *will* tell you this—the sorcerer has promised me that he will spare anyone who is with me when he takes over. Conversely, though, I'll be in a position to see that anyone…undesirable…dies. So it might be a good idea to curry my favor before we welcome the new king."

"You're not his partner." Adelaide shook her head. "You're his slave!"

"The contract I signed with him that promises me a duchy says otherwise." He gave her a self-satisfied smile. "You didn't think His Highness would seize the throne without thinking about how he would rule Monparth once he had it, did you? Even sorcerers need loyal nobles to rule successfully. Unfortunately, that falls apart if anyone alerts the king. I'll kill anyone necessary to prevent that." He leaned closer to her, and she shivered. "But not you, Adelaide. That's not what I want. I want you at my side as my duchess."

Regulus tried to push her away with his good arm, but Adelaide didn't budge. "You're out of your mind," she spat.

"You don't even love her, do you?" Mother shouted. She still knelt next to Father, who appeared to be regaining his breath.

"You'd all already be dead if I didn't love her." Nolan reached for Adelaide. Still shielding Regulus, she couldn't pull back.

"If you love me, you'll leave." Adelaide met his eyes, determined not to flinch.

"Maybe we have different definitions of love." He ran the back of his fingers down her cheek. "I *want* you, though." His voice dropped to a husky murmur. "By my sword, do I want you." She gulped against the fear strangling her and drying up her tongue.

"Adelaide—" Regulus coughed, the sound wet and concerning. "Move!" He pushed against her side. But she stayed frozen, as if Nolan's touch had turned her to stone.

"I've set my mind on having you, and now I can't get you out of my head," Nolan said, his eyes tracing the contours of her face. He returned Regulus' dagger to the back of his belt. "And so many people, including my parents—*especially* my parents—believe we're engaged." He seized her arm. "I won't be shamed by you marrying that mongrel instead."

Chapter 5

"WE MADE a deal, Adelaide." Nolan yanked Adelaide to her feet, nearly pulling her arm out of its socket. Her knee hit Regulus' side as Nolan pulled her up. Regulus moaned. Nolan pulled her away, and she stumbled after him, her left ankle aching in protest. "By denying me and accepting *his* proposal, you've broken our deal." He pushed her against the side of the couch, still gripping her wrist painfully tight. The back of her legs pressed into the couch arm. "Therefore, his life is mine to end."

Adelaide trembled. She looked to her left at Regulus panting on the floor and tried to pull her wrist free. Nolan clicked his tongue. "Can you heal your wrist if it breaks again?"

She stilled, unsure. And any magic she had, she wanted to use to heal Regulus. She couldn't agree to marry Nolan. But she couldn't watch Regulus die, either.

Nolan smiled. "I do hope you're right about your magic coming back. I was disappointed to hear while eavesdropping that the prince took it. Ah, well. That was just an extra perk. Magic or no, I desire you." He moved closer, his eyes fixed on her lips.

Adelaide stiffened and leaned away. Only Nolan's legs against hers and his grip on her wrist kept her from falling over the side of the couch onto the cushions. "You repulse me."

She bit her tongue. Hurt flickered in Nolan's eyes, but he chuckled.

"I'll change your mind." He looked at Regulus, who had managed to sit up and was holding his broken arm against his chest. "Not only is my inheritance, my family name, my home, and my pride at stake, but also sweet revenge. The chance to put a no-account bastard back in his place." He looked back at her, and the greed in his eyes turned her blood cold. "And prove I'm more of a man."

How did one defend against an immortal? How could she save herself and Regulus? With Regulus and Father injured, did they have a hope of restraining Nolan? Her mind seemed a frozen river, the thoughts moving too slow, too slow. She stared past Nolan at a bookshelf, unwilling to meet his eyes. *Etiros, help us, please!*

"Look at me, love." Nolan's voice was sickeningly gentle.

"Adelaide." Mother's voice. "Move!"

Adelaide reacted without thinking. She ducked toward the middle of the room. A fleshy thunk and then Nolan yelled. He dropped her wrist and backed away. The handle of a throwing knife protruded from Nolan's shoulder.

Nolan cursed and yanked the knife out. Blood soaked into his shirt. He gasped and fell to his knees as Mother threw another knife into his heart.

"I don't care if you're supposedly immortal," Mother said as she readied another throwing knife. "I'll kill you if you touch my daughter again!" She threw the knife, but Nolan jumped aside and it bounced off the bookshelf behind him.

Someone banged against the door and men shouted. The guards were trying to get in. Nolan looked toward the door, knife still stuck in his chest.

Adelaide spotted her dagger on the ground and dove for it, but Nolan grabbed her hair as she shot past him and pulled her back. She fell to her knees and her eyes watered from the strain on her scalp. The bookshelf blocking the door teetered as the guards tried to break down the door. She twisted around, yanked the knife out of Nolan's chest, and stabbed at his throat. He held up a hand, and the blade went straight through his palm. He looked at his hand with wide, wild eyes, and pulled away. Blood ran off the knife still in her hand and streamed out of his palm, filling the air with a sharp metallic scent. Nolan yelled and released her hair as he stumbled away.

The door rattled and thumped against the bookshelf. Adelaide pulled on the bookshelf, straining to move it away from the door. *Come on!* Why wouldn't it move faster? Nolan half walked, half fell toward the windows.

"You'll all regret this!" Nolan pointed at her with a bloody hand. "I'll be back for you. You're *mine*. You hear me, Hargreaves? MINE!" He turned and leapt through a window with a crash and a cascade of falling glass.

As three guards burst into the parlor, Nolan ran across the courtyard. One guard hurried to Father and Mother. The second asked her if she was all right. She nodded, and he went to Regulus. The third guard paused only for a moment before heading after Nolan.

Adelaide stared at Nolan and the shouting guard. She scarcely believed how fast Nolan was running for the stables with the blood he'd lost. The guard would never catch him. If he got to his horse, the only way to keep him from escaping would be to make sure the gate was closed before he reached it. She looked at Father, his face pinched as the guard and Mother helped him sit up.

Regulus sat against the back of the couch, staring at his broken arm as the guard left him to pursue Nolan. She couldn't decide which would be worse—if Nolan escaped, or if the guards caught him. Nolan might tear them apart.

Adelaide tried to control her violent shaking as she walked over to Father and Mother. "How bad is it?"

Father straightened with a groan and put a hand to his back. "I don't think anything is broken. Just blacked out for a minute there. There's definitely bruising and something is out of place." He smiled bitterly. "Were I twenty years younger, I'd be unfazed."

Mother grasped Father's face in her hands and kissed him. "Don't you scare me like that, *mareh piahre.*"

Father tapped her under the chin. "You don't have enough faith in me. It'll take more than a traitor under the influence of dark magic to kill this legend, *piahre cha mareh gehvam.*"

Love of my life. Adelaide smiled and walked back to Regulus as her parents kissed again. But as her gaze fell on the jagged bone pressing against his skin, her smile dropped. She sat next to Regulus. "How are you?"

"Nothing's bleeding, so there's that." He smiled, but the tightness around his eyes spoke to his pain as a cough rattled in his lungs. "Your father speaks Khast, then?"

"A little. Basically all he knows is curse words, terms of endearment, and some flirtatious phrases that make my mother blush."

"How do you know about that?" Father demanded.

Adelaide smirked. "Because you're so used to no one knowing what you're saying, you forget I speak Khast, too!" She rolled her eyes and turned back to Regulus.

"What phrases? Dresden says my flirting needs help." Regulus coughed and grunted, his face twisting. "Any…good ones?"

Her brows pulled together. "What are you doing?"

"What do you mean?"

"You seem…oddly calm." Her own hands still had a slight shake.

"Distracting myself." He closed his eyes and leaned his head back on the couch. "It's how I helped my men through bad injuries. Get them to think and talk about anything else." He coughed and moaned. "Just…talk to me?"

She opened her mouth to ask what hurt the most but jumped when her half-brother's shout interrupted her.

"Fath—what happened!" Landon stood in the doorway, face pinched and eyes bulging as he took in the chaos in the parlor. "I heard shouting, and a guard said a guest attacked…" He gestured at Regulus. "Who's this?"

"This is Lord Regulus Hargreaves of Arrano." Adelaide ground her teeth. "Nice to see you too, brother."

"Oh. Adelaide. I was glad to learn you're alive and well." Landon crossed to Father without a second glance at her.

She clenched her jaw and turned away. Eleven years her senior, Father's second child and eldest son had never paid her much attention—but neither had any of her other half siblings. Of course, disappearing with little explanation with her mother for several years hadn't helped.

Questioning concern reflected in Regulus' eyes. She shook her head and took his broken right arm as Father told Landon that Nolan was a liar and a traitor to the crown. "Maybe I can try—"

"Don't worry about it." Regulus shook his head. "What if you use what you have and then it's gone for good?" He coughed and a bit of blood leaked over his bottom lip.

"I'll take that risk." She held her hand over the jutting bone, hoping that would be easier and faster than his ribs, which based on his coughing, might have punctured his lung. If she healed the ribs first, she might not have enough magic left for his arm.

She dug deep for the spark of magical energy flickering in the carved-out place in her soul. Rather than removing a cork from a full flask like when she used her magic before, this felt like squeezing the last drop of water out of an empty wineskin. The familiar warmth spread across her hand, and she perspired from the exertion. Regulus relaxed as the pale-blue light spread over his arm. The bone straightened, no longer threatening to break through the skin. She focused on his arm. In the energy flowing out of her and into him, she sensed the bones and muscles and tendons pulling back together. Healing.

She could feel his arm was healed, so she moved her hand to his ribs. White spots danced in her vision, and she blinked them away. But she detected four broken ribs and internal bleeding. She focused on the bleeding first—healed the puncture and collapsing lung and forced the blood to reabsorb, then worked on maneuvering the ribs back together. Her hand shook.

Regulus placed a hand on her shoulder. "Hey, perhaps you should take a breather—"

"Shh. Concentrating." Black circled the edges of her sight. She swayed and her hand bumped Regulus' ribs. "Sorry." She shook herself. *A bit more. Come on. Give me a little more, Etiros.*

"Adelaide, stop!" Regulus sounded panicked.

The conversation behind her died as Landon exclaimed, "What in creation?"

Her eyes drifted shut as she sank into unconsciousness.

CHAPTER 6

THE LIGHT on Adelaide's palm vanished as she slumped forward, and Regulus caught her shoulders. "Adelaide?" When she didn't respond, he pushed her hair away from her face. Her eyes were closed, and her head lolled to the side.

"Adelaide!" Lord Belanger shoved Regulus aside and pulled his daughter into his arms. She slumped against him, limp and unmoving, her eyes still closed. Belanger rested the back of her head in the crook of his arm. "Ad, wake up." He glared at Regulus. "What happened?"

"She healed my arm, then started healing my ribs." Regulus touched his ribs. He suspected they were still cracked, but as usual, her magic had numbed the area. "She started looking ashen, and her eyes went all unfocused, and then she swayed and she…passed out." Tendrils of dread threaded through Regulus' heart.

"She shouldn't be using her magic at all!" Lady Belanger crouched between him and Adelaide and took Adelaide's hand.

"Wait, wait, Adelaide is a *mage*?" The wiry man with mousy brown hair Adelaide had called brother crossed his arms. "Since *when*?"

"Mages are born, so forever," Lady Belanger said, her voice rising. "We kept it a secret for her protection." She gave Regulus a look that could kill. "To prevent things like this! Like everything that has happened since she met *you*!"

He ducked his head. "The sorcerer would have found her whether she met me or not. Whether she kept her magic secret or not."

"I've half a mind to have you thrown in the dungeon, you—" She added several words in Khast that were clearly not complimentary.

Lord Belanger cleared his throat. "Tamina, this anger isn't helping."

"There's a *sorcerer* now?" the brother shouted.

They all ignored him. Regulus sat up and shifted to see around Adelaide's mother. Adelaide's lips were parted, and her chest rose and fell in gentle, rhythmic breathing. She looked peaceful, if exhausted. *Please be okay.*

A guard walked in and saluted Lord Belanger. "My lord, Nolan Carrick has escaped."

Regulus leaned back against the couch, dread replacing his relief. Their best chance had been to take Carrick while he was weakened. He remembered the fury and precision with which Adelaide's mother had thrown those knives and felt a growing discomfort about her current disposition toward him.

Lord Belanger nodded. "Double the guards. Make sure everyone knows what Nolan Carrick looks like. If he approaches the castle, attack to kill, but proceed with caution. He is a monster, not a man." The guard bowed and departed, but Belanger's last words cut Regulus to his core.

He had also born that mark. He had also benefited from strength, speed, and immortality granted by sorcery. Was that how Adelaide's parents saw him? A monster, not a man?

"She needs taken to her room," Lady Belanger said.

Belanger moved to stand, still holding Adelaide. He grimaced and dropped back down. "My back… I can't lift her. Landon, give me a hand."

The brother's eyebrows lifted. "Me?"

"No, I'll carry her." Regulus knelt next to Lord Belanger and moved his arms under Adelaide's legs and back. Something metal and sharp pressed under his chin and he froze. He looked at Lady Belanger out of the corner of his eye. She held her dagger to his throat, her mouth curled down. "Tell me why I should trust you."

"Because Adelaide trusts me."

"Tamina," Belanger said gently. She looked at her husband without lowering her blade. "Adelaide intends to marry him." His expression was unreadable. "I haven't decided if I'll allow that, but he's right. She trusts him. Maybe don't kill the man your daughter wants to marry just yet."

The tip of the dagger pressed into Regulus' skin and he tried to control his breathing. After a moment, she lowered the dagger. "All right. But if I determine you have tricked or hurt my daughter in any way, if you are anything less than the man Adelaide deserves, I will slit your throat without a second thought."

"I understand." He picked up Adelaide. Thanks to Adelaide's magic, his ribs didn't hurt, but they would doubtless complain about this later. Her head rolled onto his shoulder. "Which way?"

Lord Belanger stayed behind to talk to his son while Lady Belanger led Regulus to Adelaide's room. He hadn't been thinking about how large the castle was when he decided to carry her, but he wasn't about to let her out of his sight. And he disliked the idea of Landon, who appeared to hold little affection for his sister, carrying her.

The pain in his ribs returned faster than he had hoped, although not as bad as before Adelaide started healing them. She must have undone at least some of the damage. Still, to his irritation, his lungs soon burned, but he pressed on. He had done fine before his bond to the sorcerer, he could manage fine now. Besides, he was used to pain.

Lady Belanger pulled back the thick blanket on Adelaide's four-poster bed and Regulus laid Adelaide down as gently as possible. She didn't even stir as he moved her head onto her pillow and brushed her hair away from her face. He kissed her forehead, then winced at the hissing intake of breath from Lady Belanger. He kept his heated face turned away from her by pulling the covers over Adelaide.

"All right, that's enough," Lady Belanger said. "Out." With a sigh, he turned away from the bed.

"Reg…" He spun back, bending over Adelaide. Her eyes fluttered as she tried to keep them open. "Regulus."

"I'm here." He pulled her hand out from under the covers and clasped it in his own. She wrapped her fingers around his hand and shifted, moving over on the bed.

"Don't leave me."

"I won't." He rubbed her hand. "I promise."

Adelaide's eyes drifted shut and her breathing deepened. She still clung to him. He sat on the edge of the bed, unwilling to extricate his hand.

Lady Belanger cleared her throat. "You can't stay here."

He bit back his initial response. *I've spent the last several days and nights with your daughter unattended, I'm not going to do anything untoward now.* Might not help his case much. "She asked me to stay."

The door opened with a quiet squeak of the hinges, and Lord Belanger peeked in. He frowned at Regulus before stepping inside and closing the door behind him. Lady Belanger crossed her arms.

"He won't leave."

"She asked me not to," he repeated.

Lord Belanger raised a brow.

"She was half asleep," Lady Belanger protested.

Lord Belanger continued to survey them without speaking. Regulus focused on Adelaide. She looked serene. Unworried. And beautiful as ever.

"He's in love with her; of course he won't leave." Regulus looked up.

Adelaide's father looked resigned.

"Hmph." Lady Belanger gripped her braid. "I always feared she'd fall for someone like you. All stubbornness and passion with a warrior soul and a stupidly self-sacrificial heart."

"I'm very unsure if you're insulting me or complimenting Lord Hargreaves," Belanger responded with a grin.

"Both." She sighed and cut a disgruntled glower toward Regulus. "She needs someone to tame her wild spirit, not encourage her recklessness and put her in more danger."

Regulus frowned. "With all due respect, my lady, Adelaide doesn't need tamed. She's as dangerous as the nickname *you* gave her." He combed his fingers through her hair spread across her pillow. "She's a *shiraa*. Like a tigress, she shouldn't be caged. She's perfect as she is." He looked back at Adelaide's parents. "And I love her. I'm going to marry her."

"The last man who said that viciously attacked us in our own home," Lady Belanger said, but most of the venom had vanished from her tone.

Regulus clenched his free fist against his leg. "I would never hurt Adelaide or anyone she loves of my own free will. I would gladly die for her."

Belanger tilted his head, regarding Regulus with a thoughtful expression. "What if I challenged you to a duel?"

"What? Why?" The ache in his ribs increased as he tensed.

"For getting my daughter enslaved to a sorcerer, even temporarily." Belanger folded his arms and narrowed his eyes. "For putting her in a situation where she suffered pain and could have died. For letting a sorcerer take her magic. For calling her reputation into question by appearing with her after several days, alone." Belanger shrugged. "Take your pick. I have more reasons to challenge you than not to at this point."

"Please." Regulus swallowed back the knot in his throat. "Don't."

He couldn't argue. Even though he did everything under compulsion, even though he had tried to keep Adelaide as safe as he could when he didn't have the choice of saying no, he *had* still done all those things. His shoulders sagged.

"Whatever punishment or recompense you see fit, I will do it. Put me in the stocks, order me lashed, tell me what payment you want. But don't challenge me." He let his head fall. His chin rested against his chest. Exhaustion weighed him down. "Because I will accept, but I won't fight you. I won't harm my love's father."

"I won't give you my blessing."

"Then I'll have to earn it." He met Belanger's stare and squared his shoulders. They stared at each other for what felt like a small eternity, but Regulus refused to be the first to look away.

Lord Belanger's expression eased into a smile. "I like him, Mina." Regulus let himself relax and shifted to ease the growing pain in his ribs.

"Of course you do." Lady Belanger flung her hands out to her sides. "He's too much like you!"

"You like me well enough." Belanger moved behind his wife and wrapped his arms around her, leaning forward so his head was next to hers. "Come on, *piahre*. Leave them be."

"But—"

"You'll send for us when she wakes?" Belanger asked. Regulus nodded. "See?" He led his protesting wife out of the room and closed the door behind them.

Regulus waited only a couple minutes before he laid on top of the comforter next to Adelaide, careful of his ribs. Adelaide burrowed into his side in her sleep.

Chapter 7

REGULUS DIDN'T remember falling asleep, but as the sound of voices cut through the darkness, he pried open his heavy eyes. He moved and clutched his side, biting back a moan as a stab of rippling pain spread over his ribs. It had been awhile since he'd had to deal with lingering severe injuries. Adelaide leaned over him, her concerned face filling his field of vision.

"Easy there. The physician's on her way." She bit her lip. "I can't muster enough power to heal you again. There's something there, but...I can't reach it."

"It's really not that bad." He smiled as convincingly as possible. "Help me sit up?"

She moved back and helped him sit. He had to clench his teeth to keep from crying out as his ribs pinched. Carrying Adelaide had been a bad idea. But he would have done it again. Now upright, he noticed Lord and Lady Belanger sat in wooden chairs on the other side of the bed, near Adelaide. They watched silently as he moved back to lean against the wall at the head of the bed.

"I have good news." Adelaide beamed, her eyes twinkling. "Mother has agreed not to blame you." She winked at Regulus and he laughed, then clutched at his ribs again. Her smile faded.

"I'm fine." A lie he was used to telling. He smiled and shook his head. "Maybe a kiss would help, though."

Lord Belanger cleared his throat and Regulus' face burned. He'd been so focused on Adelaide he'd already forgotten they were there. But Adelaide grabbed the sides of his face and kissed him full on the mouth. He closed his eyes, put his hands on her waist and kissed her, not caring that her parents were watching. It took every ounce of his self-control not to pull her back in when their lips parted.

"Better?" she whispered, her eyes dancing. She still held his face in her hands.

"Better."

Lord Belanger cleared his throat again, more obviously this time.

"Please." Adelaide rolled her eyes and dropped her hands from his face as she turned toward her parents. She leaned back on her hands. "You two can't talk."

"Fine." Lord Belanger flushed. "I suppose that's fair."

A knock sounded at the door, and an older woman with a crown of gray braids walked in carrying a wool bag.

"Maggie!" Adelaide motioned the woman over with a warm smile. "This is Lord Hargreaves. He needs his ribs looked at."

The woman—Maggie, apparently—walked over to the bed, her gaze darting between Adelaide and Regulus with curiosity. She set the bag on the bed. "Take your shirt off."

He hesitated. He needed her care; but did it have to be here, in front of Adelaide and her parents? She would have to see someday, but he'd hoped it would be after they were married—when it wouldn't matter anymore. Well, he could hide the most embarrassing ones, at least. As he pulled off his shirt, he kept his back close to the wall.

Adelaide gasped, and heat rushed up his neck to his ears. He wished it was a gasp of appreciation, but he knew it wasn't. He was scarred. Several were from his time as a mercenary, like the one on his face. Many were from the last two years. The sorcery had healed him, but left scars. Some small and easy to miss. A couple were large, like the uneven white scar across most of his abdomen from the dragon's tail.

Maggie glanced up at his face, then turned her attention back to his ribs. "Hm."

He looked down. A stab of pain accompanied the movement. Blue and purple bruises marked yellowed skin over his injury. She pressed against the ribs with cold fingers. He gritted his teeth and flinched away.

"Hold still, dear." Maggie ran her fingers over his ribs.

Regulus stared at the gauzy green fabric suspended over Adelaide's four-poster bed, ignoring the ache and stabs.

"Definitely cracked," Maggie said. "And these…" She turned his arm to get a better look at the scabbed bite marks and red skin on his arm, then pulled him a little away from the wall to prod at the bite on his shoulder. He twitched against the prick of pain but tried to stay still.

"Anything you can do?" Adelaide put her hand on top of his.

"I'll salve the bites to fight infection, as I did with your arm. They should heal all right. The ribs will need salved, wrapped, and he'll need to keep movement to a minimum." Maggie pushed against his ribs again and he clenched his teeth until his jaw ached. "But they appear to be aligned and not threatening his lungs. He will heal, but it will take time."

The breaks had been worse before Adelaide started to heal them. Breathing had been difficult and agonizing, but he'd tried to hide the blood he'd coughed up. He hadn't coughed since she healed him. Adelaide looked downcast, so he gave her a reassuring smile. He couldn't say anything in front of Maggie, who he guessed didn't know about Adelaide's magic, but he hoped Adelaide saw the silent thank you in his smile. She had healed his arm, and his ribs weren't threatening to burst his lung. He counted that as a win. And Adelaide was alive and well, bigger win.

"Swing your legs over the side of the bed." Maggie fetched a stool from in front of Adelaide's vanity. She set it next to the bed and her forehead wrinkled when she saw Regulus hadn't turned. "This isn't an ideal angle, my lord."

Regulus gulped and did as instructed, his face already burning with humiliation. Maggie didn't seem to notice as she pulled a pot out of her bag, covered her fingers in sweet-smelling green salve, and began working the salve over his bruised ribs.

"Regulus…" Adelaide's fingers brushed his back, and he cringed. A chair creaked as someone shifted.

"There are many reasons someone is whipped," Lord Belanger said quietly. Maggie's fingers paused before resuming her ministrations. "Normally, I wouldn't pry, but you're pursuing my daughter. Discipline or torture?"

Regulus sighed and closed his eyes for a moment. "Mercenary discipline." He winced as Maggie bumped a tender spot on his side. "Happened once."

"What did you do that deserved a whip?"

Regulus chewed his lower lip. Would Belanger even believe the truth? But he'd promised Adelaide the truth. "Our captain was strict. My friend snuck out and missed his watch. I covered for him." *And earned extra lashes for my lie.* But Drez wasn't whipped, and that was all that mattered.

"You tried to hide your scars," Belanger said. "Why?"

He bowed his head as Maggie tended to the bite on his arm. "I am not ashamed of what I did. But…" He gulped. "My back looks like a slave's. That is unlikely to improve the opinion my intended's parents have of me." Maggie fumbled the jar, nearly dropping it as she scooped out more salve.

"Scars are nothing to be embarrassed about," Belanger murmured.

Lady Belanger cleared her throat. "Scars, especially unearned ones, are the least of my concerns."

"I don't want you ever to feel you need to hide from me," Adelaide said softly.

Their words soothed as much as Maggie's salve, but he still felt uncomfortable in the silence that followed. He looked over his shoulder at Belanger, grasping for a new subject. "We need to warn the king."

"I've already written His Excellency." Belanger rested his chin on his fist, watching Regulus thoughtfully. "I explained everything and recommended he postpone his annual birthday masque in a few weeks. I sent a falcon an hour ago."

The news brought no relief or consolation. Would the king even be able to stop the sorcerer—Kirven? The crying stone woman haunted his memories. *Death and destruction.* But they'd had to take the opal. Regulus suspected they had been seconds away from the sorcerer taking control of one of them. Now they had done the only thing they could—they had warned the king.

"Wait, his birthday masque?" Adelaide asked. Belanger nodded. "Prince Kirven attacked his parents on a Court Day, didn't he?"

"Yes…" Belanger's eyes widened. "When the castle was open and there were nobles present. He wanted a spectacle. And I was only worried about the security nightmare of a masque."

"Maybe he'll be patient enough to wait for the masque to attack," Regulus said. Maggie rubbed the cool salve over the bite on his shoulder. "That might give us more time to figure out how to stop him."

"But if the king cancels the masque, will he attack immediately?" Lady Belanger asked.

"We have warned the king." Belanger folded his hands. "And Kirven failed once before. Worry gets us nowhere."

Silence and the floral aroma of Maggie's salve filled the room. Dust particles floated in the sunlight angling through Adelaide's window between the dark, heavy curtains. Maggie put her salve away and pulled out a roll of narrow strips of white cloth. Regulus tapped his fingers against the bedspread.

"Lord Belanger—"

"Oh, Alfred. Please. Lord Belanger is a mouthful, especially among equals." Alfred raised a brow. "I hope you don't mind if I call you Regulus."

"Oh. Of course." He glanced at Adelaide, nervousness making him antsy.

"Hold still," Maggie chided as she tightly wrapped the bandages around his torso. He took a deep breath and stopped fidgeting.

"I feel the need to be more formal for this." He straightened his back, trying to look as confident as possible while sitting on a bed and having his wounds treated. "Lord Belanger, Lady Belanger. I would like to formally ask for your blessing to marry Adelaide."

Maggie froze, then wrapped more frantically. Lady Belanger frowned. Alfred crossed his arms and leaned back in the chair.

"I believe," Alfred said, eyes narrowed, "you mean to ask for my *permission.*"

"Respectfully, sir, I do not." He met Adelaide's eyes. "Adelaide asked me to marry her, and if she'll still have me, I will." Adelaide smirked, her eyes glittering.

"She…asked you?" Lady Belanger sounded incredulous.

Adelaide giggled. "I think I more told him to marry me than asked."

Maggie tied off the bandaging and stuffed her things back into her bag. "That should do. My lords. My ladies." She curtsied and fled the room.

"No," Lady Belanger said, her accent thickening. "You're too young—"

"I'm twenty-one!" Adelaide protested.

"And how old is he?" Lady Belanger flung her hand toward Regulus.

Regulus pulled his shirt back on, grimacing at the ache in his side. "I'll be thirty in two months."

"Thirty!" Lady Belanger gripped the arms of her chair. "Why—"

"*Piahre,*" Alfred patted her arm. "They're closer in age than we are."

"That's different." Lady Belanger slumped back in her chair.

"How is it different?" Adelaide waved her hands. "Father had five children and was thirty-two when he met you. You were twenty!"

"Fine, but we hardly know him." Lady Belanger huffed. "We met Gaius before he asked to court Minerva. And then he courted her for several months before he asked for her hand. And you've been through a trying ordeal. This could be manufactured emotion—"

"My lady, with respect, I knew I loved Adelaide long before the events of the last few days." Regulus put his arm around Adelaide, trying to remain as friendly as possible without backing down.

"Gaius was afraid of Father turning him down," Adelaide said. "He wanted to ask sooner. Minerva told me as much. And I wanted to marry Regulus before any of this happened. Father…what do you think?"

Alfred paused before answering. "I think you risk being shunned by society if you marry a bastard and a mercenary."

"He—" Adelaide started, but her father held up his hand. Regulus' gut twisted with the sting of Alfred's bluntness.

"Your mother and I raised you not to live your life in narrow-mindedness. Let's review what I know about Regulus. I know his past. I know he caused you pain and put you in danger." Alfred stood and clasped his hands behind his back as he turned away from them. "Yet I know that he has repeatedly put himself at risk for your sake. He has shown a concern for your safety, and a protectiveness for his friends. I know that you love him, and I can see he loves you. I know he makes you happy and you trust him."

Alfred faced them with a sad smile. "And I trust you." He looked at Regulus. "But I have two questions for Regulus first. And I want your complete honesty."

Regulus inclined his head. Nerves made him twitchy, like he should be fighting or ready to fight. With a slow exhale, he focused on looking unconcerned and honest.

"Why did you become a mercenary?"

The direct question was like a punch to the gut. His arm slipped off Adelaide as a jumble of emotions overcame him. Through the glass of Adelaide's window, he watched a flock of small birds fly in a mass, like a black wisp of cloud.

"Why does that matter?" Adelaide asked. "He was a warrior. Like you."

At least that explained why she had never asked. Unlike most people, she heard mercenary and assumed warrior—not brigand.

"No, Ad." The gentle sadness in Alfred's voice hurt worse than if he had flat-out accused Regulus of being dishonorable. "I served my king. For duty and honor and to protect my family and friends. I need to know why he fought."

The birds dove into the sprawling branches of a massive oak. Perhaps the truth would help—at least they would know he wasn't just a treasure-hungry, blood-thirsty barbarian. Her father was right to ask. But the truth would highlight his other flaw.

"He's a good man," Adelaide said. "And so are his men. They're honorable—"

"I asked Regulus." Alfred tapped his fingers against his crossed arms. "And his silence is rather loud."

Regulus sighed. He focused on Adelaide, on the way his heart ached for her companionship. "You deserve the truth."

She shook her head. "It doesn't matter—"

"Yes. It does." He picked at some lint on the covers. "My guardian—a distant cousin—reviled me. I lived with him for twelve years, and he took every chance to punish me, to mock me, to remind me my birth was an unfortunate *mistake*. But I endured for the hope that after I was knighted, I could go home. Or at least somewhere I could be accepted." He worked his jaw, ashamed of what a naïve idiot he had been.

"A couple weeks before my knighthood ceremony, my father sent a note and a gift." He smiled ruefully. "It was a sword. Plain and unassuming, but expertly made. The note said he was proud and wished me the best, but he wouldn't attend my knighting."

Adelaide placed a hand on his thigh. He shrugged.

"I hadn't really expected him to come. But I had hoped." Regulus shifted, studying the twisting carved posts of Adelaide's bed. "About a week later, Dresden and I were out for a run. Three men attacked us. We weren't armed, but we fought them off and caught one." He paused.

He'd never told this story before. "Lady Arrano had sent them to kill me."

No one made a sound, but the shock in the room was palpable. Adelaide's hand slipped off his leg. Regulus avoided eye contact. He didn't want their pity.

"I finally realized the truth," he continued. "Even once knighted, that wouldn't be my world. Dresden was my manservant, and he was my only friend. I had no idea my father wrote me into his will in the event of my half-brother dying without an heir until I inherited Arrano two years ago. At eighteen, I had no family, no home, no future."

"I'm sorry," Adelaide whispered.

Regulus ignored his discomfort and continued. "I joined the first mercenary troop I found. Dresden joined me. Later, I led my own troop. I strove to be as honorable as possible." He summoned his courage and met Alfred's inscrutable gaze. "I regret that being a mercenary affects how people see me. But I don't regret what I did. I met good, loyal men who became my friends. I killed, but I also saved people. I am not ashamed of how I led my men."

For several tense moments, Alfred stared back. Adelaide gave his hand a gentle squeeze. Regulus was about to offer to answer any further questions they might have about his mercenary history when Alfred spoke.

"Thank you for your honesty." He was relieved to see kindness, not judgment, in Alfred's eyes. "Your birth does not concern me. Your actions do. But I have one more question, and I expect an immediate answer. From you, not Adelaide."

Regulus braced himself, trying to guess what he would ask. About his time as a mercenary? About serving the sorcerer? The worst thing he had ever done? He clenched his jaw as he flashed back to his hand squeezing Adelaide's throat as the sorcerer controlled him. Although that was only the worst thing he'd been *forced* to do. He had made many terrible choices as a mercenary. Alfred's gaze bored into him, like he was looking into his very soul. Regulus fought the urge to flinch under his scrutiny.

"Did you have relations with my daughter?"

Blood drained from Regulus' face. "No! I swear it—"

"Father!" Adelaide flushed dark red.

"I respect—"

"We didn't—"

"I wouldn't—"

Alfred held up his hand, silencing them both. Regulus held his breath, ready to protest. "I am satisfied. Wary, as fathers always are, but satisfied. I give you my permission *and* my blessing."

"Thank you, sir." Regulus let the tension out of his shoulders and allowed himself to breathe again.

"Alfred," Adelaide's father said, "please."

"Thank you, Alfred." Regulus inclined his head. Lady Belanger still sat back in her chair, her lips pressed together. "Lady Belanger? Adelaide loves you. I don't require you to approve of me." He was accustomed to living under the weight of everyone's disapproval. "But I do desire your blessing."

"Mother," Adelaide said softly. "Please."

Lady Belanger blinked, her eyes moist. The tendons in her neck stood out and her temples pulsed as she worked her jaw before speaking in Khast.

"Oh, Mother." Adelaide pushed off the bed. Regulus' hand fell off her shoulder as she moved to her mother and pulled her into an embrace. She said something in Khast into Lady Belanger's shoulder. Her mother's hands clenched her hair as she responded. Regulus watched, unsure what to do or where to look. He seriously needed to have Adelaide teach him some Khast.

When they separated, both women had tears on their faces. Regulus looked to Alfred, more than a little terrified. But Alfred was looking at his family, his own eyes watering. Lady Belanger said something else he didn't understand, then stood.

"Regulus."

He moved to that side of the bed and stood. She was an inch or two shorter than Adelaide and darker, but she looked up at him with similar dark brown eyes. A few strands of silver hair stood out against her black braid. She considered him, then hugged him a little too hard and immediately stepped back.

"You better not hurt my daughter."

"Never, my lady."

CHAPTER 8

ADELAIDE SMILED as she dried her tears. *"You're my baby girl."* The tenderness and fear in Mother's voice had nearly broken her. It didn't help Adelaide was still reeling from Regulus' admission his father's wife had tried to have him killed. Even in hiding, she had never known a life without loving parents.

But she hadn't expected Mother to be so hesitant. Sure, after those years together in that cottage, they could only have become close or hated each other. Adelaide loved Father, but until Regulus, she didn't think she could love someone as much as she loved Mother. And Mother had always been protective. She should have expected Mother to fight any suitor.

"I secretly hoped you would stay with me forever." Adelaide hadn't been able to keep from crying at that. But Mother understood, even if she didn't like it. *"I'm glad you've found someone you can love like I love your father. I just don't want to see you hurt."*

"There's something else," Regulus said as he sat back down on her bed, drawing her attention. "Something the sorcerer—or Kirven, I guess—said that I've been wondering about. Something that might help you get your magic back. If that's what you want."

"What?" Adelaide sat back on her heels. Hope swelled, followed by suspicion and doubt. "The sorcerer? I don't want anything to do with sorcery."

"It wouldn't be sorcery," Regulus said quickly. "At least, I don't think so. The sorcerer wasn't much for explaining things most of the time." He sat on the edge of her bed. "One of the ingredients he had me find was the root of a neumenet tree."

"Absolutely not," Mother said, folding her arms. "No."

Adelaide looked between them. "What's a neumenet tree?"

"According to the sorcerer, it's a tree that holds a lot of magic." Regulus looked inquisitively at Mother. "He said a long time ago people would try to conceive children under neumenet trees in the hope of their children being mages. And that it sometimes worked. What do you know about neumenet trees?"

Mother huffed and returned to the armchair. "When we realized Adelaide had magic, I read everything I found, trying to understand and determine how to help her hide."

"We had books on magic?" Adelaide gaped at her mother, hurt and anger cracking through her heart like searing lightning. "You hid them from me?"

"Yes." Mother pulled her braid over her shoulder and fiddled with it. "We hoped the less you knew, the easier it would be to keep your abilities concealed. To keep you safe." She bit her lip. "Maybe that was wrong, but I stand by our decision."

"And one of these books talked about neumenet trees?" Regulus asked.

"A few of them." Mother inspected the leather tie on the end of her braid. "Every living thing has some level of magic, tied inextricably to life itself. It is a reminder of Etiros, the creator and source of pure magic. Sentient beings with high levels of magic—like mages—can use that magic to affect the world around them. For unknown reasons, some non-sentient living things are like wells of magical energy. Neumenet trees are exceedingly rare and hold more magical power than any other known thing. There are legends about its power rubbing off on sentient beings that spend time in its shade, from birds to men. Some theorize neumenets actually *are* sentient."

Adelaide stared at Mother, stinging betrayal making her throat tense. "All these years…you knew about magic and didn't tell me?"

"Adelaide." Father looked at her, his eyes sad. "I lost a good friend and a few acquaintances when the Shadow struck. If there was even a chance not using your gift would keep you safe, I was willing to try it."

Father had mage friends before the Shadow? "You never told me that." She fidgeted with her hands in her lap.

"Some things are…painful to talk about. And difficult to hear." Father scratched behind his ear and bit his lip. "How do you tell your child you…" He shook his head. "You can't tell a child you found a dear friend strangled and hanging from his own balcony because he had the same gifting your child does." His voice shook. "I wanted you safe. I didn't want you terrified."

Silence filled the room as Adelaide stared at her hands. The very air seemed to press in, smothering her. It took her a moment to get her tongue working. "So this tree could help me?"

"It felt ancient and powerful," Regulus said. "Maybe if it can give an unborn child magic, it can restore yours."

"Perhaps," Mother said. "But you can't go running off on a hunch." She laid a hand on Adelaide's head. "Powerful sources of magic attract other powerful magical creatures, both good and evil. The tree might be dangerous. More importantly, it may be best if you are powerless, at least until the sorcerer is dead and can't take further interest in you. And I don't want you leaving this castle while that monster Carrick is out there."

"Best—powerless?" Adelaide sputtered. Mother couldn't begin to understand the emptiness she felt without her magic flowing through her veins. Or the fear.

A frantic rapping sounded on the door, and they all turned.

"Come in," Father called.

The house steward stepped in, clutching his cap in his hands, his eyes wide. His graying blond hair was a mess, as if he had been repeatedly putting the cap on and taking it back off. His bony shoulders scrunched up around his neck.

"My lord, we have a problem, if I may speak with you in private."

Father frowned. "Speak, Titus."

Titus twisted his cap. "Perhaps not in front of the ladies…"

"They will find out eventually," Father responded. "Out with it."

"My lord…we received back the falcon you sent to the king."

Adelaide stood and placed a hand on Regulus' shoulder. What could possibly have upset the steward so much about whatever message the king sent back? The steward shouldn't have even read a message from the king.

"That was fast," Father said, his brow wrinkling.

"It's dead, my lord."

Adelaide dropped onto the bed next to Regulus, her mind and pulse racing. Dead?

"A peasant brought it to us with an arrow through it, your message still in the container on its back." Titus tapped his foot. "He said a man named Carrick gave it to him and paid him to deliver the carcass to Belanger castle." He glanced at Adelaide, then stared at the floor. "The man also said Carrick instructed him to give Lady Adelaide his regards and to tell Lord Belanger to desist."

Adelaide's chest constricted, as if something was pushing on her sternum. She gripped Regulus' forearm and her hands and feet turned cold. Her face felt numb and her mind thrummed with a frantic buzzing. She was vaguely aware of her father dismissing the steward as she struggled to breathe. Her vision went out of focus.

Helpless. Powerless. Useless. She ran through the most likely scenario. The sorcerer would kill the king. Nolan would be a duke with an army of knights at his command. He would storm Belanger castle. Good men would die. Regulus would be killed. Maybe even her father. Nolan would take her. Sweat ran down the back of her neck.

"Adelaide." Regulus' voice cut through her internal scream. He rubbed her back. "Breathe, Adelaide." She took a deep breath. "We'll figure this out. All right?" His hand moved in circles over her taut muscles. His smooth, deep voice washed over her like a hot bath. "Chin up, *Tha Shiraa.*"

Her breathing slowed. The tension in her shoulders eased as the weight lifted from her chest.

"We'll find a way through this together. Together, my brave tigress."

She nodded, her heart rate easing.

"Good." Regulus smiled. "Now, don't take this the wrong way, but your grip is like the jaws of a dragon."

"Hm?" She looked at her fingers digging into his sleeve. With a gasp, she released her death grip on his forearm. "I'm sorry!"

He shook his arm. "I think I was a few seconds from losing feeling in my hand." He winked and laughed nervously.

"That settles it," Mother said with finality. "You're not leaving this castle."

"I concur." Father's eyes flashed with a fury she had never seen. "I'll send another falcon tonight. Perhaps under cover of darkness it will make it. And I'll send messengers by horse and by foot. We'll have to spare a few knights to escort them. He can't stop them all. In the meantime, I'll have a guard posted outside your door. You're not to leave this room without at least two armed guards."

Adelaide's mouth hung open, but she couldn't formulate a response.

"Alfred, I understand where you're coming from, but I don't think that's going to work." Regulus continued to rub her back as he spoke. "I have experience with this. Carrick is nearly unstoppable, especially since he is eager to do his work. The sorcerer is likely stronger with the staff, and that may be reflected in Carrick's abilities as well. Your only hope is for your messengers to get past Carrick without him catching them. And we don't know if he is working alone or if he pulled some of his associates into his scheme with promises of fortune."

"What do you suggest I do?" Father said heavily.

"Send out *all* your falcons, to anyone and everyone you trust, all at once. Tell them to forward your message to the king. Hopefully one will get through, and no lives will be needlessly thrown away."

Father nodded but looked doubtful. "It's worth trying."

MOTHER AND Regulus played checkers while Adelaide laid on her stomach, hanging off the end of her bed. She tossed her dagger and caught it. Father had gone to write messages to all the dukes, several barons, and to a few lords. All she could do was wait. She hated it.

Mother had beaten Regulus for the third time, much to his clear disappointment, when the door burst open and Father flew in. "They're dead. Almost all of them."

"What?" Adelaide caught her dagger and sat up. Father's face was drawn and pale. He clutched an arrow in his hand.

"A servant went to the aviary to feed the birds." Father shook the arrow. "This was on the floor, with a small pouch and a note tied to it." He thrust out his other hand and opened it, revealing a shredded off-white wool pouch and a rolled-up piece of parchment. "The pouch was full of seed. The birds got into it." He clenched his fist around the pouch and note. "Poisoned. Most of them are dead, and a few are close. We're not sure if the others didn't eat any or if they haven't reacted yet."

Mother cursed in Khast, her eyes wide with horror. Adelaide gripped her dagger tighter. It seemed impossible. The aviary was located at the top of the south-eastern tower. Even though it had the largest window in the entire outer defense, someone would have to be a phenomenal shot to make that.

"We found a few identical arrows wedged in the moss on the sides of the window, and another inside," Father said, as if reading her thoughts. "They didn't have the pouch or note. He must have tried several times to ensure he would make the window."

"Who poisons an entire aviary?" Mother asked.

"The kind of person who orders a horse hobbled to send a message to its owner," Regulus muttered.

"I have to send messengers," Father said. He leaned back against the door. "And pray he doesn't kill them all."

"You can't send them to their deaths." Adelaide tossed her dagger onto the bed. "We have to figure out a way to send them safely!"

"Our king is in danger. Our home is under attack." Father's expression hardened. "This is war. Sacrifices must be made."

"But—"

"He's not wrong, Adelaide," Regulus said, his voice quiet.

She turned toward him, hurt and surprised. "They'll die."

"Many more people will die, including the king, if he's not warned," Father said. "It is my duty to try."

Adelaide shook her head. She *hated* Nolan. If only she had her magic. With her magic, she could keep Nolan from getting close enough to reach her. Keep him far enough away that his enhanced strength and speed and his immortality wouldn't matter. "Fine. But we need a back-up plan."

Father raised his brows. "I'm listening."

"Send the messengers." Adelaide looked at Regulus, then back at Father. "But let Regulus and I leave right after them for the neumenet tree." Mother and Father started speaking at once, so she shouted over them, "Listen!" They quieted, but neither looked pleased. "Nolan will be focused on the messengers. Send them out, and we can sneak out without him noticing us. If the neumenet tree can restore my magic, I'll be better able to defend myself. And if none of the messengers get through, then I'll go. If I have my magic back, I can get past him, I'm sure."

"That's a lot of if's," Father said with a shake of his head. "It's too dangerous."

"I'm not waiting here for him to take me!" She immediately wished she hadn't said it. But she couldn't keep her fear inside any longer, gnawing away at her heart.

No one said anything for a long moment. She stared at her blurred reflection in the dagger lying on her bed.

Father sighed. "I won't let that happen."

"Alfred." Regulus stood. "Adelaide's reasoning is sound."

"I don't care. She's not leaving this room if it means I have to chain her to her bed."

"Father!" She looked to Mother, but Mother lifted a shoulder, clearly siding with Father. "You wouldn't."

"The messengers will be sent tonight, in two groups, and will all take different routes." Father clutched the arrow and it snapped in half. "You two will be locked in your own rooms."

"Fath—"

"End of discussion." Father turned and opened the door.

"Wait!" Adelaide reached toward him, as if to stop him. He paused partway through the door. "What did the note say?"

"Nothing." Father walked out the door and she raced after him and grabbed his arm.

"Tell me."

"It's not your concern—"

She grabbed his hand and tried to pry his fist open.

"Don't make this harder, Adelaide." Father moved her aside, but she held onto his fist.

"I deserve to know." Her heart pushed against her throat. *He's only targeting you because of me.*

Father sighed and lowered his head. "It doesn't change anything if you know."

"I'd rather know than wonder." She tried to catch his eyes, but he wouldn't look at her.

Slowly, Father unclenched his fist. Adelaide took the crumpled, smashed scrap of parchment from his palm. It crinkled as she opened it. She walked closer to a small window in the hallway and held it up to the light. Nolan's handwriting looked just the same as in the love letters he had sent her what seemed a lifetime ago. Regulus walked up behind her as she read.

I'll tell you what I told Adelaide: You don't want to go to war with me. You can't stop the inevitable, Belanger. Stay out of my way. Final warning. Let's not make Adelaide fatherless if we don't have to, shall we?

Regulus reached around her and pulled the note out of her hands. He read it, then ripped it in half and dropped it to the ground.

Father wrapped his arms around Adelaide and cradled the side of her head in his hand. "It's going to be all right." He kissed the top of her head, just like he did when she was little. She leaned into his chest, taking comfort in his warmth while he stroked her hair. "I've faced many enemies. I'm still here. Don't worry." He patted her shoulder and walked away.

But none were a man who couldn't be killed. Adelaide watched him walk down the hall, back tall, but with a heaviness to his steps that betrayed the weight he carried. She had always thought Father the strongest person she knew. Believed him to be unbreakable. A war hero with laughter and love in his heart. He had never looked so ragged. So unsure. For the first time, she looked at him and didn't feel like everything would be all right.

And it was her fault.

The room was made of layered shadows when Adelaide's eyes snapped open. She listened, trying to determine what had awoken her. She must not have been asleep long; in fact, she was unsure she'd even fallen asleep. Something metallic rasped at the door. Still lying down, she gripped the hilt of her dagger under her pillow and freed it from its sheath, watching the door through half-closed eyes. The door cracked open. Faint candlelight spilled into the room. With a creak, the door opened further. The candle on the floor illuminated a kneeling figure. She blinked against the bright light as the man picked up the candle and stood, her pulse quickening. Under the pillow, she gripped the dagger tighter and prepared to scream.

The man raised the candle, and the light glittered in his eyes and made his scar shine. Her muscles unclenched and she sat up.

"Regulus? What—"

"Shh." He walked in and closed the door behind him. A bulging bag hung from his uninjured shoulder. He'd found a sword somewhere, as one now hung at his left hip. "We're going to the neumenet tree."

"What?" She squinted at the candlelight.

"Unless you don't want to."

"No, I do—"

"Then get dressed. The second group of messengers are about to leave. If we're going to do this, we need to hurry. Plus, it's only a matter of time before someone finds your guards."

Adelaide tossed off the covers and hurried to her dresser. It almost surprised her how quickly she agreed. But it was her plan, after all. Even if the clandestine, against-Father's-orders-thing was unexpected. "What did you do? How did you get here?"

"I picked the locks. And I knocked your guards out. They'll be fine, although they might have a headache when they wake up." Regulus winced. "And I don't envy them the experience of facing your parents."

Adelaide pulled an outfit she sometimes used for combat training out of her dresser and slipped behind her dressing screen. "You know how to pick a lock?"

"It's a useful thing for a mercenary to know."

Oh. She slipped out of her nightgown and struggled into the suede fitted trousers. Next, she slipped on a thin, sleeveless white undershirt and wriggled into a fitted sleeveless leather tunic she had based on a drawing in one of Mother's Khastallander books. With a hemline at mid-thigh in the front and just below her knees in the back, and slits up to her hips on the sides, it could hardly be called a dress. She tightened and tied off the laces over the bust. The back came up to her neck, but the front curved well below her collarbone.

From the dresser she grabbed tall riding boots, a black cloak, a belt, and a baldric with slots for throwing knives she had thought she would never use. Regulus' mouth fell open as she moved past him and sat on her bed to put on the boots.

"That's...you..." He cleared his throat, and she smiled to herself as she laced up her boots. "You look fierce, *Tha Shiraa.*"

Adelaide pulled her box full of weapons out from under her bed. She picked out five throwing knives and put them into the baldric before throwing it over her shoulder and across her chest. After feeding the belt through the sheathes of a couple daggers, she cinched it around her waist. She grinned as she stood and threw on her cloak.

"You're a bad influence, Regulus Hargreaves. This will be twice I've run off with you."

"It's your fault, really." The candlelight danced in his pupils. "You make me reckless." He grabbed her hand. "Ready?"

She stepped forward. "I'll lead. I know every hall in this castle. We'll be at the stables in no time."

"That's my tigress."

They snuck past the guards slumped against the wall next to her door and down the hall. Every moment they spent in the castle set her on edge, every little sound startling her, certain they had been caught. But they made it to the stables and found Zephyr and Sieger without a problem. They saddled them in a hurry, then stole through the shadows to the small servant's gate in the rear of the castle. Just large enough for a horse and rider, and easily blocked off, it presented little threat in case of attack. But it did provide an excellent way to slip out. The two guards standing in front of the gate straightened as they approached.

"Who goes—Lady Adelaide?" The guard on the right bowed. "I'm sorry, my lady, but you have to turn back."

"I command you to step aside." She put as much confidence and authority into her words as she could muster.

"Can't do that, my lady," the second guard said. "We're under orders from your father not to let anyone in or out without his express permission."

"Do you think I would be here without his permission?"

The guards exchanged a glance. "He'd be here if he wanted to give his permission," the first guard said.

Regulus stepped forward. "Look, gentlemen, you're doing a wonderful job. What are your names, so I can commend you to Lord Belanger myself?"

"Um, that's close enough—"

Regulus jumped forward and grabbed both men by the collar of their leather armor. He pushed them back into the stone wall, grabbed their helms, and knocked their heads together with a clang that was sure to draw all kinds of attention. One of the guards staggered in a daze to the side, then sagged against the wall. The other slumped to the ground. Regulus retrieved the key from the belt of the fallen man. He unlocked the door and pushed it open, then turned back, breathing hard.

"Better hurry before anyone else shows up." Regulus winced as he mounted Sieger. Adelaide bit her lip when he pressed a hand against his ribs and grunted.

She mounted Zephyr as a man shouted from further along the wall. Regulus kicked Sieger forward, and she urged Zephyr after him. They raced away from the castle, the wind from their speed pulling at her braid and cloak, the air cool and crisp on her face. She glanced back at the castle, at the cluster of torch-illuminated men near the door.

Be safe, Father and Mother.

CHAPTER 10

THEY DIDN'T dare stop while on Father's land. Too much of a risk of either Father's men or Nolan finding them. Although, if Father's men found them, they'd just be taken back. Nolan was the bigger threat. If Father's men did find them, though, they'd be even more likely to come across Nolan on their return journey. So they rode. When they had put enough distance between themselves and Belanger castle, they stopped in a copse of ash trees surrounded by large bushes. They fell asleep in each other's arms.

Adelaide awakened to pinkish light filtering through the trees, casting long shadows. Regulus was already up, digging through the sack he had brought. She stretched her sore neck while massaging her left shoulder. Regulus reached into the bag and tossed her a red apple.

"How'd you get food?"

"I wandered into the kitchen before I went to bed. Said I liked to have food in my room in case I wake up in the night. The cook seemed confused and concerned I took so much, but he's the cook, I'm the guest and the lord, so he couldn't tell me no." He ducked his head and tied the bag to the back of Sieger's saddle. "Hopefully enough to get us to Holgren and back."

"Holgren? That's a—"

"Royal forest. I know."

She stood and brushed grass and leaves off herself. "What if we're caught?"

"I guess we'll figure that out if it happens?"

That didn't sound like a plan, but she didn't have any better ideas. So she mounted Zephyr and they continued on, toward a royal forest they didn't have permission to enter and a magic tree that may or may not be sentient.

They rode for hours in silence, but Adelaide didn't mind the comfortable quiet. The laughter and squeals of children carried through an overgrown hedge, and she wondered what hers and Regulus' children would look like. They would almost certainly be tall.

"I want to learn Khast," Regulus said abruptly.

She cocked her head. "You do?"

He looked over, his expression earnest. "I want you to teach me Khast. I don't know if I'll be any good, but…it's important to you, so I want to learn."

Adelaide could have laughed with joy, but she didn't want him to think she was making fun of him. "I'd love to teach you, *mareh piahre.*"

"Mar-ay pea-aw-ruh." Regulus said each syllable as if rolling it around his mouth, trying to get a feel for the sounds. "That's what your mother called your father. What's it mean?"

Adelaide gave him a teasing smile. "My love. My father likes to call my mother *piahre cha mareh gehvam.* Love of my life."

"Pea-aw-ruh chaw mar-ay gay-vam." Regulus sighed. "It sounds better when you say it."

Adelaide chuckled. "We'll work on it, *sumdir.*"

He wrinkled his nose. "Now you're just being cruel."

"Never, handsome."

Regulus blushed. "All right, how do you say beautiful?"

"Khast doesn't have a different word for beautiful and handsome."

"So…you're mar-ay soom-dear pea-aw-ruh? My beautiful love?"

His pronunciation sounded like someone trying to speak around a mouthful of marbles, but she grinned nonetheless. "Charmer."

Toward evening, they arrived at the edge of a forest. Wooden signs nailed to tree trunks proclaimed HOLGREN ROYAL FOREST. ENTRY WITHOUT ROYAL WARRANT STRICTLY PROHIBITED in faded white paint. They looked around, but didn't see anyone, so they continued inside.

Regulus paused. "Give me a minute to get my bearings. We don't want to waste time wandering about."

She reined in Zephyr. The fresh air smelled of moss and pine. A couple birds chirped somewhere nearby. Yellow edged in on the leaves of birch trees, announcing that summer was growing old.

A strange prickling ran across Adelaide's skin from head to toe. Almost like a breeze, but the air remained calm. Something deep inside her made her look to the right. The forest looked the same over there, but a voice—more of a sensation than actual words—seemed to tell her to go that way. As if Etiros himself were prodding her deeper into the forest. The familiar warmth of magical energy shuddered through her, brushing over the empty places in her soul and calling to her. She had urged Zephyr forward before she even realized it.

"Regulus," she called over her shoulder. "This way."

"What? Hey, where are you going?" Regulus directed Sieger closer. "Do…you feel something?"

"Yes." Her voice sounded detached. The pull increased. "I can feel it. Like a current sweeping me along."

The external pull of magical energy grew until it felt like it would carry her away. Her breaths came sharper and quicker until Adelaide and Regulus broke through the trees and she saw it. The pull stopped, and her jaw went slack. It was…unbelievable.

Clouds obscured the sun, but even so, the leaves on the gigantic tree shimmered like shards of silvery glass. Some of the light bent as it reflected, sending bright spots of color into the forest. Its black branches stretched out over a meadow and trees a half dozen paces away that bent away from its shade. The trunk looked big enough to fit a bedroom inside, and its black bark was glassy, as if the tree had been carved out of obsidian. She had to look up, shielding her eyes against the glaring light on the leaves, to see the top. Who knew trees grew so enormous?

They rode forward, but their horses got skittish, so they dismounted and walked. "Do you hear that?" She moved toward the tree as if in a dream.

"Hear what?"

"The tree." She couldn't describe the sound. Soft, nearly inaudible. Somewhere between a deep thrumming and a soft, wordless singing. The sound moved through her, calming and frightening her all at once. She reached toward the shiny bark, then paused, her palm hovering inches away from the glossy surface broken by angular edges that caught the light.

Warmth flowed between her hand and the trunk, and she felt the tree. Its life. Its tremendous age. Somehow, she knew, almost as if she had gotten a glimpse of it in her mind, that this tree had been tall when the rest of the forest hadn't yet begun to grow. It seemed to both call to her and warn her. She looked up at the glittering leaves above her. So high above the surrounding forest, they swayed in an unfelt breeze, flashing without a sound. A leaf separated from a branch and floated toward her, arcing back and forth like a falling feather. She caught it in her hand and its softness surprised her. No hard edges, despite looking like glass. She let it fall to the ground and looked back at the trunk.

A noise like a stifled groan behind her caught her attention and she spun around. "Reg—" She gaped at the empty space. Sieger and Zephyr shuffled and whinnied near the edge of the trees. But Regulus had disappeared.

"Regulus!"

"Don't worry," a quiet, shrill voice said. "He's all right."

Adelaide turned toward the voice as she drew a dagger and a throwing knife. Her eyes widened, and she stepped backward. A fairy shorter than the length of Adelaide's hand flew less than a foot away from her face. A sleeveless dress of pale green embroidered with silver hugged the fairy's pale skin. Short reddish hair stuck out in all directions around her delicate face. Her wings beat the air so fast Adelaide couldn't make them out, other than to tell they shimmered with each movement.

"What?" Adelaide's voice squeaked, and she cleared her throat. "Who are…where is Regulus?" She pointed her dagger at the fairy, but the fairy tittered, her laughter like tiny wind chimes.

"This isn't about him," the fairy said. "It's about you."

Adelaide shook her head. "What do you want?"

"To help you, of course." The fairy smiled, showing pearly white teeth with sinister-looking points. Adelaide blanched.

"Where is Regulus?" She put as much force into her words as she could, even as she wondered how one fought a fairy.

"Oh, please. He's hardly the important one here, my dear." The fairy flitted side to side. "You're the mage. You're the interesting one."

Her breath caught. "How do you know what I am?"

"I can feel it, dear. Just like you can feel the neumenet tree. And I know what happened to you. I sense that, too." The fairy tilted her head and gave her a sympathetic look. "You were right to come here. The neumenet tree can help you. Reach out and take it."

Adelaide lowered her weapons. "Take what?"

"The tree's magic!" The fairy smiled again, and chills ran down Adelaide's spine. "You know how to do it, because it's been done to you."

Adelaide stepped backward. She flashed back to the feeling of her magic, her energy, her very life being drawn out of her. Even now the sensation of the tree's power only emphasized the abyss inside her where her magic had once been.

"No. Not like that."

"I'm afraid this is the only way."

"No. That's…that's sorcery. It's taking what isn't yours. It's *hurting*."

The fairy laughed again. "It's only a tree."

So were the trees around the sorcerer's tower. The ones so drained of life they turned white as bones. Trees sapped of energy until they blackened as if they had been burned. The sorcerer took their energy, their magic. And it killed them.

"I'm not a sorcerer. Sorcery takes. It steals and destroys and kills to further your own power." As she spoke, she became more certain. "That's why it's corrupted. It's been twisted from something that helps others to something that helps only yourself at another's expense. I won't get my magic back by becoming like him. Now where's Regulus?"

"Hm. Foolish girl." The fairy waved and pointed. Adelaide followed the line of her finger.

Regulus stood where she had last seen him, but his eyes were wide over his gagged mouth. Rope-like vines bound his wrists together, and more vines wrapped around his arms, tying them to his sides. Several fairies hovered around him, holding the ends of the vines that bound his torso. *Oh, Etiros, no!*

Adelaide's pulse quickened. She clutched her weapons tighter as her breathing became shallower. Not again. She couldn't watch him be hurt *again.* Her mouth went dry. "Regulus." Her voice cracked.

Regulus strained against the fairies, but somehow the tiny creatures held him without any struggle. He stilled and held her gaze, the message in his eyes clear. *Run.*

"There's your man." The fairy sounded bored. "Free him, if you want him back."

ADELAIDE DREW her dagger again and stepped toward Regulus. A blast of white light hit the dagger out of her hand.

"Free him," the fairy taunted.

With a growl, Adelaide drew a knife and threw it at a vine held by one of the fairies. The fairies on both sides of Regulus darted with surprising speed to the side, and Regulus stumbled sideways with them. Her knife sunk into his left shoulder and she cried out as he winced. Adelaide flinched and bit her tongue.

"Oh, dear." The fairy tittered, and the other fairies laughed with her. Their melodic laughter grated on Adelaide's taut nerves. "Better try something else."

She dug her feet into the ground and found every bit of magical energy left inside. It wasn't much, like a river reduced to mud. She pushed her energy out, sending blinding blue blasts at the fairies on either side of Regulus. The blasts hit the fairies, and they dropped backward, but held onto the vines and recovered quickly. Adelaide panted, sweat beading on her forehead as her vision swam. She didn't have another blast in her. She recalled the warning in the *Compendium*. Mages who drained themselves of their magic died. She looked at the first fairy.

"Please. Let him go."

"Free him."

"I can't!" She clutched her hands to the side of her pounding head. "Please!"

"Yes, you can," the fairy said in a sing-song voice. "Take power from the tree."

Adelaide shook her head. "I can't."

"You mean you won't." The fairy crossed her delicate arms. "I suppose we'll take him with us. He should make a good slave."

"No!" She held her hands out and stepped toward the fairy, her heart pounding.

The fairy flitted backward. "Lay your hand on the trunk. Pull its magic out into yourself. It has plenty to share, you won't kill it. You can't hold all the power it holds. Just take a little. Save your love."

She looked at Regulus, desperation making her heart pound. Blood ran down his arm from her knife. He struggled against his bindings, but to no effect. Even with her magic depleted, she could sense the magic holding the vines in place. She would need a great deal of magic to free him.

"I'm not a sorcerer," she whispered. Tears stung her eyes. "I won't hurt others to help myself."

"But you've already hurt your dear Regulus," the fairy reminded her. "And you could lose him forever."

No. No, no, no. She turned toward the tree and reached toward the trunk. *Etiros, forgive…* Her hand shook. This was wrong. Something deep inside whispered it shouldn't be like this. Stolen power would only leave her hungry to take more. Somehow, she knew. If she did this, she would become as power hungry as Kirven.

"I'm getting bored," the fairy said. "I think perhaps we should take our new slave and go."

"No!" Adelaide turned back to the fairy. "Please! I'm begging you!"

"Don't beg me, fight me!" The fairy thrust her tiny hands toward Adelaide.

White light slammed into her chest, pushing her backward. She had no strength to even raise a shield. The magic of the neumenet tree thrummed next to her, but she ignored it. *Etiros, I don't know what to do.*

Adelaide fell to her knees and hung her head as tears rolled down her cheeks. "Please. Don't take him." She wouldn't lose him now. Not after everything. "I won't steal power like a sorcerer. But I can't lose him." She looked at Regulus through her tears. He gave her a nod, and she knew he was agreeing with her decision not to steal magic, but it made the tears flow faster. She would watch him until he was gone. Unless…

"Take me, too," she choked out.

Regulus shook his head, eyes bulging. He tried to say something through the gag, but it was unintelligible. Adelaide looked at the fairy hovering above her.

"If you must take him, take me too. I won't leave him."

The fairy flashed a sharp-toothed smile. She flew down until she was right in front of Adelaide's face. "Give me your hand."

Regulus made more muffled grunting sounds as she held her hand out, palm up, toward the fairy. The fairy landed on her palm. She was so light; Adelaide hardly felt her. Her wings stopped beating, and Adelaide marveled at the two pairs of translucent, shimmery green wings. The fairy clapped her hands, the sound bizarrely quiet.

"Adelaide Diya Belanger, you've passed the test."

Adelaide gasped as power flowed from the neumenet tree into her. A rush of energy and life, a swelling in her very soul. If Kirven stealing her magic had felt like dying, this felt like the first breath of air after drowning. The colors around her flared with vibrancy. The smell of the grass, the pine trees in the distance, even the freshness of the dirt hit her with unexpected clarity as every nerve ending tingled with life.

The fairy fluttered back up, hovering a short distance away. Adelaide dropped onto her hands as her head spun, dizzy from the rush of magic coursing through her veins. Strong hands gripped her shoulders, and she looked up at Regulus' concerned expression. She grinned.

"My magic is back."

His features relaxed and he smiled. She pulled her knife from his shoulder and healed the hole it left behind. Then she healed his ribs. As soon as she stopped, he pulled her into an embrace.

She hugged him, then looked up at the fairy. The fairies who had been holding Regulus now hovered behind the first fairy. There were men and women wearing various earthy colors, all with the same delicate, beautiful features, but with skin tones from ebony to as white as the first fairy and everywhere in between.

"That was a cruel test," Adelaide said.

The fairy waved a hand. "But it was a good test. We are the guardians of the tree. It's up to us how we do that."

Regulus stood and helped her up. "But you didn't stop me from taking a root."

The fairy nodded. "There was strong, evil sorcery on you. A terrible corruption of protection magic. Stopping you would have been near impossible. Some things have to happen, and it is not up to us to determine why." The fairy smiled, but her fanged teeth still made Adelaide uncomfortable. "But I am glad to see you are free of your curse. It will make righting things easier."

"What do you mean?" Regulus asked before Adelaide could.

"You have made a wicked man very powerful." The fairy frowned. "The Staff of Nightfall has been broken and useless for hundreds of years. Because of you both, it is whole."

"I don't understand," Adelaide said. "What is the staff?"

"Hmm." The fairy rolled her eyes. "Doesn't anyone know anything anymore?" The fairy sighed, and Adelaide shuffled her feet, her shoulders bunching.

"You can store magical power in an inanimate object, such as a staff," the fairy explained. "When you use your magic, as you are aware, it eventually refills. Unless it's stolen, in which case, it usually takes an extra push to fully recover that magic. When a mage—or a sorcerer—puts magic into an object, that magic gets locked into the object. It can then help focus a mage's magic, making a little magic go a longer way. So while it takes an immense amount of power to create such an object, it later helps the user consume less energy to accomplish the same effect. Does that make sense?"

Adelaide nodded, although all the information made her lightheaded.

"A powerful and twisted sorceress created the Staff of Nightfall. She imbued the Staff with corrupted sorcery tinged with her own cruelty, bloodlust, rage, and thirst for destruction. Because of this, the Staff works best when used for destruction, to bring pain and suffering and darkness. It took five mages to stop the sorceress and take the Staff. But such powerful magic is difficult to destroy. So they broke the Staff and each mage hid one piece. The pieces remained undisturbed until the sorcerer Kirven started looking for them. He never would have acquired them all without both of your help."

"I didn't have a choice." Regulus sounded resigned.

The fairy looked at him with pity. "I know. You tried, dear boy. But you learned the hard way not to make deals with sorcerers."

"My men—"

"Will die at the sorcerer's hand if he succeeds," the fairy said. "But you couldn't have known that at the time. Still. The fact remains, regardless of circumstances, that you both had a hand in creating a powerful threat to all creatures and people not only in Monparth, but in surrounding kingdoms as well."

Adelaide's gut twisted. Ironically, given the tiny creatures flying before her, she felt small. "Can't you stop him?"

"That is not our place."

"Why not?" Regulus snapped. "Are you cowards?"

The fairy turned red and clenched her tiny fists. "No. We will die if we leave the vicinity of the neumenet tree. It is the link to our realm. Why do you think the sorcerer sent you to gather the root? Because he couldn't be bothered? He knew what defended the tree."

"And didn't warn me," Regulus muttered.

"Adelaide." A male fairy with dark skin and wearing indigo hose and a periwinkle jerkin flew forward. His voice was also shrill, although deeper than the first fairy's. "We can teach you to use your magic. We can help you stop Kirven."

Adelaide looked to Regulus. His eyes reflected his uncertainty. The fairies had just bound and gagged him and threatened to make him their slave. Although they helped her get her magic back and released him. But she was just one person. They said five mages had to destroy the last person to wield the Staff. How would she defeat him on her own? Was it even her responsibility? She hadn't wanted to give the sorcerer this power.

"You are one of only five mages in Monparth," the female fairy said, as if reading her mind. "The others are too weak or too young. You have strength and determination. And more magic than I have seen in a mage for decades."

"There has to be another way." Regulus put his arm around her. "Someone else who can help."

"It has to be you," the male fairy said.

Adelaide's shoulders fell. She wasn't prepared for this kind of responsibility. She had wanted her magic back so she would have a chance against Nolan and could warn the king. But then what? Did she really think the king's guards would be able to protect him? She considered how easily Nolan had incapacitated Regulus and Father. But then she remembered the sorcerer branding her with his mark. Remembered him pulling her magic out of her. She shivered. She didn't stand a chance against him.

"Don't agree to serve him, and he cannot claim you," the male said. Could fairies read thoughts?

"And the neumenet's protection is on you now," the female said. "If you had tried to steal the tree's magic, you would not have been able to. Unlike all other living things, in Etiros' mysterious wisdom, the neumenet tree's life cannot be stolen. Now your magic cannot be stolen, either. So, you see, you *are* the only one that can stop him. We will help you."

She rubbed her forehead. What else could she do? If no one else stopped Kirven… Nolan's note to Father invaded her thoughts. The king would die. Regulus would die. Her family might die. She would be lucky to die. Adelaide had told Minerva she wanted to use her magic to help people. If she refused to fight Kirven…she would have to face the possibility she had been lying to herself her entire life. That all she had truly wanted was power, not to help.

"All right." Adelaide hated how small her voice sounded. "Teach me."

The fairies smiled, their white fangs bright. "We will. But you have to come with us to our realm." The female looked at Regulus. "He must remain behind."

CHAPTER 12

"ABSOLUTELY NOT." Regulus pulled Adelaide closer.

Minutes ago, he thought he had traded slavery to the sorcerer for slavery to fairies, of all things. He might not know much about magic, but everyone knew fairies were tricky. Manipulative. He had just seen that for himself. According to the stories, they also liked to trap people in their realm.

"We're leaving."

"That's not for you to decide," the female fairy said with a hiss. The other fairies whispered to each other. "You aren't ready, mage. Kirven has honed his skills for years. If you face him unprepared, you will die."

Adelaide curled into Regulus and placed a hand on his chest. "For how long?" she asked.

"As long as it takes," the male fairy said.

"Or until we run out of time," the female added.

Regulus fought the urge to draw his sword. It wouldn't help in this instance. "Why can't I come?"

"You're not a mage." The female stated this as if it were obvious. "If you came with us, you wouldn't be able to leave."

"You wouldn't let me leave?"

The male fairy rolled his eyes. "No, you wouldn't be *able* to. You need magic to leave the fairy realm."

"Why can't you teach me here?" Adelaide asked.

An excellent question, Regulus thought. *Tricksters.*

"We can't stay here long," the female said. "We weaken the longer we are in this realm."

"Can I talk to Regulus alone for a moment?"

The two fairies looked at each other, as if having a silent conversation. Regulus glanced toward the horses. If the fairies were telling the truth about weakening while in their world, maybe they had a chance at running away.

"Fine." The female waved her hand dismissively.

They stepped away from the fairies and Adelaide folded her arms over her stomach. Regulus tapped his leg.

"I don't like it."

"But they have a point." Adelaide bit her lower lip. He blinked. He needed to focus on the problem at hand and not how attractive that was. "What if it takes a mage to stop a sorcerer?" She kicked at the ground. "And I can't…" She looked away.

"Hey." He tilted his head and moved to catch her eyes. "Look at me." She met his gaze. "I don't trust them." He rubbed her arms. "But they are right about one thing. I can't make this choice for you."

"What would you do if you were me?" Adelaide glanced at the fairies, then met his eyes again.

He pursed his lips. "I'm done making questionable deals with people or beings with magical powers."

She took a steadying breath before turning back to the fairies. He followed her, hand twitching on the hilt of his sword. The fairies watched with crossed arms, wings beating faster than Regulus could see.

"Thank you," Adelaide said, "but…I don't want to leave this realm. I'll take anything you can tell me or teach me before you have to go back."

The fairies muttered to each other. The dark male in blue pulled on his hair. "Foolish. Why are the humans always so foolish!"

The lead female shook her head. Regulus had the odd thought that the movement should sound like a tiny bell. "Fine. You must practice. Practice until you can do three things at once without thinking. Practice until you don't have to picture what you're going to do first, you just remember how to do it on instinct. You have talent and much power, but little control. The more control and focus you have, the more precise you will be, and the less energy you will waste. Wasted magic will mean death when facing someone as powerful as Kirven."

"If you came with us, we would show you how to create your own staff," the male said. "Although it can take years to learn to craft one as fine-tuned as the Staff of Nightfall. But I suppose you can teach yourself. Start small. It's easier if you use something that was once living, especially if it had magical energy while it lived. Try to store magic in leaves from the neumenet tree. Build up gradually."

"We will teach you one thing before we go," the female added. "Protection binding. You've felt the corrupted, twisted version before."

"The sorcerer's mark," Adelaide said. Regulus tensed.

"Correct." The female flew closer. "Such a mark can only be bestowed if the bearer accepts it. It binds the giver to the receiver, and the receiver to the giver."

"It's difficult." The male swayed from side to side. "It's rather like putting magic into an object, but easier since people are natural receptacles of magic. You channel the magic into a person with a specific intent—to heal, protect, and unite. Think of it like healing and raising a shield all at once, but directing that energy into the person's very soul."

"It's draining," the female fairy added. "And takes time to recover due to the amount of magical energy sacrificed. So never attempt a binding unless you're sure you have time."

"You're certain you won't come with us?" The male tilted his head.

Adelaide reached back and Regulus took her hand. "I'm sure."

The fairies muttered and shook their heads.

"Then farewell." The female curtsied, her red hair falling into her face. "Stay here and practice as long as you can. The magic of the neumenet will help you. It has a way of guiding mages it favors, but it can only do so much. Return here and call for Jara if you change your mind. You're Monparth's best hope. Possibly its only hope." She looked at Regulus. "You both are."

Regulus swallowed back the knot forming in his throat. *No pressure.* Then the fairies vanished, leaving empty air. A glittering neumenet leaf drifted through the emptiness. He followed its slow descent as it arced back and forth until it landed on the grass.

"I can't do this," Adelaide whispered without looking at him.

He shifted. If he were honest, he was scared, too. The sorcerer had always intimidated him. But now…he sounded unbeatable. No, he wouldn't think like that. Not after he had fought for so long for his freedom. One thing Regulus had learned as a mercenary—every opponent was beatable. Some were just harder. He turned her toward him.

"Remember when I told you I took over the mercenary troop after the old captain retired?"

Adelaide knit her brows and looked up at him. "Yes?"

"He retired after his arm was crushed by a troll. He and two of the other mercenaries had gone to purchase supplies, got lost, and ran into a cave troll. One of the men didn't make it, and Captain Samuelson nearly lost his arm. He was an experienced, adept fighter. So was Jack—the man who was killed. Samuelson and Ivan almost didn't escape." *And later I lost Ivan to the sorcerer.* He pushed that thought aside.

She shook her head. "Why are you telling me this?"

"Because"—Regulus took both of Adelaide's hands in his—"it was only a few days ago that *you* killed a troll. Do you remember? I do. I remember you looking fearsome and powerful, cutting the head off a mountain troll with a sword of light wreathed in flame. You can do anything, *Tha Shiraa*."

She lowered her eyes, her head drooping. "I couldn't even free you from some tiny fairies."

"First, fairies are notoriously one of the most powerful magical beings in the known world." He caught the hardness of what Dresden had termed his "captain voice" and tried to pull it back. "Second, you weren't at your full strength, so it doesn't count."

"But—"

"I'll help you. All right? I'll help you train. And then we'll stop Kirven together." He let go of her hand to lift her chin. "Who are you, Adelaide?"

"I'm...a mage?"

"You're the woman who ran at a group of armed men who were beating me. The woman who volunteered to go serve a sorcerer even though she was afraid." He smiled. She might not believe in herself, but he believed in her. "Where is the woman who killed a troll? Because that woman *knows* she's a mage. That woman is a tigress. So say it again."

"Regulus—"

"Say it like you mean it. I'm a mage."

She smirked. "No, you're not."

He rolled his eyes. "Say it, *piahre*." He felt a small amount of pride at how easily the Khast word rolled off his tongue, but this wasn't about him.

Adelaide huffed. "I'm a mage."

"Hm." He released her hand and stepped back. "I'm unconvinced."

"I'm a mage."

He forced his face to stay neutral. "Not feeling it."

"This is ridiculous." She planted her hands on her hips, her face reddening, but amusement sparked in her eyes.

At least the fear was gone, but he wasn't looking for mirth. He was looking for confidence. Her confidence had taken a hit since losing her magic and the fiasco with Carrick. More than anything, he wanted to see her as confident as she had been when she told Carrick off before the tournament. As confident as she had been when she told him she was going to marry him.

"Make me believe it."

"You know I'm a mage."

"Are you? You say you are, you tell me your magic's back, but—"

"It is! I'm a mage!" She held her hand out in front of her and her palm glowed blue. "I just healed you!"

He waved, pushing further. "You could do that yesterday. *Show* me what you are. Who are you, Adelaide?"

"I'm a mage! Reg—"

"Who. Are. You!" She stepped back, surprise at his harsh tone showing in her hurt expression. He wanted to apologize, but he didn't relent. Just like Dresden never relented when Regulus had been mired in despair. "Are you a mage or aren't you? Does your mother think you brave for nothing?" Her mouth fell open, but he pressed on. "Make me believe you're a mage! Because I'm doubtful right now. Who are you? Are you—"

"I AM A MAGE!" Blue light exploded from Adelaide in every direction, bending the grass. The light reached Regulus and knocked him backward. He scrambled to his feet. Adelaide's eyes glowed golden. She held her hands out to her sides, massive balls of flame hovering over her outstretched palms. "My name is Adelaide." She didn't shout, but her voice rang out across the meadow. "And I am a mage."

"There she is." He walked toward her. As intimidating as she looked, he had no reason to fear her. His wide smile pulled on his scar, but he couldn't stop grinning. "Yes, you are."

The fires over Adelaide's hands shrank then disappeared and her eyes returned to their normal rich brown. "You…" She scowled as he stopped in front of her. "You *scoundrel.*" She pushed against his chest, but without much force.

"Whatever works, right?" Regulus laughed. "I thought, it works on the mercenaries…"

"Don't you *ever* yell at me again." She crossed her arms.

He ducked his head. "Sorry. Never again."

Adelaide threw her arms around him and buried her face in his shoulder. "Thank you," she whispered. He wrapped his arms around her and squeezed, despite her throwing knives digging into his chest. She leaned back and met his gaze. "All right, Sir I'll-Help-You-Train. How exactly do you plan on doing that?"

"Oh." Regulus stepped back and rubbed the back of his neck. He gave her a sheepish smile. "I was planning on attacking you."

ADELAIDE BIT back a cry as Regulus sank the dagger into her left arm, halfway between her shoulder and elbow. He grabbed her opposite shoulder to steady her. Tears squeezed out of her eyes and her chest heaved with each labored breath. A crushed neumenet leaf glinted in the trampled grass at her feet.

"I'm sorry," Regulus murmured.

She nodded, unable to respond. Pinching pain surrounded the blade, while pulses of pain radiated up and down her arm in time with her heartbeat. He withdrew the dagger and she whimpered and sagged forward. Blood streamed down her arm. After being stabbed three…no, four times now, she thought she should be better able to handle it. But, by the fairy realm, it still *hurt*.

Regulus guided her right hand to the wound. "Come on. Heal it."

Adelaide's hand shook, but warmth spread across her palm, then over the wound. The area numbed so she couldn't feel the flesh knitting back together. The pain gone, she straightened and looked over. A vein stood out on Regulus' forehead, and his jaw clenched, emphasizing every angle of his temples and jawline. She finished healing herself and dropped her hand. Regulus exhaled but didn't relax.

"That's enough." He rubbed his eyes.

"I'm all right," she said to convince herself as much as him. "I can keep going."

"But I can't." He looked at her dagger smeared with her blood still in his hand. "I'm done. We'll practice another way. This isn't working. And…I won't hurt you again," he whispered.

"But it's all right. See?" She pointed to her arm. "You can't even tell."

"Yes, you can," he said, his voiced strained. "You have blood down to your hand. We need a new plan."

Adelaide was inclined to agree. She didn't enjoy getting stabbed. Not to mention the embarrassment of her repeated failures to stop him. She wasn't used to fighting with magic, but her throwing knives and daggers wouldn't prevail against Kirven. Regulus was quick, good at misdirection, and took advantage of the slightest opening. If he could stab her, what would Kirven be able to do with sorcery aided by the Staff?

"If I can't even defeat you, how am I supposed to defeat Kirven?"

Regulus mussed his hair. "Maybe you're not trying as hard because it's me? You could keep me from even getting close if you really wanted. You're sub-consciously holding back."

He might have a point. She sighed. "Are *you* holding back?" His glance away told her everything. "Great. I can't even keep you from stabbing me when you're trying not to."

"Trying not to kill you." He turned red. "To be honest, I did try to stab you."

She sank onto the grass, her confidence dwindling again. "Do you try to stab Dresden when you train?"

Regulus sat down and cleaned off her dagger. "We train with swords. And we wear armor. There are bruises involved. I cut open his leg once. He had to be stitched up and limped for a week." He handed over her dagger. "The last couple years I mostly did defense. If they hit me, I'd be okay. But I had to be careful not to…kill someone by accident."

She turned her dagger over a few times before sheathing it. At least she hadn't backslid. After regaining her magic, she had worried all her progress over the last few months of practice would be lost. She could still conjure a flaming sword, raise a shield, throw a blast, and everything else she had painstakingly taught herself. If anything, she could do them faster—the neumenet tree's presence hummed through her, strengthening her grasp on her abilities. De-spite all of that, Regulus kept winning.

"Maybe I should have taken up the fairies—"

"I'm glad you didn't." Regulus plucked blades of grass. "I would have gone crazy worrying if I'd ever see you again."

She smiled and elbowed him. "Aw. That's so sweet."

He threw a handful of grass at her. "Besides, your mother would probably have killed me if you vanished into the fairy realm. She's terrifying."

Adelaide laughed and brushed the grass off. "She's just protective."

His lips twitched toward a smile. "She threatened to slit my throat when you were unconscious."

"She did not!" At his serious expression, her chuckle died. "Sorry. She wouldn't…I don't think."

"I believe she would if it saved you." He handed her a neumenet leaf. The leaf shimmered, pinpricks of color dancing along its translucent surface. The soft and pliable leaves in contrast to their glasslike appearance still surprised her. "Here. Something you can practice that's not dangerous."

She pinched the stem of the leaf between her thumb and forefingers and rolled it back and forth. The leaf glittered as it twirled. "I have no idea what I'm doing."

"You're smart." Regulus laid back. "You can figure it out like everything else."

"Right." She stared at the leaf. Just…direct the magic into the leaf. Sure. Her palm glowed, and she imagined her power flowing into the leaf. Then she sensed it. The transfer of energy running down her hand and into the leaf. The leaf glowed blue. "Regulus."

He sat up and looked at the glowing leaf. "That was fast."

The magical energy stopped flowing, as if it had nowhere else to go. The leaf ceased glowing, and then so did her hand. *I guess an object can only hold so much power.* Adelaide spent the next hour practicing storing magic in leaves, then in neumenet twigs, and finally a couple of sticks of a pine tree at the edge of the meadow. That proved more difficult, and between fighting Regulus, healing herself, and all that magical transference, she was drained. She sensed the neumenet tree replenished her magic faster than it would otherwise come back, but she had used a lot.

"I think now's a good time for you to rest. Maybe try to sleep," Regulus said.

"I look that tired?"

He stroked her hair. "Don't worry. I'll keep watch."

"I'm not worried." She laid under the massive canopy of the neumenet tree and drifted to sleep within minutes.

Adelaide woke to a fire crackling in the darkness. Regulus sat next to her, staring into the flames. She stretched and sat up. "It's night?"

"Sun set half an hour ago. You hungry?" He held out a small cloth bag.

Inside, Adelaide found dried venison. Between bites of the tough, salty meat, she said, "I think we should only stay here one more day."

Regulus raised a brow. "The fairies said—"

"Yes, I know." She ate another bite. "But I want to find out if Father has heard anything about the progress of the messengers."

Regulus pursed his lips. The intensity of the unspoken question in his eyes made her uncomfortable.

"What?"

"I thought we were past secrets." He picked up a long stick from next to the fire and poked at the glowing embers. "Are you not being honest with yourself, or just not with me?"

Adelaide lowered the food to her lap. "I don't know what you're—"

"Why do you want to go back? Really?"

All right, there was another reason. But did she have to say it out loud? She tore off another piece of venison and tossed it in her mouth.

He sighed. "Information on the messengers will be important for plotting our next step. But it could wait. I don't want you ever to feel you need to hide from me." The softness with which he repeated her own words back to her pricked her conscience.

"I need to make sure my parents are safe." Saying it aloud somehow made the threat seem more real. "I'm afraid of what Nolan might do." She met his eyes. "Truthfully, I'm more afraid of him than Kirven. And I know that's stupid, but I can't help it. Kirven wants to rule. He'll kill the king and anyone who gets in his way. If it was only Kirven, maybe…" She trailed off, ashamed of herself.

"You'd be tempted to let him win." He didn't sound disappointed or disgusted. In fact, he sounded sympathetic. "I had the same thought. Would it be so bad? Maybe if we ignored him, he would ignore us. But he's vindictive. I doubt he'll feel satisfied with killing the king. I'm not sure anyone would be safe. And if he learns your magic is back… He'd see you as a threat. I don't think we can be free until he's dead."

"I know." She set the bag of jerky on the ground, her appetite gone, and pulled her cloak tighter around her arms. "And even if I could convince myself that wasn't all true…" She shuddered. "If Kirven gives Nolan the political and military power he wants, I'd never be safe. You and my family would never be safe. I'm more worried about that than the kingdom." She laughed weakly. "I suppose that's selfish."

"It's not selfish to want to protect the people you love." Regulus stood and offered her his hand. "Come on."

Without hesitation, Adelaide took his hand and he pulled her to her feet. "Where are we going?"

"Nowhere. But you need a distraction. So practice." He pointed at the fire.

"Put up a barrier from the fire to the trunk of the tree."

They practiced for hours. Adelaide put up one barrier after another. Straight, curved, a complete dome over her and Regulus. Then Regulus made her keep a barrier up while she conjured and used lances, knives, and swords. The neumenet's power flowed alongside hers, as if guiding her, helping her learn. By the light of one of her spheres, Regulus set up a bunch of branches in the ground and had her knock them all down while he tried to break through a barrier. She sent the last branch flying into the forest and dropped the barrier. Regulus stumbled forward as she bent over, hands on her knees, breathing hard. Her stomach growled.

"All right. That should be enough for tonight."

She smiled at the pride in Regulus' voice.

SUNLIGHT GLINTED off the neumenet tree's leaves, casting a rainbow of color into the tendrils of mist drifting over the meadow. In the early morning light, Regulus imagined he could see how thin the veil between their world and the fairy realm was under the tree's canopy. Even if the ground under magical trees still proved hard and uncomfortable.

He had always hated sleeping on the ground. But with Adelaide pressed against his chest, the ground and his aching muscles didn't seem so bad. As their eyes met, the enchanting beauty of the meadow and neumenet tree faded away, leaving only her.

The sound of her gentle breathing. The dip in her waist where his arm fit so perfectly. Her gorgeous round face and soft brown skin, her dark brown eyes that held his gaze captive and tangled up his insides. The second the sorcerer was dead, Regulus was going to marry her and make sure he woke up to her every morning.

Adelaide ran her finger along his scar, tickling his skin and sending his mind careening in a dozen directions, several of which were less than innocent. But shame about the scars covering the rest of his body tainted his thoughts.

"What are you thinking about?" she murmured.

His face heated. "Um… How to help you train today."

Adelaide laughed, her eyes glinting mischievously. "No, you weren't."

"No," he admitted. "I was thinking about doing this." He leaned over, gripped her waist, and kissed her. "Every day." He kissed her cheek. "For the rest." A kiss against her neck that made her sigh. He smiled and moved his lips back to hers. "Of my life." She met his kiss and clutched the side of his neck. Her stomach rumbled, intruding on the moment and making him laugh against her mouth. "Hungry, *piahre?*"

"Using so much magic makes me starved." She gave him a quick peck and slipped out from under him.

He collapsed onto his stomach on the grass that was still warm with her body heat with a groan. A few moments later, Adelaide's shadow fell over him.

"Are you going to eat, or should I use your back as a table?"

Regulus sat up and rolled his eyes. She sat across from him and handed him some bread and roasted nuts. He raised a brow as she tore into the bread with as much gusto as one of his men after a hard training session. Her gaze moved from his eyes to his lips to his scarred cheek before returning to his eyes.

"I know you said you like my scar, and that I don't need to hide." He tossed some nuts in his mouth, trying to appear nonchalant. "But… I heard you gasp when you saw the rest. Are they…" His throat knotted. *Repulsive?*

Adelaide set her bread down. "They don't bother me." She moved toward him. Regulus wasn't ready for the shock that went through him when she slid her hand under his shirt and pushed it up. "They sadden me." She ran her left hand over the large scar from the dragon's tail. "This looks like it should have killed you."

He had to force his mouth to work, his mind was so consumed with her touch. "It would have, if the sorcerer's magic didn't pull me back."

"What happened?" She met his eyes, her brows knit. "Unless you don't want to—"

"Dragon."

"Oh, Etiros." Her hand left his stomach. "At the Glowers' party, when I asked you about the Black Knight and the rumors about a dragon… No wonder you were upset. I'm sorry."

He shrugged. "You didn't know."

She lowered her gaze, her right hand still holding up his shirt as her fingers trailed over various scars, warming his skin and making his breath hitch. "Are they all from serving him?"

"No. Mainly the worst ones."

Adelaide let his shirt fall and touched the long scar on his cheek. "And…this one?"

He worked his jaw and swallowed. "Not that one."

Her fingers slipped off his cheek. She settled back and picked up her bread. She wouldn't push him for the story, and he appreciated that. But he couldn't pressure her not to keep secrets and then do the same.

Regulus sighed. "First and most obvious scar, over a momentary, stupid decision. The first mercenary troop Drez and I joined isn't the one we stayed with. We'd only been with them two weeks when I got in a fight with the lieutenant and a few of his friends. They were drunk and bothering some poor barmaids."

He looked at the charred remains of the fire, remembering the feel of hands pinning down his arms and knees digging into his torso, the fist yanking on his hair to hold him in place. The agony as the knife traced over his skin.

"Drunk men still understand insults. And are still strong." He massaged the scar. Thinking about it made it hurt. "I'm just glad the fool with the knife was either sober enough or drunk enough not to cut all the way through. Drez cursed enough to make a sailor blush the entire time he stitched me up."

Adelaide placed a hand on his arm. "Stopping churls from bothering girls isn't stupid." He looked at her. She watched him with a warm smile. "It makes your scar more attractive."

He laughed through a frown. "I'm both bewildered and pleased I found a woman who finds my scar attractive."

"Well, you don't think I'm beautiful in spite of being half-Khastallander…" She trailed off, her smile vanishing as she stuffed the last of her bread in her mouth.

"Who would say something like that?"

She reddened and didn't look at him as she stood. "I'm ready to train now."

They spent the day training. Regulus challenged Adelaide to see how many things she could do at once, recalling the fairies' advice. Even when she grew tired, he pushed her. The sorcerer wouldn't stop when she was tired. And with Regulus' immortality gone, the best way he could help was by making her ready.

Adelaide dropped her shield and straightened. "I need a break—"

He hurled a large stone at her. She gasped and dove to the ground, but Regulus didn't pause and ran toward her. He knocked her back down just as she started to rise and grabbed her wrists, pinning her down. She smirked.

"If you want to kiss me, you can—"

"This isn't a game!" He released her wrists and stood, pacing back and forth. "Without a staff, the sorcerer bested fifteen of the best mercenaries I've ever met. According to the fairies, the Staff will make him stronger."

"You said…I can do anything."

Regulus stopped. Fear showed in Adelaide's eyes and a pang of sorrow shot through him. He knew what it felt like to question everything you thought you knew about yourself. He knelt next to her, trying to think of what Dresden would say.

"You *are* strong, Ad. But what separates a warrior from a champion isn't strength. It's perseverance. And it's training so their skills are the best they can be when they are tested."

An idea occurred to him. He could make his point and have fun.

"There's a coastal town in Hedengal where they tell stories of—well, I won't try to pronounce it, but it translates to 'the cliff-men.' Men who were battered like the cliffs by a stormy sea, but like those cliffs, they would not break. They killed the demon sea serpents that had been tormenting the town. They fought without rest from dawn until midnight, when the last serpent fell."

Adelaide huffed. "Legends make good stories—"

"Hey." Regulus turned and pulled up his shirt just enough to reveal a small knotted scar on his lower back. "Demon serpent bites burn. They spit saltwater in the wounds they inflict. My men and I fought too hard for you to roll your eyes at us." He released his shirt.

She stared. "Are you being serious?"

Regulus enjoyed her look of astonishment. "I should mention we also are forbidden from ever entering that town again after Caleb got caught kissing our benefactor's—the mayor's—daughter." He offered her his hand. "The point is, I'm pushing you because you'll need to be a cliff-woman to win."

"Okay." Adelaide took his hand and stood with a sigh. "You're right."

They left the tree at dawn the next day. As they reentered the forest, Adelaide paused to look back at the neumenet tree. "I can still feel its energy," she murmured.

Regulus shifted in his saddle. "Should we stay another day?"

She shook her head. "No. It isn't pulling me anymore. And I want to get back."

"Okay." He nudged Sieger forward. "But you should practice everything you can while we ride."

Sometimes Regulus would point out a branch to throw a magical spear at or ask her to see how long she could keep a shield up. He hoped the practice helped keep her mind off whatever Kirven and Nolan were doing.

The sun sank toward the horizon, turning the sky pink and the clouds burnished orange. A few hours away from Belanger castle, they heard voices ahead.

Regulus had decided they should assume the worst and avoid everyone, so they moved into a copse of trees in a nearby field. The men kept talking, but no one came down the road.

"Let's keep to the field," he whispered. Adelaide nodded and followed him.

Three men stood next to a small fire on the side of the road. All wore swords and chainmail. Their horses were staked nearby.

"Sure, tell that to his face, coward." One of the men threw what looked like a bone into the fire, then wiped his mouth. "Yer more than happy to take his gold."

"His gold won't help if we're hanged!" another man said.

Regulus glanced at Adelaide and put a finger to his lips, then gestured to ride further from the small group.

"Then leave." The third man's deep voice carried loud and clear over the field.

"Yeah, if I have a death wish. Carrick's lost his mind." The second man cursed.

Regulus whipped his head around and locked eyes with Adelaide as her face drained of color. *No!* He shook his head, but she was already turning Zephyr back toward the road. Mentally cursing, he followed her.

"Carrick's got a plan," the first speaker said. His dark hair was pulled back in a short braid. "And he ain't lyin' about bein' immortal."

"Well, I don't see how that will save *my* neck if somebody finds out what he did." The man ran his hand through knotted blond hair. "His family connections won't save him or us this time."

Zephyr snorted, and the three men turned toward them, swords drawn.

"Hey." The man with the braid pointed. "That's her, right?"

CHAPTER 15

"WHERE IS Nolan Carrick?" Her heart pounding, Adelaide drew two throwing knives and readied them as Regulus stopped next to her. "What did he do?"

The men circled them and raised their swords. "We don't want to hurt you," the deep-voiced man said. "But you have to come with us."

She threw a knife into his leg. He cursed and howled as he stumbled backward. "Where is Nolan Carrick?"

The blond bolted to one of the horses. She threw a knife at his neck, but he moved to mount the horse and it hit his back, bouncing off his chainmail. She cursed in Khast and drew another knife.

"Watch out!" Regulus' sword grated against its scabbard.

She looked back at the man with the braid just as he grabbed her cloak and pulled. She twisted and stabbed the knife into his forearm as she slid sideways in the saddle. The man cursed and leapt back, yanking her cloak against her neck so she tumbled out of the saddle and fell hard on her arm. Adelaide drew a dagger and staggered to her feet as Regulus ran up next to her. Her knife still stuck out of the man's forearm, but he had dropped his sword. Regulus held the tip of his sword to the man's throat.

"The lady asked you a question."

"He's at Belanger castle!" The man glanced at his friend, but he had sat down a few feet away and was trying to stop the bleeding from his leg. "He got some men together and took the castle by force."

"By force…" She swayed, suddenly dizzy. "Lord and Lady Belanger, are they alive?"

The man nodded rapidly. "Sir Carrick locked 'em up! But they're safe. I swear it! He said none of the Belangers could be hurt." She lowered her dagger, relief mixing with fear.

"Why were you posted here?" Regulus asked.

"To keep an eye out for you." The man swallowed hard, his eyes wide. "We was ordered to kill Hargreaves and take Belanger to Carrick. And if we couldn't, to let him know you're coming."

Oh no, the blond! Adelaide whipped around, but he was gone.

"How many men does Carrick have holding the castle?" Regulus looked eerily calm as he held his sword to the man's throat. Meanwhile, panic pushed against Adelaide's lungs and squeezed her throat. Incoherent thoughts of despair and anger chased each other through her mind.

"I don't know!"

"Think about it," Regulus coaxed. Adelaide wanted to shake the man. Or scream. Or cry. Maybe all at once.

"He brought twenty with him—"

"Nolan took Belanger castle with only twenty men?" Adelaide's eyes widened. "Was there a sorcerer with him?"

The man shook his head and glanced toward her knife still embedded in his forearm. Blood dripped from his elbow to the ground. "I don't know about a sorcerer! But you ever seen a man get run through with a sword and shake it off like a punch? You ever seen a man rip an arrow out of his throat and keep walking? Seeing that does things to men's spirits. He ripped a side door off its hinges, and we walked right in. We only lost a few men before the castle surrendered. Carrick locked up anybody who didn't join him."

"Join him?" Adelaide clenched her fist. "My father's men would never—"

"Carrick can't die and keeps saying he's gonna be the second most powerful man in Monparth soon. Greed and fear get men to do a lot." The man looked from her to Regulus. "I answered your questions. Please don't kill me!"

Adelaide and Regulus looked at each other. She hesitated before she stepped forward and pulled her knife out of his arm. "Go."

Regulus lowered his sword, and the man stumbled over to his companion. They ran to their horses, as best as the other ruffian could with a wounded leg.

"They'll go to Carrick," Regulus noted.

"That's probably where the other one went, anyway." She cleaned and sheathed her dagger and pressed the heel of her hand against her temple. "What if he's wrong? What if my parents are—"

"No." Regulus sheathed his sword. "He'd be an idiot to kill them."

She paced next to Zephyr. "We have to go rescue—"

"No."

"What?" She stilled and clenched her fists.

"You can't go near the castle. Absolutely not."

"Are you insane?" she shouted. "He has my parents—"

"Exactly." Regulus' eyes searched hers. "Think. Why? What will you do if he threatens them? If he puts a sword to your mother's throat? What would you do, Adelaide?"

She opened her mouth, closed it, opened it again, then snapped it closed. She wanted to say she would save them, she'd use her magic, she'd find a way. But what if she couldn't?

"We both know what you'd do," he said gently. "Because you've done it before."

Adelaide screamed and threw her knife into the ground with such force only the tip of the handle stuck out of the dirt. "Then what am I supposed to do? I can't leave them! What if he gets tired of waiting? I have to do something! I can't—"

A sob tore from her throat and she bent over, her chest seizing. She kept picturing Nolan standing over her parents' bloodied, lifeless bodies, that cavalier smile on his haughty face.

Regulus pulled her close and Adelaide sobbed into his shoulder. They had been outwitted. Outplayed. All Nolan had to do was threaten her parents, and she would surrender. Nolan knew it, too. When he threatened to tamper with Minerva's carriage, she had caved. He had pushed her at Arrano, and she had agreed to marry him to save Regulus and Gaius. He likely overheard her telling her parents she helped the sorcerer to help Regulus. She had a history of giving in to save others. Nolan had a history of being unbothered by hurting others. If she went to the castle, she would give herself to Nolan before she watched her parents suffer or die. But for all she knew, he would kill them if she didn't go, anyway.

Adelaide cried until her stomach hurt from gasping through her tears. Regulus held her close but didn't say a word. He let her cry and rubbed her back in big circles. Even when she could finally breathe normally again, she leaned against him. She had soaked his shoulder with tears, and more embarrassing, snot. Once her face was dry, she pulled away.

"What do we do?"

Regulus cupped his hand to the side of her neck and rubbed his thumb over her jaw. "They're going to be okay. But if Carrick is there, and the sorcerer is not, there is a good chance the messengers didn't get through to the king." She nodded, even though she couldn't think about that right now. Regulus sighed. "We're going to have to split up."

"What?" She grabbed his arm. "You can't leave me! And I'm definitely not leaving you! Not after—"

"Shhh." He smiled sadly. "You need to warn the king. You have a better chance of getting there, and once there, you can probably get in. You're Lord Belanger's daughter. I'm nobody. If we want any chance of preventing the sorcerer from seizing the throne, the king must be warned."

"But my—"

"I'll get my men, and we'll rescue your parents. We're mercenaries. This is what we do."

Adelaide shook her head. "Even with your men, how will you defeat Nolan? He has more men. And a castle! It's impossible."

He gave her a look of deep hurt. "Glad to hear you have so much faith in me. The men are going to be offended, too."

"I didn't mean…" She sighed.

"It's this or we both go to the king. Carrick has too much of an advantage over you. Your parents wouldn't want you to knowingly walk into a trap. Your father would want you to warn the king. So, I rescue your parents without you, or we leave your parents until after the king is warned."

She chewed on her lower lip. All right, fine. If she ended up captured trying to rescue her parents, they would be beyond livid. Father could be chained up in the dungeons, and he would still lecture her about tactical miscalculations.

But what if he *was* chained up? What if Nolan had put Mother in the dungeons? The thought of Mother, alone on a hard, dirty dungeon floor, shackles on her wrists, made Adelaide's blood run cold. What about her half-brother and his wife and their infant? Even though she didn't like Landon and Julia, they were still family. Nolan wouldn't put Julia and her baby in the dungeons, would he? Adelaide couldn't abandon them. But she couldn't hand herself over to him, either.

"It's the best way," Regulus whispered. He leaned his forehead against hers. "The king is warned. Carrick won't kill your parents when you're not around. I've done many stealth missions. I can rescue your family. I promise you, I'll get them to safety. Trust me."

She closed her eyes. His plan, though imperfect, made sense. This was the man who had fought demon sea serpents and dragons. He could sneak her parents out, right?

He shifted, holding the sides of her face in his strong, capable hands, and kissed her forehead. "We'll see each other again, *mareh piahre*. I promise."

"I'll hold you to that."

Regulus pulled her to him and kissed her urgently. Adelaide tangled her fingers in his black curls. If passionate kisses could ensure his survival, she'd make sure he lived to be a hundred. When they finally separated, she rested her forehead on his shoulder, her chest heaving and stomach doing flips.

"I need to go," he whispered. "The sooner I get to Arrano, the better."

She didn't want to let go, but she did. They gave each other one last embrace that said everything they couldn't articulate. He handed her his satchel with the last bits of food they had, and they mounted their horses.

"Swear to me you won't go near your parents' castle."

"I swear it." She swallowed back her sorrow.

"And promise you'll keep practicing your magic, even while riding."

"I promise."

Regulus turned toward Arrano. Adelaide watched him disappear into the twilight, then she adjusted course for the palace. She had a king to warn, and as much distance as possible to put between herself and Nolan.

CHAPTER 16

REGULUS RODE through the night without stopping, and all the next day, too. Concern for Adelaide preoccupied his thoughts as the sun beat down on his back. He prayed she would truly head for the palace; that she would avoid any run-ins with Carrick or the sorcerer. While he believed separating had been their best chance at success, it would be days, perhaps weeks before he saw Adelaide again, and his anxiety for her safety added to his exhaustion.

He missed her. Her absence felt like when he reached for his sword but found he wasn't wearing it. It was a lost, unanchored sensation, and he wanted to remedy it as soon as possible. So, he shook away the drowsiness and rode on.

The sun had long set when he approached Arrano. The stars and a waning moon half-hidden behind clouds cast pale light on the outlines of his castle. Regulus rode toward the main gate, posture drooping. His dry eyes itched. A shadow on the ramparts above the gate moved.

"Halt! Who goes there?"

"Lord Hargreaves," Regulus called back wearily. He recognized the man's voice but couldn't connect it with a face. "Who's on watch? Maxwell?"

"Lord Hargreaves?" The guard sounded stunned. "Gerald, my lord. Maxwell's home with his family."

"Ah. Could you open the gate, Gerald?"

"The gate! Of course! Apologies, my lord!" Footsteps slapped hard and fast on the stone. A few moments later, a chain rattled and clacked, the portcullis lifted, and the great double doors of the gate groaned as they swung inward. Regulus nudged Sieger forward. The gate closed behind him and the portcullis settled back down with a clang. A torch bobbed toward him across the courtyard, held by a bleary-eyed stable boy, his shirt half-tucked in and twisted around his torso and his boots unlaced. Regulus dismounted and headed for the castle before the stable boy even reached Sieger. He called a thank you over his shoulder as his boots tapped against the cobblestones leading to the front door.

He didn't want to wake Harold, but he couldn't risk oversleeping. It took a couple knocks before Harold answered his door.

"My lord!" Harold blinked several times. "What—you're okay! But... I—"

Regulus half smiled. "Wake me at dawn, please. I can't sleep past then. And tell my knights to meet me in the hall for breakfast just after dawn. Oh, alert the cook, too."

"Yes, my lord." Harold's brow wrinkled. His eyes were full of questions Regulus was glad he wasn't asking, because he was too exhausted to answer.

Regulus rubbed his eyes. "Is my room locked?"

"Oh, yes, one mo—"

"Just give me the key." Regulus held out his hand. Harold's mouth twisted down, but he gave Regulus his copy of the key. "Good night, Harold." Regulus trudged up the stairs to his room.

Magnus knocked him onto his backside when he stepped into the room. "Okay, boy." He chuckled as Magnus whined and soaked his face with his large tongue. He tried to push the massive fluffy dog away, but Magnus seemed heavier and stronger than he remembered. "Down, Magnus."

Magnus whimpered, but moved off his chest. Regulus buried his fingers in the soft, fluffy brown fur on Magnus' neck as he walked past to his bed, giving him a quick scratch. He stripped down to his trousers and sunk into bed. Magnus curled up next to him. The dog wasn't Adelaide by any stretch, but his warmth brought some measure of comfort.

Morning and Harold's voice came too soon. Regulus washed his face and shaved but had no time for a full bath. He pulled on clothes and headed to the hall, Magnus close on his heels.

Dresden, Perceval, and Caleb already sat at the table. Dresden stood as Regulus entered the room, his angular features pinched with emotion. He had dark circles under his eyes and his thick black hair was a mess, but his beard looked as well-trimmed and kempt as ever. Regulus smiled and nodded. Drez nodded back, some of the tension leaving his face as he eased back onto his chair. But he sat forward with his back ramrod straight, as if too on edge to relax.

Perceval rubbed his hand over his morning scruff and narrowed his eyes at Regulus. His nose was bright red and peeling, likely from working the field around his cottage. Caleb's blond hair was even more tousled than usual, and the pitying look in his eyes as Regulus sat down made him wonder what they had been saying before he entered.

The door at the far end of the hall opened, and Estevan walked in. He smiled when he saw Regulus, creating deep dimples in his freckled tan face. They just needed—the main door swished open, and Jerrick strode in, panting like he had been running. He wore a bright orange shirt that contrasted well with his dark skin.

The men watched him intently with questioning eyes. Dresden's temple pulsed. But none spoke, respecting Regulus' right to tell them what he wanted, when he wanted. They had been called, and they knew it wasn't as friends. They sat tall and alert, focused on their captain.

Regulus opened his mouth to speak, but the door to the kitchens opened, and servants emerged carrying trays of food, plates, and goblets filled with water. He waited for them to place the trays of bread, butter, boiled quail eggs, and thick-sliced ham on the table. He loaded his plate, even though he didn't feel hungry between his worries over Adelaide and concerns for their upcoming mission. His men followed suit, albeit with more gusto, particularly Jerrick and Estevan, who were the youngest of the group.

Regulus cleared his throat as he spread butter over a piece of warm bread. "I'm certain you have questions. I will try to cover everything, but we are pressed for time." He ate a couple bites before continuing. "Much has happened since I left. Of first importance"—he set down his bread and rolled up his sleeve, showing the underside of his forearm—"the sorcerer released me. My debt is fulfilled."

Dresden, still sitting forward like he was afraid to let his back touch his chair, froze with his fork halfway to his mouth. Perceval choked on his water. Estevan grinned. Jerrick muttered something in Bhitran that sounded like a prayer of thanks to Hallilek. Caleb slumped back in his seat.

"Then it's over?" Dresden lowered his hand to the table.

Regulus sighed. "Not really, no." He took a long drink. No one moved. "Unfortunately, the sorcerer *is* actually a prince. Prince Kirven. The king's brother. He is plotting to kill the king and seize the throne."

"So send the king a message." Dresden glowered. "Who is king doesn't concern us."

"Considering the sorcerer seems bent on death, destruction, and revenge...yes, it should concern us." Regulus tapped his finger against the side of his goblet. "But more directly, it concerns Adelaide and me."

"He took Lady Belanger," Perceval said, a stated guess more than a question.

"No. Adelaide is safe, or at least she was last I saw her. But if the sorcerer succeeds, neither of us will be safe."

"Everything he made you do, everything he did to you, and he can't leave you alone?" Dresden's raised voice echoed in the hall.

"The sorcerer? Perhaps. But, unfortunately…" Regulus' hand tightened around his goblet. He drew a steadying breath. "He has a new pet. A willing servant to whom he has promised wealth and political power for accepting the mark. If the sorcerer succeeds, Nolan Carrick succeeds with him. I'll be a dead man, and Adelaide…" He cracked open a quail egg with more force than necessary and began eating its soft-boiled contents.

The men stared in stunned silence. Finally, Caleb asked, "Carrick…has the mark?"

"Yes," Regulus said around a mouthful of bread and yolk.

"He's like you were?" Perceval waved the piece of bread in his hand. "Strong, fast…immortal?"

Regulus nodded as he took a large bite of ham. Dresden cursed. Repeatedly and at length, his face red. Regulus had expected a negative response, but Dresden looked as if he'd taken Carrick joining the sorcerer personally.

"Reg." Dresden's voice was low and strained, and he glared at the table like he was considering stabbing it. "Where's Adelaide?"

"On her way to warn the king. We're not sure if any messengers got through. If she does as we agreed, she's going to the palace."

"If?" Estevan swallowed a mouthful of food and tilted his head. "Why are you here, then?"

Regulus took a drink and set down the goblet harder than intended. He focused on the goblet. He needed to keep calm. To be a captain, not an emotionally compromised fool.

"Through a series of events, Adelaide and I were headed back to her father's castle when we learned that Carrick took the castle and is holding her parents hostage." He looked up, meeting each of their eyes. "That's why I called you here. We have a new assignment. We're rescuing Lord and Lady Belanger."

"From a castle?" Drez gestured to the men at the table. "With what army? You're not immortal anymore, need I remind you, and we'd be facing someone who is! Six men can't storm a castle. And then we'll have to face Carrick?" His hands fisted on either side of his plate. "Do you have a plan? Some secret that will give us an advantage? Do—"

"Enough!" Regulus slammed his fist on the table. Drez's objections had already occurred to him, and he knew his friend had a point. But he'd made a promise. "We leave in half an hour."

Dresden's eyes flashed. "That's not an ans—"

"Sir Dresden," Regulus snapped. "Am I your captain or not? Am I your liege or not?" He hated himself even as he said it, and he hated the hard look that slipped over his best friend's face, the uncomfortable way the rest of the men averted their eyes. But he didn't have time to waste arguing.

Dresden worked his jaw. "Regulus, attacking Carrick when he has the mark, especially in a castle, is—"

"We'll aim for stealth."

"And if we're caught?" Dresden demanded. "You—"

"Sir Jakobs! Do I answer to you? Or do you answer to me?"

Dresden's face darkened. He pushed away from the table and stood, his movements stiff. "I'll be ready in the courtyard in half an hour, *my lord*." The tightness in his voice cut straight through Regulus, but he didn't soften his expression or flinch. They had an agreement. In private, Drez could say whatever he wanted, but he didn't question Regulus in front of the men. Dresden gave an abrupt, shallow bow, straightening with a momentary wince, and strode from the hall.

Jerrick leaned back in his chair with a disapproving frown. "He didn't deserve that. Especially not after what happened."

Regulus' stomach pinched at Jerrick's tone. "What happened?"

The men glanced at each other. None looked eager to share.

"What. Happened?"

Jerrick pulled at his shirt collar. "When Carrick came…we weren't here. Perceval and I didn't see them arrive. Estevan and Caleb were out hunting. When they couldn't find you, Carrick threatened to beat Dresden until you showed yourself. Sir Gaius convinced him not to."

Perceval scratched his stubble. "Sir Gaius and Lord Drummond left, but Carrick stayed to see if you would return." The men seemed fascinated with their food as Regulus' chest clenched.

"He beat him," Harold said from the stairwell. Regulus turned toward his squire. Harold's tear-filled eyes blazed. "You were gone! Carrick was angry, so he hit Dresden. He punched him, again and again. Then he had his knights tie

Dresden to a tree, and he took a belt to him. Because he knew hurting Dresden would hurt you. Thankfully, that knight arrived saying he'd seen the Black Knight and Lady Adelaide, so Carrick only used the belt a few times, but he hit hard. The bruises haven't fully healed." Harold clenched and unclenched his fists. "I should have done something."

Regulus' stomach lurched and his hands shook. He swallowed hard. "No, Harold…" Guilt choked off his words. He'd abandoned Drez. But he hadn't thought…he couldn't have known… *I'm going to cut Carrick's head off.*

Harold slunk back up the stairs, shoulders drooping.

Regulus shoved his plate away, his appetite gone, but didn't get up. He wouldn't run away. The men ate in silence, glancing at him out of the corner of their eyes. One by one they left until only he and Perceval remained.

"He doesn't blame you, Captain."

Dresden should blame him. But blame wouldn't help them rescue the Belangers. "He might have a point about trying to infiltrate a castle being a bad idea. It will be difficult, and…" He rubbed his temple. "I don't want to know what Carrick will do to you all if he captures you."

"We'd follow you anywhere, Captain. Drez is just being cautious." Perceval stood. "I trust you, Captain. You always come through."

Reluctantly, Regulus looked up. "What if I'm not sure how to do this?"

"I'd be dead half a dozen times over if not for you. You know I wouldn't have settled down and served any random lord. Even Leonora couldn't get me to do that. But I'll fight anyone you ask me to. I'd die for you." Perceval tapped his hand on the back of his chair. "We all would, Captain."

"Thank you, Perceval. But I don't want anyone to die for me."

Perceval nodded with a smile. "That's why we'd do it."

Regulus slouched as Perceval left the hall. He tossed Magnus a piece of ham and returned to his room. It didn't take long to put on a gambeson and his lightest chainmail shirt over his shirt. He needed speed and flexibility more than he wanted the extra protection of plate armor. As soon as he'd strapped a sword to his side, he headed to the stables. Dresden was there, his scimitars crossed over his back, waiting for a stable boy to saddle his brown destrier. After Regulus spoke to another stable boy, Dresden came over to him.

"Can I speak with you?" Drez murmured.

"Actually, I was going to ask you the same." They stepped out of the stables. Dresden opened his mouth, but Regulus cut him off. "They told me what

Carrick did." Dresden flushed crimson. "I'm sorry…" He struggled to find the right words.

"I told you I'd take a beating for you someday." Dresden smiled sadly and winked. "I'd say we're even, except a belt doesn't leave the scars a whip does."

"You never owed me."

"And you never owed me, but you don't listen."

Regulus ran his fingers through his hair and rubbed the pommel of his sword, his face burning. "Are you—"

"I'm fine now, Reg. Worse was not knowing if you were alive for the last week. Not knowing if you'd ever come back. Why didn't you send word?"

"We were… I… There was a lot…" He hung his head. "I should have thought to. I'm sorry."

Dresden sighed. "Now you show up, tell me the man who tried to have you killed and beat me is immortal and teamed up with the sorcerer while you're normal again, and you want to face him? I panicked." He crossed his arms. "But I apologize. I shouldn't have publicly challenged you."

Regulus sighed. "But I shouldn't—"

"No. I was wrong, and I deserved that."

Regulus shook his head. "You're my friend first, Drez."

"And you're my friend. My brother. Always." Dresden scratched his beard. "But you're my captain and my liege, too." He grimaced. "We can't be equals. No matter how much I wish otherwise."

Regulus winced. He wanted to argue Dresden's point about not being equals, but he couldn't. Not when raising Dresden to the knighthood had made his best friend his vassal. Not when he'd just exercised that authority in a way that highlighted their inequalities and probably made Dresden feel like a servant again.

"But between us, I'm concerned." Drez shifted his weight from side to side. "I don't say this to blame you, so don't hear that. Carrick hates you. Enough he took it out on me with his fists and a belt. He'd have used a whip if he had one." More guilt pricked at Regulus. "He thinks he's untouchable now he's in league with the sorcerer. If Carrick captures the men, what do you think he'll do to them? And you? He'll tear you apart."

Regulus fiddled with a strap on his gauntlet. "Which is why we won't act until we've scouted out the situation and agreed on a plan." He met Dresden's eyes. "I won't risk you all. The Belangers will have to wait until we have a plan that has a strong chance of success. But I have to try. I promised."

Drez smiled wryly. "A Hargreaves promise is a powerful thing."

Regulus sighed as the stable boys led out their horses. *I just hope I haven't made a promise I can't keep.*

ADELAIDE CONSIDERED turning toward Belanger castle several times, but each time she talked herself out of it. Thinking of Nolan leveraging her parents' lives against her made her shudder. She recalled his attack in the drawing room—his strength and speed, the lust and determination in his eyes—and fought a wave of nausea. Regulus would get them out.

After a couple hours, she stopped to sleep at the base of a birch grove. Every little sound put her on edge. The hard dirt felt more uncomfortable without Regulus' arms around her. She tossed in the prickly grass and woke from a troubled sleep at dawn, horrified at her decision.

What was I thinking? Without her there to stop him, Nolan would kill Regulus. Adelaide had been so worried about her parents, so relieved and ready to think *Regulus is a warrior, he knows what he's doing, he'll save them.*

But Nolan was immortal. She shouldn't have let Regulus try to take on Nolan. *I should go back and stop him.* And what? Leave her parents in Nolan's clutches? She couldn't do that, either. Regulus didn't need to take back the whole castle. Just get her family out. But how would he even find her family? And if Nolan caught him… *I have to stop him.*

Adelaide mounted Zephyr and headed toward Father's estate. *He seemed so confident,* part of her brain murmured. *He knows what he's doing.* But she remembered Nolan snapping Regulus' arm and hurried Zephyr on. With every mile she rode closer to home, doubt crept in. Father would want her to warn the king. She had promised Regulus she wouldn't go near Belanger castle.

She dismounted in a thicket of trees near the road and paced back and forth. *Save Regulus, risk the king and abandon my parents. Warn the king, risk Regulus.* She screamed and threw a knife at a nearby pine. It felt good, so she threw the rest.

Etiros, what do I do? She pried her knives from the tree, mounted, then dismounted again. Her eyelids drooped as she rested her forehead on Zephyr's saddle. *Regulus. My parents. The king.*

If she warned the king and Nolan killed Regulus, she would never forgive herself. If she returned to intercept Regulus, Nolan might catch her. Worse, if Father's messengers hadn't gotten through, the king would not be warned, and all would be lost.

What would Father and Mother do? Father would warn the king. Mother would save Father. She slumped against Zephyr's side. If she didn't warn the king, Kirven would make Nolan a duke and things would only be worse. The only way to stop Nolan was to stop Kirven. Her mistake in leaving Regulus couldn't be undone now.

Despite her writhing stomach, she turned Zephyr toward the palace, praying Etiros would protect Regulus and her parents.

As Adelaide tracked the sun and followed the roads toward the southwest coast of Monparth, she sent Father a mental thank-you for teaching her how to navigate and to Mother for teaching her geography. She kept her hood pulled low over her face, her hair braided and tucked out of sight, and her cloak drawn about her to hide her figure despite the warm sun. Whenever anyone approached, she left the road. That cost her time, but being accosted on the road would slow her progress more.

The supplies in Regulus' bag lasted the first day. She awoke much later than needed the second day, then had to scavenge fruit and raw vegetables from a nearby field. Every minute she wasted, she failed the king and Father.

On the third morning, she reached the royal township of Selcairn. Adelaide paused at the crest of a hill, looking over the largest town she had ever seen. Jumbles of buildings, mostly built of wood, sprawled out on both sides of a shining blue river. The narrow steeple of the township's chapel jutted above nearby slate roofs. A thin haze of smoke obscuring half the town indicated where the greatest concentration of shops must be. At least in such a bustling place, she might blend in. Maybe she could trade one of her knives for some food.

She continued down the hill, past peasants on foot, a small black carriage with a harried-looking driver and curtains pulled over the windows, and a group of brown-clad monks singing in a low drone. A young boy tossing a red wooden ball dropped his toy and chased it in front of Zephyr. Zephyr reared, and the boy screamed and scrambled backward as Adelaide struggled to rein in Zephyr. She dismounted and patted Zephyr's neck, calming him before tossing the boy his ball.

"Don't run in front of horses," Adelaide chided, her heart racing. "You could have been killed."

The boy ran off to a nearby woman, crying for his mama. Several people stared. A few pointed and whispered. Adelaide realized her hood had fallen off, and in the excitement, she had pushed her cloak back over her shoulders. She stood in the middle of the road, the knives on the baldric across her chest and the daggers at her hips on full display. She pulled her cloak around her and threw her hood up, but it was too late to stop the stares.

Someone wearing a hooded black cloak and riding a tan palfrey had stopped on Zephyr's other side when she turned to remount. She focused on her saddle, ignoring the spectator as she threw her leg over Zephyr's back.

"Where is a lovely lady like yourself going alone and bristling with blades?" a man's voice asked from under the hood. Something familiar about his voice made her pause, and she looked over.

The man looked up, his horse a little shorter than Zephyr and the man himself shorter than average. His hood shadowed the top of his face. A pale, round nose protruded over a long brown beard streaked with gray. Crimson accents stood out like blood against his layered black robes. One pale, knobby hand gripped the palfrey's reins. Her eyes locked onto the top of a gold staff, mostly hidden under his cloak. A dark opal with hints of blue and specks of red rested at the base of a hollow oval of gold spirals. Her gaze snapped back to his shadowed face as her hands went cold. A smile tugged at the corner of Kirven's mouth. Adelaide kicked Zephyr and the gelding shot forward.

"How rude!" Kirven shouted.

Something hit her side and launched her from the saddle. She groaned as she hit the ground. People on the road screamed and scattered. Adelaide lifted herself on her elbow and shook her head, trying to clear her double-vision as Zephyr bolted. Kirven's palfrey trotted up next to her.

"Where were you going, she-mage?" Kirven snickered. "Or, I suppose, just girl now."

Adelaide thrust her hands up and a blast of pale blue light sent Kirven flying off his horse. The palfrey galloped away as she scrambled to her feet and Kirven tumbled across the road. She threw off her cumbersome cloak and directed a blast of fire at him. He blocked it with a shield of lime green light before it hit him. The flames licked past him on either side of his shield as he lay on his back in the dry ditch on the roadside. She conjured a spear and threw it, then another blast of fire. *Keep him down!*

But Kirven stood, using the staff to help him up. He made his magical shield bigger and kept it steady against her barrage of hard light blasts, magical knives and spears, and fireballs. On the other side of his shield, the opal pulsed with a dark green glow. Kirven slammed the bottom of the staff into the ground. The road buckled and a ripple moved toward her across the ground that knocked her off her feet. The back of her head slammed against the packed dirt. Her pulse thudded in her ears and black dots danced in her vision.

"Interesting." Kirven's footsteps moved toward her. She blindly threw a barrage of light shards as she sat up, but his shield absorbed the shards with a soft hiss. The shield dropped in the same moment as he pointed the Staff at her, and a green blast of light exploded from the tip. Adelaide raised her own shield, but the force of the blast rattled her bones. She threw a fireball around her shield. Kirven raised a new shield in a blink.

Glowing green ropes snaked out from his free hand and curled toward her on both sides of her barrier. She expanded the shield, turning it into a dome completely covering her. The ropes stabbed at the barrier as she panted to catch her breath. Kirven let his shield fall and switched to firing a continuous stream of flames at her barrier. She knelt, chest heaving, while heat built within her little dome. Sweat soaked her neck and trickled down her forehead and into her eyes.

The barrier was getting more exhausting to maintain by the second. Worse, her dome was running out of air. Adelaide pushed to her feet, forcing the barrier into a wall. With a heave, she threw the barrier toward Kirven. He planted the staff in the ground and managed to stay on his feet. He scowled, his hood thrown back. She wanted a moment to gulp in the cooler air, but instead she heard Father's voice. *"You have an advantage, you press it. A fight is never fair."*

She charged, conjuring a sword of light and flame. Kirven recoiled. He aimed the staff at her as she swung toward him with the sword. The blast from the staff, inches away from her chest, felt like a battering ram to the sternum. She sprawled on the ground, lungs burning, unable to breathe. Nothing but a pinprick of blue sky showed in the blinding whiteness. After a small eternity, she gasped in a giant breath and rolled onto her side, coughing and panting. Her throat was raw. The whiteness faded, but black hovered at the edges of her vision.

Something grabbed Adelaide's ankle, and she kicked it away. Green, glowing ropes raced over her arms and legs and around her neck. She tried to attack Kirven, but the ropes pulling at her wrists made it difficult. She saw the blast of magic just before it slammed into the side of her head. Her neck snapped to the side, and she knew no more.

Adelaide moved her heavy head and moaned. Her heartbeat pulsed behind her eyes. She fought to force her heavy eyelids open. Walls surrounded her, windowless but with long cracks between the boards that allowed narrow strips of sunlight into the shadowy room. The warm air smelled of mildew.

Ropes—real ones, not magic ones—wrapped around her, binding her arms over her torso and digging into her skin. Her arms were crossed in an X at her wrists, with her palms against her shoulders. She attempted to move her hands but could barely rotate them. More ropes tied her ankles together. Straw poked into her arms. Her knives and daggers were gone.

The small dark room was empty, save for a thick layer of dust, old straw scattered over the floor, and a three-legged stool in one corner. Perhaps it had been a shed in the distant past. Adelaide shimmied into a sitting position. A door to her right opened, spilling blinding sunlight around Kirven's outline.

"Good, you're awake." Kirven hurried inside, letting the door rattle closed. He set the staff in the corner, moved the stool closer, and sat down. "Now. Adelaide, isn't it?"

She glared. She needed to break free of these ropes, and soon. But she used her hands to perform magic, and with them tied in place, she was at a loss.

"I haven't been truly surprised in a long time, Adelaide." Kirven leaned forward, resting his elbows on his knees. He threw his hood back, and his eyes caught her off-guard. The whites were bloodshot around coal-black irises rimmed with a thin line of green. "I wasn't expecting to see you—much less with your magic back. Now, I usually kill people when I steal their magic, so the thought that it might return had occurred to me. However, I never would have guessed it would return so quickly, or so strong. Most interesting. Tell me, how did you speed the process?"

She clenched her jaw and glanced toward the Staff. Her head still ached, but at least the pounding behind her eyes had lessened.

"Look, mage." Kirven's tone turned sharp and impatient. "This can be quick and painless, or long and painful. How did you get your magic back so quickly?"

Adelaide glowered up at him, mouth set in a hard line.

He tugged on his beard. "I drained you of your magic. *All* of it, save the drop that kept you alive. If I had pushed a little further, I would have taken your life. But I promised I wouldn't kill you, and if I don't keep my word all the time, what good are my threats?" He grabbed her chin with cold fingers. "So believe me when I say, if you don't tell me exactly how you got your magic back in such a short span without the aid of sorcery, you will experience pain beyond what you can comprehend."

She stiffened. "You didn't kill me. My magic came back gradually. That's what happens when you let someone live." Kirven shook his head.

"I know you're lying. I could barely light a candle for three days after the amount of power it took to re-forge the Staff of Nightfall. That wasn't even a complete draining of my ability—thanks to the extra power from you. You're going to tell me how to speed that process up." His fingers dug into her jaw. "I do it by stealing energy from living things. It took an entire grove of trees and two hapless satyrs to get me back to full strength this time. But I know that's not what you did. Tell me."

"I can't help you."

The sorcerer's hand warmed. Pain moved through her jaw like a screw forced into her bones. Adelaide screamed as the pain spread. Down her spine, along her bound arms, through her legs. Every bone in her body felt like it would crack at any moment. She just wanted it to stop. Her own screaming rang in her ears and tears blinded her.

The pain vanished. Her chest pushed against her bound arms as she gasped for air. Her throat ached.

Kirven rubbed one ear with his forefinger. "Women's screams are so painful on the ears. Now. The truth."

She shook, staring at the moldy straw on the dirt floor as tears blurred her vision. She wouldn't help him. If she could just do some magic...

"Stubborn." He sighed and placed his hand on top of her head.

A shield! She squeezed her eyes shut and focused on creating a shield over her body. Her hands fisted. Kirven hissed and jerked his hand back. She opened her eyes to a pale blue shimmer over her skin, but maintaining it felt like trying to hold water in her hands.

"Clever girl." Kirven fetched the Staff and touched the end to her head.

Pressure built along her head until her grasp on the barrier shattered. Pain cracked through her skull and crushed her spine. She thrashed away with a scream as tears streamed down her face. He sat back down and lifted an eyebrow.

"Ready to talk?"

Adelaide trembled. Maybe it wouldn't help him. At the tree, the fairies had said Kirven didn't want to face them, that's why he sent Regulus for the root. And she'd had to pass a test—a test Kirven would fail. Besides, she didn't want any more pain.

"I visited the neumenet tree in Holgren Forest. There were fairies. They tried to trick me into stealing the tree's powers. I refused. Then the tree just…gave me back my magic."

"Was it coming back on its own before that?"

She licked her dry, salty lips. "Only a little. I tried to heal Regulus and passed out and then couldn't do anything."

"Mm. Disappointing." Kirven sighed dramatically. "Technically, I guess you were telling me the truth when you said you couldn't help me. So," he sounded displeased, "I suppose I owe you an apology for the torture. Still, you weren't being forthcoming, so that's on you."

On me! At last she stopped shaking. Her tears dried in dirty lines on her cheeks. If she hadn't already believed Kirven would make a terrible king, she was certain of it now.

"Speaking of His Saintliness, where is Hargreaves?"

No. She couldn't betray him.

"Let's not have a repeat of your reticence, shall we? I'd like to spare my ears."

Adelaide shuddered. She understood better now why Regulus had been ready to kidnap her, with that pain being the alternative. How had he even considered disobeying for so long?

"He went back to Arrano," she said, her voice tight.

"Did you two have a falling out?" When she didn't answer right away, Kirven grabbed her braid and yanked her head back so she was looking at him. "What happened to 'I love you?' And he seemed desperate to protect you. With his constant self-sacrificing, I wouldn't have expected him to let you wander about alone. What's he up to?"

If she didn't answer or lied, he would torture her again. But if she told the truth…what if he warned Nolan? Kirven sighed and wrapped his hand around her throat. Burning lines spread from his hand over her skin.

"All right!" The pain stopped, but he kept his hand on her neck. "We split up to cover more ground. He went to get his men."

"Why?" His wiry eyebrows knit together.

"To rescue my parents." Adelaide gulped.

"Typical. And I think I know where *you* were headed, but I'd like to confirm my suspicion."

"I was riding to warn the king."

"Foolish girl." Kirven pushed her back. She choked at the force of his hand against her windpipe. He stood and clasped his hands behind his back. "You and your father are nothing but trouble. Carrick told me your father figured out my secret. I recommended he kill Lord Belanger, but no." He wrinkled his nose. "He's obsessed with having you. It's clouding his judgment. I'm letting him try his way for now, because a willing servant works better in my long-term plans, and he believes he can control you."

His voice took on a hint of impatient annoyance. "I made a deal with him and put the binding on him because of his intelligence, ruthlessness, charisma, and ambition. A man with such a craving for power, with that much selfishness and so little regard for his fellow man, is an excellent ally in a war. Not to mention terribly easy to manipulate. He will be useful in restructuring Monparth's nobility to serve me—but that works best if he's happy with our arrangement. Also, I assumed he would kill Hargreaves. I'm disappointed he's not dead yet. Perhaps Carrick is less competent than I hoped."

"Then why didn't you kill Regulus?"

"Because," Kirven sounded like he was explaining something simple to a bratty and stupid child, "I gave my word. Haven't you been paying attention?" He ran his fingers through his beard. "Ah, well. I'll alert Carrick. I must be on my way again. There's a palace to scout and a masque to ruin. But first..." He placed his hand on her forehead.

"No, please!" She tried to scoot away, but the bindings prevented much movement. Her back pressed into the wall of the shed. She hunched down, making herself as small as possible. His hand burned hot against her forehead. Nothing else happened.

Kirven frowned. "What?" He pressed harder, forcing her head against the wall. The heat from his hand made her eyes water. He dropped his hand and stared for a moment before grabbing the Staff. He placed the end of the Staff against her head, then cursed and moved the Staff to her chest. Nothing.

"What aren't you telling me?" he screeched. "Why can't I take your magic?"

Oh. That's what he's— Searing heat spread from the end of the staff, spreading invisible flames over her skin.

"Tree!" she shrieked. The burning subsided. "The fairies said the neumenet tree's powers can't be stolen! It gave me my magic, so my magic can't be stolen. That's what they told me!"

Kirven's features slackened.

Adelaide cowered against the wall of the shed. "Please. That's what they told me. I don't know any more. I don't know any more."

He drew back the Staff. His shoulders rose and fell in sharp, tense movements as his expression became dark and dangerous. "Say you'll serve me."

CHAPTER 18

THE SUDDEN command took Adelaide aback. "What?"

Kirven bared his teeth. "I can't take your power as my own, but I can still ensure your magic serves me."

Serve…no. She remembered all too well how his mark burned. And he could torture her at any time. Take control of her body. He would force her to use her magic to harm.

She swallowed back her fear and straightened. *Etiros, give me strength.* "I'd sooner die." Her voice shook, but she stared him down.

Kirven crouched in front of her. "Say you will serve me, or I will torture you again."

"Because you never tortured Regulus while *he* served you? You'd torture me sooner or later." Adelaide raised her chin, even though her lower lip trembled. "I know what you're doing. You can't put the mark on me unless I agree. I won't."

Before she could so much as flinch, Kirven placed the end of the staff on her stomach. Pain spread like ropes laced with sharp glass wrapping around her torso, then her arms, her legs, even her head. The invisible rope squeezed, and she felt like she should be bleeding everywhere. She fell to her side, writhing in mind-numbing agony. Her mouth was open, and she knew she was screaming, but she couldn't hear herself. She thrashed against the ropes, against the pain. Kirven pulled the staff back and she curled into a ball. Sobs wracked her body. Fresh tears raced down her face and neck, soaking into her tunic.

Kirven grabbed the rope around her torso and hauled her to a sitting position. She was crying so hard her eyes wouldn't focus on his face.

"Look at me!" He slapped her. She coughed, choking on her sobs. "Agree to serve me!"

Adelaide shook her head, even though she wanted to give in. A voice in her mind shouted to just say yes, it wasn't worth it, do anything to prevent more pain now, sort the rest out later. But she pushed that voice away. There would be pain later, even if she agreed. He would have to give up eventually. She had already helped this monster too much. Never again.

He grabbed her face and leaned in close. "If you don't agree to serve me, once I'm king, I'll torture your entire family. Your father. Your mother. Any siblings you have. Hargreaves. The pain you've just experienced? I'll make them feel it while you watch. Eventually, people can't take it anymore, and their minds break, like shattered glass."

A stifled cry shuddered through her. She pressed her eyes closed. *Etiros, please, no!* She couldn't serve him. But how could she refuse?

Kirven's fingernails dug into her face. "You will serve me, or you will watch your family suffer. And then you will suffer. Like this."

Ice seemed to spread from his hand, freezing and burning at the same time. Adelaide shrieked and broke free of his grip. Released from the pain, she curled against the wall.

"Serve me, or my first act as king will be to summon your entire family to their slow and excruciating deaths while you watch."

Adelaide cried silently. *Etiros, help me.* Kirven's words replayed in her mind. *"First act as king…while you watch."* To do that, he would have to leave her alive. If she lived, she would have a chance to escape and stop him. But she couldn't stop him if she agreed to serve him like Nolan had. She shivered. She would never choose the same path as Nolan.

Kirven wrenched her chin up. "Swear to serve me."

"No." It was a near-silent whisper, but enough for him to hear. Kirven snarled and backhanded her face. Her teeth cut into the corner of her mouth, and she tasted blood.

"Mages!" He threw together a string of nonsensical curse words in Monparthian, Khast, and languages she didn't know. He stopped short and looked at her, as if seeing her for the first time. "Mages…"

Kirven bent down and pulled a crimson handkerchief from his obsidian-accented belt. He dried her face, his expression calm. "I thought I had eradicated mages from Monparth, because no one knew of any." He dabbed at the blood on her lips. "You've been hiding all your life. I was surprised how much magic I pulled from you. All that power, and you hid. Why?"

"Because you killed everyone like me!"

"Not everyone." He smiled wickedly. "If I had killed *everyone* like you, I would have had to kill myself."

She recoiled, but already pressed against the wall, there was nowhere for her to go. "I'm nothing like you."

He dropped his hand and let the handkerchief fall. "I was you, once. A mage. Powerful, but clueless. Uneducated. Talented but without knowledge, just as you are. I couldn't help I was born a mage. But because of something out of my control, they took my birthright from me. Because of a centuries-old treaty, I wasn't allowed to be king.

"My *brother*," he bit out the word and spittle flew on her face, "would get everything that was rightfully *mine*. My throne. My crown. I could be his *advisor*. My brother and I studied together under the best tutors in government, military strategy, history, geography…but my parents refused to give me a tutor in magic. I was forbidden from even trying to use my power, punished when it accidentally escaped. My oh-so-loving father thought if I didn't know much about my power, I would be less of a threat." He laughed bitterly. "He was wrong. It just made me angry. When my mother caught me practicing, they forged a magic-suppressing cuff around my wrist."

New dismay contorted her face, but she shoved away the pinch of empathy. She wouldn't pity this monster.

He pursed his lips. "Your parents did the same, didn't they? Forbade you from accessing the energy burning through you, tried to force you to ignore the roar of power, to pretend you weren't what you are."

His words hit too close to her heart, and her gaze fell. Anger snapped her back to her senses, and she snarled at him. "Because of you! Because it wasn't safe!"

"Different circumstances, same lack of understanding." Kirven leaned back. "The difference between us is I didn't accept my cage. I left to find my own tutors. And you know what I discovered? Sorcery is far more interesting. More fun. More…useful." He reached toward her, and she shied away with a whimper from the torture that would doubtless accompany his touch. He grinned and leaned back. "See? Anyway, I learned quickly. Made some of my tutors nervous. I realized the best way to use a tutor was to have them teach you everything they knew, then kill them by draining their magic. Then they couldn't try to stop you, their knowledge died with them, and your power temporarily strengthened."

She grimaced as revulsion filled her.

"When I thought I was ready, I returned to claim my throne and punish those who denied me my birthright. But I miscalculated." He pulled the left side of his robe and tunic away from his neck and shoulder. Twisting white and pink scars covered every inch of exposed skin. "A gift from one of my father's mages." He shifted his collar back into place. "A burn covering most of the left side of my body. Don't worry," he said as she stared at his shoulder with horror, "after I learned how to track them all down, I killed every mage in the kingdom, including the ones who did this to me. So no one could stop me next time I tried to claim my throne. And yet"—he cocked his head—"here you are."

"Then kill me." She'd meant it as a challenge. But her voice was so weak and desperate, it sounded like a plea.

"Don't you see? I'm offering to help you. To teach you. All this power, don't you want to learn how to use it properly? Don't you want to learn everything you are capable of?" Kirven's eyes narrowed. "You have a choice, Adelaide. On the one hand, you have a future as Carrick's wench. He's immortal, you can't fight that. A future filled with your family's pain and suffering. A future of using your talents only when your husband tells you to."

Her stomach churned, and she looked away.

"On the other hand, you have a future where *you* can show the world your power. You can control Carrick, not the other way around. You could avoid marriage to him. You can't have had an easy life, being half Khastallander. If you desire, you would have the power to punish anyone who has ever treated you as inferior for the way you were born. Agree to serve me, and I will make you the second-most powerful sorcerer in the world. I haven't waited so long to assemble the Staff of Nightfall to stop at Monparth. Together, we will conquer the known world. You could be ruler of Khastalland. I could even make you my queen. My empress."

She jerked her head up, her lungs seizing.

He laughed. "All right, never fear, I wouldn't force you. But perhaps one day you'd like to be queen. I'd even let you keep that self-righteous mercenary as your lover. All the freedom, all the power, all the status, all the wealth you desire. But even without the title of queen, you will be a sorceress of astounding power. You would never lose a battle again. Even Nolan Carrick would tremble at your feet."

"I don't want that." Adelaide shook her head, hard and fast, trying to dislodge the voice that whispered she did. "I'm not a sorceress. I won't corrupt my magic for personal gain."

"Then what's the point?" Kirven moved to the stool. "Don't be unreasonable. I am offering you power beyond belief. I am offering you freedom—from Nolan Carrick, from a society that judges you for your heritage and fears you for your magic. I'm offering you the chance to save your family and friends. Don't you want to protect them?" He crossed his arms. "Or I'm promising you the pain and suffering and death of everyone you care about. I'm promising you a life as Carrick's wife and plaything."

Adelaide trembled and fought growing nausea. It felt as if Kirven had peered into her soul and found all her deepest hurts, shames, fears, and desires. He took her experiences and emotions and twisted them to make his offer, his way of thinking, seem…tempting. *No. I'm not him. I won't become a monster.* She swallowed hard.

"Do you think you can bully me into joining you?"

"And bribe."

"I don't want anything you can give me."

It was half a lie, and she knew it. Part of her would love to relax, out of Nolan's reach. She could give in, and her family would be safe. Regulus would be safe. She could learn more about her magic. But the cost was too great. She remembered the haunted look in Regulus' eyes as he told her he had stolen and killed for Kirven. To knowingly agree to help the sorcerer murder the king and any other evil actions… Regulus would never look at her the same. Minerva would fear her. Mother and Father would be ashamed. And she would hate herself.

"I will *never* serve you."

Kirven's face hardened. He pressed the tip of the staff against her chest, pinning her to the wall. Her breaths came sharper, faster. "You will."

Adelaide's throat worked, but fear locked her words in her chest. Thousands of white-hot needles buried into her, ripping her apart. She screamed and curled forward. Her mind emptied of everything except the pain. The staff moved away, taking the pain with it. She fell onto her side and sobbed.

"Last chance." She barely heard Kirven over her weeping. "Will you serve me? Or will you watch as I torture your family?"

She squeezed her eyes shut and tried to control her crying. *I'll live. I'll get free. Regulus will come. The king will have guards. Kirven won't win. He can't. Etiros, he can't win.*

"Answer me!"

"No," she whispered.

"Fine." He cursed. "Suit yourself. I'll be back." He strode out of the shed, throwing open the door so it banged against the wall.

Her throat was raw from screaming. Her head hurt, especially across her forehead. She wanted to go to sleep and wake up in a world without sorcery and evil men who hurt others to get what they wanted. Adelaide closed her eyes, curled her knees toward her chest, and prayed for the unconsciousness of sleep.

She awoke to Kirven pulling her off the ground. Her head still ached, but not as much. Her throat was swollen and parched. Kirven pushed her into a sitting position. The sunlight coming through the open door and the cracks in the walls had dimmed and taken on an orange hue. Outside, the long shadows cast by the trees had deepened to black.

"You want to be difficult." Kirven moved slower and had bags under his eyes. "Fine. But I won't have you causing more trouble." He twisted around and picked up something. Two thick half-circles of hammered iron connected by a hinge on one side. The open sides turned out a ninety-degree angle with a hole in each end. It was just large enough to encircle her neck. Her heart beat faster.

"What is that? What are you doing?" Adelaide tried to squirm away, but he closed the cold metal around her neck.

"You'll use your magic to serve me, or you won't use it at all."

She pulled against the collar. Kirven held it firmly as he slipped a small padlock into the holes where the two halves met. The lock clicked shut. He released the collar, and it settled against her skin.

Exhaustion overcame her panic as all her energy, magical or otherwise, drained away. Not like when Kirven had stolen her magic, but more like how she felt after using a lot of magic when training or fighting.

"What is this?"

"Magic suppressor." Kirven sat back and rubbed his head. "Tricky spell. Saps a person's energy. Takes a lot of power to create, which I'm not pleased about. But don't worry, I'll be at full strength to commit regicide. Fratricide, I suppose. You'll find using magic while wearing that exceedingly difficult. You could, but not for long, and you'd likely pass out from the effort." He sneered. "If you'd joined me, you would have learned how to do this yourself, instead of suffering the effects. But you're too hung up on ideas of being noble. A true match for the mercenary."

She wiggled her hands, contorting her wrists to grab the collar. She managed to lift it off her skin, but it didn't help the drained feeling. Resigned, she let it fall.

Kirven stood. "I've contacted Carrick. Someone should collect you before you starve." He paused at the door. "We'll see each other again. In the meantime, give some thought to who I should torture first—your father or your mother?" He shut the door behind him.

Adelaide laid back down. The collar weighed against the side of her neck. A single tear fell from the corner of her eye.

The plan had disintegrated. She had failed the king. She had been a fool to part ways with Regulus. If they had stayed together, maybe she wouldn't be in this mess. Perhaps if Regulus had been there, she might have won. Or escaped. And at least she wouldn't be alone. Or maybe Regulus would be dead. She shifted, trying to find a position that didn't hurt her shoulders, back, neck, or hips. That proved impossible.

With nothing else to do, her thoughts wandered. The only spot of light in her dark mind was that people had witnessed her and Kirven's magic on full display. Perhaps word would make it to the king, and he would be extra cautious. But that was small comfort against all her other concerns. Kirven was more powerful than she had feared. Would *any* amount of caution or security be enough to save the king?

And who would come for her? Would Nolan come himself, or would he send someone? What would he do when he had her? She pushed that thought away. Where was Regulus? Had he made it to Belanger castle yet? Did he stand a chance against Nolan?

"Please be safe, Regulus," Adelaide whispered. She cried herself to sleep.

REGULUS PACED, his sword swaying and chainmail rustling with his swift stride. Caleb had been gone too long. He scowled at the sun half-hidden behind the trees lining the horizon. Much too long. If Caleb had been captured, the blame fell squarely on Regulus' shoulders. And if Caleb had been captured, that meant they had even less of a chance of success than he had feared. It would mean he had done the exact thing he had sworn to never knowingly do. He had led his men on a suicide mission. And he had left Adelaide to fend for herself to do it.

Thoughts of the last time he had led his men into a trap flashed in his mind. Images of friends' lifeless bodies, of ten graves. He shoved the memory aside. That wouldn't happen this time. He wouldn't let it. And the sorcerer wasn't here.

As he paced, his long shadow moved over the rest of his men. They sat on stumps or on the ground in front of their tiny make-shift camp of three low tents, their horses staked nearby. Estevan and Perceval played with dice while Dresden watched. Jerrick knelt with his eyes closed, his lips moving silently. Praying to Hallilek. He had a faith Regulus envied. Harold remained at Arrano—Regulus refused to put the youth in Carrick's path.

"He's fine, Captain. Cal's always fine, just tardy. Stop your pacing." Perceval threw down his dice and wrinkled his nose. Regulus did not stop pacing.

Estevan whooped. "Ha! That's two homemade mince pies for me!"

"You really shouldn't gamble your wife's cooking," Dresden said, his chin cupped in his hand. "Basically gambling away her labor. That's just wrong."

Perceval scowled. "You cheated, Wolgemuth."

"How?" Estevan rattled the dice in his hand.

"Check the dice," Jerrick said without opening his eyes. "His weighted one has a tiny nick on the corner."

Amid sounds of scuffling and grunting as Perceval tried to wrest the dice from Estevan, someone crested a nearby hill, his outline black against the setting sun. Regulus tensed and gripped the hilt of his sword. Behind him, his knights stood and watched the figure approach. The man waved, and fading sunlight highlighted his shaggy blond hair. Regulus dropped his hand from his sword. Caleb walked at a languid stroll, which did nothing for Regulus' mounting impatience.

"Well?" Regulus asked as soon as Caleb reached hearing distance. He tapped his foot, arms crossed. "What's the report?"

"Got some good news, some bad news, and some news I'm going to count as great but may be up for interpretation."

Regulus grunted, but Caleb just lowered onto a nearby moss-covered log. Dresden stood next to Regulus, and the rest of the men returned to their seats, the game of dice forgotten.

"Good news is, based on what the servants around the castle are saying, all the Belangers are alive." Caleb crossed his ankles and leaned back, propping his elbows on a protruding broken branch. "Bad news, the castle's well-garrisoned. I spotted ten men on the walls. Looked like more inside. But the stars have aligned, my friend."

Regulus cocked an eyebrow and waited for Caleb to continue. He should have sent someone less prone to dramatics, but Caleb had a way of making people comfortable and their tongues loose. Made him an excellent scout.

Caleb grinned. "Sir Immortal Brute has just left the castle all alone in a spectacular hurry, with no explanation other than he would be back in a day or two and instructions to keep the prisoners in good health."

"Carrick is gone?" Caleb nodded. "For at least a day?" Another nod. Regulus smiled and returned to pacing. This would make things easier. Maybe not easy, but easier. He stopped midstride. "He gave no indication of where he was going in such a hurry? Or why?"

"If he did, it wasn't in public. Hence the up for interpretation." A dreamy expression spread over Caleb's face. "I was chatting with a lovely milkmaid in the courtyard. A braid the color of honey, round, rosy cheeks, green eyes that positively demand a song—"

"Focus, Cal." Regulus rubbed his temple.

Caleb rolled his eyes. "Carrick jogged right past me on his way to get his horse. He was shouting about finding things just as he left them when he returns and threatening dismemberment if any harm came to the prisoners."

Perceval snorted. "It's a miracle you even heard that! Why the captain trusts you to stay on task, I'm sure I don't know, you philandering—"

"Oh, philandering, did you pick that up at university?" Caleb sat forward and pointed at Perceval. "I'll have you know I was on task. That milkmaid can get us into the castle." He gave an over-dramatic look of hurt. "To think I've called such an uncivilized oaf my friend."

"Not now, you two," Jerrick said.

Regulus gave Jerrick a grateful nod. "How can this milkmaid of yours get us in?"

"She's not my milkmaid." Caleb's eyes danced. "At least, not yet. But she's not happy with the current situation at the castle, and when Carrick left, was easily convinced to let us in. Two hours from now, just after dark, at eight and a half bells."

"Well done, Caleb." Regulus turned to Dresden and motioned with his head.

They walked a short distance away, followed by the sound of Perceval and Caleb's routine bickering and Estevan goading them both on.

"This could be good, but I don't like it," Regulus admitted. "Something strange is going on."

"Agreed." Dresden looked toward Belanger castle, its turrets just visible over the tops of the trees. "I can think of no good reason for Carrick to have left so abruptly."

"The sorcerer could have called him away." He chewed on his lower lip. "I don't like not knowing what they're up to."

Dresden rubbed his beard. "Or he could somehow know we're here. It could be a trap. Caleb's milkmaid could even be in on it."

"That occurred to me, too." Regulus rubbed the back of his neck. "But, even as blinded as he can be when it comes to women, Caleb would have noted if her behavior was suspicious." His chest tightened. "There is another possibility, though." His throat dried out.

"Carrick might have learned something about Adelaide's whereabouts."

"She wouldn't leave her parents behind. Splitting up seemed the best way to keep her away from Carrick." Regulus sighed. "But now I don't know where she is or if she's okay. I think I made a mistake. I should have dragged her to the palace if that's what it took."

Dresden gazed out at the sunset. Loud laughter rose from the camp behind them, the men unaware of the turmoil and fear in Regulus' heart. Drez turned to Regulus.

"There's no point in agonizing over what's done. We focus on the mission at hand. With Carrick gone and a way in, we can take back Belanger castle, not just get the Belangers out. So, let's plan."

Like it or not, Drez was right. He didn't have the luxury of spending energy and time worrying about Adelaide. She would have to take care of herself. He just prayed he had been right in believing she could.

Darkness fell and they crept toward the side door of the castle. The same one he and Adelaide had escaped through just a few days prior. Based on the fresh wood, the same one that Carrick had broken down. The mercenaries wore dark cloaks over their armor and moved with speed and stealth across the hill leading up to the castle walls. A dim crescent moon made it easier to blend into the night.

Regulus pressed against the wall next to the door. The fresh wood was reinforced with iron that gleamed dully in the faint moonlight. Dresden moved behind him, and the knights lined up against the wall. A gentle bell somewhere in the castle pealed once, signaled half-past eight. Regulus took a deep breath and knocked. Three rapid taps. Pause. Two slow taps. Pause. Three rapid taps.

A key scraped in the lock. Regulus drew his sword, nerves taut and every muscle coursing with energy. The door opened without a sound—a blessing of new hinges. Regulus raised his sword. A small, pale hand held aloft a lantern. The flickering yellow light illuminated the wide-eyed face of a young woman with a gray shawl pulled over her head and shoulders. She stepped back and Regulus lowered his sword, scanning the darkness behind her. She beckoned them inside, and they followed.

Two guards sat slumped against either side of the door, sleeping. One snored and shifted position as they entered. Regulus grabbed the girl's shoulder and leaned in close to her ear. "Did you drug them?"

She shook her head, fear etched on her face. "The cook did."

"Carrick's men or Lord Belanger's?"

"Carrick's."

Regulus glanced down at the men. Still slumbering. But for how long? And they had aligned with Carrick. They chose violence the moment they entered this castle. He nodded at Estevan, then pointed to the men. Carrick had declared war by taking Belanger castle. He and his would reap what they sowed.

Silent as a shadow, Estevan slit both men's throats. The milkmaid pressed a hand to her mouth and the lantern shook in her outstretched hand. Regulus took it, extinguished the flame, and set it down.

"Can you lead us to the dungeon?" Regulus murmured. She nodded, still staring at the corpses. Regulus turned her away with a flicker of shame. Adelaide deserved better than a killer. But taking a castle with only six men required the ruthless mercenary. The girl stood immobile in shock. "We need to move quickly…" He looked to Caleb questioningly.

"Susan," Caleb whispered.

"The dungeons, Susan."

Susan nodded again and drew a deep breath. She clutched her shawl against her chest and led them in the shadows along the base of the wall. Something moved ahead of them, and Regulus grabbed her arm to stop her. A guard carrying a torch approached. A soft whoosh passed Regulus' head and moonlight glinted on the edge of a blade before Estevan's throwing knife buried into the guard's throat. Regulus sprinted forward, caught the body before the sound of its fall could draw any attention, and lowered it to the ground.

Susan stifled a gasp. Her knuckles whitened as she gripped her shawl tighter. "I knew him."

"He's not locked up; he's a traitor," Perceval muttered. "Good riddance."

"It's Lord Belanger's choice what happens to the traitors," Regulus hissed. He looked at Estevan. "Let's try not to kill any of them again." Estevan and the others murmured disgruntled agreement.

They continued, moving from shadow to shadow across the courtyard. At a corner, Susan held up her hand for them to stop. She peeked around.

"One of Carrick's is guarding the door," she whispered.

Regulus moved her back and glanced around the corner. A large man leaned on the side of his shoulder against a door some twenty paces away. Regulus waved Caleb forward.

Caleb pulled his bow off his shoulder and nocked an arrow as he knelt at the corner. A soft thwang of the bowstring, and a short grunt followed by a muffled thud. Caleb stood and gave a quick nod. Regulus scanned the surrounding area before they ran to the building. Jerrick found the dead guard's keys and opened the door. Susan led them down a hall, then pointed to a descending spiral stone staircase.

"The dungeon is down there. From what I've heard, Carrick is only letting his own men be on guard in the dungeon." She glanced around, her wide eyes searching the shadows. "But Lady Belanger and Lady Julia are locked in their rooms."

"Don't worry, we'll get them next." Regulus smiled, trying to reassure her. "You've been very helpful and very brave. We can take it from here."

"Good luck." Susan fled.

"Permission to kill anyone not in a cell, Captain?" Perceval asked dryly.

Regulus adjusted his grip on his sword. "Granted."

They rolled their steps as they stole down the stone stairs. Quiet, indiscernible voices echoed up the stairwell. The stairs emptied into a guardroom. A few torches in iron ring sconces lit the room in orange light. Three men wearing chainmail and armed with swords sat playing a game with bone dice at a wooden table.

The guards jumped to their feet, but not fast enough. Estevan threw, and his knife buried into the throat of the guard on the right. His eyes widened and he fell backward. Caleb shot an arrow straight through the neck of the middle guard. The man fell onto the table. Jerrick ran forward, hefting his two-sided battle-axe. The last guard fumbled with his sword, his eyes darting to his deceased cohorts. Jerrick swung. The last guard's head rolled across the dusty stone floor.

Dresden was already crossing the room, double scimitars drawn, his gaze sweeping the hallway beyond the guard room. Perceval followed, broadsword in hand. Regulus stepped over the headless corpse and snatched the keyring off the hook on the far wall with a loud jangle. The sound of footsteps bounced off the stone walls as someone ran toward them down the hallway.

"Hey, what's—" The newcomer's sentence was cut short as Dresden sliced both scimitars in an X across the guard's neck. The body crumpled to the ground.

Regulus had grown accustomed to facing battle alone. But as his men worked seamlessly together, their movements coordinated, each one knowing the others had their back, he remembered why he loved leading them. *A wolf is strongest with its pack.* What a fool he had been to forget that. Facing enemies with his men—his brothers—was the only place he had ever felt comfortable. Until Adelaide. *Etiros, wherever she is, protect her.*

Regulus grabbed one of the torches from the wall and they continued, alert for more guards, but none appeared. They passed several empty cells before the dungeon opened further, spreading to the right and left. Someone moved in the cell to their left. A shorter man stood and walked to the door of the cells. The man leaned against the bars, taking in their appearance with confusion on his weathered face.

"Who are you? What do you want?"

"Lord Hargreaves." Regulus stepped closer. "Here to help Lord Belanger take back his castle."

"Lady Adelaide's Lord Hargreaves?"

"Yes." Regulus ignored Dresden's snicker and the laugh Jerrick hid behind a cough. A couple more men hidden in the shadows at the back of the cell came forward.

"Excellent. I'm Sir Ruddard. Lord Belanger's men are in the next few cells." Ruddard cocked his head to his right. "Lord Belanger and Sir Belanger are at the other end of the dungeons." He inclined his head in the opposite direction.

"Thank you. I'll be right back."

Dresden accompanied him down the hall while the others remained behind. No more guards met them. They found Alfred and his son sleeping in two cells at the end of the hallway. Regulus tried various keys in the cell door while Dresden held the torch.

"What do you want?" Alfred's hard voice echoed against the stone.

Regulus looked up and smiled. "To rescue you like I promised your daughter I would."

The color drained from Alfred's face as he scrambled to his feet. "Adelaide is here?"

"No." A key finally fit, and the lock opened with a satisfying click. Regulus swung the door open, and Landon awoke in the next cell. "When we heard what happened, I went to Arrano to get my knights, and she headed for the palace to warn the king."

Alfred sagged against the bars. "Thank Etiros. But Carrick—"

"Left this evening and isn't expected back for a day or two." Regulus moved to the younger Belanger's cell and found the key quicker. Landon gave him an unreadable look as he strode out of the cell.

"My men—" Alfred started.

"We'll get them next," Regulus said. "The ones down here, anyway. Some of them—"

"Joined Carrick, I know." Alfred's expression darkened. "They will pay for their treachery in blood."

They freed Belanger's loyal knights, swelling their number by ten. Ten unarmed men.

Alfred's soldier instincts must have kicked in, because before Regulus could ask, he said, "The armory is in this building. I'll lead the way."

Dresden handed Alfred the torch. Several hallways and two spiral staircases later, Alfred, Landon, and the Belangers' knights rushed through arming themselves.

"Do you have a plan?" Alfred asked, buckling a sword belt around his waist.

"Depends on if you want any of the traitors alive after tonight." Regulus caught Estevan's smirk and the glint in Perceval's eyes but ignored them.

Alfred's upper lip curled back. "If they weren't in a cell, they aren't my men."

"In that case, I'm sending my men in three groups to clear out the guards on the walls. We will head to the residence to find your wife and daughter-in-law. Your men are welcome to join, but my men will not take it well if they interfere in killing the traitors."

Sir Ruddard stepped closer, his jaw tight. "That won't be a problem."

"Good. Caleb, Perceval, take the east side." The two might bicker like rivals, but they worked together in battle like they shared one mind. "Jerrick, Estevan, west side. Dresden, see to the gates. All of you, take a few of Lord Belanger's men with you. The rest of you will accompany Lord Belanger and me to rescue the ladies." He made eye contact with Alfred and inclined his head in deference. "If that sounds good to you."

Alfred nodded. As they left the armory behind, Alfred murmured, "You have an interesting assortment of knights, Regulus. I dare say only two are Monparthian."

Regulus glanced sidelong at Alfred. "They were my mercenaries before they were my knights, if that's what you're getting at."

"You trust them?"

Regulus paused, reaching for the handle to leave the tower. "Do you trust me?"

"My trust was a bit broken when you disappeared with my daughter," Alfred's voice held an edge that cut right through him. "But I believe I do."

"Good. Then know you can trust my men. I trust them with my life." Regulus gripped the door handle and looked pointedly at Alfred. "I would trust them with Adelaide's life."

"Good enough for me."

Regulus opened the door and followed Alfred into the night. They hurried toward the central residential part of the castle, a multilevel building of soaring windows and gothic points. The other groups splintered off. Stealth was no longer required, but Regulus still noted with distaste how much louder Lord Belanger's men were than his own.

The front doors were locked. Alfred banged the pommel of his sword on the door. When no one answered, he banged again.

Regulus looked around the courtyard, catching sight of a man falling from one of the gate towers. "Is there another way—"

The door opened, revealing a bleary-eyed servant. "Lord Belanger?"

Alfred pushed past. "Where. Is. My. Wife!"

"In your rooms, my lord."

Regulus followed Alfred across the foyer as two men wearing only loose-fitting trousers ran in from an adjoining hallway, swords drawn. Regulus intercepted them while Alfred continued toward a door in the back corner of the foyer. The men hesitated when they saw Alfred, but Regulus did not. He drove his sword through the first man's stomach, turned as he withdrew his blade, and sliced across the second man's torso. Both men fell to the ground. Regulus followed Alfred up the flight of stairs behind the corner door. Landon headed in the opposite direction with a few of the knights. He did have his own wife to rescue, after all.

They ran up the stairs, Alfred taking the steps two at a time and Regulus close on his heels. The light of the torch in Alfred's hand sputtered, casting eerie shadows from suits of armor as Alfred sprinted down a hall. A man sat in a chair next to a closed door, head resting against the wall. He looked at them, then jumped up.

"You…Carrick said there was no way you could breach the walls!"

Before they reached him, the man unlocked the door and bolted inside. The door slammed in Alfred's face and the lock clicked. Alfred bellowed and jammed his shoulder against the door. It shook but didn't budge.

Regulus motioned for him to step aside. Alfred hesitated, but moved over, his face pinched. Regulus lifted his foot to kick at the door just as the door swung inward, and he nearly fell forward through the door. He stepped back in surprise. Lady Belanger stood in the doorway in a midnight-blue nightgown, eyes wild and shoulders heaving.

"Alfred!"

"Tamina," Alfred gasped out and dropped his sword. She ran into his arms and he lifted her off the ground, kissing her with such passion, Regulus turned away. He peered into the bedroom. The guard's body lay in a heap on the floor next to the massive four-post bed, just visible in the dim light from a gap in the curtains. The handle of a dagger protruded from his neck.

After a small eternity of tear-filled kisses, Lady Belanger turned toward Regulus. "Hargreaves." Her dark brown eyes flashed. "Where is Adelaide?"

"Hopefully safely on her way to the palace." Heat crawled up Regulus' neck as she stared him down.

"Alone!" She slapped him across the face. His mouth fell open as he touched his stinging cheek. Alfred grabbed Tamina's shoulders and pulled her back.

"Troll take you, you—"

"Mina!" Alfred held his wife back. "Regulus just saved us and ensured Adelaide didn't come—"

"I heard Carrick talking to that man," Tamina pointed in the direction of the body. "He said Kirven had sent word of where he could find Adelaide, and that Regulus might attempt a rescue." Her tone softened. "He didn't think you a threat against a garrisoned castle. And while part of me is pleased he was wrong"—her hands formed fists—"Adelaide is out there *alone* with Carrick after her. His exact words were, 'I'm going to *collect* Adelaide.' Like paid-for goods. Why aren't you with her!"

Regulus stepped back, shaking his head. "No…she's on her way to warn the king. Her magic is back. Adelaide is strong and smart. She's okay. She has to be."

Tamina pointed at him. "First you run away with her when you were told to stay put. I suppose I should be thankful, because otherwise she would have been here when Carrick attacked. But then you leave her alone?"

"She wouldn't abandon you," Regulus said, his voice hoarse. "It seemed like the best way to keep her safe from Carrick."

"When did you last see her?" Alfred demanded.

"Three days ago? She's safe," Regulus said, trying to convince himself more than Adelaide's parents. He stared down at the blood giving his sword a red sheen. "I…" He swallowed. "I have to find her." He looked up, determination replacing his fear. "I have to go." He turned and pushed past the gawking knights blocking the hall.

"Where?" Alfred called. "You have no idea—"

"I'll head for the palace." Regulus clutched the grip of his sword until his fingers hurt. "I'll follow the route Adelaide most likely would have taken. Or I'll track Carrick. One way or another, I will find her." He lowered his voice, guilt carving a hole in his chest. "I have to."

BETWEEN THE memory of the torture, the collar leaching her magic, and the gnawing in her stomach, Adelaide felt lightheaded and dizzy, even lying on the ground. A night and most of a day had passed since the sorcerer had left her in the shed. She'd slept poorly. It was impossible to get comfortable, and fear of Kirven and his torture haunted her dreams. She grew weaker with each passing hour. Worse, she reeked, although she could now ignore the scent of urine. So far, she had managed to avoid defecating on herself. But she had begun to worry whether her magic would return when she got the collar off. How she would remove it, she didn't know, but she would find a way.

At this point, she was even too exhausted to be angry. She had spent part of the morning trying to escape the ropes, or even to stand up and hop her way to the door with the idea of breaking it down. When that proved futile, she had sat with her back against the wall, her rage building, lashing out at everything that had gotten her to this point. At the center of which, in the moment, had seemed to be Regulus. Adelaide finally understood why Mother had been so angry with him.

Regulus had gotten her involved with the sorcerer. Regulus had made an enemy of Nolan Carrick. Regulus was the reason Nolan had found Kirven and was now unstoppable. Regulus had the idea to split up, hadn't been there to help her when Kirven attacked. But as the pain in her empty stomach increased and the day dragged on, her anger cooled.

Regulus hadn't wanted to serve Kirven. He hadn't wanted to take her to Kirven, either. And Adelaide had made an enemy of Nolan, too. She had agreed to splitting up. Maybe the person who deserved the blame for her predicament was herself.

In the end, she decided to blame Kirven. He was behind all this pain. Everything—her years of hiding her magic, Regulus' pain, her capture, Nolan's immortality—came back to him. That spark of righteous anger kept her from utter despair. Sooner or later, someone would come, that's what Kirven said. They'd have to untie her, and she would make her escape. She would find Regulus. And somehow, someway, they would see that Kirven didn't hurt anyone else.

Adelaide was lying on her back, watching a bat trying to find its way out of the rafters, and wondering what it would be like to fly and if insects tasted any good, when the door to the shed opened. She squirmed to a sitting position and squinted at the influx of evening sunlight and the figure outlined in the doorway.

No. Not him.

"Gracious, Adelaide!" Nolan dashed forward and knelt next to her, brow wrinkled.

"Don't touch me!" Her voice croaked. *Why did he have to come himself?* Adelaide wriggled away, her heart racing. He grabbed her shoulders, looking her up and down. She hated the involuntary whimper that caught in her throat. But unlike Kirven's, Nolan's touch didn't hurt.

"Did he hurt you?"

"As if you care." Her stomach twisted and emitted a strange groaning sound.

"I care. He left you like this?" Nolan sounded surprisingly upset. "Have you eaten?"

"Yes, he left me like this. And how could I have eaten?" She wiggled her fingers by her shoulders.

"Hold on." Nolan darted out of the shed and returned a moment later with a bag in hand. He pulled Regulus' dagger from the back of his belt and cut the ropes off her torso. Adelaide groaned as her arms fell to her sides. She would have clawed his eyes out if her cramped muscles had allowed her to move her arms.

He took a wineskin from the bag and offered it to her. "Water?"

She tried to reach for it and moaned. Her muscles prickled everywhere they weren't numb. Her arms didn't want to obey.

"Here." Nolan poured water over her chapped lips. She felt ridiculous, but thirst got the better of her pride and she gulped down the water. He placed the wineskin on the ground and picked up her right arm.

"What are you doing?" She jerked her arm, her eyes widening, but he didn't let go.

"Relax, love." He started rubbing her arm from the shoulder down.

She tensed, but then eased as feeling returned to her arm. Fine, let him help. It would only restore her strength faster.

"Better?"

Adelaide didn't want to admit it, but it was. She nodded, and he moved to her other arm.

"Kirven told me your magic is back. I'm happy for you." He stopped massaging her arm and brushed his fingers over the collar. "You wouldn't have to wear this if you joined us."

She shifted away. "You're not happy for me. You think having a wife with magic will make you more powerful."

Nolan returned to massaging. "What can I say? I'm attracted to power." He finished rubbing her arm and kissed her shoulder. She jerked away with a shudder. Nolan sighed and pulled a few pieces of jerky out of his bag. She devoured them, not caring they were dry and tough.

"I like your attire." He handed the water over, and she begrudgingly accepted. His gaze wandered over her. "Very enticing."

She threw the open wineskin at him. Water splashed his face, and she smiled with satisfaction at his irritated frown. She lifted her chin, trying to look as dignified as possible. "I need to relieve myself."

His nose wrinkled. "Pretty sure you already have."

She blushed and he snickered, making her face heat more. "Laugh when you've been left bound in a shed," she muttered.

"All right, all right." He picked up a long piece of rope from the ones he had cut off her torso and tied it to the loop in the side of the collar, next to the lock. "I'm not going to let you just run off," he said in response to her withering look. He cut the ropes off her ankles.

It took Adelaide a couple tries to stand on her aching legs and numb feet, but she managed it with a little assistance from Nolan. He picked up his bag and wineskin and waited outside the door while she relieved herself.

"Done yet?" he called. She scowled as she exited the shed.

A few maple trees were spaced between little groves of ash and birch. A soot-blackened wooden frame of what might have once been a cottage stood several feet away. She sucked in a deep breath of the fresh air, appreciating anew the warmth of the sun and the coolness of the evening air on her skin.

Nolan gave her a once-over. "Come on. You need to clean up." He strode off, the rope attached to the collar leading her after him. "There's a stream down here."

"Fine," she said through gritted teeth. However, she was thankful for the opportunity to rinse off her clothes.

Nolan stood on the bank next to her boots while she sat in the shallow stream and attempted to wash off some of the smell. He leered. "This might be easier if you took your clothes off."

Heat covered her head from scalp to collarbones. She turned away and scrubbed more furiously at her fitted trousers. He just laughed.

"I'm going to kill you." The words spilled out before she thought better of it.

He stopped laughing. "First, that's a rude thing to say to your knightly rescuer and future husband. Second, you must have missed the part where I can't die."

She glared over her shoulder. "I'll try cutting your head off. I'd like to see Kirven heal that."

His lips pursed. "We really need to work on your attitude. Plotting to kill your betrothed is frowned upon."

"We are *not* betrothed."

"Yes, we are. You agreed, remember? Besides, if we're not, why am I sticking my neck out for you?"

She stood with her back to him and squeezed excess water out of the skirt of her suede tunic and tried to press water out of her trousers. "What are you talking about?"

"Prince Kirven would have killed you if not for me. You're welcome." He paused, as if waiting for a thank you, but he was not about to get one. "But His Highness isn't interested in threats to his power. I told him I can control you, but if you misbehave, he won't hesitate to kill you. And that's not what I want."

Adelaide turned, water dripping from her trousers. "Don't pretend this is you being self-sacrificial."

"I can protect you easier if you marry me."

"I don't need or want your protection!"

"Really?" He lifted his brows. "If that's true, why were you bound on the floor of an abandoned shed?" He pulled on the rope. The collar pressed against the back of her neck, and she stumbled out of the stream toward him. "If you didn't need my protection, you wouldn't have a magic-suppressing collar around your neck." He drew her in until she was standing in front of him. She stared down at the grass poking up between her toes.

"Look at me, Adelaide," he pleaded. She clenched her jaw, annoyed at his constant playacting. "Please." With a huff, she looked at him. "Stop fighting

Kirven and marry me, and I can and will give you anything and everything you can possibly desire. You won't have to wear this collar. You can use your magic. You want tutors in magic? I'll send to every kingdom to find the best ones. You want silks? I'll order dresses in every color in any style you choose. You want exotic fruit? I'll send to the edges of the known world for them. You want to travel? I'll take you anywhere. You want to meet your mother's family? I'll find them for you. What do you want, Adelaide? I'll make sure you have it." He looked at her, his eyes gentle, begging. His love-sick puppy act sickened her. "Just love me."

She crossed her arms. "I want this collar off."

"Once we're married. After you've sworn your loyalty to me in front of witnesses."

"Now."

Nolan sighed. "I try to be your knight in shining armor, and you act like I'm the dragon. You'll see. I can be cruel, I know, but only when necessary. I won't be denied or disrespected. But I can be kind." His blue eyes shone with affection that caught her off-guard. "I can be the man you deserve, Adelaide. The man you need." He rubbed the back of his fingers down her arm in a soft caress.

She shivered, and not just from the cold of her wet clothes.

"I will give you all the riches of the world. I will fill you with ecstasy and live for your pleasure, if you let me."

He ran his thumb over her cheekbone. Adelaide swallowed back the bile pushing against her throat and turned her head away. She stepped back, but the collar dug into her neck, keeping her close to him.

"Stop fighting me." Nolan's voice dropped to a seductive murmur. "We could be unstoppable. We could do anything. Let me in, Adelaide." For a moment, the tenderness of his tone took her aback. Gentle longing filled his eyes. His ability to lie, to play a part, astounded her. No wonder he had seduced so many. Only because she denied him did she have the displeasure of seeing his true nature.

"Untie the rope at least. Please." She tried to look harmless and innocent as he regarded her, lips pursed.

He shook his head. "You're not ready yet."

"I'm not going to marry you!" Adelaide grabbed the rope and turned to run. Nolan's grip was too strong, even with her sudden movement. She released the rope and stood erect with her back to him.

"I am your destiny, one way or another." His voice hardened as he grabbed her elbow, his fingers digging in around the joint, and wrenched her back around. She bit her tongue to keep from crying out. "You can sit in splendor at my right hand, or you can kneel at my feet. The choice is yours. But either way, you will be mine."

Nolan lifted her chin, placed his other hand on her back, and pressed his lips to hers. Her skin itched with disgust as she stood momentarily frozen. He kissed her softly, then more forcefully when she tried to pull away. She pushed against his chest, but he locked his arms around her. His hand on the back of her head held her in place. She squirmed and thrashed, her arms pinned between their bodies, trying to break away. Her lips hurt from trying to deny the press of his mouth. His lips left hers and she gasped in a deep breath. He brushed a kiss against her jaw.

"Be mine, Adelaide." He kissed the side of her neck above the collar.

"Stop," she rasped. She shook as she pushed against him. She couldn't breathe.

Nolan lifted his head. His eyes glinted with hunger. "Why don't you want me? How can I be driven mad with the thought of you, and you won't spare a glance my way?" He kissed her shoulder, ignoring her struggling. "You fill my dreams; your smile steals away my concentration. I see you when I close my eyes, and it's not fair."

His mouth hovered above hers. With his hand still holding the back of her head like a vise, Adelaide couldn't turn away. Her heart pounded against her chest, and she pressed her eyes and mouth closed.

"You've gotten under my skin," he murmured. "Some half-Khastallander girl with skin the color of dark amber, the product of an alliance between a lord rich with the spoils of war and a merchant's daughter. You aren't topping any list of most wanted maidens."

How flattering. She pushed her head back against his hand to no avail.

"You were just the answer to my marriage predicament, but I can't stop thinking about you. I desire you with every fiber of my being, with every bone in my body." He gave her a quick peck on her closed lips, then pulled back. She risked opening her eyes.

Nolan watched her, his eyebrows pinched. "Does no part of you desire me?"

Adelaide clenched her jaw. "No."

She sent a burst of magical energy out of her palms and into his chest. It was tiny for how much effort it took, but he stumbled back, his arms slipping and allowing a small space between them. She sent another shockwave, and he let go as he staggered backward. Dark spots danced in her eyes, and she shook her head, trying to clear away the dizziness. She swayed and leaned forward, supporting herself on her knees.

Nolan straightened, face flushed and eyes dark. "I'm tired of you!" He pulled on the rope, and she fell to her knees on the grass. "I'm tired of you fighting me! I'm tired of you choosing that scarred bastard mercenary over me! I'm tired of losing to that stuck-up mongrel nobody who doesn't deserve his title or castle and certainly doesn't deserve you. I'm tired of wanting you and being denied. I'm tired of you acting like I'm some cruel monster."

"Then stop behaving like one!" She sounded braver than she felt. Those small uses of her power had drained her, and she didn't have much energy left to so much as stand, let alone fight. That scared her, because she didn't know what Nolan would do next. *Etiros, protect me.*

"You think me cruel?" He strode toward her. Adelaide tried to crawl backward, but he drew in the rope, stopping her. "So be it. If that's what you want, I can show you cruelty." He backhanded her face, making her cheek sting and throb. "I can be your monster."

"Nolan, please…" In spite of herself, a sob tore from her throat and tears squeezed out of her eyes.

He knelt in front of her, his expression softening. "It doesn't have to be like this." He wiped a tear off her cheek with his thumb. "Stop fighting me." He grabbed her waist and pulled her closer.

The truth sank into Adelaide's chest like a rock. She couldn't fight him. Not right now. Not for long, anyway. She wanted to be strong, but she was exhausted. The collar drained her, leaving her weak. Weak, tired, and scared. She hadn't recovered from Kirven's torture yet. Nolan's strength dwarfed hers, and even if she wounded him, he would heal. This wasn't a fight she could win.

She wanted Mother. She wanted to be a little girl again, watching with fascination as Mother sewed a new dress for her in a Khastallander style and told her Khastallander fables. Back before she knew the extent of the world's cruelty. When she climbed too high in the trees and cried and Mother crossed her arms and said if her brave little tigress, her *shiraa*, could get up, she could get down.

Nolan's hand gripped her thigh as he forced her onto his lap. As numbness settled into her chest, she didn't feel like a tigress. She didn't feel brave. Mother had raised her to defend herself, and she couldn't. *Give me courage*, she prayed. *Give me strength. Protect me.* Her mind raced, searching for a way to stop him. Suddenly, she remembered Regulus' dagger, stuck in the back of Nolan's belt. She needed to stall him. To distract him long enough to get ahold of the dagger. His hands roamed as he leaned toward her.

"Nolan." Her voice came out in a croak. She cleared her throat. "Nolan, I…I'll marry you." He froze. "I just need—more time." She gulped against the lump in her throat. "I'll marry you."

He narrowed his eyes. "I've heard that before."

"Please." She blinked back a few stray tears and edged her hand toward his waist. "You're right. I'm not ready. But I won't… I won't fight you. On, on our…" She exhaled slowly to steady her voice, even as the words killed a part of her soul. "On our wedding night. If you wait." She met his eyes. "Please." *Please don't let him notice*, she prayed as her hand hovered near the back of his belt.

His eyes narrowed. "What about after our wedding night?"

"I'll…" She licked her dry lips. She would have to lean toward him to reach the dagger. "I'll be a dutiful…affectionate wife." Cold clawed at her insides.

A slow, self-assured smile pulled at the corner of Nolan's lips. "Swear it."

"I promise." Adelaide leaned forward as she reached around behind him. Her fingers brushed the hilt of the dagger. With a quick pull, she freed it from his belt and slashed toward the rope, her heart pounding. Nolan caught her wrist, stopping her before the blade met the rope. She looked from the dagger to his eyes, her moment of bravery spent. He watched her with eerie calm, his mouth drawn into a hard line. His hand clutched her wrist so hard she feared her bones would snap.

"I'm sorry," she whispered, his silence more unnerving than shouting. "I…I panicked. I'm sorry."

He pulled her hand away and she dropped the dagger, hoping he wouldn't break her wrist again. "Why, Adelaide? Why don't you want me? Why do you continue to fight me?"

She shook her head, too tense to say anything. Nolan pushed her back onto the ground with force that hurt her shoulders. He grabbed the dagger and stood, still holding the rope. The sun had nearly set; dusk gathered around them. The first stars stared down from the darkening sky; cold, distant, and uncaring.

Nolan turned the dagger over in his hand. "I'm of two minds, Adelaide. Part of me wants to keep trying to be your knight, to show you I can be compassionate. To give you time to accept the inevitable." He crouched and put the edge of the dagger to her throat, right above the collar. "The other part of me is done trying to win you over."

You were trying? She tried to move her neck away from the blade, but his hand followed her. She lost her balance and fell back, propped up on her elbows. He crawled over her, the knife still pressed to her throat. The metal rested there, one faulty move away from opening a wound that, in her weakened state, she wouldn't be able to heal. Her stomach twisted, threatening to push up the jerky.

"Nolan, please…"

"Do you have any idea how frustrating you are?" He released the rope to trace the top edge of her tunic. His fingers stopped at the ties of the bodice.

Adelaide curled her fists, her nails digging into her palms. Her breaths came in rapid, shallow gasps. *Stop, please, make him stop.* "I'm sor—"

"You're maddening. I've had ladies throw themselves at me. I've had women beg me *not* to stop." He tilted his head. "But the problem isn't me, or even you. You want me, you just don't realize it yet." He leaned back, returned the dagger to his belt, and picked the rope back up.

Every muscle in her body was taut as a drawn bow as she watched him, hope a weak spark in her shuddering chest.

"When Hargreaves is dead, when he's no longer confusing you, you'll finally see me. When I'm the only thing between you and Kirven's wrath, you'll realize how generous I've been. You'll come crawling. You'll beg me to take you. And when you do…" Nolan leered and leaned closer, his voice teasing. He ran his fingertips down her spine, and she shivered. "You'll wish you had given in sooner."

Not likely. Adelaide bit back the retort, careful not to stir his anger again. She fought to keep her expression blank and not betray her disgust and terror. He seemed to have decided to stop, at least for the moment, and she wouldn't risk antagonizing him into changing his mind.

"CARRICK!" REGULUS' shout boomed through the twilight air. A flock of birds in a tree beyond Carrick and Adelaide took flight, their wings rustling as they soared into the pink-tinged sky. Adelaide was lying on the ground, propped up on her elbows. Carrick leaned over her, holding a rope tied to a collar around her neck. Indignation boiled Regulus' blood. He kicked Sieger forward and raced down the hill toward them. Dresden and Alfred followed close behind.

Nolan sighed as he stood, pulling Adelaide up with him by the arm. "What are *you* doing here? How did you even get here?"

"Turns out you're not the only one good at hunting," Regulus snarled as he jumped off Sieger's back and drew his sword. In actuality, one of the servants had overheard the sorcerer telling Nolan where to find Adelaide. Drez and Alfred had insisted on coming, too, and they had pushed their horses hard to catch up. Sweat frothed on Sieger's neck.

Nolan wrapped his arms around Adelaide and held her against his chest. A human shield. Regulus ground his teeth.

"Lord Belanger?" Nolan frowned. "How…unexpected. I really didn't think you could actually pull off a rescue, mercenary."

"Unhand my daughter!"

Adelaide looked at them, eyes wide—with hope or fear, Regulus wasn't sure. He stalked closer. Why wasn't she doing something? Had she lost her magic again? His gaze flicked to the iron collar around her neck. Did that have something to do with it?

"Ah, and the Carasian servant." Carrick grinned. "Did you give your master my message?"

Regulus glanced at Dresden. Dresden had turned dark red.

"I wish I'd had the time for a more comprehensive belting," Carrick said. "Did he tell you those stripes were for you?"

"Enough!" Regulus' voice shook.

"Three against one," Carrick said. "And I'm not wearing armor and they are. Don't you think that's unfair, love?" He kissed Adelaide's shoulder, just below the collar, maintaining eye contact with Regulus. Adelaide flinched as his mouth pressed against her skin, and Regulus focused in on a bruise on her cheek. *He hurt her.*

"Let. Her. Go." Regulus took an offensive stance, ready to sprint forward at the hint of an opening.

Carrick raised a brow. "All right." He dropped his arms, then hit Adelaide hard on the side of her head. Alfred screamed as Adelaide crumpled into Carrick's arms. Regulus' heart fell like a stone. Carrick lowered her onto the ground. "Don't worry, she's just unconscious. I wouldn't kill my bride." He stepped over her still form. "What are you waiting for?"

Regulus lunged forward and swung at Carrick's neck. Carrick dove under the blade with unsettling speed and pummeled into Regulus' torso, wrapping his arms around Regulus as they toppled. Regulus grunted, the air knocked out of him. His sword slipped from his grip as he landed hard on his back with Carrick on top of him.

"I'm going to finally kill you, mercenary." Carrick punched Regulus in the face, and Regulus groaned as his cheekbone cracked. He wrapped his legs around Carrick, gripped his shirt, and twisted, rolling Carrick onto his back. He punched Carrick's mouth, and blood seeped from Carrick's lips.

Carrick growled and caught his fist. Regulus punched with his left hand, catching Carrick in the temple. Carrick shouted and wrenched Regulus' arm, then threw him to the side. Regulus jumped up, his right shoulder aching, as Carrick scrambled to his feet and picked up Regulus' sword. He barely escaped Carrick's manic thrust. Carrick sliced and Regulus jumped back. The tip of the sword scraped across his chest, the sword clinking against the chainmail.

Two curved blades protruded out of Carrick's chest. Carrick stared at Regulus, mouth hanging open in a silent scream. *Good job, Drez.* As Carrick fell to his knees, Dresden withdrew his scimitars. He swung at Carrick's neck, but Carrick met one scimitar with Regulus' sword and grabbed Dresden's other hand. Dresden strained against Carrick. Regulus grabbed Carrick's shirt and tossed him to the ground. Carrick groaned but rolled onto his back as Regulus reached for his sword, moving too fast. His fingers dug into the grass. *Too slow. I'm too slow!*

Carrick kicked his ankle, and Regulus collapsed to one knee as Carrick rolled away and sprung to his feet. A little pain couldn't stop him right now. He needed to *get up!* Drez blocked Carrick's desperate swing. But then Carrick released his grip on the sword with his right hand, reached forward, closed his hand around Dresden's neck, and shoved. Regulus scrambled to his feet as Dresden fell onto his back, coughing and wheezing. *Not my best friend, cur.*

Regulus aimed a punch at the back of Carrick's head. Just before his fist made contact, Carrick leaned forward and turned. His boot rammed into Regulus' gut, knocking him backward. Regulus gasped, his abdomen throbbing and lungs struggling to pull in air. Dark spots flickered in his vision. Carrick sneered and thrust the sword at Regulus' heart. The blade pressed into the chainmail, but Carrick kept pushing until he fell onto his back. His chest ached. Carrick stomped on his sternum, and something cracked. Regulus sucked in air against the suffocating pain as his vision blurred.

"Let's see what my new strength can do." Carrick stood over him, straddling his middle.

I have to move. But his body wouldn't listen. Carrick raised the sword and brought it straight down with the speed of a viper. Against the superhuman impact, and with no give as Regulus lay braced against the ground, the chainmail broke.

The sword ripped into his gut with hellish pain, its momentum stopped only when it hit the chainmail on his back. Regulus gasped; strangled, staccato groans of agony as tremors ran up and down his body. He'd nearly died enough times to know—he wouldn't survive this. But all he could think about was Adelaide. *Get her away, Alfred.*

"No!" Drez screamed. "Regulus!"

Carrick released the sword and turned in time for Dresden to bury both scimitars in Carrick's stomach. Carrick bellowed in pain as Dresden withdrew his blades. Regulus' hands shook, but he grabbed the blade and tried to push it out. The sharp edges cut through his leather gloves, stinging as it split open his palms. Shallow, pain-inducing breaths wheezed in his throat. Through his blurring vision, he saw Carrick throw Drez aside like a rag doll. *No…* He tried to call Dresden's name but couldn't speak. Darkness encroached along the edges of his sight.

"I told you I would kill you, mercenary," Carrick panted.

He grabbed the hilt and twisted. Regulus' scream came out strangled. The blade scraped out of his stomach as Carrick withdrew it. Tears ran down his temples into his hair. Carrick dropped the sword and stumbled away, pressing his hand against his blood-soaked middle as he headed toward Alfred and Adelaide. *No!* Panic forced Regulus' dying body into action.

"Carrick!" He coughed up blood, but he fought through the pain and managed to get to his knees. He'd endured worse. "I'm not dead yet."

Carrick glanced over his shoulder, then laughed. "You're good as."

Regulus tried to stand and fell back to his knees. He was dying, and this time, there was no stinging sorcery dragging him back from the brink. He had failed to protect Adelaide. *My fault…* He fell forward. He raised his head and tried to warn Alfred, but his tongue wouldn't work.

Pain overwhelmed his senses. The world went in and out of focus. *I'm sorry, Adelaide. I'm sorry. I love you, and I'm sorry.* His eyelids felt heavy. He had the odd thought of being terribly thirsty. He looked at Alfred, trying to see past him to Adelaide. To see her one last time.

Alfred moved aside. Adelaide sat up, and Regulus wondered if he was dreaming, or maybe already dead. Or halfway between the realm of the living and the afterlife. Adelaide's eyes glowed golden as she leapt to her feet. Wings of fire spread out behind her back and a sword of light and flame appeared in her hands. His avenging angel. The world faded into darkness. He let his face fall onto the grass.

Goodbye, Adelaide.

NOLAN'S FACE turned ghostly white. With the collar gone, Adelaide felt lighter, but also furious. All fear vanished. She raised her flaming sword to swing for his neck. Before she got the chance, Nolan fled. She sliced the sword through empty air. An arc of flame flew off the glowing magic blade and singed Nolan's back as he ran. She started after him, but movement in her periphery caught her attention.

Dresden ran through the dark, weaponless. Not after Nolan, but somewhere else. She traced his trajectory to a mound in the grass.

No, not a mound.

Regulus.

The scream she emitted hardly sounded human. The magic sword vanished. She raced toward his still body. Dresden beat her to him and rolled Regulus onto his back as she slid to a stop. Even in the dim light, she could see the blood that covered his abdomen and had pooled on the grass. His eyes were closed, his features deathly pale and still. His chest wasn't moving.

"No, no, no," Dresden muttered. "Regulus? Can you hear me?" He touched Regulus' neck, searching for a pulse. "Please, Reg."

Tears burned her eyes and soaked her cheeks as she knelt next to Regulus. She reached out tentatively. "Regulus…"

Dresden made a strangled noise in his throat. "Don't you abandon me now, Regulus. Please." He adjusted his fingers on Regulus' neck, pressing as if that would induce a pulse. "Reg?" His hand slipped away as he sobbed.

"No!" Adelaide grabbed Regulus' blood-soaked chainmail, choking on her sobs. Her chest burned with the effort of breathing and her stomach muscles tensed and knotted to the point of pain. Mucus ran out of her nose and mingled with her tears. "Regulus, you hang on!" She placed her hands over the wound on his stomach. Soft blue light illuminated the ragged tear in his chainmail and blood-soaked gambeson.

"He's gone, Adelaide." Dresden's voice was deadened and hopeless.

"No." She shook her head. She could feel it. The tiniest bit of life. A spark of energy deep in his chest. "He's hanging on. Just barely." But she detected the wound, too. She sensed the hole through his body and the damage done to his organs. "Please, Etiros. Please."

Her palms glowed brighter as she focused all her magic on Regulus. From deep inside working out, she pulled him back together.

"Come back to me, Regulus," Adelaide whispered. "Don't leave me." *Don't leave me. I'm sorry I blamed you, even for a moment. I'm sorry I didn't stay with you. I'm sorry I didn't stop Nolan. I'm sorry your pain is because of me again. But don't leave me.*

Her tears dripped onto her hands and mixed with Regulus' blood. She sensed the wound closing, healing, the blood reabsorbing, but the flicker of life in his chest sputtered on the edge of going out.

"Come on," she muttered. "Etiros, please. COME ON." The light glared brighter. "I love you. I love you. I love you." The wound closed, but still he didn't move. She moved her hands, searching. His sternum was cracked. She healed his chest, then his battered cheek and pulled off his gloves to heal his cut hands. Still he showed no signs of improving. "Regulus?"

Dresden felt Regulus' neck again. "Reg…?" He shook his head. "He…he's lost too much blood." Tears traced lines down the blood marring the side of Dresden's face.

"No…he can't…I can't… Regulus." Her voice cracked. Adelaide laid across his chest, holding on to his shoulders. "I can't…stop. Can't stop them. Not—not without you," she whispered between sobs and gasps for air. "I love you." She broke down weeping onto his shoulder, numb to everything. Numb to Regulus' limp body beneath her, to the tears on her face.

"Can't…breathe…" Regulus' voice was so quiet she almost didn't hear it over her crying. She gasped and straightened. His eyes were open, and she sobbed again as they met hers.

"Regulus?" Dresden choked out.

"I'm…tired." Regulus blinked sluggishly. She placed her hand on his chest. The spark of life shuddered, losing the fight to hold on.

"No, no, don't you go to sleep!" She grabbed the sides of his face. Her lower lip trembled. A tear fell from her chin onto his cheek.

"I love you, too." Regulus sounded thin and reedy. Completely unlike himself. "I'm…sorry."

"No, you have nothing to be sorry for." She stroked his hair, her hands shaking. "I'm sorry! I—"

"Shhh." He closed his eyes. "You didn't…do…anything…wruh…"

"Regulus!" Adelaide pulled his head toward her, and he opened his eyes.

An idea occurred to her. She didn't know if she could do it, and she'd already used so much magic, but she had to try. She had to. "You want to marry me, right?"

"Yush…"

"You want to bind yourself to me forever?"

"Ad…I would—have…"

"I am yours." Her voice trembled. "Say you're mine. Forever."

"Yes. I…your…sh." His eyes fluttered shut.

"No, you don't." Adelaide wiped away her tears and set her jaw. She pushed up the sleeve on his right arm and placed her hand over his scars.

Warmth spread across her palm as energy pulsed from her chest down her arm. *Protect him. Heal him. Tie his life to mine.* She put every ounce of healing power, all the energy she would use to create a protective barrier larger than any she had conjured before, into him. Her power drained away, emptying out of her and filling him. Even if she poured herself out and her magic was gone forever, she didn't care, so long as it worked. Even if it killed her. It *had* to work. *Etiros, let this work. Please!* Regulus' arm glowed blue under her hand.

The flicker of life in Regulus' chest flared back to full strength. She felt a bond between them, like a cord connecting her heart to his. Felt him like he wasn't just next to her, but he was in her heart, in her very soul, and she in his. Her hand slipped off his arm and weariness made her sway, her vision clouding over. A black mark stood out on his skin, over the white of his scars.

The overlapping knot design had no beginning and no end, just one never-ending line, crossing over itself to form two interlocking hearts connected by a diamond. White spots drifted through her sight as she stared at the mark. She closed her eyes. She just…needed…a moment…

REGULUS SAT up with a gasp, nearly hitting his head against Dresden's in the dark. Every muscle vibrated with energy. He felt like he had just jumped into a freezing lake while half-asleep, and the jolt to his system had erased any feelings of tiredness. He grabbed at where the sword had pierced his abdomen. His chainmail was sticky with blood, but it was like the wound had never been there.

"Regulus." Dresden sobbed and hugged Regulus to his chest, his body shaking as he squeezed so hard Regulus couldn't breathe. When Dresden pulled back, his face was streaked with tears.

"Are you hurt?" Dresden shook his head, and Regulus looked around. "Where is—" *Adelaide.*

Alfred held her across his lap, leaning over her ashen face. Regulus' heart nearly stopped until her chest rose with a small breath. He moved toward them.

"Adelaide?"

Alfred didn't look up as he stroked her head. "She did something to heal you, and then she just…fell over. I think she fainted, but she's barely breathing."

"What?" Regulus touched her braid where it fell across her shoulder.

Alfred sniffed, and Regulus realized he had been crying. "She healed your wounds, but you were still dying. And then she put her hand on your arm. I don't…" He drew in a ragged breath and kissed her forehead.

"You were nearly gone," Dresden said. "I thought you—" His voice cracked, and he broke off.

"She wouldn't let you go," Alfred murmured.

Dresden snuffled. "She said… Your arm… Oh, no. No. I know what she did." Regulus looked back, surprised by the horror in his friend's voice. "Look at your arm, Reg."

Regulus frowned down at his arms. His right sleeve was pushed up to his elbow under the chainmail.

"The underside." Drez sounded resigned, almost bitter.

He turned his right arm over and lifted it. The chainmail slid back to his elbow. A new black mark stood out against his skin; an intricate knot of inter-locking shapes formed from an unbroken line. He squinted in the dim moon-light. Two triangles, their points extending toward the sides of his arm, formed a diamond shape between two…hearts?

He ran his fingertips over the mark. A comforting warmth spread up his arm at the touch and the strangest humming sensation nestled deep in his chest, almost in his soul. The humming drew his gaze toward Adelaide. He took her hand. Something inside him tugged toward her. An ethereal connection he couldn't explain, but that made him feel at ease and energized at once.

"She marked you," Drez said angrily, "just like the sorcerer."

"No." Regulus smiled and caressed the side of her face. "Not at all like the sorcerer."

"She made you agree you wanted to be bound to her forever. She used magic to put a mark on your arm, and somehow that kept you alive when you should have been dead. Doesn't that sound familiar?" Frustration laced Drez's voice.

"This isn't sorcery." Regulus turned toward Drez. "This isn't about control. It doesn't hurt. It feels completely different. Less one-sided. It even looks different. This isn't slavery." He looked back at Adelaide's face. Even in sleep, exhaustion pulled at her features. "This is love."

"I hope you're right." Drez sighed. "At least you're alive. I…"

"I'm okay." Regulus clapped Dresden's shoulder. "Thank Etiros you are. If I'd woken up and you…" He swallowed hard.

Dresden crumpled and rubbed at his beard. "I thought I lost you. You looked like—" He stopped himself with a shake of his head, but Regulus could imagine what he was going to say. Like any of the friends they had lost as mercenaries. "I won't forgive you if you die," Dresden muttered. "I won't forgive *me* if you die."

"Drez—"

"I couldn't save you." Dresden's head sank further. "I kept staring at you, trying to think of what I should have done differently so you wouldn't be lying there. My friend. My *brother*. Always there to protect me, and every time it matters, I can't protect you!" He looked up, his eyes brimming with tears.

Regulus stared at Dresden, at a loss for words. Part of him wanted to point out he wasn't always there. He hadn't been there when Carrick beat Dresden. And it wasn't Dresden's fault Carrick was immortal and unstoppable.

"I can't see you like that again." Dresden forced a smile. "You're not allowed to die. Ever."

"Okay." Regulus smiled weakly. "Only if you never die."

Dresden laughed, the sound tight and pained. "Deal."

CHAPTER 24

As THE sun rose the next morning, clearing away the fog rising off the nearby stream, it became clear Adelaide would not awake anytime soon. Regulus washed the blood off his clothing as best he could and put his chainmail and his gambeson in his saddlebag. His long-sleeved gray shirt now was blood-stained and had a hole over his stomach, but they had no thread or needles with which to mend it. They found a shed nearby where Adelaide had clearly been held, and the fury in Alfred's eyes rivaled Regulus' own. They let Adelaide sleep through the day, exchanging concerned glances and wondering if they should move her. And wondering when they should continue to the palace.

Alfred wanted to warn the king, but he also wouldn't leave his daughter. Regulus had determined never to part ways with Adelaide again. Dresden didn't stand a chance of convincing anyone to even let him in the palace. Besides, they were exhausted from riding through the night and all day to find her. So they waited and prayed as the day turned to night and another day dawned and Adelaide still did not wake.

At least Regulus had convinced Dresden that Adelaide wasn't a sorceress and hadn't enslaved him. The marks looking nothing alike helped. Dresden teased him about how it looked like hearts. But he still looked at Adelaide with a mixture of distrust and fear. Not that Regulus could entirely blame him—Drez and Alfred had confirmed that he hadn't been hallucinating. In her fury, Adelaide had sprouted a pair of fiery wings.

Unfortunately, though, Carrick had escaped. Regulus blamed himself. If Adelaide hadn't left her pursuit of Carrick to save his life, perhaps she would have succeeded in killing the villain. If anything could break the bond to the sorcerer, it would probably be a weapon of pure magic. Maybe cutting him in half would do the trick.

Regulus sat next to Adelaide, watching an eagle circling high above the trees. Alfred had left to stretch his legs. Dresden had gone in search of fresh food as midday approached. Adelaide stirred, the grass rustling against her tunic. He laughed with relief and wetness rimmed his eyes as she stretched out on the grass with adorable soft grunting noises. She squinted against the bright sunlight.

His grin pulled at his scar. "Morning, *sumdir*."

She smiled groggily and propped herself up on her elbow. "You're alive." She eyed his torn, stained shirt. "A mess, but alive."

"All thanks to you." Regulus cupped his hand to the side of Adelaide's face and caressed her cheek with his thumb. Her smile vanished and fear flooded his mind. She flinched, pulling away from his hand. He drew his hand back, his stomach dropping. "What's wrong?"

She shook her head and forced an unconvincing smile that made his heart twist. "Nothing, everything's fine. I'm sorry."

"What aren't you telling me?" he asked quietly. Uncertainty lingered in her eyes.

"Nothing." She rolled her shoulders and looked around. "What time is it?"

"Approaching noon. It's been two days since we found you, though."

"Two days! I slept that long?"

He shrugged. "When the fairies told you about how to do a binding, they did say you would need a lot of time to recover. How are you feeling?"

"Still—" She yawned. "Still tired. But better. I can feel my magic returning. Strengthening. And I'm not drained anymore, it's a relief to…" She faltered, her eyes going out of focus as her fingers drifted to her neck.

"The collar," Regulus said, confirming his suspicion. "The one your father broke off. It somehow suppressed your magic, didn't it?"

Adelaide's gaze fell. "Kirven… I met him on the road. He defeated me. Bound me. When he failed to steal my magic or convince me to serve him, he put that collar on me." She shivered. "It sucked away my power, my energy. Just…a constant drain."

"Hey, it's okay." He moved closer and put his arm around her, pulling her in as he kissed her cheek. Instead of relaxing, she stiffened and inhaled sharply. Hurt pierced his heart. "Adelaide?"

"I…I'm sorry." She quivered in his arms.

Inexplicable sorrow and fear coursed through him. It was when a sensation of a name, more than an actual thought, accompanied the surge of anxiety that he understood. *Nolan*. Somehow, he was sensing Adelaide's emotions.

His jaw tightened. Anger and regret fought for dominance in his soul. "What did Carrick do?"

"Nothing." She pulled away and stood, her back to him. But not before he saw the tears that glistened in the corner of her eyes. "Nothing happened."

"Then why are you afraid?" He kept his voice gentle, even as he wanted to shout and fume. "I can sense your fear. Your sadness."

Adelaide glanced over her shoulder at him. "What?"

He stood and walked around in front of her. "The bond you created…it's different from the sorcerer's. When I touch you, I can…feel you. Your emotions. Your soul."

"You feel it, too?" she whispered. "This…connection. Like we're…"

"Part of each other," Regulus finished. She nodded. He inclined his head so their eyes were at the same level. "So why can't you be honest with me?"

She turned and took a couple steps away. "Where's my father? And Dresden?"

"They'll be back shortly."

"You got my family out." She didn't look at him. "My mother? And Landon and Julia and their son?"

"They're safe and unharmed." He hoped that was all she was worried about. "We took back Belanger castle. They've taken precautions; Carrick won't get in again."

She glanced back and said, "Thank you," before she turned away again.

Dread that Adelaide blamed him for her capture grew in the pit of Regulus' stomach. But he hadn't detected anger, only fear. And he didn't like not knowing why she was afraid. He couldn't help if he didn't know the problem. "What's wrong? Talk to me, *shiraa*."

"Don't…" She hugged herself and ducked her head.

Regulus furrowed his brow. Something had happened. And he didn't want it to be what he thought it was. "Don't what?"

"Call me that," she whispered.

He took a step back, stunned. "What? Why?"

"I'm…" She shook her head. "I need… I'll be back." She walked toward the stream, but he strode after her and caught her elbow. Adelaide whimpered and pulled away, drawing into herself. For the moment their skin touched, Regulus felt her spike of panic. She looked at him, eyes wide and face red. "I…I didn't… I'm sorry. I don't know…" She reached toward him, then dropped her hand.

He eyed the yellow-green bruise on her right cheek. "He hurt you." When she lowered her gaze to the ground, her chin resting against her chest, that was all the answer he needed. He exhaled through his nose. "You're safe now."

"Am I?" Adelaide didn't look up. "I couldn't fight them. I was…weak."

His heart broke. "Adelaide." He reached for her again, then stopped, remembering her reaction. "You aren't weak."

"I *am* weak." She sank onto the grass.

He couldn't stop himself. He sat next to her and pulled her into his arms. She turned and leaned against his shoulder.

"It's okay," he said. "You don't have to tell me."

"I lost, and… I was helpless. And then the collar…" She hugged his waist like she was holding on for her life. Her chest heaved. "When Nolan… I was afraid and weak. I'm not—brave." She hiccupped and tucked her face into his shoulder.

Regulus rubbed her back, rage a fire in his veins. *That…* A slew of vile names for Carrick raced through his mind.

Adelaide turned her head to speak again. "He didn't even… I'm all right, really." Her hands clutched the back of his shirt. "He just scared me."

"He's a monster," Regulus said through gritted teeth.

Adelaide shuddered. "I antagonized him. He…" She buried her face in his shirt, her voice muffled as she continued. "I prayed he would stop. Maybe that's why he did. But I…I didn't help matters. I was stupid. Reckless. Defiant. And now…when…when… I'm sorry."

Every word she spoke ripped him apart, piece by piece. Her tears finally broke through, seeping into his shirt. She didn't need to finish the thought. He sensed her regret, her fear, and he knew. Knew that when he had touched her, she had flashed back to Carrick touching her.

"Oh, Adelaide." Regulus swallowed against the swelling in his throat. "No. It's not your fault. You didn't do anything wrong. He shouldn't have laid a finger on you. His behavior is his. Do you hear me?" His chest shook with each jagged breath.

"It's not your fault," he continued. "Don't blame yourself and don't you dare feel guilty. You did nothing wrong. Nothing you did excuses his actions. And you're not weak for being scared or upset." He stroked her back as her breathing deepened, becoming more regular.

"And I'm not angry with you," he added, sensing her dread. "I don't blame you for shying away. *I'm* sorry. I wouldn't have…" His anger threatened to break into tears. "You have every right to not want to be touched."

Adelaide didn't respond, but her storm of emotions calmed.

"You did nothing wrong," he whispered. "But I did. I never should have left you. I should have been there. I should have protected you." His throat tightened so much he felt strangled. "I failed you. I'm sorry. I'm so, so sorry."

After a moment, Adelaide mumbled into his shoulder, "It's all right."

"No, it's not." He took a deep breath, steadying himself against the growing ache behind his forehead. "I—"

"No." She shifted, turning so her cheek laid on his shoulder. "It's not your fault, either."

"But—"

"I did blame you." Adelaide's admission cut deeper than the sword that nearly killed him. "Briefly. I was alone, and scared, and…angry. But I realized it wasn't your fault." She drew in a long, shaky breath. "You said it yourself. Kirven's actions, Carrick's behavior," her voice hitched, "it's theirs. Don't take blame that isn't yours."

Her words released a chain Regulus hadn't even realized he'd placed around his heart. He'd been blaming himself for the sorcerer's actions for two years. How could he tell her she wasn't responsible for other's evil while blaming himself? She never blamed him. His men never blamed him. But he still blamed himself.

"Regulus." Adelaide's voice was soft, timid. "If it's not my fault, it's not yours, either. You have to stop blaming yourself."

He exhaled slowly and rested his cheek on top of her head. "I know," he murmured. "Still, I should have been there. I promise I will be in the future. No more splitting up."

"Yes." She linked her fingers behind his neck and snuggled closer. "No more splitting up."

Her fear and hurt abated. He wanted to kiss her forehead but didn't dare. Not yet. He would gladly give her all the time she needed. He wouldn't so much as hold her hand if that's what it took for her to overcome any lingering fear. So help him, he would not remind her of Carrick. Adelaide relaxed, and Regulus thanked Etiros that she trusted him enough to let him hold her.

CHAPTER 25

WHEN ALFRED returned from his walk, he didn't say anything about finding Adelaide on Regulus' lap. Maybe he was too relieved she was awake. Or maybe he didn't care. They hadn't spoken much while Adelaide was asleep, but Regulus sensed an increased respect from Alfred that he suspected had much to do with nearly dying and Adelaide pulling him back.

Alfred hugged and kissed his daughter, although Adelaide shied away even from her father's touch. He told her how relieved he was she was alive and how much he loved her. But he didn't ask any questions or pressure her to talk about what had happened.

Dresden returned carrying two rabbits and several fish while Alfred was telling Adelaide how impressed he was with her magical abilities. Regulus went to help Dresden with the fire and preparing the kills. Adelaide left to relieve herself, and Alfred came and sat next to Regulus. He pulled a knife from his belt and took one of the fish.

"Did she say anything about what happened?" Alfred asked.

"Why are you asking me and not her?"

Alfred paused, his knife halfway down the trout's belly. He scowled at the limp fish like it had threatened him. "I didn't want to ask her questions she might not be willing or able to answer. But I thought maybe she would have told you, if she was going to talk to anyone." He opened and closed his mouth a few times, like he wanted to say more. As he gutted the trout he said quietly, "Have you ever been captured?"

"Other than by the sorcerer? No."

"Right." Alfred glanced at him. "You mentioned he'd use the mark to punish you. Adelaide may not have the mark, but somehow, he tortured her."

"What?" Dread made Regulus dizzy. "What makes you—"

"I *have* been captured."

Regulus looked up in surprise. So did Dresden from the rabbit he was skinning.

"Most people don't know." Alfred looked around before continuing. "I was acting as King Olfan's double." He turned and pulled up the edge of his shirt with his pinky, the knife still in his hand. White scars crisscrossed his back and a large, knotted scar marred his side. He let the shirt fall back down. "I know what happens when you anger vengeful, powerful men."

He returned to the fish, but Regulus stared. Alfred looked calm as ever, but now Regulus realized his strength wasn't from never being weak. He had earned his strength through survival.

"Some things are difficult to speak aloud," Alfred said, his voice strained. "She was smiling, but I recognized the pain and fear in her eyes. The nervous energy. The hesitation to be touched. The way she's standing, making herself smaller. Something more happened to her than whatever caused that bruise on her cheek. Whether she healed it, or whatever Kirven did left no marks…" He shook his head. "I want to know she's all right, but I can tell she's not."

Regulus caught Dresden's eyes as Dresden tied the first rabbit over the fire. Dresden looked as shocked as he felt. Alfred was intent on cleaning the trout. But his jaw tightened, and wrinkles deepened around his eyes and across his forehead.

Regulus focused on scaling his own fish. He should have known. He thought only Carrick had hurt her. That the sorcerer could torture someone who didn't bear his mark hadn't occurred to him. And who would torture a woman? After everything else the sorcerer had done, he shouldn't be surprised. But he was still furious. He squeezed the fish and a scale sliced into his palm. He winced and held his hand up to inspect the cut, but the pain vanished as it closed in front of his eyes. As if by magic.

"When they realized you were just a lord…" Dresden started, pulling Regulus' focus back to Alfred's story. "Why didn't…" He shook his head and started on the second rabbit.

"Why didn't they kill me?" Alfred asked without looking up. "They still hoped for a ransom. I escaped by pure luck and some sheer stupidity on my captors' part. But I would have been caught again if it hadn't been for Tamina."

What? Alfred set aside the cleaned fish and grabbed another. His worried features had softened, a hint of a smile pulling at the corner of his mouth. But Regulus saw Adelaide returning, so he dropped his questions and returned to preparing the fish.

Adelaide sat on the opposite side of the fire. Whether because she didn't want to watch them gut the fish and rabbits or because she wanted space, Regulus wasn't sure. She'd healed the bruise on her cheek, and he wondered if her magic had hidden anything else. Or if, like when the sorcerer tortured him, she had nothing to show for her suffering.

"Adelaide?" Dresden looked up from the rabbit. "Thank you. For saving Regulus." Adelaide nodded, and he tied the second rabbit over the fire, looking uncomfortable. "So. Fiery wings, huh?"

"Fiery wings?" Adelaide frowned and shook her head. "Did I miss something?"

"Wait, you're saying that wasn't on purpose?" Drez whistled. "I don't know if that's better or worse. Either way, it was terrifying."

"Who, me?" Adelaide looked to Regulus, her face drawn and anxious. "What did I do?"

"Ad, you…" Alfred added his fish to the stone. "When you got up…"

"You went all avenging angel," Drez said, settling back on the grass. "With these huge wings of fire at your back and a flaming sword and everything."

"I suppose that's why Nolan ran away as fast as he did." She drew her knees up to her chest and stared at the fire.

Alfred's right, Regulus thought with a stab of shame. Her shoulders hunched forward, her chin tucked behind her knees. Making herself small. A hollow look had settled behind her eyes.

"I barely saw it," Regulus said. He willed her to look at him. "But you looked incredible." She finally lifted her gaze to meet his. "You were incredible."

She bit her lower lip. "I didn't even realize… That seems like a waste of energy."

"Anything that scares your enemy isn't a waste," Alfred said. "It's a tactical advantage."

"So is having a soldier who can't die," Drez said. The suspicion in his voice was impossible to miss. Regulus gave Dresden a look of warning, but Drez was focused on Adelaide. "I can't be more thankful my best friend is alive. But what did you do to him, exactly?"

ADELAIDE WRAPPED her arms around her legs, glancing back and forth between Dresden and Regulus. She didn't like the accusation in Dresden's tone. Regulus' eyes widened, then his features hardened.

"We talked about this, Drez."

"You say it's not sorcery, I want to hear from her how she did it and what she did." Dresden didn't take his searching gaze off her for a moment.

The cooking rabbits sizzled, filling the air with savory aroma and making her stomach tighten. She was too tired and too hungry to argue.

"She saved you, and I'm grateful," Dresden said. "But how? She was captured by the sorcerer, who could be controlling her—"

"She doesn't have the mark, Drez!" Regulus sounded on edge.

"We don't know how easy it is for a mage to become a sorcerer," Dresden countered, challenge in his tone. "I won't watch you be a slave all over again! I want proof—"

"I'm not a sorcerer." Adelaide rested her forehead on her knees. "If I were, I wouldn't have…" The memory of Kirven's torture returned, and phantom pain slid over her body.

"Wouldn't have what?" Dresden asked.

"Enough." Father used his commanding officer voice, and Dresden's mouth slammed shut. Father was no poet, but he had his own way with words. "She saved Regulus' life. Why isn't that enough for you?"

"Because the sorcerer saved his life a lot, too." The agitation left Dresden's voice, replaced by resignation. "For two years he tried to earn his freedom or break free in another way. Do you have any idea what it's like for your friend to—" He shot a glance at Regulus. "The point is, I don't want to see him suffer again."

"I would never hurt Regulus." She met Dresden's eyes, hoping he would see the truth in hers. "Surely you know that."

After a moment, Dresden relaxed. "I know you love him. But what if you don't even know what you did? Will you remove it if it harms him? *Can* you remove it?"

"I told you, it's different, Drez." Regulus sighed. "Less one-sided. More like we're both connected to each other. And there's another difference." He held up his hand, showing his palm for some reason. "I cut this hand on a fish scale a little bit ago. It healed almost instantly—and there wasn't a chance of it being fatal. And the healing process didn't hurt."

"Hm." Dresden waved a hand. "But that's tiny. Maybe that's why it didn't hurt."

Regulus picked up the knife he'd used to clean the fish and wiped it off on his pant leg, then stuck it in the fire to finish cleaning it. "Fine. Let's check."

"Regulus!" Adelaide gasped and stood. "Don't you dare!"

"It's a protection enchantment, right?" He looked at her, completely calm.

She did *not* feel calm. "I mean…yes, but I don't know how…or what…"

"Well, if it doesn't work, you can always heal me anyway." Regulus grinned. "Besides, it can be payback for misguided training at the neumenet tree." With that, he plunged the knife into his upper arm.

"Regulus, this is—" At the exact moment the knife cut into Regulus' arm, just as he winced, Adelaide grabbed her own upper arm and winced. It wasn't like when he had stabbed her at the neumenet tree. More like an echo or memory of that pain. Still sharp, but not as painful as the real thing. He pulled the knife back out. As his arm healed, the pain in her own arm subsided and a tiny amount of her power left her.

Regulus looked down at his arm and wiped away the bit of blood smeared over his skin and the edges of the hole in his sleeve. "Good as new."

"I…felt that," she whispered.

All three men looked at her.

"What do you mean, you felt it?" Father's brow furrowed.

"Not like actually being stabbed, but a softened version. An echo of the pain."

Regulus looked horrified. "Are you sure?"

Adelaide hesitated. Maybe she *was* just remembering the pain of being stabbed in nearly the same place. She needed to know. "I'm going to turn around, and then you do it again, somewhere else. I don't want to ask you to hurt yourself again, but—"

"Okay," Regulus said, his expression grim.

She turned around. A moment later, something slashed across the back of her right calf. Deep, too, but more of a quick stinging sensation than an actual cut. She grimaced and grabbed at her calf, but it was unharmed. The pain subsided, and she turned back around. Regulus had turned white as the clouds drifting above them. Dresden's mouth hung open. Father's expression was stoic and unreadable.

Regulus looked at her, the blood on the back of his right calf, then back. "That's…no." He shook his head. "No." He stood and charged past Dresden toward her, rolling up his sleeve. "Take it off."

"What?" She drew back. "No!"

"I'm not letting what hurts me hurt you, too." He shoved his arm toward her. "You have to remove it."

"But…" She stared at the mark on his arm, her mind racing. "It's a small amount of pain. And I don't bleed. It's all right—"

"No, it's not!"

"I agree with Regulus," Father said. She shot him a hurt look.

"You said this thing is more two-sided," Dresden said. "So what happens if she gets hurt?" She hadn't thought of that.

Regulus turned toward Dresden. "I don't really care—"

Adelaide snatched the knife out of Regulus' hand and jabbed it into her thigh before Regulus could stop her. She sucked in a breath through clenched teeth. Compared to the pain Kirven had put her through, this was minor. She pulled the knife back out. The wound continued to bleed down her thigh, showing no signs of healing. She tossed the knife toward the fire and held her glowing palm over the throbbing cut until it closed.

"I…didn't feel anything." Regulus sounded ashamed.

"So not completely two-sided then," Dresden said. "But it seems like the benefit is all yours right now, Reg. Which I'll admit doesn't seem like sorcery's methods."

Adelaide glared over Regulus' shoulder. "I told you. I'm not a sorceress."

"So you can't hurt him, or force him to do something—"

"No!" She crossed her arms. "At least…I don't think so."

"It doesn't matter," Regulus said. "I want it off."

"And I don't want you to die!" Tears pricked her eyes. Why couldn't she just be angry without feeling like she was going to cry? She was too tired for this. "Nolan can't die. It's only fair you have the same advantage."

Dresden stood and walked over next to them. "What if you tell him to do something? If he disobeyed the sorcerer, that mark caused him pain."

"I know that," Adelaide snapped. Still, Dresden's worrying was getting to her. "Regulus, Dresden is annoying me. Punch him in the face."

Regulus blinked. "What?"

"Punch him!" She didn't want Regulus and Dresden to fight. She hated it. But she needed to prove to herself Dresden's concerns were unfounded.

"Adelaide…" Regulus rubbed the back of his neck. "I've never laid a hand on Dresden." He winced. "Not by choice, anyway."

Her gut twisted as she remembered that Kirven had made him attack Dresden twice. "Does the mark hurt?"

"What—oh. You were testing…" Regulus half chuckled as relief eased his expression. "No pain. Nothing."

Dresden pursed his lips. "Good. But I still don't like that it works similarly."

"Sorcery is corrupted magic," Father said. "That's hardly surprising." He still sat next to the fire. "But I don't like that you're feeling his pain, either, Adelaide."

"See?" Regulus held his arm up. "Please."

"If it didn't hurt me, would you still want it off?"

Regulus shifted and averted his eyes.

"I thought you agreed it wasn't sorcery?" Her self-assurance faded.

"No! It's not that." Regulus sighed. "No, I wouldn't. I wouldn't care either way, if it stayed or not, so long as I have you. But it *does* hurt you, so I want you to remove it."

"I thought I lost you." Adelaide released a shaky breath, trying to stay in control of her emotions. "I can't—I won't go through that again." She pushed his arm away, his concern hitting her mind as she touched him. "Please."

Regulus looked down at her hands on his arm, then back at her eyes. "Okay." He pulled the sleeve back down.

"And you," she pointed a finger at Dresden. It shook, undermining her anger. "Don't you ever accuse me of sorcery again."

Dresden glanced away, but otherwise looked unapologetic. "Only if you don't do anything sorcerous."

"If I wanted to be a sorcerer, I already would be!" She bit her tongue. She didn't want to talk about this. Not in front of Father. Not to Dresden. She turned toward the fire and sat down. "The fish are burning."

Regulus sat next to her. Dresden and Father turned their attention to the fish while Adelaide stared at the flames. Her own screams echoed in her memory. *Stop thinking about it, stop.* But she imagined Kirven's mocking black eyes in the ash. A weight pressed against her back. Adelaide leapt aside with a short, strangled scream. Everyone froze.

Regulus stared, his mouth hanging open, his hand still suspended midair where he had tried to rest it on her back. To comfort her.

"Sorry," she mumbled. "You startled me."

They ate in silence, but she didn't miss Father's poorly disguised concerned glances or the questioning, pitying looks Dresden sent her way. Regulus sat close, a deep line between his eyebrows. She didn't need their pity. It just made her feel weak all over again.

Full for the first time in what seemed an eternity, Adelaide laid back in the grass and suppressed a yawn. "We need a plan. To stop Kirven."

"You need to rest," Father said. "We can worry about that later."

"We have to warn the king. Kirven mentioned the masque, but the sooner the king is warned, the better." She sat up, even as her mind begged for sleep. "We should leave immediately."

Regulus and Father looked at each other.

"I'm fine." She swallowed a yawn.

"We can leave tomorrow morning," Father said. "That still gives us enough time."

"But—"

"Please, Adelaide," Father pleaded. "Rest. For me."

"So what if I'm a little tired? If it was one of you, you wouldn't wait."

"You're exhausted." Father pointed to himself and Regulus. "And we are, too. We've hardly slept. We could all use the rest." He gave her another look of deep concern. She got the feeling that, somehow, he knew she'd been hurt far worse than a bruised cheek.

"All right." With a huff, she laid back down. It didn't take long for the warm sunlight to lull her to sleep.

When Adelaide opened her eyes, dark pressed around her. Kirven stood over her, his face illuminated by a sickly green glow from the opal in the Staff of Nightfall. She screamed and went to blast him back, but her hands were bound behind her back. *No. No, no…*

She stood and ran, but every leaden step only covered a few inches. Something pulled against her neck and she fell backward. The collar. Oh, Etiros, he put the collar back on. Panic pressed against her lungs. She looked around, frantic, as Kirven moved closer, holding the rope tied to the collar in one hand and the Staff of Nightfall in the other.

"Where's Regulus and my father?" Her voice sounded raspy and weak.

Kirven shook his head. "You cause so much trouble, you and your mercenary. You couldn't just go with Carrick, could you? Couldn't be a good little girl." He pointed the staff to her right. Father was tied to a tree, his mouth gagged and his head hanging forward like he was unconscious.

"Father!" He didn't move. *No...* She tried to stand, but Kirven pushed her down with the end of the staff.

"I promised I would torture your family if you didn't join me." Kirven knelt before her.

Nolan stood behind him, leaning on the pommel of a sword and watching impassively. Blood ran down the blade, soaking into the ground. Some instinct told her it was Regulus' blood. Her heart seemed to stop beating. Kirven squinted, then looked over his shoulder, following her line of sight.

"Oh. He's just waiting his turn." He placed the end of the staff on her chest. Ice spread from the edge of the staff, freezing and burning all at once. She screamed.

"Adelaide!" Kirven shouted. "Adelaide!"

Something gripped her shoulders and shook her. She continued to scream, writhing on the ground.

"Adelaide!" Kirven's voice morphed into Regulus'. "Adelaide, wake up. WAKE UP!"

Adelaide bolted upright and fought free of the hands holding her shoulders and her hand. "Let go!" Her chest heaved as she gasped for air and struggled to bring the faces hovering over her into focus. "Don't hurt me!"

Regulus released her shoulders and sat back on his heels, his expression terrified and pained. Kneeling on her other side, Father released her hand. He looked like he had aged ten years, his face was so drawn. Dresden stopped midpace behind Regulus. Faint sunlight still lit the pale blue sky, and the few clouds had an orange tint. No sign of Kirven or Nolan.

"You're safe." Regulus' neck corded. "Just a dream. You're safe. No one's going to hurt you."

"Reg?" Her voice broke on a sob.

"Ad." Regulus pulled her into an embrace.

Adelaide wrapped her arms around him and cried. It didn't matter it was embarrassing. The tears had decided to fall and would not be stemmed. She sobbed into Regulus' chest for several minutes, and her stomach and chest ached when her tears were finally spent.

"I'm sorry," she murmured as she pulled away.

"There's nothing to apologize for," Regulus said.

"For you," Dresden said. Adelaide looked up in confusion. Dresden sighed. "There's nothing you need to apologize for. But…I do." He crossed and uncrossed his arms. "I…shouldn't have doubted you. You've clearly been through a lot. I'm sorry."

She nodded, unable to say anything. Dresden strode away. She pressed a hand to her pounding skull.

"I wouldn't agree to bear the mark again." Waking up screaming like a child felt foolish. Even though she didn't want them to know, she owed them the truth. "Kirven—"

A violent shudder made it difficult to speak as she recalled the pain he had inflicted on her. That he had threatened to inflict on her family. She curled in on herself. Words failed her. How could she tell Father the truth? That she hadn't known a person could experience that much pain and live?

"You don't have to explain." Father knelt beside her and stroked her head. "They'll fade." His voice was barely a whisper. "The memories. The dreams. And the pain. They won't last forever."

He already knew. A sob tightened her throat as she met Father's gaze. "When?" She focused on the love in his eyes and let his calm wash over her.

Father shook his head, still stroking her hair. "I don't know. But they will. I've…been where you are. This feeling of—being broken. It's a lie. You will heal." He kissed the top of her head. "You're so, so strong, my dear. Don't doubt that, all right?"

Adelaide nodded, even though she didn't feel strong. She felt worthless; useless and used. *Broken* seemed right. *It's a lie.* But right now, she didn't know how to heal. How to wait for the memories and the dreams and the pain to fade.

"I think I'll sleep easier when he's dead. When they both are."

Father's lips drew into a hard line. "You don't have to be the one to face them—"

"Yes, I do." She looked down, fiddling with the edge of her tunic. "You don't know what he can do. It's going to take more than some knights to stop him."

Father obviously wanted to argue, but there was nothing he could say. He stood with a sigh. "Your mother will blame me for your insistence on being the hero, but that stubbornness is all her." He patted her head, then walked away.

Regulus rubbed her back. "I wish I could blot out what Kirven did to you," he whispered, his voice hoarse. "I…" His strong arms wrapped around her. Protecting her. Shielding her.

Adelaide leaned against him. "I'm all right."

By the way Regulus tightened his grip on her, like he could hold her tightly enough to press all her broken pieces back together, she knew he didn't believe her.

REGULUS DIDN'T let himself sleep until Adelaide was sound asleep in his arms, which took a while. He didn't care to know the specifics of her nightmare. That she had mumbled for him and her father and then screamed like she was being burned alive was more than enough for his aching heart and guilty conscience.

When she asked him not to leave her side, he swore he wouldn't. He didn't care that Dresden looked amused when he curved his body against Adelaide's back. Or that Alfred tightened his mouth so much his lips turned white when he wrapped his arms around her, and she curled her hands around his forearm. He only cared that Adelaide felt safe, that she slept comfortably, even when his own arms fell asleep.

He was thankful to be the first person awake in the early dawn. During the night, they had shifted. Regulus was on his back, and Adelaide lay on her stomach across his chest, her head resting on his shoulder and her left leg hooked around his left leg. The fingers of her left hand had intertwined with his right. Her heart beat a gentle rhythm against his ribs. A hot stone seemed to burn in his stomach and his skin tingled. He hardly dared to breathe, afraid he'd disturb her slumber.

Birds sang nearby, their chirps competing with the gentle flow of the stream. The air was crisp and cold, more like the beginning of harvest than the end of summer. He stroked Adelaide's unraveling braid, undoing the strands as the sky turned from a dusty pink to a washed-out blue. Green leaves swayed in a breeze that didn't reach the ground, revealing the occasional tinge of yellow and orange.

He smiled, relishing this moment of peace. Adelaide's warmth, the gentle beauty of a new day. This was what he wanted, every day for the rest of his life. Well, maybe inside, on a bed with pillows. A pinch had developed in his neck.

Drez tossed onto his side on the other side of the ash-filled fire pit. More important than Regulus' discomfort, it seemed wise to get up before Alfred. He eased his hand out of Adelaide's, but she stirred as he tried to move out from under her.

"Five more minutes," she mumbled as she wrapped her hands behind his neck.

Regulus chuckled. "You make a compelling argument," he whispered in her ear, "but—"

"Too cold." She turned her head, hiding her face in his shoulder, and mumbled something he couldn't make out.

"Okay, but only to protect you from the cold."

"Good," she said, her voice still heavy with sleep.

A sparrow flitted through the air above him, catching insects. No part of him wanted to get up. He wanted to stay like that forever. Sorcerers and immortal creeps be damned. He put his hands on her waist, thinking he would just pick her up and move her over. Instead his hands developed a mind of their own and moved over her waist, tracing up her back and tangling in her hair. She filled his mind, all other thoughts sinking into blurry shadows.

Adelaide shifted, and he sensed her sleepiness fall away. Her love and desire shot through him, mixing with and heightening his own. Regulus closed his eyes and breathed in, trying to calm his racing heartbeat. She turned her head and her breath slid over his neck. His right hand wandered up and over the back of her neck, her skin warm and soft under his fingertips as he brushed his fingers through her hair. He gripped her waist with his other hand. A flare of anxiety and fear edged into his mind as she tensed. Guilt and sorrow squeezed at his chest and he released her waist and opened his eyes.

A dark shape hovered above him as something hard dug into his side opposite Adelaide. He grunted and Adelaide gasped. Regulus squinted against the light as Alfred bent down and pulled his arms off her back. His face burned like he'd been sitting inches from a roaring fire. Alfred's eyes flashed, his face and neck flushed. Adelaide scrambled off Regulus, her cheeks darkening. Alfred drew his arm back, his hand curled into a white-knuckled fist. But instead of punching him, Alfred reached down, gripped the front of Regulus' shirt, and pulled him up so his mouth was next to Regulus' ear.

"You go too far," Alfred whispered, voice tense. "I won't have you taking advantage of her weakened state. Even without what she's been through, show some restraint." He pulled back so they were eye-to-eye. Regulus' tongue stuck to the roof of his mouth, his fists pressed into the dirt. It took all his courage not to bow his head in submission at the withering look Alfred gave him.

"I'd give you a proper beating instead of just a boot to your side," Alfred said, "but I can't hurt you without hurting her." He shoved hard against Regulus' sternum, pushing him backward.

Adelaide stood with her arms wrapped over her stomach. "Father—"

"No." Alfred pointed at Adelaide. He opened his mouth, shut it again, then dropped his hand. "You're not married to him yet," he said as he strode past.

Regulus rubbed his sternum, wondering if Adelaide had felt that, too. She met his eyes apologetically but didn't look like she felt the throb in his own chest. The dull ache dissipated quickly, however. Points to Adelaide's magic for ensuring he didn't have a bruised side or sternum.

Alfred glared every time their paths crossed while they ate some apples and fish for breakfast and prepared to leave. Dresden had awoken just as Alfred landed a swift kick in Regulus' side, and every time their eyes met, he looked on the brink of laughter.

The sun had breached the horizon when they were ready to depart, their scarce supplies packed up and the horses saddled and bridled. With Zephyr gone, Adelaide headed toward Sieger with Regulus close behind. As she reached for the saddle, Alfred cleared his throat.

"No." Alfred's tone left no room for argument, but that didn't stop Adelaide. "No, what?"

"You can ride with me, or Regulus can ride with Dresden."

Dresden wrinkled his nose and lifted an eyebrow.

"Fath—"

"Or someone can remain behind." Alfred's glare made Regulus' blood run cold. Adelaide looked to Regulus.

Regulus glowered. "Respectfully—"

"Respect?" He recoiled at the intensity of Alfred's voice. "Respectfully, Lord Hargreaves, you push the limits of propriety with my daughter, and I've had quite enough." Alfred held out his hand. "Ad, let's go."

After a tense moment, Adelaide spun around and mounted Sieger. "Regulus?"

"Uh…" He looked from her to Alfred's red face.

Alfred stalked over and snatched Sieger's reins. "We're not leaving. Not until I am certain you're away from his wandering hands."

Adelaide fidgeted. "Father."

"I apologize for any impropriety," Regulus said, "but I promise—"

"Promises are easily broken when opportunity abounds." Alfred narrowed his eyes. "Your choices are to ride separately, or Regulus can have his hands tied behind his back."

"Father!"

"Final." Father and daughter stared at each other for several moments. Regulus was torn between saying he could ride with Dresden and agreeing to have his hands bound when Adelaide lowered her head, her shoulders slumping.

"Yes, Father." She looked miserable as she went to dismount.

"Wait." Regulus put his hand on her knee, then drew it back as the corner of Alfred's mouth turned down in displeasure. He took a step away from Sieger's side, his face burning. "Sieger is the biggest horse we have. You two can ride him, my lord." He hadn't meant to sound so disappointed, but truthfully, he was.

Alfred nodded, and Regulus mounted Alfred's gray stallion, ignoring the disbelieving judgement in Dresden's eyes. They had enough concerns without making his betrothed's father hate him. As much as he resented Alfred's harsh turn, he understood. Alfred had barely forgiven him for sneaking Adelaide out of Belanger castle. Not to mention that Alfred had to wonder, if Regulus was willing to get that…comfortable with Adelaide with her father a few feet away, how comfortable might they have gotten when they were alone?

It didn't matter the answer was they had been focused on things like not dying or getting kidnapped by fairies and when Adelaide practiced magic she slept like a hibernating bear. Alfred was her father, and if years of managing mercenaries had taught him anything, it was that fathers tended to be fiercely, even irrationally, protective of their daughters. Assurances of self-control and respect rarely soothed an outraged father.

They rode in silence. The tension was palpable, making the morning stretch on. Guilt weighed on Regulus' shoulders. He had embarrassed Adelaide and seriously offended her father. Far worse, he had scared her. The sensation of her anxiety had lasted only a moment, but it was enough to sink claws into his heart.

They stopped to eat around noon. Adelaide tied Sieger near a half-dried up brook while Alfred approached him, his face stern.

"Can I trust you for two minutes?"

Regulus ground his teeth. "Yes, my lord."

Alfred wandered off to relieve himself, and Regulus approached Adelaide, although he resisted the urge to touch her.

"I'm sorry," he said quietly.

"Don't be." Her smile both lifted the weight on his shoulders and made the pang in his heart worse. She placed one hand on his chest and touched the ends of his hair with the other.

"I got carried away. And…" He hung his head. "I scared you. I felt it."

Her hand pulled back from his hair, her smile fading. "I'm sorry. I didn't—"

"Hey, you don't have anything to be sorry about. And don't step on my apology." He forced a smile. "I don't ever want to scare you."

Adelaide shook her head. "No, it's not… I'm not afraid of you, Reg. I'm not sure I ever could be. Not after everything." She leaned her cheek on the top of his shoulder while her hand drifted to the side of his neck. "I didn't mean to react like that. It's not your fault."

As her skin touched his, her conflicting emotions skidded over his consciousness. Sorrow. Doubt. Nervousness. Anger. Guilt. Fear. But not of him. His hand fisted at his side. Of Carrick. Regulus closed his eyes and attempted to steady his nerves. Instead, his mind jolted. Shadowy, disjointed glimpses of scenes through Adelaide's eyes flickered behind his closed eyelids.

Carrick leering as he pulled Adelaide toward him out of the stream. Carrick holding her immobile against his chest as he forced a long, rough kiss on her. Adelaide pushing him away, her magic bright against the darkness of the memory. Carrick grabbing Adelaide's waist and thigh and pulling her to him. Regulus experienced her fear, her panic, her hopelessness as Carrick held a dagger to her throat, then changed his mind. Carrick leaned over her, his eyes lustful and expression gloating. Adelaide's remembered terror seeped into Regulus. Carrick's words slipped into his mind, muffled and distorted. *"When Hargreaves is dead… Come crawling… Wish you had given in sooner."*

Regulus stumbled backward, his eyes flying open. His pulse throbbed in his head. The ground tilted. He was aware of Adelaide shouting his name and Dresden running over as he teetered and fell onto all fours, shaking. He pressed his eyes closed against the double image of grass floating in his vision.

"What the hell did you do?" Dresden shouted. "Tell me what you did!"

"I—I didn't! I don't understand—"

"What is going on?" Alfred demanded.

"*She* did something to him!"

"No, I—"

Regulus held up a trembling hand, silencing them as he took several deep breaths. When he finally opened his eyes, the world stayed level. He rocked back onto his heels and wiped his hand across his forehead. He opened his mouth, to tell Adelaide he was okay, to tell Alfred everything was fine, to tell Dresden not to yell at his betrothed. But all that came out was a broken, "Adelaide."

"Regulus?" She wrung her hands.

"I saw," he said hoarsely. "I saw what Carrick did."

Adelaide paled and took a step back. Her jaw quivered as she shook her head. "No…that's not… Oh, Etiros. No."

"I'm so, so sorry, Adelaide. I'm sorry. I'm sorry."

"Stop—stop saying that." Her eyes glistened with unshed tears.

"I…" Regulus slammed his fist into the ground. "I don't know what to do! I don't know what else to say!" He punched the ground again and released a deep-throated scream. "I should never have left you. I failed you, and I'm sorry." A tear raced down the side of his nose while he stared at the grass stuck to his knuckles.

What would she want? For him to listen? To hold her? To leave her alone? He couldn't forget what he saw, what he felt of her emotions. He wanted to help, and he didn't know how.

"Tell me how to make it right." His voice cracked. "Tell me what to do!"

Adelaide knelt in front of him. Her fingers lifted his chin. He wasn't prepared to feel her emotions, but they hit him anyway. Humiliation she had no reason to bear. Grief that struck at his heart like a hammer. Rage that had turned ice cold. And love he didn't deserve.

"Nolan Carrick owes me an apology." The strength in her voice belied the tremor of her lips. "You're not the guilty party."

She placed her hands on his shoulders, then moved them up to the back of his neck, her thumbs rubbing back and forth behind his ears. "You really…" Her lips parted. "You don't think I'm weak. You don't blame me for being afraid."

Regulus pushed her hair out of her face. "I would never. And you're so much stronger than you realize. So much stronger than I am." *I don't know how you're holding together.*

Adelaide laughed through her tears. "Please. Where do you think I'm getting my strength?" She embraced him, her body pressing against his. As he hugged her back and tucked his face into her shoulder, he promised himself that so far as was in his power, he would never leave her alone again.

After a while, she pulled away. "I need to, um…you know. I'll be right back." His hand slipped down her arm as she stood and walked away.

Alfred watched her go, his expression pained. "Did Carrick…" Alfred's neck bulged as he swallowed.

"He kissed her and put his hands on her." Regulus stood, feeling weary, ill, and murderous. "He threatened her. And he…got too close. But no."

"I suppose I should be thankful for that," Alfred said, his voice hollow. "But I'm too angry and heartbroken to care. He violated her mind, if not her body." He met Regulus' eyes. "Carrick has to die."

ADELAIDE WASHED her face in the brook. The cool water somehow eased some of the emotional strain. She didn't understand how this bond she had created worked. Why and how had Regulus seen her memories? When she first realized what had happened, she had thought she might either faint or vomit.

Regulus not only knowing but watching what Carrick had done…her failure to stop him… It added to her humiliation. She had feared he would see her as broken and used and worthless as she felt. Yet when she touched him, she sensed no judgment or disappointment. Just understanding, sorrow, and love. And fury.

She splashed water onto the back of her neck and massaged her tight muscles. She had also sensed his pride as he told her she was strong. If only she could agree. Simultaneously wanting Regulus' touch and dreading it didn't feel strong. Neither did the way the involuntary memories of Nolan's assault or Kirven's torture sent her pulse racing. But Regulus and Father looked at her and called her strong.

The gnawing in her stomach drove her back to the others. Dresden intercepted her and held out a handful of fresh-picked black berries.

"We just found them. Over there." He gestured to the left, not meeting her eyes. "They're sweet and refreshing." He pushed his hand out further.

"Oh…thank you." Dresden didn't look at her as she scooped berries out of his hand. Her fingers broke the thin skin on some of them. Purplish-red juices stained her fingertips and the flesh of his palm.

"Listen, I…" Dresden sighed as he closed his fingers around the remaining berries. "I'm sorry for yelling." He scratched his beard. "Reg is…he's my brother. Not by blood, but he's my brother all the same. He's protected me since we were children, and I will always protect him. I nearly lost him, and…" His throat corded.

"You were afraid."

"I can't thank you enough for saving him. But his soul was dying under the sorcerer. I can't watch that again. I can't." Dresden took a deep breath and met her eyes. "I wasn't afraid; I was terrified. If he'd died fighting for you, or if you'd enslaved him, even by accident, it would be my fault. But I shouldn't have doubted you, and I'm sorry."

Adelaide stared. "I forgive you, but…how would it be your fault?"

"Ah, he wouldn't have told you that." A sly smile spread over Dresden's face. He looked over as Regulus approached. "Reg, you didn't tell her my part in enabling your romance, and frankly, I'm offended."

She expected Regulus to scoff and brush Dresden's comment off. Instead, he turned bright red. "Drez—"

"Regulus almost didn't go to the Drummonds' party." Dresden tossed a couple berries into his mouth with a toothy smile. "I talked him into going." He elbowed Regulus. "Forced him to talk to you, too. The frowny-faced coward. Talked him out of giving up on pursuing you several times. Plus, there's our little secret." He winked, much to Adelaide's bewilderment.

"Secret?" Regulus demanded.

"Aw, don't tell me you've forgotten about the pastries." Dresden arched a brow.

Pastries? The nalotavi. Regulus' sweet and slightly ridiculous note. Dresden's postscript confiding that Regulus thought he had thrown that note away in favor of a more restrained message, but Dresden had thought she'd like that one better.

Adelaide smiled, then giggled. Regulus looked affronted, which for some reason made her laugh more. All her stress welled up and bubbled out of her in gut-squeezing, shoulder-shaking laughter.

"You were right, you know," she wheezed, her hand pressed against her stomach. "It was sweet; and I liked it."

"See?" Dresden slapped Regulus' shoulder. "I always have your back."

She wiped a tear from the corner of her eye while Dresden sauntered away. Her laughter died out, but her smile remained. Especially as Regulus watched her with a deep crease between his eyebrows and an expression like a lost puppy.

"Dresden exchanged the letters you wrote when you sent me the nalotavi." She slipped her hand into his. "He wrote at the bottom he thought the original was more honest."

"Oh, great." Regulus' embarrassment crept into her mind through their connection. "Just…excellent."

Adelaide giggled and leaned against his shoulder. "I liked it. In fact, I hope you don't stop writing me sentimental letters when we're married. Or giving me nalotavi."

"Marry me and I'll ask Sarah to bake you nalotavi every day if you want."

"You do know how to charm a girl." She kissed him as his abashed delight traveled through their bond.

Dresden hadn't lied—the berries were ripe and juicy. They walked hand-in-hand over to the horses. Father handed her some leftover cold fish. He looked calmer than when she left, but she still caught the flicker of pained worry in his eyes. They ate quickly and prepared to continue their journey.

Adelaide planted a kiss on Regulus' cheek while Father's back was turned before mounting Sieger. Regulus moved toward Father's horse, but Father stepped up to the stallion's side and mounted before Regulus could. Regulus stood stock-still. He gave her a helpless, confused look.

Father looked down at Regulus. "Don't stand there. We don't have all day, and I doubt you'll keep up long on foot." He turned his horse toward the road.

Relief and joy washed over Adelaide. Regulus turned toward her, looking unsure. With a grin, she motioned him over with her head. He cast one more look at Father riding in the direction of the road, then jogged to Sieger's side.

Once he settled into place behind her, he plucked the reins out of her hands. His torso bumped against her back as he whispered in her ear, "Can— would you mind…if I kiss your forehead?"

She didn't know if she wanted to laugh or cry, the gentleness in his voice almost too much to bear. Unable to force a response past her tied tongue, she nodded. His lips pressed against her temple. With the contact of their skin, Regulus' love and desire to protect her sank into Adelaide like an ache. He leaned back and prodded Sieger to follow Father.

The rest of the day passed more comfortably, with Regulus' arms around her while they rode. After they stopped for the night, it didn't take her long to fall asleep, tucked against Regulus' side.

The next morning passed in the same manner, but in the early afternoon they crested a hill and Adelaide's mouth fell open like her jaw had unhinged. The rolling green hills continued before them, but beyond, stretching into what seemed like an eternity, was an expanse of glittering deep blue. A cool, salty breeze tugged at her hair.

"Is…is that…?"

"The Ismuire Sea," Father said.

She leaned back against Regulus, staring. The expanse of the water beckoned her. When Adelaide was little, she had told Mother she wanted to visit

Khastalland. Mother had asked if she wanted to go by land or sea. She had said she didn't care, she just wanted to see all the places in Mother's stories.

But as Adelaide looked across the lush hills at the water glittering like diamonds and sapphires, she wanted the sea. She wanted to touch the sea, to step in it and see what it felt like. To sail out into it until the land disappeared from view. She wanted to know the sea and find out if it would accept her.

They rode to a path that followed the coast. As they neared the water's edge, the sound of the sea built. She had always assumed the sea would sound like a river, but somehow bigger. It was nothing like a river.

The water pushed and pulled at the shore, the rushing swoosh of the waves building until they fizzled out before receding and smashing against a new, incoming wave. Stones along the shore clacked against each other as waves moved over them, making the water whisper. The rhythmic rustle and crash of the waves held a melodic beauty that would make a musician envious, with an unpredictable wildness that was both exciting and alarming. White-crested waves broke along the shore, bubbling and swirling between massive boulders as the sea breathed.

Regulus placed his hand on top of hers. She sensed his curiosity, then his amusement as he said, "It is incredible, and beautiful. I can't believe you've never been to the sea." He removed his hand. "Dangerous, too."

Sir Ruddard had told Adelaide and Minerva about the one time he traveled on the sea. It was a favorite story of his, because he got to dramatize how close he was to death in an abrupt, terrible storm. He always insisted he saw mermaids that day. Or maybe sirens, he would say. The howling wind sounded too much like singing for his comfort.

The sea passed in and out of sight as the trail wound through pines and birch trees and across gentle valleys and hills. They entered a grassy valley with a stream running through it that emptied into the sea. Between two protruding rock cliff-faces topped with pines, a sand and pebble beach surrounded the stream's outlet.

"I think we need a quick break," Regulus said, turning Sieger toward the sea. She looked at him over her shoulder. His eyes danced. "I don't need the bond to know what you want. Your entire body is straining toward the sea."

"We're nearly to the city," Father protested, but Regulus followed the stream, urging Sieger to a canter.

Adelaide couldn't suppress her giggle. Regulus halted Sieger at the edge of the beach and hopped down. He reached toward her waist, then paused, his concern reflected in his eyes. *Oh, Etiros, I love him.* She grabbed his hands and guided them to her waist. He smiled, his scar pulling one side of his upper lip higher in that lopsided way she loved, and lifted her off Sieger's back and set her on the ground.

She pulled off her boots and pushed her trousers up to her knees. The water was colder than it looked, but not unpleasant. Careful not to slip on the loose pebbles, Adelaide waded into the sea. The waves, smaller here in this protected little beach, pushed and pulled on her legs, messing with her balance. She continued until the water was sloshing onto her thighs, soaking her trousers. A receding wave pulled a pebble out from under her foot and her arms pin-wheeled as she leaned to the side.

Regulus caught her arm, steadying her. She grinned up at him. His loose black hair swayed in the sea breeze as he laughed, rich and deep. The sunlight reflected off the rippling water, flickering over his face and making his light gray eyes sparkle. He was so attractive it made her heart physically hurt.

His eyes met hers, his hands still holding her arm to keep her steady. She didn't need the bond to tell her what he was feeling. She felt it too. The sound of the waves filled her mind, soothing her nerves. She turned toward him. Before Adelaide could even raise her lips to his, Regulus' arms wrapped around her and he lifted her into the air. She leaned over him, cradled his face in her hands, and kissed him like she had been waiting her whole life for his salty kiss.

SOMETHING SLAMMED into Regulus' ribs, jolting him awake. He reached for his sword as the shapes in the shabby inn room clarified in the dark. The beds where Alfred and Drez were sound asleep, the hole-ridden curtain over the discolored glass window, and the table and two chairs beneath it. Satisfied it was just Adelaide's elbow that had awoken him, he set the sword back down on the rough wooden floorboards.

The old inn wasn't pretty, and the flat, straw-stuffed mattresses stank of body odor. The thin wool blankets itched. But it was indoors and boasted one of the cleanest taverns Regulus had seen. Rain had started shortly before they arrived at the royal town of Crelburgh at dusk, and they had arrived exhausted. Anything was better than sleeping in the rain.

Adelaide shifted beside him. "Won't." He squinted at her in the feeble light. She curled into a ball, her eyes squeezed shut. "No." She tossed over on her back and kicked his knee.

"Ad?"

"Please," she whimpered, her eyes still closed.

Oh. A deep heaviness settled into his chest. He gently shook her shoulder. "Wake up. Come on, wake up."

"Leave him alone," Adelaide mumbled. Her terror tickled his mind as he touched the bare skin of her arms.

Regulus sighed and closed his eyes, trying not to panic. Instead, his panic increased when her nightmare leapt into his mind. Figures stood outlined in eerie green light as he looked out of Adelaide's eyes.

A rope bound Adelaide's hands together, the palms against each other, and disappeared into the darkness. The sorcerer stood before her, both hands gripping the Staff of Nightfall. Carrick stood next to him, one hand on Alfred's shoulder, the other on Tamina's shoulder. Alfred and Tamina knelt with their wrists chained.

"I made you a promise, mage." The sorcerer extended the staff toward Alfred.

"No! It's not their fault! You can't do this!" Adelaide lunged toward her parents, but something caught on her neck and yanked her backward. "You're not king yet." Desperation rang in her voice as she stared at the tip of the staff hovering over her father's chest. "You said after you were king!"

"I *am* king."

Adelaide's eyes flicked up to the sorcerer. To the crown on his head that hadn't been there a moment before. "No. No!"

Regulus forced his eyes open and the nightmare vanished. "Adelaide! You have to wake up." He shook her, but she didn't open her eyes. "Wake. Up!"

Her eyes opened wide, the whites stark in the darkness. She grabbed his arms and her fingers dug through his sleeves as she looked around.

"Hey, it's okay. You're safe. Your father and mother are safe. The sorcerer and Carrick aren't here."

Her face relaxed and she leaned into him. He stroked her back, her chest heaving.

"Wha goin' on?" Alfred mumbled.

"Nightmare," Regulus said. "You can go back to sleep."

Alfred mumbled something, and a few moments later, his breathing deepened again.

"Wait." Adelaide pulled back to look into his face. "My parents?" She bit her lip. "Did you…see my dream?"

"I closed my eyes while touching you. I didn't mean to," he added, hoping she wasn't offended. "It just happened." She didn't respond. "Do you want to talk?"

She shook her head.

"Okay." He wrapped his arms around her. He could feel her heart still racing. "If you change your mind, I'm here." He held her while her breathing and heartrate slowed and wished he could do something more.

"Kirven…" Adelaide's voice was barely a whisper. "He promised to torture my family in front of me until they went mad from the pain. And you. But not until after he's king, so I thought we could stop him. But… I don't know if we can."

His fingers brushed against her bare arm. The fear and hopelessness he sensed seemed so unlike the woman who just a couple weeks ago looked at him and said she would help free him. Who said if the sorcerer went back on his word, they would find another way together. She had been through so much, and it made his heart feel squeezed and hung out to dry.

"I'm not giving up." Regulus rubbed her back. "You have endured so much. Don't give up now."

She nestled closer to his chest. "It's just…hard."

"I know." *Etiros knows just how much.*

Adelaide reached under his right sleeve and her fingers rubbed the scars from his attempts to remove the sorcerer's mark. "How did you stay strong and keep hope for two years?"

"I didn't." He sighed. "Dresden wouldn't let me give up. He…"

Honesty. He needed to be honest. He had seen all Adelaide's fears, all her pain. He couldn't hide his from her. Maybe it would help, somehow, to know she wasn't alone.

"Shortly after I took the oath, I refused to rob a cathedral. The sorcerer…if he'd maintained control a few seconds longer, I would have murdered Dresden. Harold barely escaped, too." Regulus gulped against the lump lodged in his throat. "I went to the cathedral after that. Killed an innocent monk. While I was gone, Dresden somehow convinced Harold to stay. Later, Dresden found me after I tried to cut out the mark, and when that failed repeatedly, tried…" His mouth felt dry. "I tried…"

His throat closed as the locked-away memory came crashing back, along with the recollection of his pain. His wretched hopelessness, fear, and self-loathing.

"Please, Drez."

"I won't. Don't ask me to."

"I've tried everything else! I—I need you to behead me. Please. Please."

Dresden had taken Regulus' bloody sword and tossed it aside. Bits and pieces of what Dresden had said echoed in his mind. *"This isn't how you win. I'll help, Regulus, I promise. This is temporary. You're more than your failures, mistakes, your worst moments, or the sorcerer's actions. You can't leave me. I'm not abandoning you. You're my friend, my brother. The world is a better place because of Regulus Hargreaves, and I won't see the world become worse by losing you."*

Adelaide sucked in a breath and pulled away, but before her skin left his, he sensed it wasn't out of shock or disgust. She simply couldn't bear feeling his emotions.

"Reg…" She clapped her hand over her mouth and looked toward Dresden. "I didn't mean to…" Her voice was jagged and raw, and a hint of moonlight caught in the silent tears on her cheeks.

Oh. No. "You…saw?" He wiped away his own tears.

She threw her arms around him. "I'm sorry."

Regulus now understood how horrified Adelaide had been when he accidentally spied on Carrick's attack. The realization she had not only seen him at his lowest and most vulnerable, but lived his memory of it, crushed him. But Adelaide didn't turn away. He leaned into her embrace, but avoided touching his skin to hers, careful not to flood her with his emotions again.

"I lost hope," he said past his tight vocal cords. "I saw no way forward, and the guilt…"

She rubbed his back and arms and moved closer against his chest. Comforting and accepting him as his emotions choked him. Her unflinching love soothed his battered heart.

"But Drez didn't abandon me or judge me," he continued quietly. "He never stopped believing in me. He was always nudging me forward, insisting I keep living my life like it was normal, because it would be someday. He came up with a mantra to ground me when my thoughts got too dark. And he got me Magnus. To 'give me a reason to leave my room.'" *Which did help, actually.*

Regulus shifted. Part of him felt exposed and ridiculous. Part of him was relieved to tell her, to talk about it.

"I'm glad you have him," Adelaide whispered.

"Me too." He licked his lips. They still tasted salty from the afternoon of sea breezes. "No one is strong all the time, Ad. Even tigers run from fire and hunters." He kissed her hair. "That's why we all need each other. I thought I was being strong by separating myself and putting up walls. I thought I was protecting my friends. But Dresden was right. Being a lone wolf made me weaker, not stronger, and only hurt the people I care about."

Adelaide squeezed him tighter.

"I don't expect you to be fearless." Regulus stroked her hair. "But I hope you'll stand with me and try to do what's right. Together."

After a moment, she responded. "Thank you. For being honest." She felt for his hand in the dark and gripped it, and her determination, heartache, and love poured into him. "I think I can manage together."

Chapter 30

IN THE MORNING they ordered a tub of hot water brought to their room. Alfred gave Adelaide coin to purchase new clothes for herself and Regulus while the men washed up. Even though Regulus had argued against Dresden and Alfred coming to rescue Adelaide, he was thankful they had insisted. Thankful to have Dresden, and thankful Alfred had had the foresight to pack a good amount of coin.

He wished he had the rest of his men with him, too, but it was better this way. Safer to travel in a smaller group. Better that he hadn't endangered their lives any further. And comforting to know Caleb and Perceval had stayed to help protect Belanger castle while Jerrick and Estevan had returned home to keep an eye on Arrano.

Regulus was scrubbing his back when someone knocked at the door. Dresden, his hair still dripping, finished fastening his trousers and threw the door open. Adelaide's eyes widened and her face turned dark red as she looked from Drez's bare chest to Regulus sitting in the wooden tub to the ceiling. Regulus tensed, his skin on fire even as a traitorous grin pulled at his lips. She shoved a pile of clothes against Dresden's chest and spun away.

Alfred slammed the door closed, one boot half laced. "Do you have a brain, man?"

Drez laughed. "I'm not sure which surprised her more, Reg. My excellent olive-skinned physique and masculine chest hair, or the fact you're naked."

Alfred whacked the back of Drez's head and stomped back to his bed to finish putting on his boots. Drez held the bundle of clothes with one hand and rubbed the back of his head with the other. He mouthed "ow" to Regulus as he dropped the clothes onto a bed.

"This should look fetching on you, Reg." Dresden held up a deep green dress.

"That's clearly Adelaide's, you egotistical, bearded nit-wit."

Drez laid the dress out on the other bed before he finished dressing. Once Regulus had shaved and dressed in the new clothes—a pair of black trousers that were a touch tight, a blue tunic, and a black belt—the men left the room. The inn's staff changed out the water for fresh heated water, and Adelaide went in to get cleaned up. Alfred stood watch outside the door while Regulus and Dresden got food and drink from the tavern on the ground floor of the three-story wooden building.

The vegetables were mush and flavorless, but the bread was fresh and the mead decent. They got more than a few stares and curious glances. Regulus' scar and Dresden's Carasian complexion and nose often drew attention, so it wasn't new.

Regulus and Drez split up, talking to other tavern guests and fishing for information about if anyone had seen or heard anything about the sorcerer or Carrick. People either didn't care to talk or didn't know anything. Regulus intimidated the barmaid, judging by the way she kept looking at him then away, and she seemed suspicious of poor Drez.

Accordingly, they hadn't discovered anything when Alfred came down the creaky stairs with Adelaide. She looked lighter, as if some of her turmoil and pain had washed off with the dirt and grime. Her dark green dress brushed the floor. Fitted sleeves covered her arms, but the wide neck left the tops of her shoulders bare. A silver cord tied around her hips hung down the front of the dress, swinging as she walked. She had pulled her hair into a thick braid that cascaded over her shoulder.

Drez nudged Regulus' arm with his elbow. "Stop gawking."

Adelaide swept across the floor and kissed Regulus' cheek. "You can gawk if you like, *piahre*." She stepped back to look him up and down with an appreciative smirk. "So long as you don't mind me gawking in return." It was difficult to restrain himself from kissing her in front of a tavern full of strangers.

The entire time Alfred and Adelaide ate, Regulus was acutely aware of the stares Adelaide received. Ladies didn't frequent inns or taverns, so the patrons' curiosity wasn't surprising, but it put Regulus on edge. Especially the roving looks some of the more disreputable-looking men gave her.

The moment Adelaide and Alfred finished eating, Regulus rushed them out the door. They rode to the towering palace walls, where Alfred gave the guards his name and showed them his ring with his rearing unicorn crest. One of the guards led them inside the walls.

Compared to the palace gardens, the garden in Arrano's courtyard was a peasant's bean field. Trees Regulus had never seen within Monparth's borders stretched toward the sky. Flowers in every color and shape with strong fragrances bloomed amid all the greenery that grew along winding paths of white stone. They passed three marble fountains, one with a woman pouring water from a jar over her nude body, another of three leaping dolphins, and one of a crane with its long neck extended into the air and water shooting out of its beak.

He glimpsed a chapel between the trees that looked more like a miniature cathedral with its high arches. White plaster covered the walls of the palace so that they shone in the light, even with the partial cloud cover.

The guard spoke to a servant who led them inside the palace. Rose marble bannisters curved next to granite steps covered with a long red carpet. The servant didn't lead them up the steps, instead turning into a narrow hall to the right that ran through several rooms. Tall stained-glass windows of nature scenes, knights, ladies, and magical creatures illuminated each room. They walked through the first few rooms too quickly for Regulus to register anything other than each room appearing to have a specific color scheme and lots of opulence. Another red carpet ran down the length of the hall, through all the open doors.

The servant left them in a room with several plush armchairs upholstered in turquoise with bronze legs. A rug embroidered with a floral pattern covered the floor and a tapestry of a stag hunt covered most of the long wall opposite the windows, except for a plain door. A rose marble fireplace nestled in the wall to their right, a mantel held over it by two bronze statues of kneeling women in gauzy dresses. A huge painting of a noblewoman with rosy cheeks and a small dog at her feet hung on the wall opposite the fireplace.

Alfred sat in one of the chairs and Adelaide followed his lead, but Regulus felt awkward in all the finery and just stood near the empty fireplace with his hands clasped behind his back. Dresden was apparently fascinated by the tapestry and stood squinting at it.

After several minutes that dragged on, the door next to the tapestry opened. A thin, tall man in a deep blue doublet with silver embroidery on his belt, cuffs, and boots entered. He bowed as Alfred stood.

"Lord Belanger. I am His Excellency's steward, Sir Michael." Sir Michael clasped his hands in front of him. "I am told you are asking for an audience with His Excellency?"

"That is correct, Sir Michael." Alfred bowed, but not as deeply. "I am afraid I come bearing grave news. It is a matter of life and death that I speak to His Excellency immediately."

"Life and death?" Sir Michael raised an eyebrow. "Perhaps if I had more information—"

"The king's life is in danger," Alfred said, his tone sharp. "If you tell him I said so, I am certain he will want to speak with me. I *must* speak to him directly."

Sir Michael looked uncertain. "His Excellency is quite busy. But I will pass on your message and see what the king would like to do." He left, the door clicking shut behind him.

Adelaide sat on her hands and swung her legs. "Well. I don't think we'd have gotten an audience with the king on our own, Regulus."

"Seems that way." Regulus pursed his lips. "Do you think he will listen?"

Alfred sat back down. "Yes."

They waited for an hour. When Sir Michael returned, he threw the door open. Sweat glistened on his forehead as he motioned them through the doorway. "His Excellency will see you immediately."

Regulus and Dresden looked at each other. Maybe he shouldn't be surprised. Alfred had nearly given his life for the king's father, after all.

Sir Michael rushed them down hallways with paintings of royals and showed them into a small room with no furniture save for an empty small wooden throne with red cushions. After collecting their weapons, the steward left them, closing the door behind him. Against the throne leaned a sword with a gold hilt formed in the shape of a dragon's head in a scabbard of gold, ivory, and onyx.

Behind the throne, a floor-to-ceiling clear glass window illuminated the room. The fireplace to their right had a gold mantel supported by statues of gold dogs. A door opposite the fireplace opened and the man from the portrait Alfred had shown them walked in.

The king, like his brother, was short. No silver had yet touched his short brown beard. A simple gold crown sat on his head, holding his long brown hair in place. He wore a crimson cloak with gold edging over a black doublet embroidered in gold and black hose. Every finger bore a ring. Gold embroidered his belt and gold buckles shone on his boots.

Alfred dropped to one knee and bowed, and Dresden and Regulus did the same behind him while Adelaide curtsied low.

The door closed behind King Gawain as he walked to the throne. "Rise, Lord Belanger and companions." Regulus waited for Alfred to stand first. The king sat down. "We are glad to see you, old friend."

Alfred inclined his head. "I wish it were under better circumstances, Your

Excellency."

"Yes. Our steward told us you fear for our life." The king rested his chin on his fist. "Explain."

"Your brother is alive, Your Excellency. He has obtained a powerful magical weapon and plans to kill you at your birthday masque."

King Gawain paled and leaned back in the throne. When he spoke, his voice was quiet and tense. "How do you know this?"

"My daughter and her betrothed have met him." Alfred gestured back toward them. "And he told my daughter as much."

The king shifted his piercing gaze to Regulus, then Adelaide. "Kirven told you his identity and plans?"

Adelaide offered another small curtsy. "Yes, Your Excellency."

"And how did you come into contact with a sorcerer?" The suspicion in the king's voice made Regulus wince. He stepped forward and bowed.

"Your Excellency, she met him because of me."

The king raised an eyebrow. "And you are?"

"Lord Regulus Hargreaves of Arrano, Your Excellency. And for two years, I served the sor—Prince Kirven."

King Gawain's expression turned cold. "He was stripped of his title."

Regulus bowed his head. "He still fancies himself a prince. He did not tell me his name, but he called himself the Prince of Shadow and Ash."

The king's eyes widened, but he quickly recovered. "You served him? Why?"

"To save my men's lives, Your Excellency."

"And how did Lady Belanger meet him?"

Regulus winced. He knew this would come up, but it didn't make it any easier. He glanced to Adelaide. "He needed a mage. He demanded I bring Adelaide to him to help recover a relic." His collar suddenly felt itchy. "The last piece he needed to re-forge a powerful weapon, the Staff of Nightfall."

"You are certain?" The king leaned forward, gripping the arms of his throne. "He has the Staff of Nightfall?"

"You've heard of it?" Alfred asked.

"Rumors. I thought it was a myth." Regulus noted Gawain's abandoning of the royal we. The king dragged a trembling hand across his brow and his eyes shot over to Adelaide. "Wait. A mage? You're a mage?"

"Yes, Your Excellency."

"Prove it."

Adelaide held her fist out in front of her, her palm glowing a faint cerulean while she conjured a sword of blue-white light. The light sword vanished as she dropped her hand.

"Your name is Adelaide?" The king asked. She nodded. "Approach us, Adelaide." Adelaide approached, her footsteps hesitant. "Kneel."

She knelt, and the king stood and drew the dragon sword. Adelaide's hands shook at her sides. Regulus reached for his own sword, but his scabbard hung empty and useless at his side. He stepped forward. Alfred stopped him with an arm against his chest. He looked at Alfred, panic clawing at his heart. Alfred shook his head, but his features were drawn and afraid.

"Lady Adelaide Belanger, as your king, we request that you join our personal guard," King Gawain said solemnly. "We ask that you live and die to protect us. Do you agree?"

Wait, what! Regulus' mouth fell open.

Adelaide looked up at the king. "I…"

"Your king requests it," the king repeated with a stern expression. "Will you heed our call?" With a sinking feeling, Regulus understood. It was not a request.

"Yes, Your Excellency." Adelaide's voice quivered.

The king nodded. "Very good. Please repeat these words. I, Adelaide Belanger."

"I, Adelaide Belanger."

Regulus wanted to intervene. To pull Adelaide to her feet and tell the king he couldn't force her into his service. But to do so would be treason. His hands fisted. The king continued, Adelaide repeating each line.

"Swear to uphold the laws of Monparth, and to serve my king and the royal family. My will and aim are now and forevermore to serve and protect the king."

Adelaide swallowed, stumbling over the words.

An ache settled behind Regulus' forehead. He was going to lose her. What if the king wouldn't permit them to marry? What if he couldn't even see her?

"I swear before the king, before Etiros, and before those gathered here," the king continued, Adelaide repeating. "That I will give my life and death to protect the king of Monparth."

Her shoulders dipped as she repeated the oath.

"Until my death or the king's word release me."

"Until…" Adelaide took a shaky breath and Regulus' heart snapped in half. "Until my death or the king's word release me."

King Gawain raised the sword. Only now did Regulus notice the gold script running down the length of the blade, but he couldn't make out the words. The king touched the sword to Adelaide's shoulder. "We hold you to your vow, Lady Adelaide Belanger, member of the royal guard and shield to the king." He sheathed the sword and let it fall against the side of the throne. "Arise, Lady Belanger."

Adelaide stood and moved back. She glanced toward Regulus and Alfred, her eyes big as a frightened deer's. This wasn't how this was supposed to go.

The king looked to Alfred as he sat back down. "Thank you, Alfred." Then he looked at Regulus. "Lord Hargreaves. You spent two years in Kirven's service. Any information you can give is desired."

Regulus had to clear his throat before speaking. Anger at the king's selfishness flared hot on his skin. King Gawain hadn't given Adelaide any more of a choice in serving him than Kirven had given Regulus. "He was secretive and told me only what was necessary to fulfill his commands."

"Why for two years?" The king strummed his fingers against the arm of his chair. "You said you served him to save your men. Did he capture them?"

"No…well, yes. He threatened their lives but released them when I agreed to serve him."

"And you continued to serve him because…"

Because, like you, he puts people in agreements they can't get out of. "He put a mark on my arm that bound me to him. It caused me great pain if I did not obey. And he could use it to control me. To force me to hurt my men. After he received the last piece of the staff, he released me for payment of the life-debt he claimed I owed him."

"A mark?" The king leaned forward, curiosity in his expression. "Where? Show us."

Regulus shook his head. "It disappeared when he released me, Your Excellency."

"Hm. So no proof, then. Your story seems questionable. We wonder if we can trust you, Lord Hargreaves."

Alfred answered first. "I assure you, Your Excellency, he is honest and loyal."

"I have the scars to prove my *story*, Your Excellency." Regulus hesitated. According to the laws of Monparth, he owed the king his allegiance and thus his complete cooperation and honesty. Even if he didn't believe he owed this self-absorbed monarch anything. "And…I have another mark. One put there by Adelaide's magic. It is different, but—"

"Show us."

Reluctantly, he stepped forward and rolled up his sleeve. The king inspected the mark.

"Interesting. What is its purpose?"

"Protection and healing," Adelaide said. "He was dying from a fatal stomach wound inflicted on him by Kirven's lackey, Nolan Carrick. It was the only way to save him."

"Carrick? The baron's son?" The king frowned when Adelaide and Regulus nodded. "Troubling news indeed. Is the baron aware?"

"We do not believe so, Your Excellency," Alfred said. "But I cannot say without a doubt." The king stroked his beard.

The seconds dragged on while the king stared into the distance. Regulus rolled his sleeve down and stepped back, thinking about how underdressed and out of place he was amidst all the gold and splendor of the private audience chamber. It made him once again feel like a fake. A mercenary pretending to be a lord.

As if he suddenly remembered they were still in the room, the king looked back at Regulus. "Protection and healing? What does that mean?"

Regulus didn't want to answer, but when the king asked a question, you answered, and you told the truth. "If I'm hurt, I heal. When I had the sor—Kirven's mark, I couldn't die. I don't know if that's the case with Adelaide's, but it seems likely. I also have noted some increased strength."

The king tilted his head. "Indeed. Lord Hargreaves." By the glint in the king's eye, Regulus knew what he would say before he said it. Resentment surged. "As your king, we request that you join our personal guard. We ask that you live and die to protect us. Do you agree?"

Regulus stiffened, his jaw clenching. So this would be his lot. He would exchange servitude from one brother to the other. One thing comforted him as he knelt before the king. At least he would be with Adelaide. He met the king's eyes as he knelt, not caring if the king saw his fury. "I agree, Your Excellency."

THEY SPENT the next hour and a half in the king's audience room answering his questions and telling him everything they knew about Kirven, Nolan, and their plans. Which wasn't much. Adelaide's feet and lower back ached from standing. Regulus had looked even more unhappy about being drafted into the royal guard than she felt. At least the king hadn't taken his title. King Gawain had explained Regulus would be Lord of Arrano in name, but so long as he was in the guard, his position as a guard trumped any other responsibility or title. But he had been demoted from the nobility in practice, if not on parchment. It was completely unfair.

The king had asked Dresden what his story was, and his curt response of, "I'm a mercenary. I'm just an armed escort, Your Majesty," did not impress the king. Adelaide suspected that was purposeful. A way of avoiding the fate that had befallen her and Regulus.

When King Gawain was satisfied that they could give no further information, he left them with instructions to wait for a servant to escort them out.

Father's perfect posture crumpled the moment the door closed. He rubbed his temples. "I'm sorry. I didn't think—you're a *woman*. I thought he might ask for your help, or accept if you offered, but I never… I would have had you both wait in town if I had known. I'm sorry." His brows pinched as his eyes filled with worry and sorrow.

"Self-righteous, egotistical, arrogant…" Regulus threw out a few less savory words.

"Someone could hear you," Adelaide hissed.

"Let them." Regulus crossed his arms. "I'll do what I swore. But I never swore to be happy about it or act grateful to be made a slave all over again."

"You'll be paid," Father said, his voice weary. "That's technically not slavery."

"Who cares about technicalities," Dresden muttered.

"It's also not my choice." Regulus turned and looked at Adelaide, a wretched sadness undercutting the rage in his eyes. "Can I even marry you now? Is that allowed?"

She couldn't believe that hadn't occurred to her. She had been too surprised by the king's non-request, too frightened and confused by the sudden change in her life trajectory to think through all the consequences. Then getting through the questions about Nolan and Kirven had reopened her emotional scars, especially when she had to admit to Kirven torturing her. At least she hadn't been forced to talk about Nolan's intentions. Regulus and Father had avoided the issue, and she had been more than happy to do the same.

"Royal guards are permitted to marry, although they rarely do." Father shook his head. "Marriage can present difficulties when you're required to live in the palace with the other guards. But…surely the king doesn't expect Adelaide to live in the barracks." She didn't like the uncertainty on his face.

"Out of the question," Regulus said. "You seem to know a decent amount about this. The vows mentioned the king could release us. How often does that happen?"

The pained look Father gave her nearly made her sick. Adelaide leaned against the golden fireplace mantel, fighting a bout of dizziness. Regulus rushed to her side and slipped his arm around her waist.

"There are typically two reasons a royal guard is released from service." Father spoke slowly. "Old age or injury that renders the guard unable to perform his duties."

Dresden cursed, and Father cast him a disapproving scowl.

"This isn't fair," Regulus protested. She didn't need to touch his skin to detect his fury. "He's using us! Just like—"

"Enough," Father interrupted with finality. "What's done is done. Perhaps once Kirven is defeated, the king will release you. There have been instances of kings releasing guards from their service with a generous pension for service beyond the normal purview of the royal guard."

A small spark of hope ignited in Adelaide's soul. "Really? When? Recently?"

"King Gawain has never done so, but his father did, once."

"Oh." Regulus sounded like something had clicked in his mind. Like he finally understood something she still couldn't even see.

"Oh, what?"

Father sighed. "Adelaide… You know I don't like talking about the war." She stared at him, uncomprehending. "I knew what the king wanted as soon as he asked you to kneel and drew that sword. Because King Olfan did the same thing to me."

"You…were a royal guard?" He was a warrior, everyone said. A general.

"For a time, yes. I paid for my release with my blood." His eyes filled with sorrow, pity, and pain. Her heart twisted. "It was only afterward that I led his armies."

She leaned against Regulus. Why was Father being so vague? "I don't—"

The door they had entered through opened. A young woman entered wearing a simple black dress, her hair drawn back in a bun, accompanied by a boy holding Regulus, Father's, and Dresden's swords.

A middle-aged man with red-blond hair and a powerful build followed just behind them. A red sash hung across his chest over a cobalt coat with brass buttons. The man turned toward her and Regulus.

"Lady Belanger and Lord Hargreaves of Arrano?"

They answered in the affirmative. Regulus removed his arm from her waist so he could bow, and she could curtsy.

"I am Captain Russell of His Excellency's Royal Guard." Captain Russell inclined his head toward them. "Welcome to the guard. Come with me."

The woman curtsied toward Father and Dresden. "If you will please follow me, my lords, I will escort you out of the palace."

Panic gripped Adelaide's chest. Wait, this…was goodbye? Regulus took his sword from the page while Adelaide walked to Father.

"I…" The sudden fear she would never see him again cracked down her sternum. "I—"

"Disobedience and tardiness are not tolerated in the Royal Guard regardless of your gender, Belanger," Russell barked.

She gulped back her fear. "I love you, Father." She hugged him tightly. His returned embrace nearly squeezed the air out of her lungs. She held on longer than she should have, but she couldn't bring herself to let go. Neither, apparently, could Father.

"I love you, too," Father whispered. "My brave daughter, my *shiraa*." He kissed the top of her head. "It's going to be all right." She clutched the back of his shirt.

Russell cleared his throat. "I'm not accustomed to being kept waiting, Belanger. This is your last warning."

She let Father go and blinked back her tears. She would not cry in front of Captain Russell. Russell strode out of the room. She followed, slipping her hand into Regulus' as they followed him down the hall. She cast one last glance over her shoulder at Father and Dresden following the servant woman in the opposite direction.

"His Excellency told me you both are assigned to his personal guard, but he didn't specify why." Russell looked back at them, his expression halfway between curious and disgusted. "I don't know what use a woman can be in his guard." He eyed their joined hands. "I guess that's why you two are to have your own room separate from the barracks. Ridiculous."

He looked back in front, keeping up his rushed pace. Adelaide cast Regulus a relieved glance. At least they wouldn't be separated. The scarred side of his mouth pulled up in a slight smile and he squeezed her hand.

"I will show you to your room and explain how the guard works," Russell continued without looking back. "Lieutenant Beale will orient you later. You will be notified of your schedule once I've worked that out. Apparently," he said with annoyance, "the king wants one of you on his personal detail as often as possible, but he had a meeting to attend and couldn't explain."

Russell opened a door to a plain spiral stone staircase and led them down, instructing them to close the door behind them. Archer's loops in the wall provided the only light and let in the outside air. They were in the back of the palace, based on the glimpses Adelaide caught out the narrow slits as they passed them.

At the bottom landing, Russell paused. His gaze trailed over her from head to toe and back. "What's the truth? Seems there should be an easier way to disguise a royal affair. And that doesn't explain"—he pointed at their joined hands—"this."

Adelaide gasped. "That's not—"

"She's not his mistress!" Regulus' grip on her hand tightened.

"What, not yet?" Russell raised his eyebrows. "You don't have to keep up the act with me. I know every secret the king has, including the ones the queen doesn't."

Regulus' indignation melded with Adelaide's horror and embarrassment through their bond. "The king needs my protection." She hated how high-pitched her voice sounded.

Russell snorted. "I'm sure you have many useful skills." He eyed her in a way that made her want to hide behind Regulus, but she stood her ground and scowled.

"In fact, I do." She threw a small ball of fire at the stone wall less than a foot away from Russell. He jumped.

"You…you're a…"

"Mage." The fear in his eyes pleased her more than it should have.

"And you're…?" He looked at Regulus.

"Her betrothed. And maybe immortal."

"Right…" Russell nodded slowly. "Right." He opened the door to a cob-blestoned courtyard bordered by wooden buildings.

Servants rushed back and forth. Some carried baskets, boxes, and sacks. A few led livestock. Russell led them behind the palace, then entered another door. The hallway here was undecorated, the stone floor barren. They walked past several doors, passing male and female servants from small children to older women with silver hair tucked under headscarves, then turned down another corridor. Finally, Russell opened a door and motioned them inside.

The small room had a worn green rug, a simple wooden dresser, a small square wooden table with two worn chairs, and a bed covered with a faded green comforter and two flat pillows. Nothing hung on the bare stone walls, none of which had windows. The only light came in through the open door. A glass oil lamp sat on the table next to a couple pieces of flint.

A servant's room. Disappointment pinched her gut, but Regulus squeezed her hand. At least it wasn't a dirt floor and wasn't the barracks. Russell stood near the table, hands clasped behind his back.

"You have taken a solemn oath to serve and protect the king, whether that be by your life or your death." He looked quizzically at Regulus as he said *death*. "I have no idea if this will work differently, so for now I'll give you the usual orders. You will report for meals in the barracks mess hall when assigned. You will be assigned a time to report to the barracks courtyard for training. You will not speak to any members of the royal family unless addressed first, and you will keep your answers short and refer to the king as Your Excellency, the queen as Your Majesty, the crown prince as Your Highness, and the princesses as Your Grace.

"You will address the members of the court as my lord and my lady. You will report to me or the officer on duty before and after each shift with your fellow guards. You will follow all orders given by myself, Captain Matthews, and Lieutenants Beale, Breck, and Antar promptly and without question. You may not leave the palace grounds without the consent of the officer on duty. You will address your captains and lieutenants as sir.

"Disobedience will be punished according to the severity of the offence and if it is a repeat offence, ranging from withheld meals to time in the stocks to lashings to execution and other punishments at the discretion of the assigning officer. Is that clear?"

"Yes, sir," they said in unison.

"Someone should come measure you for a uniform at some point today, Hargreaves. I don't know what we're doing about clothes for you, Belanger." He shook his head, then continued. "Lieutenant Beale has been notified to find you here and should arrive presently. Any questions you have may be directed to Lieutenant Beale, as I will be off duty for the remainder of the day." Russell turned on his heel and headed out. He paused in the doorway.

"One other thing," Russell said over his shoulder. "I don't know why the king didn't tell me about the…um, magic. Maybe His Excellency wants it kept secret. Until we're told otherwise, keep your cards to yourselves." He departed, leaving the door open.

Adelaide sank onto the bed, relieved to be off her feet. The frame creaked under the thin mattress as Regulus sat next to her. "Well. At least we're together."

Regulus gently held the side of her head and pulled her toward him. "My life has taken some unexpected turns since meeting you." He kissed her temple. "But you're worth it."

Her face warmed. His sincerity pulsed through their connection, comforting her and loosening the knots in her back. He rubbed her shoulder and kissed her forehead, then her cheek. She turned toward him, meeting his lips with hers. Her arms circled around his waist.

Someone cleared their throat. They leapt apart and stood. A man dressed in the same uniform as Russell but with a black sash instead of red stood in the doorway, arms crossed and mouth turned down. His brown hair was cut close to his head. He had a stubbly beard, thick eyebrows, and light brown skin that might have just been a dark tan.

"I'm Lieutenant Beale. You must be Hargreaves and Belanger." They confirmed as Beale continued to scowl. "Follow me."

CHAPTER 32

LIEUTENANT BEALE led them across the cobblestone courtyard to a stone wall, through a set of open double doors into a dirt-floored courtyard that extended to the palace wall. A two-story wooden building stood in the far-right corner with rows of small windows without glass and with open shutters. A one-story building occupied the far-left corner. Shirtless men were everywhere she looked. Some sparred with each other while others hefted and tossed stones. A few fired arrows into dummies stuffed with straw. Some stretched or ran in place. A few at a time, the men noticed their arrival. Whispers went around the courtyard as Beale lead them toward the smaller building. Men stopped what they were doing to stare at them. At her.

Adelaide hated it. She wanted to hide. Regulus put his arm around her shoulders, drawing her into his side. A couple men let out a low whistle. Someone said, "What's a lady doing here?"

Another man said, "Her handler's awfully protective. Must be expensive." Heat rushed up the back of her neck.

"So, what, officers get a pass on the no women in the barracks rule?" another man muttered.

Beale halted and turned around. "Since your attention is off your training anyway." His raised voice carried over the courtyard. "Meet the two newest members of the king's personal guard. Regulus Hargreaves and Adelaide Belanger."

"Sir, you're saying the woman's…one of us?" A man with bulging muscles wiped sweat off his glistening forehead.

"No," Beale said tersely, "His Excellency says she is."

The men glanced at each other, whispering. Adelaide gripped her skirt and fought the urge to flee the courtyard. She wanted to press into Regulus' back to hide from their stares. Instead, she lifted her chin and looked around the courtyard, daring them to challenge her.

"She need a sparring partner?" A lanky man who looked a little younger than Adelaide leered. "I'll volunteer."

"You aren't even that good, Tom," called out another man. Adelaide couldn't find him in all the staring faces. "We all know I'm the best at hand-to-hand combat. I could give her some pointers. Demonstrate some moves." This was greeted by snickers and exclamations of agreement and offers to teach her. Adelaide clenched her teeth so hard she feared they might crack.

"Enough." Beale started back toward the low building. "Back to your exercises, men."

A chorus of "yes, sir's" answered him, but the men only half-heartedly returned to their training, their eyes still following her. Beale opened the door and walked inside. Long rows of tables bordered by wooden benches ran the length of the mess hall. Some twenty men sat at the tables, chatting and eating.

"This is the mess," Beale said. Eyes turned toward them, widening when they saw Adelaide. "You'll eat your meals here." He pointed toward a counter with a window into the kitchen at the far end of the hall. "You'll give your name and get your food there during your time slot."

Regulus shuffled his feet. "Perhaps it would be better if Adelaide—"

"You arguing with me, Hargreaves?" Beale rounded on Regulus, stepping up so they were face-to-face. Or close. Beale's head ended at Regulus' eyes.

"No, sir, I just think barracks discipline might suffer—"

"Well, if your lady didn't want to eat with the guards, she shouldn't have joined."

"She didn't have a choice!" Regulus glared down at Beale.

"What was that?" Beale squinted. "Didn't Captain Russell tell you the rules?"

Regulus looked lost for a moment, then said, "She didn't have a choice, sir."

"Well, she doesn't have a choice about eating in the mess, either, unless and until the king or Captain Russell or Captain Matthews say otherwise."

Adelaide felt Regulus about to protest again, so she squeezed his hand hard. She could handle it. It wasn't like she couldn't protect herself. She wouldn't be collared. Not this time.

Regulus grunted. "Yes, sir."

"Good." Beale led them to the other building, which she guessed must be the barracks. The men watched her all the way.

"They'll get used to it," Adelaide whispered to Regulus, hoping she was right. "It's just novel now." Regulus worked his jaw in response, the veins in his neck bulging.

Inside the barracks, Beale took them into a room with a large desk, a wall covered in parchment with schedules written on them, and a round table with four chairs. Two men sat at the table playing cards, both wearing the same outfit as Beale, including the black sash. The one on the right had a small scar running through his left eyebrow. His brown hair fell in a thin braid down his back. The other man had thick, wavy black hair and the same dark olive complexion as Dresden but was taller and much huskier.

"This is the officer's command center," Beale explained. "Assignments and schedules are posted here. You will report to this room to debrief before and after every shift protecting the king. Do you understand?"

"Yes, sir."

"This is Lieutenant Breck," Beale continued. The man with the scar nodded. "And Lieutenant Antar." The olive-skinned man waved. "These are the new recruits, Hargreaves"—Beale jutted his thumb at Regulus—"and Belanger." He jutted his thumb at her.

"So, it's true." Breck stood and looked them both over. "Don't get why the king wants some foreign girl to protect him."

"Hey, I'm foreign," Antar said.

"Well, at least you're a man and a soldier."

"I'm Monparthian," Adelaide said with rising indignation. "My father is Lord Alfred Belanger."

"Don't much care who your father is," Breck said, his eyes narrowing. "But I *do* care about you following protocol, woman or no. Did you get the full run-down of the rules or what?"

Dammit. "I apologize, sir." She bowed her head, hoping that would show enough deference to stay his wrath. "And we did, sir."

"Ah, you know new recruits, Breck." Antar propped his boots on the back of one of the other chairs and crossed his ankles. "Always takes a little while to adjust. Slip-ups happen." Antar smiled. "I'm sure you'll work on it, right, sweetheart?"

She managed not to let her irritation show as she replied, "Yes, sir."

"You call all your soldiers sweetheart, sir?" Regulus asked. *Oh. Great.*

Antar's expression darkened. "I could if I wanted to, sweetheart."

Adelaide sensed Regulus' anger rising, and she grabbed his arm with both hands. He looked at her, eyes flashing. She gave a small shake of her head. He took a deep breath and relaxed.

"Guess the girl's got more brains than you," Breck said. "That attitude you're showing has no place here. It'll get you in trouble. But by the look of that scar, you're acquainted with trouble. Where'd you get it?"

"As a mercenary," Regulus said flatly.

"You were a mercenary?" Breck looked surprised, and Antar looked impressed.

"For nine years. A captain for five of those." Regulus glared back at Breck, a hint of pride in his voice.

"Ah, so that's the cause of the disrespect in your tone." Breck's mouth curled down. "You think you're better than me."

"I mean no disrespect, sir." Regulus sounded unconvincing as he stared down Breck.

Adelaide looked to Beale. "Sir, is there anywhere else we need to know how to find?"

"Don't change the subject to protect him, girl," Breck said.

"Breck," Antar said with an easy wave of his hand. "Let them be."

"Sure." Breck tilted his chin up. "Soon as scar-face apologizes to his superior for his disrespectful tone."

Regulus tensed. *Please,* she thought, remembering Russell's list of punishments. *Just get it over with.* She heard Regulus grind his teeth.

"I apologize, sir." He sounded almost sincere. Almost.

"I still feel disrespected." Breck crossed his arms. "Kiss my boot to make it up to me, guardsman." Adelaide stared at the lieutenant in disbelief. Regulus didn't move. "If I have to tell you again, you won't get dinner." Still, Regulus didn't move. He probably figured going hungry for a while was worth skipping the humiliation of kissing Breck's dust-coated boot. To be honest, she didn't blame him. "No dinner, then. Kiss my boot, or I'm taking your supper, too."

Regulus stood immobile. This was insane. She looked at Beale and Antar, but Beale just watched and Antar looked mildly amused. She gave Regulus' arm a gentle tug. This was getting out of hand. He didn't even look at her.

Breck shook his head and tapped his foot. "One more chance, but this time you're looking at a night in the stocks."

Adelaide's mouth fell open. That wasn't a legitimate order. That punishment did not fit the crime. But she didn't dare say so, not with the gloating expression on Breck's face and the disinterest Beale had in the whole situation. She slid her hand from Regulus' sleeve to his hand, hoping he would receive her desire to give in. Her fear of being without him that night.

Regulus started at her touch. Some of the fire left his eyes, but his expression remained tense. "Yes, sir."

Regulus got down on his knees and kissed the tip of Breck's boot. As he straightened, Breck kicked him in the chest. Regulus fell back against the wall next to the door. Adelaide yelped, both at the unexpected attack and the ache in her own chest that indicated just how hard Breck had kicked him. She leaned over Regulus, praying he wouldn't lose his temper and make things worse. His chest heaved, but he didn't say anything.

Breck nodded, a self-satisfied smile on his face. "Still no dinner or supper for you."

"I'm sorry," she whispered as she helped Regulus up.

His face was red, but he whispered back, "Don't be."

A hand grabbed her upper arm. Adelaide shied away and scrunched her shoulders toward her ears. *Pull it together. It's just your arm.* All the same, fear made her rigid. Regulus thumb rubbed her hand. His love and even somehow his anger gave her more confidence and she relaxed.

"I don't get it," Breck said as he squeezed her arm. "More muscle than I expected, but not enough to be much use. And seems skittish." He released her and sneered. "A week's wages says the king requests her on night shifts."

Beale laughed. "Do I look like a fool to you? I'm not betting against that." Adelaide's face burned. "Ah, look. You've upset her." He laughed again.

"That's enough," Antar said, his voice quiet but firm. "I apologize for my fellows. You're free to go back to your room."

"Thank you, sir." She pulled Regulus out of the barracks, Breck's complaining about Antar's sour attitude fading behind them. They kept a rapid pace until they were back in their room with the door closed. She hovered a sphere of light in the center of the room.

"The king's an idiot," Regulus spat. "He didn't pause for a moment to consider what a bad idea putting a woman in the guard was."

"Being angry won't change it." She pulled him down next to her on the bed and gripped his shirt. "I understand, but please, don't do something like that again."

"I've done enough groveling and being pushed around in the past two years to last me a lifetime."

She couldn't argue with that, but her own irritation with his stubbornness continued to grow. "I know. But—"

"They don't scare me." Regulus' eyes narrowed. "I—"

"It's not only about you!" She shoved his chest and released his shirt. "Did you consider how your actions affected me? Now if I want to eat, I have to face the mess hall alone. I almost had to spend the night alone. Did you think about that? Did you think of me? Well, did you?"

"I…" His face fell. "No. I didn't."

"No. You didn't." She huffed and stood. "Together, Reg. That's what you said. Together!"

"I'm sorry—"

"You're not a lone wolf, Reg, you—"

"Ad." He grabbed her hand. "I know. I'm truly sorry." The genuine regret on his face and the sorrow roaring through their bond made her anger deflate. "It won't happen again. I swear."

"Thank you."

Someone knocked and Adelaide groaned. "Two minutes. Can't we have two minutes to process?"

The person knocked again, so she stepped toward the door before she remembered Russell's orders to keep her magic secret. She crossed to the table, lit the lamp with her magic, and vanished the glowing sphere before answering. An older man with a mustache stood at the door, holding a large cloth bag. He stepped back as he saw her.

"I…may have the wrong room." He glanced past her to Regulus, then looked back at her. "I'm Phillip, the tailor? I'm here to fit Hargreaves for a royal guard uniform and was told to tell Belanger to report to the mess hall anytime within the next hour for dinner?"

Adelaide sighed. "I'm Belanger." She stepped aside to allow the tailor to enter and nodded toward Regulus. "He's Hargreaves."

"I…don't understand." Phillip's brow wrinkled. "You're a royal guard?"

"That's correct." She looked at Regulus, then back at Phillip. "How long will getting his uniform fitted take?"

Phillip set down a bag and started pulling clothing out of it. "We should be done within half an hour."

She turned around while Regulus changed into the uniform Phillip had brought, then sat on one of the chairs and watched while Phillip measured and pinched and pinned and smoothed and re-pinned. When he finished, he had Regulus maneuver out of the pin-filled uniform.

"I should get this back to you by this evening," Phillip said with a nod, then left.

Concern etched Regulus' face as he pulled his boots back on. "Are you going to eat?"

Adelaide wanted to say if he wasn't eating, she wouldn't, either. However, she *was* hungry. And, more importantly… "For all I know, I could get in trouble if I don't." She kicked at the floor. "Do you think…they'll let you in, at least? Even if you can't eat, you could just sit there, right?"

"Well, we can try."

Fewer men were training in the courtyard, but they still stared and whispered. She kept her chin up and avoided their stares, her fingers intertwined with Regulus'. They entered the mess hall. Regulus pointed at an empty table.

"I'll wait there."

The boy behind the counter looked no older than fourteen. He looked at her in surprise as she stepped forward after the man in front of her moved down the counter.

"Belanger," she said. The boy gaped for a moment, then checked a list tacked to the wall just inside the window.

"Uh…guess you are on here." He handed her a long wooden plate and a rough iron fork. "Help yourself."

"Thank you." She loaded some potatoes, beef roast, and peas onto the plate. She felt the eyes of every man in the mess hall on her as she walked back to Regulus and sat. "That was the most awkward walk of my life," she whispered, trying to lighten the mood. Regulus cracked a halfhearted smile.

Footsteps alerted her to the approaching men before four guards sat down, one next to her, the others with clear disappointment opposite her. Their plates clattered as they set them down. Regulus straightened, but Adelaide focused on eating her dinner.

"So," the man across from her said. He was wiry and looked to be about thirty, with lots of freckles. "How'd you become a guard? Thought they didn't take women."

"King's request," she said between bites. Perhaps if she answered some of their questions, their curiosity would abate.

The man whistled. "Why? That's rare. I don't get what you can do that we can't." He grinned. "Well, other than the obvious."

"I'm sworn to protect the king, same as you." Adelaide worked to keep her voice even. "Nothing more and nothing less."

"Maybe you're a spy, or something?" This from a man in his mid-twenties, with a blond ponytail and pencil-thin lips. "You'll blend in with the nobles, so they don't know you're a guard. Is that it?"

She shrugged.

"Told you." Ponytail reached behind Freckles to slap the third man's shoulder. "Pay up."

"Hey now." The third man had a deep baritone voice that somehow made him less ridiculous than his balding head made him appear. "A shrug doesn't count." He leaned his elbow on the table. "You know some foreign language, is what I think. You'll be a stealth interpreter. When people think the king can't know what they're saying."

She was so surprised, she said, "You think the king made me a guard so I could listen to people gossip in other languages?"

"Ha," Ponytail said. "That's pretty clearly a no. At the very least, you're wrong, so I should still win."

"That's not how it works, Rob."

"You just don't want to keep your end of the bet." Ponytail—Rob, apparently, made a grabbing motion with his hand.

"No one's right or wrong yet," Baritone said before shoveling an oversized bite of potato into his mouth.

The man to her left scooted closer until his thigh touched hers. She gripped her fork in her fist. "You want a fork in your eye? Back. Off." He made a sour face but shifted back over so they had a small space. Regulus snorted.

"Hargreaves!" Adelaide nearly spilled peas everywhere as Breck's shout echoed through the mess hall. Breck cursed as he tramped toward them, his boots clacking. "—do you think you're doing in mess?"

"Not eating, sir." Regulus kept his tone even and respectful, but irritation stormed in his eyes.

"Get out."

"Sir?" Regulus' brows drew together. "I haven't eaten, sir—"

"You want to miss breakfast, too?" Breck grabbed the back of Regulus' shirt and pulled him off the bench. "Get out!"

Regulus blew air out his nose, gave a clipped, "yes, sir," and left.

Adelaide sat frozen, watching Regulus stomp out. The side of the fork cut into her fingers, she squeezed it so tight. She could have eaten more, but she picked up her plate and stood. Breck's hand gripped her shoulder and pushed her back down as he sat next to her.

CHAPTER 33

ADELAIDE'S THICK tongue stuck to the roof of her mouth. She couldn't think of anything other than Breck's hand on her shoulder.

"You didn't finish your food."

"I'm not hungry anymore, sir."

"Don't take more than you can eat, then." Breck still gripped her shoulder. "I don't like to see food wasted. Finish eating. That's an order."

"Yes, sir." She took another bite. Her heartrate rose, but she breathed easier when Breck removed his hand.

"Here's the thing, Belanger." Breck rested his elbow on the table and turned toward her. "I don't know what's going on. I don't know why you're here, or what the king's playing at. I don't know if this is some crazy test, or if you made someone powerful very angry, or if it's an elaborate and pretty transparent way to cover up that you're in the king's bed. But you're not an exception because you're a woman. You have to follow orders, same as everyone else."

She stared at her plate. "Yes, sir. I know, sir."

"And tell your lover or handler or whatever Hargreaves is I don't care if you two were chosen by the king for whatever mysterious reason. That doesn't make you better than us."

"No, sir."

Breck grabbed her hand holding the fork and stabbed the tines into a piece of roast. "I said to eat." He moved her hand toward her mouth. Her face burned as she bit the roast off the fork. "Good." He released her hand.

Adelaide shoveled down food, but her appetite was gone. She finally finished and picked up the plate. Before she could stand, Breck slung his arm over her shoulders, keeping her on the bench. A tremor ran down her spine.

"Got somewhere important to be?"

She chose her words carefully. "I should return my plate, sir."

"Lewitt can take care of that. Can't you, Lewitt?"

"Yes, sir." Freckles reached across the table and took her plate, stacking it on top of his own before carrying them to the tub in the corner.

"Tell me about yourself, Belanger." Breck smiled, and it made her stomach churn. She was going to lose her dinner. "Tell me a secret."

"I don't like being touched, sir." She sat still as a statue, staring at the empty space where Lewitt had been sitting.

"Hargreaves' attitude isn't rubbing off on you, is it? I'm leaning more and more toward you two angered someone. Who was it? Was it the king himself? What'd you do? Ah, you *didn't* get in his bed, is that it?"

"Sir, I want to protect the king." Her fingers curled against the tabletop. "I want to be a good royal guard, sir. To do that, I need rest. May I please go, sir?"

"Rest? How boring. Or are you just wanting to bed Hargreaves?"

Adelaide felt her face and ears go red. In that moment, she truly understood Regulus' earlier actions. She twisted free and jumped off the bench.

"I didn't say you could go!" She stopped midstride and slowly turned around. Breck had stood, a cruel smirk twisting his mouth. "Come back here."

She took a deep breath and stepped toward him.

"Closer."

Another step. She could see the rings of brown in his murky green eyes.

"Closer." Breck grinned, taunting her.

"May I please go, sir?" She stepped closer, her boots nearly touching his. He grabbed her hips and pulled her to him, and she bit back a cry. A couple of the men watching snickered. She leaned back, her heart thumping in her ears. *Don't cry.* "Sir, this is hardly appropriate."

"You being here isn't appropriate." His hands moved up her sides.

No. No, not again. Consequences and punishments be hanged; she was through. She wasn't weak this time, and she wasn't powerless. Adelaide grabbed Breck's wrists and pulled his hands off her. The surprise on Breck's face almost made her smile.

He yanked his hands away. As she turned and headed toward the door, he grabbed her braid and pulled. She winced but didn't turn around. Anger burned in the pit of her stomach.

"Sir, respectfully, if you don't let me leave right now, I will embarrass you in front of all these men."

Breck laughed. "I think it's going to be the other way around, girl." He grabbed her shoulder and turned her toward him. "Making threats against an officer. Tsk, tsk." He leaned forward, his gaze drifting to her mouth as his fingers dug into the back of her shoulder. "Kiss me to show how sorry you are."

Never. She slammed her palms against his chest, releasing a blast of magical energy. Breck flew backward two table lengths then skidded across the packed dirt floor before his shoulders knocked into the wall under the counter. Adelaide didn't wait for him to recover, she rushed out the door. Regulus was leaning against the wall just outside.

"Hurry." She grabbed his hand as she sped past.

"What happened?" Regulus strode next to her. "Is everything—"

"BELANGER! Stop right there!"

She closed her eyes, her shoulders slumping as she stopped.

Regulus glanced at Breck. "What. Happened."

"Both of you, on your knees!" The guards in the courtyard stared.

Adelaide cursed in Khast and lowered onto her knees in the dirt. Regulus did the same beside her, but his anger built alongside her own

"I don't know what just happened." Breck stopped in front of them, his face red and lips pulled back in a snarl. "But the punishment for attacking a ranking officer is twenty lashes."

"What?" Regulus gripped her hand so hard it hurt.

"Someone bring me the whip!" Breck shouted. "Before I decide to flog each and every one of you dawdlers!" He sneered. "Policy is bare-backed."

"I'll take her punishment, sir." Regulus' rage and panic mingled with her fear.

"Not the way it works." Breck cocked his head. "But you can get some lashes, too, if it will make you feel better."

"Sir, please." Regulus bowed his head. "Give me as many lashes as you want. She…she can watch. But—"

"But nothing!" Breck glowered down his nose at her. "She attacked me; she'll be stripped and lashed."

Adelaide's chest heaved. She was not about to be stripped in the middle of a courtyard full of men. She didn't deserve any lashes, and Regulus definitely didn't. Not to mention she would feel both whippings. "You wanted to know a secret, sir?"

Her fury overpowered her dread, leaving a reckless storm in her chest. Maybe Mother and Regulus were right. Maybe she was a *shiraa*. She didn't even care if she was breaking Captain Russell's order to keep her magic secret.

"You wanted to know why the king wanted me in the royal guard?" She smiled. *Let the tigress play.* "Be careful what you wish for, sir."

She let go of Regulus' hand and stood, taking a few steps away. Breck watched in confusion and outrage. She had no idea if this would work, but if she had done it before subconsciously, she could choose to do it—right? The familiar magical warmth spread across her palms against her dress. *Come on. Fire and flames.* Adelaide pictured what she wanted, and heat flared at her back.

"Oh…" Breck cursed and stepped back. Shouts and whispers echoed across the courtyard. She glanced to the side and smiled when she saw red and orange flames fanning out in the shape of a massive wing.

"Any other questions, Lieutenant?" She summoned a sword of magic light in her right hand, just for the fun of it.

"What are you?" Breck took another step backward.

"I'm a mage." Satisfied that Breck looked sufficiently terrified, Adelaide let the wings and sword vanish. Silence filled the courtyard. Regulus stood, and they headed toward the gate, every royal guard within the wall watching them, unmoving. But the men's stares didn't make her feel small anymore.

"You think you get a pass because you're a mage?" Breck said, snapping out of his stupor. "You still swore an oath! You still have to obey me!"

She cast him a cold glare. "Take it up with His Excellency."

"I'm still your commanding officer!"

At that moment, Lieutenant Antar strolled in from the entrance to the courtyard. "What's going on here?"

"Belanger disobeyed a direct order, assaulted me, and is trying to avoid punishment." Breck sounded manic.

"Sir." Adelaide tried and failed to keep her anger out of her voice. "Lieutenant Breck assaulted *me* and I defended myself. He ordered me to kiss him, and I did not comply. I will not be accepting a punishment I do not deserve."

Regulus made a disgusted sound in his throat and started to turn around, but she grabbed his hand and stopped him. She had already defended herself. He didn't need to further stoke Breck's rage and get them in more trouble.

"Huh." Antar looked at her, clearly impressed, then looked at Breck. "What do you mean, she assaulted you? You're at least twice as strong as she is."

"She's a filthy mage!"

Antar raised his brows. "A…what? No, no, wait. That makes so much more sense." He shook his head and chuckled. "Did you actually order her to kiss you?"

Breck opened and closed his mouth. "She was being insubordinate and insulting."

"Breck, you're a disgrace." Antar nodded at her and continued across the courtyard. "Have a good day, Belanger. Hargreaves."

"But—" Breck started.

"Don't make me report you to Captain Russell," Antar said. "You've already got two strikes this month for abuse of power."

As they walked to their room, Regulus leaned over and murmured, "That was risky."

"It was riskier not to."

"I'm proud of you."

"Well, maybe hold off on the praise until we determine if I've just made our lives a living hell." Her stomach still felt uneasy.

"I'm sorry," Regulus said quietly. "That should never have happened. I should have been there, like I promised."

"It's not your fault." They turned into their little room. "And it wasn't..." Her voice dropped. "I've been through worse."

"Doesn't make it okay." Regulus closed the door, plunging the room into darkness.

She created an orb, the soft blueish light filling the room, and sat on the bed.

"Are you sure you're all right?"

"I had the opportunity and means to fight back." Adelaide laid on the bed and rested her hands on her midsection. "Somehow, that helps."

He shifted and his brows pinched. "If I ever make you feel uncomfortable, if you need me to back off... You know you can tell me, right?"

Sorrow accompanied a swell of love. "Thank you," she whispered. She shifted over and patted the bed. He hesitated, then laid next to her and wrapped his arm around her. Adelaide nestled against him, thanking Etiros for Regulus.

"I always want you to feel safe with me."

"In your arms is the only place I feel safe right now," she murmured.

A guard arrived shortly with orders to give them an exhaustive tour of the palace. Regulus got his uniform that evening, and a servant delivered several dresses for Adelaide. Adelaide skipped dinner, opting to stay with Regulus. A servant delivered a parchment with their schedule for the next day. They would have breakfast together, but the rest of the day one would be on duty when the other wasn't. The following days were similar, and often they had late night and early morning shifts. The king wanted one of them on guard whenever possible, which made it difficult to see much of each other.

Adelaide asked for a set of throwing knives and dagger and wore them on her belt, which seemed to help some more with the other guards' opinion of her. They still stared, but they gave her space. The king didn't care if the guards knew she was a mage, but wanted it kept a secret from the nobles, so she practiced magic behind the mess hall.

Breck glared whenever he saw her, took every opportunity to make suggestive comments when the other officers weren't present, and relished every order he gave, even if it was, "Tie your boot laces, Belanger." But he didn't try to touch her again.

Guard duty was boring. She hung back, standing in the shadows, observing anyone the king interacted with. Listening to him talk and talk about harvests and food supplies, trade routes, taxes, approving marriage arrangements, and laws and bylaws. She practiced forming her magic into various shapes behind her back or while guarding the king's chambers at night to pass the time.

Despite having a son and two daughters, the king and queen rarely interacted. Adelaide discovered Russell had been telling the truth when she watched a lady-in-waiting her own age enter the king's chambers one night. It made her sick.

The king held a meeting with the officers of the royal guard, a few of his top knights, and Regulus and Adelaide on the third day, four days before the masque. Breck turned pink when he saw them in the council chamber. The king elected not to cancel the masque. He hoped to catch Kirven and wouldn't be dissuaded. Captain Russell suggested a double, but the king said his brother would know, and wouldn't reveal himself to a double.

After the meeting, Adelaide secured permission to go into town and buy masque-appropriate clothes for herself and Regulus. She had managed to convince the king that if she and Regulus blended in with the crowd, they stood a better chance of finding Kirven and Nolan before they could attack. She found a dress she would only need to alter slightly and bought matching material to make Regulus' outfit. More importantly, the trip gave her an opportunity to visit Father.

They sat in the inn's tavern, quiet during the mid-afternoon slump, sipping on ale. The place smelled of spilt food and drink mixed with soapy water as a maid scrubbed the dented wood floorboards. Occasional clatters rose from the kitchen, and whenever a worker passed through the door to the back, the scent of preparing stew drifted through. Adelaide wrapped both hands around her tankard and gazed at the candle flickering on the table between them. They'd tucked themselves into a shadowy corner where Adelaide drew less attention.

"You don't have to go," she said. "Weapons aren't allowed; what could you—"

"The king has granted me permission to bear my sword. Sir Jakobs, too." Father leaned back in his chair. "Jakobs has an unfortunate lack of respect for his king and takes his cavalier attitude a bit far sometimes, but I rather like the fellow. Yesterday, he—"

"This isn't about Dresden." She stared at the lingering foam along the wall of her tankard. She still hadn't told Father about Kirven's threats. But she couldn't risk him falling into Kirven's hands. "Even if you have a sword, Nolan is still immortal, Kirven is—"

"Adelaide." He reached across the table and pulled one hand away from her tankard and held it. "Do you have so little faith in me?"

She looked up and softened at the gentleness and determination in his green eyes. "I'm just…afraid."

"Fear is a healthy emotion, in its place. Fear helps prevent recklessness. Warriors don't face battle unafraid. They face battle because they are fighting for something they value more than they fear the battle." Father squeezed her hand. "What are you fighting for?"

"You. Mother. Regulus, Minerva, everyone. My own freedom. But mostly to protect the people I love." *To protect you from Kirven's wrath.*

"Love." He nodded. "Love will always conquer fear, my tigress."

She drew in a ragged breath. "I don't feel like much of a tigress lately."

Father rubbed his thumb over the back of her hand. "When your mother and I told you about The Shadow, you hid under a blanket and cried. But when we told you about the cottage and learning to hide your magic, you were so upset about leaving your siblings you said you weren't scared of shadows, even mean ones. You still had tears in your eyes, but you lifted your chin and crossed your little arms and said you didn't need to hide."

"I was four; I barely understood."

Father just smiled. "You've always had the heart of a tigress. That heart is still in there. That determination. That boldness."

Adelaide worked her throat. "But if I fail—"

"If you fail, the outcome will be the same as if you don't try. But you have a real chance to succeed." Father's head bowed as sadness overtook his expression. "Adelaide… I won't apologize for trying to protect you. I did what I thought I had to, but I was wrong. I wish I could have helped you be more prepared. But I've never doubted you. I am in awe of the things you can do."

He met her eyes. "I'm proud of you. Proud of you for doing what you know to be right, even when it's dangerous. Proud of the kind, strong, selfless young woman you are. Proud of the dedication you're showing in learning to use your power. Whether you defeat Kirven or not, I'm proud you're my daughter. And I believe in you."

"Thank you." Her choked words came out in a whisper. She wiped at her eyes. "I should go. I need to get back before my next shift."

He released her hand and they both stood. Father pulled her close. "I love you."

She leaned her head on his shoulder and embraced him. "I love you."

Father kissed the top of her head. "It's going to be all right." He couldn't know that. And yet, for some reason, when Father said it, it felt true. He patted her back. "I'll see you at the masque."

Between guard duty and practice, Adelaide and Regulus struggled to find time together as the masque approached. In her spare moments, Adelaide worked on their masque attire. Regulus often fell asleep watching her sew. When she crawled into bed, he'd pull her close in his sleep. She'd often wake to find him already gone, and every time, she hated it.

The day of the masque, Adelaide's nerves buzzed and exhaustion dragged her down. Sleep had evaded her the night prior, and when she had slept, she had nightmares. Dresden weeping over Regulus' mangled corpse. Minerva, heavily pregnant, trying to run from Kirven. Mother screaming, but Adelaide couldn't find her. A giant Nolan towering over her, laughing as he locked a collar around her neck and dragged her away. But Regulus had been there, holding her together every time she woke up.

Regulus couldn't sit still, so they walked through the gardens, holding each other and not saying a word. They didn't need to. What their bond didn't convey, they shared with a look. They would face Kirven and Nolan together. If they won, they would win together, and if they fell, they would fall together. But that night, Adelaide knew, either Kirven would die, or Monparth would fall.

CHAPTER 34

REGULUS LEANED against the wall outside their bedroom door, waiting for Adelaide to finish changing. He pulled at the edge of the dark turquoise doublet Adelaide had made. The material was velvety and rich, and not really his style. He would have been satisfied with the black long-sleeved shirt he wore under the doublet, but Adelaide insisted he needed to look the part. At least she wasn't forcing him to wear hose, just narrow-legged black trousers, and he wasn't wearing his uniform. He hated that uniform that declared his choices had been stolen.

He rubbed the pommel of his sword. It would make him stand out a little, as the guests would be required to surrender any weapons. But, bewilderingly to Regulus, it wasn't unheard of for lords to wear fake swords to these events, bladeless hilts attached to empty scabbards, just to keep up appearances. His weapon wouldn't completely undermine their plan to move unnoticed through the guests, looking for the sorcerer and Carrick.

The bedroom door squeaked open and Regulus pushed off the wall. Adelaide swept out in a matching turquoise dress of the same velvety material as his doublet, her hands behind her back. The wide, low vee of the neckline bared her shoulders. The sleeves split open at the middle of her upper arms and hung to her thighs, lined with satiny gray material. A narrow gray cloth belt embroidered with twisting silver circled her hips, the long ends hanging down in the front. A thin silver chain hung from her neck with a small, teardrop-shaped crystal. Her dark hair fell in loose curls over her shoulders and down her back.

Regulus opened his mouth, but his tongue stuck in place. She smiled. "Tigress got your tongue?"

"You…" His voice cracked and he blushed. He cleared his throat. "You are breathtakingly beautiful. I don't know that you'll really be blending in as the prettiest girl there."

She laughed and pulled two narrow black masks decorated with turquoise swirls from behind her back and gave him the larger one. "You look striking, too, *sumdir*. Ready?"

"Almost." He placed his hand on her back and pulled her close, brushing his fingers across her cheek. He sensed her flutter of giddy nerves and anticipation. "I love you, Adelaide Belanger. Whatever happens today, I love you until the sun fails to rise."

He kissed her, desperately and tenderly. Her hand gripped the side of his neck, her fingers cool against his skin. Between the delight rippling through him and the sensation of her desire, he barely managed to stay standing.

"And I love you, Regulus Hargreaves." Her eyes shone up at him. "No matter the outcome. Until the sea swallows the land, I love you."

He kissed her nose between her eyes, then tied on his mask. It only surrounded his eyes, and for a moment he regretted it didn't hide his scar. But Adelaide liked his scar. He smiled. "Let's go to a ball."

They walked arm-in-arm across the servant's courtyard to the side livestock gate, Adelaide carrying her skirt up to keep it clean. As part of their objective of blending in, they would enter with the other guests, starting their surveillance in the reception line. If they could catch Kirven and Nolan before they even made it into the palace, even better. As they approached the wall, Breck stepped out of the shadowy recess of the closed gate.

"About time you two were leaving. Thought you were going to be late." His gaze traveled slowly over Adelaide.

Regulus tensed and pressed his hand against his thigh to keep it from curling into a fist. "We'd best be on our way then, sir."

"The point is for you to blend in." Breck circled them. "I'm just checking that you look up to the task." He walked back around and nodded. "I suppose you look like guests, but Belanger's going to be useless with all the men that will be trying to plaster themselves to her and talk her out of that dress."

"Sir, we need to join the guests," Adelaide said, her tone dark.

"All right, all right." Breck opened one side of the double doors and held it open for them to pass through. He picked the door on Adelaide's side, so she would have to walk past him. Regulus wanted to move her to his other side, but Breck would find a way to make that into some grave offense. As they passed, Breck said, "Remember, your only concern is to protect the king. Not to see how many nobles you can lure into dark corners."

"Substitute servant girls for nobles and you've given yourself some great advice, sir," Adelaide said. Regulus nearly tripped over the cobblestones. "See you in the ballroom, sir."

Breck called her a couple words that made Regulus' hair stand on end, but

Breck turned back inside and slammed the gate closed behind him. Regulus grunted. "So I get scolded for making him angry, but you get to do it?"

She didn't answer right away. "I'm going to face Kirven and Nolan today. Breck and his pettiness seem pretty insignificant right now."

"Oh." He moved his arm around her waist. "How are you feeling?"

"I'm scared, Reg. I'm terrified I'll fail again." She looked up. "But I'm determined. I'm ready to face them. For you, for myself, for Father and Mother. For Minerva and Gaius and their unborn baby. For Dresden and Perceval and Estevan and…" She frowned.

"Caleb and Jerrick and Harold," Regulus said.

She nodded. "Even for Landon and Julia. Even for the rest of my half-siblings. Just because I don't like them doesn't mean I want them and their families to live in a world where Kirven is king and might hurt them because of me. But I'm afraid I'll fail them all."

Regulus spoke quietly. "You're not solely responsible for protecting all of Monparth."

"I think I am. I think we are. And we don't even have a plan. Just…" She sighed. "Find each other if we see them. Get the staff, kill Kirven and Nolan. That's not a plan. That's a goal."

"Well, think of it this way: without a plan, we don't have to worry about if things don't go according to plan."

She scowled. "That's the worst attempt at positivity I've ever heard."

He smiled. "Sorry. Why do you think I keep Caleb around?"

"And I thought you just liked his music," she said with a laugh.

They rounded the front of the palace walls and found the reception line already stretched to the front gate. Men and women of all ages in ornate outfits and masks of every color stood gossiping and laughing. Regulus scanned the crowd as they joined the line. The masks further complicated their task. Everyone had tried to talk the king into at least changing the party so it wasn't a masque, but the king said that would signal that something was wrong, and he didn't want to worry his people or alert Kirven. Regulus believed the king was an idiot, but he was also the king, so idiocy ruled the day.

A group of three men in their early twenties stood in front of them, chortling and holding small open flasks. Apparently, they'd decided to start the party early. They wore ridiculous hose and doublets in flashy and obnoxious colors. One looked over his shoulder, sunlight glinting on the silver inlay on his violet mask.

"Hey." The man nudged one of his fellows. "Look at what just fell from the heavens."

Regulus rolled his eyes as the other two men turned toward them. His arm was still around Adelaide's waist, but either the young noble didn't notice or didn't care.

"I actually crawled out of hell," Regulus said. "But thanks for the compliment." Adelaide giggled.

The noble squinted at him, then laughed too. "This your husband?"

"Betrothed," Adelaide replied.

One of the other men wiggled his eyebrows. A vivid green mask covered the right half of his face. "What I'm hearing is I still have a chance." He held out his flask. "I'm Will. Care for a drink?"

"No thank you, Will," Adelaide said with an amused snort.

"I'm Thomas," the first speaker said. He pointed at the third noble, who wore a crimson mask. "That's Sean. And the angel's name is…?"

"Adelaide," she said, before Regulus could say *none of your business*. "But I'm quite human."

"Where are you from, Lady Adelaide?" Sean asked. "Carasom? Khastalland?"

Regulus felt her stiffen as she said, "Nueres Duchy."

"Oh." Sean pointed at Will. "Will has relatives in Nueres. But where were you from before that? Khastalland, right?"

Regulus winced. He'd seen Dresden lose his cool over similar lines of questioning in the past. Jerrick and Estevan hadn't been born or raised in Monparth, so it didn't bother them unless someone implied they didn't count as Monparthians, despite their status as knights of Monparth.

"My mother's womb," Adelaide said flatly. "Who was in Nueres." She shuffled her feet. "But she was from Khastalland."

"Ah, see?" Sean snapped his fingers. "I knew it."

Regulus looked around, scanning the growing line behind them. No one looked like Nolan or the sorcerer. He turned back to the intoxicated young men. "Do you know anyone else coming to the masque?"

"Sure," Will said. "Lots of nobles. None that could wear that dress so well, though." He winked at Adelaide. Regulus could have punched him, but he restrained himself.

"Have you heard if any of the Carricks are coming?" Adelaide asked.

"Duke and Duchess Carrick come every year," Thomas said. "Not sure if any of their sons are coming."

"Henry said he saw the youngest, what's his name?" Sean said. "Nathaniel?"

"Nolan," Will said.

"Yeah, that's it. Said he saw him carrying some boxes for some older man over in the merchant's district a couple days ago. Said he planned on coming. Why?"

Regulus and Adelaide glanced at each other. She placed her hand on his chest. "Regulus used to be good friends with the Carricks. He was hoping to reconnect and introduce us."

"I wouldn't do that." Will laughed. "Or if you do, keep a close eye on your lovely lady. Nolan Carrick has a reputation for charming the ladies."

"Does he?" Adelaide murmured.

"Well," Regulus said, "at least I don't have to worry about the three of you."

Thomas and Will laughed, but Sean turned red as his mask. "At least we've still got our looks." Sean traced his finger down across his cheek to his chin, mirroring Regulus' scar. Regulus' mouth turned down and the tops of his ears burned.

"Don't worry, Sean," Adelaide said. She turned toward Regulus and ran her fingertips over his scar, making his skin tingle. "Maybe one day you'll grow out of those boyish features and look like a man, too." Regulus couldn't help himself. He leaned over and kissed her.

"Well, then." Will pulled at his collar. The young men turned around and returned to their flasks, commenting on the ladies they could spot ahead of them in line.

The line moved forward at a slow but steady pace and continued to grow behind them. They scanned the crowd, looking for any sign of Kirven or Nolan, but couldn't get a good enough look at anyone. Captain Russell and Lieutenant Beale stood just outside the doorway, checking for weapons and scanning the passing faces for anyone who matched the descriptions Regulus and Adelaide had given them.

"See anything?" Russell whispered as he pretended to check Regulus' sword.

Regulus shook his head. "Too many people. Too many masks."

"Masquerade." Russell cursed. "I hope you have better luck than we're having once you're inside. They're passing us too quickly."

They continued inside, up the red-carpeted staircase and into the cavernous ballroom. Massive crystal chandeliers with dozens of candles hung from the vaulted ceiling. Candelabras with intricate metalwork covered in gold leaf stood on pillars between the towering stained-glass windows. Tables covered with food arranged into the shapes of animals, flowers, and magical creatures lined the sides of the long room. A group of musicians played softly in the far corner.

The royal dais stood empty, but the hall was filling with guests and a low buzz of constant conversation mixed with the sounds of the harp, lutes, and flutes. Royal guards stood on either side of every entrance and exit, and in front of every window. Servants carrying trays of silver goblets filled with deep red wine wove through the guests. Regulus realized he had frozen, gawking at the overwhelming opulence.

"We should probably split up to cover more ground," Adelaide whispered before kissing his cheek. She slipped out of his arm and breezed away, looking unconcerned and like she wasn't bearing the weight of the world on her shoulders. He watched her move among the guests, her above-average height helping him track her.

With a sigh, he turned away. He wasn't much for talking at parties, but he was a good listener. He meandered through the hall, listening for Carrick or the sorcerer's voice or for anyone to say anything about Nolan Carrick or anything suspicious.

ADELAIDE WANDERED the ballroom as discretely as possible, but she couldn't avoid people's eyes, their whispers, or sometimes their conversation. She faked politeness and, as the hall filled and the music changed from peaceful background music to dances, gently turned down a couple offers to dance.

The afternoon sped on. The angle of the sunlight through the stained-glass windows changed and dimmed as evening approached. She saw Regulus several times, but no sign of Kirven or Nolan. Part of her felt relieved, as if nothing would actually happen. But deep down, she knew that was ridiculous. They would be here. Sooner or later.

She nursed a goblet of wine and scanned the crowd. Breck stepped up next to her, far too close for her comfort. "Getting intoxicated on duty, are we?"

Adelaide snorted. "Blending in as per your orders, sir."

"Right." He put a hand on the small of her back. She couldn't repress her shudder, and her involuntary reaction made Breck snicker. He leaned in to whisper, his breath tickling her ear. "Don't get carried away. If you get drunk while on duty, that'll be that lashing I owe you." He walked away.

She pressed her eyes closed, then left the goblet on a nearby table and continued to meander. Couples twirled around the dance floor, making her wish this was just a party, and she was in Regulus' arms. She looked across the dancers, searching for Regulus. Just seeing him would help calm her jittery nerves.

Someone stepped up behind her and a gentle hand brushed her hair behind her shoulder. A slow smile pulled at her mouth.

"You look ravishing, love," Nolan whispered close by her ear.

An invisible rope coiled around her chest. In spite of how much she had thought about being strong when she saw him, she trembled. Something sharp pressed against her ribs as he kissed the side of her neck. Her stomach lurched. Her breath stuttered and the muscles in her neck and back went taut.

"How'd you get a weapon in here?" Adelaide whispered, trying to control the pounding of her heart.

"Oh, it's just a tiny blade I had up my sleeve." Nolan ran his knuckles over her jaw in a caress that made her skin crawl. "But it's enough to do some decent damage. Nothing you can't heal, based on the fact Hargreaves is alive. I'm disappointed, but I suppose I'll simply kill him a second time."

"I'm surprised you had the mettle to show up after you ran away last time." The tip of the knife pressed deeper into her side, threatening to break through her dress.

"I had been run through with a sword four times," he snapped. "I knew it was pointless to waste my time fighting you in that state. It was a tactical decision."

"Right. I'm going to turn around now." She turned slowly, but he didn't stab her. Nolan wore a black doublet with gold stitching, and a matching mask. Facing him made Adelaide flash back to the last time she saw him, and it made her dizzy. *Focus. It's different this time.* She kept her voice low. "As a member of the royal guard, I'm placing you under arrest for treason."

"Really?" Nolan laughed. "So, the rumors around town a woman joined the royal guard are true. I suspected it was you." He adjusted the knife's point against her side. "But if you arrest me, you'll be too busy with me to find Kirven."

"Where is he?" She looked around. "Is he here?"

Nolan clicked his tongue. "What would be the fun in telling you that?" He took her hand. "May I have this dance?"

"Are you going to stab me if I say no?"

"It's just a dance." He smiled. "Don't say no and we won't have to find out."

"Fine." She lifted her chin, determined not to let him see her fear. "But put the knife away or I'll step on your feet."

He chuckled. "Maybe I want to keep it out to make sure you don't try anything stupid."

"Maybe I'm trying to keep a low profile until I find Kirven and think dancing is as good a way to do that as any." She met his eyes, even as her stomach twisted in on itself.

"Deal." Nolan's hand left her side and he slipped the short, thin knife up his sleeve then showed her his empty hands. "Satisfied?"

"I will be when you're either dead or in prison."

Nolan took her arm. "With that mouth, you're awfully lucky you're so attractive." A crooked, leering smile replaced his frown as he pulled her against him on the dance floor. "But at least your mouth is excellent for kissing." He pressed his lips to hers. Adelaide gasped and pulled back, but he yanked her forward again.

"Ah-ah," he murmured against her mouth. "Don't cause a scene, love. You wanted to blend in." Her legs shook and she squeezed her eyes shut, the blood draining from her face as he kissed her. He pulled back and moved her hands into position for the dance.

She stumbled over the first several steps, her mind numb. She could still feel him, taste him. Her knees shook. She tripped and mumbled an apology. *We should have had a better plan.* As they brushed past other couples, she searched for Kirven to keep her mind off Nolan. Why did Kirven have to be so short? She caught glimpses of Regulus on the other side of the room, his head rising above most of the other guests. She focused on him.

"I feel like you're ignoring me, which makes you a poor dance partner." Nolan pulled her closer. "Give in, Adelaide. I know you want to."

Panic squeezed at her throat. *I'm not helpless. I'm not trapped.* But it didn't feel true, and her heart hammered against her ribs like it wanted to escape its cage. She stared over his shoulder; every ounce of her shaking concentration focused on moving her feet in time to the music.

Captain Matthews and Lieutenant Breck stood conversing near one of the servant entrances, near two other royal guards. She wondered how to lead their dance toward them without being obvious. Surely the five of them could restrain Nolan. She purposefully mis-stepped so Nolan's foot landed on top of hers. She gasped and dropped her hand from his shoulder, exaggerating her limp.

Nolan steadied her. "Are you all right?"

"I think I just…need to sit down for a moment." She put some weight on the foot and stumbled, wincing and sucking in a breath to sell it. Not that it didn't hurt—her big toe throbbed—but it wasn't *that* bad. She put a hand on his shoulder. "Help me off the floor?"

"Least I can do." He beamed as she leaned on him and took the opportunity to loop his arm around her waist. She tried not to let her aversion show while she hobbled toward a bench near Matthews and Breck. She kept her head turned toward the bench but looked toward the officers. Breck caught her gaze and rolled his eyes, looking disgusted. Adelaide glanced toward Nolan, then back at them. Breck just shook his head.

Nolan helped her onto the bench. "Here, let me look at it." He knelt and pulled her boot out from under her dress.

Adelaide risked looking over her shoulder at the officers and pointed at Nolan. She dropped her hand and looked back just as Nolan looked up from her boot.

"Feels swollen. But, you know," he said, massaging her foot through her boot, "it wouldn't have happened if you'd done the proper steps."

"I know."

"I am sorry, though." His hand moved to her ankle, wandering up her calf as he smirked, his eyes filled with desire. Her throat constricted. "Let me make it up to you."

"Belanger," Breck said, approaching with Matthews. Nolan looked at them, his brow creasing. "If you're trying to point out that you're doing the exact opposite of what I said—"

"It's Nolan Carrick." Adelaide's palms glowed blue. *Time to try something new.* Nolan stood, but the ropes she formed out of her magic curled around him, tying his arms to his sides. Matthews and Breck drew their swords. The people standing near them gasped and moved away.

"I'm disappointed, love." Nolan strained against the glowing ropes. Keeping them in place felt like trying to maintain a barrier against Kirven's attacks. "But you're too late."

Trumpets bugled, signaling the royal family's arrival. Adelaide looked toward the dais, her heart sinking as the crowd turned toward the end of the hall. The king walked to the large gilded throne in the center of the dais, trailed by the royal family. Guards stood in a line in front of the dais. The king raised his hand in a welcoming gesture.

The windows imploded. Women screamed and men shouted as colored glass crashed across the room. Most of the candles went out. Nolan kicked Adelaide in the face, and she catapulted backward over the bench. Her mask cracked in half and fell. Pain exploded over her face and blood poured out of her nose. She lost control of the ropes binding Nolan as her vision blacked out; her pulse hammered in her face.

Her head weighed her down and her eyes watered. Adelaide's hand shook as she held it to her shattered nose, unable to see anything as she healed herself. The ringing in her ears added to the cacophony of the hall. The pain subsided, her nose making sickening snapping sounds as it returned to its normal shape. Her vision cleared.

By the time she straightened, which couldn't have been much more than a minute, Nolan was gone. Breck lay on the floor, his eyes glazed over and his head at an impossible angle. Matthews slumped against a glass-covered food table, blood trickling out of his mouth and pouring out of his stomach. Breck's sword was missing. Worse was the chaos in the ballroom.

Kirven floated over the crowd, a swirl of green light around his feet. His flowing black and blood-red robes glittered with gold embroidery. He held his arms out to his sides with the Staff of Nightfall in his right hand. Green lightning crackled from the top of the staff, reaching into the panicking crowd. Screaming echoed in the rafters as men and women, young and old, nobles and servants, were struck by the grasping tendrils of lightning and fell to the glass-strewn floor, their lifeless bodies smoking. She could never shield them all, and despair tugged at her soul. Nobles ran past, but cries of anguish dragged Adelaide's attention toward the exit. Kirven had blocked it. The lightning stopped, leaving behind the smell of burned bodies.

"Hello, brother." Kirven's voice resounded over the hall and the crowd quieted, too shocked to say anything. A shudder raised goosebumps on Adelaide's arms. This wouldn't be like last time. She was more prepared.

Guards huddled around the royal family. Barriers of shimmering green light and blocked the doors behind the dais. Father and Dresden stood among the guards shielding the king from Kirven, their swords drawn. Her gut pinched. *No.*

"I have no brother." The king's voice carried through the hall.

"Now that's just cruel," Kirven said. "But then, I *am* here to claim my throne and kill you and your family, so fair." The opal in the staff emitted an emerald glow.

Adelaide shoved her hands forward. The blue light barrier rose in time to block the fireball Kirven threw at the cluster of guards. She expanded the barrier until it reached from floor to ceiling and wall to wall. Kirven cursed. People screamed and shouted about sorcery and magic as they pushed to get through Kirven's barrier.

"The windows!" someone shouted. Guests and servants scrambled out the now-empty windows.

Kirven barraged Adelaide's barrier with bursts of green light, flames, and more lightning. The guards attempted to break down Kirven's barriers over both rear doors. Satisfied she could keep the barrier up, Adelaide conjured a spear and threw it at Kirven's back. At the last moment he turned and knocked the spear away. He looked around, face twisted in anger, searching the surging mass of bodies escaping through the windows.

"Belanger!" He hurled a massive fireball into the crowd, and she barely managed to shield the fleeing innocents. "Where are you?"

Adelaide opened her mouth, but before she could answer, she gripped her side and doubled over in pain. It felt like someone had stabbed through the side of her abdomen, just above her right hip. *Regulus.* The link hurt more than usual. Maybe because maintaining the gigantic barrier and healing Regulus at the same time strained her power. Maybe because it was a worse wound. She panted, grimacing as she forced herself to straighten.

A barrage of green shards flew at her and she erected a barrier over herself and the guests escaping near her. Her magic drained as the barriers and Regulus' wound pulled her power in three directions. Her grip on the larger barrier was slipping. Kirven turned back toward the dais.

"You're wearing my crown, brother." Kirven pointed the staff at the dais. A steady stream of green light pummeled into Adelaide's barrier. She dropped the barrier over herself and fought past the retreating crowd, intent on keeping the barrier up. The king had to live. Father had to live.

"Kirven!" She broke through the last guests, glass crunching under her boots. "I'm ready to try again."

Chapter 36

THE GAPING sword wound in Regulus' side pulled together and his breathing steadied. The light from Kirven's assault and Adelaide's barrier at his back cast the glass-strewn hall in an eerie teal glow. Regulus glared back at Carrick and squared his shoulders as he raised his sword, dripping with Carrick's blood. Carrick tilted his head, his face furrowed with pain from the deep slash healing across his torso.

"Are you…" Carrick eyed him. "Healing?"

"Looks like you're not the only immortal on the battlefield today." Regulus inched his right foot forward, pushing away broken glass to get more secure footing.

"She can do that too, huh?" Carrick looked impressed, but also outraged. He moved into a defensive position. "You have a mark, too?"

"Not like yours. Mine doesn't make me a slave." Regulus thrust his sword toward Carrick's chest, but Carrick parried the attack.

"Kirven!" Adelaide's voice rang out. Regulus and Carrick looked toward her. "I'm ready to try again."

Regulus swung for Carrick's neck, taking advantage of his split focus. Carrick blocked and countered with a thrust of his own. Their swords clanged together as they circled, glass sliding beneath their boots while they avoided the charred bodies of masque guests.

Out of the corner of his eye, Regulus caught glimpses of Adelaide and Kirven battling with flashes of blue and green light and red flame. He couldn't worry about her right now. He had his own fight.

Adelaide raised her shield just in time to stop another blast of crackling green lightning. Her hair clung to her sweat-soaked forehead and neck. She yelled and sent two streams of flame toward Kirven, but he just held out the staff and extinguished the flames. How did he make it look so effortless? She conjured several spears of blue light and hurled them toward Kirven, followed by a blast of light and another stream of fire.

Kirven raised a shield that easily absorbed every attack. Meanwhile, her breathing grew more labored by the moment. Movement on the dais caught her eye. She threw a haphazard barrage of knives to keep Kirven focused on her. One of Kirven's barriers, the one blocking the exit to the left of the dais, had vanished. The guards hurried the royal family out the door, followed by Father, Dresden, and the guards, including Captain Russell. *Thank Etiros.* Now she just needed to keep her barrier up long enough for them to escape.

"You're tiring, girl." Kirven pointed the staff at her. Half a dozen fingers of lightning cracked toward her, and she surrounded herself with a barrier. The assault continued for seconds that felt like hours. The lightning stopped, and she dropped the shield. Adelaide conjured ropes of blue light and snapped them toward the Staff of Nightfall. If she could pull it out of his hands…

Kirven laughed and sent a stream of fire at the ropes. He clicked his tongue. "Theft is a serious crime, Adelaide."

With a grunt, she let the ropes vanish. She raised her hands, conjuring a shield above Kirven's head, then slammed her hands down. The shield crashed into Kirven's head. He cursed as he fell, but shoved the tip of the staff toward her before she could attack again. She raised a shield, but the blast from the staff knocked her backward. She tripped over the hand of a charred body and fell onto her back.

"Guess you actually have some skill, mongrel." Carrick dodged Regulus' thrust and countered, but Regulus blocked the blow. Carrick aimed a cut at Regulus' leg, which Regulus parried. "Too bad it won't be enough."

"I'm going to cut your head off," Regulus said through gritted teeth as Carrick blocked his attack.

Carrick flashed a cocky grin. "Funny, Adelaide said something similar—just before I kissed her. She has such soft, sensuous lips."

Rage rushed over Regulus like fire on his skin. He lunged, but his heel slid on glass and he slipped to one knee. Carrick sliced toward his neck. Regulus blocked, the impact shuddering down his arms. He pushed Carrick's blade away and jumped to his feet.

Adelaide cried out. Instinctively, Regulus looked toward her. She had fallen onto her back, and she raised a bleeding hand with bits of glass glittering in the cuts. Carrick's sword sliced across Regulus' abdomen. Regulus moaned. Adelaide yelped and clutched her stomach. Blood seeped out of Regulus' gut, and he stumbled backward as his vision swam.

Instead of seizing his advantage, Carrick ran for the dais. Regulus turned in confusion. Adelaide's barrier was gone, but so were the royal family and their guards. Carrick ran through the door to the left of the dais. Regulus grunted and pressed a hand to his stomach as the numbing warmth of Adelaide's magic healed his wound. How long ago had the king left? Only human, mortal guards stood between Carrick and the king. He had to—

"You stupid, annoying, nuisance of a mage!" The sorcerer shouted.

Regulus glanced over his shoulder. The sorcerer stood on the ground, the top of the Staff of Nightfall aglow. He lifted the staff and a blast of jade light exploded toward Adelaide. She raised her hands, a sapphire shield covering her. But her elbows bent, her hands lowering under the constant barrage of the sorcerer's attack. Regulus ran toward the sorcerer, his only concern helping Adelaide. The blue light of Adelaide's shield faded. Regulus launched into the sorcerer, knocking him to the ground.

The sorcerer thrashed, but Regulus crawled over him and reached for the Staff of Nightfall. His fingers brushed the staff. He just needed to pull it out of the sorcerer's grip… A snap of greenish lightning cracked off the tip of the staff and slammed into his chest.

Regulus felt like he was being ripped apart with white-hot claws and pushed back together by searing hands at the same time as the lightning traveled through his body. He went rigid, unable to even scream to process his pain. But he could hear Adelaide screaming, and that was almost worse. His sight gave out, going completely white. Then cool numbness pushed back the searing pain, starting from his feet and moving up toward his chest, as Adelaide's healing magic fought the sorcerer's destructive magic in his body, gaining ground inch by excruciating inch.

The sorcerer shouted, the crackling sound of the lightning intensified, and a strangled scream escaped Regulus as a fresh wave of torment pushed through him. *Just let me die.* But the comforting healing sensation shoved back, chasing the jagged rending of the lightning out of his convulsing body. *No, no dying today.* He latched onto the soothing sensation of Adelaide's magic, focused on their bond and his love for her. The pain faded as the searing sorcery fled from Adelaide's magic. A resounding crack split the air as the lightning released

Regulus, and he collapsed onto bits of sharp glass.

The sorcerer screamed curses between cries of pain. Regulus blinked and his vision cleared. The sorcerer knelt in the dimly lit hall, cradling his right hand. Giant red blisters covered his palm. The Staff of Nightfall lay on the ground between Regulus and the sorcerer, its light extinguished and smoke rising off the entire length of the staff.

"What is this?" the sorcerer shrieked. "What is this? What did you do?" He looked at Regulus, his eyes wide and bloodshot. "This isn't possible. The spell rebounded onto the staff. That's not possible!" His palm glowed green, and the skin repaired itself.

Regulus shook his head as feeling returned to his limbs. Adelaide lay sprawled across the floor, her eyes closed but her chest rising and falling. He wanted to go to her, but he had an opening to kill the sorcerer. Spotting his sword, he moved toward it. He grabbed the hilt just as green ropes wrapped around his wrists. The sword slipped from his hand.

"Why aren't you dead?" The sorcerer stood. A third glowing rope curled around Regulus' neck, cutting off his air. He gasped and tried to reach toward his neck, but the ropes holding onto his wrists wouldn't let him. The sorcerer clenched his fist and a glowing moss-green sword shimmered into existence in his hand as he walked to Regulus.

"It's high time you died." The sorcerer ran the sword through Regulus' chest. The pain nearly made Regulus pass out. His scream stuck in his strangled throat, coming out in a thin moan. The sorcerer withdrew the sword. Sword and ropes vanished, and Regulus fell face-forward onto the ground. His chest was on fire. He couldn't breathe. Blood pooled beneath him. From where he lay on the ground, he saw Adelaide bolt upright, her hand clutched over her sternum.

"Regulus!"

Slowly, the fire blazing in his chest cooled and the pain numbed. Adelaide ran toward him. At the last moment, she changed direction and snatched the staff off the ground. She slid across broken glass until she stood in front of him, the staff clasped in both hands.

"He's not yours anymore." The challenge in her voice forced a smile to Regulus' face.

The sorcerer laughed. Regulus pushed himself to his knees, and the sorcerer's laugh died on his lips. "What… Oh." He slapped his forehead. "You put a bond on him. Idiot."

"Your Highness!" Carrick ran into the hall, panting. "The king has escaped. I can't find him."

Relief filled Regulus as the sorcerer cursed.

"I'll take that back." A coil of green rope shot from the sorcerer's hand and ripped the staff away from Adelaide, pulling her forward.

Adelaide conjured a flaming sword. Kirven held his hand forward, but Adelaide blocked the blast of flames with a shield of magical light. Regulus turned his attention to Carrick—right as Carrick slammed the pommel of his sword between Regulus' eyes.

Adelaide panted, sweat trickling down her back as she braced herself against Kirven's fiery assault. She maintained the shield with her left hand, the flaming sword still held in her right. Pain exploded between her eyes, but she couldn't look back at Regulus as she focused on withstanding Kirven's attack. Kirven raised the staff, then slammed the end into the ground. A small tremor raced toward her, enough to knock her off balance. Kirven cursed and fumbled the staff. Her foot slid across glass, and she fell onto one knee.

"Should we go, my lord?" Nolan said.

Kirven waved his hand and a blast of green she didn't have time to block knocked her sideways. "Yes, but not empty-handed."

He sent a dozen ropes toward her, leaning heavily on the Staff of Nightfall and looking pale. She raised a barricade around herself and tried not to worry how much strength she had left. A rope broke through her barrier and grabbed her wrist.

"Hargreaves is unconscious?" Kirven asked. Carrick answered in the affirmative and Adelaide looked toward Regulus. He lay in a heap on the floor. Her heart twisted, her concentration breaking. Another rope got through and circled around her waist.

"Good." Kirven wiped his forehead with his sleeve. "Take him and go."

"What?" Carrick sounded as stunned as Adelaide.

"Are you stupid, boy?" Kirven shouted. "Take him and get out of here now!"

In her surprise, she lost all control of the barrier. The ropes wound around her arms, her legs, her waist, her throat. She strained against them, watching helplessly as Carrick ran past her, Regulus thrown over his shoulder.

"No," she choked out past the rope tightening around her neck. She let a blast of magical energy radiate off her entire body. The ropes disintegrated. She gasped in air.

"You've gotten better," Kirven panted as he walked toward the entrance to the hall. "I'm too tired to continue fighting you right now."

She stumbled to her feet and threw an arc of fire, but a green barrier stopped it. Kirven raised his left hand. Emerald light swirled around his legs, lifted him off his feet, then sped him toward the entrance. Adelaide darted around the barrier Kirven had left up. It disappeared as she passed it while Kirven floated out of the hall doors. She hitched up her dress and chased him.

A green shimmering barrier blocked the door behind him. She ran into it and was pushed back. "No!" She threw a fireball at it, but it held. "No, no, no!" She conjured a sword and attacked the barrier, but still it held. "Regulus!" She pounded the barrier with the sword, then stepped back and threw a stream of fire at the door. It flickered but didn't break.

"No!" Wait. The windows. *Idiot!* She turned and ran to the nearest window and climbed up onto the sill, ignoring the shards of glass cutting into her palms. She fell three feet to the ground outside and twisted her ankle. "I don't have time for this!" She tried to run without healing her ankle, but it slowed her progress and every step was excruciating. She cursed in Khast and stopped to heal her foot.

She didn't see a trace of Kirven, Nolan, or Regulus in the front garden, so she hurried on. One of the royal guards knelt over a bleeding guard on the ground next to the open font gate.

"Where are they?" she screeched. "The sorcerer and Nolan Carrick and Regulus Hargreaves! Did you see them?"

The guard looked up, eyes wide, and pointed a shaking hand out the gate. She ran past into desolate streets. Kirven and Nolan were gone. And so was Regulus.

She fell to her knees on the cobblestones and screamed. A blast of flames flared around her, turning the stones black. Another shrill scream ripped up her throat, leaving it raw, and echoed against the palace walls.

EVERY PART of Adelaide felt numb as she dragged her feet back inside the palace. She stood in the middle of the empty, silent great hall as night fell, dark and lifeless as the emptiness that had settled in her chest.

The king had escaped. Kirven had said something was wrong with the Staff of Nightfall. She had stood her ground, and Kirven had run away. These things should have comforted her. They didn't.

She had failed. Kirven and Nolan had escaped. The bodies of those she had failed to protect littered the floor of the hall. Kirven had taken Regulus, and she didn't understand why. Her bond would heal a lot if they hurt him, at least. But it wouldn't spare him from pain—or her from experiencing an echo of whatever pain he felt. It wouldn't prevent Nolan from cutting Regulus' head off his shoulders. Her stomach turned and she swayed. Footsteps sounded on the dais and someone entered holding a lit torch. She looked up, her mind blank.

Dresden stood on the dais, staring into the shadows. Blood stained his torn sleeves and covered his shirt and the bandage wrapped around his middle. He pressed his left hand against his side.

"Anyone here?" He held the torch high. "Regulus? Adelaide?"

She couldn't even find the energy to respond. As he walked further into the hall, the edge of the torchlight reached her.

"Adelaide?" Glass crunched under his boots in the stillness. "Adelaide?" He stopped before her, looking around in confusion. "Where's Regulus?"

She shook her head. Dresden paled. "D-dead?"

She shook her head again.

"I don't under… Captured?" She nodded. Dresden stumbled back as if slapped. "No… Reg…" He cursed and kicked at the glass.

"I tried…" Her throat constricted. She stared at the glass glittering in torchlight on the floor between them.

Dresden took several deep breaths. "I'm sorry, Adelaide. I need to tell you something." His voice was too low, too gentle. Her stomach knotted. "There's not an easy way to say this. It's…your father."

She jerked her head up, her throat closing. The drawn look on Dresden's face sucked away her breath.

"Adelaide…" Dresden sighed. "He's—"

"No." She shook her head. He couldn't be about to say what she feared. Tears burned in the corners of her eyes. "Where is he?"

Dresden's expression was pained. "He died a noble—"

"No!" She shoved Dresden's chest. *Died. Died.* "No, you're lying. You're wrong!" Her shrill voice wavered as her shoulders shook. "He's not… No." She pushed him again and felt a twinge of remorse as he groaned and clutched at his bloodied side.

He dropped the torch onto the floor and grabbed her shoulders. "Adelaide—"

"He can't be dead." Her head hurt like it had been hammered. She pictured Father's face, his eyes crinkling as he laughed. A sob shook her entire body. "He's not dead!"

Not Father, who was always there. Father, who had kissed her head and told her not to be afraid when he told her about the Shadow. Father, who always made her believe that somehow, everything would be all right.

"Adelaide—"

"No, you're wrong." She was supposed to save him. To save them all. "Where is he?" She broke free of Dresden's grip, sobbing as tears made his face difficult to see. "Where's my father?"

"I'm sorry. Your father is gone."

She rubbed her eyes and his face came back into focus. In the shadowy light of the torch on the floor, she saw the truth in his eyes. *No.*

"Take me to him. I—I can—" She gulped back her sobs, trying to talk past the ache in her throat. "I can save him. I can heal him. You have to take me to him!" She'd heal him, and he'd laugh and say she was as stubborn as Mother.

Dresden shook his head. "I'm sorry, Adelaide. It's not like Regulus. He's gone. I don't think even you can resurrect the dead."

"No, please…" What was left of her heart broke with a pain that was physical. Father's green eyes filled her mind. The sound of his voice as he teased Mother. The love and protectiveness in his face every time he called her *my daughter.* She had failed him.

Light flickered in the doorway behind the dais. "Clear," someone said. "Lay them out on the dais."

Adelaide stared at the doorway as guards carried bodies into the hall. Her chest constricted. Dresden tried to turn her away. "Adelaide, don't—"

She released a blast of light against his chest, knocking him to the ground, and ran to the dais, ignoring Dresden's cry of pain. She recognized the faces of the guards on the ground but didn't know their names. Another guard carried in a body not wearing a royal guard's uniform. She froze while the man placed the body on the dais next to the others. She stumbled forward as Dresden came up behind her, holding his torch in one hand and clutching his side with the other.

"Adelaide…"

She stared down at Father's ashen, lifeless face. His glassy eyes stared at the ceiling. The blood covering his chest glistened in the light of Dresden's torch.

Adelaide sank to her knees. "Father? I—I'm…here." She brushed her fingers over his cheek. His skin was too cold. His unseeing eyes didn't move. Her jaw quivered. "No, you can't, you have—you have…to stay."

She moved her trembling hands over his body. Her palms glowed as she searched for a spark of life. Nothing. She could sense the wound that went through his still, unmoving heart. She tried to heal it, to pull his heart back together and force it to beat again. "Tell me it—it's going to be all right. Pl…please, Father."

His heart didn't beat. His lips didn't move. Adelaide lifted his stiffening torso and cradled him in her lap as she rained tears on his unblinking face.

"I'm sorry, Father. I—I—I… I tried—" A sob swallowed her words. Her soul shattered like the stained glass covering the hall floor. She clenched his shirt and buried her face in his shoulder, choking on the sharp and bitter scent of his blood.

Dresden pulled her to her feet and Father's body fell back to the floor with a sickening thud. She screamed. Dresden dragged her away. Her legs shook and she collapsed, nearly pulling Dresden down on top of her. Her wails echoed in the vaulted ceiling. She howled her pain into the air until her throat was so raw, she couldn't make a sound, and then she pounded her fists against the floor.

Bits of broken glass cut her hands and her blood dripped onto the floor, but she didn't care. She couldn't feel the pain. There was too much pain in her heart for her body to feel anything. Dresden knelt and pulled her against his chest, preventing her flailing. She wept silently into his shoulder until she fell asleep, too exhausted to keep her eyes open.

When Adelaide awoke, she was lying in the dark on top of the bed in her and Regulus' little room. Her head throbbed. Everything came back at once. Regulus had been taken. Kirven and Nolan had escaped with the staff. And Father was… Father was…

Dead. The word bounced around inside her skull, making it pound more. She turned onto her side and curled into a ball. Her throat felt like it had been tied in knots and then untangled. She made a sound like an injured dog. Movement somewhere in the room made her freeze.

"Adelaide?" Dresden's sleepy voice. "Are you awake?"

After a moment, she said "yes," but no sound came out of her mouth. She cleared her throat. "Yes." Her voice sounded scratchy and thick.

"Do you need anything?" Dresden murmured. "I have water…"

She licked her dry lips. They tasted of tears. "Water would be good."

She managed to conjure a small orb of light. The light hurt her eyes and made her headache worse, which seemed impossible. Dresden sat in one of the chairs by the table, squinting. Dark bags circled under his heavy eyelids. He picked a large canteen up off the table and handed it to her. Swallowing was almost painful, but the water soothed the tightness in her throat.

Adelaide stared at the canteen in her hands as the question she both wanted and dreaded to ask burned in her chest. She took another drink. The water helped her headache, if only a little. Blood from her broken nose had dried on her chest and the bodice of her dress. Cuts and scrapes covered her hands, especially the fleshy sides of her palms. Parts of her skirt and sleeves were singed. And none of it mattered.

It took a moment to find her voice. "What happened?" The words came out in a croak. She took another drink and cleared her throat again. "How did my father…." Her eyes filled with tears. "How'd he die?" She finally met Dresden's eyes. "Were you there?"

Dresden hesitated. "We followed the royals. A guard or two was left every so often to slow down anyone who might try to pursue. We got to a locked brass door. The king unlocked it, and the guard captain and a few other guards accompanied the royals inside. It leads to some underground maze with several exits for the royal family to escape if need be."

He took a deep breath. "Three guards, your father, and I remained to guard the door. Good thing, too, because Carrick ripped the door off its hinges—

after he caught me in the side"—his hand drifted to the new, clean bandage on his left side—"cut off the hand of one of the guards, and severely wounded the other two. Your father stood his ground the longest. He bought the king time to escape."

She swallowed back a whimper.

He shook his head, admiration sparking in his eyes. "I would never have expected someone of his age to move so fast. He didn't think. He just fought." Dresden sighed heavily and his gaze left hers. "But Carrick was too fast and too strong. Alfred didn't stand a chance. He was stabbed through the heart. He died quickly."

Against her will, an image of a sword thrusting into Father's chest filled her mind. She tightened her jaw against traitorous sobs. She pressed her eyes closed as her stomach roiled.

"I was supposed to keep him safe," she whispered.

"He wouldn't want you to blame yourself," Dresden said quietly. "I spent several days with him, and I know how much he loved you."

His words meant to comfort just made her loss more acute.

"Your father never thought you needed to protect him. He just wanted to protect you. He would gladly have given his life for you, and he would never blame you."

She trembled as tears dripped off her chin. She wanted to tell Dresden to stop, stop talking, stop trying to make her feel better. Where once had been a father's love, now was an aching, empty loneliness. She didn't want him to try to ease her pain. But she couldn't make herself speak.

"He made his choice to stand his ground and defend the king." Dresden's eyes met hers, but instead of pity she didn't want, she saw unexpected understanding and determination. "He knew the risk. He didn't have to bring a sword or follow after the king. He didn't even have to come to the masque."

"If you think he didn't have to come," Adelaide whispered, "you don't...didn't know him very well at all."

"That's my point." Dresden leaned forward in the chair. He winced and clutched his side with a sharp intake of breath.

"What am I doing?" She wiped at her eyes and moved over to Dresden. "You're hurt. And I'm...I'm..." *Useless.* She held her hand over his side. The cut was long, but didn't touch any of his vital organs, and whoever had stitched him up had done a good job.

"Adelaide—"

"Almost done." She wasn't sure she wanted to hear what he had to say. Every word was just another strike, the hit of a hammer against an anvil, forging Father's death into an inescapable reality.

She finished healing his side. "You'll have to pull the stitches out." She headed back toward the bed, but Dresden caught her hand.

"Thank you. But you need to listen. Because if you can't forgive yourself, you're going to break. I've seen it before."

She pulled her hand away and sat on the bed.

"Your father knew what he was doing; he was aware of the danger, and he did it anyway because that's who he was. He was a good man. A brave man. He deserves your pride, not your self-blame."

"I don't want to be proud." She rubbed away a tear with a shaking hand. "I want him back." *I want my Father back. I want him to embrace me and tell me everything is going to be all right.* Her teeth chattered as she tried to stop crying.

Dresden didn't respond, and she was thankful. She didn't want platitudes or expressions of pity or pointless apologies. If she had resented Nolan before, that rage had frozen over into stone-hard hatred that threatened to drag her down and drown her in the storm-tossed waters of her hopelessness and sorrow. But some part of her whispered it wasn't really Nolan she hated; it was herself. Maybe Dresden was right. If she couldn't forgive herself and accept Father's sacrifice, she was going to crack. She clenched the worn blanket in her fists. Father was dead, and Regulus was gone, and Mother was—*Mother.*

"How am I supposed to tell my mother…?" Adelaide buried her face in her hands. How could she even cry this much? How could her heart hurt this much and not just kill her?

She didn't know how long she cried. Ten minutes, twenty, thirty, five. Time had ceased to have meaning. When she stopped, she took several deep breaths. "I think I'm going to go for a walk."

"Um…" Dresden cleared his throat. "A…Lieutenant Bell? Ball? A lieutenant said you're to report to him as soon as possible. Technically, he said the minute you wake up. He wanted to wake you, but I wouldn't let him."

She should have known. Duty first. "Can…can you come with me?"

"Of course."

They walked through the dark night to the barracks, an orb floating above them to light the way. She guessed it to be around three in the morning. A guard on duty at the entrance to the courtyard said Beale was in his chamber, but had left orders that if she came, to show her straight in. The guard led them to the end of the first floor of the barracks and knocked on a door. No one stirred inside, so he knocked again, harder and longer. A muffled voice shouted for them to enter. The guard bowed and departed, and Adelaide pushed the door open.

Beale sat on his bed, rubbing his eyes. His uniform coat was on but open over a white undershirt. His boots laid on the floor, but thankfully he was still wearing his trousers.

"Ah, good. Belanger." He rubbed the back of his head. "I need a report of what happened in the hall after the king left."

"Where is the king?" Weariness made her voice small.

"Safe. The royal family have been escorted to various places to hide. The king wants you to join him at once. But first I need to know what happened and what we're looking at going forward." He glanced toward Dresden. "I got a report from Sir Jakobs about what he knows about the attack. But I was knocked unconscious by Kirven's initial blast. I'm working blind here."

She relayed everything that happened. Her fight with Kirven. How Kirven tried to kill Regulus and she passed out, but something had happened to the Staff of Nightfall. How it seemed to not be working properly and be causing Kirven pain. Kirven and Nolan taking Regulus. She hung her head.

"I'm sorry, sir. I failed."

"You gave the king a chance to escape," Beale said. "The king is alive because of you. You did your duty. And you tried. And survived, which is more than I can say for…far too many of our men." He dragged his hand down the side of his face. "Captain Russell accompanied the king. Lieutenant Antar is gravely wounded and may lose his leg, possibly his life. Captain Matthews and Lieutenant Breck are dead. Five guards sustained minor injuries, five are critically wounded, ten are dead, and seven are missing, suspected desertion. Best guess, they panicked when attacked by a sorcerer, ran with the guests, and are too afraid to come back."

Adelaide nodded. The punishment for abandoning your post was at minimum thirty lashes and two days in the stocks without food or clothes.

"That leaves us with only twenty-five guards." Beale clasped his hands together. "And the threat is still out there. So I need you to pull yourself together, Belanger. We don't stand a chance without your help."

"Where are the wounded?" She sounded more tired than she had hoped. "I can help them."

Beale perked up at that. "Most are in the infirmary, at the beginning of the hall." He stood. "Lieutenant Antar is next door."

He led them into Antar's room. Antar lay on his bed, his damp hair plastered to his head. He muttered incoherently under his breath. Blood soaked through a thick bandage wrapped around the top of his right leg. Beale moved to unwrap the leg, but Adelaide stopped him.

"I don't need to see it."

And truthfully, she didn't want to. She held her hand over the bandage. Her magic flowed out and into Antar, and she got a sense of his wound. The wide cut went deep, partway through the bone. A sensation she hadn't encountered before surprised her until she realized what it was. An infection was already spreading through his body.

"I don't know if I can heal this," she admitted. "Why didn't they amputate already?"

"He insisted they wait until morning. I think he was hoping to die first."

She focused on mending the bone, the torn muscles and severed veins and nerves. Antar stopped muttering and his breathing deepened. The infection was harder—she had never dealt with that before. She tried to kill it, as if burning the infection out. When she had done everything in her power, she turned to Beale.

"He's technically healed, but I don't know if he will live. He's lost a lot of blood."

"I understand. Thank you for trying." Beale led the way to the infirmary, and she spent the next hour healing the guards. By the end, she felt more like a ghost than a person.

"I need to sleep," she mumbled. "I have to…to…have to regill. Refain." She shook her head. "Regain my energy. Wait for my magic to rurn…return."

"Yes. Yes, of course." Beale looked like he thought she might topple over at any moment. "We need you at your best, Belanger. Get some sleep."

She fell asleep within moments of collapsing on the bed. She only barely registered that Dresden had followed her and settled back into a chair. Somehow, his presence made the ache in her soul a little more bearable. But Regulus' absence next to her felt like a hole in her heart as she slipped into a deep sleep.

Light was stealing into the room in the cracks around the door when Adelaide bolted awake with a scream trapped in her lungs. She arched her back and flailed her arms and legs but couldn't break free of the bone-crushing pain pummeling her body. She rolled off the bed and hit the ground hard. Dresden jumped off the chair and grabbed her shoulders as she pulled in a wheezing, strangled breath.

"Breathe!" He dodged her wildly swinging hands. "What's wrong?"

She found her voice, and a single word leapt from her throat in a shriek. "Regulus!"

CHAPTER 38

SOMETHING ROUGH poked into Regulus' back as he groaned awake. He shifted. Metal clanked, aggravating his throbbing head. What was going on? Something weighed down his arms. He pried his eyes open. Pale, early morning sunlight illuminated the trees and meadow around him. The almost inaudible crash of waves sounded in the distance. The blackened bark of an oak tree pushed into his back. He recognized the dull, lifeless black of the tree and the shriveled, charcoal leaves curled on the edges of the branches. He'd ridden past the same thing on his way to the sorcerer's tower too many times.

Carrick and the sorcerer sat on stumps on either side of a small fire several paces away, turned away from him and eating something that smelled savory and made his stomach growl. Regulus went to move his arms and found he couldn't. He looked down.

A thick chain wrapped around his chest and the tree several times. Another chain connected to shackles around his wrists, then wrapped around his forearms before also wrapping around behind the tree. The right sleeve of his shirt had been cut off. He strained against the chains, but only succeeded in bruising his chest and making his wrists hurt. He glared at Carrick and the sorcerer, but they continued eating and paid no attention to his grunting and the clinking of the chains.

"Hey!" He tried to use his legs to push himself up, but the chains were too tight. "What am I doing here?"

They finally looked at him. Carrick's mouth curled into an irritated snarl as he chewed, but the sorcerer just wiped his fingers on his robe, picked up the Staff of Nightfall, and stood. Carrick glared up at the sorcerer, then tossed down the last bit of meat in his hand and followed the sorcerer toward Regulus.

"You are here," the sorcerer said, thinly veiled fury in his voice, "because of this." He held the top end of the Staff of Nightfall in front of Regulus' face.

At first, Regulus didn't understand. But as he looked closer, he saw the source of the sorcerer's rage. Two deep, jagged cracks ran through the opal mounted in the top piece. Spots of murky white marred the shiny black surface. The purple, blue, and red flecks looked dull instead of glittery. The sorcerer tossed the staff aside.

"I don't know how to fix it," the sorcerer spat. "Every time I use it since I tried to kill you with it, it doesn't work properly and burns my hand. But perhaps, if I can better understand this"—he bent and placed his fingers between the chains on Regulus' right arm, on top of Adelaide's mark—"I can understand exactly what happened and fix it."

"Well, if you're hoping I can explain," Regulus said with a glare, "I can't. I was unconscious when Adelaide put that there, and I know nothing about magic."

"Oh, I don't need you to explain." The sorcerer straightened. "I know what that is, even if I've never seen one before. Honestly, I thought the lover's bond to be purely hypothetical. First time I've been wrong in quite a while."

The way Carrick clenched his fists and tightened his jaw at *lover's bond* lit a satisfied spark in Regulus' chest. Let the cad try to argue he could win Adelaide's heart now.

"There are three known bonds," the sorcerer said. "The servant's bond, sometimes called the slave's bond, which I perfected and with which you're well acquainted." Carrick frowned at that, and Regulus nearly laughed. "The protection bond, which is the most common but still not widely used because few people are so selfless as to let another essentially borrow some of their magic. Finally, the lover's bond. Obviously the rarest, since I didn't believe it existed outside of legend."

The sorcerer stroked his beard. "But the lover's bond is also the strongest, the hardest to break, and most closely unites the bearer and the giver." He sat cross-legged next to Regulus. "So you don't need to explain what it is or how she put it there, or even how it works because I'm aware your stupid brain doesn't understand it. But I do want you to explain what you have experienced since receiving it. What are its effects? What changes have you noticed?"

"Let me say this plainly and simply." Regulus rested his head against the tree. "As Adelaide said: I'm not yours anymore. I don't answer to you."

The sorcerer shook his head. "You always make things so difficult." He placed his palm against Regulus' chest. The pain was immediate, and worse than anything Regulus had experienced when he had the sorcerer's mark. Somewhere in the back of his mind he wondered if it was because of the direct proximity of the sorcerer, but he was too consumed with the pain to think clearly. He screamed, struggling against the chains but unable to do more than kick his legs. His boot hit the sorcerer's side, and the sorcerer's hand left his chest. Regulus gasped for air as the world tilted and shifted before his vision cleared.

The sorcerer rubbed his side and cursed. "All right. Let's try this again. Tell me about the effects of the bond."

Regulus glared. He wanted to tell the sorcerer to go to hell. But he also didn't want to experience that pain again. More importantly, when what hurt him hurt Adelaide, he couldn't go asking for punishment. But would that information help the sorcerer fix the staff? A malfunctioning weapon would help Adelaide defeat him.

"This shouldn't require that much thought, Hargreaves." The sorcerer stood. "If you won't tell me, I suppose we'll just have to do some research. Carrick." He motioned toward Regulus. "Have fun."

Carrick grinned and pulled a dagger from the back of his belt. "My pleasure."

"No, wait." Regulus struggled to sit up straighter as Carrick crouched next to him.

"Afraid of a little blood, mongrel?" Carrick laughed. "Where should I start? Maybe I'll reopen that scar of yours." The blade glinted as it moved past Regulus' eyes.

He squelched his rising panic. It would be better to pretend to play along, give obvious information, than let them hurt Adelaide. And he didn't want to be tortured, either. "I heal."

"Tell me something I don't know," the sorcerer spat.

"Little things heal, too. Nicks, bruises."

The sorcerer squinted. "And that's it? You're holding out on me, Hargreaves. Do it, Carrick." Carrick grinned and moved the point of the knife to the top of Regulus' scar.

"No!" The chains clinked as Regulus fruitlessly tried to raise his hand to stop Carrick. "That's it, it works like yours, but without the pain! Please! I heal, there's no pain, she can't control me, that's it." The point of the knife touched his skin. "Don't! That's it, I swear. Please!"

The sorcerer held up his hand, and Carrick scowled as he lowered the knife. "Hm." The sorcerer tilted his head, his gaze drilling into Regulus. "You're not afraid of pain. You know you'll heal, so it's not a fear of a wound. What are you so afraid of?"

Dammit. He met the sorcerer's gaze and tried to keep his expression closed, to betray nothing. The sorcerer's eyes narrowed as he thought. "You only have ever begged me to spare others, never yourself. Others… Wait. The mage cried out like she was in pain, but I hadn't hit her." He looked to Carrick. "But you hit *him*." He looked back to Regulus. "What aren't you telling me, mercenary?"

Regulus set his jaw and glared right back.

"Cut his face open."

"Finally." Carrick brought the knife back up. From the way the corner of the sorcerer's mouth twitched upward, Regulus suspected he already knew the truth.

"All right!" Regulus lowered his gaze. "Adelaide feels my pain."

Carrick froze, the point of the knife hovering just above the top of the scar. "What are you talking about?"

"When I'm hurt, she feels an echo of my pain. Not as intense as actually receiving the wound herself, but she still feels it." Regulus looked up at the dead branches above him. "When we realized, I tried to get her to remove the mark. But she wouldn't." He looked back at Carrick. "Please. Anything you do to me, you do to her."

Carrick tilted his head. "So it doesn't actually wound her?"

"There's no mark or blood, no."

"But she feels your pain? Your injuries?"

"Yes!" He knocked his head back against the tree. "Do you not understand, or do you not believe me!"

"No, I believe you. And I understand." Carrick's eyes glinted. "I understand that when I do this," the tip of the dagger cut into Regulus' face as he pulled the blade down the length of the scar while Regulus screamed, "she'll know exactly what is happening to you."

Regulus clenched his teeth, his chest heaving and eyes watering. Carrick stood and moved back to give the sorcerer an unobstructed view of Regulus' mutilation. He had cut deeper than the original scar, slicing all the way through the cheek so that the skin curled away from the side of his face. Regulus moaned, the pain like fiery needles over the side of his face. Then the pain faded away. He breathed deeper. The skin curled back and pulled together. Regulus unclenched his jaw and opened his eyes.

The sorcerer stood stroking his beard, expression impassive. Carrick's brows lifted toward his hairline. Regulus spat blood toward Carrick's feet. Carrick stepped back, his top lip pulling up.

"Interesting." The sorcerer tugged on his beard. "All very interesting."

Regulus sighed. Sooner or later, the torture would break him, and he would have put Adelaide through all that pain, just to give in. He couldn't let them hurt her. "Please. I'll tell you anything I can. Just…stop hurting her."

Carrick looked to the sorcerer, who nodded. With clear disappointment, Carrick crossed his arms.

"You said you were unconscious when she bound you," the sorcerer said. "That shouldn't be possible. You should have to agree to a binding."

"I did, apparently. I don't really remember." Regulus glowered at Carrick. "Carrick had run me through with a sword, and I had mostly bled out. Adelaide healed the wound, but I was still fading. She asked me if I wanted to be bound to her for life, and I didn't really understand what she was asking, so of course I agreed. Then I blacked out. I came to a couple minutes later, Adelaide had passed out, and I had this mark."

"How long was she out for?"

"About a day and a half, two days."

The sorcerer clasped his hands. "Any other side effects?"

When Regulus hesitated, Carrick twirled the knife in his hand.

"When we touch—actual skin contact—we can feel each other's emotions." Regulus shifted against the tree trunk, but there was no getting comfortable. "Any skin contact, I can sense her emotions. And a couple times, I've seen what she's thinking about when I close my eyes while touching her."

"Examples," the sorcerer grunted.

Regulus fixed Carrick with a withering stare. "She was scared and upset, and I was trying to comfort her. I closed my eyes, and I saw her memories, as if looking through her eyes. You know what I saw, Carrick? I saw *you*. I know what you did."

Carrick reddened and glanced away, then recovered his neutral expression. At least he had some sense of shame.

"And you." Regulus turned his attention to the sorcerer. "She has nightmares. About what you did to her, what you threatened to do to her family. I tried to wake her one night and closed my eyes, barely more than a blink, and my mind was pulled into her nightmare."

"No wonder my spell backfired," the sorcerer muttered. "This bond is stronger and deeper than I would have dreamed possible. But then, magic born out of self-sacrifice is always strong, because the price paid for it is so high."

"Sacrifice?" Regulus' brow wrinkled. "Why, because I nearly died?"

"That's part of it, yes. You sacrificed yourself for her, but the amount of energy she put into you to create *that* mark—she was ready to give up her power entirely to save you. She could have killed herself with the effort."

What? Regulus' mouth fell into a silent *oh.* A surge of love and gratitude fought with guilt. *No wonder she slept for so long.*

The sorcerer crossed his arms and shook his head, his features sagging and weary. "When I used the staff on you, the sorcery in it tried to overpower the magic in you to kill you and failed. All that destructive magical energy had to go somewhere, so it did—back onto my staff." He snarled the words. "I had hoped it said something about her power, that she might have the strength to repair the staff. But this"—he pointed at Regulus' arm, his disgust apparent— "this isn't because of the power of her magic, just her love. It's a cyclical strengthening based on your sickening affection for each other. Your love strengthens the bond, the bond strengthens your love, and so forth, making the protection magic in you stronger than the destructive magic was in the staff. It's useless to me, unless I want to use you as a shield."

"Oh, yes," Regulus said with a scowl, "how *dare* something exist you can't twist to use for your own selfish needs."

The sorcerer lifted an eyebrow, then waved his hand. "Carrick, he's all yours."

"What?" Panic crawled up Regulus' spine. "I answered your questions! I won't beg for myself, but for Adelaide? Please. Don't." He desperately looked at Carrick. "I'm begging you. Don't hurt her."

"Actually," the sorcerer said, "what I want more than anything right now is to hurt your precious mage for making a mess of all my plans. I'd do it myself, but I'm tired, and need to rest and think so I can figure out where to find my stupid brother."

Regulus clenched his fists in a useless gesture of defiance. "But—"

"Carrick, don't cut any appendages off, especially not his head." The sorcerer sounded bored. "Other than that, go ahead and let all that rage and resentment that's been making you insufferable out on him." The sorcerer started back toward the fire, then paused. "And for the love of sorcery, gag him so I don't have to listen to his screams and protestations."

"I answered your questions!" The chains dug into Regulus' chest as he strained against them. "No, you can't—I answered your questions!"

Carrick pulled off his blood-stained doublet and cut a long, thick strip, paying no attention to Regulus.

He switched tactics. "Carrick, you have to realize this won't help you win her. She won't forgive you."

Carrick shoved the fabric into Regulus' mouth and tied it behind his head. "I'm not trying to win her heart anymore, mercenary. She doesn't want me, and she likely never will. She won't forgive me, anyway." Uncertainty flickered over his expression. "Not after I killed her father."

Regulus stopped straining against the chains. Her father… His eyes bulged. Alfred Belanger was…dead? Carrick killed him? *Oh, Adelaide.*

"He got in my way." Carrick shrugged, but from the tone of his voice and the pinch of his brows, he was troubled. "I'd kill you, too, but apparently I'm not allowed." He shifted over to Regulus' right arm. "I had hoped once you were dead, she would be free to want me. But I see now…" He dug the dagger into Regulus' forearm and began cutting around the mark. Regulus screamed into the gag. "She's given her heart too completely to you for it to ever be mine. She could have had my love. Now she will know my vengeance."

Carrick pried the chunk of flesh bearing Adelaide's mark, the mark of a lover's bond, out of his arm. Regulus sagged against the tree, black spots clouding his vision. Bile rose in his mouth but had nowhere to go against the gag, so he swallowed it back down. He closed his eyes and bit down hard on the gag.

Numbing warmth spread over his forearm until the pain faded away. Still, tears soaked into the gag pulling at the sides of his mouth. He let his head fall forward and leaned in exhaustion against the chains. Carrick rubbed at his arm, and Regulus opened his eyes as Carrick pulled his hand away. On his arm, beneath the smeared red, Adelaide's mark stood out as clear as ever.

"Hm. Unsurprising, but disappointing." Carrick flicked a spray of blood off the dagger. "I want to be clear, though." He used the dagger to lift Regulus' chin, forcing him to look at Carrick's face. "I've admitted I can't force her love. But I will still have her. I've never been one to walk away. My parents said my reckless, bull-headed determination was cute when I was a child, but is…what was it? Boorish now. But then, I was always their least favorite son." He turned the dagger so the edge sliced into the underside of Regulus' chin. "I don't like losing. Adelaide will be my wife, even if I have to keep her collared and chained."

Regulus pushed his tongue against the gag, trying to force it out of the way so he could tell Carrick off. His face burned from his neck to his scalp. He pulled at the chains, willing them to break even as the shackles cut into his wrists and the effort pulled at his shoulders. He kept his eyes locked on Carrick's and hoped Carrick could see his rage.

"I never liked you, mercenary. A peasant masquerading as a lord." Carrick lowered the dagger. "But trust me, at this point, I hate you as much as you hate me." He stabbed the dagger into Regulus' thigh. Regulus grimaced, then groaned as Carrick dragged the dagger down several inches. "Maybe His Highness will let me keep you. If Adelaide misbehaves, I can just hurt you." He twisted the dagger. Regulus shook as he bit back a scream. "Knowing that her bad behavior will spill your blood and cause you both pain might help keep her docile." He pulled the dagger out of Regulus' leg with a sickening squelch. "Should help with holding her to her promise."

Promise? Regulus raised his eyes from his leg to Carrick.

Carrick laughed. "Oh, she didn't tell you? Before you came barreling in and nearly got yourself killed, she promised me that once she and I are married—and we will be—she will be, and I quote, 'a dutiful, affectionate wife.'" He sneered.

Regulus felt like he had been punched in the gut. Was that the only reason Carrick had stopped that day? He pulled at the chains, his muscles bulging. He pictured his hands closing around Carrick's neck. The chain made a squeaking groan as it pulled against the tree. But it wouldn't break. There was no point, so he stopped struggling and sagged against the chains, his head hanging as guilt crushed him.

"That's right." Carrick examined the blood-soaked tip of the dagger. "Be a good mongrel dog and accept your leash."

ADELAIDE GRIPPED Dresden's arm, steadying herself as she nearly fell over in the middle of the entrance to the guards' courtyard from the pain in her leg. There had been a short window without pain—meaning Regulus wasn't in pain. She had changed her dress during that window, then headed to the barracks to ask Beale if he had heard anything about where the sorcerer might have gone. But getting there was proving difficult. Every wound inflicted on Regulus not only caused her pain but drained some of her energy to heal him. The pain in her leg faded. She let go of Dresden's arm and straightened.

"Why are they doing this?" Her voice trembled.

Dresden shook his head, his eyes pinched. "Maybe to see how much he can take. Or to keep you weak. Maybe just for the fun of it."

Her stomach clenched. She could see Nolan hurting Regulus just to hurt him. But surely Regulus would have told him that it hurt her, too. She remembered Nolan kicking her face and shattering her nose. And then he killed her father. Clearly, he didn't care about not hurting her. At least there was a twisted upside to that. Maybe it meant he didn't want her anymore. But, no. She recalled the glint in his eyes as his hand slid up her leg. He simply no longer cared if she wanted him.

They had only gotten a few yards into the courtyard when she grabbed her throat. *Can't...breathe...* Stabbed. They had stabbed Regulus in the throat. Dresden wrapped his arm under hers, supporting her. A tear slid down her cheek as she dropped her hands from her throat.

"The pain is that bad?"

"It does hurt. But not as much as it's hurting him. And that's worse than the actual pain." She pulled away and ran across the courtyard. "I have to find him!" She clenched her teeth and tried to ignore the stab of pain in her left hand.

She threw open the door to the barracks. Beale and Antar sat in the briefing room. They looked up as she entered, stopping mid-conversation.

"Has any information come in about where the sorcerer might be?"

Beale shook his head. "No, but that's not—"

"*Someone* had to have seen something!" She stomped her foot. "Someone must know—" She gasped and clutched her stomach as something prodded, pinched, and twisted. She grimaced against the pain, against the knowledge of what was happening.

"Are you okay?" Beale stood and reached toward her.

She held up her hand and he stopped. "I'm fine," she said through gritted teeth. "It's Regulus. We have this bond. I can feel—" She leaned against the doorframe as pain sliced down her bicep. "His pain. They're torturing him."

Beale and Antar exchanged a look. "I don't understand," Antar said. "Why don't they just kill him?"

"They can't." She had forgotten they had never explained Regulus' abilities to the officers, only to the king. "The bond. It constantly heals him so he can't be killed."

"He…what?" Beale shook his head. "That's impossible."

"How're you feeling, Lieutenant Antar?" She looked pointedly at his leg.

Antar flushed. "Tired, but otherwise fine. Thank you. I should have said that already."

"You're welcome, but that's not my point. My point is, why should it be impossible?" She pushed off the doorframe. "Now, I *have* to find Kirven and Regulus. This torture is a constant drain on my power. The longer they hurt him, the less energy I'll have to fight Kirven." *And the more pain Regulus will experience. And me.* Something stabbed between her ribs. She groaned and grabbed the spot.

"She feels only a fraction of his pain," Dresden said behind her, his voice tight. "If she's in this much pain, Regulus is…" He gulped. "He needs help."

Beale shook his head. "I'm sorry, Belanger. My orders are to send you to the king, not out looking for the sorcerer."

"Fine." She straightened. "I'll find them without your help." She turned and nearly ran into Dresden standing in the doorway.

"Belanger." The tone of Beale's voice stopped her. "If you leave now, it won't just be abandoning your post. It'll be counted as desertion. You'll be hanged."

She hesitated. An invisible blade sliced across her jaw. *This can't continue! Kirven, Nolan, whoever is doing this, they have to get tired of it, right?* She whimpered as pain dug deep into the front of her shoulder, just above her armpit, and twisted back and forth. Dresden grabbed her shoulders as her eyes watered and she moaned. The knife or whatever it was dragged out of Regulus and she felt her power healing him as the pain abated. She squared her shoulders. Without looking back at Beale, she said, "So be it," and pushed past Dresden out of the room.

They were only a few feet from the barracks when Beale's voice rang over the courtyard. "Adelaide Belanger, you are under arrest for desertion, a crime of treason against the king. Men, seize her."

She stopped mid-stride. The dozen or so men around the courtyard looked over. No one moved. Adelaide grabbed Dresden's hand and sprinted toward the gate. Beale shouted at the men, and they drew their weapons and started after them.

"Stay back!" Adelaide threw an arc of fire behind her as she ran. The guards slowed but didn't stop. They were almost to the gate when two men stepped in front of them, their faces white. With a wave of her hand, she blasted them out of their path. Their pursuers were all behind them now. She blindly threw a blast of energy behind her and heard a couple men grunt. They ran through the gate and she skidded to a stop and whirled around. She raised her hand, and a shimmering blue barrier filled the open gate. The closest guard tapped the barrier with his sword. A burst of energy pushed him back.

"Let's go." She strode away from the barricaded gate, her jaw set.

Dresden hurried after her. "Do you have a plan?"

"Get out of the palace. Find Regulus." She turned toward the livestock gate, the closest exit, and dodged a servant boy leading an obstinate goat. "Kill Kirven and Nolan."

"Remind me never to let you and Regulus plan anything alone," Dresden said. "He's a great fighter, a firm but understanding captain, and an inspiring leader, but his plans usually need some help to be actual *plans*."

"I'll figure it out." She strode toward the gate and ignored the shouting voice in her head agreeing with Dresden, telling her she was making the same mistake they had made before the masquerade. The guard on duty glanced between them.

"Um, no one told me—"

She cut him off, conjuring a ball of flames above her right hand. "Unlock the door."

The guard paled. "I…I can't without orders—"

"Then give me the keys and I'll do it." The flames flared larger and hotter.

"I really wouldn't try her if I were you," Dresden said, a flicker of amusement in his voice. "The love of her life has been taken and she's on the war path."

The guard backed toward the gate. "I'll be thrown in the stocks."

Adelaide groaned. She dropped the flames and shoved her hands forward. The blast pushed the guard back and up against the gate with a crash. He slumped to the ground, unconscious. She pulled the keys off his belt and opened the lock holding the crossbeam in place. She pushed the gate open and tossed the keys on the guard's chest before striding out of the palace. Once they were well away from the palace walls, she stopped. She needed a direction. Walking with no destination would waste precious time. And every minute she wasted was another minute that Regulus—

Wait. She stared at Dresden.

"They stopped."

"What?" Dresden looked around the narrow, shadowy alleyway between two tall wooden buildings. His hand gripped his sword as he watched the townspeople walk by the opening of the alley, busy with their lives and their shopping as if their king wasn't on the run. "Who—wait. The pain? It stopped?"

"Yes. What does that mean?" She should have been relieved, but irrational fear clawed at her mind. They couldn't have found a way to kill him—could they? No. No, she wouldn't lose Father and Regulus. She couldn't.

"It means he's okay for the moment," he said, his voice calm. "Now, we need a plan. We can't just wander around, hoping to stumble across them before the guards find us." He stroked his beard. "If they're torturing him, they're unlikely to be in town. Even with a gag, that would make a lot of noise and draw too much attention. If the sorcerer was worn out from your fight, they wouldn't have gone terribly far. He must have needed to regain his energy, just like you did, which is probably why they didn't start on Regulus until this morning."

He spoke so matter-of-fact. It reminded her of the way she once heard Father and some of his friends discussing how to find and corner a hobgoblin that had been causing havoc in the gardens. Methodical, dispassionate. But this was *Regulus* being tortured he was talking about.

"They'd likely want to stay close enough to town that they could sneak in and listen for gossip on where the king is," Dresden continued. "But they wouldn't want to be too close to the palace in case of search parties while they're recovering and getting whatever it is they want from Regulus."

She leaned against one of the buildings. The rough wood snagged on her dress, but she didn't care. "How are you so calm?"

"I'm not calm!" Dresden slammed his palm into the wall. "I'm trying to be *controlled.* Controlled keeps you from making stupid decisions and wasting time or getting killed. Regulus might not be great at coming up with plans, but he never meets the enemy on their ground without stopping to think. You know how many mercenary troops had as high a success and survival rate as ours? Not many. Because he never made a move without sending out scouts. He never broke camp until he had consulted with his lieutenants. He tried to avoid going in somewhere when he didn't have a way out." He sighed. "Until the sorcerer. He gave up and got reckless after that. It's part of why he would never let us go with him. But that's irrelevant."

Adelaide looked up at the sliver of blue sky peeking through the narrow space between the wide top floors of the buildings. Some kids ran past the alleyway, laughing as adults shouted at them. She massaged her forehead. "All right. Do you have an idea?"

"Just…give me a minute to think!"

She closed her eyes and leaned her head back against the building. *Where are you, Regulus? Where would they take you?* His face filled her mind. His intense gray eyes. His lopsided smile from the pull of his scar. The gentleness in his strong hands as he held her. She needed his strength right now. The way she felt protected when curled against his side. *I need you, Regulus. Where are you? Please, Etiros. I need to find him.* Something tugged at her gut. A gentle current, almost like the pull of the neumenet tree, but different. Her eyes flew open.

"Dresden." She stepped into the alley, heading toward the back of the buildings. The pull grew, and she knew in her heart. "I can find him."

Adelaide raced through the twisting streets of the town. A couple times she had to back up and retrace her steps when the pull shifted, and she realized she had missed a turn. Dresden tried to tell her to slow down, that they should form a plan, but the thrum of energy leading her toward Regulus overpowered his protests. *I'm coming, Regulus. I'm coming.*

They left the town behind. Farmers watched in confusion and irritation as they cut across fields and leapt over low stone walls. But for whatever reason— perhaps their clothes marked them as nobles, or the farmers thought with sorcerers on the loose it was better to ignore strangers—no one tried to stop them. The air cooled and smelled of salty sea air. The pull of their bond strengthened, but she forced her feet to slow.

"We're getting close," she said.

Dresden grabbed her arm, forcing her to stop. "How close do you think we are?"

She tugged on her hair. "It's difficult to explain, and it's inexact. I know he's that way," she pointed toward the trees on the other side of an apple orchard just ahead of them. "I don't know how much past the orchard. Could be a couple feet. Could be ten paces."

Dresden pinched the bridge of his nose. "Okay. We need to go slowly. I want to rush in, too, but our best bet is to surprise them, and to do that, they can't hear or see us coming." He pointed to the hedge circling the orchard. "We should keep to the outside of the hedge, stay low, instead of cutting across the orchard. If we can, we need to get Regulus *before* confronting the sorcerer and Carrick. That will make our chances better and prevent the possibility of them hurting Regulus and making you both useless."

His bluntness made her wince, but she nodded. "Once Regulus is free, we need to prioritize Kirven. So long as he's alive, we can't kill Nolan. And the best way of stopping Kirven is to get his staff."

"Good thinking." Dresden sighed. "That will have to do. There are too many variables with all this magic involved. No point in making a plan that might fall apart."

They crept along the outside edge of the hedge at a maddeningly slow pace. They were so close to Regulus it made her skin tingle. But that also meant they were close to Kirven and Nolan. And that made her stomach churn, which reminded her she hadn't eaten breakfast. The gnawing in her stomach added to her nervous energy as they darted across the empty space between the hedge and the trees, as quickly and quietly as possible. She led the way toward Regulus through the trees. She wanted to hurry but forced herself to move slowly, watching the ground to avoid any dead leaves that looked crunchy or sticks that might snap and give their approach away.

"—honestly, I should be torturing *you* for letting Gawain escape!" Kirven spat. Adelaide dropped into a crouch and moved away from his voice and closer to where she sensed Regulus.

"Then get it over with," Nolan said. Adelaide's breath caught as grief and anger slammed into her at the sound of his voice. "You're the one who said you could easily take care of Adelaide if she was there. Besides, if you had taken your shot faster, she wouldn't have had time to raise that barrier." Nolan groaned. *You deserve that and more*, Adelaide thought as she edged toward an opening in the trees.

"And if we had just killed her, she definitely wouldn't have been able to." Nolan grunted. "Not the agreement."

"If she gets in my way again, I'm killing her," Kirven said, his words heated.

Adelaide and Dresden crouched behind a couple of trees. Regulus sat chained to an oak tree that looked like it had been through a fire. His head rested against the black tree trunk. A blue gag pulled against his mouth and his eyes were closed. Dried blood stained his right arm and the chains binding it and covered his legs, his neck, his torso, even his face. She leaned against the tree, light-headedness making her vision black out until her head cleared. Oddly, the Staff of Nightfall lay in the grass at Regulus' feet. Kirven sat several paces away, his back toward them. But Nolan stood across from Kirven. If they left the cover of the trees, he would see them.

"Didn't you already try that at the palace?" Nolan clenched and unclenched his fist, his face red. "You couldn't even manage it then. And we should have taken *her*. What was the point of taking Hargreaves? You made a mistake—" Nolan screamed and doubled over. Adelaide ran out of the trees, Dresden close on her heels. She slid across the grass to the side of the oak furthest from Kirven and Nolan. The air reeked of Regulus' blood.

Chains. How to break chains? Fire? No. Cut through them with a magic blade? It might work. She looked at the chains around Regulus' chest, then at the shackles around his wrists. Which should she try to remove first? Both needed to come off, but the moment they did, they would make noise. Nolan had stopped screaming. She risked leaning out around the tree. Nolan stomped away from Kirven, his back to them. Good. The Staff of Nightfall lay on the grass, so close. Staff first, or Regulus first? Regulus first.

She moved closer to Regulus and touched his shoulder. His eyes snapped open, full of silent pleas for mercy that made her heart bleed. He relaxed when his eyes met hers, the terror in his expression replaced with joy. She smiled and held a finger to her lips, then untied the gag. He moved his jaw as she dropped the rag to the ground. She leaned close and murmured in his ear, "I thought we agreed no more splitting up."

"I'm glad to see you," he whispered, "but you shouldn't have come."

"You would have come for me." She pressed her hand to the side of his face, against the blood caked over his jawline. "Together, remember?"

He glanced toward Kirven and Carrick. "Alright, but we need to hurry."

"Hey." Dresden crouched next to her. His face tinged with green as he looked at Regulus, but he shook his head and looked in control again. Regulus looked exceedingly displeased to see Dresden. "Isn't that the staff? Should we take it?"

"What are you doing here?" Regulus hissed. "This is magic and immortals. They could kill you."

Oh. She hadn't even stopped to think of that when Dresden followed her. She had been too focused on Regulus. Too focused on herself.

Dresden grinned, but it was full of sorrow and pain. "Somebody had to watch your girl's back with you off getting captured."

An idea occurred to Adelaide. She had no idea how to break the staff, or if she even possessed the power to do so. But they could at least ensure Kirven didn't have a chance to use it against them—and keep Dresden safe. "Dresden, you should take the staff and run." She glanced toward Kirven and Nolan. They still weren't looking. She kept her voice low. "Take it far from here."

"It's a good idea." Despite his hushed tone, Regulus' words held urgency.

Dresden shook his head. "And leave you two?"

She placed a hand on Dresden's arm. "I can't lose anyone else."

"I won't abandon my brother," Dresden whispered fiercely.

"Look at me." Weariness laced Regulus' voice. "I won't let this happen to you. I can't let Carrick hurt you again."

Again. Adelaide recalled Nolan's taunt. *"Did he tell you those stripes were for you?"* Her hands fisted.

"Please, Drez. I need to know you're safe."

"And I need you safe," Dresden shot back. "We protect each other, remember?"

Adelaide sighed. "Regulus can't die. I can defend myself from Kirven's magic, and Nolan won't kill me. You have to go."

"I can help," Dresden pleaded. "Reg, you know I can—"

"Drez..." Regulus rested his head against the tree. "Don't make me order you."

Dresden's expression turned stony. "Please don't do this."

Adelaide looked helplessly between them and glanced toward Kirven and Nolan. They were still turned away from the tree, but it was only a matter of time.

"Sir Jakobs." Regulus looked apologetic as he locked eyes with Dresden. "As your liege, I command you to take the staff and flee immediately, and don't come back." He hung his head. "As your brother, I'm begging you. Please go."

Dresden worked his jaw. "Fine. I'll find you when you return to the palace." With one more glance at Kirven and Nolan, Dresden grabbed the staff and ran.

Good. She watched Dresden disappear among the trees, taking the Staff of Nightfall where Kirven couldn't reach, then turned back to Regulus. "Can you grab the chains on your arms, so they won't fall when I unlock them?"

In response, Regulus gripped the chains. *How…maybe like closing a wound, but opposite?* She held her hand over the shackle on his left wrist and closed her eyes, but couldn't sense the lock. She detected Regulus and the blood pumping in his veins. *No.* She knit her brows together, concentrating. This wouldn't work. She needed… *Key.*

Such an obvious answer. She conjured a rough key shape and inserted it into the lock. At last, she sensed the inside of the lock, and she morphed the key until it fit, then turned it. The shackle made a click that sounded terribly loud to her ears. She glanced toward Kirven and Nolan, but they still weren't looking. She moved to his other side, closer to Kirven. *Okay, focus. Form the key, shape it…* The lock clicked and she smiled.

"I hoped you'd show up, mage."

CHAPTER 40

T HE SOUND of Kirven's calm voice slithered down Adelaide's spine. She whirled around and stood, shielding Regulus. Kirven moved toward her, a self-assured smile on his face. Carrick followed, his sword drawn. The clink of metal indicated Regulus had released the chain on his arms.

"I'm glad you're here, Adelaide." Kirven nodded. "We can have a nice talk."

"I'm not here to talk." She conjured a sword and hoped she looked intimidating. Nolan eyed them both but didn't attack. Probably waiting on an order from his master. "Where's your staff, Kirven?"

Kirven frowned, then looked down. His head jerked back up. "What did you do with it?"

"It's long gone. A friend took it; I don't know where. He might have thrown it into the sea for all I know."

Kirven's eyes flashed. He clenched his fists, his shoulders scrunching toward his ears. He relaxed and his expression returned to bored neutrality. "You're protecting him with your life when that's not necessary. Standing over him, placing yourself in harm's way, when he can't die because you already protected him with your bond."

When he said it like that, it did sound stupid. She *could* die. "I won't let you hurt him anymore." She looked at Nolan. At the blood staining the ends of his sleeves and splattered on his shirt, trousers, and boots. Regulus' blood. Guards' blood. Father's blood. Anger and sorrow kicked at the inside of her chest, a caged and wounded animal that wanted out.

"Why?" Her voice broke. She hadn't meant to say that. It just came out.

Nolan's cocky, unconcerned façade cracked. For a moment, she saw regret in his eyes. Then it was gone. "I'm sorry. He shouldn't have gotten in my way."

His careless words hit her like fists. Her emotions built, threatening to crush her. Adelaide willed back her tears. *No. Not now. You can't fall apart right now.* She saw the green light out of the corner of her eye too late. She'd been too focused on Nolan and her hurt to stay on guard. The blast knocked her sideways, throwing her several feet from Regulus and the tree. She grunted as she hit the ground. *Stupid!*

Nolan held his sword to Regulus' neck. Regulus glared up at Nolan but didn't try to move. Cautiously, Adelaide walked closer, her hands at her sides as Kirven watched her with an impassive expression.

"Ready to talk?" Kirven stroked his beard. "Or should I have Carrick find out if your precious Hargreaves can regrow limbs?" Nolan stepped on Regulus' right hand and held the sword at his wrist.

"No!" Adelaide held up her hands submissively. "I'll talk."

"You owe me, mage." Kirven crossed his arms. "Your lover's bond caused my spell to rebound and cracked the opal in the Staff of Nightfall. I could, with some effort, replace the opal. But I fear the damage runs deeper than that. Your friend may have taken the staff, but it was already useless to me. You owe me a replacement weapon."

"I can double-check under my bed, but I don't think I have another staff imbued with sorcery lying around."

Kirven rolled his eyes. "I had something else in mind." The look in his eyes, the sly half-smile, and she knew. A lump grew in her chest. "You."

She swallowed. "I've already given you my answer."

"Carrick, remind her what's at stake—but nothing that might not heal yet."

"No, wait—" She reached toward Nolan and Regulus, but Nolan jabbed the sword into Regulus' side. Regulus groaned and Adelaide stumbled forward, grabbing at her own side and biting her tongue against the pain. Nolan pulled the sword further down into Regulus' hip. Adelaide moaned and fell to her knees as Regulus screamed.

"Stop!" She struggled to stand. Nolan withdrew the sword. Regulus' blood dripped off the blade and she turned her face away.

"You took my greatest weapon from me," Kirven said. "One I worked for nearly twenty years to find and reassemble. You owe me a new weapon."

Energy drained out of her to heal Regulus. A new thought occurred to her. The warning in the *Compendium*: *"drained of magic until they perished."* Might she reach a point she couldn't heal Regulus, even with the bond? Would Regulus die if they kept this up? Would *she* die? She needed to find a way to stop them, and soon.

Adelaide shoved her hands toward Nolan. A blast sent him flying. She ran toward Regulus, but Kirven put up a green-tinted barrier between them. *Fine.* She conjured a sword and turned toward the tree. With all the strength she could gather, she brought the sword down on the chains. *Please, work.* The glowing sword of magical energy carved deep through the chains and the blackened trunk. With a clatter, the chains fell to the ground. Regulus leapt to his feet and lunged at Kirven as Adelaide ran around the barrier.

Nolan intercepted Regulus before he could reach Kirven. His blade protruded from Regulus' back, glistening crimson in the sun. Pain tore through her body. Regulus bent forward, and Nolan's stone-hard face appeared over his shoulder. It was too much. The pain, the sight of Regulus impaled on Nolan's sword. The fact it felt like watching a repeat of Nolan killing Father.

Adelaide fell to her hands and knees and dry heaved, her stomach clenching. Nolan tossed Regulus down next to her. The retching stopped, but her entire body trembled, and tears wet her face. Her energy drained further as Regulus healed. Her fists closed around grass. Dirt rolled under her fingernails. This had to stop. She couldn't take much more. She raised her head.

Kirven cocked an eyebrow. "Have you figured it out yet?" She nodded.

Regulus grunted as he sat up next to her. "Figured what out?" He rested a hand on her back. His touch comforted her despite her hopelessness.

"Tell him." Kirven jutted his chin toward Regulus.

"Tell me what?" Regulus gently pulled her up until she sat back on her heels.

The realization of Kirven's plan made her heart twist with guilt. She met Regulus' eyes. His anger melted, replaced with concern. She took a shaky breath and tried to force her hands to stop trembling. "I'm running out of energy…out of magic. To—to heal you."

Regulus' face went slack. "What does that mean?"

"You really are dense," Kirven cut in. "Magic, like energy, gets used. You run, you have to rest. You use magic for any reason, you have to rest. Hargreaves, you get hurt, your bond heals you by stealing magical energy from Belanger. With no time to rest, she'll run out. And when she does…" He smiled maliciously. "One of three things will happen. One, the bond will break, and Hargreaves will die. Two, the bond will leach off Belanger's own life until she dies. Or three"—he shrugged—"you'll both die."

Her headache returned, and she closed her eyes against the throbbing behind her forehead. Regulus grabbed her hand. She felt his confusion, his fear. Then his sadness. His guilt. There had to be a way to win. If she could just get them to leave Regulus alone long enough to defeat Kirven, then maybe they would stand a chance.

"There is another option, though," Kirven said.

Adelaide opened her eyes. She wouldn't do it. She'd die before she served him again. And she knew Regulus would, too.

"You don't have to run out of energy." Kirven held his hand toward the closest tree, a birch sapling a few feet away. Green tendrils of light stretched from his hand to the tree. The leaves curled in on themselves and blackened. Black veins crawled up the tree trunk and spread until it was totally black. Still Kirven didn't lower his hand. The tree shuddered, and its leaves all fell off at once with a soft whoosh. The bark disintegrated, leaving behind wood as white and dry as old bones. Kirven lowered his hand. He took a deep breath that swelled his chest. "Ah…" He smiled. "That's a bit better."

She stared at the tree. She could sense Regulus' disgust. That…was wrong. Kirven didn't just use the tree, like cutting down a tree for a building. He…consumed it. His sorcery reached into the tree and sucked its life, its energy, right out. Just like the fairies had tried to trick her into doing at the neumenet tree. Just like he had done to the forest surrounding his tower. Just like he had done to *her*.

"Try it," Kirven coaxed. "You'll like it."

"No."

"Tens of thousands of people in Monparth," Kirven muttered, "and I had to find a mage with a conscience." He held out his hand and glowing green ropes snaked over the ground. She conjured a domed barrier over herself and Regulus.

"Adelaide." Regulus' voice was heavy. "Is that true?"

She plucked blades of grass. "I don't know. But I know I'm tired. And it gets more exhausting every time you're hurt."

"Oh, Ad." She felt his wish through their connection as he guided her hand to the blood-covered mark on his arm. "You have to remove it."

"This is my choice." Adelaide pulled her hand off Regulus' arm and cradled his face in her hands. "Forever. That's what I asked you. Did you want to be bound to me forever, and you said yes. I'm yours, and you're mine. Is that still true?"

His heartbreak rushed through her. "Of course it is."

She pressed her lips to his. "Then stop asking me to do what I cannot."

"You can't stay in there forever, you know," Kirven said as he and Nolan circled the dome in opposite directions, hunters on the prowl. "You might as well give up now."

Regulus brushed his fingers through her hair. "I'm ready to fight when you are."

"Fighting isn't worth it," Kirven said. "You'll lose."

"What you fail to realize," Regulus said, his gaze never leaving hers, "is that we will die before we serve you." She smiled sadly. *Together. Love conquers fear.*

Kirven made a sound like a growl. "What you fail to realize is I won't stop at killing you. You think your family and friends will be safe when you're dead? You think just because I can't make you watch I won't still enjoy torturing them for all the trouble you've caused me?"

Adelaide released Regulus' face as her hands went cold. Fear tore up her insides. She dropped the barrier.

REGULUS STARED at Adelaide. She couldn't be giving up. She wouldn't… But then, he had seen her nightmares. "What are you doing?"

Adelaide slowly stood and faced the sorcerer. "I make you a counter-offer."

The sorcerer stroked his beard. "Speak quickly."

"You think your sorcery makes you so strong. Then fight me—fair and square. No hurting Regulus to hurt me. No help from Nolan." Regulus stood and grabbed her hand. She pulled it away, but not before he sensed her determination. "Chain Nolan and Regulus up and have a fair fight."

The sorcerer laughed, but it was sharp and angry. "Why would I do that?"

"You defeated me before, but you were cheating, using the staff. You've already cheated today." She held her hands out to her sides. "I'm tired and weakened. So what are you afraid of? Do you think my magic is stronger than your sorcery?"

"Of course not! And it's not cheating to use every tool at your disposal. Why would I waste energy when I can just continue to torture your mercenary lover until you break?"

Regulus flinched. *Please, no!* But a warning bell went off in his mind. She wouldn't. He had to be wrong, she—

"Because if you win and I survive, I'll serve you," Adelaide said quietly.

"Adelaide!" Regulus turned her toward him. "Absolutely not." He would rather Carrick cut him to pieces than Adelaide enslave herself. Ideally, though, the bond would break and let him die first. He understood why she wouldn't remove it, but he wished she would. He was tired of the pain.

Sorrow made Adelaide's eyes look dull and lifeless. "My father is…dead." She swallowed. His heart clenched at the brokenness in her voice. "I can't let any more of my family die because of me." She turned back to the sorcerer, leaving a hollow ache in Regulus' chest.

"But if you win," Adelaide said, "whether I live or die, you have to promise no harm—no pain, no capture, no killing—will come to my family or Regulus' men." Carrick snorted.

The sorcerer raised a brow. "And if you win?"

"I'll kill you."

Adelaide and the sorcerer glared ice daggers at each other. Regulus eyed the distance between himself and the sorcerer and tried to judge how far behind him Carrick stood without looking. He could still remember the feel of Carrick's blade through his heart. The excruciating feeling of dying without the release of death. Until Adelaide's magic had eased the pain. Until he had stolen her magic, weakening her.

It wasn't fair. If Regulus could just reach the sorcerer, maybe he could break the monster's neck. But if either the sorcerer or Carrick attacked him first, all he would accomplish was weakening Adelaide further. Despair pressed against his lungs. No. He wouldn't give up; not on Adelaide.

The sorcerer fiddled with his belt. "You know what you're agreeing to, if you lose and don't die?"

"I'll accept the mark." Adelaide's shoulders slumped.

No. Regulus wanted to say they should take their chances fighting together, fight until death if need be. But if they lost, her family would suffer. Dresden and the rest of his men would suffer. *Etiros, help us!*

"You realize I'll marry you off to Carrick," the sorcerer continued. "You're too annoying and wearisome to have around all the time. Besides, in a moment of shortsightedness, I technically did promise he could have you."

Regulus bristled. "You can't force her to marry him!"

"What about the mercenary?"

"Let him go."

The sorcerer scoffed. "Unacceptable."

"If you lose, he dies," Carrick said, as if he thought he were the one giving orders.

Relief surged in Regulus. *I'd be free at least. No more pain. No watching Adelaide suffer and be corrupted by sorcery. Please. Kill me.* He shook his head to dislodge the invasive thought. He would never abandon her.

Adelaide gulped. "A compromise. If I die, you can kill him—only him, no one else. But if I lose but live, I'll remove the bond. Then you let him go."

"Hm." The sorcerer looked past her to Carrick. Regulus looked back at Carrick, not bothering to hide his rage—or his heartbreak.

Carrick glowered. "Fine. I can live with that."

Regulus was about to protest when Adelaide grabbed his hand. Her fear slammed into him. She would sacrifice herself with the hope she protected everyone else. But hope simmered under her desperation. She wanted to win and believed she had a chance. She was just preparing for the worst. It was a daring plan. The plan of a tigress. He squeezed her hand, and hoped she felt his admiration and belief she could win, and not just his fear. But he hated this plan didn't include him.

"I'm supposed to fight for you. I'm supposed to protect *you*."

"We're supposed to fight for each other." Her fingertips lifted his chin. "And you already have fought for me and protected me. When you came for me after we separated. When you nearly died for me. When you came to my aid in the palace. And every time you pulled me out of a nightmare. Every time you didn't let me feel alone. You fought for me. It's my turn to fight for you." Her thumb rubbed his chin, flaking off bits of dried blood. "You've fought enough today, Regulus."

The surge of affection and gratitude from her wasn't enough to erase his anguish. Her fingers left his chin as she turned back to the sorcerer. Regulus' chin drifted downward.

"Do we have an agreement?" She held out her hand.

After a moment, the sorcerer took her hand. "We do."

The cold metal of the shackle pressed against Regulus' wrist as Adelaide closed it, her jaw clenched and apology in her eyes. He sat against the oak tree again. She wrapped the chain a few times around his forearm, then pulled back and chained his other hand. On the opposite side of the fire, Kirven used the other chain—which he had melded back together—to bind Carrick to a tree.

"I'm going to win," she said softly.

"I know you are." Regulus smiled. "You're a mage and a tigress. You can do anything."

She smiled, but her eyes were sad and harbored the same doubts he felt. "I love you."

"And I love you. After you win, I'm going to spend the rest of my life showing you just how much." She laughed, but it ended in a sob. "I believe in you, Adelaide."

Adelaide gripped his face and kissed him. Her tears wet his face. Regulus knew he was covered in blood and disgusting, but that thought faded as he kissed her. The chains held his hands back, preventing him from holding her like he longed to. He tried to push all other thoughts away and just be here, with her, alone in this moment. But tears slipped down his cheeks anyway, because he couldn't stop the thought—this might be the last time he kissed her.

"If you're quite done," the sorcerer said brusquely, "I have a fight to win."

Adelaide's mouth left his far too soon.

"Adelaide…"

She didn't meet his eyes as she stood and turned away.

Adelaide's insides felt scrambled, as if they had been rearranged and turned inside out. But she squared her shoulders and faced Kirven anyway, the memory of Regulus' kiss soothing some of the ache in her heart. *"Love,"* Father's voice echoed in her mind. *I'm not losing anyone else today.*

"I'd like to check you put those on properly." Kirven strode past.

"Fine. Then I'm checking you didn't cheat with Nolan's."

"Certainly." Kirven reached down to check the shackles on Regulus' wrists. She ground her teeth and stomped over to Nolan.

Nolan had stuck his sword in the ground a couple feet in front of him, and the sight of it tied her stomach in knots. Seemingly oblivious to her revulsion, he smiled.

"Comfortable?" she snapped. "I hope not."

"Not particularly." His smile took on a wolfish quality. "But it's not bad when I think about how comfortable I'll be tonight with you in my arms."

She shuddered as ice slid through her veins. *Focus. Only the fight matters.* She walked around the tree, tugging on the chain in various spots, then stopped in front of him again. The chain looped around him bound his arms against his sides. He shouldn't be able to move or break free. Hopefully.

"You killed my father." She stared at Nolan's hairline, unable to look in his eyes. "The thought of you touching me should be enough motivation to ensure I either win or don't survive this fight."

"Ouch." His voice softened. "I am sorry, Adelaide. I was focused on getting to the king. I didn't even realize it was your father until it was too late."

"Likely story."

"It's the truth."

She pressed the heel of her palm to her forehead. "If—when I win, I'm going to kill you."

"Love, I truly am sorry about your father." Carrick offered the sincerest expression of sorrow. Ever the convincing actor. "I didn't want to kill him. I had orders, kill anyone who got in my way. You know what happens if I disobey Kirven. I wasn't paying attention to who I was fighting. I wish he hadn't been there. Honest. I never wanted your family hurt. I wish I could change it."

Adelaide's chest tightened as her throat constricted. "Liar. You didn't kill the other guards."

"Hm, must have thought I did."

"You…" No. There was no time to force him to admit he was lying. She needed to forget about Nolan and the pain of Father's death and focus on winning this fight. And failing that, figure out how to make sure she died.

"Adelaide, love—"

"Don't call me that!" She clenched her hands and forced herself to meet his eyes. "I wish killing you would rid me of the memory of you. But at least you'll be dead."

"Oh, Adelaide." Nolan rested his head against the tree and stared up at the branches, like he hadn't a care in the world. "I admire your confidence. But I'm not going to die, because you're not going to win. And when you lose, you're going to marry me." He leered. "And then you're going to keep your promise."

She flushed and turned away, trembling so hard she feared she would start retching again. *Not now. Focus.*

"Don't worry, love." Nolan's honeyed tone was like sweets on an upset stomach. "I'll be gentle."

You don't know the meaning of the word. Adelaide straightened. She wouldn't cower before Father's killer. With her head held high, Adelaide strode back toward Kirven, who stood waiting for her halfway between Regulus and Nolan. Halfway between the man she loved and the man she loathed. Between the future she wanted and the future she dreaded. She looked at Regulus. She would focus on the future she wanted to give her strength to make it through this fight. Because if she thought about Nolan…she swallowed back the hopelessness that tried to drag her to the ground.

"You look tired." Kirven looked her up and down. "You should surrender now and save yourself the pain."

He was right. She was tired. But she smiled and forced all the confidence she didn't feel behind it. "Having second thoughts? I guess all that Prince of

Shadow and Ash business was posturing to make up for your insecurities."

Kirven snorted. "You have a sharp tongue for a slave." He whipped his hand up so fast she barely had time to raise a shield before the line of razor-sharp shards of green light slammed into it. The impact pushed her back. She shoved her shield at Kirven. He sidestepped it and threw a fireball at her head.

Adelaide ducked. The heat of the fireball made her dizzy, but she threw her hand across as if throwing a knife to the side. A volley of small blue throwing knives rushed at Kirven from her fingertips. He put up a shield of his own before they reached him. Already she could feel herself tiring. Her eyes darted from Kirven over to Regulus. He watched with wide eyes, his worry clear, but he caught her gaze and smiled encouragingly.

"Is that the best your sorcery can do?" she taunted. *Wear him out.*

Kirven responded with a wicked smile and held his hands out to his sides. Several spears of green light flashed into existence around him, then spread until they pointed at her from the front and sides. She surrounded herself with a barrier as they zipped through the air toward her. The spears sizzled out of existence as they rammed against her shield. Kirven paced back and forth, throwing attack after attack from every side and driving her back toward the trees while she struggled to keep up with his pace. She bent over, breathing hard with her hands on her knees, and sealed herself inside a dome of shimmering translucent blue.

Kirven laughed and stole some more energy from trees on both sides of her dome. "Out of power already? Taking energy from living things will have to be our first lesson. This is pathetic."

She didn't respond. She had convinced herself that somehow, someway, she would win. But her limbs wearied, and she couldn't bring Kirven down to the same level of mental, emotional, physical, and magical fatigue that plagued her. Not when he kept replenishing his energy when she couldn't.

She was going to lose.

Regulus strained to see around the sorcerer's back. Adelaide leaned forward under her barrier, like she was catching her breath. *Come on, Adelaide.* After a moment, the dome disappeared, and Adelaide straightened and threw a blast of blue light toward the sorcerer. The sorcerer leaned forward, arms crossed in front of him as he raised a shield, but Adelaide's blast still pushed the sorcerer backward. His feet slid across the grass.

That's right! Adelaide threw a blast of fire, but the sorcerer lifted into the air and away from her in a swirl of green. The fireball just missed the bottom edge of his robes. *Press your advantage, Ad! Don't let up now.* She walked forward, sending blasts of light and fireballs one after another. The sorcerer dodged or blocked each one, and the space between each of Adelaide's attacks lengthened. She was tiring.

Regulus couldn't help feeling that yet again, he was at fault. If he had been more level-headed when fighting Carrick, he might not have nearly died, and Adelaide wouldn't have needed to bind them. If he hadn't gotten captured, Adelaide wouldn't be here, and she wouldn't be weakened. She would doubtless disagree with him. The fact she didn't and wouldn't blame him was the only thing that kept him from completely breaking as he watched her switch to defense and give ground again against the sorcerer's aerial assault.

He had felt her sincerity when she refused to remove the bond. She wouldn't risk sacrificing him to save herself. Which made him feel guiltier that she would sacrifice herself to save him—even though he would do the same for her in a heartbeat if given the chance. If only he could give her back everything she had given him. If only he could give every ounce of energy and strength he had left to her, the way she had given her magic to heal him.

Come on! You're strong, Ad; stronger than you know. As she threw a reckless barrage of magic knives toward the sorcerer that went wide, Regulus wished he could get her to sense his thoughts without touching her. That she could understand how much he believed in her. One of the sorcerer's spears grazed her hip as she raised a barrier a moment too late. She yelped then glared at the sorcerer, but her posture betrayed her weariness.

Oh, Etiros. Give her strength! Why can't I help her? Why can't my strength be hers? What good is this bond if it helps only me and not her! He would give up the bond to give her back all the power his wounds had stolen. He would give his life if it gave her life. Blood stained the side of her dress as she held up a barrier against the sorcerer's attacks with one hand and healed her hip with the other. He might be chained and physically useless, but he wouldn't let her fight this battle alone.

"Adelaide! Who are you?"

She looked toward him, panting. Sweat gleamed on her brow. *If I could give you any strength I have, I would do it. But I'll give you my belief.* "Tell me who you are!"

Adelaide straightened behind her barrier. "I'm a mage."

"I can't hear you!"

The sorcerer glanced back at him and hovered closer to the ground as his focus wavered. "Shut up, Hargreaves!"

Regulus strained against the chains. *You're so strong. Any strength I have at this point is yours. All yours.* "Who are you!" He felt a strange draining sensation. Utter exhaustion hit him with the force of running straight into a stone wall. If he hadn't already been sitting and chained, he would have collapsed. He sagged against the tree but kept his eyes on Adelaide.

Adelaide lifted her chin. Her eyes shone with golden light. "I am a mage!"

Regulus realized then he had never understood what it meant to be in awe. But as flames arched up behind Adelaide and unfolded into the shape of gigantic wings and blue light swirled around her feet and lifted her into the air, as a sword as big as the one he had carried as the Black Knight flashed into existence in her hands, he knew what awe felt like. It felt like his heart leaping for joy and plummeting to the ground in shock, somehow at the same time. It felt like his jaw hanging down like it had come unhinged. Like his mind struggling to comprehend what he saw. And awe felt like an overwhelming flood of pride and love as Adelaide soared toward the sorcerer, her wings of flame trailing behind her.

Adelaide pulled the sword back over her head as she leapt, propelled by her magic and Regulus' faith in her. Kirven's face went white. He raised his hands, conjuring a barrier as he looked up, but he had misjudged where to place it. She passed over his barrier as she came back toward the ground. Kirven raised trembling hands. He created a shield just above his head right as she swung her sword down. The impact of the sword against the shield make a crack as loud as a thunderclap. Kirven's shield stopped her sword from cutting into his skull but couldn't stop her momentum. Shield and sword slammed into the top of his head. He crumpled and fell.

She landed on the ground next to Kirven's still form. Adelaide dropped the sword, her sudden burst of energy spent, then turned from Kirven's body toward Regulus. Regulus looked pale, but he grinned. Relief and joy bubbled up inside her as she ran to him.

"That's my *shiraa*!" Regulus sounded like he was cheering for the champion at a tournament. "That's my mage!"

She laughed and wiped a tear from the side of her nose as she dropped to her knees next to him. She hastened to remove the shackles. The moment his arms were free, he wrapped them around her and started kissing every inch of her face.

"You did it. You did it. I knew you would."

For the first time in what felt like forever, the tears that snuck down her cheeks were tears of joy.

He pulled her close. "My mage."

"My mercenary." She kissed his blood-covered scar. He brushed his fingers through her hair, but then his gaze darted away from her face and his eyes turned stormy. "What?"

"Carrick." Regulus scowled.

Oh. Right. Her heart sank. She didn't want to deal with him right now. But she stood anyway and held her hand out. Regulus took it, and she gasped.

"Reg!" As he stood, she gripped his forearm. It was still stained rust-red from smeared, dry blood, but... "The mark...it's gone."

Chapter 42

"WHAT?" REGULUS pulled his arm out of Adelaide's hands and looked closer. She was right. No black lines traced an intricate knot on his arm. The mark was gone.

"How…what—what does that mean?" Adelaide's voice trembled. "He…Kirven called it a lover's bond. Why…?"

"Hey, no." Regulus pulled her against his chest and cradled the back of her head in his hand. "It doesn't mean we stopped loving each other."

Carrick's laugh carried over the space between them from where he still stood chained to the tree. "How tragic. Guess that love wasn't as deep as Kirven or either of you thought."

Regulus' face heated. "No one asked the opinion of a dead man!"

That shut Carrick up. Regulus moved back to see Adelaide's face. "Don't listen to him." He ducked his head sheepishly. "I think…I may have—somehow—given it back?"

"Given it back?"

"I was praying I could give you my energy, my strength, the way you give me your power to heal me. Thinking I would give anything, even my life, so you could live and win." He scratched the back of his neck. "And then…I suddenly felt exhausted, like all of my energy had been sapped away. Honestly, I feel like I haven't slept in days."

Adelaide's lips parted. "And I got a sudden rush of energy. Oh, Etiros…" She pushed his hair off his temple. "I don't understand. But thank you."

The squeak of metal on wood and a grunt drew his attention back to Carrick. The villain strained as he tried to squirm out of the chains. Regulus walked around Adelaide, and she fell into step next to him. Carrick struggled more at their approach, his face red. Regulus pulled Carrick's sword out of the dirt as they passed it, anger overpowering his exhaustion.

Carrick stilled. "All right; let's talk about this. Is killing me necessary? We can just…go our separate ways."

"No, we can't," Adelaide said quietly. "Not after everything you've done."

Blue light flickered as Adelaide conjured a dagger of solid light in her hand and raised it toward Carrick's throat. But her hand shook, and her expression was strained. Regulus understood her hesitation. Killing an unarmed man felt different. Killing someone you knew…any decent person struggled with that. Unfortunately for Carrick, being a mercenary hammered a lot of decent out of a person. Regulus had no intention of letting him live.

Carrick paled, but quickly regained his irritatingly relaxed expression. "If I could go back and spare your father's life, I would. And I'm sorry you can't see how much I care for you. I'm sorry you won't accept that I just wanted to keep you out of the hands of this mercenary dog."

"You're the only dog here," Regulus growled.

Carrick ignored him. "I'm sorry you can't see that even when I was cruel, it was only because I didn't know how else to process that I love you, and you don't want me."

"You don't love me." Adelaide's hand bobbed, and the magic dagger softened on the edges. Regulus considered moving Adelaide out of the way and beheading the churl, but maybe she needed to confront him.

"Of course I do!" Carrick slammed his head back against the tree. "Love you, need you, crave you. You've made me mad with desire. You can't blame me for going to extreme lengths to make you mine. I'm willing to do whatever it takes to win you."

"To own me." Adelaide moved the tip of the dagger of light under Carrick's chin. "You killed…" She shuddered. "Part of me wants to kill you now. Part of me wants to drag you back to the palace so you can be hanged in front of everyone."

"An interesting idea," Carrick said. "Public execution is probably more just."

Regulus frowned. "He's just trying to buy time, think of ways to escape. We should kill him now. We're royal guards. We have the authority to deal with a threat to the crown with deadly force."

"I'm *so* threatening right now." Carrick rolled his eyes.

"You should hang." Adelaide lowered her hand and the dagger vanished. "A quick death is too good for you, anyway."

"I'll gladly do it slowly," Regulus growled.

"Slowly." Carrick smiled, cocky and self-assured. Regulus gripped the sword hilt so tight his fingers ached. "Slowly is how I plan on doing you, love."

Regulus raised the sword, but Adelaide had her dagger back at Carrick's throat.

"I don't know what the right thing is to do anymore. My father…" Her voice cracked. "He would say justice."

"Well…" Carrick smirked. "The thing is, justice doesn't rule. Power does."

Adelaide shook her head. "What does—"

Something curled around her neck and pulled. She reached toward her throat as Regulus cursed. Her fingers brushed against a rope at her neck. *No…* She'd killed him. *Never let your guard down until you are certain the fight is won.* She should have put her sword through his heart.

"First rule of combat," Nolan gloated. "Make sure your opponent is actually dead."

Adelaide choked as Kirven yanked on the rope. She stumbled backward and turned around, clawing at the suffocating rope around her neck. Kirven held his hands outstretched, a rope trailing from both hands. She traced the other to where Regulus had fallen to his knees, his face turning blue as he tried to free himself. She sent a blast of fire through the ropes.

The ropes vanished, and Regulus gasped and fell onto his hands, coughing and sputtering. Adelaide collapsed to her knees, dragging air down her raw windpipe. Glowing green ropes wrapped around her arms and bound them to her sides. She looked up as Kirven aimed a spear of sorcerous light at Regulus.

"No!" She pushed to her feet, arms still bound, and jumped in front of Regulus.

Kirven dropped the spear. "That close to being out of power are you, girl?" He strode forward and pulled on the ropes, tossing her onto her side.

"You were defeated." Regulus rubbed his throat as he looked up at Kirven. "You lost. It's over."

"It's over when I say it's over," Kirven snarled.

"Leave him alone!" Adelaide maneuvered onto her knees and blasted away the ropes. She raised a shield between Regulus and Kirven. Even such a small, simple barrier proved more difficult than it had in ages. Her head pounded. Her limbs weighed her down.

Regulus picked up Nolan's sword and rose unsteadily to his feet, his movements slow.

"Oh, very interesting." Kirven's gaze fixed on Regulus' arm. "You broke the bond to give her strength. I'm impressed, honestly. But"—he smiled—

"that technically counts as helping. That means you broke our agreement. According to the ancient and sacred rules of combat, cheating results in a forfeit."

"Mercenaries have never cared much for the rules of combat," Regulus snapped.

"Well, anything goes now, at the least," Kirven said with a wicked grin. He sent an arc of green light toward her. She raised a second shield, but the arc of solid light went right past the edge of the shield. She allowed herself a small smile. At least that blow to the head had weakened him and affected his aim. She had a chance, despite her exhaustion.

Regulus moved into a ready stance, the sword gripped in both hands, and looked toward her. She nodded at Regulus, but his eyes widened. "Adelaide!"

A strong arm wrapped around her as Nolan pulled her back against his chest. Kirven hadn't missed. He'd freed Nolan. The tip of a blade pressed against her side. She stiffened as Nolan pulled her away from Regulus.

"Drop the sword unless you want to see how well Adelaide handles the treatment I gave you earlier," Nolan said, his soft tone in glaring dissonance with his words.

Regulus dropped the sword, his face red. "You would torture the woman you claim to love? What sick kind of love is that?"

Kirven sent ropes around her shield. The ropes wrapped around Regulus' wrists and throat. Adelaide let the useless shield fall, conjured a dagger, and stabbed it into Nolan's thigh. He cursed, but didn't let go, so she stabbed again. Nolan released her and stumbled back.

"Let him go!" She burned through Kirven's ropes, the effort making her dizzy. Regulus coughed.

Kirven grunted. "Here's my offer, mage. Swear to serve me now, and I'll let the mercenary go. Otherwise, I'll have Carrick carve his heart out."

Adelaide glowered at Kirven, even though she didn't feel particularly defiant. "I beat you."

"Yet I'm still alive."

"She still won," Regulus protested.

"By cheating!" Kirven clenched his fists.

Nolan grabbed her arm, but Adelaide turned and sent a blast into his chest, knocking him to the ground. White spots sparked in her vision and she swayed. She shook her head then ran to Regulus, pulled him to the ground, and threw a dome over them. Her muscles twitched as magical energy leeched from her.

"Regulus." She had meant to sound more certain, but her voice came out small and weak "I…I'm going to surrender."

"Smart girl," Kirven said.

"What?" Regulus gripped her shoulders. "No!"

She lowered her head. "He's right. I would have lost without your help."

"That's ridiculous, and you know it." Regulus shook his head, his tone gentle. "It was your magic to start with, and what is some extra energy if you don't put it to good use? He stole energy from the trees! How is that different?"

"Because she can't repeat that trick, imbecile." Derision laced Kirven's voice. "I, on the other hand…" Green light covered the ground around the sorcerer and the grass withered and crumbled to dust.

Adelaide rubbed the heel of her hand over her eye, desperately trying not to cry. "I can't watch you die again. I can't." She bit back a sob.

"Ad—"

"I'm not strong, Reg." She let the tears come. Too much sorrow. Too much loss. Too much fear and failure. She had been so close and ruined it by one stupid mistake. "I'm scared, and I'm tired, and I don't want my family to die because of me. I—" A sob cut through her words. Kirven would make her do unforgivable things. But she pictured Minerva laughing with Gaius, her hands holding her swollen belly. "I have to save them."

Regulus pulled her close. She leaned into him. "Ad…" His cheek rested against her forehead, but his emotions didn't hit her.

The bond is gone, she reminded herself. Another whimpering sob burned at her throat.

"Hargreaves," Nolan said. "Kindly unhand my wife."

Adelaide shivered and clenched Regulus' shirt as his grip on her tightened. She wanted to fall asleep against him and wake up in a world where Father wasn't dead, where Regulus hadn't broken their bond, where she wasn't on the verge of collapse. She should fight. Fight until her last breath. She should die before she helped Kirven kill the king and subjugate Monparth and its neighbors. It was what Father would do. *But Father isn't here.*

"My mage," Regulus murmured. "Don't give up, *shiraa.* We'll fight—"

"I don't have any fight left." She wasn't the seasoned warrior he was, wasn't the tigress Father had thought her. Despair ate away at her heart. She could stop running, stop fearing. All it took to save her family, to save Regulus, to finally *rest,* was to give in and become a sorceress.

It would make her a monster. She would corrupt her soul until she enjoyed others' pain as much as Kirven did. But maybe the ache in her heart would go away. The people she loved would live.

And she'd be married to Nolan.

She couldn't surrender. She couldn't fight.

"Help me," Adelaide whispered. Whether she was asking Regulus or Etiros, she wasn't sure.

Kirven laughed. "Only I can help you now."

"I won't leave you." Regulus swallowed hard. "I'll serve him, too."

"No!" Adelaide pulled back to look him in the eyes. "Regu—"

"Forever, *piahre*." He held her gaze. "That's what you asked me. That's what I agreed to. Forever. No more splitting up."

She shook her head as her stomach twisted. "But—"

Regulus held her face in his hands. "We fight together, we die together, or we serve together. I'm not abandoning you."

"Not an option," Nolan spat. "Adelaide is mine."

"She's mine," Kirven said. "I'm just letting you borrow her. You can share."

Adelaide stared at Regulus and tried to block out Nolan and Kirven. They no longer shared their emotions with a touch, but she could read his face. His love and unwavering belief that she didn't deserve. But also pain and fear and anger. He didn't want to serve Kirven again. But he would. For her. For a woman who was too broken to keep going. How did he love her enough to give up the freedom he had worked so hard to earn? To go back to that life of pain?

"Love conquers fear," Father's voice whispered.

"Stop doubting yourself," Regulus murmured. "I love the woman I see."

She blinked. How could he know? Only one thing to do. "Together."

CHAPTER 43

CONFUSION WELLED in Regulus as Adelaide's barrier dissolved above them. She pulled away and took a shaky step toward the sorcerer.

"We surrender. You win. My family and Regulus' friends are safe."

Regulus' shoulders caved. For a moment, the spark in her eyes, the way she said together… He thought she had changed her mind. So that was it then. A lifetime spent serving the sorcerer. Spent watching Adelaide taint her soul with sorcery and suffer under Carrick's control. But the alternative of abandoning her to bear that alone was worse.

"Could have saved us both a lot of trouble and me a splitting headache if you'd given in earlier," the sorcerer grumbled.

"No harm will come to my family or Regulus' friends?" Adelaide pressed.

"So long as they don't interfere with me, no harm will come to them."

The sorcerer would provide himself a loophole.

But it must have been good enough for Adelaide, because she pushed her sleeve up over her elbow. "You'll take Regulus, too?"

The sorcerer huffed. "Fine. Give me your arm."

"What?" Carrick sounded offended. "You can't—"

"*I* can do whatever the hell I want," the sorcerer snapped. "Now stop whining before I change my mind about keeping my word."

Carrick grunted, but shut up.

This is wrong. Regulus gripped the hilt of Carrick's sword. If he could cut off Carrick's head…

"Drop it, mercenary." The sorcerer's voice was cold. "Now, mage. Your arm."

Adelaide hesitated, and hope sparked in Regulus. But then she held her arm out to the sorcerer. Regulus looked away. He couldn't watch.

"Do you know what *shiraa* means, Kirven?" Adelaide asked. Regulus frowned up at her.

The sorcerer shrugged. "It's Khast. Tigress." He placed his hand over her forearm.

"Tigers," Adelaide said softly, "don't like being caged." Her palm glowed a soft blue. A shaft of solid blue light appeared in her grip and extended into the sorcerer's stomach.

The sorcerer shrieked. A blast of green light knocked Adelaide to the ground. Regulus seized the sword and leapt up. The sorcerer was focused on healing the hole Adelaide had put through his abdomen, paying no attention as Regulus rushed him. Carrick shouted a warning, and the sorcerer's head whipped up.

Regulus swung with every ounce of energy he had for the sorcerer's neck. The sorcerer gaped and lifted his hands, his palms glowing green, but too late. Regulus screamed a battle cry, all his anger and heartbreak lending strength to his wearied arms. The sorcerer's head tumbled to the ground.

The sorcerer's body fell.

Regulus' chest heaved. It was over. Really, truly, over.

He lowered the sword. For the first time in two years, he felt free. He squared his shoulders as an immeasurable weight lifted off him. But then he looked for Adelaide, and his rage threatened to rip him apart.

Kirven's blast knocked Adelaide to the ground. Blackness crowded out her vision and her arms shook as she tried to push herself up. She lurched to her feet, but before she could turn to aid Regulus, Nolan wrested her to the ground and shouted a warning to Kirven.

Nolan rolled over on top of her, pinning her in place. She tried to send a blast of magic off her body, as she had done before to break free of Kirven's ropes, but was too drained. Nolan's legs trapped her hands against her thighs and his hands on her shoulders wouldn't let her shift enough to see what was happening with Regulus and Kirven.

"You won't want to see that, love." He pressed his forearm across her chest as she struggled.

Regulus bellowed a war cry. Adelaide slammed her head into Nolan's mouth. The impact hurt more than she had anticipated, and her eyes watered. Nolan cursed and pushed against her until she feared her sternum would crack. Regulus' shout stopped. Nolan gasped and pulled away, his brow furrowed.

"What…" He shook his head and shifted enough she could pull one hand free.

She blasted Nolan backward as Regulus shouted, "Get off her!"

Adelaide sat up, her body shaking and stomach roiling as her eyes fought to focus and her head ached. Regulus kicked the side of Nolan's head and held the point of the sword to Nolan's throat. Adelaide's gaze locked onto a mound of black and red robes.

Kirven's head was not attached to his body. She pressed her fist to her mouth, transfixed by the horror before her. Her stomach clenched. *Look away, look away...*

"Ad," Regulus said. She tore her eyes from Kirven's grotesque head to Regulus standing over Nolan. "I want to run him through." His voice was so low and gravelly she hardly recognized it. "I want to do more than that. But not if..." He grunted. "If you want him to hang."

She wanted to curl into a ball somewhere dark and cry until she fell asleep, then sleep until this was all a distant memory.

"Um...I vote hanging," Nolan said.

Adelaide stood, her legs shaking. "Why? So you can try to talk your way free?"

"To be honest, yes." Nolan's voice lacked its usual confidence. "I was tricked! And then he used me! He controlled me and tortured me and forced me—"

"Did he force you to kiss me?" Adelaide shouted. She conjured a throwing knife, even though the effort made her sway. "Did he compel you to assault me?" Her voice shook. She raised the throwing knife. This wasn't what Father would want. The king would appreciate a prisoner to make an example of. And it might help with her desertion problem. She sighed and let the throwing knife vanish. "I need a peace offering for the king."

Regulus shook his head. "What are you—"

"I..." She kicked at the grass. "I sort of deserted."

"What?" The rage vanished from Regulus' voice, replaced by fear. "To come find me?" She nodded. "You'll be hanged!"

Nolan laughed. "Fancy that."

"Shut up, or I'll run you through."

Adelaide raised her head and tried not to flinch at Regulus' appalled expression. "A prisoner the king can execute to remind his people he's in charge might help my case."

"Okay," Regulus sounded panicked. "Okay, that might work. Okay." His voice leveled as he calmed himself. "Looks like you're good for something,

Carrick. Ad, can you get the chains with the shackles?"

Adelaide hurried to bring the shackles from the oak tree. She crouched next to Nolan, careful to avoid looking at his face. She closed a shackle around his wrist, then moved to his other side and closed the other shackle. Regulus used the chain to pull Nolan to his feet.

"Try to run," Regulus said. "And I'll slice open your ankles. Understood?"

Adelaide stepped next to Regulus and looked up at him as he stuck the sword in his belt. His stormy expression softened as he gazed at her.

"Are you okay?" he murmured.

She nodded, although her lower lip trembled. "You did it. We're…"

"Free." Regulus looked tired, despite his smile. "*We* did it, *mareh piahre*. We defeated him together."

She smiled, unsure what she was feeling in the wreckage of her emotions. Relieved, certainly. The echo of *failure* still resounded in the back of her mind. She doubted she deserved Regulus. But as she looked into his piercing gray eyes, she felt overwhelming love.

"Can we save the adoring looks for when I'm not around?" Nolan muttered.

"You should apologize, cad," Regulus growled.

Nolan glared at Adelaide. "I'm sorry." He pulled his lips back in a snarl, contorting his handsome features into the monster he really was. "I never should have let you leave that morning after I took you from Arrano. I'm sorry I didn't break into your room that night and make you my—"

Regulus' fist connected with Nolan's jaw with a sharp crack as Adelaide paled.

Nolan spit blood and grinned, his teeth smeared with red. "Too bad you can't kill me, since the wench got herself in a predicament."

Anger burned away Adelaide's exhaustion, mixing with her fear. She clenched her fists as she tried to stop shaking.

"Bet you can't make her tremble like that, mercenary."

Rage and humiliation knotted her insides and squeezed her throat. Regulus punched Nolan's stomach, and Nolan stumbled back, coughing. Nolan straightened and stepped back as far as the long chain would allow.

"Want another kiss, love?" He licked his bloodied lips as his eyes roamed over her. "Maybe a bit more?"

She shuddered. "Gag him."

Nolan gave her a mocking smirk as Regulus moved toward him. "I'll convince the king I was ensorcelled, and Hargreaves entrapped you. And when I marry you, I won't waste time—"

Adelaide screamed and threw a knife she didn't recall conjuring at Nolan. The glowing blade buried deep in his neck. His face went slack as he choked. *What did I just do?* The blade vanished and Nolan fell to his knees, pressing his hands against his throat. She stared in mute shock, rooted in place. *Your bargaining chip. You need him alive!* But she couldn't move as his face whitened. He fell forward with a clatter of chains.

Adelaide dropped to the ground. He might still be alive. But she didn't have the energy or desire to save Nolan's life. She stared at Nolan's body as tension built behind her forehead. Regulus knelt next to her and held her against his chest.

"He deserved it, Adelaide."

She sobbed and wrapped her arms around Regulus' neck.

"He was guilty and dangerous," Regulus whispered. "And he deserved so much worse."

"I murdered him." She buried her face in his shirt. "Justice…"

"This is justice." He rubbed her back. "Even your father told me Carrick deserved to die. Now or later, why does it matter? We're royal guards. We have the authority to kill a traitor to the crown."

"Well…you are," she mumbled. "Oh, Etiros, what have I done?"

Chapter 44

*E*TIROS, *I* DON'T *know how to help her.* This wasn't the first life Adelaide had taken; Regulus knew that. But this wasn't a random bandit. And she wasn't a mercenary. The things he usually said to help a man struggling after his first battle didn't seem right. He wasn't even certain if she was more upset that she had killed Carrick, or worried about her desertion.

"You defeated the sorcerer," Regulus said tentatively. He rubbed her back. "And you saved the king's life at the masque. He would have to be an idiot not to see that you hunting down the sorcerer was a good thing." But a part of him worried, because in his opinion the king was an idiot. *But surely not that much of an idiot.*

"Is it wrong I'm relieved he's dead?" Adelaide whispered.

"To be honest, I'm happy he's gone."

They didn't say anything for several moments. Regulus wished he still had the ability to feel her emotions. He could ask her. But he didn't know if she wanted to talk about it, or if she could even be honest. He didn't want to pressure her. So he held her as exhaustion and relief pulled on his eyelids. He rested his head against hers and let his eyes close. But then he pictured Carrick straddling her.

"Ad?"

"Mm."

"Are you…" He knew she wasn't okay. And he didn't want to ask outright if Carrick had kissed her again. Part of him didn't want to know. But after last time…he didn't want to overstep when he no longer sensed her fear. "Is this okay? Me?"

She shifted, burrowing closer. "What do you mean?"

Regulus worked down the lump in his throat. At least she had moved closer. That was a good sign. "I don't want to… Carrick…" He bit his tongue. "Just… Tell me if I go too far?"

"Oh, Reg." Adelaide's voice cracked. She pulled away. The departure of her warmth left him hollow. Her deep, rich brown eyes were full of love and heartbreak.

He looked away. He had failed her; left her alone to mourn her father and almost caused her to become enslaved to the sorcerer and Carrick. He was supposed to protect her, and he had failed. Again.

"I'm sorry." He drew in a shuddering breath. "I'm sorry you were hurt because of me. I'm sorry I wasn't able to keep you from despairing—"

"Regulus Hargreaves, stop that." He looked up in surprise at the hardness of her tone. "If anyone should apologize, it's me." She looked down at her hands and twiddled her thumbs. "You wouldn't have been tortured if it wasn't for me."

"I—"

"But it wasn't our fault," she said softly. "And I would have given up without you. Any strength you see in me…it's from you."

Regulus couldn't stop the chuckle that escaped him. Adelaide looked up, her expression half offended and half confused. "And I was thinking my strength was all yours." He smiled and reached for her cheek, then hesitated.

"I'm not afraid of your touch, *piahre*." She laced her fingers behind his neck.

Regulus leaned forward, but didn't meet her lips, giving her a chance to pull back. She moved closer and pressed her lips to his. He kissed her, matching her gentleness at first, but then grabbed her and pulled her close, holding nothing back. He poured all his love, his gratitude, all his passion into kissing her. She broke away. He opened his eyes to see her crying silently. A weight settled in his stomach and he released her, his heart heavy.

"I'm sorry—"

"Don't be. It's not…" She wiped tears from her cheeks. "Would you really have served Kirven?"

Oh. "I won't leave you alone." He rubbed her shoulders. "I love you."

She wiped at her tears. "But I failed—"

"No, you didn't." He stroked the top of her head as he tried to find the words to comfort her in the midst of his own aching heart. "And even if you did, I don't love you because you won or lost. I love you because you're kind and good and smart and independent and strong—"

"I wanted to surrender!" Her voice was thick with tears. "How is that good or strong?"

Regulus wanted to shout at her, to shake her until she understood, or kiss her until they both forgot her pain. He wanted to bring the sorcerer and Carrick back just to hurt them for what they had done to her. He wanted to slip into unconsciousness until the tension behind his forehead eased. Until the memory of Carrick's torture and his fear as he watched Adelaide surrender faded.

He recalled Adelaide's irritated rebuke as they made their way to retrieve the opal what seemed ages ago. *We don't always get what we want!* He lifted her chin so he could look into her eyes. *Give me wisdom, Etiros.*

"There are many kinds of strength. Love isn't weak. Surviving isn't weak. Wanting to surrender doesn't make you less worthy, it makes your final victory more impressive. You felt defeated, but you kept fighting anyway. You're amazing, and I wish you believed that." He stroked her messy hair. "I love you, Adelaide. More than you can know."

"Thank you." She looked more at peace, her face more relaxed. She touched the tips of her fingers to his arm where her mark had been. "I'm too weak now, but I'll put it back—"

"I don't need it." He took her hand in his. "I know you love me. No one's trying to kill us anymore. And I never want you in pain because of me again. But…" He grinned. "Estevan has been trying to talk me into getting a tattoo for years. I have a design in mind now."

She laughed, and even though her laugh was weak and broken, it was real. And it told him she was going to be okay. They both were. "Maybe I can get one, too. The horror on my half-siblings' faces would be priceless."

He chuckled. "They'll probably be shocked enough when you marry me."

Her gaze roamed over his face, and her expression saddened as she touched his scarred cheek. "I'm sorry they hurt you. But—maybe this is selfish of me… I'm glad my magic didn't erase your scar." She smiled. "It's a reminder. Scars mean we survived."

"I could kiss you for that."

"Then why don't you?" Her eyes danced, even though she looked exhausted.

He leaned forward to kiss her but glimpsed the sorcerer's severed head behind her. He grimaced. "The corpses are kind of killing the mood."

"Eugh." Adelaide winced. "We should probably get back to the palace, anyway. Let them know Kirven's dead."

"Agreed. I hope whoever's in charge lets you sleep before they start in with all the questioning." He picked up the sword and headed for Carrick's body.

"What are you doing?"

He looked over his shoulder. "We'll need to bring the heads back to the palace as proof of death. And then at least the king can display them if he wants."

Adelaide blanched. Her revulsion made his stomach twist. He lowered the point of the sword to the ground and turned toward her.

"Ad…"

"No, you're right." She still looked uncomfortable.

"Did you not realize this is what a mercenary did?" he blurted before he thought better of it. An irrational fear screamed in his mind as he watched her pinched expression. The fear she wouldn't want this side of him. He shouldn't make it worse, but cruel, taunting doubt pushed the words past his tongue. "I'm a killer, Adelaide, I've never pretended I'm not. Not to mention a bastard and social pariah. You're so worried you're not good enough, when I'm the one who can't ever deserve you."

Her face went stony. She stomped toward him. "Regulus, if you say anything like that ever again…" She clenched her fists, looking like she wanted to punch him. "I *love* you. And I'm too hungry and tired to tell you why you're amazing. So just…stop!"

"Okay." Regulus laughed. *Etiros, I love this woman.* "Easy, tigress. I think there's some food by the fire pit."

Regulus cut off Carrick's head while Adelaide consumed the last of the sorcerer's food. He could have eaten, too, but she ate like she had been starved. The least he could do was let her eat. He made a makeshift bag and padding for both heads out of the sorcerer's clothing, slung it over his shoulder, and they headed for the palace.

When they arrived at the palace gate, Regulus requested to see the officer on duty immediately. A guard ushered them straight to the royal guard barracks. Beale and Antar met them in the courtyard.

"Belanger," Beale snapped. "You—"

"Are a hero." Regulus dumped out the heads and they rolled across the dirt. He tossed down the sack and glared at Beale.

"The hell, Hargreaves?" Beale blanched and stepped back.

"The heads of the sorcerer Kirven and Nolan Carrick." Regulus nodded toward the heads. "Adelaide and I killed them. You're welcome."

Beale blinked. "The sorcerer is dead?"

"Unless he can survive as only a head," Adelaide said unsteadily. "I served my king and removed the threat to his crown. I—"

"You're still a deserter," Beale said curtly.

"Are you serious?" Regulus motioned to the heads. "She defeated the sorcerer! And killed his lackey! Who, I might remind you, killed a lord. And many royal guards, I understand."

"And Captain Matthews and Lieutenant Breck," Adelaide added. Beale glared at her.

"She disobeyed a direct order from a superior, abandoned her assigned post, and attacked fellow guards." Antar pushed at Kirven's head with the tip of his boot. "But she also saved my life. And, I'd say, the kingdom." He looked up. "Well done, Belanger."

"We don't have the authority to pardon her, Antar." Beale crossed his arms. "And I already sent a messenger to the king informing him of her desertion. The king will have to decide what to do when he returns. Until then, you're under arrest."

"That's ridiculous!" Regulus stepped forward, his fists clenched at his sides. He wanted to beat someone senseless, and as Breck was apparently dead, Beale would do almost as well. "You should be thanking her, not arresting her!"

"The king will likely pardon her," Antar said.

"But only the king *can* pardon her," Beale added. "Belanger. Are you going to come without any trouble this time?"

"Come *where*?" Regulus demanded.

"Yes, sir." Adelaide's voice was soft.

"Do I need cuffs or are you going to come along willingly?"

"No." Adelaide shook her head. "I'll come."

Beale motioned for her to follow him and headed out of the courtyard.

"You can't seriously be putting her in the dungeon?" Regulus stepped in front of Adelaide, panic squeezing him. He had promised not to leave her alone again.

"That's the law, Hargreaves," Beale said sullenly.

She patted his shoulder. "It's all right, Reg. It won't be for long." She kissed his cheek. "You said it yourself. I saved the king's life. He'll pardon me. Behave. Please?"

Regulus whirled toward Beale. "I want to stay with her."

Beale rolled his eyes. "Not protocol."

"Hang protocol! Look at her!" He pointed to Adelaide. "She was wounded, she's drained herself of her magic to kill the sorcerer, she nearly died, she's exhausted. She could have run, but she came back! If you were a decent person, you'd let her stay in her room! Post a guard if—"

"Enough!" Beale's expression darkened. "Your attitude grows old, Hargreaves. As does your inability to call me *sir*. Now back off, or you can spend the rest of the day in the stocks."

Regulus clenched his jaw. "Yes, sir." He stepped aside and watched Beale lead Adelaide to the dungeons with a heavy heart.

Regulus glared at the wall of the mess hall with enough intensity to burn a hole through the wood. He clutched his fork. Just when things seemed to have finally looked up, Adelaide was taken from him again. Most likely not permanently, but he didn't like it.

The other guards in the mess hall avoided him. Whether because he'd brought back the sorcerer's severed head, because he was the mage's betrothed, or because of the murderous look on his face, he wasn't sure. But he was thankful to be left alone. After lunch, he laid on their bed in the dark room, unable to sleep in the empty bed while Adelaide slept alone in a cell.

He wandered around the gardens until he was too tired to walk anymore. A spot under a willow tree, hidden by well-manicured bushes whose leaves were starting to show hints of red called to him. He hadn't meant to doze off, but it was early evening when he awoke to the rustle of willow branches and buzz of bees. His stomach drove him to the mess hall, and then his heart drove him to the dungeons. The guards wouldn't let him see Adelaide and threatened to throw him in a cell far from hers if he persisted. He left, muttering and cursing under his breath.

Their little room felt empty and harsh. He would have given anything to be lying in bed, sleep pulling at his eyes while Adelaide crouched over a formless blob of fabric, her brows drawn close together and absently biting her lower lip as she moved the needle and pulled out a staggering number of little pins. So help him Etiros, this was the last time they would be separated unnecessarily. He pulled off his boots and belt and tossed the dagger Carrick had stolen from Adelaide on the table before he blew out the lantern.

He'd only been lying on the bed a few minutes when someone knocked. *This can't be good.* He stumbled toward the door and slammed his foot into a bed post. Biting back a curse, he hopped on one foot. He survived mutilation and torture; he wouldn't be brought down by a couple stubbed toes. The person in the hall knocked again.

"You in there, Reg? Adelaide?" *Dresden.*

Regulus opened the door so quickly it banged against the wall. "Drez!"

"Oh, good." Drez peered inside the room. "Where's Adelaide?"

"In the dungeons." He stepped aside to allow Dresden to enter.

"What?" Dresden stared, rooted in place. "They're not still charging her with desertion, are they?"

"Wait, you *knew*?" Regulus crossed to the table and lit the lamp, filling the room with flickering orange light. "Drez, I swear—"

"Hey, you ever tried stopping her from doing something? She was throwing magic and fire and telling people off. Besides which, I was on her side. If she was doubling over in pain at what they were doing to you, I can't imagine…" Dresden gulped. "I was worried." He sat in one of the chairs by the table. "I like Adelaide's light better. Makes the corners less shadowy."

"What? How would you know that?"

"Come on, Reg." Drez leaned back in the chair. He looked worn; his beard considerably less well-kempt than usual. "She lost you; then her father died, and she couldn't save him. And she tried, Reg. It…was rough." He rubbed the side of his beard, his eyes distant. "I wasn't about to leave her alone."

Regulus sank onto the edge of the bed and a pang of sorrow went through his heart. "Thank you," he whispered.

"What are friends for if not to sleep on uncomfortable chairs and take care of your girl because you're too busy being captured?" Dresden gave a forced laugh. "Oh, also, if we ever run away to become mercenaries again, please take her with us. That mage healing is excellent."

"Wait, you were hurt?" If Dresden had been hurt, that meant he had fought Carrick, and that meant… *I could have lost him.* "How bad—"

Dresden snorted. "Compared to you? A scratch."

"Is that what Adelaide will tell me if I ask her?"

"I'm alive, you muscular nursemaid, relax. It was definitely nothing compared to Antar's leg." He straightened. "Which reminds me. As soon as I heard that you two had shown up at the palace with a couple of severed heads— nicely done, by the way, I heard you dumped them out and disgusted the guards, excellent style—I came straight to the palace with the aim of giving the staff to Adelaide. A pretentious Lieutenant Beale who's very concerned with protocol confiscated it."

Regulus plopped back on the bed. "Sounds about right. He insisted on locking up Adelaide until the king can decide if she should be charged with desertion."

Drez shook his head. "This is why I was on board when you decided to become a mercenary. No tradition and nonsense, just whoever fights best and whoever comes through when they need to. Justice is simple, effective, and fair."

Regulus laughed. "No nonsense, says the man who is still sore he lost his collection of lucky rabbit feet."

"And look where we are now." Dresden spread his hands. "Bet you we never would have met that sorcerer if I'd still had 'em."

"That is the definition of circumstantial and you know it."

"We both know I'm never wrong." Dresden laced his fingers behind his head. "And I bought those as a laugh, but we had the best luck for the month I had them."

Regulus rolled his eyes. It felt good to have this easy banter with Drez again. To laugh and have some normalcy. "I'm glad you're here." He laid back on the bed. "I just wish Adelaide was, too."

Another day and a half passed before the king arrived. Regulus tried several times to see Adelaide, but every time the answer was no. He watched the entrance to the dungeon and only ever saw servants enter with bags of bread and buckets of water. It infuriated him, and he told Beale off twice. The first time Regulus was denied dinner. Drez snuck in food from town. The second time Beale wanted to put Regulus in the stocks for two hours, but Antar convinced Beale to give Regulus a warning. Beale agreed, but told Regulus his next offense of any kind would get him five lashes. Regulus kept his head down and grumbled only to Drez—particularly when the king didn't call them in for a hearing the moment he arrived back.

ADELAIDE AWOKE from a nightmare, a scream on her tongue and a pinch in her neck. Her body ached from lying on the hard stone. The cell was only around four feet deep and five feet wide. Bars separated her from empty cells on either side. The only item in the entire cell was a stained and odious wooden bucket shoved back in the darkest corner. Water dripped somewhere, and some other prisoner coughed in a distant cell.

She had naïvely hoped her incarceration would give her time to rest and process. Rest was difficult to come by on the cold stone floor with mice burrowing into her skirts. A few times she had caught herself wondering what Father would say or do when she saw him, how he would react to her being thrown in the dungeon. Then she would remember, and the pain in her heart would start all over again. But the nightmares were worse.

Once she dreamed of Nolan killing Father. She was stuck on the other side of one of Kirven's barriers, able to see but unable to help as Nolan ran his sword through Father's heart. In another nightmare, she stumbled past Father's corpse to where Nolan and Kirven were torturing Regulus. By the time she reached Regulus, she was so weak she couldn't even conjure a barrier. This time, she had awoken from a dream of Kirven burning his mark into her arm and handing her over to Nolan.

Every time, she woke to her screams echoing in the dungeons. No one checked on her. No one cared. She longed for Regulus' comforting arms around her. She curled up alone on the stone, surrounded by the unfeeling darkness and iron, and cried into her arm. *I'm safe,* she reminded herself. *They're dead. They can't touch me, or Regulus and my family. We're safe.* Except for Father. Father's words about her nightmares after her rescue seemed prescient.

"They'll fade. The memories. The dreams. And the pain. They won't last forever." When? *"I don't know. But they will. You will heal. You're so, so strong, my dear. Don't doubt that, all right?"*

She wished Nolan and Kirven's power over her life didn't feel like it extended past their deaths. But even with their shadow hanging over her, she was alive. *"Surviving isn't weak,"* Regulus' voice whispered in her mind. Still, Kirven and Nolan had changed her in a way she didn't quite understand yet. She felt like she had been broken and put back together a half dozen times over the last weeks, and she was different for it. More tender. Her heart more easily bruised. But also more resilient. A survivor.

Her empty stomach clenched. How long had it been since a servant had delivered a loaf of bread? Time was strange with no sunlight. She couldn't even hear the chime of the chapel bells under all this stone. It could be morning. Could be the middle of the night. Or the middle of the afternoon.

Her heart longed for sunlight, and she was on the verge of insanity from not knowing the time. Adelaide had tried to ask the guards a couple times, but they ignored her. The servants practically threw her bread at her, then hurried away without speaking.

And oh, what she wouldn't give for fresh air on her skin and dirt and grass under her feet. She might never wear sleeves again, Monparthian fashion sense be hanged. How did people live in dungeons for longer than a few days? It was torment.

And Regulus. Oh, Regulus. The only thing she wanted more than the open sky above her and nothing but trees, sunlight, and a misty morning all around her was Regulus. She wished he was with her. But she also didn't. Somehow, knowing he was free up there made a part of her free, too. Even though he wasn't there to comfort her, thinking about him helped.

As she watched the flicker of the torches stuck in the walls every few feet, Adelaide knew a few things for certain.

Father's death would always leave an ache in her heart. That pain might fade, but it would never disappear.

It was going to take her a long time not to become nauseous or afraid when she thought of Nolan, even with him gone. But Regulus was right—his actions were his own.

She wouldn't ever be separated from Regulus so far as she could help it again. And she was going to marry him at the earliest opportunity.

Heavy footsteps echoed down the hall and she sat up, even though it sounded like a guard, not a servant. A man carried a sputtering torch to her cell.

"Belanger." Antar smiled as he unlocked the cell door. "Time to go. The king would like to see you. You have an hour to get presentable and be back in this cell."

"In the cell?" Adelaide stood and brushed off her dress, only smearing the grime further. "The king is…coming to the dungeon?" That made no sense.

"Oh, heavens, no." Antar swung the cell door wide open. "It didn't seem right, you being…you know." He gestured at her bloodied and disheveled appearance. "Not after all you've done. Beale's out purchasing supplies in town." He winked. "What he doesn't know won't hurt him. Or at the least, he can't stop."

She stepped out of the cell and followed Antar down the hallway. "He doesn't seem to like me much."

"Yeah, well." Antar cleared his throat. "He was good friends with Breck. Some of the guards saw you with Carrick just before everything went to pieces. Saw Carrick kill Breck first and you not helping. He has this harebrained notion you wanted Carrick to kill Breck, since you two didn't get along." He shrugged. "I talked him out of thinking you were on Carrick's side, but he still thinks you didn't care if Carrick killed Breck."

"Oh." She didn't know what else to say. Just thinking about teaming up with Nolan for anything made her lightheaded. Even if she hadn't given Breck's death a second thought, she wouldn't have conspired to kill him.

It was morning—late morning. The sun was blinding, and she had to shield her eyes. Antar led her to her room. To Adelaide's extreme disappointment, Regulus wasn't there. Antar didn't know where he was. But there was a tub of water. "I'll be right outside the door when you're done. I mean, I know you won't run, but…"

"I understand." She locked the door nonetheless.

A bar of soap sat on the table, next to the lantern—and the ivory-accented dagger. She stared at it, frozen as she remembered the sensation of the steel pressed against her neck. She shuddered and pushed her fear away. Nolan was dead. But she still hated that dagger. She threw a dirty shirt Regulus had left on the floor over the dagger.

The water felt amazing, if only a little warm. She used her magic to heat it further, then sunk in and rested her chin on her knees. She healed the bruises from the night on the stone, then scrubbed off the filth and stench. Her hair was such a disaster she climbed out of the tub before cleaning it. She couldn't finish lacing her sky-blue dress on her own. The tangled knots in her hair fought her comb as she worked through her long thick hair. She was nearly finished when she heard voices in the hall.

"Lieutenant? What's wrong?"

Her heart rejoiced at the sound of Regulus' voice. She tossed the comb on the bed and made for the door.

"Ah, I can't let you open that door," Antar said. "For decency's sake."

"What?" Regulus sounded bewildered and flustered.

Adelaide unlocked the door and threw it open to a view of the back of Antar's head. Regulus stood across from Antar, arms crossed, his mouth curved down, pulling on his scar. Dresden stood at Regulus' side, a look on his face like he was sizing Antar up for a fight. Regulus looked past Antar as she opened the door. He broke into a wide grin. Etiros above, that smile made her heart dance.

Antar glanced over his shoulder and stepped out of the way. She barreled past him and slammed against Regulus' chest. Regulus grunted, then laughed as he wrapped his arms around her. She closed her eyes and breathed him in. He smelled like linen and pepper and leather. And like he had been training, but she didn't care. She held him like she might never get the chance again.

"Hey," he murmured. His breath tickled the top of her ear. "You okay?"

"Yes. I am now." She pulled back so she could kiss him and didn't stop until Antar cleared his throat—twice. Regulus looked dazed. She turned and pointed at her back. "Can you finish lacing me up?"

"Huh?" Regulus said. "Oh, yeah."

Deep red suffused Antar's face, and he turned and faced down the hallway. Regulus grabbed the laces, but the dress didn't tighten around the top of her torso. Instead, his lips pressed against her back between the laces. She blushed.

"I missed you, too."

"I'm standing right here," Dresden complained.

"Then turn around or something," Regulus grumbled. The dress pulled closer around her shoulders and down her torso as he finished tightening the laces. He tied off the bottom and her breath caught as his mouth brushed over the base of her neck. "Is this okay?" he whispered.

She nodded, her heart running away in the best way possible. "More than okay." His fingers stroked the side of her neck as he pulled her hair over her back.

"Marry me, Adelaide." He kissed her cheek and slipped his arms around her waist.

"Great," Dresden said. "In case you're wondering, he likes to be called Captain or My Lord when he gives orders."

"It's not an order, you idiot," Regulus said with a laugh.

Adelaide turned in his arms with a chuckle and curled a strand of his hair around her finger. His clear gray eyes were the most beautiful thing she had ever seen. "I thought we already agreed?" She leaned forward to kiss him again, but Antar cleared his throat like he was trying to get the attention of an entire courtyard.

"You should, ah, finish brushing your hair. I need to get you back to the dungeon before Beale gets back."

Regulus frowned. "What? Why?"

"Rules are rules to Beale. Rules are…bendable when Beale's away." Antar motioned her back into the room. "Compromise so she can look like a lady in front of the king."

With reluctance, she left Regulus' arms and returned to combing her hair.

"The king has asked for her?"

"And you," Antar confirmed. "Couldn't find you, but I figured you'd show up. I have a servant boy looking for you, though."

Regulus reddened. "I, um…"

"Snuck out?" Antar asked.

Adelaide froze with the comb in her hair. Surely he wouldn't have done something so reckless, not now.

"Oh, no! Drez and I maybe…kind of…practiced our swordplay in the king's private training yard." Regulus shrugged. "No one ever uses it."

Adelaide held her breath. Then Antar laughed. "This is selfish of me, Hargreaves, but I hope the king keeps you two around. You keep things interesting."

Adelaide finished combing her hair and braided it. She slipped on clean boots and tied a narrow navy cloth belt around her waist, then stepped out of the room. Antar led her back to the dungeon. Regulus accompanied them, holding her hand until they reached the guard room, at which point Antar wouldn't let him continue.

"I'll see you soon, *mareh piahre.*" Regulus ran his fingertips around the edge of her face.

"And then no more splitting up. For real this time." She kissed his cheek and whispered in his ear. "The sooner I can call you my husband, the easier that should be."

She left Regulus staring after her with a ridiculous boyish smile as she followed Antar back to her cell. She paced back and forth to keep herself from sitting down or leaning against the bars and soiling her dress. Finally, footsteps echoed down the hall—but it was a servant bringing food. Nervousness about seeing the king reduced her appetite, but she managed to eat most of the bread before more footsteps approached.

Beale opened the cell door and wrinkled his nose as she stepped out. "How'd you get cleaned up?"

She smiled and waved a hand. "Magic."

He stared for a moment, then shrugged. "Come on. You've been called to an audience with the king." She followed him back to the guard room. Beale selected a pair of manacles off the wall and walked toward her.

"Seriously?" Adelaide stared at the shackles.

"It's protocol." He grabbed her hand and closed the cold manacle around her wrist. "You're not above the rules." He locked the other manacle in place. The round metal bars laid heavy on her wrists. "Let's go, Belanger."

Regulus stood waiting outside. His face clouded as he strode toward her, eyes flashing. "Manacles, sir? Really?"

"Protocol," grunted Beale.

Regulus ground his teeth and wrapped his arm around her shoulders.

"No touching the prisoners." Beale glowered at them.

But Regulus didn't let go. "What're you going to do? Shackle me? Fine, but we'll be late." Adelaide had to purse her lips to keep from smiling at the irritated look Beale gave Regulus.

"Fine." Beale motioned them forward. "Just keep walking."

THE ENTIRE time they made their way through the palace, Adelaide stayed nestled against Regulus' side. Beale led them to a room a little bigger than where they had first met the king. The furnishings were ostentatious, with candelabras covered in gold leaf and black marble statues of rearing horses that framed a large fireplace. A wood throne with cushions covered in deep purple cloth sat unoccupied on a small dais under a stained-glass window of a white hart in the woods. The front legs of the throne were carved with a dragon on one side and a knight on the other.

The door to their right, next to the fireplace, opened. They all bowed as the king strode in, his crimson cape brushing the ground behind him. The dragon-hilt sword hung at his hip and a gold crown rested on his head. He did not look at them as he crossed to the throne. It made Adelaide feel small and nervous.

After he sat on the throne, the king finally looked at them. "Adelaide Belanger. Step forward."

Adelaide moved forward, Regulus' arm slipping off her shoulders and leaving her cold. She knelt before the king and lowered her head, the shackles on her wrists clinking a reminder of her tenuous position.

"Adelaide Belanger, you stand accused of desertion from the ranks of the royal guard, of disobeying a direct order from your commanding officer, of attacking other members of the royal guard, and abandoning your sacred oath to us, that you would protect us first and foremost. What defense do you give?"

The forbidding coldness in the king's tone wasn't promising. Adelaide took a moment to answer, praying for the right words.

"Your Excellency." She looked up at the king's hard expression and fought to keep her tone measured and even. "The night of the masque I did everything in my power to protect Your Excellency and your family. I gave my energy; I gave my strength. And against my will, I sacrificed my betrothed to capture and torture and I lost my father to the next life." Emotion gave her voice a slight tremor, and she had to push aside her heartache to continue.

"I did not disobey orders because I wanted to turn my back on Your Excellency or my duty," she continued. "I did not want to wait for Kirven to come. Nor could I. The bond between Regulus and I meant that the longer they tortured him, the weaker I became. If I had done as ordered, Kirven would have come and I would have been drained of power and Your Excellency's life would have been in danger. I set out to rescue Regulus and stop Kirven and Nolan Carrick before they hurt or killed anyone else, including Your Excellency. And that's what I did. I do not regret my choice." She lowered her head. "I humbly beg Your Excellency's pardon for my disobedience. I did it out of regard for my duty, not disdain."

The king sat silent while sweat beaded on her brow. "Sir Michael," the king called.

The side door opened. Sir Michael the steward scuttled in, the Staff of Nightfall in his hands. So Dresden had made it back to the palace, she realized with relief. Sir Michael held it out to Adelaide. She took it, confused why he had given it to her. The steward stepped away.

"What would you recommend we do with our brother's weapon?" The king rested his chin on his ring-laden fingers.

There was only one thing to do with it, but Adelaide doubted she had the strength. She lowered her head and gripped the Staff, letting her magic flow into it, exploring it. She flinched at the anger and destructive sorcery her magic brushed against in the Staff, but she also found weaknesses. Kirven had been right—the rebounded spell had caused fissures all along the Staff of Nightfall.

She closed her eyes and channeled her magic into the fissures, concentrating on hardening the magic into solid light, like driving a wedge into a crack. Light glowed in front of her closed lids. Then, with a sound like a crack of thunder, a flash of light, and a rush of her power, the staff shattered in her hands. Adelaide collapsed forward and pressed her trembling hands against the floor, panting, but allowed herself a slight smile. Gold and opal pieces littered the carpet.

"I would throw the pieces into the sea, Your Excellency," she said, breathless.

Several moments passed before the king spoke. "Sir Michael, please gather the pieces and have them thrown into the sea at three different points." Sir Michael gathered the pieces as the king continued. "Lieutenant Beale remove her shackles. Adelaide Belanger, you have asked for our pardon, and we freely—and gratefully—give it."

"Thank you, Your Excellency." Adelaide swayed as she stood and curtsied to the king, then drew back next to Regulus. Beale didn't look pleased as he removed her manacles, but she was too relieved to care.

"You are dismissed, Lieutenant Beale." The king waved a hand. Beale bowed to the king and departed with a quick glare at Adelaide.

Regulus placed his arm around her shoulders, and Adelaide slumped against his side, exhausted.

"We owe you both our life and our kingdom." The king inclined his head. "What reward would you ask of us?"

Could they ask to be released from the guard? She didn't want to appear dismissive of the king's generosity, but would asking be impertinent? Regulus also seemed unsure since he didn't speak. She had just been pardoned; maybe humility was best.

"Your Excellency," Adelaide said with a wobbly curtsy, "your continued rule is a reward in itself."

The king smiled. "A noble answer, but please. This is your chance to ask anything." His eyes danced. "We grant you two boons to show our gratitude. The first is our choice, the second is yours. First, in recognition of your service and your sacrifice, we release you, Lady Adelaide Belanger and Lord Regulus Hargreaves of Arrano, from our service. You are free to return to your former lives."

She curtsied and heard Regulus sigh with relief as he bowed.

"What would you ask of us?" the king pressed.

Before Adelaide thought of an answer, Regulus whispered in her ear. She smiled and nodded.

"Your Excellency, there is only one thing I want in this entire world." Regulus squeezed her hand. "Would Your Excellency perform our marriage rites?"

CHAPTER 47

"MARRIAGE? RIGHT now?" The king's forehead wrinkled. "Here?"

"If it pleases Your Excellency, yes." Adelaide tapped her toes, impatience restoring some of her drained energy. They could find a priest or lord or someone if the king said no, but she was ready now.

A slow smile spread over the king's face. He stood. "Very well." He looked around the room. "I shall send for a unity cord."

She untied the thin midnight blue cloth belt from her waist. "We can use this, Your Excellency."

The king took the belt. "Face each other and take each other's right hand."

They did as instructed, and Adelaide could no longer stop her wide smile. Regulus grinned until the skin wrinkled around his scar. She fixed her gaze on his sparkling gray eyes and her pulse quickened in eager anticipation.

"Lord Regulus Hargreaves, Lady Adelaide Belanger." The king began looping the belt over and around their clasped hands. "Today you declare before Etiros, before man, and before your king, that you shall henceforth be united. As we now bind your hands, may this cord symbolize that you shall be bound to each other, heart, mind, body, and soul." The king tied the ends of the cords together and rested the knot on top of their hands. "Let this knot never be undone, nor the bond between this man and woman severed."

The traditional Monparthian marriage blessing placed a dull ache in her heart. Her gaze drifted down to Regulus' right sleeve. He squeezed her hand. When she met his eyes again, they were brimming with joy and not a hint of doubt. The ache abated and she waited impatiently for the king to finish the blessing.

"May love and joy mark your days." The king clasped his hands. "When darkness falls, may you be each other's light. When light abounds, may you increase each other's joy. When storms come, may you be each other's strength. When you disagree, may you remember you started this journey hand in hand. And when tensions arise"—the king tugged on the sides of the knot and tightened it further—"may they serve only to bring you closer together." He looked at Regulus. "Would you like to add your own vows?"

Regulus nodded. "I…" His voice broke and he cleared his throat. "I promise to respect you, honor you, love you, and protect you so long as I live. I will stand by your side as you stand by mine. I will love you and you only, wholly and completely. You are my home, my life—*mareh piahre*. I choose you to be mine and give myself to you. I would not change you, but I cherish you as you are, my mage, my *shiraa*." He rubbed her hand with his thumb, sending a spark dancing over her skin. "The bond that exists between us, connecting us heart to heart and soul to soul, shall never be broken."

The king looked to her, but she had to try several times to speak as she blinked away tears. *The bond that exists.* Not existed. Exists. They didn't need magic to bind them any more than her parents did. *I wish Father were here.* She swallowed back her sorrow as her mind drifted to the vows Mother had written for her wedding and framed in their cottage in the woods. A combination of Monparthian and Khastallander tradition. She adapted what she could remember of them now.

"From this day forward, I walk beside you." Her voice strengthened as she continued, echoing the resolve in her heart. "We will walk together, we will share our strength, our happiness, and our trials. I will walk beside you in love and sacrifice. What is mine is yours, and what is yours is mine." She paused, remembering his full acceptance of every part of her. "*Naem vishodah rohpe ahpek sanerpat hohn, aor haem ahp mareh kusheh.*" Regulus' brows drew together, but his smile didn't fade nor did the sparkle in his eyes. She repeated herself in Monparthian. "I am purely devoted to you, and you are my joy."

The king waited a moment to ensure she was done, then spoke. "Lord Hargreaves, do you take this woman to be your wedded wife, to serve and protect and cherish her, from this day until you breathe your last?"

"I do." Regulus responded almost before the king had finished speaking.

"Lady Adelaide, do you take this man to be your wedded husband, to serve and respect and cherish him, from this day until you breathe your last?"

"I do." She bounced on the balls of her feet.

"Then by the power we hold as king of Monparth, we solemnly charge you to keep these vows, and we pronounce you husband and wife. From this day forward, you will be known as Lord and Lady Hargreaves of Arrano. Lord Hargreaves, you may kiss your bride."

Adelaide grabbed the back of Regulus' head as he placed his hand on her waist and they kissed, their hands still clasped between them with her belt loosely tying them together. She could tell Regulus wanted to pull her closer, but instead he let his lips leave hers.

"May Etiros bless you and your marriage." The king gathered up the top of the belt and they slipped their hands out. He handed the tied belt to Regulus.

Regulus bowed and looped the belt over his arm. "Thank you, Your Excellency."

The king sat back down on his throne but did not dismiss them. Regulus slid his arm around her waist as they waited.

"We would recognize you in front of all our people," the king said. "Tomorrow night, we will host a banquet in your honor." He smiled. "After that, you are free to return to Arrano."

Adelaide curtsied and Regulus bowed as they murmured their thanks. The king rose and left the room. Regulus turned and swept her off her feet and kissed her with all the passion he had held back in front of the king. "My wife."

"My husband." She took his hand and they exited the way they had come in. A servant escorted them out of the palace, casting incredulous looks over his shoulder as they giggled like children and once nearly walked into a display of armor because they were too busy staring into each other's eyes. The servant left them in the rear courtyard in a hurry. They were so busy hanging onto each other, she didn't notice Dresden running toward them until he skidded to a stop in front of the entrance to the servant's wing.

"What did the king say?" Dresden demanded as they straightened and pulled apart slightly, heat rushing to Adelaide's face. "No shackles, so is everything…" His eyes narrowed at Regulus' arm, and he pointed. "What—wait. Is that…a unity cord?" He staggered back, jaw hanging open and brow pinched over wounded eyes. "Regulus Daveth Hargreaves, did you get married without me?"

Adelaide blushed and looked away, hoping she looked less awkward than she felt.

"Ah… We, I mean…" Regulus cleared his throat. "The king released us from the guard and then he…we were…Drez—"

"Oh, I see." Dresden threw his hands up. "I get you two together and I'm not invited to the wedding!" He rolled his eyes. "It's fine, I'm just waiting, mad with worry, while you're getting married without me, not even thinking about me, headed to your room clinging to each other like a couple of…" His eyes widened. "Oh great Etiros above and all the world below. I—I should go…" He edged away from the door into the courtyard. "Totally forgot, I need to…uh, see a man about, um…a goat?" He gave Regulus an exaggerated wink and left.

Regulus and Adelaide looked at each other, then doubled over laughing. Regulus looped his arm around her waist and drew her close as they made their way inside. At their door, Regulus stopped.

"Ah, wait. I've always wanted to do this." He pushed the door open then swept her into his arms. Her head bumped the doorframe and her boot caught on the wall. He stumbled into the room, both of them shaking with laughter.

"Well, that went differently in my head." He set her down on the bed and caressed her cheek. "How are you feeling? You looked drained after breaking the staff. Do you…need food? Water?" He hesitated. "Sleep?"

"Are you joking?" She grabbed his shirt and pulled him down to kiss him. Her heart danced as they tumbled onto the bed, tangled in each other's arms. "Right now?" she whispered, breathless. "I just need my husband."

CHAPTER 48

THE EARLY morning sun warmed Regulus' back, and his chest grazed Adelaide's back as they rode toward home. Her braided hair smelled of honey and flowers. A light breeze whispered through the yellowing leaves of the orchard to their right and the field of grain to their left. The horses' hooves kept a steady beat on the rutted dirt road. Dresden rode to their right, and a white mare from the king trailed along behind carrying their saddlebags.

"Zephyr was a gift from Father," Adelaide had murmured. "I'm sure I'll love her eventually. But not yet."

Regulus didn't mind riding together in the least. Since their marriage, he found he always wanted to touch her. Hold her hand, stroke her hair, put his arm around her waist or shoulders. Just to know she was there, and to let her know he was there. To reassure himself that she was his, and he was hers, and this bliss wasn't just a dream. Currently, he had his arms looped around her middle, Sieger's reins held loosely in his right hand.

They didn't have much to pack. Other than food, the saddlebags carried the gifts the king had given them at the banquet, in front of the court. Nobles had clapped and cheered and raised their glasses when the king toasted them and made certain to shake their hands and congratulate them. Many seemed genuine. Regulus pretended not to notice the others' occasional murmurs of *illegitimate*, *mercenary*, *non-noble*, and *foreign*. Their judgment hurt, but when Regulus looked at Adelaide, he knew they were stronger than any narrow-minded, insecure nobles.

The rich gifts made Regulus nervous to travel across Monparth alone. A sack of gold coins as a reward for killing the sorcerer. A small wooden box engraved with running deer with antlers carved from actual antlers that held their unity cord. A delicate sword, about a foot long and made of pure silver with a handle of gold as a gift for Lady Tamina Belanger in recognition of Alfred's sacrifice. Adelaide had cried when she accepted the sword.

The king had also given them the sword that hung at Regulus' side and a set of throwing knives and a dagger Adelaide had hidden in her boots. At least their riches were hidden in an average-looking saddlebag. Besides, between the three of them, any would-be bandits would regret targeting them.

"I still don't know how I'm going to tell Mother," Adelaide said, breaking the silence. "And Landon…he's going to blame me."

"It's not your fault. If he can't see that, if he doesn't see you as a hero like the king does, that's his problem." Regulus sighed and rubbed her upper arm through her soft sleeve. "And I'll be with you. You won't have to do it alone."

She shuddered against his chest and took a shaky breath. "Promise?"

"I already did." He kissed her cheek. "Forever and always. No more splitting up."

She laughed and wiped away a tear. "Thank you."

"Anything for my wife." He kissed the back of her neck. And then behind her ear, making her giggle.

"Again, I am right here," Drez said. "Save the newly-wed shenanigans for when you're alone. Gracious." But his complaining sounded a lot more like amusement than disgust.

"First on the agenda after we get to Arrano," Adelaide said. "Find Dresden a lady so we can get some peace."

"Now that," Drez said with a chuckle, "is an idea I can get behind; especially now that I have somebody to keep an eye on Regulus. Which is exhausting, I hope you realize. Say, you sure you're fresh out of unwed sisters?"

Adelaide laughed. The genuine, lighthearted laugh he loved so much, that reminded him no darkness was inescapable. "Quite sure." She leaned her head back on Regulus' shoulder and reached up to play with his hair. He had to fight the urge to close his eyes instead of paying attention to where Sieger was going.

Not that he cared much where they went. They needed to see Tamina, and he wanted to bring his wife home to Arrano. He could already imagine the congratulatory heckling the men would give him. But he was in no rush. He didn't care where they traveled or how long it took to get there.

Regulus was free to do what he wanted, not only what he was told. Free to face his men without worrying if he would hurt them. Free to love Adelaide and choose to fulfill her every wish. He rested his cheek against her temple and watched the sky turn from pink to brilliant blue.

He had everything he needed right here.

Servant, Mercenary, Brother

A Dresden Jakobs Vignette Collection

Volume I

Dresden, Age: 10
Location: Lanure Duchy, Monparth

A LOUD THUD sounded from the tiny kitchen, and Dresden paused outside the back door. His grip tightened on the basket of eggs as Da's agitated voice filtered through the uneven gaps in the rough wood door of their mud cottage.

"I don't know what else to do!" Da snapped in Carasian. Whatever they were arguing about, it was bad if Da wasn't using Monparthian. Da had a rule: between breakfast and supper, only Monparthian. He wanted his family to do well in Monparth.

Wanted. Dresden didn't understand the specifics, but he knew they weren't doing well. Ma and Da argued more all the time. It scared little four-year-old Tatya, and Dresden hated that. But he didn't know what the problem was, other than they were in trouble, so he didn't know how to fix it. He knew that they didn't have the coin to replace the trousers that showed his ankles, that Ma had added fabric from an apron to the sleeves and sides of Tatya's dress when it got too tight instead of replacing it.

"But the animals are the only thing keeping us going," Ma said quietly, also in Carasian. "What will we do without selling the milk and eggs? How will we feed the children? We will have nothing."

A shudder went through Dresden. He brushed dark hair out of his eyes as he glanced back at the little pen, where Tatya was cooing under her breath to the goat while stroking its black hair. The nanny goat mostly ignored her, contentedly chewing on grass. Da wanted to sell the animals? *But…what will we eat? And Tatya is going to cry.*

"We'll still have a home," Da said roughly. "They keep increasing the interest, saying there's a new fee. They're robbing us, and I can't…no official will listen to a Carasian peasant. If I don't sell the animals now, they'll take them and throw us out." Da drew a ragged breath. "I'm sorry. I failed you. We shouldn't have left Carasom. I shouldn't have taken us so far into Monparth—"

"My beloved, hush." Soft footsteps sounded on the dirt floor of the kitchen, and Dresden leaned closer to the door. "Our children have been spared the violence we suffered."

"We could have gone somewhere else," Da mumbled. "Other parts of

Carasom have better rulers, who keep better peace. Or we could have—"

"We are here now. We cannot move forward by dwelling on the past, be-cause we cannot change it. You did what you thought was right. I trusted you. I still trust you."

Dresden nudged the door, and it inched open. He peered through the nar-row gap. Ma stood next to Da, who sat at the rough square table, his head in his hands. She tenderly stroked his thick dark hair, but her olive brown face was drawn and oddly pale.

"You believe this is best?" Ma murmured. "It will be enough silver?"

Da's shoulders heaved. "If we sell them all? The cow, the chickens, the goat… I think so. We'll find a way to survive. It will be easier without them taking every spare coin."

Ma's lower lip trembled, but she nodded. "Then that's what we'll do."

When they didn't say anything more, Dresden finally pushed open the door and walked in, pretending like he hadn't just heard that Da was selling all their animals, that they weren't about to lose almost everything. He smiled as well as he could.

"I got all the eggs," he said in Monparthian. "Twenty today. How many should I put aside for the market?"

Da lifted his head. "None of them, Dresden." His Monparthian was thick and heavily accented. His dark eyes looked tired. "Leave them on the table for your mother. I need you to help me take the cow and goat into town. We'll be taking the chickens in tomorrow."

Dresden froze. He wanted to ask why, to know what was happening. But demanding answers of his father would not be respectful. "Yes, Da."

Tatya did cry when Dresden took the goat from her pen and Ma explained the goat had to leave and not come back. She clung to Ma's skirts, snot running from her little button nose. It twisted Dresden's heart.

They led the red heifer and the black nanny goat into town and walked the three miles along the worn, rutted road in silence. Da's scimitars across his back glinted in the midday sun. Dresden wished he could wear his. Da looked so intimidating wearing them. But despite Da giving him his own set last year, Dresden wasn't very good with them yet. They were still big for him to use and made him tired.

The tangle of wooden buildings forming the town of Wiltsley spread out ahead of them. The air took on a stench of bodies and waste that Dresden hated as they drew closer. Da sighed.

"Dresden… I want you to understand. So you never do what I did." Da rubbed the back of his neck with his free hand, the other holding the lead to the heifer. "I borrowed coin to get us started here. Too much. And I took too long to pay it back. We desperately need coin—" Da drew in a sharp breath and stopped short. "Dresden. Stay close to me."

Dresden took in his father's tense expression, then traced his stare to two Monparthian men walking toward them. One was broad-shouldered, dressed in rich linens dyed deep blues and greens, his blond hair drawn back in a greasy tail. The other was slim, with an overly wide smile, wiry brown eyebrows, and closely-shorn brown hair.

"Jakobs, fancy seeing you here," Blond said, a mocking edge to his voice. "This must be your son?" He looked to Dresden. Dresden drew closer to Da's side.

"Where are you going with those fine animals?" Skinny asked.

"Market," Da said flatly.

"I see." Blond stopped, entirely too close for Dresden's comfort. "Hopefully they fetch a good price, if you're to pay back the two hundred and fifty silver you owe."

"Two—it's one hundred and eighty," Da exclaimed.

Skinny shrugged. "Pretty sure with your current interest and fees for our time, I have two hundred and fifty written down. You might be in luck, though." Skinny stepped closer. "How old are you, boy?" The man reached toward Dresden, and Da stepped between them.

"Don't touch my son."

Dresden peered around Da's shoulder, squeezing the goat's lead so hard the rope dug into his palms.

Skinny held up his hands. "Easy, I'm not threatening. Just thinking." He nodded toward town. "There's a man in town from the Kimberly estate. They're looking for a boy between the ages of nine and twelve to be a personal manservant to some noble boy."

Dresden wrinkled his nose. *A servant to some stuck-up noble?*

"Hey, that's smart, Jeffrey," Blond said. "Come on. We'll take you to him."

"I'm not interested," Da said. He started forward, and the men blocked his path.

"Wearing your weapons again, I see," Skinny—Jeffrey, apparently—said.

Da shifted. He wasn't nervous…was he? Da was never nervous. Dresden peered up at Da's strained expression.

"Surprised you haven't sold those yet," Jeffrey continued. "Hardly proper for a peasant to be caring them around. Someone might think you're trying to cause trouble. Mightn't they, Trenton?"

"Aye, they might."

"No trouble." Da's throat bobbed.

"Good," Trenton said. "Then you'll happily accompany us." The men started forward. Da hesitated, then followed. Dresden trailed after him, the goat nudging his hip with her head.

These were the men Da owed? *Why would Da ever make a deal with people like that?*

The men led them past the marketplace to a tavern. A few people stood around under the wood awning stretching across the front of the tall, narrow building. Blond waved at a middle-aged man with a pinched expression who was shaking his head at a couple of young men. He shooed the young men away and crossed over.

"Can I help you?"

"You're the man from the Kimberly estate, yes?" Trenton asked.

The man lifted a brow. "I'm Steward Harreldon, yes."

"Heard you were looking for a servant boy." Trenton jerked his thumb toward Dresden. "Might have found one. Depends on the deal."

"No," Da said, his voice steady. "This is a misunderstanding."

"Might change your mind depending on the deal," Jeffrey said.

Harreldon ran a palm over his flashy bright green doublet, looking down his nose at all of them. "Lord Kimberly has in his care a young…nobleman. He's eleven and requires a servant of a similar age. Someone to do his cleaning and wait on him, accompany him, do whatever small tasks the young man might require. The terms are a ten-year indenture, purchased for four hundred silver, paid to the boy's family."

Dresden's eyes went wide. *Four hundred silver!*

"Well, that seems excellent." Jeffrey turned toward Da. "You can send your boy to serve some rich nobleman's son, keep your animals, get a little extra coin, and we get our three hundred silver."

"Three hundred?" Da's voice squeaked.

Trenton grinned, the look somehow savage. "Middleman fee for arranging this deal."

"And if I say no?" Da said quietly.

"Well, we still went to all this trouble," Jeffrey said with the fakest expression of concern Dresden had ever seen, "so you'll still owe us three hundred."

Dresden coiled and uncoiled the rope in his hands. Would…would Da send him away? For ten years? *Tatya could get a new dress. Ma and Da could stop fighting. Da wouldn't have to sell the animals.*

"What is indenture?" Dresden asked. His voice sounded small and high, and he tried to cover it by standing up straighter.

Harreldon clasped his hands behind his back. "A contract that binds you to your master until you've repaid the debt, fulfilled the terms of your contract, and your master signs your release. In this case, ten years in exchange for four hundred silver. If you leave before you are released, you will be hunted, and your master can choose to take you back or have you imprisoned or executed."

Dresden swallowed hard.

"Thank you for your time." Da inclined his head, but Dresden caught the slight tremor in his voice. "We are not interested."

Jeffrey looked askance at Trenton. "Shame. Hope you can get three hundred silver for your animals. Better sell the foreign swords, too. Maybe that will get you close." He lifted a shoulder.

Da just nodded and turned back toward the market. Dresden followed slowly. "Da?"

"Yes?"

"Can you get three hundred silver for the animals?"

Da's shoulders slumped. "No."

Dresden's feet dragged, his worn boots catching on the uneven street. *Da wanted to sell the animals so he wouldn't owe coin. And he still will.* "Da?"

"Yes, Dresden."

"Will they really make us leave the house?"

Da stopped short and gave Dresden a sharp look. "Were you listening to your ma and I talk?"

Dresden's cheeks heated, and he ducked his head.

"Possibly," Da said with a sigh.

And Tatya won't have a safe home. Dresden straightened and lifted his chin. "I can be a servant."

Da's eyes widened. "Dresden, no—"

But Dresden dropped the goat's lead and ran back to the man in the fancy doublet. Harreldon lifted a brow as Dresden stopped in front of him. "I will do it."

"No." Da's hand clamped his shoulder and pulled him back.

Dresden turned on him. "Tatya should be able to get a new dress. And Ma is right. You need the animals. Please, Da."

Da's eyes glistened. "You don't understand what you're saying."

Maybe he didn't. He wasn't sure. He'd heard nobles could be rude. Mean. But those men were mean to Da. And Dresden could make them leave Da alone. "I will do it."

Harreldon grunted. "Your father has to agree. You both have to sign the papers."

"And the silver coin?" Dresden asked.

"Locked up in the tavern."

Da shuffled his feet. "So if we agreed…you would give me the coin today?" He shook his head. "No. I can't. Dresden, your ma will never forgive me."

"What will happen to Ma if you can't get the coin?" Dresden asked.

Da's face twisted. "*Yuldesh, hir isad.*" *Alright, my son.* Da dropped to one knee and pulled Dresden to his chest, nearly strangling him in a tight embrace. Dresden buried his face in Da's shoulder as he clutched his father's shirt. "*Yuldesh, hir lodde tam,*" Da murmured. *Alright, my brave boy.*

They tied up the cow and goat and followed Harreldon into the tavern, through a crowded room that smelled of pipe smoke, up rickety stairs into a tiny room with a sagging cot and table hardly big enough for Harreldon to lay out what he explained was the contract of indenture. Da signed his name with an X, and Dresden clumsily wrote his own name under the lines of Monparthian text he couldn't read. Harreldon handed Da a bulging sack of coin and looked at Dresden.

"Let's go. I want to leave this disgusting place."

Da made a strange noise in his throat. "Right now?"

Harreldon waved the parchment. "Yes, now. His life is not his own. Assuming he doesn't do anything to increase his debt, he'll be his own man again in ten years."

Dresden wiped his sweaty hands on his ratty trousers. Ten years was so long.

"Can…can I send him something?" Da asked, his voice strained. "To the Kimberly castle?"

The man shrugged. "So long as his master allows him to keep it."

Da nodded and hugged Dresden again. "I'll bring you your scimitars," he whispered in Carasian. "I'm sorry, Dresden. This shouldn't be your burden to bear. You're too young…" Da shook his head and firmly patted Dresden's back. "Do well. Serve well. Stay out of trouble. Make us proud. May Etiros protect you and keep you."

The final goodbyes were a blur. Harreldon mounted a horse and pulled Dresden up behind him. Dresden clutched Harreldon's belt as he watched Da fade away into the distance. *What have I done?*

DRESDEN'S MOUTH fell open as they approached the castle. He'd never gone near it before. It was so big, with its towering gray stone wall and central stone tower. Several multi-story wood buildings that looked far more solid than the ones in town flanked the tower. They stopped in the courtyard, empty except for a few servants going about their tasks. Harreldon dismounted and lifted Dresden down.

"I'm going to present you to Lord Kimberly and Master Hargreaves," Harreldon said gruffly. "Bow when you see them. Keep your eyes lowered, don't speak unless you are asked a question, if you must answer a question, refer to Lord Kimberly as my lord and Master Hargreaves as master. To be clear for the future, you will call Lady Kimberly my lady, and everyone else mistress or master. Understood?"

Dresden nodded, unable to speak. Harreldon escorted him inside. Dresden gawked as they walked down a hallway covered with a crimson carpet, past vases and carved busts on pedestals. Harreldon ushered him into a side room with plush armchairs.

"Wait here. Don't touch anything. Just…stand still." Harreldon slipped out of the door. Dresden stood stiffly and studied the paintings on the walls. Some kind of serpent with icy-blue scales and spikes around its face in a snowstorm. A giant cat that had tusks like a boar, prowling toward a deer. He shuddered and stared at the ground.

My lord, master. My lord, master. As the moments ticked by, he wondered what his master would be like. Would he be kind? Cruel? *Etiros, let him be kind.*

The door creaked open. Harreldon looked at Dresden with distaste. "This way, Jakobs."

He led Dresden into another little room, this one with smaller cushioned chairs arranged in a semi-circle. A brown-haired man wearing clothes that looked even finer than Harreldon's sat in one of the chairs, his muscular build lounging casually. He wore a bored expression. *Must be Lord Kimberly.*

A boy with a round, earnest face stood near the man, but not too near. He'd left a healthy gap between himself and Lord Kimberly. Black hair curled around his ears and over his pale forehead. His light gray eyes fixed on Dresden, his expression curious. In contrast to the vivid dyes and layers of Lord Kimberly's clothing, the boy wore only a simple navy tunic with a plain black belt and gray trousers.

They stopped in the middle of the room, and Dresden did his best bow. Lord Kimberly snorted, and Dresden hoped his face wasn't as red as it felt.

"Lord Kimberly, Master Hargreaves," Harreldon said with a bow. "This is Dresden Jakobs." He handed the boy a rolled-up parchment. "That's the signed indenture."

Master Hargreaves tucked the parchment into his belt.

"He's foreign," Kimberly said.

"He speaks Monparthian fine." Harreldon shrugged.

Kimberly's upper lip curled. "And he's a mess. You'll have to get him cleaned up, Hargreaves, I won't have some peasant running about my estate looking like a beggar."

"Of course, my lord," Hargreaves said quietly.

"And you're responsible for him. Make sure he knows how to behave. I can't imagine he knows anything, so you'll have to make sure he knows his duties and doesn't cause trouble." Kimberly drummed his fingers on the arm of his chair.

"I will."

Kimberly glared at Hargreaves, and the boy flinched.

"I will, my lord."

Dresden's forehead wrinkled. *That seems odd.*

"What are you gawking at?" Kimberly snapped. Dresden quickly bowed his head. "Discipline might be a problem," Kimberly mused. "You might want to purchase a whip."

Dresden's hands went cold. *What?*

"A—a whip, my lord?" Hargreaves stuttered. "He's not a horse or a slave."

"He's indentured, he might as well be a slave." Kimberly sniffed. "Besides, foreign servants are always troublesome."

Terror coiled around Dresden's chest and squeezed. *A…slave?* His knees wobbled. *Da was right. I was foolish. I can't do this.* His gaze flicked to the contract in Hargreaves' belt, and he remembered what Harreldon had said about being hunted. *I have to. I'm trapped.* Understanding of his situation crashed over him. He was entirely at the mercy of this boy and Lord Kimberly.

You're doing this for Tatya and Ma. But even that thought couldn't stop the fear gnawing at his stomach. Fear that soured and turned into resentment toward his new master.

Kimberly stood. "I better write my cousin and tell him I did as requested and got his mistake a servant." Hargreaves' shoulders inched toward his ears. Kimberly strode out, and Harreldon followed. The moment the door closed, Hargreaves' entire body relaxed.

"Hello." Hargreaves smiled. It was a kind, open smile. The kind of smile Dresden would take as an invitation to be friends from one of the village boys. *Keep your eyes down.* Dresden lowered his gaze.

"Hello, master."

"Oh, please, don't do that." Hargreaves cleared his throat. "I mean, in front of Kimberly, probably do. He'll expect it. But…you can call me Regulus the rest of the time."

Dresden's gaze snapped up. "Master Regulus?"

"I suppose that works." Regulus sighed. "Come on. I'll show you around."

Dresden followed him out of the room. He didn't trust his new master's friendliness. Nobles were supposed to be self-obsessed, dismissive of their servants. But…

Could they be friends?

Kimberly's mention of a whip made him shudder. *No, I won't trust him. Not when he's getting a whip to use on me.*

Dresden felt numb as Regulus lead him through the castle, explaining where things were. They ended the tour at Regulus' small room. Dresden had a tiny side room attached to Regulus', just big enough for small cot and a chamber pot. That night, he cried himself to sleep.

DROWN

Age: 10

Location: Kimberly Estate, Monparth

WHEN DA BROUGHT Dresden his scimitars a week later, Regulus let them go for a walk together. Da told him how well they were doing with the extra silver and no longer owing any coin. It made the ache in Dresden's chest dull a little. When Regulus caught Dresden trying to hide the scimitars in his room, he told him not to worry about it. In fact, he'd been fascinated and begged Dresden to tell him about them. He let Dresden keep the blades in his room. And as far as Dresden knew, Regulus didn't buy a whip.

Still, Dresden didn't trust him. Kimberly and his son, Hendrick, were mocking and cruel, to both Regulus and Dresden. Dresden didn't imagine Regulus could be around that and not become equally malicious. But every time Dresden got in trouble for not looking humble enough, or being in the wrong place, or speaking out of turn, Regulus defended him.

"I don't care how you act when Kimberly and Hendrick aren't around," Regulus said one day. "But please, keep your eyes down and don't talk unless you have to around them. Someday, I might not be able to stop them."

Of course, that was easier said than done. Servants were supposed to be quiet, unobtrusive, to stand still and not gawk. Dresden quickly grew restless. Being a servant was harder than anticipated.

But he didn't know what to make of the genuine concern in his master's eyes. *I can't trust him. He's one of them.* But he wasn't—not really. The other servants told Dresden that Regulus was the illegitimate son of Lord Arrano, Lord Kimberly's distant cousin. Kimberly barely tolerated Regulus. The more time Dresden spent around them, the more he hated how the Kimberlys treated Regulus. Except for Brigid Kimberly, who was the same age as Dresden. She sometimes teased Regulus, but not in the malicious way Hendrick did.

Still, Dresden wouldn't get his hopes up that Regulus truly cared about him.

One morning three months into his indenture, they went for Regulus' morning run. He always had Dresden come along. Dresden kept a respectful distance behind Regulus, despite Regulus trying to get him to run alongside him.

As they neared the river that cut across Kimberly's fields, the morning mist thickened, and the sound of rushing water filled his ears. Dresden tensed. He didn't like crossing the narrow wooden bridge over the river, especially when the river was swollen and rushing from recent heavy rainfall. He'd never learned to swim, and the railing-less bridge terrified him, but he wouldn't let Regulus know his weakness.

Fog swirled over the river and clouded the banks. Regulus ran across, his longer legs stretching effortlessly as Dresden struggled to keep up. A twinge went through his side as he neared the center of the bridge. His steps wavered, and his foot caught on a part of the bridge slick with morning dew. He twisted and fell, his feet plunging into freezing water. He clawed at the edge of the slippery, worn wood as the current tugged on his feet. With a scream, he fell, and the river dragged him under.

Dresden thrashed, darkness swirling around him. *Which way is up?* His heart hammered. He kicked as his lungs constricted, making it harder to hold his breath. His head broke water, and he tried to breathe, but got a mouthful of water as he sank back under. He sputtered, only drawing in more water through his nose and mouth. He flailed about looking for something, anything to grab onto. His hand hit something, and he tried to grab it, but it shifted. Something tugged on his arm.

He struck out, trying to free himself from whatever was pulling him down. Somehow, he managed to get his head above water. He blinked stinging water from his eyes as he coughed and gasped, his lungs burning, and continued to fight the river. Something tightened around his chest. He kicked and thrashed.

"Dresden! Stop fighting me!"

Regulus' voice cut through his fuzzy thoughts. He whipped his head around. Regulus' face was inches from his, strained with concentration.

"Calm down so I can swim!"

Dresden forced his trembling limbs to stop flailing. Regulus pulled Dresden's back closer against his chest and dragged him toward the bank, his legs bumping into Dresden's as he kicked. Dresden coughed up water that burned his throat and nose. Regulus pushed him up onto the bank, then climbed up and dragged him away from the river's edge. Dresden rolled onto his side and vomited water. He gulped down air, shivering from the cold.

"Dresden!" Regulus seized his shoulders and searched his face, his eyes wide. "Are you alright?"

Dresden nodded wearily and tried to speak, but his voice came out in a croak. He cleared his throat. "Fine. I'm fine."

"Blessed Etiros above, Dresden. You scared me! You can't swim?"

"No." He coughed again and scrunched his shoulders.

"Well, I'll teach you." Regulus laid back on the grass, his chest heaving. "I'm glad you're alright."

Dresden shivered again. "You…saved me."

Regulus threw his arm over his eyes, hiding the top half of his face. "I was afraid I wasn't going to reach you in time."

"Why did you save me?" Dresden looked at him warily.

"Why?" Regulus removed his arm from over his eyes and frowned. "Someone needs help, and you can help, you help them. And you're my only friend."

"Friend?"

Regulus sighed and sat up. "Look, I know—good gracious, you're shaking. Come on." He pulled Dresden to his feet and led him back to his room, where he forced Dresden to dress in dry clothes. As Dresden dressed, Regulus stoked the fire.

"That's my job, master—"

"I saved your life, maybe you can just call me Regulus now." Regulus added another log to the fire, still wearing his own soaking clothes. He only changed once Dresden was settled in Regulus' single armchair in front of the fire, wrapped in one of Regulus' thick, soft blankets.

"Thank you…Regulus." Dresden clutched the blanket around his shoulders.

Regulus grinned as he peeled off his wet clothes. "I'd hoped we could be friends. I don't really need a servant. All my fath—" He winced. "Lord Arrano's idea. But a friend? I'd like to have a friend."

"You're not like the Kimberlys at all."

Regulus drew back as if slapped. "I hope not. Is that why you've been distant? You thought I was like them?"

Dresden flushed. "You kind of bought me. That's what the other servants say. I was afraid you'd become like them, or that you were pretending to be nice."

Regulus pulled on dry clothes and sat on the floor next to the armchair, his chin cupped his hand. "I'm sorry. I hadn't thought of it that way. You…agreed, though, didn't you?"

"Yes. My Da owed some bad men lots of silver." He shrugged. "Now Da doesn't have to sell the animals, and Tatya has two new dresses, and Da said he is going to replace the doors with ones the wind can't get through."

Regulus looked up at him. "Who's Tatya?"

"My little sister."

"Oh." Regulus' face fell. He looked at the fire. "I'm sorry you had to leave your family. I guess it makes sense you don't want to be my friend."

Dresden sank deeper into Regulus' armchair. "Maybe…we could be friends."

Regulus straightened. "Really? I've never had a friend." His face went crimson and he looked away.

"I guess you have one now." Dresden smiled.

Thank you for letting him be nice, Etiros.

TROUBLE

Age: 13

Location: Kimberly Estate, Lanure Duchy, Monparth

"I WAS ONLY following my lady's orders." Dresden lifted his chin and glared at Hendrick. Morning sunlight shone through the branches of one of the many trees in the walled-in garden next to Lord Kimberly's castle, making him squint. Not really the unafraid look he had hoped would hide his inner dread.

Hendrick was older, taller, and more muscular. Not to mention a lord's son. At thirteen, Dresden was a scrappy servant. The smart thing would be to grovel and beg forgiveness. But Dresden had never been particularly good at groveling, and he'd done nothing wrong. Well, nothing terribly wrong.

"Really, Hendrick." Brigid tugged on her older brother's sleeve. Her silky chestnut hair was wound in braids above her round, pale face and wide eyes. She was short, even for a thirteen-year-old girl. Which was why she'd asked for Dresden's help. "I told him to—"

"Go inside, Brigid." Hendrick gently but firmly pushed her away. "The servant boy should have known better, so he's either a cad or an idiot."

Dresden glowered and forced his hands not to curl into fists.

"Either way, a beating should get through your thick Carasian skull."

Dresden didn't even have time to get angry at Hendrick for using his foreign heritage as an insult, because Hendrick was already pulling his fist back. Again, the smart thing to do would be to stand still and take it. But instinct took over, and Dresden reflexively raised his hands to shield his face. He squeezed his eyes shut as he realized the beating would likely be worse for trying to thwart it.

The blow didn't land.

There was a sharp smack and someone grunted, but it wasn't Dresden. Dresden opened his eyes to a head of thick black hair.

"Move, bastard," Hendrick growled. "That blow wasn't meant for you, but this one will be if you don't get out of my way."

Regulus didn't move, still shielding Dresden with his body. "Dresden is my servant. Any discipline he may need falls to me. We've discussed this." Regulus' voice was steady as he looked up at his cousin. He was barely fourteen but already tall, only a few inches shorter than seventeen-year-old Hendrick. "Now. What happened?"

"He put his hands on Brigid." Hendrick glared at Dresden over Regulus' shoulder.

The disappointment in Regulus' sigh stung far worse than Hendrick's insults. "My lady Brigid, is that true?"

Brigid glanced at her brother uncertainly. "I wanted to see over the wall to watch the horses. Dresden was just helping me balance on the back of the bench. I asked him to."

"And he should have refused!" Hendrick crossed his arms. "Good thing I happened by, because your filthy servant had his hands on my sister's waist."

Dresden winced. Okay, he hadn't thought it through. He should have said no. Or at least only held her hand. But it had felt natural to support her by her waist. And then maybe he did stand a bit closer than he should have…she was really pretty.

Regulus shifted and turned slightly so he could see Dresden without turning his back on his cousin. "Jakobs. Do you understand what you did was wrong?"

Dresden lowered his head. "Yes, master."

"Then what do you do?"

Dresden sighed and bent low toward Hendrick. "I made a mistake. It should not have happened, and I swear, it will not happen again. I humbly beg your forgiveness, Master Kimberly, Mistress Kimberly." Ugh, groveling. He'd find a way not to be a servant one day. He'd earn enough to buy a freeman's holding far from any pompous nobles.

"Your servant is presumptuous and has an attitude problem," Hendrick said coldly. "He needs a beating. If you won't do it, I will."

"Wait." Regulus blocked Dresden from Hendrick. "He's useless to me beaten. I'll deny his next meals—"

"You're soft, Hargreaves," a new male voice intruded.

Dresden glanced up, still bowed, his hands going cold at Lord Kimberly's voice. Regulus offered a quick, stiff bow to his father's cousin as Lord Kimberly approached. Kimberly always looked severe, with his lean, muscular frame and heavy brow. But the disapproving scowl slashed across his mouth made him look more unapproachable than usual.

"Hendrick is correct. Your servant overstepped his station. You must learn to control him, or he will continue to be a rotten servant."

I'm not a rotten servant. Indignation rippled through Dresden, but he kept his head respectfully bowed as he watched the others through his lashes. *I do my job.*

"Yes, my lord." Regulus inclined his head. "I will speak—"

"Speak?" Lord Kimberly's eyes narrowed. "He's your servant. You don't reason with him; you punish his wrongdoing."

"My lord…" Regulus swallowed audibly. "It was a mistake."

"And when he's been properly punished, he will make fewer mistakes." Lord Kimberly turned his cold eyes on Dresden. "Take off your belt, boy, and give it to your master."

Brigid gasped. "Father—"

"Go inside, Brigid." Kimberly, as usual, would allow no argument. Brigid fled the garden, her pink dress rustling as she ran. "Now, boy."

Dresden's hands shook, but he complied. He kept his eyes on the ground as he offered the belt to Regulus. He supposed three years as an indentured servant without a single beating was more than he could have hoped for. Regulus did not take it.

"My lord, please." Regulus' voice had lost its confidence. "It was a first offence."

Hendrick snorted. "Your servant often offends, he just does it differently every time. And you allow it, *Reg*."

Dresden winced. So, Hendrick had overheard them. He knew that Regulus let Dresden call him Regulus, or even Reg, instead of *master*. At least, when they thought no one was listening.

"He is my servant," Regulus said with a shrug. "No one else calls me master, and my name is more respectful than bastard."

There was a terrible moment of silence. Regulus had gone too far, Dresden was certain.

Kimberly sighed. "Hargreaves, Lord Arrano saw fit to give you a servant. If you don't discipline him properly, you do my cousin further discredit. Now take the belt and punish your wayward servant."

Further. Because to some, Regulus' existence did his father discredit. Kimberly refused to even refer to Lord Arrano as Regulus' father, and wouldn't let Regulus do so, either. *I may be foreign and a servant, but at least no one thinks I shouldn't have been born.*

Regulus took a deep, slow breath. He took the belt. Dresden tried not to let his fear or resentment show as he turned and stepped over to brace himself against a nearby oak. He should have known better than to hope his master could be a true friend, even if he was kind.

"My lord, you are right," Regulus said slowly. "The fault is with me, not Jakobs. I have not kept a close enough eye on him or disciplined him enough. His failure as a servant is merely a reflection of my failure as a master. A dog cannot be blamed for stealing from the table if his master feeds him scraps. I will do better in the future. But for now, the problem is me, and the just punishment should be mine."

Dresden's breath caught. He looked over his shoulder. Regulus held the belt out to Kimberly, his eyes downcast. Hendrick smirked. The corner of Kimberly's mouth twitched. He wouldn't—Kimberly took the belt.

"If that's what you want, Hargreaves."

Dresden nearly choked. "Master—"

"Step aside, Jakobs." Regulus' spine was rigidly straight, but he wouldn't meet Dresden's eyes. "Now."

Dresden moved several steps aside, more out of fear of making things worse than any desire to watch Regulus be beaten. Regulus placed his hands on the oak trunk, bracing himself.

"You want your tunic ruined, bastard?" Hendrick taunted.

Regulus grimaced. "A wise consideration, cousin." He pulled off his loose tunic and tossed it to Dresden. Dresden caught it, staring dumbly at Regulus' bare back. He looked frightfully pale compared to Dresden's rich, dark olive skin. Pale and exposed. The shirt was unlikely to have been ruined. But it might have softened the blows. Regulus braced himself against the tree again.

"What's this?" Kimberly stepped forward and hooked his finger on the thin leather cord around Regulus' neck and drew it back. Regulus clutched the necklace in his fist.

"It's mine. From my father—I mean Lord Arrano."

Kimberly stilled. "What is it?"

Regulus' shoulders shook. "A ring." Why he should be afraid of showing the ring, Dresden didn't know. He'd thought Regulus kept it always on his person for safekeeping.

Kimberly's face darkened. He dropped his hand. "Show me."

Regulus turned from the tree, his expression drawn. Slowly he eased his fist and lowered his hand. Kimberly snatched up the ring, the cord taut against Regulus' neck.

"He gave you this, boy?"

"I swear it." Regulus' lower lip trembled. "Before I left. He said to keep it in case I ever had need of it, but to keep it secret. Not to tell a soul. I know I shouldn't have it, but he gave it to me. I didn't steal it, and I don't intend to use it, my lord. Just keep it."

Dresden looked between Regulus and Kimberly, uncomprehending. He'd never looked closely at the tarnished silver ring. Kimberly let the ring fall back to Regulus' bare chest.

"My cousin is more of a fool than I thought." Kimberly looked furious.

"That could cause trouble. Only an heir should carry a signet ring."

Dresden clutched Regulus' shirt in his clammy hands.

"I know, my lord." Regulus lowered his head. "I don't know why he gave it to me. But I've never shown it to anyone."

"Never speak of it again." Kimberly stepped back. "Turn around! Let's get this over with."

Regulus' hands had barely touched the bark when Kimberly drew his hand back. The belt whirred through the air and slapped loudly against Regulus' skin. Regulus twitched and his hands curled against the trunk, but he didn't make a sound. A red line blazed across Regulus' back. As Kimberly drew back again, Dresden squeezed his eyes shut. *Whir. Smack. Whir. Smack.* Again, and again. Regulus cried out. Dresden opened his eyes, afraid to see the aftermath. But Kimberly wasn't done. *Whir. Smack.* Regulus sagged against the tree and whimpered. Again Lord Kimberly pulled back, and it took every ounce of Dresden's resolve not to interfere. It would only make things worse.

The belt hit and Regulus screamed; his knees buckled. Tears squeezed from Dresden's eyes as Kimberly hit Regulus again and Regulus cried, leaning against the tree on his knees.

Kimberly looked at Dresden. "I hope that taught you a lesson as well, boy." He threw the belt at Dresden, and Dresden fumbled it, dropping it and Regulus' shirt to the stone garden path. Hendrick snickered.

"Get up, Hargreaves," Kimberly said with a sigh.

Regulus whimpered and his body trembled, but he pulled himself up on the tree and turned toward his guardian. He managed a small bow, his face pinched with pain. "Thank you, my lord. I will do better."

Kimberly grunted. "You better. I'd hate to have to tell Lord Arrano his mistake can longer reside here. Remember, Hargreaves. You're lucky. Things could be worse. So make the most of your situation, and don't abuse my hospitality by allowing your servant to subvert his station. And keep that signet ring hidden."

"Yes, my lord," Regulus said quietly. "I'm grateful for your kindness."

Kindness? Dresden clutched the shirt and belt. *He just beat you!*

Kimberly nodded, then turned away. Hendrick followed his father out of the garden, and Dresden rushed to Regulus' side.

"Reg," he whispered. "What the hell were you thinking?"

"I couldn't do it." Regulus reached for his shirt and grimaced. He spoke so softly Dresden barely heard him. "I wouldn't hurt my only friend."

Guilt twisted Dresden's stomach. "I'm sorry. If I hadn't been stupid—"

"It's in the past." Regulus pulled on his shirt with a stifled cry. "Go ask Luke for some salve. Say it was a training accident. I'll meet you in my room."

Dresden got the salve as quickly as he could. Regulus was sitting slumped over the back of a chair, his shirt tossed aside. The red lines crisscrossing his back were dotted with dark blue bruises, and pinpricks of crimson showed where the belt had split his skin. Dresden immediately began slathering the lines with the pungent salve, praying to Etiros it would somehow help.

"I can't believe…" He shook his head.

Regulus chuckled drily. "I think he's wanted to do that for some time. He just didn't have a good excuse." He flinched as Dresden touched his back again. "I'm an embarrassment to have around. As if my disgrace taints them. He keeps me for my father's coin. Both the money my father sends for the inconvenience of raising me, and the part of my allowance I know he keeps."

Dresden shifted uncomfortably. Regulus had never talked about his situation. He always bore the insults from Hendrick and the thinly veiled jabs from Lord Kimberly without comment, even in private, and Dresden had never dared to broach the subject.

"But…it's not your fault," Dresden said.

"I know that!" Regulus jerked. "Etiros above, don't tell me things I already know!" He shoved out of the chair. "I didn't ask to be born, or to be sent here! I am polite, I stay out of trouble, I train hard to earn my knighthood so I can leave! But it's never good enough! I'm never good enough."

Regulus leaned on the table, his shoulders trembling. The salve glistened over the dark red lines from the beating that should have been Dresden's. Dresden clutched the little clay jar, unsure what to do as shame gnawed at his skin.

"And now…" Regulus' head sank lower. He looked so young and lonely. "The bastard and his servant friend. You know what they'll say? I'm too comfortable with you because I should be you. They'll say I know deep down I'm more my mother's son than my father's. Maybe they're right."

Dresden stared at the jar. He should apologize for making Regulus' life worse. But for the first time in years, he was afraid of how Regulus might react to him.

"Lord Kimberly and Hendrick will be watching more closely." Regulus sniffed, his voice hoarse. "We're going to need to be more formal. Even in private, so we don't slip up. Master and Jakobs. Understood?"

A hollow ache settled in Dresden's chest. "Yes, master."

He tried to tell himself it was worse for Regulus. At least the other servants were friendly. Regulus had no other friends. But it felt like Dresden was being punished; pushed down to his station, as Kimberly said.

Regulus took a deep breath. "Good." He moved back to the chair. "Finish, ple—" He grunted. "Too friendly," he muttered under his breath. "Finish, Jakobs."

"Yes, master." Dresden returned to applying the salve as anger fought his guilt. "I'm sorry. I won't get you in trouble again."

Regulus flinched as Dresden's fingers brushed a bit of ripped skin. Dresden finished and stepped away. Regulus remained slumped over the back of the chair, letting the salve dry. With nothing else to do and unable to stare any longer at the bruises, Dresden set about tidying up Regulus' small room. Not that there was much to clean. Regulus didn't own much. But the desk could use dusting.

"Drez," Regulus said softly.

Dresden looked up from arranging a stack of books on warfare. Was the use of the nickname to see if he would fail to remember his new instructions? "Yes, master?"

"It won't be forever." It was hard to hear Regulus, he spoke so quietly, with his forehead resting on his arm on the back of the chair. "When I'm knighted, my father will allow me back. I'm sure of it. And if not, we can travel. Find another lord I can pledge to, who won't care who I call my friend."

Dresden wasn't sure how to respond to that.

Regulus sighed. "Just…don't hate me, Drez—Jakobs." He sniffed and wiped at his face. "Please don't hate me."

"You took a beating for me." He stared at Regulus' welted back. "I don't think I could hate you, Reg—master."

"Good." Regulus stood with a grunt and moved to his bed. As he carefully laid on his stomach, Dresden heard him mutter, "I need one person who doesn't hate me."

THE RIVER

Age: 16

Location: Kimberly Estate, Lanure Duchy, Monparth

"OKAY, FIRST of all, that was a dirty and underhanded move, and you know it." Regulus shoved Dresden's shoulder hard enough to make Dresden stagger a step sideways, but he was grinning. Sweat glistened on Regulus' face and stuck in his patchy stubble. It was a constant source of disappointment to Regulus that, at seventeen, he could barely manage a decent layer of stubble, while Dresden's beard was already thick at sixteen. They both stank from their afternoon of training. Training in the heat of the day was awful, but Hendrick and his friends avoided the training yard when the sun was hottest, providing Regulus and Dresden a chance to train unbothered.

"No, see, there's no such thing as a dirty and underhanded move in a fight." Dresden would have pushed Regulus right back, but they couldn't risk someone seeing him appear to attack his master.

Kimberly castle towered not far behind them as they walked across the field at the rear of the castle. Any guard on patrol or servant going about their tasks or even one of the Kimberlys could see them, and Kimberly seemed to always be waiting for another chance to humiliate or hurt Regulus. Thankfully, Regulus was good at denying Kimberly any openings, and Dresden had learned to do the same.

"Hmmm, sounds like something a cheater would say." Regulus laughed. "Admit it, you cheated, Jakobs."

"Yes, master."

Regulus flinched. "Not like that," he whispered. "It wasn't an order."

Dresden's face heated. Over the last three years, the response had become rote. Regulus said Jakobs, Dresden said yes, master. Or, on occasion, no, master. They still blurred the lines between servant and friend, more so as the belting became a distant memory, but Regulus strictly enforced the Jakobs/master rule of address. It *did* help deter Kimberly's wrath. And had become so normal, it didn't bother Dresden anymore. Most of the time. If he didn't dwell on it.

"Well, then, no, I didn't cheat. My father said, if you're fighting to survive, you do what you have to in order to live. Anything is fair in war, so there's no such thing as cheating in a fight."

Regulus chuckled. "Your father is a philosophical farmer."

"No, he's a practical one." Dresden shrugged. "My parents grew up in a borderland in Carasom, between feuding warlords. Dangerous area, everyone knew how to fight to protect their family. That's why they moved to Monparth. And why he started training me with the scimitars at six, as his father trained him."

"Hm." Regulus' expression sobered. "In such a situation, when you're fighting to protect your family…" He nodded. "You do what you must to survive and save others. Protecting those you care about is more important than your personal honor."

Regulus frowned, his brows pinching as he looked lost in thought. Dresden wondered if he was thinking about that awful belting. Regulus shook his head and smiled.

"But, when it's not a matter of life and death, honor matters, which is why I'm giving you three seconds' head start to the river."

Dresden scowled. "Now that's insult—"

"Go! One—"

Dresden took off at a run, grinning over his shoulder as Regulus counted off two and three and followed. A stitch in his side developed almost immediately, his aching body protesting running after three hours of sword practice. He pushed past the pain, determined to win this time as he leapt over a low dry-stone wall and skirted a bush. The sound of his own labored breathing filled his ears. He wound through a grove of trees. The wide and deep bend of the river came into view across the grassy pasture. A couple cows were drinking on the far side. Poor things were going to have quite a fright. Dresden leaned forward, fighting his burning calves and the pinching in his side.

"So close," Regulus shouted as he sped past.

Dresden tried to catch up, but Regulus' legs were too accursedly long. Regulus leapt into the river with a terrific splash. The cows lowed and skittered. Dresden leapt into the river. The water was startlingly cold, and he resurfaced with a yell.

"Nope!" Regulus wrapped his arm around Dresden's shoulders, wrestling him back under. "Losers get submerged!"

Dresden dunked under and broke out of Regulus' grip. He burst back up and splashed Regulus, laughing. "Unchivalrous!"

"Says the man who kicked up dirt in my face!" Regulus laughed, a wide grin on his face as he jumped on Dresden's back and pushed him back under.

Dresden grabbed Regulus' shirt and pulled him under, then climbed up Regulus until he was sitting on his shoulders. "You're a sorry loser."

"You're a sorry runner." Regulus pushed Dresden off his shoulders, sending him tumbling back into the water with a splash.

Dresden came up sputtering and found Regulus leisurely floating on his back. "You have an unfair advantage, and you know it." Dresden splashed Regulus' face, and Regulus blinked rapidly. "You want to grow up to be a troll or something? You done growing yet?"

"I gave you a head start." Regulus ducked under, and when he came back up, he spit a stream of water into Dresden's face.

"Ugh, charming." Dresden wiped off his face but couldn't stop smiling. Times like this, hidden from view from the castle, just for a moment, they weren't master and servant. They were friends. As much as a master and servant could be friends.

"What do you think," a light female voice said, "if we ask, will they take off their shirts?"

They spun toward the bank they'd leapt from. Lady Brigid, looking like a dream in a pale blue dress that hugged her curves and bared her shoulders, stood near the bank. Her brown hair fell in soft waves down her back. One of her friends was with her. Lady Margaret's ginger hair was half up in intricate braids and she wore a peach-colored gown with a maroon belt that accentuated her waist. One of Lady Brigid's handmaids, her black tresses tied back in a bun, trailed behind them. *Kiara.* Dresden sent a smile Kiara's way as his thoughts wandered to a lovely night a few weeks ago, involving a bonfire and a stolen kiss...

"I think if we ordered Jakobs to, he'd have to obey us, wouldn't he?" Brigid grinned wickedly, her eyes sparkling.

"That seems right to me." Margaret laughed. "Take off your shirt, Jakobs."

Dresden flushed and looked helplessly to Regulus. Regulus looked una-mused, but then a relaxed smile slid over his features.

"Ladies, my servant need only obey me. But more importantly, it is my duty to ensure your innocence is protected."

Brigid's smile twitched like she was trying not to laugh. "Come, Regulus. As soaked as you are, we won't be seeing that much more."

"We did walk all the way out here." Margaret winked. "And not to see cows."

"Um..." Regulus cleared his throat. "Pardon?"

"I know you often come here after training." Brigid's smile turned teasing.

Dresden mentally cursed. If the ladies knew of their swimming routine, Hendrick might as well. Regulus would realize this, and insist they act more formal and distanced.

"And"—Brigid blushed—"we can't get a good look at you in the training yard."

Dresden's face burned so hot he wanted nothing more than to duck under the water. He glanced over at Regulus. Regulus had turned cherry red.

"Such admissions are inappropriate," Regulus said quietly.

"Oh, stop being so chivalrous." Margaret stepped closer. "You'd be more comfortable with your shirts off instead of weighing you down with all that water, wouldn't you?"

Dresden glanced at Kiara. She was blushing, but also looked like she was trying not to laugh…and a little eager. Well, if that's what it took to get another kiss… He looked at Regulus, waiting for some indication of what to do. Regulus looked as uncertain as Dresden felt.

Brigid stepped close to the bank. "Oh, it's just some harmless fun!"

"My lady," Regulus' voice was firm, "your father would not approve."

"Please." Margaret rolled her eyes. "Scared of Lord Kimberly, Master Hargreaves?" She fluttered her eyes at Regulus.

Brigid's smile faltered. Regulus lowered his head, not looking at the girls. Dresden could practically hear the echo of the belt slapping against Regulus' back.

Brigid took Margaret's arm. "Let's leave them be."

"What?" Margaret frowned. "But—"

"Let's go, Margaret!" Brigid pulled Margaret away.

Kiara stalled, still standing near the riverbank. She looked at the retreating ladies as Dresden flopped back to float on the calm surface, feeling relieved but also a little disappointed to be denied the chance to show off. Kiara looked back at them.

"I have to admit, I'm disappointed. I was curious, Master Hargreaves."

Regulus made an odd squeaking noise.

"What, not me?" Dresden straightened to stare at Kiara, offended.

Kiara grinned, her eyes twinkling with mischief. "Oh, that's a sight I've already managed to glimpse." Her smile turned seductive. "Not that I'm uninterested in taking a closer look." She spun away and hurried after the ladies.

Dresden gaped at her back. *Wait…what? When?*

Uproarious laughter invaded his thoughts. Regulus splashed him. "She *likes* you! I wonder if it was all her idea." Regulus splashed him again. "What's her name?"

"Kiara," Dresden mumbled.

"Kiara." Regulus laughed. "As awkward as that was—especially now that every time I see Brigid and Margaret, I'm going to be self-conscious—this is wonderful. Now I can tease you about *Kiara*."

"Tease away." Dresden pushed Regulus over. "I already kissed her."

"You *what*?" Regulus chuckled and pushed him back. "Scoundrel!"

Dresden grinned. "I'm pretty sure Lady Margaret would gladly kiss you—"

"Shut up." Regulus shoved Dresden under.

"—if you're interested," Dresden finished as he popped back up.

"One year, and we're free. I'm not risking that by kissing a pretty girl." Regulus made little waves with his arms, staring at the ripples.

"So you admit she's pretty? Because she definitely thinks you're handsome."

Regulus scowled and splashed him again, but amusement showed in his eyes. "Come on. We need to get cleaned up before supper."

They moved to the bank, but as Dresden started to climb up, Regulus grabbed his shirt and yanked him back into the river. When he resurfaced, Regulus was standing on the bank grinning while squeezing excess water out of his shirt. "What are you still splashing around for?"

Dresden rolled his eyes and clambered onto the bank. "I've half a mind to push you back in and make a run for it."

"Bad plan." Regulus shook his head, his expression serious as water sprayed from his hair. "You run too slowly for that."

"Rude. You'll see. I'll win one of these days."

"Sure. The same day you beat me without scimitars or cheating." Regulus headed back toward the castle, and Dresden followed.

He wouldn't admit it, but he knew he couldn't defeat Regulus with a broadsword. He could barely hold his own against him with his scimitars, and they were lighter, faster weapons and had the advantage of two blades to one. Which was why Regulus loved fighting Dresden when he used the scimitars. He said it was a better challenge.

"I am sorry about getting dirt in your eyes."

Regulus chuckled. "Only be sorry that I'm not afraid to use that move on you now."

Dresden sighed. *Oh. Great.*

"Oh," Regulus said, "Lady Margaret being here likely means Lord Hatan is here, too, so I won't be able to sneak off from supper early. You'll have a little extra free time. You know, if you wanted to see if Kiara still wants to see your muscled chest."

"Shut up." Dresden quickly glanced around, hoping no one had heard him silence his master. No one seemed to be around as they walked into the castle's shadow.

"But I'll need these clothes cleaned and hung out to dry first, Jakobs."

"Yes, master." He smiled as they went in the servant's entrance so as not to drip water in the halls, and started making plans to pick some flowers before paying a visit to Kiara.

Let's Be Mercenaries
Age: 17
Location: Kimberly Estate, Lanure Duchy, Monparth

DRESDEN WATCHED silently as Regulus paced back and forth, his long legs carrying him the length of his small room in a couple strides. He wondered again how tall Regulus' parents were. Lord Arrano had to be taller than his cousin Lord Kimberly, since Regulus had several inches on both Kimberly and Hendrick. Regulus kept muttering curses under his breath, his expression flickering between frightened and outraged. He stopped abruptly and turned on Dresden.

"Pack my things. Essentials only. Some clothes, my weapons. Get some food from the kitchen. I'm leaving."

Dresden gawked. Sure, someone hadn't just tried to murder Dresden, and the attempt on Regulus' life had shaken him, too. Still, leaving a week before Regulus' knighting ceremony seemed rash. "But—"

"Did I ask for your opinion or give an order?" Regulus sat at his desk, his movements hard and furious as he searched through a drawer. Dresden tried not to take the snapping personally. Regulus was kind, although sometimes he pretended to be harsh in front of the Kimberlys. But this was different. He was legitimately angry.

"Apologies, master." Dresden started up from the chair and immediately began pulling clothes out of Regulus' small oak dresser.

Regulus sighed. "I'm sorry; I'm not upset with you, and that was uncalled for." He mussed his hair. "There's no point in staying. The Kimberlys don't want me here, and I don't want to stay here. I was a fool to think I could return to Arrano, that my father would want me once I was knighted, that Lady Arrano…" He growled. "I'll never be accepted by nobles who think I don't deserve to live. Even the knighthood won't change their minds when they find out what I am."

Dresden winced. "There are lords other than your family, who might—"

"I'm done trying to impress nobles." Regulus snatched up his quill. "I'm releasing you from your service; you're no longer indentured and are free to seek employment elsewhere. You'll get a week's worth of severance pay from my funds, assuming I can convince Lord Kimberly to release it to me instead of keeping it for himself."

"I…what?" Dresden froze and stared at Regulus. He worked his throat.

"But…my contract was for ten years. I owe you three more years."

"And I have the right as the holder of your indenture to decide your extraordinary service has earned you an early release." Regulus finished writing something, then set the paper on the edge of the desk. "That reflects the terms of your indenture have been satisfied and you're a free man. I will write you a letter of recommendation." Regulus grabbed a blank sheet of parchment and scowled at the quill. "For whatever good it will do from an untitled bastard."

Dresden stared at the contract of indenture, his mind numb. *I'm…free? No longer bound as a servant?* He should say thank you. But he also wasn't sure he wanted to say goodbye to Regulus. "Where are you going?"

"I've heard of a mercenary troop that's currently passing through Lageness. I'm going to join them, if they'll take me." He glanced up, and something sparked in his gray eyes, his expression almost hopeful. "You could join me. Not as my servant, you're still released. But…as my friend." He glanced away.

"As…your friend?" Dresden stood rooted in place.

Regulus was his friend, no matter how distant they acted in public, and despite the respect Regulus demanded even in private as a precaution. Because when it came down to it, Regulus didn't treat him like a servant. He had been more worried about Dresden than himself in the immediate aftermath of the attack that morning. And over the years, Regulus had saved Dresden's hide on multiple occasions. Still, calling a friend "master" all the time and obeying his every order rankled, and could cause strain.

"Yes." Regulus paused in his writing and looked up, his brows creasing. "Unless…we aren't friends?" He swallowed hard and looked back down at the letter. "Which I would understand. You are free to take this letter and go as soon as I leave, if that's what you want." He dipped the quill again. "But I would miss you, Drez."

Drez. It had been years since Regulus had used the nickname. Dresden's mind spun. Mercenaries? They would be equals. And he could travel. Put his sword-fighting skills to good use. All those years of Regulus filling their days with endless training could pay off. And they could be friends. Real friends, with no social constraints.

"Of course I'll go with you, Reg."

Regulus' head jerked up. "Are you sure?"

"Sounds like an adventure. Let's make a name for ourselves as mercenaries."

"Wait, then what am I writing this letter for?" Regulus grinned, his eyes crinkling, and stuck the quill back in the bottle of ink. "Better pack up your things, too. I have to go talk to Lord Kimberly. Be quick."

"Yes, master." Regulus frowned, and Dresden flushed. "Habit. I'll take care of it, Regulus."

Dresden had their packs ready with clothes and food by the time the door opened again some fifteen minutes later. Regulus' scowl could turn milk. A red mark covered his right cheek.

"Good, you're ready. Let's go." Regulus snatched his pack from Dresden and strode out. Dresden hurried after him.

"He struck you?"

Regulus grunted. "Apparently asking for my next month's allowance was impertinent. Better pray these mercenaries are looking to hire, because we're broke."

Dresden gulped and did send up a prayer, even though asking Etiros to help them get hired as mercenaries felt wrong.

The mercenary troop captain was a short and stocky man named Fletcher. Beady eyes watched them under a mess of greasy hair that shone in the firelight in the smoke-filled tavern. He sat back in his chair with his feet propped on a table. "Age?"

"Eighteen," Regulus said.

"Seventeen." Dresden shifted his pack on his back.

Fletcher grunted. "Bit young. No experience."

"Give us a chance to prove ourselves," Regulus said.

"Hey, Kensen!"

A man nearly as tall as Regulus looked up from his tankard. His massive arms bulged under his discolored gray shirt, and scars that looked like claw marks ran down the side of his neck. "Aye, Captain?"

"These upstarts say they want to prove themselves. How's about a little duel?" The smile that split the captain's face was full of cruelty.

Kensen shrugged and walked over. "Sure, Captain." He eyed Regulus and Dresden. "One at a time, or both?"

The captain rubbed his chin, then pulled a coin out of the pouch at his belt. "Heads, both, tails, one at a time." He flipped the coin, caught it, and slapped it on the table. The king's crest rather than his profile stared up at them. He hooted. "One at a time!"

"I'll go first," Regulus said. He glanced at Dresden, and Dresden understood. Regulus was the better swordsman. If he was beaten, Dresden was free to back out.

They headed out, most of the other mercenaries coming to watch. The sun was sinking, and the air cooling rapidly. The captain claimed an empty livestock auction pen as a sparring ring, and Regulus and Kensen squared off. Dresden gripped the fence, every muscle tense.

Regulus was cautious at first, taking the defensive and avoiding as many blows as possible. He darted around the pen, his brow furrowed with concentration. The mercenaries jeered and laughed. *Come on, Reg.* Regulus blocked a blow, tilted his head slightly. He blocked another. A flicker of a grin pulled at his mouth, then vanished. Dresden smiled.

"What are you smiling about, boy?" A lanky mercenary with several missing teeth laughed. "He's losing."

"Is he?"

Regulus parried a cut and switched to offensive in a blink. He stopped giving ground, pushing Kensen back with controlled, precise cuts and thrusts. The mercenaries quieted. Regulus kicked the mercenary in the gut, batted aside a poorly-aimed thrust, and put the tip of his sword to the man's throat. The mercenary dropped his sword.

Fletcher gaped at Regulus, then clapped. "You're hired. Your friend, too, I don't even care. If he's half as good as you, I'll be happy."

It took a moment for the reality to sink in. *We're mercenaries.*

Dresden slipped into the tent he shared with Regulus as quietly as possible. He'd been out far later than he'd realized, and he didn't want to wake his friend. He stole through the dark toward his thin sleeping mat. He could just make out the outline of Regulus' slumbering form on the left side of the tent.

"Have fun out shirking your duties?" Regulus muttered. Not asleep, then.

"Shirking? …oh." Dresden cursed. "I had watch tonight. I forgot."

Regulus grunted.

"Did the captain notice?"

"Ha." Regulus snorted. "He's not a slob like Fletcher. He always notices."

They'd left Fletcher's troop after only three months. The group had quickly proved to be too dishonorable for Regulus' conscience. Not that anyone would have been eager to continue fighting side-by-side with the men who scarred their face. Dresden had stitched up the cut from the outside corner of Regulus' right eye down to his chin as best he could, but the scar was obvious. Regulus was ashamed of it despite Dresden's assurances it was masculine and intimidating. They'd been with Captain Samuelson's troop for nearly ten months, and even Regulus had made friends with the other mercenaries.

Dresden sighed. The captain was strict. There'd likely be some punishment for his missed shift. Hopefully not the lash. He winced at the thought. Samuelson was overall a good captain, but he had an over-strong belief in the effectiveness of the whip. But it was a first offense. Surely Dresden would only be put on manual labor, maybe struck with the rod. On the other hand, Samuelson had whipped a man last week for spilling a pot of stew. Granted, enough food for the entire troop had been lost to the cooking pit, but that had seemed harsh for an accident.

"I'll see the captain in the morning. Maybe if I go in bowing and scraping, he'll go easy."

"Don't bother." Regulus stayed comfortably reclined on his mat, but his words were short and clipped. "I talked to him. Just…keep your head down for a while. And pay better attention to your shifts, Jakobs."

Jakobs. Dresden recoiled. Regulus was ticked.

"And maybe invite me next time you run off to have fun," Regulus muttered.

"See, I would, but your stiffness around the ladies is off-putting." Dresden sat on his own thin mat and pulled his boots off in the dark. "Your refusal to get too close to a lady you see no chance of marrying ruins all the fun."

Regulus grunted. "Excuse me if I don't want to bring any more bastards or fatherless children into the world."

Dresden rolled his eyes, even as he felt a twinge of sympathy. He scratched at his beard. "Kissing a girl won't get her pregnant, you stick-in-the-mud."

"Just go to sleep."

He pulled off his belt, and his small coin pouch spilled as he tossed the belt aside. "Damn." He fumbled in the dark. "Where's the lantern?"

"Clean it up in the morning." Irritation rang in Regulus' low tone.

"Yeah, if I want to put a hole in my foot." Dresden found the lantern and the steel and flint next to it. "She gave me her brooch, and if I step on that pin in the morning, I won't be happy." He struck the flint, trying to light the lantern.

"Then feel for it," Regulus snapped. "I'm tired, and I don't want a light."

"Then turn your head," he snapped back, still working on the flint.

"Leave the light and go to sleep!" Regulus didn't move, but fury and something else tinged his rushed words. Something almost like apprehension. The wick finally caught, and the lantern slowly blazed to life.

"What is your…" Dresden trailed off as he looked over at Regulus.

Regulus lay on his stomach on his mat, shirtless and without his cloak that doubled as a blanket, his head turned away toward the tent wall. Dresden's abdomen clenched sharply as he took in the blood covering Regulus' back. Much of it had dried and clotted, but some of the stripes were still oozing.

"I told you to leave the light," Regulus mumbled.

Dresden dropped the flint, his stomach lurching and face burning. "Were you lashed?"

"Whatever gave it away."

"Why?"

Regulus was silent and didn't move. Finally, he sighed. "Find your precious brooch and go to sleep."

He'd tried to hide his lashing. Which was ridiculous. Even if he could have left the tent before Dresden woke in the morning, he couldn't hide it long. Which meant Regulus just didn't want to talk about it right now. Regulus was a model mercenary, and Captain Samuelson seemed to like him. What in creation could he have done that he was so ashamed to admit? It wasn't like Regulus would chide Dresden for forgetting guard duty if he'd done—

No.

"Don't bother. I talked to him."

"Regulus." His voice was choked and weak, and he had to clear his throat. "Tell me those weren't my lashes."

The only answer was the slow rise and fall of Regulus' back. The flicker of the lantern glittered in the blood. Dresden's breathing went shallow, his lungs seizing. *No.*

"Why would you do that, you idiot?"

"Go to sleep."

Dresden gulped. "I'll be back. I'm getting fresh water to clean your back. You still have that watered wine? I'll cut up some bandages once you're clean. I…" He rubbed his forehead. "Regulus, why?"

A pause. "I'm working on a full-body scar collection."

"That's not funny."

Regulus didn't respond, so Dresden pulled on his boots and left to get water, mentally cursing himself the whole way. He nearly ran into Ivan returning from his watch. Ivan blocked his path, which wasn't hard. The blond was built like a wall.

"Lieutenant Ivan." Dresden moved to go around Ivan, but Ivan shoved him back. "What's—"

"Where the hell were you?" Ivan's Segiledan accent, all choppy consonants and indistinct vowels, was extra clipped tonight.

Dresden's face heated. "I—"

"Have you seen Regulus?" Ivan shoved him again. "Have you?"

"Yes." He hung his head. "I'm—"

Ivan snorted. "Twenty lashes. Ten for the missed watch. Five for leaving camp without permission. Five for lying to the captain and saying he was the one who forgot his shift. He could have had just the five. He convinced the captain to give him yours, too. Said he could handle it better, and that it'd still convince you to mind your watches."

Dresden grimaced. *Regulus, you colossal idiot.* "I need water for his back."

"I like you," Ivan growled. "But Regulus might be the only truly honorable man I've ever met. Not to mention one of the best swordsmen I've ever seen. And he saved my life against that berserker tribe last month and saved all our hides when he figured out that Vaneltian ice serpent's weakness and killed it. So let me tell you." Ivan seized Dresden's shirt and pulled him in close. "None of the men are pleased with you right now."

"If it helps," Dresden said quietly, "I'm not pleased with myself."

Ivan grunted and shoved him back. "I've half a mind to beat you—except Regulus would probably pay me back in kind." He shook his head. "I don't know how you earned his loyalty, but I hope you're grateful for it." Ivan strode past, letting his shoulder knock into Dresden.

Grateful, and ashamed.

Dresden hurried back to the tent with the water and dunked the only clean rag he had into the bucket. He eyed the caked layer of blood. "Did no one clean it?"

"I came straight here. I didn't want to look weak."

Dresden's mouth went dry. "Trust me, no one thinks you're weak." He began to rub at the blood and Regulus convulsed, then gripped the edges of his mat. Dresden continued to wipe away dried blood, wincing as some of the worse lines bled afresh. "They're all angry with me, though."

"Wha—" Regulus sucked in a sharp breath and jerked as Dresden washed away more crusted blood. His hands shook as they held the mat. "What?"

"I ran into Ivan. Sounds like everyone thinks I don't deserve a friend like you." A pang in his chest accompanied the admission. As he cleaned Regulus' back and thought about every time Regulus stood between him and Hendrick or Lord Kimberly, he thought he might agree. None of those had been this bad, though. He'd thought that belting so many years ago had been terrible. This was far worse.

Regulus didn't respond. Maybe he agreed, too. Dresden finished wiping off Regulus' back as best he could with new blood seeping out. He dug the watered wine out of Regulus' belongings.

"This is going to sting."

Regulus' hands tightened on the mattress and his entire body tensed. Dresden carefully poured a little wine over the cuts. Regulus groaned through clenched teeth, his muscles bulging as he braced against the pain. Every twitch, every anguished moan into the mat, stabbed at Dresden's heart.

He set aside the wine bag and grabbed his spare cloak. He had no bandages, so he'd make some. The sound of ripping fabric filled the tent.

"You're going to have to sit up so I can wrap these around you."

Regulus sighed. He pushed off the ground with a stifled whimper. "Thanks."

Dresden gripped the wide, long strips of dark fabric, staring at the raw lines crisscrossing Regulus' back. "Thanks? Damn it, Regulus, this is the least I can do. You shouldn't have—"

"You're my friend," Regulus said quietly. "Don't listen to the others. They don't understand."

"Understand what?"

"Why I can't watch you be hurt." Regulus shifted and grunted in pain. "You've stood by me when I was alone. They don't know… I have to…" He fell silent.

Dresden sighed and wrapped the strips around Regulus' torso and over his shoulders, tightly binding his back. Regulus kept wincing and clenching his hands, but he sat still despite the gasps and grunts.

"Done."

To his surprise, Regulus didn't lay back down. Instead, he turned around. "Any of the men give you grief, tell me?"

"I don't need you to protect me."

Regulus winced. "I know. That's not what I meant. I don't…" He pursed his lips, then shook his head. "Can you make sure I wake up on time for the dawn shift?"

"What?" Dresden gawked. "Captain didn't take you off watch?"

"He was going to. I said I could handle it."

"What exactly are you trying to prove?"

Regulus glanced away. "Habit, I guess."

Dresden frowned. Under Kimberly's guardianship, Regulus had trained harder and longer than anyone, pushed himself constantly, refused to show weakness. He'd finally admitted he thought if he could be strong enough, he'd prove his blood didn't make him inferior. They said his mother's peasant blood had diluted him. Made him less. Regulus insisted it made him stronger. He was always trying to prove he wasn't just as good as his cousins; he was better. Regulus had been trying to prove himself and admit no weakness for so long, he couldn't stop.

Dresden scratched the side of his head. "You don't need to prove anything. I'll take your shift in the morning. And any others until you're healed."

"You don't owe me—"

"Don't I? Your prideful self took a lashing for me and Etiros only knows why!"

Regulus slumped, then gasped and straightened again. "I couldn't watch you be hurt."

"And what, I'm a terrible friend who won't care that you're hurt?" Dresden massaged his forehead. He was being harsh for no good reason, but he couldn't comprehend why Regulus would do this. "Ivan said you told the captain you could handle it better. Do you think I'm too weak to survive a lashing?"

Regulus grimaced. "No, of course not. I just thought… I owed you."

"You…owe me?" Dresden blinked.

"Seven years," Regulus mumbled without looking at Dresden. "How many 'yes, master's does each lash erase? I don't know. Not enough. Maybe none. But old instinct, regardless. Protecting you. I don't have anyone else."

For a moment, Dresden didn't know how to respond. He stared at Regulus' downcast face, his tongue thick in his dry mouth and his chest tight. "Reg. I wouldn't have come with you if I resented you. I was your servant. That's just how it was. You could have treated me however you wanted, and you treated me like a friend."

"A friend doesn't go by master."

"A master doesn't take a beating for a servant, either," Dresden snapped. "Yes, I hated calling you that. I didn't like being the servant boy, I hated that my contract made me little more than a slave. But I hated the Kimberlys, never you. You released me from my contract when you could have forced me to come with you." Regulus glanced up and frowned, looking puzzled. Dresden shook his head with a dry chuckle. "But that didn't even occur to you, did it? That's why I'm still here. Because you're my friend, and I swear, one day, I'm going to take a beating for you and we can be even."

"I hope not." Regulus offered a wry smile. "If I earn my own beating, my reputation as a straight-laced stick-in-the-mud will be ruined." He adjusted a bandage. "But I meant it, Drez. I don't want to see you hurt."

"And I don't want to see you hurt. I hate it." *I hate myself for causing it.* He moved back to his own mat and cleaned up his spilled coins and the little brass circle brooch. Regulus slowly laid back down, poorly muffling his grunts and moans. With one last regret-filled glance at Regulus, Dresden snuffed out the lantern. "I suppose I just will have to be on my best behavior, so neither of us ends up lashed."

CHANGES
Age: 21
Location: Geirah

"LIEUTENANT HARGREAVES, I want to talk to you." Captain Samuelson motioned for Regulus to stand with his left hand. His right arm was back in a sling across his torso, as it had been often since the troll attack a couple months ago. "In my tent."

Dresden stopped laughing at a joke one of the other men had told. Ivan stood as well, but Samuelson shook his head.

"Just Hargreaves, Lieutenant Cheznik."

Ivan's thick blond brows wrinkled, but he sat back down. The campfire quieted as Regulus followed the captain. Dresden gulped down the watery slop the cook dared to call stew. In four years, Regulus hadn't landed himself in trouble once—other than the time he took Dresden's lashing. Dresden had done a good job of not earning another since. Seeing Regulus' raw back was enough to convince Dresden he never wanted a lashing, and more importantly, he wouldn't risk Regulus sacrificing himself again because of some pig-headed notion he needed to earn Dresden's friendship.

Regulus had more than just not gotten in trouble, though. A year past, Samuelson had made Regulus his second lieutenant. But the fact Samuelson wanted to talk to Regulus alone, in his tent, without even Ivan, his first lieutenant… An unsettled feeling coiled in Dresden's gut.

"I thought Regulus and the captain were on good terms," Perceval mused. A muscular twenty-eight-year-old Monparthian man who'd recently joined with another Monparthian named Caleb, Perceval scowled more often than he smiled, but he got on well with Regulus. "What did he do?"

Everyone looked at Dresden. "Nothing, so far as I know."

That made him more nervous. Was there something Regulus hadn't told him? He finished his meal quietly, not even listening to the conversation around him as he kept glancing in the direction of the captain's tent. As he listened for the crack of the whip.

Someone rounded a tent, and Dresden sat up straighter. The captain walked over with Regulus. Regulus' face was impassive, but he looked fine. He walked at the captain's side, not following in subservience or being driven ahead.

"Gather round, men! I need everyone's attention!" The captain waited while word spread, and the mercenaries crowded in with low mutters.

Dresden tried to catch Regulus' gaze, to determine if everything was okay. But Regulus looked straight ahead, his arms folded over his chest. His sword still hung at his side. That was a good sign.

The captain held up a hand, and the men quieted. "Can everyone hear me?" he called. "This is important."

A low murmur of yeses passed through the crowd of twenty men. Regulus watched the captain, his expression still unreadable. What was going on?

"I'm afraid my arm has continued to worsen," Samuelson announced. "And I'm getting old. Accordingly, I'm retiring."

There was a startled murmur at this, but the captain held up his hand again.

"Regulus Hargreaves will be taking over as captain."

Dresden's mouth fell open.

"I'll stay for a couple weeks to help with the transition," the captain continued. "But Hargreaves is your captain, from this moment forward."

"Why don't we get a say?" a man shouted.

Ivan shoved the man over so quickly, Dresden wasn't sure who it was. "Idiot," Ivan scoffed.

"If you don't like it, you're free to leave," Regulus said with a shrug.

"Do you have a better idea?" the captain asked drily. "Someone else you would rather see take my place?" He looked around the men, his gaze challenging them.

A slight smile tugged at the scarred corner of Regulus' mouth. "If anyone does think they would be a better captain, they are free to challenge me for the right to lead. I will step down if anyone beats me in a fair fight."

Dresden barely managed not to laugh. Some of the men grumbled under their breath. Perceval stood, and everyone went silent. Dresden's mirth vanished. Perceval and Regulus had dueled only once—and ended the match in a tie when Samuelson called it off.

"Stop grumbling," Perceval said. "You all trust him, and you all know it makes sense." He nodded at Regulus. "Pardon the interruption, Captain Hargreaves." No one spoke as Perceval sat back down.

"That's what I thought," Captain—no, just Samuelson—said. He looked to Regulus. "Anything to add, Captain?"

"Plan's still to head out just after dawn tomorrow." Regulus nodded at the men. "As you were."

The men returned to their various campfires and conversations as Regulus and Samuelson said something to each other, then clasped hands. Samuelson headed back toward his tent. Ivan went to Regulus and clapped him on the shoulder, said something that made Regulus laugh, then returned to the fire. Regulus left for their tent, and Dresden followed.

"A minute of your time, Captain?"

Regulus paused halfway into their tent and grinned, his scar puckering near his mouth. "Come on in."

They ducked into the tent, and Regulus settled on his mat. Dresden sat next to him, then wondered if that was proper. Fear shot through his excitement for his friend. For four years, they had been equals. Would their friendship change?

"Bit unexpected," Regulus said. "Right?"

Dresden shrugged. "I didn't see it coming, but as much as the cap—I mean, Samuelson relies on you, I should have. Congratulations, Reg. Captain." He smiled, but suddenly *captain* tasted an awful lot like *master*.

"So, Drez, I have a question for you." Regulus clapped his hand on Dresden's shoulder. "I need lieutenants. I was thinking you first, and Ivan second. What do you say?"

"I…" Dresden gaped at Regulus. It wouldn't be equals. But it would be close. "Won't the men accuse you of favoritism?"

Regulus snorted. "Let them. You're one of the best fighters in the troop, Drez, and your insight is valuable. Ivan won't argue with me. You'll do great, and they'll respect you. And if not, they'll learn to."

Dresden frowned. "You've never been much for…discipline."

"I can be." Regulus dropped his hand from Dresden's shoulder. "And there are more ways to discipline than a whip."

"Are things…going to be different?"

"What do you mean?" Regulus frowned, looking genuinely confused. "I plan on running things about the same. Maybe a bit tighter, but with fewer lashings. Going to have more stringent rules about behavior and who I let in or let stay; and might be pickier about contracts. But otherwise, it'll just be that Samuelson is gone. Don't plan on kicking a bunch of men out or anything, if they're worried about that."

"No, I meant…" He shifted. "Us. Not quite equals, right?"

Regulus' brows lifted. "Oh. We won't need to act different. I mean, I guess I can't have you question me in front of the men, because that might undermine my authority, but you can always speak freely."

"Can I call you Reg?"

Regulus opened his mouth, then closed it. His shoulders slumped. "I hadn't thought about it." He shook his head. "No, it's fine. It's what I prefer. I mean, Captain would be good in an official capacity. In front of benefactors or in response to orders, but...it's not like someone is going to... There's no Kimberly here."

"Okay. Good." But Dresden's mind was stuck on *in response to orders*. He'd gotten used to not being ordered around by his best friend. Even as a lieutenant, Regulus had rarely had to give him orders. He mostly just supported and advised Samuelson. But now Regulus' word would be law. It felt like backsliding.

"You'll always be my friend," Regulus said quietly. "I had you when I had no one."

"I know." Dresden bit his cheek. *Please don't forget it, Regulus.*

Please don't change.

Crime & Punishment
Age: 21
Location: Hedengal

DRESDEN TOOK a deep breath, his hand tapping against his leg. This was going to be bad. He'd put it off long enough. Another deep breath, and he lifted the flap to Regulus' tent. "Captain?"

Regulus sat on his low cot, reading a letter. He looked up and grinned. "Drez! Run into any trouble? Thought you'd be back a while ago."

Dresden gulped. "I'm sorry, Captain." He hung his head as Regulus' smile slipped. "I…take full responsibility."

"Re… For what?"

"We made a quick stop. At the tavern." His stomach churned as shame made his hands slick. Only six months since Regulus had become captain, six months of Dresden being lieutenant, and he'd messed up. Badly. And their new roles had been going so well. "I got distracted. The men followed my example. The supplies were not properly attended. We were…robbed." His throat stuck.

"How bad?" Regulus asked quietly.

"We brought back one sack of supplies. And…no coin."

For a moment, Regulus didn't speak. Then he cursed, more than Dresden had heard him curse in nearly eleven years combined. He threw something, and Dresden closed his eyes, too ashamed to look Regulus in the eye. The tent went silent.

"Drez…" Regulus cursed again. "Do you know what I'm most upset about? Losing the supplies and coin is bad. It's going to cause problems, including discipline problems. But that's not the worst. You're right in taking responsibility."

I know. Dresden scuffed the toe of his boot into the ground. *Because taking full blame is what you would have done, even if it wasn't your fault.*

Regulus sighed, sounding unhappy. "I can't let this go, Drez. This kind of negligence…"

Dresden nodded. He'd known before he walked into the tent. "You'll need to make an example."

Regulus cursed. "I don't…" He groaned and kicked something, but Dresden kept his eyes locked on the ground. "I can't take this one for you! I'm the one that has to do it!"

"It's okay, Reg. I deserve it." He forced down the lump in his throat.

Regulus exhaled loudly and rubbed his hand over the side of his face. His face was flushed, his eyes anguished. He'd been a merciful captain. The whip had left his tent once in six months. But losing supplies through negligence was tantamount to stealing. And the punishment for stealing was clear. Regulus glanced toward a bag in the corner of his tent. A bag Dresden knew held the whip.

"No. No, I can't." Regulus shook his head fiercely.

"The men will talk." Dresden rubbed the back of his neck. "You'll look weak. You can't afford that right now." He stared at the packed dirt. "Samuelson would have done it already if it were you, and you wouldn't have argued."

"I didn't take beatings for you in the past so I could beat you myself now." Regulus sank onto his cot and held his head in his hands. "If I wouldn't do it to you, I shouldn't do it to anyone. I'll replace whipping entirely. I've already been moving in that direction."

Dresden worked his throat, trying to get his voice to cooperate. "The men need to fear their captain."

"The men need to respect their captain." Regulus looked up. "I don't want you to fear me, Drez. I don't want you…" He turned away. "To hate me."

"I won't hate you. And will they respect their captain if he plays favorites?"

Dresden didn't know why he was advocating for his own lashing. Maybe it was old guilt over watching Regulus take his punishments. The lashing had been the worst. But Regulus had often stepped in front of Hendrick's fist or accepted a kick or slap when he claimed responsibility for something Dresden had done—spilled wine, a broken vase, unpolished armor. There had been other times as mercenaries when Regulus had taken a rod across the shoulders that should have been Dresden's.

"I know the punishment for what I've done, Captain." Dresden forced his feet to the corner and pulled out the whip. He flashed back eight years as he held it out to Regulus. *We are not equals. Again. A servant and his master. A captain and his soldier.* But this time, Regulus couldn't take his punishment. And Dresden wouldn't want him to. "I brought this on myself. And it's overdue, anyway."

Regulus took the whip, making Dresden's heart twist. "Outside, Jakobs. Tell the men to gather on the east side of camp."

Dresden nodded and slipped outside. The other men from the trip into town waited not far off, looking terrified. They eyed him sympathetically as he instructed them to gather the rest of the mercenaries. His feet felt heavy as he walked across camp, stopping to leave his scimitars in the tent he shared with Ivan. It had been folly to think they could be friends as they had before Regulus was captain. Just as it had been folly to think they could be true friends when Dresden was an indentured servant.

The rest of the mercenaries gathered in a group, keeping their distance from Dresden. He stared at a fir tree. Its lowest branches were a few feet above his head, and dead needles covered the ground at its base. The trunk was narrow, but probably wide enough he could brace himself against it. He rolled his shoulders, trying not to wonder what the whip would feel like.

"The men who accompanied Lieutenant Jakobs to town, step forward." Regulus' voice was hard, authoritative. His captain voice.

The men who had accompanied him shuffled forward. Dresden glanced at Regulus, then blinked. Regulus held a rope, but no whip.

"You all failed me and failed this company by allowing our supplies to be taken." Regulus' gaze roved over the men; his scarred lips curled down in displeasure. "Accordingly, you will have no supper. But as Lieutenant Jakobs has assumed full responsibility, he will take the full punishment for the crime of depriving his company of supplies.

"Negligence that results in loss to this troop cannot be tolerated," Regulus continued. "Misuse of funds is theft, and careless stops at taverns while on duty is unacceptable. And my lieutenant in particular should have done better. You all know the punishment for stealing."

Low murmurs.

"You also know I've never liked the whip. Which is why I will no longer use lashings as punishment."

Dresden jerked his head up. "Captain?"

Regulus turned his scowl on Dresden, but there was sorrow in his eyes. "You said you were distracted in the tavern. Tell me, Jakobs, was she worth it? She must have been very pretty."

The men snickered. Dresden's face heated.

"She was beautiful, Captain. And not worth it." *Not worth our friendship.*

"I've decided your punishment. Take off your clothes."

"What?" Dresden blinked, then lowered his head. "I mean, yes, Captain." He stripped down, his face burning as the rest of the men joked and laughed. Regulus silenced them with a look.

Regulus stepped forward, holding up the rope. "You'll spend the night here." He tied the rope to Dresden's wrist, then led him over to the fir tree without meeting Dresden's eyes. He tossed the rope over a low branch and tugged, pulling Dresden's right arm above his head. He grabbed Dresden's left wrist and tied it to the other end of the rope above his head. "No food, drink, or fire. He is to be left here, unbothered, but unaided, until dawn.”

Dresden let his chin fall to his chest. It was a mercy, in a way. The Hedengalese nights this time of year were chilly, but not unbearable. He would be cold and uncomfortable. He wouldn’t sleep, and if he did, he’d likely be awakened by pulling on his wrists and shoulders. His shoulders would ache in the morning even if he managed to stay firmly on his feet all night. The effects wouldn’t last as long or be as painful as a lashing. But the humiliation as he stood there stripped down to his thin, short braies was almost worse.

“Dismissed,” Regulus barked. The men laughed and a few tossed out some insults as they turned back to camp. Regulus stood still and silent. Probably trying to figure out what to say.

“Thank you.” Dresden curled his toes into the dead fir needles and cool dirt. “It’s less than I deserve.”

“It’s more than a friend should do.” Regulus rubbed the back of his neck. “But I’m your captain, too.”

Never equals. A rueful laugh escaped before Dresden could stop it. A chill breeze stirred his hair, and he shivered. It was going to be a long night.

“I gave orders to be careful of the coin and supplies.” Regulus sounded irritated. “I trusted you with this. And as you said, you knew the punishment, you brought this on yourself. If you’d just followed orders, Jakobs…”

“Yes, master.” Dresden’s eyes widened as he realized what he’d said. He had spent so long as a youth and young man responding to Regulus saying “Jakobs” with a rote *yes, master.* Apparently that habit wasn’t dead so much as buried. “I… I didn’t…”

Regulus went rigid. For a moment, he hardly seemed to breathe, then his posture crumpled. He gulped. “I’m sorry, Drez. I’m truly sorry.” He strode away, leaving Dresden with the rope around his wrists, the fir needles poking the soles of his feet, and the growing shadows as the sun slipped toward the horizon.

☙❧

Light had scarcely begun to chase away the darkness and the sun had yet to breach the horizon when Regulus strode across the grass. Early morning fog swirled around his legs. Dresden watched his approach, shivering. His arms ached and shoulders pinched. His fingers were stiff with cold. Exhaustion weighed down his heavy eyelids, but every time he’d come close to falling asleep, pain in his shoulders or wrists had woken him.

Regulus held a dark bundle under one arm. His expression was unreadable. But as he drew closer, Dresden noted the hard line of Regulus' shoulders. The tension along his jaw and temples, indicating he was clenching his teeth. And the shadows under his eyes, suggesting he'd hardly slept. He set down the bundle on the dew-moistened grass and drew his dagger. Dresden shivered violently.

"I'm sorry, I'm hurrying," Regulus whispered. He cut free one wrist, and Dresden groaned as his arms fell to his side. His muscles prickled and his arm felt heavy. Regulus cut free his other wrist. Dresden's teeth chattered. "I'm sorry, one second."

"S-st-stop ap-apol-apologiz-izing." Dresden tried to rub his hands over his arms, but his muscles didn't want to cooperate.

"Here." Regulus snatched up the bundle and shook it open. He wrapped the thick wool blanket around Dresden and pulled it tight.

Dresden gripped the blanket, holding it as close as possible. Warmth enveloped him, easing his tight muscles despite the chill air nipping at his ears and face and creeping up under the blanket.

"Come on." Regulus gripped Dresden's shoulders and led him toward camp.

Dresden stumbled into a tent, and Regulus vanished, only to reappear a moment later and shove Dresden's clothes at him. The clothes were hot—Regulus must have placed them near the fire burning outside his tent. Dresden was tempted to just hold the bundle of warm fabric against his chest and curl up on his mat, but he forced himself to get dressed. Regulus watched, his mouth pressed into a thin line. Dresden moved to sit on his mat to pull on his boots, but instead saw Regulus' cot. He sunk onto the edge of the cot as a wave of exhaustion hit him. His arms were so tired.

"Drez?" Regulus ventured quietly.

He just nodded, staring at his boots next to his stockinged feet.

Regulus shifted. "Do…you want breakfast?" Dresden shook his head. Eating porridge sounded like more work than it was worth. Regulus nodded, uncertainty in his eyes. "Okay. Just…try to sleep, then. Your shift was moved to this evening."

"Wrong…tent—"

"No. Lie down. Sleep." Regulus' tone didn't allow an argument, even if Dresden had felt like giving one.

Dresden gratefully collapsed onto Regulus' cot and curled up to preserve his body heat. Regulus sighed and stepped forward. Only when Regulus pulled the wool blanket over him did Dresden realize he'd forgotten about it on the ground. Regulus moved to leave.

"Reg…" Dresden's voice croaked, and he cleared his throat. "Reg." Regulus froze before the tent entrance. "I don't blame you."

Regulus' shoulders sagged, an expression like relief softening some of the hard lines of his face. Dresden wanted to say more, but he felt so warm and comfortable, his eyes drifted shut. He tried to talk, but his words slurred.

"You did the right thing. Thanks…blanket. Warm clothes. Cot. Didn't have to… Not necessary, Captain…" He let his weariness and the ache in his back and arms pull him toward sleep. After a moment, he heard Regulus whisper.

"Drez?"

He was too tired to respond.

Regulus was so quiet for so long, Dresden thought he must have missed him leaving. He was nearly asleep when Regulus whispered again.

"I know I don't deserve to call you my brother," Regulus murmured. "But that's what you've always been to me. I'll keep trying. I'm sorry for failing you again, brother." The tent flap rustled shut.

Brother? Dresden pulled the scratchy wool blanket in closer. *Of course you're my brother…*

HORSE THIEF
Age: 24
Location: Bhitran coast

DRESDEN STUMBLED sideways into a display of colorful, ornate carpets. The merchant waved him away, talking agitatedly in Bhitran, his teeth flashing starkly white next to his ebony skin.

"Apologies—"

The merchant cut him off with what sounded like an epithet and another emphatic wave of his hand. Dresden pushed away from the rolled-up carpets, careful not to upset the display, and adjusted his heavy pack. His legs felt gelatinous, and the hard dirt of the dusty street seemed to tilt. As if fighting down the crowded street, through the alternating glaring sunlight and shade from tasseled awnings and tall sandstone buildings, wasn't difficult enough without the strange feeling in his legs after two weeks at sea.

"Don't worry." Perceval clapped Dresden on the shoulder and he nearly sent Dresden off balance again. "You'll get your land-legs back soon enough."

"How are you fine?" Dresden grumbled as they pushed through the crowded Bhitran marketplace. They jostled past dark-skinned Bhitrans and Motus, brown-skinned Khastallanders, red-headed Hedengali, and other olive-skinned Carasians. Perceval's pale complexion stood out the way Dresden did in Craigailte or inland Monparth.

Perceval shrugged. "I lived near the coast of Monparth, and my father owned a ship."

Dresden shook his head at a wrinkled old woman hawking dates. "Your father *owned* his own *ship?*"

Perceval grinned over his shoulder. "My father is a very wealthy lord."

"He what?" Dresden stopped. Someone walked into his back and muttered in what sounded like Geiran.

"Lord Isaac Williamson the Third," Caleb said, appearing on Dresden's left, "is only disappointed in two things: that he still isn't a baron, and the disgrace that is his second son, our own miscreant, Perceval."

Perceval spun around, his eyes narrowed and crooked nose wrinkled. "Rathburn! If you're going to spill my life story, at least do it *right*. He's not disappointed in me, he's disgusted and horrified."

"No, because *your* father would take you back. Mine forgot I existed. 'Did I have four sons? Nope, just the three, stop the will there.' He—hang on." Caleb ran a hand through his shaggy blond hair and licked his lips. "I spy a *beauty*. Wish me luck." Caleb slipped behind a cart drawn by a braying donkey and made for a young woman, her mess of black curls tied back with a bright pink scarf.

"Good luck." Dresden smirked and continued through the marketplace, the sharp scent of dried peppers assaulting his nostrils.

They passed a bare-chested Bhitran man with thick braids down to his trousers, entertaining a crowd for tossed coins. Dresden slowed as he passed the crowd. The Bhitran wove blue light into a castle, then more light into a dragon. Fire exploded from the light-dragon's mouth and razed the castle. Dresden rolled his eyes. He'd seen a few mages since leaving Monparth. Most of them worked for wealthy households as healers, warriors, or horticulturists. Maybe it was just because Monparth hadn't had any mages since before Dresden was born, but using a gift that powerful for cheap tricks seemed a disgusting waste.

He and Perceval found their cook, a Craigan man named Lawrence, and a few of the other mercenaries as they wound through the busy marketplace. The crowds lessened as they approached the edge of town, and without the shade of stall awnings, the heat increased. They found Regulus and most of the rest of their company setting up tents near a busy well, surrounded by camels, horses, and even a few saddled desert eagle gryphons. Several horses were staked among their groups' tents.

Regulus finished hammering down a tent stake and straightened. As Dresden approached, he wiped the back of his hand across his glistening forehead. Dresden nodded toward the horses.

"Got the horses, then?"

"Had to haggle to get a halfway decent price, but I *refuse* to ride those long-legged beasts." Regulus jerked a thumb toward some sleeping camels.

"Honestly," Dresden said with a chuckle, "I would pay to see you ride one."

The scarred corner of Regulus' mouth twitched. "How much?"

"Fine, I wouldn't pay, but I might dare you."

"Probably for the best, captains shouldn't take bribes." Regulus turned and lugged his belongings inside his tent.

As Etiros-forsaken hot as the Bhitran day was, the night was downright chilly. Dresden huddled beneath his cloak, tossing and turning as Ivan snored on the other side of the tent. He didn't resent Regulus for taking the captain's tent alone, and it made sense to have both lieutenants in one place should Regulus need to find them quickly. But Dresden liked to think Regulus wouldn't have made them share a tent if he'd had any idea how loudly Ivan snored.

Some other sound caught his attention. He strained to hear it over Ivan's snores. A light clinking. Whispers. A horse's snort. Dresden threw back his cloak, snatched up his scimitars, and burst out of the tent without putting on his boots. A sliver of moon and countless stars provided dim illumination, but he caught the outline of a horse moving between tents, followed by another. He frowned. Why wasn't he hearing the hoofbeats?

He stole across the now cool sand-covered ground, keeping close to the tents. Who was on guard? The whisper of muffled footsteps drew him on. Dresden darted around a tent and raised his scimitars.

A Bhitran with close-shaved hair drew up short, his eyes going wide as Dresden raised his blade to the man's throat. A rope trailed from the man's hand to the horse behind him, with two more of their expensive horses tied in a line behind the first.

"Funny, I don't recall the captain giving an order to move the horses." Dresden tilted his head to the side. "Actually, I don't recall having a Bhitran in the troop."

The man dropped the rope and raised his hands. He shifted sideways.

"Ah, no moving!" Dresden brought up his other scimitar and positioned the blades on either side of the Bhitran's neck. "Mercenaries don't take kindly to theft of their belongings."

"I will go. Leave horses. Not return." The man's accent was thick, but he spoke clearly. He sounded young. In fact, as Dresden's eyes adjusted further to the dim light, the clean-shaven Bhitran looked no older than twenty.

"You speak Monparthian."

"Yes. Please. I am sorry. You take the horses, and I leave."

The tent behind Dresden rustled. "Who is talk—what is going on here?" Regulus yawned and walked over next to Dresden, his bare feet rustling across the sandy ground.

"Attempted theft of the horses, Captain."

The Bhitran lowered his head, careful of Dresden's blades. "I am sorry, Captain. Please. I leave the horses and go, and not come back again."

A moment passed, and the Bhitran looked up. Regulus tapped a bare foot against the sand. "You speak Monparthian well. What else do you speak?"

The Bhitran shrugged. "I speak Bhitran, Motu Bhitran, Khast, a little Hedengali, a little Geiran, and Monparthian."

"You got past my guards." Regulus spoke quietly, his tone revealing nothing. "How?"

The man flashed a quick smile. "The night is my friend. It hides me. I know how to move silently."

One of the horses pawed the ground, hardly making a sound. Dresden looked closer. He chuckled. "He wrapped the horses' hooves. No wonder I didn't hear hoofbeats."

"You got three horses to let you wrap their hooves without being caught?" Regulus couldn't entirely hide the impressed tone from his voice.

The Bhitran nodded. "Horses trust me."

"I see. If I tell my lieutenant to lower his swords, will you promise not to run?"

"Will you promise not to kill me?"

Regulus laughed. "No, I'd like to talk, and men talk far better with their heads attached to their bodies." He motioned for Dresden to lower his swords, and reluctantly, Dresden did so.

"What are you thinking?" Dresden kept his gaze on the horse thief, ready to move should the man try to run.

"That we need a translator."

Dresden's brows pinched. "He's a thief."

"Half the men in our troop are some brand of criminal, Drez."

Dresden opened his mouth to protest, but he wasn't wrong. Lawrence had killed a man in a barroom brawl. Perceval and Caleb seemed to be running from something, Etiros only knew what. The way he and Regulus had left Kimberly, some might argue they were acting like fugitives, too. Not to mention how many people equated mercenary with criminal, anyway.

"What's your name?" Regulus asked.

"Why?" The Bhitran shuffled his feet and glanced to the side. Dresden lifted the tips of his scimitars, just enough to be vaguely menacing without being directly threatening.

"I'm Regulus Hargreaves. This is my lieutenant, Dresden Jakobs. I'd like to know who I'm talking to."

The Bhitran's mouth twisted to the side, then he shrugged. "Jerrick Faras."

"Why were you stealing my horses, Faras?"

The man gulped loudly. "It's my job."

Dresden barked a laugh. "Thief is not an occupation."

"I steal, I get paid. Job." Faras shrugged.

"Why not get an honest job?" Regulus folded his arms. The horses shifted behind Faras. Dresden eyed them, worried they might run off while they were talking to this lowlife.

"Ha." Faras shook his head. "Get honest job, says the mercenary. Tell me, if you decide to be something else now, who would hire you? You have particular skill, and people distrust you, yes? It is the same. Once you steal, only criminals will hire a criminal."

Dresden snorted. "Why steal in the first place?"

Faras' eyes gleamed in the faint moonlight. "My family was poor, with many children. My father had great debt. I stole little things to help, got bolder. My father boarded horses, they trust me. I stole horses. Then I got caught, and I ran. But hard to find work. I was desperate, so I work for…you would say criminal lord, I think. Steal horses. People know, but I have not been caught. No one will hire me."

Trapped. Dresden felt a twinge of sympathy for the young man. Maybe Regulus wasn't crazy. Often mercenaries were running from a life they no longer wanted—just like Regulus did.

"Any good with a sword?" Regulus asked.

Dresden's gaze snapped to Regulus, but he quickly returned his attention to Faras.

Faras licked his lips. "Not exactly. I fight with a double-sided axe. I have won a few…how you say? Illegal street fights. With fists and with axe."

"I see." Regulus looked to Dresden. Dresden sighed and nodded. Regulus was going to do it regardless of if Dresden thought it was a good idea, anyway. Regulus turned back to Faras. "How would you like a new job? Travel, see the world? Be my translator and interpreter, use your axe and stealth as one of my mercenaries?"

Faras stuttered in Bhitran. "I mean…you…I…" He spoke Bhitran again, then switched back. "I tried to steal your horses?"

"Yes, and I'm impressed you got as far as you did." Regulus uncrossed his arms. "I could use your talents. We have a strict code that you will have to agree to. Break it, and you'll be thrown out. But—"

"Yes!" Faras fell to his knees before Regulus, making both Dresden and Regulus take a step back. "I will serve you."

"Now, hold on, it's more a contractual—"

Faras held up his hands in supplication. "If you had given me to guards, punishment for stealing horses is death. I owe you my life, Captain Regulus Hargreaves."

Regulus hesitated. "Well…that's a bit much." He yawned, reminding Dresden just how tired he was. A shiver went through Dresden as the threat passed and the excitement wore off, and without something else to occupy his mind, the cold pressed in again. Especially on his bare feet.

"Will…you be leaving soon?" Faras asked hesitantly. "Orem—my employer—will be unhappy that I am leaving. Better if he does not know."

"We're leaving in the morning, escorting a Hedengali merchant who is nervous about the tales he's heard of giant scorpion-snakes and aggressive desert gryphons and other Bhitran monsters—not to mention bandits." Regulus offered Faras his hand and pulled the man to his feet. "I'm going to sleep. We'll talk in the morning." Regulus disappeared back into his tent.

Dresden shook his head. "Leaves me to take care of things, I see. Let's put those horses back. I'll be checking on the guard to make sure they watch them. You'll have to find your own place to sleep tonight."

Faras shifted from foot to foot. "He…really will take me? A horse thief?"

Dresden held both scimitars in his left hand so he could pick up the lead to the first horse. "Yes, well, Regulus believes people are more than their circumstances. He'll give you a chance to show through your actions you can be a better man. But you fail that chance…you likely won't get another."

"That seems fair." Faras scratched his closely shorn hair. "He is good man."

"That he is." Dresden smiled. "As the men like to say—that's why he's the captain." *And it's why Regulus will always be my best friend.*

I just hope he's right about Faras.

PICKING UP STRAYS
Age: 26
Location: Segiledus

"THIS IS UNACCEPTABLE!" Regulus' shout echoed through the Segiledan noble's hall. "You lied about the nature of the contract."

Ivan, standing to Regulus' left, quickly translated. Dresden stood still and alert to Regulus' right, his arms hanging loosely at his sides but ready to draw his scimitars from their scabbards across his back if necessary. He glanced at the cluster of chained Segiledan men in the corner of the large wood hall. Guards kept them pressed close together.

Lexan, their Segiledan benefactor, steepled his fingers, his eyes steely. He spoke in Segiledan, his tone dismissive.

"You have your payment. Go," Ivan translated.

"I agreed to bring in criminals," Regulus snarled. "These men are not criminals, and now I have the blood of those who resisted on my hands."

Ivan translated, and Lexan responded coldly. Ivan looked to Regulus helplessly. "He says refusing to serve in his army is a crime, so they are criminals."

"They are farmers!" Regulus thrust his hand toward the group. "You told me a dangerous band of criminals was hiding in your forest, terrorizing your people. They *are* your people!"

The men hadn't spoken since they'd caught them. Not even to answer Ivan's questions as Regulus and Ivan grew more concerned with how the small group didn't look like criminals. Some were old. A couple were young boys. They were clearly afraid. But when Regulus handed them over to Lexan, one of the captives had fallen to his knees and begged. And when Ivan had translated for Regulus, it had been with rage that made his Monparthian thick and broken.

The men hadn't been terrorizing the people. They had hidden from a draft and were sneaking out at night to plough their families' fields and visit their women and children. Lexan's defense was he had to answer an affront from a neighboring lord and needed men for his army.

"Temporary," he had said. As if short-term conflicts didn't take lives.

"They are my people," Ivan translated sullenly, "and I will deal with them as suits me. Leave, mercenary, before I change my mind about permitting you to leave."

Regulus chuckled darkly. "What will you do with them?"

Ivan translated, and Lexan looked over at the peasant men. He shrugged.

"Young men, fighters," Ivan translated. His face was red beneath his shock of blond hair. "Old men, care for wounded. Boys, labor."

Regulus worked his jaw. His sense of justice was liable to screw up another contract. "And they will not be punished for resisting?"

Lexan leaned back in his ornate chair with a dismissive look as he responded.

Ivan hesitated. He looked at Regulus, anger in the hard line of his mouth, but worry in his eyes. "They will be."

Regulus looked at Ivan. "Did he say how? His answer was longer than yours."

Ivan sighed. "Lashings, Captain."

Dresden's mouth twisted to the side. Well, that did it. They weren't getting out of here without drawing steel.

"Lexan," Regulus said in a low voice, "the boys and the old cannot be whipped."

Ivan winced as he translated. Lexan scowled and clutched the arms of his chair as he shouted a response.

"You tell me what to do in my own hall, mercenary?" Ivan supplied.

Regulus crossed his arms. "Release the old men and the boys. Or I will not leave until I have released them all." The rest of the mercenaries shifted behind them restlessly. Ready. Dresden's fingers twitched in anticipation, but they were under orders not to draw weapons unless the Segiledans did so first.

Ivan nodded, for a moment looking concerned, then eagerness sparked in his eyes as he translated.

Lexan stood with a shout, and the Segiledan guards drew their weapons. Dresden drew his scimitars and spun them as the rustle of weapons being drawn sounded behind them. Regulus said calmly, "Strike to wound."

Dresden ran at the closest Segiledan guard. The man blocked Dresden's right scimitar, but as often happened, was unprepared for the second blade, which Dresden buried in the man's thigh. The Segiledan dropped his sword with a scream and fell back, clutching his bleeding leg. Dresden turned and dodged the axe of another guard. A few blocked blows, then Dresden spun around the man and sliced open his calves.

Lexan shouted something, and the few Segiledans still standing dropped their weapons and raised their hands in surrender. On the low dais, Regulus stood between two bleeding Segiledan guards, the point of his sword at Lexan's throat.

Lexan muttered something. Regulus looked around, and Ivan stepped around a guard who was clutching his arm to his stomach. Ivan returned his mace to his belt. "He says he will tell everyone Regulus Hargreaves turns on his benefactors."

A grim smile tugged on Regulus' scar. "Oh, no, Lexan. You will tell everyone that Regulus Hargreaves bested you in your own hall. You will tell everyone that Regulus Hargreaves protects innocents and will not serve corrupt men. And you will tell everyone that Regulus Hargreaves has the honor not to slit your throat just because he has the opportunity."

Ivan translated. Lexan clenched his jaw. The fury in his eyes said he would do no such thing. But the guards standing around with wide eyes? The chained men in the corner? The servants cowering along the walls and the handful of courtiers waiting in the back of the hall for their turn to speak to their liege? Oh, they would tell. And the type of men Regulus did not want to work for would likely avoid him. But benefactors looking for a mercenary troop with honor? They would be impressed, and they would hire Regulus.

It was a game Regulus had played before. It was why men who had never hired mercenaries hired Regulus. The troop's reputation for accomplishing contracts with deadly skill, and even more, Regulus' own reputation as a fearsome swordsman, got benefactors' attention. Regulus' honor earned their trust—or their distrust, in some instances.

A Carasian warlord had once hired them and been pleased to say he could do so while his rival desperately searched for another troop. "My enemy had the opportunity first," the warlord had said. "But he could not hire the righteous mercenary for fear you would smell out his corruption and destroy him." The warlord had grinned. "You will destroy him anyway." And they had. The man had been ruthless and made his wealth off the slave trade. It was an instance were Regulus expressly told his men not to hold back.

Regulus' voice cut through Dresden's thoughts. "Someone get them out of those chains." Regulus sheathed his sword, his focus on Lexan. "This lord you have a quarrel with. Why, and what were your intentions?"

Dresden set about helping with freeing the prisoners while Regulus and Lexan talked with Ivan translating. Dresden removed the shackles from a thin boy of some thirteen or so years with knotted straw-colored hair above a suntanned face.

"Thank you, sir," the boy whispered as he rubbed his wrists.

Dresden's head jerked. "You're not Segiledan."

The boy shook his head. "I'm Monparthian. I came with my parents over the pass to sell wool."

"Where are your parents?"

The boy stared at his feet. "Dead. Troll. I hid."

"And the Segiledans took you in?"

The boy nodded, but he shuddered and glanced at a farmer standing near him. Dresden looked to the tall Segiledan. The man watched the Monparthian boy, lips pursed beneath his reddish-brown beard. He said something in Segiledan. The boy whimpered and nodded.

"You speak Segiledan?" Dresden asked the boy.

"Only a little." He glanced at the glaring farmer. "I've learned enough for orders."

"Orders?" Dresden crouched down to be at eye level with the boy and put a hand on his bony shoulder. "What—"

The farmer snapped something in Segiledan and grabbed the boy's shoulder, pulling him back and stepping between him and Dresden. Dresden straightened with a frown. The Segiledan said something else, his tone angry.

"What's he saying, boy?"

But the boy just shook his head.

"What's going on here?" Regulus strode over next to Dresden. "Why's this one look angry?"

"Don't know." Not that he didn't have his suspicions. He pointed around the Segiledan at the boy. "I was trying to talk to that Monparthian boy, and this one seems displeased."

"Monparthian?" Regulus' eyebrows rose. "Come here, lad."

The boy looked up at the Segiledan's back and shook his head. The Segiledan said something, his tone challenging.

"He says the boy belongs to him," Ivan said, coming up on Dresden's other side. "The boy stole from him, so he works to pay off his debt."

Regulus frowned, then stepped to the side to see the boy. "What's your name?"

The boy hesitated. He looked at Regulus, at the farmer, then stared at the ground. "Harold."

"How'd you come to steal, Harold?"

"Orphaned."

Regulus' jaw tightened. "Do you like working for this man?"

Harold winced. "Yes." It couldn't have been a more obvious lie.

The Segiledan put a hand on Harold and said something. Dresden looked to Ivan.

"He thanks you for freeing them, but if Lexan allows them to return home, he will need the boy's help with the harvest."

"They're going home." Regulus nodded. "We will be retrieving the money Lexan's rival owes."

Dresden frowned. "You took another contract from Lexan?"

Regulus smiled wryly. "I convinced him it was better to pay us to fight his battle than try to get these hapless souls to do it. Wasn't hard after he saw us in action."

And that's why Regulus is the captain.

"Ivan, tell them they're all going home. No more draft."

Ivan translated Regulus' news, and the men looked stunned, then overjoyed. Regulus looked back at the boy.

"Do you want to go back to the farm with this man?"

Harold glanced nervously at the farmer, then nodded. "It's the closest I have to a home. It's pretty. By the mouth of the Ureld River."

Regulus pursed his lips. "Near the Darbot Forest?" Harold nodded. "Very well." He looked at the Segiledan. "Treat him well. And give him more food." Regulus turned as Ivan translated. "Move out men! We have another mission."

❧

Raiding the other Segiledan lord's treasury proved easy. His men were unprepared for an attack, especially from a mercenary troop of fifteen. Regulus took half the Segiledan's treasury for Lexan. "Lexan won't know we didn't take it all," he said.

Lexan was borderline mousy when they returned. He clearly wanted them to take their payment and leave without any further trouble. Regulus was happy to oblige.

"Where to next?" Dresden asked.

"I fancy visiting Monparth," Regulus said. "Been nearly two years since our last contract there. I miss it sometimes. Is that ridiculous or what?"

"I'd like to see home again."

"Home?" Regulus looked at him in surprise.

"It's where we grew up. Doesn't that make it home?" Dresden frowned. "But I mean Monparth. Not the Kimberly estate. Never care to set foot there again."

Regulus laughed. "Agreed. Monparth it is. But first, we're going to swing slightly out of our way. There's something I want to check on."

The moss-covered small stone farmhouse standing in the middle of the field of bright green grass looked picturesque. A clear blue sky stretched above the field of still-green grain behind the farmhouse. The fir trees of the Darbot Forest rose up beyond the fields, a shadowy backdrop to the pastoral scene. Regulus and Dresden rode next to the Ureld River, the creak of their saddles drowned out by the gurgle of water over river stones. They'd left the men at the camp closer to the pass, and the day of riding alone had been peaceful. Times like this, Regulus felt like Dresden's friend more than his captain, and Dresden treasured those moments.

A shout split the calm air, followed by a cry. Regulus kicked his massive black warhorse to a gallop, and Dresden followed, racing toward the sound. They rounded the farmhouse as another cry echoed.

The tall Segiledan farmer stood over a small hunched form next to a basket of spilled eggs. The Segiledan shouted something and raised the thick stick in his hand. Regulus leapt off his horse with a roar. The farmer looked up, his eyes wide and brow pinched, as his makeshift club slammed into the boy's back. Regulus lunged into the man, shoving him to the ground. Dresden jumped down and went to the quaking body curled on the ground.

"Harold?" Dresden laid his hand gently on the dirty straw-colored hair. The boy twitched, then raised his head tentatively. Regulus knelt on Harold's other side.

"You…" The boy rubbed away his tears. "Why are you here?"

"I came to ensure you weren't being mistreated," Regulus ground out. "How long has he been hitting you?"

Harold whimpered and ducked his head. Dresden's hands curled into fists. The Segiledan farmer had risen to his feet, and he said something that sounded furious. Dresden stood, drawing one of his scimitars.

"I'd stay back if I were you." The man might not have understood his words, but he eyed the sword, clearly understanding that.

"Harold," Regulus said. "I'm in need of a baggage boy. How would you like a job?"

"A…job?"

"You won't make as much as the mercenaries, since you won't be doing the fighting," Regulus said. "But you'd be paid. Plenty of food." His face darkened. "No beatings."

Harold nodded rapidly. "Yes. Yes, please, sir, yes." He pushed off the ground and cried out, gripping his side.

Regulus' eyes flashed. He lifted the boy's tunic, revealing a large black-and-blue bruise. He touched the bruise and Harold jerked with a cry of pain, but Regulus continued to prod the bruise. "Just bruised. Feels like your ribs are intact." Regulus shifted and picked Harold up, holding the boys' thin frame to his chest as he carried him to his horse.

Back at the camp, Regulus went to plan their route through the mountains, leaving Dresden to take care of Harold. Dresden brought extra food, and Harold consumed it all like he'd been starved. Considering how bony the boy was, it seemed possible. After Harold had eaten, Dresden made him remove his tunic and slathered the bruises in numbing salve. The boy's ribs and spine jutted out from under his skin, and old and new bruises dotted his upper body.

"Dresden," Harold said uncertainly.

"Yes?"

"Why did…" Harold frowned. "What's his name? Reginald? The scary big man with the scar. He said it at the hall, but I can't remember."

Dresden laughed. "The scary…" He fell into another fit of laughter. "Reginald!" He tried to hold back his laughter when he saw the embarrassed blush on Harold's cheeks, but he couldn't help it. "Regulus Hargreaves. But you'll call him Captain."

"Oh." Harold pulled his tunic back on and winced. "Why did Captain help me?"

Dresden sobered, even though he wanted to laugh again at Harold saying Captain like that was Regulus' name. "The captain has a big heart, and he doesn't like cruelty."

"But…" Harold looked away uncomfortably. "Aren't you all mercenaries? Don't you…you know…kill people?"

"Yes." Dresden laid back on the ground. He'd given Harold his mat. He'd have to get a new one. "But we try to only kill bad people."

Harold nodded slowly. "That's why the captain was angry at Lexan. He thought the farmers were bad people, and they weren't?" He grimaced. "Most of them."

"Yes."

Harold looked deep in thought. "I think I like the captain."

Dresden chuckled. "Well, good. Disliking the captain is the fastest way to make sure you have no friends in this troop."

THE LETTER

Age: 26
One month later and one week after Regulus swears to serve the
Prince of Shadow and Ash
(as revealed in the novel Prince of Shadow and Ash*)*
Location: Thaera Duchy, Etchy Barony, Monparth

"REG. REG, talk to me. What's it say?"

Regulus didn't move. He stood in the exact same position he'd been in for the last few minutes, his back rigidly straight, his wide eyes glued to the letter in his hands. Dresden eyed the seal. A gryphon. He'd never paid much attention to the seals of the various noble families of Monparth, and he hadn't had cause to think on them in years, other than a few trips into Monparth for mercenary contracts. Like the one they had recently finished.

"Etiros above, Regulus, if it's not about a contract, what is it?"

"I…my…" Regulus blinked. The parchment trembled in his hands. "I'm…" He shook his head and his eyes scanned the letter yet again. "My brother is dead."

"Your…wait, your half-brother? The one you've never met?"

Regulus nodded. "It's from Baron Carrick. My father wrote me into his will."

"Your father…what?"

"He died a few years ago, apparently. My father." Regulus' hands tightened on the letter. "According to my father's will, if his legitimate son died without an heir, the Arrano title and estate is to fall to…me. And my half-brother is dead. Some horse-riding accident." He finally looked up from the letter, his brow pinched over shocked eyes. "I'm…Lord of Arrano."

Dresden gaped, his mouth stuck hanging open.

"They've been trying to track me down for nearly a month." Regulus shook his head. "Baron Carrick is currently in Lerilton on business for the next week. I can report to him there to pledge my fealty and accept my…my title." Regulus swayed. He ran his fingers through his hair, then rubbed the pommel of his sword.

"You're a lord." Dresden stared at Regulus. "Lord of Arrano."

Regulus laughed, but it was bitter, angry. "I always wanted to be welcomed at Arrano. But this…I never dreamed of this." His eyes flashed and the parchment crinkled as his hand fisted. "If this had come three weeks ago…" He growled in irritation. "I wouldn't have taken that job. I'd be free."

Dresden's gaze darted to Regulus' right arm, but the mark the sorcerer had placed there was hidden beneath his sleeve. "Well…" he said slowly. "You'll be a lord regardless. And once your debt is repaid, you'll just be a lord."

Regulus snorted. "Assuming sorcerers keep their word."

"He sounded sincere. And he's kept his word so far."

Regulus refolded the wrinkled letter. "Gather the others." His face momentarily twisted with sorrow. There were so few of them left.

Once the remaining four mercenaries plus Harold were gathered, Regulus stood before them with his hands clasped behind his back. "Men, I thank you for standing with me these last couple weeks." He worked his jaw. "I know I've only just returned, but…I will be leaving again."

Perceval swore. "He's sending you away again already?"

"No." Regulus smiled tightly. "This is a personal affair. I need to go into Lerilton." He licked his lips. "I will no longer be your captain."

"What?" several men cried at once.

"Captain—" Perceval started.

"I do not understand," Jerrick said, his arms crossed.

"Because of that Prince of Ash?" Estevan demanded.

Shadow and Ash, Dresden thought, but he didn't say anything.

"No." Regulus shifted. "I received a letter. Assuming this is not a trap, and I can convince Baron Carrick of my identity, I will no longer be a mercenary. I will be Lord of Arrano."

The men stared at Regulus, dead silent and clearly puzzled.

Regulus cleared his throat. "I have never talked about my past. My father was lord of a modest estate here in Monparth. Not far from here, actually. My mother was…" He tugged on the collar of his shirt. "A servant." He hurried on.

"My father and half-brother are dead, and I'm the only remaining heir. There is a chance Baron Carrick will seize the opportunity to take Arrano for himself by denying me. Which is why I will be going alone. If Carrick tries to kill me…" He swallowed. "I will be exposed and will have to go into hiding. If all goes well, I'll return. And at that time, I'll ask again if you wish to remain under my command."

Dresden started. He hadn't considered… If Regulus was a lord, where did that leave him? A guard? A freeman? A…servant?

"I know some of you have reasons for leaving life among the nobility behind." Regulus' gaze flicked over to Caleb and Perceval. "Some of you are used to lives of travel." He looked to Estevan and Jerrick. "So I will not blame you if settling down at Arrano is not for you." Regulus' left hand strayed to his right arm. "Or if you have second thoughts about staying under my command, given my…condition. Dismissed."

The mercenaries hesitated, then dispersed, except for Harold. Harold stepped forward uncertainly, his youthful face twitching with nervousness. "Captain?"

"Yes, Harold?" Regulus' expression softened.

Harold glanced at Dresden. Dresden wasn't sure what the boy wanted to say, but he nodded encouragingly. Harold looked back to Regulus. "Will there be a place for a baggage boy at Arrano?"

"No, I don't think so."

Dresden stared at Regulus, shocked. The boy had nowhere to go. Harold's shoulders fell. Dresden opened his mouth to ask Regulus what his problem was, but Regulus smiled.

"But if I'm going to be a lord, I will need a squire."

Harold choked. "A…squire?"

Regulus walked over and clapped the boy's bony shoulder. "Think about it. If I come back, you can give me your answer. Now go on."

"Thank you, Captain." Harold darted into the camp.

Dresden tried to ignore the discomfort in the pit of his stomach. "And what about me?"

"What about you?"

He hesitated. Their relationship was shifting yet again, and he didn't know what to do about it or how to treat Regulus now. "I suppose you'll be…needing servants."

Regulus looked horrified. "Etiros, no, Drez." He glanced toward the tents and lowered his voice. "I didn't want to say anything, not before they've had a chance to think about it. To take the chance to leave. If they're not here when I get back…I won't blame them. If I get back."

"Say anything about what?" Dresden eyed Regulus suspiciously, trying to figure out what his friend was thinking.

"If I'm a lord…I can knight you, Drez."

Dresden gasped. "Reg, I—"

"Wait." Regulus held up a hand. "I'd want you to think about it. You'd be a knight. You'd have more rights. I'm not sure what the situation is at Arrano, but I could hopefully give you some land. But…" He turned away slightly. "I'd be your liege. You would owe me fealty. You would be tied to Arrano, and to me. I don't want you to feel trapped or…to come to resent me."

Dresden laughed. "You left me tied to a tree naked a few years back. If I was going to resent you, I think I already would. I can't resent you for ennobling me."

"You wouldn't really be noble. Not in the eyes of the lords." Regulus looked to Dresden. "You would be to me. The others, too, if they accepted."

"You…would knight them all?" *Of course he would.* Because that's who Regulus was.

Regulus nodded. "If they agree. I'll need knights. Loyal men who know my secret. And friends. I'm going to need friends if this works out." He swallowed. "The bastard mercenary is unlikely to win many friends among the nobility."

"I don't need to think about it. I would have gone with you if you'd offered me a place as a gardener." Dresden smiled at the affronted look on Regulus' face. "You're my oldest friend, Reg. And the fact it wouldn't even cross your mind to offer me anything less than a knighthood, and that you would be concerned about making me subservient…" He shook his head. "You're a good man. Besides, you know how many times you've saved my life?"

Regulus chuckled. "Twelve. Well, nine. Three of those weren't mortal danger."

"Twelve?" Dresden blinked. "Hold up, that—"

"First, the time you fell in the river."

"The…I had that under control." Dresden's face heated. He hadn't. Not even a little. "You've been counting since we were children?"

"Not right away. I started counting after I took your belting." Regulus reddened. "I don't mean it like that. I…" He gulped and looked away. "I hoped you remembered…when I had to scold you in front of Lord Kimberly, or when you were wounded because you became a mercenary with me, or when I had to…discipline you as your captain. I counted the times I'd saved you, protected you. And I hoped that it somehow made up for the rest."

Dresden stared at Regulus. Ice settled into his stomach. "You've been afraid I'd resent you. Stop being your friend." Awareness weighed heavily on him. "You are my friend, Reg! You have been since that day you pulled me out of the river, and I realized you weren't like the other nobles. You cared. And even when I've been mad at you, even when I've resented that we aren't equals, I've never hated you. You're more than my friend. After everything we've been through, everything we've done for each other—don't forget, I've saved your neck on the field a few times, too—you're my brother, Regulus."

Regulus jerked. His gaze locked on Dresden, frozen. His throat worked and his jaw tightened. He blinked, opened his mouth, then slammed his quivering jaw closed. The emotion in Regulus' eyes twisted Dresden's heart, threatening to make him an emotional wreck, too.

"Brothers," Regulus whispered. "I'd make you a lord if I could do it, Drez."

Dresden smiled. "I don't need it. I'd be abominable at it, anyway."

Regulus chuckled, shaky and unsteady as a tear escaped from his eye. "I doubt I'll be any good at it."

"Anyway." Dresden clapped his hands, feeling uncomfortable with the raw honesty. "I'm coming with you to Lerilton. Things go well, I want to be there. Things go poorly, you're not going into hiding without me."

Regulus paled. "No. If things go poorly, you could be killed."

"I'm still going. My brother could need me."

"Dresden, please. I…I need to know you're alright. If I'm found out, I need to know you're safe, and I need to know you'll take care of Harold."

"Harold and Jerrick get on well, and none of those men would abandon Harold. I'm coming."

Regulus frowned. "I could order you to remain behind."

That hurt, but Dresden shrugged nonchalantly. "I could disobey."

"Oh, perfect, then my first act as a lord can be to tie you to a tree." But his words held no force, and Regulus' hand tapped nervously against his leg.

Dresden lifted a brow. "I'll take my chances that you'll forgive me."

Regulus cursed. "Fine. I'll be glad for the company, but if you get killed…" His hand fisted. "Just…don't get killed."

"I'll keep that in mind," Dresden replied dryly. But he saw the haunted look in Regulus' eyes. If Dresden was killed, Regulus would never forgive himself. *Best not die.*

My Lord

A couple days later

DRESDEN FOLLOWED Regulus and a guardsman into a private room at the tavern. The air smelled of ale and bodies kept too close together and straw mattresses that had suffered in the unusually humid summer. Dust mites floated in the air. The guard stepped to the side, his hand on his sword. Another guard stood in the room, and he straightened as they entered. His gaze swept over Regulus and Dresden, taking in their weapons, and his hand went to his sword as well. It was mildly amusing. Dresden cast an appraising glance at the guards. Either he or Regulus could take them both, easily.

"My lord Baron Carrick," their escort said, "this man claims to have business with you. Says his name is—"

"Regulus Hargreaves." Carrick stood from behind a tiny wood table covered in nicks, setting aside a piece of parchment and a quill. He nodded, his lips pursed as he examined Regulus. "I admit, I had rather hoped you either wouldn't show or would be an imposter. But you look more like Kenneth than his own son did."

To his credit, Regulus didn't so much as flinch or show a flicker of emotion at Carrick referring to his half-brother as his father's own son. As if Regulus wasn't really his father's son. Regulus gave a small bow.

"Baron Carrick." Regulus reached into the pouch at his belt and withdrew something metallic. "I wouldn't presume to attempt to claim my inheritance based on a passing similarity to Lord Kenneth Arrano." He held out his hand. The signet ring sat on his hand. "I would wager my father's will specified I would have that?"

Carrick's brows rose in surprise as he picked up and inspected the ring. "Yes…it did. Although, I didn't really expect you to have it after all these years."

Dresden tried not to gape. He didn't know Regulus still had that ring.

"Well then," Carrick handed the ring back. "You'll just need to swear your fealty, and I'll authorize the will, and legally, everything will be yours." Carrick stepped back. "Take a knee, Hargreaves."

Regulus' hand twitched, but he lowered to one knee and inclined his head. Dresden tensed, prepared to draw his scimitars if needed. But Carrick walked Regulus through the oaths of fealty to himself and to the king of Monparth, and no one made any threatening movements.

"Rise, Lord Hargreaves of Arrano."

Dresden held his breath as Regulus stood and bowed.

"Thank you, Baron Carrick."

Carrick nodded, then returned to the table. He sorted through some papers, pulled one out, and signed it. He handed it to Regulus. "You'll find the Ladies Arrano still living at the castle."

"Ladies?" Regulus asked.

"Your father's wife and your brother's wife." For the briefest moment, a dark smile flickered over Carrick's face. "I wouldn't be surprised if they challenge you."

"Challenge me?"

"In the case of your death, the estate would go to the elder Lady Arrano. As a woman, she cannot stake a claim while you live." Carrick shrugged. "But if she can find a man to challenge you on her behalf, she is permitted to do so."

"Oh." Regulus shuffled uncomfortably. "Thank you for the warning." He bowed again, and they left the small tavern room.

Once outside town, Regulus visibly relaxed. "That went better than expected."

"Congratulations, my lord." Dresden smiled, but Regulus tensed.

"Please, don't do that." Regulus' face contorted in distaste. "My lord reminds me of Lord Kimberly, or all these lords we've worked for who grow fat while they pay us to do what they're too lazy to do themselves. Or the sorcerer. And feels too much like master. Just Regulus or Reg. Please."

A warm feeling spread in Dresden's chest. "Sure, Reg."

Regulus frowned. "Might have Harold call me my lord, though. Last thing I need is for my squire to slip up and call some other noble 'sir' or something." He shrugged. "I'll let him choose."

The men were watching for their return and had gathered around before they had even dismounted.

"So?" Jerrick prodded. "Things didn't go completely wrong, since you're here."

"Am I looking at a mercenary or a noble?" Caleb asked.

Regulus held up the will. "According to this, a noble."

The men whooped and cheered. Regulus held up his hand to quiet them. "You're all still here." His voice was tight was emotion. "Will you...come with me? Serve me as Lord Hargreaves of Arrano?"

Perceval spoke first. "No one else I'd rather serve, Captain. Besides, Leonora will be thrilled. She's been trying to convince me to give up the life.

Months to years gone at a time with no guarantee I'll return, or that she'll know if I won't, doesn't suit her. Or me, for that matter. She'll move to Monparth if it means I'm staying with her."

Jerrick grunted. "Honestly, I'd rather settle down. Maybe I'll meet a nice girl. If you'll have me, Cap—my lord."

"I've rather missed living in a castle," Caleb mused. "Besides which, you can't get rid of me that easily."

Estevan shrugged. "What else would I do? And I'd be dead a few times over if not for you. Or at least in prison somewhere." The men all chuckled at that.

"You already knew my answer, my lord," Harold said. He lifted his chin, determination in his eyes. Dresden noted his *my lord* with amusement. He was eager to prove he could be a good squire, and Dresden guessed Regulus would have difficulty getting Harold *not* to call him my lord.

Regulus looked over the small band, his eyes glistening. "I may be a lord, but I'm not my own man." His hand strayed to his right arm, rubbing at the mark under his sleeve. "You would continue to serve a slave?"

A chorus of yeses and protests that Regulus wasn't a slave answered. Regulus' shoulders sagged as he swallowed back his emotion. Dresden smiled. Regulus never believed he was good or worthy. Maybe he would see it now.

"I don't deserve friends like you." Regulus cleared his throat. "Dresden Jakobs." He turned toward Dresden and drew his sword. The men made sounds of confusion. "Kneel."

"What?" Estevan gasped.

Dresden smiled reassuringly at the men and dropped to one knee.

"I, Regulus Hargreaves, Lord of Arrano"—Regulus touched the flat of the blade to Dresden's shoulder—"by the authority invested in me as a lord of Monparth, hereby bestow upon you the title and bond of knighthood." He moved the sword to the other shoulder, looking hesitant. "Do you swear to uphold the laws of Monparth, the code of chivalry, and to…serve me faithfully as your liege?"

Dresden smiled, trying to let Regulus know it was okay. "I swear it."

Regulus lifted the sword as relief flickered in his eyes. "Arise, Sir Dresden Jakobs."

Sir Dresden Jakobs. Dresden's throat tightened with joy. He might never get used being Sir Jakobs. He bowed. "Thank you, Regulus."

The men applauded and a couple started to congratulate Dresden, but Regulus held up his hand. "Step forward and kneel, Perceval."

Perceval's face went slack. "Captain?"

"Not Captain, Perce. Regulus." Regulus motioned him forward. "Unless you want to serve me without a title, step forward."

Perceval quickly stepped forward and dropped to his knee. Regulus knighted him, then looked to Caleb. "Caleb, step forward and kneel."

"I…thank you, my lord."

Regulus smiled. "Regulus. Please. I want my knights…I want my friends to call me Regulus."

As soon as Caleb had been knighted, Regulus looked to Jerrick. "Step forward and kneel, Jerrick."

Jerrick's eyes widened. "Captain… My lord… Regulus?"

"Come on, man."

"But…" Jerrick shuffled his weight from foot to foot and looked down. "I'm Bhitran."

"And if you'd get on your knee, you'd be a knight of Monparth, too." Regulus lowered his sword. "I have no hesitation about knighting you, my friend. But if you would rather not—"

Jerrick quickly moved to kneel before Regulus. He looked up with tears in his eyes. "I would not have thought…I would have no other lord as liege."

Finally, Regulus turned to Estevan. Estevan looked uncertain. Nervous. "Step forward—"

Relief spread over Estevan's face and he practically lunged to kneel in front of Regulus. "Thank you. I won't let you down, Regulus."

"Did you think I would leave you out?" Regulus asked, his brow knit and gaze puzzled.

"I'm young and…a nomad with a criminal past." Estevan flushed. "I hoped…but I wouldn't presume."

Once Estevan was knighted, Regulus sheathed his sword and looked around at his men. Dresden's chest swelled with pride. What a long way Regulus had come from the boy who had wept against a tree trunk while his own cousin beat him. An accomplished and feared mercenary captain. A lord with loyal knights.

Perceval chuckled. "If ever I were to reenter the nobility, I couldn't have hoped for more deliciously scandalous fellow knights. This is going to be fun."

For a moment, Dresden worried Regulus would be offended or concerned, but Regulus laughed.

"The bastard and his group of misfit knights." Regulus looked over his men with a grim smile. "This should be interesting."

SERVANT, MERCENARY, BROTHER

A DRESDEN JAKOBS VIGNETTE COLLECTION

VOLUME II

PART I
Before the Mage

UNEASE COILED in Dresden's stomach the longer they followed the distraught boy. He couldn't say what had put him on edge—the boy's hysterical pleas for help, the quiet forest, or that a small, scared boy was racing toward what he claimed were goblins harassing his village. The barefoot Monparthian boy had taken off the moment Regulus had promised to help. They had abandoned their half-made camp and ridden after the lad so they wouldn't lose him. He wouldn't even slow to let Regulus lift him onto his black destrier, even though Regulus had offered.

Ivan drew his muscular bay stallion next to Regulus as they passed through a clearing. Dresden pushed his own horse up on Regulus' other side. As first lieutenant, he should know whatever the captain and second lieutenant discussed.

"Something about this feels off, Captain." Ivan's whisper emphasized the sharp consonants of his Segiledan accent.

Regulus nodded. "I don't think this boy has ever seen a goblin in his life, and not only because this part of Monparth hasn't had trouble with goblins in at least a decade."

"Why are we following him, then, Captain?" Dresden asked.

Regulus glanced at him. "Because *something* is still wrong. He needs help." Regulus pulled ahead as the trees grew closer around them.

Ivan fell in next to Dresden and lowered his voice. "Watch. This will be a trick. We'll get back to a ransacked camp."

"I don't know." Dresden eyed the dirt-covered boy racing ahead of them. "Regulus is a good judge of character."

"True." Ivan grunted. "Still think it's a trick."

A sly smile spread across Dresden's lips. "A wager. If the camp is ransacked, you get the tent to yourself for two nights. If not, *I* get the tent to myself for two nights." He grinned. "Two blissfully quiet nights without your snoring."

Ivan grunted. "First, I do not snore, and second, if the camp is ransacked, we may not have a tent, so not a fair wager."

Before Dresden could respond, they rounded a copse of birch and came upon a single wood hut. No smoke curled from the chimney. No sound came from inside. Cords of wood were stacked against the side of the hut, but no one was there. The hair on the back of Dresden's neck stood on end. Ivan's heavy blond brows furrowed.

"This isn't a village," Jerrick said. The Bhitran fingered the battle axe at his belt. Jerrick's instincts were good; it didn't bode well that he was on edge, too.

Dresden dismounted as the boy ran into the hut. No goblins. No villagers in need. He drew his scimitars anyway as his nerves wound tight. What in hellfire was going on?

"Something's off, Captain," Perceval said with a threatening scowl.

Regulus' frown pulled at the pinkish scar cutting across his right cheek. He started toward the hut, and Dresden and Ivan fell into step behind him. As they approached the darkened doorway, Regulus drew his own sword. Inside the house, the boy sobbed and spoke quietly.

"Mama, Papa."

Dresden peered over Regulus' shoulder into the house and went cold.

A man and woman sat tied to wood chairs in the middle of the dim room. The boy sniffled as he fumbled with the gag on his father's mouth. His mother looked at them with wide eyes, her face pale as a sheet around the cloth digging into the sides of her mouth. The boy loosened his father's gag.

"Trap!" the man shouted.

Dresden whirled around and a flash of green light blinded him. He staggered sideways, blinking away dark spots. His heart raced.

"Who is your leader?" A short man with a gray-streaked brown beard stood alone several paces away. His black hood shadowed his face, and flowing midnight robes trimmed in crimson swayed around his ankles as he walked toward them.

Regulus took a step forward, the idiot. "I'm Captain—"

"Excellent." The man's teeth showed through a vicious smile as he lifted his hands, the wide sleeves of his robes falling back to reveal knobby fingers. Shards of green-tinged light shot from his hands and slammed into several of the men, straight through their armor. Their bodies fell.

Dresden's stomach churned as he dragged his gaze from his fallen friends to their attacker. The closest Dresden had ever seen to something like this were a few mages giving performances, and he'd never witnessed one fight. Were they facing a sorcerer? Haversham lunged at the man, sword swinging. The man turned his left palm and a burst of orange flame engulfed Haversham. The mercenary screamed and staggered sideways, catching a couple bushes on fire as he rolled to the ground.

Definitely a sorcerer. Dresden shook off his shock and charged with his scimitars raised. The sorcerer flicked his wrist and a blast of light knocked Dresden sideways.

Men grunted and cried out. Regulus roared, but his battle cry turned into a scream. Dresden's heart thundered as he launched to his feet and looked for his captain. Regulus dropped his sword, cradling his right hand. "Reg—"

"Drez!" Estevan shouted. "Behind you!"

Dresden spun around. A rope of green light shot from the sorcerer's hand toward him. He sliced at the rope, but it evaded his blades and wound around his throat. The rope tightened, and Dresden dropped his weapons to claw at the rope as it dug into his windpipe.

"No!" Regulus shouted.

"Come here," the sorcerer commanded. "Without the sword, or they die."

Dresden choked and fell to his knees as the rope squeezed tighter.

"What do you want?" Regulus' voice warbled.

Dresden strained to turn his head toward Regulus. He watched Regulus approach the sorcerer out of the corner of his eye. *Run, you idiot.* Every breath was harder to draw in, rasping down his strangled throat. His vision blurred as he thrashed against the strangling rope. The roar of blood in his ears muffled the voices of Regulus and the sorcerer.

Dresden's panic mounted as his lungs burned. The rope tightened. *No, I'm not ready. I'm not ready to die.* But his movements slowed, and his hands fell away from the rope as he lost the energy to fight. Some desperate part of his brain told him to hold on as the world went black.

Regulus will come. He won't let me die.

He drifted toward unconsciousness.

Hurry…

Reg?

Please.

The crushing pressure on his neck vanished. Air rushed down his throat. Every muscle shook as Dresden collapsed onto his stomach, coughing and gasping. His neck burned where the rope had touched his skin. His throat ached. Someone screamed, but he couldn't move. Large black spots wavered in front of his eyes. Although his head still pounded, his sight cleared and the roaring in his ears faded. Boots ran toward him, then Regulus knelt in front of him.

Relief at surviving and seeing Regulus alive overwhelmed him, and he closed his watering eyes. *Regulus won.*

"Are you okay?" Regulus gripped Dresden's shoulders and pulled him up. "Dresden!"

Dresden opened his eyes as Regulus shook him.

"Drez, talk to me!"

"Re—" A wheezing cough cut Dresden off. He swallowed and cleared his throat. "I'm okay. What happened?"

"Mercenary!" The sorcerer's voice broke through Dresden's daze like a punch to the face. The sorcerer still stood a few paces away, his arms crossed. "Come back here!"

Dread slithered down Dresden's spine. He looked back to Regulus.

Regulus set his jaw, vengeance in his glare. He gasped, eyes going wide, and dropped Dresden's shoulders to claw at his right forearm. Dresden snatched up Regulus' arm, pulled away his hand, and pushed up his sleeve. Instead of the expected injury, a black tattoo stood out against the pale skin on the underside of Regulus' forearm.

A tattoo that hadn't been there that morning. Dresden dropped Regulus' arm and blinked, but the mark remained. Two hollow diamonds placed end-to-end, with a V open toward his wrist at the end. A chain of two hollow diamonds placed end-to-end, with a V open toward his wrist.

"What's going on?" Dresden forced the words past his lips.

"It's burning…" Regulus winced.

"Yes; it's not for decoration." The sorcerer sneered beneath his hood. "You swore an oath. You disobey me, you'll suffer the consequences. Now come back here; I wasn't done talking to you."

An oath? What had Regulus done?

Regulus clenched his fist and looked around. Dresden followed his gaze. Most of the men were dead. The handful still alive gawked at either Regulus or the sorcerer. Ivan's blood-drenched body lay contorted, his glassy eyes staring unseeing into the tree branches. Dresden's chest spasmed. Regulus' face twisted and indignation lit his eyes before his entire body jerked.

"Reg?"

His friend screamed and arched his back. Still screaming, Regulus fell and writhed on the ground. He looked to Dresden, frightened and helpless in a way that made Dresden's blood freeze. Dresden reached forward, trying to avoid Regulus' flailing limbs. Regulus gasped in air and stopped screaming, his body going still as a tear slid down his sweat-drenched face.

"I don't tolerate disobedience, mercenary." Wicked amusement cut through the sorcerer's words. "Come here."

Dresden watched in stunned horror as Regulus pushed himself up on quivering arms and walked to the sorcerer, his head down.

"Yes?" Regulus asked quietly.

"Yes, *my lord*," the sorcerer snapped. "I am the Prince of Shadow and Ash. You'll address me with proper respect." Regulus didn't respond, then he cried out and gripped his forearm again.

"Yes, my lord." Regulus inclined his head.

This can't be happening. Dresden jumped up and grabbed his scimitars as he prepared to charge. Regulus wouldn't let him die, and Dresden wouldn't stand by without helping his brother. Nearby, Perceval also stumbled up, sword in hand.

The sorcerer glanced at them. "Tell your men to stand down."

Regulus looked over his shoulder. "No!" He lifted his hands. "Stand down. Stay back! Put your weapons away." He turned back to the sorcerer.

Indignant, Dresden sheathed his scimitars. What else could he do? Even if he disobeyed Regulus' direct order, the sorcerer would overpower them again. Or torture Regulus. Dresden was going to be sick.

"What's your name?" the sorcerer asked.

"Captain Regulus Hargreaves."

"And you understand the terms of our deal, Hargreaves?"

Regulus slumped. "I am your servant. Until I've repaid you for sparing their lives."

"What?" Jerrick gasped.

Dresden was too dismayed to speak. Regulus had made himself a servant? To save their lives? He gulped. *To repay a debt.* Regulus might as well have signed a contract of indenture—branded on his arm.

"More like my slave." The sorcerer shrugged.

That couldn't be right. The words replayed in Dresden's mind, their weight settling on his chest as he realized this sorcerer had the power to make those words a reality. He hadn't felt so helpless since he was a boy.

"But yes," the sorcerer said. "I'll have tasks for you to complete in order to repay your debt. Once you've repaid me, I will release you and remove that mark. You will answer when I call, you will go where I say when I say. If you disobey me, I'll kill them all."

Dresden staggered back. Regulus' posture fell further.

"I believe in only two things in this world: vengeance and my own word. When I say I will release you, my word is my bond. And when I say if you defy me, you and yours will suffer, that is not an idle threat. Understand?"

"Yes." Regulus' voice was terse and quiet. The sorcerer tilted his head, and a glimmer of green flickered in the shadow of his hood. Regulus grunted and flinched, his right fist clenching. "Yes, my lord."

The sorcerer sighed dramatically. "We'll have to work on your respectfulness. Now, I want you to go to Mount Yarob." He pulled a rolled-up parchment from his robes and handed it to Regulus. "This will help you find a tunnel into the mountain. In the cavern at the end, you should find a magical relic—a gold rod, flared at one end. Retrieve it alone. That's important. *Only* you can enter the tunnel—"

Perceval snorted. "Like hell we're letting our captain face danger alone—"

Regulus cried out and fell to one knee. Dresden clenched his hands so tightly they ached. Caleb stepped in front of Perceval and shoved against his chest, holding Perce back from attacking.

"Alone, I swear it," Regulus panted.

"Hmm." The sorcerer pointed at the parchment in Regulus' fist. "If you succeed, follow the map to my tower here in the Tumen Forest."

"And if I fail? My lord?"

The sorcerer's beard twitched. "You won't come out of the mountain."

Dresden's lungs seized.

"However…" The sorcerer reached out and hooked a knobby finger under Regulus' chin, forcing him to look up. "I think I've finally found someone who won't fail." He rose into the air on a cloud of green light and flew away through the trees.

For a moment, no one moved or spoke. Dresden gaped at Regulus, at a loss for what to do or say. There was nothing he could do. His neck still stung, reminding him just how useless he was.

Regulus clutched his head, his breaths short and shallow. Just as Dresden moved to step toward him, Regulus threw his head back and screamed, a low, guttural sound that built while his red face contorted with rage and heartbreak. He dropped onto both knees and bent forward, his hands covering his face.

Dresden's heart twisted. He couldn't get Regulus out of this nightmare, but he could ensure Regulus wasn't alone. As he wove around the bodies of his fallen comrades toward Regulus, he tried to ignore their lifeless faces. But every face, every name, every accompanying memory of laughter and having each other's backs sent a bitter pang through his chest. Ten friends, gone. *But Regulus is still here.* He knelt next to Regulus and laid a hand on his shoulder.

"They're dead." Regulus' voice shook, full of anguish. "Dresden, they're all…they're…" He trembled under Dresden's hand, and Dresden had to fight his own tears. "I failed them. And you…I almost…" Regulus looked toward the rest of the men standing nearby.

Dresden followed his gaze. Little Harold, pale and looking far younger than his fourteen years, stared at the bodies. Dresden wondered if the boy was remembering seeing his parents die, and he wished he knew how to comfort him. Estevan's dirt-streaked face pinched as his mouth hung ajar. Perceval scowled, his fingers white around the hilt of his sheathed sword. Tears glinted in Caleb's eyes. Jerrick, ever in control, maintained a stoic expression as he held a gash in his side.

"I couldn't…I couldn't lose any more," Regulus whispered. "I couldn't watch… I'm sorry I didn't save them. I'm sorry. I'm sorry."

"It was a trap," Jerrick said quietly. "A trap, Captain, you—"

Regulus shook his head. "No, I don't deserve… I'm no captain. Look!" He thrust his hand out at the bodies. "I failed! If he'd wanted, he could have finished it, I couldn't…" He screamed again through clenched teeth.

Dresden flexed his fingers as he struggled to find the right words to soothe his friend, even as his own heart shattered.

"It was a sorcerer." He kept his tone gentle. "We had no idea what to expect. We've never faced a sorcerer. And you still saved us; you did everything you could. It's not your fault, Regulus."

"Samuelson wouldn't have done any better." Perceval released his sword and crossed his arms. "And you wouldn't have blamed him. We'll figure out how to help you."

"You…" Estevan stared at Regulus like he was a specter. Most of Estevan's right sleeve was gone, his arm singed by the sorcerer's flames. "You bound yourself to a sorcerer…to save us?" He blinked and shook his head.

Dresden rubbed the back of his neck. He knew that feeling of inadequacy mixed with gratitude; the confusing mixture of emotions that came from someone suffering to protect you. Regulus had sacrificed himself for Dresden too many times, and he still didn't know how to process it. He just knew he would do the same for Regulus in a heartbeat.

Jerrick gulped, his blank expression cracking. "You could have let us—"

"No." Regulus locked eyes with Jerrick. "I would have sworn anything. Anything. I'm your captain. Your friend." He lowered his head and ran his thumb over the mark on his arm, silent for a long moment. He wrapped his hand around his forearm, covering the mark. "But you all are right. I'm still your captain. A captain doesn't abandon his men." He straightened and released his arm. "I won't just give in."

Regulus pulled his knife and before Dresden could stop him, sliced under the mark. Dresden gasped. Regulus screamed through clenched teeth and shoved the knife at Dresden as blood pooled on his arm. "The fire."

For a moment, Dresden didn't understand. But a nearby bush ignited during the fight still smoldered. Dresden ran for the smoking bush and plunged the blade into the dying flames as his heart raced. They needed to cauterize the wound quickly—

Regulus hissed through his teeth. "This doesn't feel right." Another sharp intake of breath. Dresden ran back, ready with the glowing knife. Regulus frowned at his arm as he rubbed his palm over the smeared blood.

Dresden stopped short. Regulus' arm was whole. Uninjured. And the mark was back in the same spot.

"What? No, no!" Regulus snatched the blade away from Dresden and pressed it over the mark. The stench of burning flesh filled the air as Regulus stifled a scream. Dresden pressed his hand over his mouth and swallowed back bile. Regulus threw aside the knife.

The flesh was red and blistered, the skin mostly gone, and with it, the mark. But as Dresden watched, Regulus' skin healed. Some scarring showed, but Regulus' arm was uninjured again—and the mark was back in crisp black lines.

"No…" Regulus slumped. After several moments, Regulus spoke without looking up, his voice resigned. "You're all dismissed and free to take whatever you can from the supplies. I'm…a slave. Not a captain."

"You're our captain," Perceval growled. "We're not turning our backs on you after you saved us. Are we?" He glared at the others.

Regulus lifted his head. "No, you—"

"You idiot." Dresden crouched and gripped Regulus' shoulder. "The rest of the men can do what they like, but I'm with you. I'm not abandoning you, now or ever."

"There's sorcery in me."

"So? You're still the same man, aren't you? Still my friend." Dresden shook his head. "Still the kind of fool who just swore his life away to a sorcerer, and the first thing he does is come make sure I'm okay."

"You took my life-debt," Jerrick said. "Saved my life. I owe you my life." He held his right fist over his heart and bowed, despite clear pain from the cut on his ribs. "By Hallilek, I will serve you, Captain."

Caleb nodded slowly, his solemn expression beneath his mess of blond hair so unlike his usual jocular attitude. "You know I'm hardly religious, Captain, but I'm not risking Etiros' wrath by turning my back on the man who saved my life at the cost of his own."

Perceval frowned. He took a deep breath, grinding his teeth. "I'll say this once and once only, so mark it—I agree with Caleb."

"I'll certainly mark it." Caleb tapped his head with a small smile.

On any other occasion, Perceval agreeing with Caleb would have sparked laughter and incessant teasing until Perceval threatened bodily injury to Caleb, at which point Caleb would have patted Perceval's head and run away laughing. The men's only reaction was a few tight smiles, but Dresden's heart lightened.

"I…" Estevan glanced at Dresden. "I don't know if you were really thinking about all of us, Captain, but…" He scratched his freckle-covered nose, his light brown skin taking on a hint of red. "You've always been kinder than I deserve. The only one who would take me in. I'm staying."

Harold dragged his gaze away from one of the fallen mercenaries. His jaw trembled. "Please don't send me away. Please, Captain."

Regulus gaped at his men. Finally, he nodded. "Okay. Okay. Thank you." With a deep sigh, he stood. "We should…" The muscles in this throat strained. "We should check on the boy and his parents. And see if they have…shovels."

The forester and his wife and son met them before they even reached the door of the hut, and immediately started thanking Regulus for helping them, for answering their son's plea for help, over and over again. The family clung to each other, laughter and tears mingled between kisses and tight embraces. Regulus' haggard expression softened as he watched them, relief in his gray eyes. His sacrifice had saved that family, and Dresden knew that would comfort him.

But Dresden's gut twisted, old feelings he had long buried about his own family threatening to resurface. Memories that hurt too much to recall, so he pretended they didn't exist. Right now, he had other concerns. He cleared his throat to catch Regulus' attention and nodded toward the corpses.

The forester agreed to let them bury the men in the woods nearby and scrambled to give them a few shovels and hoes. With a final expression of gratitude, the family left them to bury their fallen brothers in peace. Estevan and Jerrick tended each other's wounds and watched the rest of them dig. Ten graves for ten friends. Lost for no good reason. They worked quietly, their grief too keen for words and too deep for weeping. Regulus worked like the labor revitalized him more than it drained him, digging at a pace none of them could match. Until they got to Ivan.

Ivan, Regulus' second lieutenant, who had been with them for nearly ten years. Regulus sobbed and turned away as they threw the first shovelful of dirt over Ivan's corpse. Regulus' muffled crying shattered the ice behind which Dresden had buried his own mourning. Tears raced down his cheeks. Caleb sniffed. Harold sat nearby, his arms wrapped around his legs, rocking back and forth and staring straight ahead. Regulus took several deep breaths and wiped his face. He didn't make a sound as they buried the remaining men, but his eyes were watery, and he kept a white-knuckled grip on the forester's shovel.

Once they finished the last grave, they all looked to Regulus. When they lost one of their own, the captain usually said a few words of remembrance or a traditional blessing. Regulus shook his head and turned away. Dresden bit his lip, fighting between trying to coax Regulus into saying something and realizing the responsibility probably fell on him as first lieutenant. Someone cleared their throat.

Perceval stepped forward. "To our fallen brothers, we wish you peace."

Although Perceval taking responsibility relieved Dresden, it also surprised him, as did the choice of a traditional Monparthian blessing for fallen knights. The fallen hailed from Vanelt to Geirah and had beliefs as far ranging.

"You fought gallantly in life," Perceval continued. "May you find rest in your valiant death." Regulus shuddered.

"Your name and memory will be remembered in the hearts of your brothers who fight on. We, your brothers-in-arms, thank you for your sacrifice. May you be welcomed to your eternal home in the light." Perceval left off the Monparthian "of Etiros," and bowed his head, as did the others. Dresden bowed his head and closed his eyes.

After a moment of silence, Perceval spoke. "We bid—"

"We bid our brothers farewell with the hope we may yet meet again," Regulus finished in a soft voice.

Dresden opened his eyes. Regulus had turned around, and he tapped his right fist over his heart, crossed his right arm over his stomach, and bowed to the graves. Dresden and the others repeated the action.

After they returned the shovels to the forester, everyone collapsed in a nearby clearing, dirt-streaked and exhausted. Except Regulus. He hardly looked exerted. Dresden's brows knit. The way Regulus had moved dirt twice as quickly as the rest of them, he should have been worn out. And yet…Regulus' posture reflected none of the exhaustion Dresden felt. He had supposed Regulus was working out his anger and sorrow through the labor. But something seemed off. Judging by how Regulus stood staring at his hands as he slowly opened and closed them, Regulus thought so, too.

Regulus turned and walked over to a large boulder. He considered it for a moment, picked it up, and threw it. Dresden's jaw dropped as the boulder crashed through the bushes. Regulus rolled his shoulders and slowly turned around. He'd gone pale.

"You threw a boulder." Estevan blinked. "That's amazing."

"Amazing? It's unnatural!" Regulus looked back at the flattened brush from the boulder's trail. "I'm…a monster."

"And I'm a fish because I can swim." Perceval crossed his arms. "You are the same person you've always been. No sorcerer can change that."

"Maybe. We'll see. But I have to go." His left hand drifted to the mark. "It's…burning. Like it knows I haven't left yet."

"Wait." Dresden stood. "We'll accompany you to the mountain. You can go in by yourself," he said before Regulus could protest. "But we're going with you as far as we can."

Because I'm afraid you won't come back.

Arrano

Four weeks later

Location: Arrano Estate, Etchy Barony, Thaera Duchy, Monparth

DRESDEN SAT taller in his saddle as they rode up the hill to Arrano castle.

After Regulus had retrieved the relic for the sorcerer—and in the process, discovered that he couldn't be killed—they had camped out a short distance from Tumen Forest. A messenger had found them there and delivered a shocking letter from Baron Carrick, lord of Etchy barony.

Regulus had inherited his father's estate and title.

Dresden and the rest of the men followed Regulus through the gate into the main courtyard of Arrano. He looked around with curiosity, taking in the towering, square stone keep surrounded by trees, gardens, and small wood buildings, all protected by the thick outer wall. *So…this is where Regulus was born.*

And where I will be a knight. Not a servant. Not ever again.

When Dresden and the other mercenaries had refused to leave Regulus, he had knighted them all. Except Harold, who Regulus had made his squire, to the boy's delight.

Servants and knights around the edges of the courtyard watched them dismount. Some shrunk back, their fear obvious. Others scowled and watched them through narrowed eyes. Dresden tried for a smile, but that just seemed to put the small crowd more on edge.

Regulus' persistent frown wasn't helping. Baron Carrick had warned Regulus that Lady Arrano might challenge his claim, and if the grim look on his face was any indication, Regulus wasn't looking forward to seeing her.

The doors of the castle opened, and a woman with a stern face under a crown of silver-streaked blonde hair strode out, her rich blue gown swishing around her legs. A red-haired young woman dressed in black and a knight in full plate armor trailed after her.

Regulus stepped forward and bowed. "Lady Ar—"

"I challenge your claim to the title and lands of Arrano." The older woman turned up her nose as she spoke in clipped, agitated tones. "Sir Gerwalt shall be my champion. The fight shall be to the death." She made eye contact with Regulus. "I shall not be satisfied until Regulus Hargreaves' blood waters my land."

Dresden had to bite his tongue to keep it in check. Based on the muttered obscenity and his red face, Perceval was having a harder time controlling himself. Jerrick put a hand on Perceval's shoulder and whispered something. Perceval nodded.

Regulus merely inclined his head. "I agree to the terms."

Dresden jogged over to Regulus' side before the match began. "Be careful."

"I will."

Sir Gerwalt was a skilled swordsman, and perhaps he might have lasted longer had he fought Regulus a month prior. But now, aided by the sorcerous mark on his arm, Regulus moved with unnatural speed. If the spectators discovered Regulus' secret, he'd be hanged or beheaded for the crime of consorting with a sorcerer, even though it wasn't his fault. His knights' lives would likely be forfeit, too. Dresden's hands ached from clenching them. *Just…slow down, Reg.*

Regulus slammed his sword into the helm of Lady Arrano's champion. The man collapsed to his knees. The ladies gasped as Regulus drove his sword through the man's throat. Regulus withdrew his sword, and his opponent's body fell sideways. Dresden wiped his clammy hands on his trousers and hoped no one noticed that Regulus didn't look exerted.

Regulus turned toward his stepmother and sister-in-law, bloody sword still in hand. Dresden leaned forward, curious how Lady Arrano would react. The law only allowed one champion. She would have to accept Regulus' claim, but her wild expression as she gaped at Gerwalt's body did not promise a graceful admission of defeat. Dresden glanced at the knights around them. Most of them were unarmed. Hopefully, there would be no further bloodshed.

"My ladies," Regulus said. "Your champion is defeated. But I do not wish to drive you—"

"You filthy, disgraceful *bastard!*" Lady Arrano grabbed the redhead's hand. "Fine! Keep your philandering disgrace of a father's old castle! Hazel, we'll accept your family's offer and join them in Craigailte." She turned and dragged Hazel back toward the castle.

Regulus' throat bobbed. "That's not necessary—"

Lady Arrano whirled, her face red. "You think I would live under the same roof as *you?* I should have smothered you in your cradle!"

Dresden clenched his teeth until they ached. Across from him, Jerrick and Caleb restrained Estevan and Perceval.

Regulus took a step back. The point of his sword drifted to the ground. "I... I—I will see you have enough coin—"

"I don't want charity from you!" Lady Arrano shook with fury. "And you won't trick me! We will take our own small funds and jewels, and not touch what your *father*," she spat the word, "legally left to you. Even though you shouldn't get any of it!" She released Hazel's hand and stepped toward Regulus. "Where is it! Where is the signet ring?"

"Why?" Regulus asked. "It's mine."

Lady Arrano stepped back as if slapped. "So you do have it. You've had it all these years. When did he give it to you? With that stupid sword?"

"No." Regulus' tone bit like sharpened steel. "When I left at six."

Lady Arrano's face turned a deeper shade of crimson. "If your father was still alive, I'd kill him." She stormed back inside the castle, Hazel stumbling after her.

Regulus' shoulders rose and fell with a deep breath. He turned around, a deep weariness in his eyes that had nothing to do with physical exhaustion. "I've brought my own knights. Any of the previous Lord of Arrano's vassal knights, come by this evening and see me about getting severance pay, recompense for your land, and a letter of release. You have a week to vacate Arrano."

Perceval offered Regulus a handkerchief, and Regulus cleaned off his sword.

The knights whispered as they dispersed, looking displeased. Dresden scowled. *They should be grateful.* Regulus easily could have thrown them out with nothing. But Regulus was better than that.

Regulus, his sword now sheathed, stared at the great front doors of the castle. He didn't move to enter. Dresden went to his side.

"Reg?"

Regulus opened and closed his mouth. "I can't. I can't go in," he whispered.

Jerrick stepped up on Regulus' other side. "It is your right—"

"You don't understand." Regulus shook his head. "I've never been inside when she was here. My mother and I lived in the servants' building behind the keep. I went inside a handful of times. Only when invited by Lord—by my father. Only when she was out."

Dresden placed a hand on Regulus' shoulder. He didn't know what to say.

"The last time I was here... I..." Regulus' jaw pulsed. "I was six. I thought maybe I was going to meet my infant half-brother. Instead, my father pressed the signet ring into my hand, told me to keep it safe but secret. He told me to be strong, to be the best I could be, to be *excellent*, because I was his son. Then he told me to pack my things and bid my mother farewell, because I was leaving within the hour to live with a cousin."

Dresden's mouth pressed into a line. He gently squeezed Regulus' shoulder. Regulus stood rigid, staring at the castle door.

"My mother tried to stop the knight who came for me," Regulus continued, his voice quiet and strained. "She locked the door to our room and held onto me, even though she was exhausted from whatever had infected her lungs. My father convinced her to open the door. He held her while one of his knights dragged me away. My mother cried and cursed my father while he kissed her hair and told her it would be better for me and her. She died three months later. I hate that that moment is one of my only clear memories of her."

Perceval spat. "You're just getting what always should have been yours. And she's not even getting half of what she deserves." He added some colorful insults that made even Dresden raise his eyebrows. "We're with you, Captain. This is your moment of triumph."

Regulus didn't respond.

"Regulus." Dresden searched for words. "You did what your father asked. You are strong and brave and good. But even without all that, he left you that ring and wrote you into the will. You're meant to walk through that door with your head held high."

The silence stretched on. Regulus mussed his hair. "When I arrived at Kimberly's castle, he told me I had no father. I made the mistake of referring to my father once. Kimberly made me spend the night in the pig pen. It was snowing."

Estevan cursed under his breath. Dresden's mouth fell open. When Regulus was *six*? No wonder Regulus had already been afraid of Kimberly by the time Dresden arrived five years later.

"He would say I'm a fraud to stand here and claim the Arrano title as my own."

"He'd be wrong!" Indignation coursed through Dresden. He turned Regulus toward him. "This is your castle. Your title. And you deserve it, probably more than any noble has ever deserved anything. Kimberly was cruel and selfish, and you *know* you shouldn't believe a word he ever said. He would have had you see me as a slave. You didn't listen to Kimberly about me. Don't you dare listen to him about you."

Regulus smiled weakly. "Thank you." But he didn't move toward the castle.

"Take your time." Jerrick nodded. "When you're ready, we're behind you. Your castle, your knights."

The rest of the men added their assent.

"Lord Hargreaves?" A kind, feminine voice intruded from the side. An older woman took a tentative step closer. Her rough-spun brown dress hugged her ample figure. A hint of gray wove through her brown hair, pulled back in a messy bun. She gave a small curtsy. "My name is Alaina."

Dresden stepped out of the way as Regulus turned toward the servant.

"Forgive me for the interruption, your lordship. You probably don't remember me, though I remember you." She smiled, but there was sadness in her eyes. "You've grown so tall. And are the image of your father."

"You…" Regulus' throat bobbed. "You knew me?" She nodded. "So…you knew my mother?"

"I did. We grew up together. She loved you so much. Loved your father, too, despite everything." Alaina blushed, as if fearing speaking out of turn about Regulus' father. "Would you like to visit her grave?"

"Her grave?" Regulus tapped his hand against his leg. "I…yes."

Alaina turned, and Regulus started after her. Dresden forced himself to stay behind. He wouldn't intrude on Regulus visiting his mother—

"Drez?" Regulus paused and looked back at him, and a warm feeling rose in Dresden's chest. "Would you…follow? Watch my back? I don't want to let my guard down while Lady Arrano is still here."

Dresden's initial sentimental surge that Regulus wanted him along to support him as he grieved gave way to disappointment. Regulus only wanted a bodyguard. He chided himself for being ridiculous. Regulus had asked only him, no one else, because he trusted Dresden enough to let him in on this private moment. He trailed behind Regulus, giving him a respectful amount of space.

Alaina led them around the castle, past a long wood building behind the keep that Regulus glanced at with sorrow. They walked through a grove of apple trees heavy with small, green apples. Some wildflowers grew among the roots of the trees, adding pops of yellow, blue, and pink among the green grass and filling the air with a subtly sweet scent. The soft buzz of honeybees added to the peaceful atmosphere. But the pastoral scene had no effect on Regulus, who walked with his shoulders scrunched and head down, every step tense.

They emerged from the orchard into a grassy area running up to the outer wall surrounding the castle. Ahead of them, a thick hedge taller than Regulus grew in a half circle, ending on both sides at the outer wall. A wood gate stood in the center of the hedge, its rusty latch padlocked shut. A carved inscription decorated the frame. Dresden drifted a touch closer than respectful so he could make it out.

"May Etiros' righteous wrath descend with fury on any who desecrate or harm this place of eternal rest and peace."

"Your father used to visit her," Alaina murmured. Her hand slipped into her dress pocket. "I don't know what happened to his key. But he gave me a key before he died. In case you ever returned." She held out a simple iron key.

Slowly, Regulus took the key with what sounded like a mumbled thank you. Alaina curtsied and left back through the orchard. Regulus turned the key over a few times in his hand, then squared his shoulders and unlocked the gate.

The gate's hinges squeaked and groaned as Regulus pushed it open. Dresden couldn't see around Regulus standing in the opening. Regulus dragged one foot forward, then the other. His entire body shook. Dresden forced himself to stay back, to give Regulus his privacy. He should turn around, watch for any threats...

Regulus fell to his knees and leaned against the square base of a white marble statue of a female angel. The woman's right hand stretched down, as if she were reaching for Regulus' head, but her smiling face looked up toward the top of the hedge. Her other hand was clasped over her heart. A simple dress tangled around the statue's legs as she seemed frozen mid-step. Her wings stretched up behind her, and her hair fell in carved ringlets over her shoulders.

A strangled whimper came from Regulus. His shoulders heaved. Dresden turned around but still heard Regulus weeping. Tears pressed at the corners of Dresden's eyes, and he wiped them away, unsure why he was even crying. Because Regulus was in pain? Or because it made him wonder where his own parents were?

Thoughts he usually kept locked away, hidden behind jokes, shoved aside by a night on the town, forgotten behind another girl's pretty face and inviting lips, broke to the surface. He had chosen not to go looking for his parents when Regulus released him, but sometimes, in quiet moments, he wanted to know— did they ever wonder what had happened to him? Did they care? Were they even alive?

He stared at the orchard. So many complicated emotions, usually ignored with a smile, threatened to overwhelm him. He had acted rashly, leaving without saying goodbye. Out of anger, out of bravado, out of the rush of newfound freedom, out of concern for Regulus…out of fear. Fear of disappointing them, of a sister who likely wouldn't remember him, of a life as a farmer. He had feared if he had even visited, he would have felt too guilty to leave again, and was afraid Regulus wouldn't wait for him. If he were honest with himself, he regretted not trying.

But as the sounds of Regulus' weeping carried through the open gate, he didn't regret staying with Regulus. For all Regulus' strength, he was also still that lonely boy who so desperately needed a friend.

Maybe Dresden could try to find his parents now that he was in Monparth to stay. Now that he was a knight. But not yet. Not while Regulus was still trying to find his feet. Not while the threat of the sorcerer loomed over them. But maybe, once they'd settled in… The thought of facing his parents sent a sudden stab of fear through him, so he pushed it away. A decision for another day. For a day when his brother didn't need him.

Several minutes passed while Regulus cried, then quieted. When Dresden heard footsteps, he turned back around. Regulus' eyes were red and puffy, but his expression had lost the nervousness it had held earlier. The gate stood open behind him.

"I'm going to have the hedge torn down," Regulus said. "She shouldn't be hidden away." He walked past, heading back into the orchard.

Curiosity drew Dresden to the open gate in the hedge. If the angel was meant to be Regulus' mother, she had been beautiful. He decided it must be, because her smile reminded him of Regulus—warm, crinkling her eyes, yet somehow mournful. An inscription had been chiseled into the square base.

Here lies Marcella Eryn Hargreaves, a lover and a mother, beloved and cherished forever in our hearts, her grace taken from this world too soon. May she light the next life as she brought light to this one.

Forgive me, my love.

A curse and torment on any who desecrate this place of rest.

Dresden gawked at the inscription. No wonder Lord Arrano had put a curse on the memorial and over the gate. A fear of divine retribution was probably the only reason Lady Arrano hadn't destroyed it as soon as her husband passed. Lord Arrano, it appeared, had truly loved Marcella Hargreaves. And yet she had died *Hargreaves*, not *Arrano*. A lover, not a wife. Her child taken from her while she watched her son's father raise another woman's child. Then she was buried and hidden from view.

Yes, Dresden thought as he followed Regulus, sorrow and anger struggling within him. Lord Arrano had much to apologize for—and an epitaph was too late.

Regulus strode back to the front of the castle, and Dresden had to jog to catch up, then hurry to keep pace with his long strides. Gone was Regulus' hesitancy as he approached the front door, his head held high, his back straight. He was doing this for his mother, Dresden realized.

"Sir Jakobs," Regulus said, stopping just in front of the door. "Would you please announce me?"

Dresden smiled. There likely would be no one to hear, but Regulus needed this. He nodded and moved past Regulus to open the door. Two curving staircases led up to a low balcony with a central set of double doors at the rear of a simple, large foyer. A couple servants bustled past, but they slowed as Dresden held open the door and called, "Lord Regulus Hargreaves of Arrano."

Regulus stepped inside—just as a woman stepped through the doors on the balcony. Lady Arrano screamed, high-pitched and outraged, and flung her arm forward. Something glinted as it flew through the air. She leaned against the railing at the edge of the balcony, chest heaving and face flushed. Whatever the metallic object was, Regulus reacted a moment too late. He moved to dodge, but it still clipped the side of his head.

"There," she huffed. "He wanted you to have that, now you have it!" She spun away and pushed through the doors.

Rubbing the side of his head, Regulus turned and picked the object up. The silver medallion gleamed in the sunlight, the Arrano crest—a rose over crossed swords—embossed on the surface.

"At least it wasn't a weapon?"

Regulus winced. "Don't give her ideas."

The door Lady Arrano had left through reopened, and Dresden prepared to leap in front of Regulus in case she *had* come back with a weapon before he remembered Regulus couldn't die. Although maybe that was more reason to block him.

But it was the younger Lady Arrano, Hazel, who was very weaponless.

"Here to throw something at me, too?" Regulus snapped. "I'm not in the mood for further insults."

"What?" Hazel paled. "N-no. I…um… I'm sorry. That she is so awful to you." Her consonants were hard, a bit of her Craigan accent coming through. She wrung her hands. "I tried to convince her not to challenge you. She said letting you take Arrano without a fight was an insult to Theodore. But Lord Kenneth Arrano wanted you to inherit, and I think it's insulting to him to try to stop you. You know, Theodore told me Lord Arrano had wanted you to come back, but Lady Arrano wouldn't hear of it. Theodore wished he could have met you. He was always curious what you were like. You're taller than he was—he probably would have been jealous." She laughed nervously, but her eyes glistened with unshed tears.

"You were gracious to offer to let us stay. I just wanted you to know I'm grateful. I was afraid…" She blushed.

"Afraid?" Regulus asked.

"They said you are a mercenary, ruthless and dangerous."

Dresden suppressed a smirk. Technically, Regulus was those things. He was just also good.

"Lady Frewin told us to leave before you came. She thought you might try to kill us or force me to marry you."

Regulus' eyes widened. "Never!" He held up his hands, still clutching the medallion. "So long as you remain in Arrano, I promise, you are safe."

"And…once we leave?" Hazel's voice trembled.

"I won't be protecting you," Regulus said, his tone gentle. "It wasn't a threat. Just an acknowledgement that the trek to Craigailte is dangerous. I meant it. You're free to stay."

Hazel looked around the foyer. She was young for the heaviness in her eyes. "There's nothing left for me here." She sighed. "You seem kind. I'm sorry…just sorry." She went back through the door.

Regulus looked around, his expression clouding and posture starting to sag. Dresden cleared his throat.

"What were the other memories?"

"What?" Regulus furrowed his brow.

"You said the last time you saw your mother was one of your only clear memories of her. What were the others?" He offered an encouraging smile. "Surely you have a happy memory here."

A smile trembled on Regulus' lips. "I do have one other clear memory of my mother. Of her and my father, laughing and flirting and kissing in the garden while I played. A rare moment where we felt like a family." His ghost of a smile faded. "But of course, then he left us to go back to his castle, to his pregnant wife. My mother deserved better." He glanced toward the door the ladies had gone through. "So did Lady Arrano, honestly."

Dresden snorted. "I don't care how awful your husband is, you don't get a pass for attempted murder, especially of an innocent boy."

A dry, crooked smile tugged at Regulus' scar. "Well, when you put it like that, I feel a lot less guilty about driving her out of her home."

"Your home," Perceval noted, strolling through the open front door. He looked around and gave a satisfied nod. "Not bad, Captain." He turned and gave Regulus a quick bow. "With your permission, Captain, I'd like to go get my wife."

An honest laugh erupted from Regulus. "Can you give it a week? I'd like to have you around in case there is any trouble."

Perceval nodded. "Probably for the best. I can send a messenger ahead of me. Leonora will be furious if I show up and she hasn't had time to pack her things." He wandered inside, followed by Estevan and Caleb, who raced each other up the stairs, saying something about finding the best rooms.

"Don't go opening any closed doors!" Regulus hollered after them. "And leave any women you come across alone!"

"No promises on the second, Captain!" Estevan said with a grin.

"Yes, promises, and I told you to call me Regulus! Repeatedly!" But Estevan had already disappeared through the large double doors.

Caleb winked. "You know us, only if the lady is interested." He followed Estevan.

Regulus shook his head and groaned. Dresden pulled in his lips to avoid laughing. Regulus should have known better than to expect decorum from those two.

Jerrick wandered in, taking in everything, a contemplative expression on his face.

"Something the matter, Jerrick?" Regulus fiddled with the medallion but kept his gaze on Jerrick.

"Oh, no, Cap—Regulus." He grinned sheepishly. "Just…first time I've had a real home since I was a child. First castle I've been in while having a title in front of my name." He shrugged. "A little stupid to get sentimental over, I suppose—"

"No," Dresden cut in. "Not stupid." He looked up at the vaulted ceiling, his own emotions stirring. "First time in a castle not as a servant or a mercenary is kind of a strange feeling."

"You feel strange?" Regulus chuckled. "You don't own the place." His brows pinched, and he turned slightly green. "I own a castle. Etiros above, I'm a lord. I have to…do lordly things and run a castle and…" The fingers of his left hand brushed against the inside of his right sleeve.

Jerrick clapped Regulus' shoulder. "Don't worry. You'll be as good a lord as a captain. And you've got us to help, don't forget. We all have your back."

Regulus still looked like he might be sick.

"He's right, you know," Dresden said. "You can do this. And what you can't, we'll help with. That's what we do."

Maybe someday, he'd look for his parents. But for now—he had a family right here.

DRESDEN DISMOUNTED in the cobblestone courtyard of the Russelthorn spired castle. A lanky servant boy ran up and bowed to him and Regulus before taking the reins of their horses. Regulus patted his big black horse, Sieger, as the boy led the beasts away. Early evening sunlight cast an orange-tinted glow over the nobles making their way through the towering open doors of the castle.

"Ready?" Dresden whispered.

Regulus gave a curt nod and set out, moving with the flow of guests. Other nobles glanced at them, some looking back to stare for a moment. Dresden trailed Regulus through oak double doors carved with a forest scene. Flowers in massive vases decorated the foyer that led to the great hall where the stream of guests bottlenecked. A servant dressed in neat livery of forest green and satiny black lifted a brow when they reached the entrance.

"Pardon, my lord, your name?"

"Cap—" Regulus cleared his throat, and Dresden felt a twinge of second-hand embarrassment. "Lord Regulus Hargreaves of Arrano. And Sir Dresden Jakobs."

The servant's jaw slackened, but he quickly recovered his calm, professional expression. "Lord Regulus Hargreaves of Arrano and Sir Dresden Jakobs," he announced.

The giddy rush of hearing himself announced as a knight faded as people across the hall turned to look. Noblewomen craned their necks to watch them enter. Servants sent furtive glances their way between rushing around to fill goblets and place food on the long tables spaced throughout the massive room. Noblemen pulled their wives closer or pushed daughters behind them. *Spoilsports.*

What in Monparth had these people heard? They'd only been at Arrano for two weeks; the rumor vine in Etchy Barony must be efficient.

A man with flowing waves of blond hair and a sharp grin beneath an impressively thick, short blond beard strode toward them, guests moving out of his way. His forest green doublet sported silver buttons, and his polished black boots shone in the candlelight illuminating the hall.

He stopped before Regulus, bent slightly at the waist, then extended his hand. "Lord Kesper Russelthorn. A pleasure to make your acquaintance, Lord Hargreaves."

Regulus returned the partial bow and clasped Russelthorn's forearm. "The pleasure is all mine, Lord Russelthorn. Thank you for your hospitality in hosting this banquet."

"It is my honor," Russelthorn said as he released Regulus' forearm.

Some of the tension building along Dresden's shoulders dissipated.

"How are you finding Arrano?"

Regulus lifted a shoulder. "It's well."

"Adjusting well, then, to your new position?"

Dresden suppressed a frown. It was a fair question. Russelthorn didn't necessarily mean anything negative or condescending by it.

"Yes."

Ah, so they were at one-syllable answers. Regulus was already uncomfortable, and they hadn't even sat down to supper.

"Pleased to hear it." Russelthorn smiled, but there was something stiff about the look. "If you'll excuse me, I must greet my other guests, but I do hope to speak with you more before the night is out, Lord Hargreaves." He inclined his head and walked away. Regulus visibly relaxed.

They made their way to a table near the back corner, near the entrance to the hall and far from the dais, but they didn't sit down—that would have been rude. They both gratefully accepted when a servant offered to fill their goblets with wine.

A reedy man with silver-streaked hair bobbed over to them. "Lord Hargreaves." He gave a sharp, stiff bow. "Sir Orthwell. I hope you don't think me impertinent, my lord, but I must confess, we are all quite curious—is it true you were a mercenary?"

The nobles and servants nearby did nothing to hide their eavesdropping, many inching closer.

Regulus gave a curt nod. "That is correct."

"A captain, the rumors say."

"Correct."

Dresden looked around, hoping supper would begin soon and they could sit down—and hopefully everyone could fill their mouths with food instead of questions.

"And your knights…" Orthwell cast a glance toward Dresden, distaste poorly concealed. "They were mercenaries under your command?"

"Correct." Regulus crossed his arms. "Although two of them were previously knights of Monparth."

Orthwell's eyebrows shoved the skin of his forehead up into deep wrinkles. "Indeed? And…erm…have you heard…from the ladies Arrano? Since they left?"

"No." Regulus stood stiff as a tree. "I pray they arrived safely in Craigailte, but they have sent no word. I don't expect they will."

"I see." Another odd bob of Orthwell's head. "Well. A pleasure to meet you, Lord Hargreaves." A bow like the snap of a green branch, and the man walked away and promptly fell into hushed discussion with a small cluster of nobles.

"This was a mistake," Regulus whispered.

Dresden offered an encouraging smile and whispered back. "They'll get used to you. And try smiling; you look ready to fight the whole hall."

"It'd be easier than standing here," Regulus muttered.

Mercifully, Lord Russelthorn called for them all to be seated, and dinner began. But now they were seated in close quarters with other nobles, and food did not stop their tongues.

Not that anyone spoke to either of them. If anything, their neighbors made a point of talking to others so they wouldn't have to talk to the mercenaries. But some whispered words at their table—and not whispered from other tables—occasionally cut through the low drone of conversation and clatter of utensils. Words accompanied by glances their way, or otherwise clearly about them.

Mercenary. Murderer. Bastard. Foreigner. Disgraceful. Commoners. Shocking. Killer. Several insulting words about Regulus' parents that Dresden sincerely hoped Regulus didn't hear. *Demon-possessed* was a concerning one, though.

After dinner, they remained seated while the guests at their table got up and mingled. Regulus spun the signet ring on his little finger. "How soon is too soon to leave, do you think? Or maybe it doesn't matter, since I'm judged regardless of what I do."

Dresden pursed his lips. "Well…maybe we should try to talk to some people. Let them get to know you." He nudged him. "Maybe find a pretty girl to talk to?"

A condescending feminine laugh sounded behind him, and Dresden twisted around on the bench. A young woman, her auburn curls framing a pale face with a haughty expression, raised one thin brow. She held a goblet aloft in one hand, her other wrapped over her slender waist.

"Forget about pretty girls. It seems a beautiful woman has found us." Dresden gave her his best charming rogue smile as he stood and bowed.

"Amusingly confident." She sipped from her goblet and looked over to Regulus, who had also stood. "*Lord* Hargreaves of Arrano."

"My lady." Regulus bowed. The young lady's gaze roved up and down him, a touch of appreciation in her eyes, even though her nose wrinkled when she lingered on his scar. She held out her empty hand, her curved fingers inviting a kiss. Regulus stiffly placed his fingers under hers and brushed his lips to her knuckles.

"Lady Geneva Hatan."

Regulus jerked away his fingers as he straightened. "Lady…Hatan." The name did sound familiar, but Dresden couldn't place it.

"It has been an awfully long time, hasn't it? Not that you ever paid me much mind back then, being eight years older than I." She swirled her goblet. "I'll have such delicious gossip to bring back to Lanure. Lord Kimberly will be scandalized."

Dresden's stomach knotted, and Regulus stiffened.

Hatan, Hatan… Friends of the Kimberlys, Dresden finally recalled. Margaret Hatan was Lady Brigid's closest friend. The one who had tried to get them to remove their shirts when they were swimming. This must be a sister. Dresden hadn't counted on coming across anyone who knew him when he was a servant, and his skin went cold. He did some quick math. She would have been ten when they left…maybe she wouldn't remember him.

She looked to Dresden, and that hope faded. But all she said was, "Sir Jakobs, was it?" He nodded. "They say you were one of Lord Hargreaves' mercenaries. Is that true?"

Awfully forward. But at least she didn't remember him. He'd rather not have everyone in Etchy Barony know he had been a servant. "Yes, that's true. A respected mercenary, due to being a talented swordsman." A lopsided smile, and he let his voice drop to a low, husky register. "I'm also a talented kisser."

He added a wink.

Red suffused Geneva's cheeks. With an outraged gasp, she flung the contents of her goblet onto his face. "Impertinent upstart pig!"

Dresden blinked burning wine out of his watering eyes. Conversations around them fell silent.

She tossed the empty goblet at Regulus, who caught the vessel with ease. "Control your knight, *Lord* Hargreaves." She strode away while Dresden wiped wine off his face with his sleeve.

"I think it's time to go," Regulus muttered. He set the goblet on the table with a heavy thud.

They left, walking past nobles who snickered or frowned and servants who whispered and glanced at them out of the corners of their eyes. But the darkest scowl belonged to Regulus.

As they rode away in the dusk, Dresden slouched in the saddle, stewing over how poorly the evening had gone. After several minutes of nothing but the sound of their horses' hooves on the packed dirt and the chirp of insects and trill of nocturnal birds, Regulus broke the silence.

"I wish I could tell Kimberly myself. Would be something to see the look on his face when he learns that in spite of everything he ever said, I am lord of Arrano." He shrugged. "Or he'd just mock me. Kimberly at least had the spine to call me a worthless bastard to my face."

Dresden grimaced. He was about to say it didn't take much spine for a lord to insult a child, but Regulus spoke again.

"Been a while since you've had a drink thrown in your face." He chuckled. "If it hadn't been so awkward, I would have been laughing. Maybe you've lost your touch."

Dresden opened his mouth to protest, then shook his head. "I'm sorry. That was stupid of me and reflected poorly on you."

"I'm pretty sure *I* reflected poorly on me." Regulus' shoulders dipped. "And I rather expect Lady Hatan was looking for an excuse. But still, maybe don't use lines you would use on tavern girls on noble ladies."

"Noted," he grumbled. "A shame I won't get the chance to practice at more parties."

"Why not?" Regulus rubbed his horse's neck. "You aren't going to make me go alone because of one failure, are you?"

Dresden blinked. "You...plan on going to more?"

"If I'm invited," Regulus said. "I ran away at eighteen because I didn't think they'd ever accept me. It seems I was right—but I'm not going to let them win. I'm not going to run away now. I think my parents wouldn't want me to surrender. Besides, with all the rumors, if I stop going, I'll look guilty." He shifted in the saddle. "I need to look like I'm not hiding."

"So…does that mean you will reciprocate invitations…?" Dresden guided his horse around a sapling sprouting out of the road.

"Ha, no." Regulus' voice held no mirth. "So someone could sneak around and find that accursed armor or mirror? So they can come into my home and insult me under my own roof? Never happening."

"Well then." Dresden glanced at Regulus in the growing dark. "You should probably work on your smile, frowny-face." He laughed when Regulus scowled. "Good, now do the exact opposite of that."

"You're lucky I can't reach you, or I'd push you out of that saddle."

"So rude," Dresden exclaimed. "Also false, as I know you wouldn't."

"Fine, but you're still impertinent."

"And you're a grump."

"Braggart."

"Troll."

"Shorty."

"Baby face."

"Hey now, I think the scar makes up for the lack of facial hair." Regulus rubbed the lower half of his face, and Dresden laughed.

They might have had an inauspicious introduction to noble society, but Dresden wasn't worried. So long as they had each other, they'd be fine.

ATTACK
Three months later
Location: Arrano, Thaera Duchy, Monparth

"See?" Dresden pushed on Harold. "Harder to knock you off balance with proper footing."

Harold nodded enthusiastically. "So then—"

The stairwell door in the corner banged open, echoing in the main hall. The falling sleet had driven them inside to train. Regulus stepped into the hall, glaring at them, his mouth twisted into a snarl.

"Ah. Finally. *People.*"

"Reg?" Dresden straightened. "What's wrong?"

"Reg is awfully familiar," Regulus said, his voice low and mocking as he stalked closer. "We must be close."

Dresden's face heated. "Excuse me?"

"Friends?"

What? Dresden frowned at the fury in Regulus' eyes. "You're like my brother. You know that. Did I—"

Regulus' hand shot up and wrapped around Dresden's neck. "Like a brother. Oh, perfect." He lifted Dresden until his feet dangled above the ground. Terror replaced Dresden's outrage as he tried to kick at Regulus.

"Reg...stop..." He clutched Regulus' wrist, fighting to breathe. Regulus squeezed harder. Shadows stole into Dresden's sight as his kicks weakened into twitches of his feet. No...air...

"No! Stop!" Harold slammed into Regulus, low and driving his shoulder into Regulus' diaphragm, just as Dresden had taught him. Regulus' hold weakened as he stumbled back, and Dresden pried off Regulus' fingers and fell to a heap on the ground, coughing and gasping in air that burned down his throat. His trembling hands went in and out of focus as he fought to recover. His neck ached. What had come over Regulus? This wasn't right. His friend would never—

"And the boy." Regulus grabbed a fistful of Harold's hair. "Cut out his heart? No, no. Bash in his head." He threw Harold aside. "But first, the bearded one."

The bearded one? Doesn't he know me? Dresden rubbed his throat and scrambled to his feet while Harold shakily pushed himself off the stone floor. Regulus turned toward Dresden, cruelty all over his face. He hardly looked like himself.

"Regulus, what are you doing?"

"Actually… Perhaps better to save the *brother* for next time." Regulus turned back toward Harold. "Good motivation."

"Harold, run!" Dresden didn't understand what was happening, but that wasn't his best friend. That was a monster, as if the cruelty of the sorcerer had wormed inside… *The sorcerer.*

"Run!" Dresden launched himself at Regulus' back. "Regulus, whatever the sorcerer did to you, come out of it!" He wrapped his arm around Regulus' neck, choking him.

Regulus pulled on Dresden's arm with so much force Dresden had to let go or risk his arm breaking. Harold threw open the main hall door and darted out. *Good. At least he'll get away.* Regulus shoved Dresden down. *Assuming Regulus comes to himself.*

Dresden crawled backward and lurched up. He turned to run.

"Oh, no. Someone is dying today," Regulus snarled. He grabbed the back of Dresden's shirt, pulled him back, and tossed him onto the stone, making Dresden gasp with the impact. Regulus straddled Dresden's chest and drew back his fist.

"Regulus! It's me!" Dresden barely got his arms up in time to block the blow. Something in his left arm cracked, and he cried out. He punched Regulus' mouth.

Regulus reeled back just enough for him to slip out and scurry to his feet. He ran toward the hall door, pushing himself to go faster as Regulus roared. Something hard slammed into his back, and he sprawled across the floor. The dining chair Regulus had thrown clattered on the stone. Pain covered Dresden's back and his left arm. Before he could regain his footing, Regulus grabbed his hair and pulled him to his knees. Dresden trembled as tears dripped down his cheeks.

"It's me, Regulus. Please. Remember me, Reg, please!"

"Oh, he knows, boy." Regulus grinned, vicious and deadly. "He's aware. I can feel him screaming. He just can't fight me."

"Fight you…" Dresden shuddered. "I'm talking to the sorcerer?"

"Prince of Shadow and Ash!" Spittle landed on Dresden's face as Regulus wrapped a hot hand around his throat again.

No. No, this couldn't be how he died—strangled by his best friend, by the only family he had anymore. He tried to tear away Regulus' iron grip. "Regulus…see me. Stop. Please, don't."

A tear rolled down from the corner of Regulus' eye, even as he laughed and his lips twisted into a mocking grin. "Don't worry. Regulus is watching and listening."

Dresden stilled. There was no point in fighting. "You didn't do this, Regulus—brother. I forgive you."

Another tear squeezed out of Regulus' eyes. "Oh, but he…no!" To Dresden's shock, Regulus' grip loosened on his neck. Hope swelled. "This took too long," the sorcerer snarled through Regulus' mouth. "Damn—"

Regulus abruptly stopped speaking, his expression going from malicious to stunned in an instant. He released Dresden's hair and neck and scrambled backward, tripping over his own feet in his haste.

"No…" Regulus' jaw quivered. His face tinged green. "No…" He looked down at his violently shaking hands, fell to his knees, and vomited.

Dresden stood, then swayed as his vision wavered. He gripped his throbbing arm and inched toward the door, ready to run again. "Regulus?"

Regulus turned from the puddle of sick and clutched his arms over his stomach as he cried. Dresden had seen Regulus cry only on a few occasions. But never like this. Regulus went pale as tears flooded his cheeks and snot leaked from his nostrils. He gasped in air, sounding like he could scarcely breathe.

"Reg?" Dresden took a tentative step closer.

Regulus gasped and closed his eyes. He took several deep breaths.

"Who am I talking to?"

After a moment, Regulus opened his eyes and stared at the floor. "It's me, Drez."

Dresden relaxed but couldn't make himself get any closer. "What happened?"

"I…" Regulus rubbed the heel of his hand against his temple. "I refused to obey. The sorcerer—tortured me." He swallowed. "He wants me to get some magical artifact from a monastery. I told him I wouldn't rob a monastery. When the torture didn't change my mind fast enough…he took over my body."

He looked up, eyes wet and terrified. "He said he would make me kill someone I care about. I told him no amount of pain could force me to do that. He laughed, and then… I couldn't do anything. He controlled me. And he'll try again." Regulus sobbed, then stood. "I have to go. Help me with that accursed armor?"

Dresden nodded.

Putting on the oversized black armor was difficult with his hands shaking from the fright of nearly dying at Regulus' hands and the pain in his left arm. He tried not to let it show. But as Regulus lifted his elbow to allow access to a buckle, he bumped the arm, and Dresden bit back a sharp cry.

"You're hurt?" Regulus sucked in a breath. "That punch…"

"I'm okay." Dresden finished buckling the armor in place and stepped back. "Or I will be. I think it's a minor break."

"Minor…" Regulus gulped. The grotesque black armor clinked as he walked to the door, his steps dragging. He paused with his hand on the knob and leaned his forehead against the door. "This monastery is far. I won't be back for several days. Don't be here when I get back. All of you." He straightened and strode out.

Don't be here? Dresden stood frozen. *He can't… Regulus can't mean that.* He shook his head and hurried after Regulus. He wasn't in the hall. Dresden raced down the back stairs, to the wood-walled corridor Regulus had ordered built to hide his passage to and from the stables. He glimpsed Regulus' hulking black armor disappear into the stables.

"Regulus!" Dresden ran in after him.

Regulus had Sieger's saddle in his hands. "What are you doing? You need to have that bone set—"

"I need you to know I'll be here. When you get back."

"Then…then I won't come back."

Anger and panic mixed, setting Dresden's skin on fire. He reached over the saddle and jabbed his forefinger against the black breastplate, searching for what to say to convince Regulus to come back. "Brothers."

Regulus' jaw trembled as he placed the saddle on Sieger's back.

"We help each other," Dresden said, practically begged. "So I'll be here."

"I nearly killed you!" Sieger shook his head as Regulus' shout echoed in the stable. Regulus patted the horse's neck and cinched the saddle.

Dresden's quivering hand drifted to his still raw throat. "It wasn't you—"

"Yes, it was! It was my hands! I could see you; I could feel your neck. It *was me.* And I couldn't stop it. I couldn't fight it, couldn't do anything but watch you die as *I* squeezed the life out of you! If I hadn't refused—"

"You didn't know he would do that, or that he even could. So stop. Stop feeling sorry for yourself and trying to drive me away." Dresden moved to Sieger's other side to stand across from Regulus. "I need you. We're brothers, and the sorcerer doesn't get to change that."

A tear raced down Regulus' cheek along his scar. He nodded and led Sieger to the hidden trap door to the escape tunnel in the corner of the stables. Dresden trailed after him, an uneasy feeling in his stomach.

"I'll see you in a few days," he said as Regulus led Sieger down into the tunnel.

"In a few days," Regulus said. "I promise."

FOUR WEEKS had passed since Regulus returned from the mission to the monastery. Almost four weeks since Dresden had found Regulus attempting to end his own life after trying over and over to remove the mark. Since his best friend had begged Dresden to behead him. The moment was at once a haze of tears, of reassuring words he barely remembered, of Regulus crying into his shoulder, and a sharp memory of blood and pain and heartbreak seared forever into his mind.

For a week afterward, Dresden had slept on a cot in Regulus' room, determined not to let Regulus feel alone. He'd since moved back to his own room down the hall, but he lay awake at night worrying and woke early to spend the day with Regulus. Especially since some days, Regulus wouldn't even get out of bed. Sometimes Dresden had no choice but to leave Regulus to sleep the day away. At least for the last week, Regulus had gotten out of bed every day and had more good days than bad.

The men worried. Dresden had told them about the sorcerer's control when Regulus left for the monastery, and how Regulus had asked them to leave Arrano. Only Harold considered leaving.

In the end, Harold had stayed once he understood that Regulus had been horrified and didn't want to hurt him. The boy knew what it was like to be alone and hurt by someone who thought they owned you. A few days after Regulus' attempt, Harold had come into the room to empty the chamber pot. Regulus asked Harold why he hadn't left. Harold said, "you saved me, so I wasn't alone anymore. I can't save you, but I can stay." Dresden had been proud, but after Harold left the room, Regulus had wept.

However, Dresden didn't tell the men about the monk Regulus had accidentally killed at the monastery. And per Regulus' wishes, they didn't know about the blood stain on Regulus' floor that Dresden had tried to clean and then covered with a rug. As weeks dragged on and Regulus refused to leave his room, all Dresden could tell them was that Regulus was fighting the darkness in his mind. Every day they asked how Regulus was. Every day, Dresden told them the same thing—he was holding on. Some days better, some days worse.

Regulus' anxiety over Dresden and the other men's continued presence showed in his darting eyes, in the way relief and dread mingled in his expression every time he saw Dresden. How his gaze constantly went to the splint Dresden still wore on his left arm. Guilt lingered in his shadowed face. He had agreed to let Dresden help him, to keep fighting, but his shoulders sagged in defeat. His left hand strayed to the scars around the mark when he thought Dresden wasn't looking. Every time Dresden suggested spending time with the knights, Regulus reacted with frozen panic. Even though Regulus had made Dresden promise not to tell anyone what he'd attempted, he acted as if they knew, and he couldn't bear for them to see him as weak.

It was hogwash, all of it, Dresden thought as he watched Regulus across the checkerboard. Regulus' twitching fingers hovered over the game pieces. The winter sunlight coming through the tall window behind Dresden made Regulus appear extra pale. But if there was a word Dresden would never apply to Regulus, it was weak.

The truth was that Regulus had felt he had no other option. The tragedy was that Dresden hadn't fully realized what Regulus was feeling and intervened sooner. He refused to let Regulus believe the lie that he had nothing good left to offer.

Regulus picked up a piece, moved it, and removed one of Dresden's. "I had an idea."

"Oh? About what?" Dresden moved a piece, getting his revenge by removing two of Regulus' pieces from the board.

"The mark always comes back, but it's always in the same place." As soon as Regulus mentioned the mark, Dresden's nerves wound tight. "So maybe…I need to cut my arm off entirely."

Dresden's hand jerked so hard he nearly upset the gameboard. He stared at Regulus, but his friend wouldn't meet his eyes. "What?"

"If losing an arm—"

"No." Dresden shook his head. "I thought we were in agreement."

"It's not my head," Regulus mumbled.

Dresden leaned back in the cozy armchair and ran his hand through his hair. "Let's say we do that, and your arm grows back. That's a lot of pain and me doing something I don't want to for nothing."

"We don't know it would grow back."

"Let's say it doesn't, then." Dresden tried to keep his voice calm. "What if the mark moved to your left arm? Shall we cut that off, too?"

Regulus shrugged. "Maybe. I'd be useless to him—"

"And then what? You can't fulfill the terms of the agreement. What happens then?" Dresden clenched his fists, trying to soften his voice. "You don't fulfill your debt. What happens?"

Regulus sagged. "He'll kill you." He ran his forefinger around the edge of a checkers piece. "Maybe he will eventually, anyway." His strained whisper barely reached Dresden's ears. "Maybe it would…be better if—"

"No!" Dresden jumped to his feet, causing the checkers pieces to jolt. He took a deep breath and knelt next to Regulus. "Look at me."

Slowly, Regulus met his eyes.

"I want you to make me a promise. Promise me you won't hurt yourself anymore. Not intentionally. Promise me you'll endure. I'll help you and won't ever abandon you; I solemnly swear it on the life of my parents and sister, wherever they might be."

Regulus' eyes widened.

"Now promise me. Please."

"I…" Regulus' gaze dropped to his right arm.

"That's not all you are." He searched for the right words and grasped at the first argument that occurred to him. "What's the punishment for horse theft in Bhitra, Regulus?"

Regulus frowned. "What's that—"

"What is it?"

"Death," Regulus whispered.

"Right. Shall I go cut off Jerrick's head, too? Or what about Estevan? He tricked people out of their money, which was theft. Some places would take his hand. I could cut off Estevan's hand while I'm removing body parts." Anger cut through his words. "Caleb's probably done something that some lord somewhere would like his head for. Perceval's gotten into enough barroom brawls to warrant at least some time in the stocks. And me? Well, I'm going to have to get someone else to give me the beating and the two lashings I earned and never received."

Regulus turned red. "What's your point?"

"My point? My point!" Dresden stood and waved his hands. "Your men, Regulus, what are we? A collection of mistakes, of crimes, of punishments we never received, of blood-drenched weapons, of disgrace and shame—"

"That's not what you are!"

"Then it's not what you are, either!"

Regulus worked his jaw and looked away.

Dresden sighed. "You're more, too, Regulus. Was I less worthy when I was your servant than I am now?"

"No."

"If it was me…would you kill me?" He gulped, suddenly afraid of the answer.

Regulus closed his eyes. "No."

Dresden sat back down in the armchair across the board from Regulus as he fought to make his voice work. "Your circumstances, your mistakes, none of it determines who you are, what you can be. You're more than a slave or a monster. You're my brother."

After a long, tension-filled moment, Regulus sighed and looked across the table. Slowly, his eyes lifted to meet Dresden's. "I promise. I won't hurt myself again. And I won't ask you—"

"Or anyone else," Dresden added.

"Or anyone else to do so," Regulus said quietly. "I'll try to endure. I swear it on my mother's grave."

They sat in silence, Regulus staring down at the checkers board, unmoving. "I don't deserve you," he said at last.

Dresden scratched his beard and affected a thick, sarcastic tone. "Yes, aside from the—what was it you claimed? Twelve times you've saved my life? Your all-around self-sacrificing behavior? The way you help people every chance you get? Aside from the fact you're a person, and at least according to what I remember the priests saying, that means something?" He shook his head. "Sure, Reg."

Regulus wrinkled his nose. "You get too much enjoyment out of being right, I think."

Was…that an attempt at humor? Dresden tried to hide his elated grin as he moved his piece. "I have an idea. You need something to keep you grounded. To remind you who you are. Like a mantra."

Regulus managed a dry chuckle, but even that warmed Dresden's heart. "I'm not repeating some ridiculous phrase."

"Even if it helps? You won't know if it will until you try it."

"Fine."

"Hmm." Dresden moved his piece. Soft clacking of wood on wood filled the room as they took turns and Dresden turned over the idea in his mind, looking for the right words in the right order, something that would be meaningful, easy to remember, could give Regulus some semblance of hope when he needed a reminder. "How about this? 'My circumstances don't define me. I choose who I am, not the sorcerer.'"

"The sorcerer kind of does choose, though."

"Oh, yes, the sorcerer definitely chooses that you're the kind of person who would do anything to protect his friends." Dresden rolled his eyes. "Your personality and morality have *totally* changed, and you have no thoughts of your own."

Regulus pursed his lips, but amusement flickered in his eyes. "You're sarcastic and annoying, you know that?"

"Just two of my innumerable charms." Dresden grinned. "Now, say it. My circumstances don't define me. I choose who I am, not the sorcerer."

Regulus sighed but echoed the phrase. "I choose who I am," he repeated in a whisper. He moved a piece on the board and removed two of Dresden's. "Thank you, Drez."

"I told you I'd help."

"I meant for being terrible at checkers."

Dresden looked down at the board and groaned. There was no way he could win at this point. "Bah, I was focused on helping you."

"True, can hardly expect you to do two things at once."

Dresden narrowed his eyes as he moved a piece in a futile attempt at turning around the game. "Are you mocking me now? I'm not sure if I'm offended or relieved."

"Well, I"—Regulus moved a piece and removed another of Dresden's—"have just relieved you of a piece."

"Terrible jokes are my thing. Your thing is being foolishly self-sacrificial; leave my thing alone." He stood. "Come on, this game is boring, and your horse is restless. Let's go for a ride."

"You just don't want to lose." Regulus leaned back in his chair with a flicker of a smile.

"So? Point stands."

"It's snowing."

"Again—so?"

Regulus sighed and shook his head. "Go ahead. I think I might sleep for a bit."

It's the middle of the afternoon. Dresden swallowed the words and nodded. "Okay. Supper at six bells?"

"Mm." Regulus looked up as Dresden stood. "Thank you. For everything."

"Always, Reg." He punched Regulus' shoulder. "At least dream of something fun. You like brunettes, right?"

"Get out." Regulus lightly shoved Dresden toward the door, but he was smiling, and that was what mattered.

MAGNUS
Several days later
Location: Town of Palion, Etchy Barony, Monparth

"MMM." DRESDEN licked butter off his fingers as he walked through the town, then pulled his woolen gloves back on to block the cold. "I must say, I am pleased your 'delicious baked goods' excuse to see your flame is true. Those rolls are, in fact, heavenly."

Jerrick sighed, the sound so lovesick it made Dresden shake his head. The Bhitran was bundled up in a thick coat with a scarf wrapped around his neck. He held a roll in one gloved hand and carried a basket in the other. Steam drifted through the towel covering the fresh loaves of bread. "Sarah is heavenly. Did you see the flour on her cheeks? So cute. I could just stare at her."

"And, you did," Dresden reminded him. "Every second that her father's back was turned."

"She's just… I mean, the way she moves…and smiles…and laughs…especially laughs. I love when I can get her to laugh." Jerrick gazed at the roll in his hand like he wanted to kiss it.

"If you are going to make out with that roll instead of eating it, please give it to me."

Jerrick scowled and bit into the roll. He closed his eyes and made a contented sound. "But this is the best bread in Monparth, possibly the world."

"As you said to Sarah and her father. Multiple times." Dresden licked his lips, savoring a bit of butter. "Not sure I can argue, though. So, are you going to ask to court her?"

Jerrick's dark cheeks took on a reddish hue. "I'll keep visiting, buying bread. See if Sarah really seems interested—"

"Oh, she's interested, or I'm blind." Dresden laughed.

"—and get her father used to me."

"He really didn't seem to mind you, Jerrick… Huh." Dresden backed up, staring down at the fluffy shapes that had caught his eye.

A little make-shift pen had been tucked into the corner of the sheltered porch of the cobbler's shop. Tails wriggled from the mound of black, brown, and white fur in the middle of a blanket.

"Huh, what?" Jerrick turned and walked back to Dresden. "Dogs?"

"Good deal on 'em." The gray-haired man sitting next to the pen in front of the rickety wooden building pulled his thick wool cloak closer about himself. "Unplanned litter."

Dresden picked up one of the pups. Its fur was incredibly soft, black by its face and floppy ears, brown along its back, and nearly white at its fluffy tail. It licked his face with a sloppy pink tongue. He held it at arms' length and realized just how heavy it was. "How old?"

"Oh, 'bout two months."

"Seems big for two months." He hefted the large puppy to emphasize his point.

"Heh. Big dogs." The man jutted his thumb toward the other end of the porch.

The mother lay inside a large crate placed on its side and padded with a blanket. She looked perfectly comfortable in the cold under all her shaggy dark brown and white fur. Dresden gaped.

Jerrick whistled. "No kidding."

"Strong, too," the man said. "Pretty smart. Good for training. And affectionate," he added as the puppy licked Dresden's face again and whined for attention.

"Didn't think you were a pet person," Jerrick said.

Dresden looked into the puppy's golden eyes. "Not really. But Regulus always wanted a dog as a boy."

Jerrick laughed. "The man could use a lovable distraction. Not a bad idea."

"Why, thank you." Dresden looked to the old man. "How much?"

∞•∞

Dresden knocked on Regulus' door. The puppy shifted in the sack he had hidden it in and whined behind his back. Wiggly thing. He was liable to drop it. "It's me, Reg."

"Come in," Regulus called.

The puppy writhed and whimpered as Dresden pushed the door open. Regulus reclined on his bed under the covers, a book in hand. It looked like he'd read three pages all morning. Dresden ignored the pang in his heart, deciding to be happy Regulus was even trying to read.

Reg set the book aside. "Yes?"

"Got you something in town." Dresden gently deposited the bag on the bed next to Reg's legs. Regulus looked at it curiously and leaned forward, then paused with a frown when it moved.

"What is—"

The puppy yipped and wriggled in the sack. Regulus pulled the drawstring open, and the puppy tumbled out. Dresden couldn't repress his grin, but Regulus just stared at the dog like he'd never seen one before. The puppy took a few clumsy steps around, tripped, and got back up. It looked at Regulus, wagged its tail, then jumped onto Regulus' chest and began whimpering and licking ferociously at his face.

Regulus scowled, but his eyes twinkled as he grabbed the puppy and held it away from his face. "What is this?"

"A puppy, obviously." Dresden plopped onto the end of the bed.

Regulus rolled his eyes, but the corner of his lips twitched toward a smile. "Why is it here?"

"Thought he might cheer you up. And give you a reason to leave your room."

"Hm." Regulus set the puppy down, and it immediately climbed back up his chest to lick his face.

Dresden laughed. "I think he likes you."

"Or he likes salty things," Regulus mumbled as he pushed the puppy down.

"Salty…oh." *Regulus was crying again.*

The puppy flopped over on Regulus' lap and decided that was a good place to curl into a ball for a nap. Regulus stroked the puppy from its floppy ears down to its fluffy tail. A smile eased his face as his stiff shoulders relaxed.

"What's his name?" Dresden asked.

"Hm." Regulus buried his fingers in the dog's fur. "I could always take a cue from you and name him Dog."

Dresden groaned. "Look, I didn't want to get attached in case anything happened. We were mercenaries! Mercenary horses don't always last long! And my da said it was ridiculous to name animals because you might have to eat them someday…" Regulus grimaced and Dresden held up his hands and rushed on. "He's used to Horse now, anyway."

"Mm-hmmm." Still stroking the dog, Regulus chuckled to Dresden's immense satisfaction. "He's kind of a big boy."

"Only two months old," Dresden said. "You should have seen his mother.

He's going to be huge."

Regulus looked up with an unconvincing glower. "You got me a huge dog?"

"Well, it was what I found." Dresden smirked and reached for the puppy. "If you don't want the big dog, I could take him back to that dirty, hole-filled doghouse covered in snow—"

"Oh, hush." Regulus smacked his hand away. "Maybe a huge dog will get along well with Sieger."

Regulus *would* worry about his horse and dog getting along. The puppy stretched with a yawn that curled its tongue. A full smile lit Regulus' face.

"Magnus. I think I'll call him Magnus."

❦

Two months later

"You almost had it that time, boy." Regulus sighed and walked back to the puppy, coaxing him back to a sit. "Now wait." The puppy wagged its tail, its tongue hanging out of its mouth as it watched Regulus back away. It started to stand, and Regulus held up his hand. "Ah-ah." The puppy lowered its haunches, its tail wagging furiously.

Dresden stifled a chuckle. He was hidden behind crates of supplies that had recently been delivered and the servants hadn't put away yet. He'd meant to watch for a moment. Instead, he had been half crouched behind the crates watching Regulus trying to train the dog for so long his back was aching.

"All right, Magnus, now come!" Regulus' voice was encouraging and full of excitement. Nothing like his commanding captain voice. Or like the sad murmur he often spoke in lately. With a little yip, the puppy ran straight for Regulus, who had crouched with open arms. Regulus laughed as he caught the puppy, and Magnus licked Regulus' face. "All right, all right!" Regulus tried to move his face back, but Magnus rested his enormous paws on Regulus' chest and kept soaking Regulus' face with drool.

Dresden bit his lip to keep from laughing.

"Are you spying?" Dresden jumped at Harold's voice at his right shoulder. "No, just…watching in hiding."

Harold frowned, but amusement showed in his eyes. He was looking stronger; healthier and fuller. Made him actually look his fourteen years.

"I think that's the definition of spying." Harold peered between a couple crates.

Regulus used a piece of bread to get Magnus to twirl in circles. Dresden grinned, relief and joy combining as he took in the carefree smile on Regulus' face.

"He's letting the dog sleep on the bed," Harold said.

Dresden looked over at him. "Hm?"

"Regulus. Every morning, I find Magnus curled against his side on the bed."

"Good." He chuckled. "Although, that might be a problem when Magnus is grown."

"Is…he okay?"

"What do you mean?" Dresden turned to lean against the crates and watch Harold.

Harold shifted, his cheeks flushing. "I was cleaning yesterday, and…I beat out the rug in the middle of the floor. It was covered in fur, and it needed done, but when I went to put it back, I noticed…" He gulped and glanced about.

Dresden knew what he'd noticed. Try as he might, he hadn't been able to remove the bloodstain. The wood had absorbed too much. "He's okay. It's from months ago. Just…don't mention it to him. Or anyone else."

Harold nodded quickly. "But…was it his, then? Did the sorcerer make him hurt himself? Or did he hurt you—"

"No, Harold." Dresden sighed. "You have to act like you don't know this, okay?"

Harold glanced toward Regulus, now running around as Magnus chased him. "Okay."

"He would rather hurt himself than us."

Harold's eyes went wide. "Oh… Oh."

Regulus' laughter carried over to them. "Alright, you got me, boy. Down, Magnus. Good—" He inhaled sharply. Dresden looked back through the crates. Regulus clutched his right arm, pain and anger mixing in his tight expression while Magnus whined at his feet. "I'm sorry, Magnus. No more playing." Regulus' shoulders caved, his left hand still gripping the sorcerer's mark.

Dresden rounded the crates. "Hey, Regulus."

Regulus looked up, and relief crossed his face, followed by what looked like shame. "Can you keep Magnus out of trouble? I have to…" He looked toward the castle and rubbed his arm. "My master calls," he muttered.

"Come here, Magnus." Dresden hefted the dog. Even after only a couple months, the puppy had grown larger. He scratched behind Magnus' ears. "Remember, your circumstances don't define you. You decide who you are, not the sorcerer. And every mission gets you closer to being free."

Regulus nodded. "At least he left me alone for a couple months. Can you let Lord Endover know I regret I am unable to attend their dinner party as planned?"

"I'll take care of it." Dresden watched Regulus head inside.

Harold came up next to him and rubbed Magnus' furry chest. "I hope he's free soon."

"Me too, Harold. Me too."

PART II
The Mage

DRESDEN NODDED at a passing servant as he walked through Arrano's garden. Well, it had been a garden when they arrived. It was mostly weeds now. He should try to talk Regulus into—wait. He spun back toward the man.

"Is that a letter?"

The older man stopped and turned back with a half bow. "Aye, Sir Jakobs. A messenger just delivered it for his lordship."

"I'll take it up to his room." Dresden held out his hand. The servant handed over the letter and continued on his way. Dresden waited until the servant was gone before sitting on a nearby stone bench half hidden in ground vine.

He flipped the folded parchment over and checked the wax seal. A raven's head over an axe, whatever that meant. Why was he so terrible at remembering the noble families' seals? Good thing he wasn't a herald. He bent the seal to crack it open.

"You know he doesn't like you opening his letters."

Dresden jumped at Harold's voice. "And yet he always forgives me." He resettled on the bench and unfolded the letter as Harold came and stood next to him.

"Anything interesting?"

"The Drummonds are hosting a banquet because Lady Tamina Belanger and her daughter Adelaide are visiting." He frowned. "I wonder why?"

"I don't recognize the name Belanger." Harold sat on the edge of the bench and peered at the letter. "It's not a family in Thaera Duchy." Harold had studied all the noble families in the duchy as part of his squire duties. If Harold didn't know this Belanger family, they had to be visiting from another duchy…but why?

"It seems familiar, though. And they must know the Drummonds…" Dresden snapped his fingers. "Lady Minerva Drummond! She's a Belanger. She married Gaius Drummond shortly after we came to Arrano."

"Why do you remember that?"

Dresden refolded the letter. "Because Lady Minerva's mother is a commoner from Khastalland. That's unusual. I think Lord Belanger is a Monparthian knight who got rich in the Trade War." He nodded as he recalled a recent conversation with another knight at a tavern. "That's right. Sir Rengel mentioned Minerva Drummond is pregnant, and her sister was coming to stay with her during the pregnancy. He was going on about how he'd heard Minerva had a generous dowry, and if he were younger, he'd try for her sister. Honestly, I was focused on the barmaid and wasn't really listening."

An idea formed in his mind. More of a plot, really. He reopened the letter and checked the date. Regulus had been gone on this mission for the sorcerer for three days. He should be back before the party. And the sorcerer usually waited at least a couple weeks between summoning him again, so Regulus should be available.

"Harold, I have a brilliant plan."

Harold frowned. "Why does that worry me?"

"Hey." He shoved Harold's shoulder playfully. "The goal when Regulus returns is to convince him to attend this party."

"Why?"

"Because Lady Adelaide Belanger is *single*, Harold. Her mother isn't noble. Her father is a warrior. Plus her sister's pretty, so I imagine she is, too." He leaned closer. "Who do we know who is single, has a non-noble parent, and is a warrior?"

Harold's lips parted and his eyes widened. "You're trying to find a wife for Regulus?"

"Exactly." Dresden tapped the side of his nose. "Lady Belanger stands a good chance of not shunning Regulus on account of his past. If it doesn't work out, it gives Regulus something to think about other than the sorcerer for a while. If it does work out, it gives him another reason to live. Something to look forward to. Might help with his confidence among the nobles. And…I'd like to see him truly happy again."

He did have one reservation. Regulus loved fiercely. If he fell in love with this girl because Dresden pushed him into it, and she didn't reciprocate, it might crush Regulus. But Regulus was so nervous about girls, he wouldn't develop feelings unless the girl in question encouraged it. This could be brilliant.

"I don't know…" Harold scratched his ear. "Regulus hates parties. He's declining more often again."

"Oh, I'll convince him to go. And talk to her."

"I suppose if anyone could, it'd be you. What do I do?"

"You just make sure he wears something that showcases his physique." Dresden smiled and Harold shook his head with a chuckle.

A girl wouldn't heal Regulus, Dresden knew that. But love couldn't hurt.

THE BANQUET
One week later

Location: Drummond Estate, Etchy Barony, Thaera Duchy, Monparth

A SERVANT CLEARED away Dresden's plate, and Dresden gave him a friendly nod of thanks. The older man blinked at him in surprise and hurried away, and Dresden stifled a sigh. He hated how servants never expected to be thanked or even acknowledged—unless it was to berate them for an error. He remembered how it felt, trying not to draw attention to himself, how much he resented the nobles who treated him like a moving fixture of the Kimberly's castle. Not Regulus, though. He looked over at his friend, but Regulus was looking at Lady Adelaide Belanger again.

She was gorgeous. Smooth brown skin and flowing dark hair and eyes so deep a brown they seemed to pull you into them. Lips that often curved into a smile. No question about it, if Regulus didn't act on his obvious infatuation, Dresden was going to gamble on trying himself.

He locked that thought away. This was about *Regulus*, not himself. And he doubted Regulus had noticed, but Adelaide had practically tripped over herself when she met Regulus. Adelaide's gaze cut across the hall, landing on Regulus before looking away. Was that a slight blush? Oh, this was excellent. He just had to ensure Regulus talked to her. Easier said than done.

The crowded hall quieted as Lady Adelaide Belanger stepped forward to recite, and Regulus leaned subtly forward. Dresden smirked. *Or not so difficult. And Harold thought this would never work.*

Adelaide recited a romantic poem—a tragic one, but romantic, nonetheless. Hopefully that put Regulus in the right mood. The poem concluded, the guests politely applauded, and Adelaide stepped away from the dais as guests rose and mingled. Regulus, however, made no move to leave his chair. And he was frowning again. Just a pinch to the corners of his mouth, but enough he looked broody and not at all approachable. *Would it kill the man to smile?*

Dresden punched Regulus' shoulder. "So, are you going to sit here frowning, or are you going to go talk to her?"

Regulus' expression eased. "I'm not frowning."

"You're always frowning." He motioned toward Adelaide. "Go. You gave your word."

Regulus rolled his eyes with a grunt, but he shoved away from the table and stood. Dresden didn't hide his triumphant grin, not that Regulus could see it as he walked toward Adelaide. Or marched. He had that straight-backed, purposeful stride he used to approach a potential benefactor as a mercenary captain. This should prove interesting.

Regulus slowed as he approached Adelaide, who had fortuitously moved off to the side by herself and was…looking at the stained-glass window? Strange woman. A good match for Regulus. Dresden snickered. Regulus' stride lost its confidence until he slowed to a stop near Adelaide. He looked back at Dresden, indecision in his wide eyes.

Dresden threw his hands up. *What are you waiting for?* The man had more courage addressing a warlord than a girl. Regulus faced Adelaide. She turned around, but Regulus shifted, blocking Dresden's view. After a minute passed and they were still talking, Dresden congratulated himself and left the table. He had given Regulus a shove, that was all he could do. Now, time to find some fun of his own.

His gaze caught on a heart-stopping young lady with silky blonde hair falling in gentle curls. She stood far to one side of the room near a wall, and laughed with another young woman, full lips stretched in a wide smile. He didn't recognize her from any previous parties. Visiting from outside the barony, perhaps? He watched her out of the corner of his eye as he wove through the guests.

Her bright blue dress with fitted long sleeves hugged her figure. A bracelet of silver squares with intricate floral patterns connected by a thin chain glinted around her wrist, sliding up around her sleeve and then down practically around her hand as she gestured. *Perfect.*

He slipped behind the girl, deftly pulling the loose bracelet up and away from her sleeve just enough he could unhook the simple clasp and steal the bracelet from her wrist. He darted away, the bracelet clutched in his fist. She continued to talk with her friend while Dresden waited for an opening. The friend saw someone across the room and excused herself. *Finally.* He ambled over with an easy smile.

"Pardon me, fair lady." He bowed and held out the bracelet on his upturned palm as the young woman turned toward him. "Did you lose this?"

She gasped and clutched her wrist. "I—I must have. Thank you!" She reached toward the bracelet, but Dresden closed his fingers around it as he straightened.

"Please. Allow me." He swept up her hand and fastened the bracelet around her wrist, making a show of checking the clasp was fastened. He released her hand and inclined his head with a smile. "My lady."

He turned and took leisurely, measured steps away.

"Wait."

He grinned, then schooled his expression into a polite smile as he turned back. "Yes, my lady?"

A hint of pink crept into her cheeks. "It's Katherine. Maid Katherine Rowland." *Maid.* Unwed daughter of a knight, which made them of approximately equal social standing. Most excellent.

"A lovely name. Sir Dresden Jakobs, at your service, Maid Katherine."

Katherine smiled. "And whom do you serve, Sir Jakobs?"

"Well, between you and me." He stepped closer. "I serve my heart first and foremost." Her smile twitched as her eyes crinkled. "My heart, sadly, has no lady to serve. But my sword is sworn to the lord of Arrano."

"The mercenary?" Her expression turned wary. "Are you a mercenary?"

"I was." Dresden let a little feral creep into his smile as he leaned toward her and lowered his voice. "Why? I'm afraid if you prefer soft men, I might be a bit too dangerous for you."

"Dangerous?" Her eyes locked on his. She took a step back and bumped into the wall.

"Mmm." He stepped closer. "Rather like a cat. I have claws and sharp teeth and am capable of violence, but I'll be honest." Another step. "I much prefer lying on a sun-warmed couch."

Katherine smirked. "I suppose next you'll say you'd like it even better if there were a lady on the couch."

"Well, I wouldn't object." He chuckled. "Cats and I both enjoy a lady's fingers brushing through our hair."

She laughed, somewhere between amused and incredulous as her eyes darted to his hair, his beard, then settled on his eyes again. "Scoundrel."

"No, just honest." He shrugged. "Unlike you."

Her lips parted. "I beg your pardon?"

"As I am a man of chivalry now"—he gave her a crooked grin—"I shouldn't reveal a lady's secrets." He glanced around and leaned over her, then spoke in a whisper. "But if you want to touch my hair so badly, I won't stop you."

"I do not!" But her gaze went to his hair again.

He straightened, giving her plenty of space to slip away if she so wished. "As you say." He winked. Her lips twisted in a suppressed smile as she rolled her eyes.

"But, as I am not a liar, I must confess something." He moved to the side and leaned his shoulder against the wall next to her. "I stole your bracelet off your wrist. You didn't lose it."

Katherine gasped but didn't move away. "You…what? How? I would have noticed!" She touched the bracelet but didn't look away from him.

He chuckled. "I might be a strong knight and dangerous mercenary, but I'm also gentle." Dresden reached up and brushed a strand of her hair behind her ear, then slowly combed through her hair before twisting the lower part of the strand around his forefinger. "And I so badly wished to talk with you, Maid Katherine," he murmured.

Her face flushed. "Talk, hm? That's all?"

Dresden lifted his brows. "Why? Did you have something else in mind?" He continued to toy with her hair, still leaning against the wall.

She huffed. "The sun is set, so no lying with your head on my lap in the sun for you."

"I never said anything about putting my head in your lap." He smiled deviously. "Although that does sound lovely. I like your thinking."

"Why, you…" She slapped his hand away.

Dresden laughed. "Apologies, my lady, I didn't mean to offend."

"And what did you mean to do?"

He lifted his shoulder. "You looked bored. I was bored. I thought we could be less bored together. So. Shall I leave, or am I amusing enough to beg your leave to remain and continue talking with you?"

Katherine pursed her lips. "I will allow it."

"You are too gracious, my lady." He bowed. "I don't believe I've seen you before. Are you new to Etchy Barony?"

"No." She sighed. "I'm the youngest of four daughters, and my mother is old-fashioned and wouldn't allow me to attend parties until my sisters were wed, even though I'm twenty."

"So, no suitors, then?"

She blushed. "Well, I mean, no, not exactly, no."

"Not exactly?" He tilted his head. "I am fascinated, do explain."

"I don't have to explain myself to you."

He clutched at his heart. "I'm wounded. And here I thought we were having such a pleasant conversation."

Katherine scowled, but the look broke into a smile. "Well…you did say you wouldn't share a lady's secrets."

"Never." He moved closer and leaned down. "Your whispers are safe with me."

"Well, now I don't want to tell, you scoundrel."

Dresden brushed his thumb over his lower lip. "You say *scoundrel* like you like the sound of it."

"I—why—you…" She huffed as her eyes fixed on his thumb stroking his mouth. Even after he dropped his hand, it took her a moment to move her gaze back to his eyes. "You're frustrating."

"Is that a compliment?"

"No."

"Ah, good, because it would have been a terrible one." He rubbed his beard. "You're beautiful. Your hair is soft as an angel's feathers, your eyes as bright as jewels. Your voice makes me want to curl up on that couch I mentioned and bask in the sound." He pushed her hair over her shoulder and murmured, "That's how you give a compliment, Maid Katherine."

She opened and closed her mouth a few times before speaking. "Sounds like flattery."

"Flattery is untrue. Now." He adjusted himself against the wall. "How do you 'not exactly' have suitors?"

"I haven't had a suitor, but…" Her voice dropped to a whisper. "I kissed the stable boy. A few times."

"And I'm meant to be the scandalous one?"

Katherine swatted his arm with a giggle.

"Stable *boy*, hm?" He waved his hand dismissively. "Shame. Boys don't know what they're doing."

"And I suppose you do?" She crossed her arms. "You think I should kiss you?"

Dresden grinned. "*I* didn't say that. But I would be interested if you're asking me to kiss you."

"I am not!" Her hands fisted at her sides. "You're impertinent!"

"I'm *honest*." He took her hand and pressed a kiss against her fingers, slow and gentle. "I'll stop bothering you, Maid Katherine. I'm feeling a touch sleepy, anyway. I think I'll take a little catnap on the settee in the alcove in the foyer. Looked comfortable, quiet, and secluded." He dropped her hand and strode away, running his hand through his hair as he moved around guests.

He glanced around, looking for Regulus and Lady Adelaide Belanger. His steps slowed when he didn't find either of them. Interesting. It would be most out of character for Regulus to have already found a dark corner with Adelaide, but then, he seemed smitten with her… Dresden could always hope.

So long as they hadn't occupied the settee he had claimed.

To his relief, the foyer hall and the little alcove were empty. He sat on the settee and leaned against the wall, one ankle tossed over his opposite knee. If Regulus and Adelaide had wandered off to be alone, Dresden might have a heart attack. He'd be proud, but…what was she, a sorceress? And if they hadn't, where in Monparth was Regulus? He wouldn't leave without telling Dresden…would he? Maybe he should look for Reg. He'd made up his mind to check with the page at the front door to see if Regulus had left when soft footsteps approached. He did his best to smother his victorious smirk.

Katherine glanced over her shoulder before standing in front of him. She looked all around before her gaze settled on Dresden.

He lifted a brow. "Looking for something?"

Her mouth curved in a teasing smile. "A cat."

"Ah, sorry to disappoint." He scooted over to make room on the settee. "I'm afraid it's just me. But I can be excellent company."

Katherine perched on the settee next to him. "Your beard was softer than expected."

So, his lingering kiss on her fingers had served its purpose. "My hair's even softer."

"You're very forward, you know that?" She frowned, but her eyes sparkled.

"I haven't even started being forward yet." He shifted closer and slipped his arm around her waist. "Do you want me to stop?"

She bit her lower lip. "Not yet."

"Let me know if you change your mind," Dresden murmured as he brushed his lips against her cheek.

"Are you just playing with me?" Katherine whispered.

Dresden stilled. "Is a little fun such a bad thing?"

"You really *are* dangerous, Sir Jakobs."

He removed his arm from her waist. "If—"

"I didn't say I changed my mind." She turned toward him and cupped the side of his head. He leaned into her hand. "You better kiss me now, Sir Dresden, because I may not give you another chance."

"Is that so?" He placed his hand lightly on her waist and leaned in, drifting toward her lips. "Maybe you're the dangerous one, Maid Katherine."

She closed the space between them and kissed him. Maybe that stable boy hadn't been so innocent, because her kiss wasn't. Her hands worked into his hair, and Dresden smiled before he deepened the kiss and pulled her closer.

They had to take a moment to straighten up their hair and clothes after they finally separated. Katherine stood and looked down at him.

"Are you certain fun is all you're interested in?" She cocked her head as she reached out and smoothed the top of his hair.

Part of him was tempted to say no, but he just winked. "I'm not sure serious suits me."

She smiled but sadness touched her eyes, and Dresden's buoyant spirits fell. "A shame. I think I could have liked you." She went back into the main hall.

Dresden remained on the settee, waiting so they wouldn't reenter too close together. The delight of kissing Katherine faded as he wondered what it would be like to pursue her, or any girl. To try to win her hand for a lifetime, not her lips for one evening. As much as he enjoyed flirting and kissing—and he very much did—he liked the idea of settling down. Of having a woman who was happy every time he came home, someone he could enjoy without any guilt, and that he could truly love.

Kissing random girls was fun. But there was something special about the way Jerrick and Sarah looked at each other, something untouchable and dazzling about the way Leonora kissed Perceval, something incomprehensibly strong about the way his mother had followed his father from Carasom to Monparth.

He shook the thoughts away. Thinking about his parents made him either gloomy or irritable, depending on if he became angrier with them for neglecting to visit or with himself for not looking for them. Just like he did as a youth, it was easier to forget he had a family other than Regulus than to wonder what might have been had things been different.

Besides, what would happen if he tried to court Katherine? Two years of knighthood, and her first response was *mercenary* and distrust. Talking girls into a dance or flirtatious banter or even into kisses wasn't that hard. Some women, especially the higher-ranking ones, wouldn't talk to him. But for others, the combination of being a Carasian, a former mercenary, and a knight to the mysterious lord of Arrano was enough to capture their interest. But it was usually a passing interest, and the reason he had learned to capitalize on the allure of his dangerous side. Even if the ladies might be interested in more…finding a girl whose father wouldn't laugh in his face might prove harder.

Maybe not. Sarah's father loved Jerrick. But Dresden was nervous to try. Which he would never admit to Regulus, not when he spent so much time trying to convince Regulus people wouldn't react as negatively as Regulus feared.

Speaking of Regulus…

Dresden headed to the front entrance. A young page bounded up from a stool.

"Can I fetch your cloak, sir?"

"No, I was just wondering, has Lord Hargreaves of Arrano left? Tall, scar?"

"Oh, yes." The boy nodded, and Dresden's spirits fell further. "A while ago."

"Thank you." Dresden sighed and trudged back toward the hall. It hurt more than he cared to admit that Regulus had left him behind, without so much as a word.

What went wrong? Did Adelaide find out who and what he was and throw a glass of wine in his face? Dresden should have been there for him, not sequestered in a corner with a girl. Maybe that was why Regulus was angry with him.

He shook his head. No, they were brothers; he shouldn't assume Regulus was angry with him. But that Regulus was upset enough with how the romantic escapade had progressed to run away wasn't good.

Even if Katherine really was interested in more and her father didn't toss Dresden out on his backside, he couldn't think about a serious relationship until Regulus was taken care of.

He returned to the main hall, wondering if he should go after Regulus or if Regulus would want space. He spied Adelaide talking with her mother and a couple guests. *What did you do to my friend?*

Adelaide's gaze landed on Dresden. Her brows pinched and her head tilted to the side. She glanced around him, as if looking for someone, but then another guest said something and she turned her attention back to the conversation.

Dresden pursed his lips. Had she been looking for Regulus? Did the frowny-faced coward run off for no reason?

"You there. Carasian."

"Hm?" Dresden turned toward the male voice, forehead furrowing. A man with blond hair, fine clothes, and a dismissive air stood nearby, holding a goblet of wine. Oh, excellent, the impertinent noble snob who had interrupted Regulus in the foyer before the party. Dresden knew he'd seen him before but couldn't seem to think of his name. "I'm Sir Jakobs; can I help you?"

The noble snorted. "It seems your *lord*"—his upper lip curled—"has left early. Without all his things." He eyed Dresden over his goblet.

Dresden clenched his teeth. "Have a good evening—"

"I have a message for him." The man sipped his wine. "Think you can manage to relay a message?"

"From who?"

"From *whom*, uneducated peasant." The noble sniffed. "Sir Nolan Carrick."

Dresden stiffened, glad he hadn't said or done anything too offensive to the son of Regulus' liege. Baron Carrick hadn't struck Dresden as the forgiving sort.

"Tell the mercenary lord I've warned Lady Adelaide of him, and he would do well to keep his distance from her. Understand?"

"Yes, of course, Sir Carrick." Dresden smiled, although it probably looked like more of a snarl.

"Hm." Carrick turned on his heel and strode away.

Dresden moved over to a table set with small desserts and picked up a jam-covered pastry as he sorted through the information he had. Adelaide had seemed attracted to Regulus. Regulus had left. Adelaide had looked confused to see Dresden and had appeared to be looking to see if Regulus was with him. Carrick was warning Regulus away from Adelaide, and men only told another man to back off of a girl if they felt threatened. He licked jam off his fingers, winning him a disapproving frown from a middle-aged woman in a heavy brocade dress that was probably so hot it was putting her in a bad mood. He ignored her as he came to his conclusion.

Adelaide was at least curious about Regulus, but Sir Carrick had expressed interest and Regulus had surrendered. To be fair, Dresden would probably do the same if he had to compete for a lady's attentions with the son of a baron. But he wasn't about to let Regulus give up.

When the night ended, Dresden made sure to stop to speak with Adelaide on his way out.

"Lord Hargreaves asked me to tell you he enjoyed your conversation and regrets he had to leave early to attend to other business. He hopes your paths cross again soon." Dresden smiled as he lied through his teeth. "Might I bring him a message from you, my lady?"

"Oh." Adelaide glanced away for a moment, as if considering her words. "I wish Lord Hargreaves hadn't left so soon. I would have liked to continue our conversation. It was the only real conversation I had all night."

Dresden bowed and hoped his glee wasn't too obvious. "Excellent. I wish you the best, Lady Belanger."

"Wait!"

Confusion replaced his short-lived victory.

"Can…can you tell him I know?" she asked softly. "And I don't care about lineages, either?"

Dresden couldn't stop his smile. "I will, my lady."

He had a spring in his step as he left the Drummonds' house and went to his horse. He'd been right. She didn't care that Regulus was a bastard. He ran her words back through his mind as he rode through the night back to Arrano, making sure he didn't forget anything.

Sorry, Carrick. I have a message for Regulus, and it's not from you.

"You've already asked Sarah to bake the nalotavi and bought the ingredients, you can't back out now." Dresden sprawled in one of the armchairs in Regulus' room, his legs stretched out toward the empty fireplace. Magnus pushed his big head up under his hand, begging for ear scratches.

"I could eat them myself," Regulus muttered. He plunked the quill in the inkwell and slumped back in his desk chair. With an exaggerated sigh, he ran his fingers through his hair.

"You need a haircut." Dresden closed his eyes, still rubbing Magnus' ears.

"You need a haircut."

He snorted. "I keep my hair well-trimmed. You're the one with a mess of loose curls."

"When it's to my shoulders, I'll cut it. Longer hair makes up for my lack of beard."

"That makes no sense, but sure, Reg."

Regulus' chair creaked, and the quill clinked against the side of the inkwell. Dresden opened one eye. Regulus hunched over the desk, quill suspended over the blank parchment. A drop of ink splashed onto the page. Regulus speared the quill into the inkwell, wadded up the parchment, and threw it at Dresden.

"Hey!" He batted aside the parchment and frowned. Regulus ignored him, pulling another piece from a desk drawer.

"I don't know what to say," Regulus groaned. "I like you a lot, so I had this nalotavi made for you—I hope you like it, I hope you like me?"

Dresden laughed. "No, probably not that."

"You're no help."

"I could get Caleb—"

"Don't you dare." Regulus withdrew the quill and scowled at the parchment.

Several long moments ticked by with no sound of quill scratching on parchment. Dresden straightened, pulling his hand away from Magnus, who laid down with a dramatic huff.

"Okay, start with the basics. 'Dear Adelaide.'"

Regulus tossed a quick glare over his shoulder but put quill to page, murmuring, "Dear Lady Adelaide Belanger."

"So formal." Dresden shook his head. "But at least you started. Now, say you liked talking to her. Maybe say some nice things about your conversation. Tell her you're sending her a token of affection. Mention how beautiful she is, and how you're looking forward to seeing her again. It's not that hard."

"You can say that. You're not the one writing it." Regulus thought for a moment, then wrote in fits and starts, but kept writing. He replaced the quill in the inkwell, held up the parchment, and read aloud.

"Dear Lady Adelaide Belanger, I greatly enjoyed your company at the Glowers' feast. Your conversation turned an evening that would have been long and trying into an enjoyable night that passed far too quickly. I am impressed by your wit, your honesty, your thoughtfulness, and your bold heart. I hope I am not being too forward in sending a small token of my admiration. I hope my little gift reminds you of home—and keeps me in your thoughts, as you are in mine. I look forward to when our paths cross again. Until then, I shall have to settle for fond memories of your gentle face framed by silky black hair and the deep warmth of your dark brown eyes. Sincerely yours, Regulus."

It was good, and surprisingly forward coming from Regulus. But before Dresden congratulated him, Regulus groaned.

"It's ridiculous! Far too sentimental, like I'm trying too hard." Regulus scowled at the letter. "No, it's too unrestrained. She'll think me a cad!" He tossed the parchment over his shoulder and set about writing a new letter.

Dresden shook his head as he went and retrieved the letter from the floor. It was perfect, because it was imperfect and genuine and very…Regulus. He folded the letter and slipped it up his sleeve as he returned to the chair.

Regulus stopped writing. "Dear Lady Adelaide Belanger, thank you for the pleasure of your company and excellent conversation at the Glowers' feast. Please accept this token of my admiration until I have the good fortune to speak with you again. Respectfully yours, Lord Regulus Hargreaves." His nose wrinkled. "That's not right, either." He crumpled the parchment and tossed it aside.

Five drafts of varying quality later—while Dresden considered throwing Regulus out the window, as a fall couldn't kill him, anyway—Regulus had settled on Monparth's worst love letter.

Dear Lady Adelaide Belanger,

It was an honor to spend an evening in your company. I send my most humble regard and this simple gift, along with the hope that we will meet again.

Respectfully,

Regulus, Lord of Arrano

"Why the Lord of Arrano bit?"

"I don't know!" Regulus groaned and slid down the chair. "I'm sending her pastries! Like—like a servant! Stupid!" He jolted to his feet. "I'm going for a ride. Please eat the pastries before I embarrass myself." Magnus followed Regulus out, and the door slammed shut after them.

"Remember how I feared if Regulus fell in love and the girl didn't reciprocate, it might break him?" Dresden mused aloud to the empty room. He pulled the first letter out of his sleeve and sat at the desk. "Well, she had better reciprocate."

He wrote a quick postscript, a little amused about using a skill Regulus had taught him to undermine Regulus' will—but for the good of Regulus' heart.

P.S. Regulus threw this note away because he feared it was too sentimental and forward, but I switched out the letters because this one is a more accurate representation of his heart. Perhaps it can be our secret? I should very much like to live.

—Dresden Jakobs

He knew he could have sent the letter without the postscript, but this way, he could tease Regulus about it at the wedding. Because there had better be a wedding after all this trouble and living with Regulus' moody pining. He pulled Regulus' wax and Arrano seal out the top drawer and sealed the letter with a smug grin.

DRESDEN CURSED under his breath as he leaned against his closed bedroom door. He shut his eyes and rested his head against the wood. He wanted to be happy. His plan had gone better than hoped. But this…this was out of control.

When he had decided to play matchmaker with Regulus and Adelaide, he had expected one of three outcomes.

One, Adelaide snubbed Regulus, or they didn't like each other, and it went nowhere. Little to no harm done.

Two, Regulus and Adelaide flirted for a while, but ultimately the relationship ended for whatever reason. For a time, Regulus got a little harmless fun and a reason to anticipate instead of dreading parties, and Dresden could enjoy himself at parties without feeling guilty about leaving Regulus alone. Maybe it ended in heartbreak for Regulus, but Dresden had judged the risk worth it.

Or three, they fell for each other and eventually got married. In that scenario, Dresden had pictured them slowly falling for each other over several months. He should have known better.

Regulus was too respectful and modest for casual flings, and he had been too reserved and self-deprecating to look for love. But Dresden had always known—when Regulus did finally fall in love, it would be head-first, complete, and consuming. That was how Regulus loved and did everything. Never by half-measures. He just…hadn't expected Regulus to fall so *fast*.

But seeing Regulus' hope, his joy…seeing how Adelaide truly appeared interested… Dresden had pushed. Perhaps he shouldn't have.

Interested. Heh. Dresden knew from talking to ladies that they often found Regulus attractive. Far more attractive than Regulus considered himself. Adelaide had stars in her eyes the first time she laid eyes on Regulus, and Regulus hadn't even noticed, the poor man. He'd been too busy falling for her.

But this…this was dangerous.

Dresden opened his eyes and shoved off the door. He dragged a trunk out of his closet and began packing for the tournament. It had always been a dangerous game. The possibility of Adelaide getting hurt was more real than he liked. But was it so bad to want to see Regulus truly happy again?

A tournament, though? He cursed again. Adelaide was supposed to give Regulus a reason to *live*, and she was certainly doing that, but to stay alive, Regulus needed to keep his secret. Dresden had refused to behead him. If Regulus' secret was uncovered, someone else would do it. Worse, if Regulus made a mistake and revealed himself at this tournament and was killed, it would be Dresden's fault.

His meddling was going to get Regulus killed.

"Damn it!" He hurled a shirt into the open trunk, which wasn't at all satisfying.

The bedroom door squeaked open, and he spun around. Harold walked in and raised a brow at the clothes haphazardly strewn in the trunk.

"Going somewhere?"

"We all are," Dresden muttered. He stopped to consider. "I think. I don't know; ask his love-struck idiotship." He kicked the sleeve of a shirt inside the trunk.

Harold blinked. "What?"

Dresden sank onto the end of his bed. "Regulus entered the Etchy Tournament. Because Adelaide is going to be there."

"Wait, truly?" Harold grinned. "That's great!"

"Great?" Dresden grunted. "Fool's going to get caught! You know what Baron Carrick will do to him if he's seen healing? Or lifting something he shouldn't be able to? If they realize he has a bond to a sorcerer? They'll execute him."

Harold paled. "But…it's not his fault."

"They won't care," he snapped. "Regardless of *why*, Regulus is working with a sorcerer. That's illegal. And most of the nobles don't like him much to start with."

"But…" Harold fidgeted with his hands. "He won't get caught. He's smart and careful. Regulus must believe he can hide it, or he wouldn't enter, right? You trust Regulus, don't you?"

Dresden sighed. "Yes. I'm just worried."

"You're worried?" Harold chuckled. "I have a big responsibility. I have to pack for him."

"What—"

"Making a good impression on Lady Adelaide falls on me." Harold winked.

A smile tugged at Dresden's mouth. "Maybe try to favor shirts that hug his arms a little…"

"On it." Harold laughed, but his smile faded and he shuffled his feet. "I also…don't really know what to do…as his squire. I've never been to a tournament."

"Oh." Dresden stood. "Come on." He walked past Harold out the door and headed down the castle hallway.

"Where are we going?"

He glanced over his shoulder. "I went to a tournament once, but I was fourteen and Regulus wasn't competing. I can tell you a lot, but not everything. So, we're going to do something I've always wanted to." He rubbed his hands together. "We're going to go poking into Perceval's and Caleb's pasts."

MY TURN
About three weeks later
After Regulus and Adelaide leave for the sorcerer's tower together
Location: Arrano

"WHERE IS SHE?" Carrick's upper lip pulled up in a sneer. "And where is your mongrel lord?"

Dresden glared, his arms crossed as he blocked the closed front doors into the castle.

Gaius and his father stood behind Carrick. Gaius shifted, looking like he had tasted something sour. "Sir Carrick, I think this line of inquiry is both needlessly crass and futile. Why would your betrothed leave your side to visit another man unescorted?" There was a note of suspicion in Gaius' tone, and accusation in his eyes. Gaius Drummond was no fool.

Confusion pinched Lord Drummond's brows. The seven knights behind them waited, looking impatient as Dresden continued to block the entry.

"Yes, Sir Carrick," Dresden said, his tone mocking. "Surely you don't fear your betrothed is with another? If you love each other, it would be nonsense to suspect such a thing."

Carrick reddened. "I don't think she came here; I think Hargreaves must have followed us and taken advantage of her being out alone to kidnap her. Now where is Hargreaves!"

Dresden leaned back against the doors, keeping his voice level. "Your betrothed was out alone? Why didn't you accompany her? Did Lady Belanger not wish for your company?"

Lord Drummond cleared his throat. "I'm confused as well. Why do Gaius and this knight seem…suspicious of your engagement, Sir Carrick?"

Gaius clenched his jaw like he wanted to say something but couldn't.

"I, for one," Dresden said, locking eyes with Carrick, "suspect he threatened and forced the Lady Belanger into an engagement she doesn't want."

Carrick's fist connected with Dresden's jaw before he had a chance to react. Dresden's head whipped to the side and cracked against the door. He blinked spots from his eyes and rubbed his aching jaw as he straightened. "Strike a nerve, Carrick?"

"I will not tolerate such slander," Carrick snarled. "Especially not from a

Carasian peasant. Make another claim like that, and I'll have you dragged before the court for bearing false witness against a nobleman."

Dresden gulped. For a common-born knight like him and a foreigner at that, such a charge could receive a death sentence.

"Now. Where. Is. Your. Master?"

"My *lord* is not home at present." Dresden lowered his hand from his throbbing jaw, trying to look unconcerned.

Carrick chuckled. "Please, Jakobs, no need to pretend. My father did his research. I know what you really are. Hargreaves shows his coarseness well by knighting a former indentured servant."

Lord Drummond gasped, and Gaius' eyes widened. The other knights frowned. Heat flared over Dresden's neck and face. He didn't need their acceptance, but their disdain still made him angry. He focused on Regulus. Regulus needed time to escape. And Regulus never let the nobles know they had gotten to him. So, Dresden kept his voice as calm as possible.

"My previous employment doesn't change the fact that Lord Hargreaves is not at home and is not expected back for some time."

"Fine." Nolan lifted his chin, a triumphant gleam in his eyes. "In the name of my father, Baron Carrick, acting as his authorized representative on account of suspected criminal activity, I hereby compel you to allow us entry, or be found in breach of Hargreaves' oath of fealty."

Dresden had no idea if that was something Carrick could do, but he sounded confident, and Dresden wouldn't risk calling Regulus' loyalty to Baron Carrick into question. Hopefully Regulus and Adelaide had gotten out by now.

"Very well, Sir Carrick." He bowed, opened the door, and stepped into the foyer.

"Hargreaves!" Carrick shoved Dresden aside as he strode in. "Come out! Search every inch of this place," he growled to his knights.

Dresden stepped forward. "You have no right—"

Carrick turned and kicked Dresden in the gut. Dresden gasped and leaned forward, shocked by the sudden attack.

"I have every right, peasant. My *betrothed* is missing!" Carrick backhanded Dresden's face, then punched his stomach. Dresden coughed and stumbled back, wishing he'd put on his scimitars that morning. His stomach ached along with his jaw.

"Sir Carrick!" Gaius pulled Dresden aside by the elbow in a surprising gesture of camaraderie. "I know you are…concerned about Adelaide's wellbeing, but show some restraint."

"You're right." Carrick inclined his head. "I'm on edge with worry. That was uncalled for." He looked at the other knights. "Search the castle and grounds. Kilcurn, stay with me. Everyone else, spread out. Quickly!"

The knights, including Lord Drummond and Gaius, although he looked reluctant and unhappy, dispersed into the castle and back out into the courtyard. A muscular knight with stringy brown hair stayed behind.

Carrick drew his sword and used it to motion Dresden further inside. As soon as Dresden moved deeper into the foyer, Carrick pressed the tip of the sword to his back. "Now. Show me to your master's room. And no delays or wrong turns, unless you want a prick."

Dresden clenched his fists. "Fine."

"Yes, my lord." He could hear the sneer in Carrick's voice.

"If you want to call me that," Dresden said with a shrug.

"Imbecile." Carrick pushed the blade into Dresden's back, and Dresden lurched forward to avoid the sharp tip.

"Right this way." He led them directly to Regulus' room. Which was, of course, empty. To his surprise, it wasn't locked—Harold must have been too distracted to remember to lock it. Thankfully, the mirror was put away, and he thanked Etiros Magnus wasn't there. The dog had probably gone down to the kitchens, as he often did when Regulus was gone. After what Carrick had ordered done to Sieger, he didn't want to know what Carrick would do to Magnus in his current mood.

"This is Hargreaves' room?" Carrick sounded incredulous. "Not very lordly. Are you lying to me?"

Dresden sighed. "I have a sword pointed at my back; why would I lie? You want proof? There's dog hair everywhere. You think Regulus' dog sleeps in a spare room? No, this is his room. And as you can see, he is not here."

Carrick brushed past him, looking around as if Regulus and Adelaide might be hiding somewhere. He even checked under the wide bed and inside the wardrobe.

"If Hargreaves isn't here"—Carrick turned on Dresden with a snarl—"where is he?"

Dresden lifted a shoulder. "He left on business. Didn't tell me where."

"Business? What business?"

"Didn't ask. He would have told me if he wanted me to know."

"Kilcurn, bring him along. We'll check the other bedrooms on this floor."

Kilcurn shoved Dresden down the hall. Carrick threw open a door to a room with drawn curtains and a few pieces of furniture covered in sheets. He marched in and searched every nook and cranny anyway, checking under the bed and inspecting the dusty sheet covering it as if it might be a ruse.

"My, my," Dresden said drily after Carrick slammed the door behind him. "You must really be worried your betrothed would rather slip between the sheets with Regulus than with you."

Carrick stopped short and turned slowly. "Know something I don't, peasant?"

"Only noting that you seem oddly concerned with checking beds." Dresden rolled his eyes. "But even if they were here, you wouldn't find them in a bedroom. Regulus has far more honor than you do."

Carrick stepped closer. "I tire of your attitude. Grab him."

Kilcurn seized Dresden's arms as Carrick drove his fist into his stomach. Dresden bent over, unable to draw in a breath. He could barely struggle in Kilcurn's grip. Carrick hit him again, and Dresden gasped for air as his knees buckled, but Kilcurn held him on his feet.

"Apologize, peasant." Carrick looked down his nose.

Dresden glared at Carrick and straightened. He kept his mouth firmly closed. Carrick punched his mouth, making his gums bleed, then hit his kidneys, his ribs, his stomach. Dresden stared at the floor, sagging in Kilcurn's grasp as he took Carrick's rage. He held his moans behind clenched teeth while he hoped Adelaide and Regulus had made it into the tunnel unseen.

"Stop!" Harold cried. Dresden lifted his head as Harold ran down the hall toward them. "What are you doing? Leave him alone!"

Carrick frowned. "That's no way to address a nobleman."

Harold bowed. "I'm sorry, my lord—" Carrick slapped Harold so hard he stumbled sideways into the wall.

"Hey!" Dresden pulled against Kilcurn's iron hold.

"Don't interfere unless you want a beating, too, boy." Carrick looked back at Dresden. "Where was I? Oh, yes." His fist flew into Dresden's stomach. A groan betrayed Dresden's pain.

"Wait." Carrick lowered his fist. "Boy."

Dresden glanced over at Harold, pressed against the wall and watching with horror. His mouth went dry. "I'm sorry, my lord. Leave the lad out of it. I apologize."

Carrick grunted. "I'm unconvinced you're sorry, but this isn't about your insubordination. Boy, is your master here?"

Harold shook his head. "No, he's away on some business, my lord."

"So everyone keeps saying." Carrick pointed at Dresden. "This one. He's Hargreaves' favorite, isn't he?"

Harold looked at Dresden, his eyes wide and jaw trembling.

"I'll take that as a yes. Where does your master keep his whip?"

Dresden chuckled, even as his legs shook. "Regulus doesn't keep a whip."

Harold shook his head. "Regulus hates the whip."

"What?" Carrick sighed. "Fine, I'll make do with a belt. Kilcurn, take the peasant outside. Boy, if your master is here, he has five minutes to show himself before I beat Jakobs."

Harold paled. "My lord, please, he's not here! He left! You can check the stables; his horse is not here."

"You can't do this," Dresden said as Kilcurn dragged him backward. "It's against the law! And Regulus isn't here! If he was, he would have presented himself already."

Carrick shrugged. "I'll believe he's not here if he doesn't show when your cries echo off the walls of his castle."

Dresden let Kilcurn drag him outside. Carrick wouldn't dare. And if he did, Dresden wanted to save his strength to fight then. In the courtyard, Kilcurn forced him to his knees. He stared straight ahead at a half-dead bush. Harold had visited the stables to ensure Regulus and Adelaide left and to slip some food in their saddlebags, so his return meant they were safely away. But would the sorcerer keep his word? Dresden had kept hope all these years, but now Regulus' fears wormed into his own heart. And what if something happened to Adelaide? Regulus would never forgive himself, and he might never forgive Dresden for pressuring him to court her or to take her to the sorcerer.

"Here." Carrick's voice. "I found this. Should be enough to fit around that tree."

Kilcurn yanked Dresden to his feet and shoved him forward. *Oh, no.* He wasn't about to be tied to a tree and beaten. He twisted and lunged to the side, slipping out of Kilcurn's grip. Another man ran up, and Dresden raised his fist, but someone knocked him down from behind. Three pairs of hands grabbed his arms and hair.

"Get your hands off me!" Dresden lashed out with his feet and tried to pull free, but too many hands held him, dragging him toward the tree. They shoved him against the trunk and his face scraped against rough bark. Bodies pushed against him as he struggled and hollered. Someone fastened a rope around his left wrist, and a few moments later, around his right wrist. The men released him with his arms now fastened around the trunk of the tree.

"Carrick, you—" Dresden unleashed a string of curses as the bark pressed into his chest.

"Sir Carrick!" Gaius sounded appalled. "What is the meaning of this?"

"The bastard won't come out, so I'll draw him out." Venom filled Carrick's voice. "Cut open his shirt."

"Sir Carrick, I will not allow this!"

Dresden strained to peer over his shoulder. Gaius stood behind him, shielding him. A noble…that wasn't Regulus…was protecting him. Maybe there were more good men in this world than he thought.

"What do you care, Sir Gaius?" Carrick made a sound of disgust. "He's a peasant and a Carasian."

"He's a knight," Gaius shot back.

"Raised to that position by a bastard."

"By a lord," Gaius said. "Lord Hargreaves is of higher rank than you, might I remind you, Sir Carrick. He could bring charges against you for striking his man. Nor can you legally beat a knight in this manner. Furthermore, you cannot succeed in your aim. Lord Hargreaves and Lady Belanger are clearly not here. We have looked everywhere and not found a sign of them. Lord Hargreaves' horse is missing, and my sister-in-law's horse is not here."

"I will not abide this either, Sir Carrick," Lord Drummond said, sounding ill at ease. "I doubt your father would approve."

Carrick crossed his arms. "So they're not here. Doesn't mean they weren't here and left and are just waiting for us to depart before returning. Let me beat the truth out of the servant."

"Absolutely not, Sir Carrick." Gaius' tone was firm. "You have yet to ask Lord Belanger's permission to marry his daughter. Do this, and I will ensure Lord Belanger knows you are not a fit suitor for his daughter, as you will have demonstrated a propensity for violence and a lack of honor and self-restraint."

There was a tense moment of silence. Dresden held his breath.

"Very well," Carrick said. "Help me release him then, Sir Gaius."

Gaius set about untying Dresden's right hand. His expression was a mixture of concern and outrage, and he met Dresden's eyes apologetically. Carrick spoke softly as he untied the rope from Dresden's left wrist.

"I would not place yourself between me and Adelaide, Sir Gaius. Be a shame if Lady Minerva experienced any complications so late in her pregnancy. Am I clear?"

Gaius tensed, his temple twitching as he slipped the rope from Dresden's wrist. "Very clear." His throat bobbed.

Carrick finished loosening the rope. Dresden pulled back, clenching his fists until his fingers ached, but he knew better than to strike and give Carrick an excuse to punish him. Where were the rest of the men? Perceval and Jerrick lived on their holdings just outside the castle. If they were inside or busy behind their homes, they wouldn't have noticed Carrick's arrival. Estevan and Caleb…Dresden ground his teeth as he remembered. They'd gone hunting. And the guard on duty at the gate was only a hired freeman who would fear acting against a baron's son. He was on his own.

Carrick looked around. "Well. New plan. If I'm correct, Hargreaves is waiting for us to leave to return. So, we need to make it look like we've left." He looked to Lord Drummond. "I'll remain with my knights. Everyone else will depart."

Dresden gulped. With Gaius gone, there would be no one to stop Carrick from releasing his fury. "You'll be disappointed. My lord will not be returning for some time. Possibly days."

"Then I will remain until tomorrow, and if he has not shown himself, I will believe you."

"I will remain as well," Gaius said.

"I think your wife will miss you," Carrick said, his tone light. "That seems unnecessary." He cast a meaningful look at Gaius. Gaius lowered his gaze and nodded.

Lord Drummond looked uncomfortable, but he agreed. The Drummonds and all but three of the knights departed. The moment the gate closed behind them, Carrick snorted.

"Tie this peasant fool back to that tree."

Dresden didn't bother to fight. What would be the point? He couldn't hold them off forever, and he wouldn't try to hide like a coward. They bound him to the tree and cut open his shirt.

"Huh." Carrick sounded astonished. "Some scars, but these are battle wounds. How many years as an indentured servant and a mercenary, and you never once felt the sting of a whip?"

Dresden stared at the ground, his cheek pressed against the trunk as shame heated his face. "As Harold and I told you, Regulus loathes the whip."

"You must have been an exceptionally well-behaved mercenary to never earn a taste of it. The mongrel wasn't your captain the entire time, was he?"

"No." Dresden's throat tightened.

"Your prior captains also loathed the whip?" Carrick sounded truly confounded.

Dresden took a deep breath, making the bark dig into his torso. There was no point in earning a harsher beating by refusing to answer. "No, Regulus is the only captain I know who didn't use lashings as discipline."

"Why?"

"I suppose he didn't like how it felt on his own back," Dresden bit out.

Carrick stared at him a moment, then laughed. "Does he have the scars? Does Half-Breed's back look like that of a slave?" He shook his head, still laughing. "Oh, as much as I hope he's not currently with my bride, the thought of her discovering his shame…" He chuckled. "Almost makes me less angry. Almost." He grinned viciously. "Well, it will be my honor to acquaint you with the concept of a proper beating, Carasian."

Dresden braced himself as Carrick stepped closer and drew back the belt. A commotion at the gate drew their attention.

"Hargreaves?" Carrick said as the gate swung open.

"Regulus Hargreaves! Please, I need to speak to a Regulus Hargreaves of Arrano!" A harried, frightened-looking lone man rode into the courtyard. Lather covered his horse's neck and foam dripped from its mouth. The rider, dressed like a noble out for a hunt, complete with the bow and quiver strung over his back, must have pushed the beast hard. The man gaped at Dresden. "What…" He shook his head and looked at Carrick. "Sir Carrick, right?"

"Sir Nolan Carrick, yes."

"Oh, good!" The man sagged in his saddle, his features relaxing. "She told me to find Regulus Hargreaves and Nolan Carrick."

"She?" Carrick asked. Dresden stared at the man, fear writhing in his stomach.

The man dismounted, his entire body shaking. "I was hunting, a few miles north of here, and I fell behind my party." He spoke quickly, tripping over his own tongue. "I heard something and thought it was my party, but it was…it was…" His eyes bugged, and he licked his lips and swallowed hard. "The Black Knight. Dear Etiros above, I saw him, I saw him with my own eyes, taller than any mortal man, a voice like thunder in that horned helm. Like a demon astride a massive black horse. He caught the arrow I shot. Caught it in his hand!"

He'd definitely seen Regulus and Adelaide. Thank Etiros Regulus had worn that stupid armor.

"He'd taken a lady captive," the man said. "She said her name was Adelaide, and to find Regulus Hargreaves of Arrano and Nolan Carrick and tell them the Black Knight had taken her." He wiped a trembling hand across his glistening forehead. "That's all she said before he silenced her."

"Explain," Carrick demanded. "What do you mean, captive? Silenced her?"

"Her hands were bound, her horse tied to his," the man said. "And after she cried out, he covered her mouth so she couldn't speak; treated her roughly."

"The Black Knight," Carrick muttered. "No. She was never here. She was taken, and I've been wasting time while she was in danger…" He shook his head. "Wait. He silenced her, but she was not gagged. Did she appear injured?"

"No, not gagged, just her hands bound." The man hesitated. "She appeared frightened, but unharmed. I noticed no wounds, although…there may have been blood on her skirt. Or dirt, as her clothes didn't look torn. I don't know. It happened so fast."

Carrick nodded slowly. "Someone take this man inside and get him some water. Find him a fresh horse. Sir…?"

"Hostland," the man said with a slight bow.

"Sir Hostland, will you lead me to where you saw them?"

"Of course." He glanced around. "Is Regulus Hargreaves here as well?"

Carrick grunted. "He is away on business, apparently." One of the knights led Sir Hostland inside, and Carrick turned back to Dresden. "Where is Hargreaves?"

"I told you. I don't know where his business was taking him." Dresden frowned. "But it seems you know where Adelaide is, so why do you care where Regulus went?"

Carrick moved over to stand across from Dresden's face and tilted his head. "You want to know what I think? I think Adelaide would not allow herself to be taken without a fight. You know she carries blades." A wicked smirk curved his mouth. "Based on how quickly Hargreaves, that boy, and the horse healed, I'm going to guess you know she's a mage."

Dresden's lips parted. Carrick knew?

"Ah, but you didn't know that I knew." Carrick looked thoroughly amused. "Adelaide is a fighter. The first time I threatened her, she nicked my face with her blade. She wouldn't be taken unharmed, her clothes dirtied but not damaged. Why bind her hands but not gag her? Why let her be on her own horse at all? Why even take her? The Black Knight has never taken a maiden before. And Hargreaves is gone, as is his large black horse. So tell me, *Sir* Jakobs—is your master the Black Knight?"

Dresden laughed and hoped it didn't sound too forced. "Oh, I hope so. Would explain some things. And I hear the Black Knight can't be killed, so if Regulus is the Black Knight, I'll look forward to him going after you." He sobered. "But more importantly, I like Lady Adelaide. If the Black Knight has her, I hope to Etiros that the Black Knight is Regulus."

"You're smarter than you look, Carasian." Carrick tapped the belt against his leg. "Option one. The Black Knight really has taken Adelaide, Half-Breed is uninvolved, and Sir Hostland just didn't notice her injuries. Or perhaps the Black Knight caught her unawares. Seems unlikely. Option two, Adelaide arranged for the Black Knight to capture her in order to avoid me, and it has nothing to do with Hargreaves. Possible, but exceedingly unlikely, don't you think?"

Dresden glared at Carrick in response.

"Option three. Hargreaves has been the Black Knight this entire time, which is why the Black Knight appeared shortly after Hargreaves took over Arrano and why Hargreaves randomly disappears. He's pretended to kidnap Adelaide as the Black Knight to clear his own name. Whether she came here or he found her, I don't know, but that's the most logical explanation. Now tell me." Carrick used the folded belt to lift Dresden's chin. "Where are they going?"

Dresden knew where the sorcerer's tower was. He could tell and let the sorcerer finish Carrick off. He could deny that Regulus was the Black Knight, but Carrick wouldn't believe him. Or he could admit Regulus was the Black Knight, but claim he had no idea where they were going. That was true since he didn't know if the sorcerer might send them somewhere else. Which answer would be least likely to earn him a beating while still protecting Regulus as long as possible?

"I don't know."

A grim smile darkened Carrick's face. "I was rather hoping you'd be difficult." He stepped back, and a moment later, the belt cracked against Dresden's back. Dresden grimaced and clenched his fists. "Where are they headed?"

"Regulus didn't say," Dresden muttered.

"Hm." Carrick chuckled. "But you don't deny *they* headed out together?"

He closed his eyes. *Damn it.* Carrick hit him again. The sound of the belt against his skin echoed in his ears.

"That's for lying. Now. What's their plan?"

"I swear, I don't know. I can't tell what I don't know."

The belt slammed into his back again, making his skin smart and burn and sending pain down to his ribs.

"Um…Sir Carrick?" Sir Hostland interrupted. "Does the servant's beating need to happen while the lady is in danger?"

I'm not a servant. There was no point in voicing the thought aloud. He looked like a servant. Weaponless, foreign, tied to a tree and being beaten by a knight. There was no one around to verify his status.

"True." Carrick hit Dresden again, and Dresden bit back a cry as he flinched against the trunk. "We must depart. Bring my horse! The *servant*," Carrick said with delight, "can receive the rest of his beating another day."

The belt whirred and bit into his skin once more, and Dresden's eyes watered as he clenched his teeth, determined not to reveal his pain. Carrick moved in close to Dresden's back.

"If I'm wrong," Carrick whispered, "or if I miss Hargreaves and he makes it back here, do tell your master—those stripes were for him."

Carrick and his men departed with Sir Hostland, leaving Dresden tied to the tree. The moment the gates closed, Harold appeared, tears on his face as he fumbled with the rope.

"I hope Regulus kills him!" Harold sniffed, then cursed at the rope. He drew a dagger from his belt and cut through the binding.

Dresden pulled away from the tree and winced, the smarting and aching in his back joining the throbbing of the bruises forming from Carrick's punches. And that was only five lashes. Regulus had borne more at fourteen. The humiliation hurt far more. Part of him was glad the rest of the knights weren't in the castle.

"Harold, tell the guardsmen not to allow anyone else in unless they're one of Regulus' knights or Regulus himself. Or Lady Belanger." He held his other wrist out to Harold, and Harold cut through the rope. "Then meet me in my room. I'm going to need help with some salve."

Harold nodded and turned to go, but Dresden caught his arm.

"And Harold…" He swallowed hard. "No one else needs to know."

"No." Harold shook his head and pulled away. "They do. And you should tell them."

"What?"

Harold sighed. "The guard knows, some of the servants know. The others are likely to find out. You're always telling Regulus he doesn't need to pretend to be fine. Don't be like Regulus. Not in this."

Dresden gazed across the courtyard, fighting with himself. He didn't want them to know his failure. But would he judge any of them if they had been in his place? No. And hiding his pain would be near impossible. He sighed and immediately regretted it as a stab of pain accompanied the heave of his lungs.

"You're right, Harold."

"Of course I'm right; it's what you'd tell me." Harold grinned, but the look faded, replaced by worry. "Go on. I'll be up with the salve shortly."

WAITING
Five Days Later
Location: Arrano

EARLY MORNING sunlight provided dim light from the single window at the end of the hall as Dresden left his room and headed toward Regulus'. Harold stepped out of Regulus' room, a downcast look on his face and Magnus at his side. Dresden stopped and slumped against the wall. He winced as the worst bruise, just below his left shoulder, pinched. Most of the bruises on his ribs and abdomen from Carrick's fists had faded to yellow splotches. When he'd checked his back in the mirror last night, the welts had healed, but the bruise beneath his left shoulder still had blue spots and ached when he moved his shoulder. Harold looked up from locking Regulus' door and met his eyes.

"He will come back, right?"

Dresden almost lied. But he wouldn't do that to Harold. "I don't know."

Harold's entire body crumpled. "I think he will," he whispered before heading to the stairs to the kitchens.

Every morning, Dresden headed straight for Regulus' room, hoping to find him asleep in his bed. Five days had passed since Regulus had taken Adelaide to do the sorcerer's bidding—and Carrick went after them. The earliest Dresden supposed they could have returned was the third day. A day to get to the sorcerer's tower and another back, and a day to do whatever the sorcerer needed. Which meant one of two things. The sorcerer had sent them somewhere far, or…they weren't coming back. Whether because the sorcerer hadn't kept his word or because Carrick had found them. Although if Carrick had killed Regulus, surely someone would have confiscated Arrano by now.

Magnus rubbed against Dresden's legs and whimpered. He petted the big dog's fluffy head absently. Every day that passed killed more of Dresden's hope. For so long, he had focused on getting Regulus through. On the promise of freedom. What if he had been wrong? What if the sorcerer had killed Regulus and Adelaide? *Maybe I should have cut his arm off. If it worked, at least they'd both still be alive.* But the thought turned his stomach.

Etiros…I know I have no right to ask. I'm not very faithful. But for Regulus' sake…protect them. Bring them back safely. Please.

He sighed and continued down the opposite staircase to the great hall. The rest of the men were waiting there when Dresden arrived. He shook his head. Their expressions fell, and they trudged out of the hall in silence.

Regulus wasn't back the next morning, either. The seventh morning, Dresden stared at the ceiling in the dark. Was it worth checking? A sinking feeling warned him Regulus wouldn't be there. He might never be there again. Dresden didn't think he could bear to be alone.

He'd left his family. Even if he went to Lanure Duchy and looked for his parents, he didn't know if he would find them. At this point, they might not want him back. He'd made Regulus his family when he chose to leave with him. If Regulus died, he would have no one. No family.

No, he would have Harold. But they were a family now, Regulus and Harold and Dresden and the others, and Regulus was its heart. *I need you to come back, Reg.*

Rapping sounded on his door. Dresden frowned. The rapping intensified, and he rushed to the door without bothering to put on a shirt. He flung open the door to Harold's smiling face. Harold. Smiling. His hopeful question stuck in his throat.

"My lord has summoned you and the other knights to a meeting over breakfast. You're to go at once."

Dresden closed his eyes and rested his forehead against the doorframe. "He's alive. He's back."

"Yes."

Dresden grinned and opened his eyes, but his smile fell when he saw the uncertainty in Harold's eyes. "What's wrong?"

Harold shifted. "He wasn't wearing the armor. And…the Lady Adelaide is not with him. I didn't dare ask…"

"Oh."

Regulus had returned without Adelaide and called a meeting with his knights. His stomach twisted in on itself. Something had gone horribly wrong.

"I have to go tell the others." Harold darted away.

Dresden got ready and rushed to the hall, his mind troubled. He considered going straight to Regulus' room, but surely Regulus would explain everything. He tapped his hand impatiently on the table. The main door swung open and Perceval hurried in.

"You know anything?" Perceval took a seat. "Harold didn't tell me anything other than that Regulus summoned us. Whatever prompts the captain to *summon* us to a meeting at dawn after he's been gone for a week…" He shook his head. "Gives me a bad feeling."

Dresden nodded. "I agree. Harold mentioned Regulus arrived with his armor gone…and without Adelaide."

Perceval stiffened, then scratched his cheek. "I don't like the sound of that."

"Me neither."

They fell silent. Dresden watched the stairwell door, his nerves buzzing.

The main door behind him swung open, and Caleb walked in, mid yawn. He mussed his shaggy blond hair. "You talk to him yet, Drez?"

"No."

"He returned without his lady," Perceval said as Caleb sat down.

Caleb grimaced. "Etiros have mercy."

Finally, Regulus entered the hall. Dresden shot to his feet. Dark circles shadowed Regulus' tired eyes, and he was frowning, but he seemed uninjured…although with the sorcerer's powers, that didn't mean much. Regulus smiled slightly and nodded. Dresden nodded back, some of his worry melting away. Regulus didn't seem frantic. He'd been able to smile. *It's all right.* Dresden eased back onto his chair, perched forward to avoid putting pressure on a couple bruises still healing on his back. They didn't hurt anymore—unless he bumped them.

He wanted to ask Regulus questions, but knew they had to wait for the others. Estevan finally came in, and shortly after, Jerrick ran in, but then the servants brought in breakfast. Dresden wouldn't have thought he could eat, but as the savory aromas filled his nostrils, he changed his mind. While he and the men ate, Regulus spoke.

"I'm certain you have questions. I will try to cover everything, but we are pressed for time."

Dresden tried to control his impatience as Regulus took a bite. If Regulus was worried about time and still eating, he must be starved. Still, Dresden wanted to know what had happened as quickly as possible.

"Much has happened since I left," Regulus continued. "Of first importance"—he rolled up his right sleeve—"the sorcerer released me. My debt is fulfilled."

Dresden froze with his fork midair and stared. The mark was gone; only the scars remained as a testament to the hell his friend had been through. He barely noted the other men's responses as joy rose in his chest. "Then it's over?" He lowered his fork.

The look of pain that flashed through Regulus' expression made Dresden's heart clench. "Not really, no. Unfortunately, the sorcerer *is* actually a prince." Regulus focused on his goblet. "Prince Kirven. The king's brother. He is plotting to kill the king and seize the throne."

Dresden didn't see what that had to do with them. Regulus was finally free, and Dresden was not about to let him throw away his life a second time. "So send the king a message. Who is king doesn't concern us."

"Considering the sorcerer seems bent on death, destruction, and revenge…yes, it should concern us." Regulus' fingernail clicked against his goblet. "But more directly, it concerns Adelaide and me."

Dread choked down the curse Dresden wanted to utter.

"He took Lady Belanger," Perceval growled.

"No. Adelaide is safe, or at least she was last I saw her."

Dresden's relief was short-lived as Regulus continued.

"But if the sorcerer succeeds, neither of us will be safe."

"Everything he made you do, everything he did to you, and he can't leave you alone?" Dresden was aware he was shouting, and he didn't care.

"The sorcerer? Perhaps. But, unfortunately…" Regulus' hand tightened around his goblet. He drew a steadying breath. "He has a new pet. A willing servant to whom he has promised wealth and political power for accepting the mark. If the sorcerer succeeds, Nolan Carrick succeeds with him. I'll be a dead man, and Adelaide…" His jaw clenched as he trailed off and attacked a soft-boiled quail egg.

It took a moment for Regulus' dire words to sink in. Dresden's back smarted with the remembrance of Carrick's belt, the slap of leather on his skin echoing in his ears. Sweat trickled down the back of his neck. No. This was supposed to be their triumph; their family was supposed to be whole and safe once Regulus was free. But if Nolan Carrick was immortal and the sorcerer became king, Regulus would be dead. They would all be dead—at best. He was going to be sick.

Caleb's tentative voice sounded small. "Carrick…has the mark?"

"Yes."

"He's like you were?" Perceval demanded. "Strong, fast…immortal?"

Regulus nodded, and something in Dresden snapped. After everything, after two years of torture, two years of fighting for hope, when Regulus was *finally* free, when they should have been celebrating, Regulus gained an immortal for a nemesis? The man who had tied Dresden to a tree and gleefully beaten him in his own home was bound to the sorcerer and possible future king?

His frustration exploded in a volley of incoherent cursing. He caught his breath in the stunned silence following his outburst and glared at the table. Wait… Why wasn't Adelaide with Regulus? His throat tightened. Surely Regulus wouldn't be so calm if Carrick had her. "Reg. Where's Adelaide?"

"On her way to warn the king," Regulus said levelly. "We're not sure if any messengers got through. If she does as we agreed, she's going to the palace."

Some measure of calm settled over Dresden. At least Adelaide was safe. For now. Adelaide was too kind and good for a snake like Carrick to ever touch. A surge of protectiveness for the girl that helped and loved his brother rose in him, followed by dismay. Regulus was right—she wouldn't stay safe for long if someone didn't stop Carrick and the sorcerer. But facing Carrick *and* the sorcerer? That frightened him.

"If?" Estevan asked. "Why are you here, then?"

An excellent question. Dresden looked to Regulus, who was avoiding meeting any of their eyes.

"Through a series of events," Regulus said, "Adelaide and I were headed back to her father's castle when we learned that Carrick took the castle and is holding her parents hostage."

Just when Dresden thought the news couldn't get worse.

Regulus finally looked around at each of them with determination. "That's why I called you here. We have a new assignment. We're rescuing Lord and Lady Belanger."

"From a castle?" Dresden struggled to control his panic as he motioned at the others. "With what army? You're not immortal anymore, need I remind you, and we'd be facing someone who is! Six men can't storm a castle. And then we'll have to face Carrick?" He clenched his hands as he tried to block out the humiliating memory of his beating and focus on the current problem. "Do you have a plan? Some secret that will give us an advantage? Do—"

"Enough!" Regulus slammed the table, startling him. "We leave in half an hour."

"That's not an ans—"

"Sir Dresden," Regulus snapped. Dresden stiffened, his insides going cold. "Am I your captain or not? Am I your liege or not?"

Every word pummeled him, but he understood. Ever since Regulus had been a captain, their rule had been that Dresden wouldn't argue with him in front of the men—it undermined troop discipline and morale. But anger and worry marked Regulus' every word. He might not be thinking clearly. They couldn't undertake a mission like this on emotional responses, surely Regulus knew that.

"Regulus, attacking Carrick when he has the mark, especially in a castle, is—"

"We'll aim for stealth," Regulus said simply.

"And if we're caught?" Dresden hid his trembling hands under the table. "You—"

"Sir Jakobs! Do I answer to you? Or do you answer to me?"

Dresden swallowed a dozen hurt responses. Regulus didn't mean it. He couldn't. But Regulus gazed at him with a stony expression, his eyes cold.

I didn't take a beating for this side of you. Dresden shoved away from the table and regretted the sharp movement as the bruise on his shoulder blade smarted. "I'll be ready in the courtyard in half an hour, *my lord.*" He offered a mocking bow and hoped no one noticed his twinge of pain. An angry tear squeezed from the corner of his eye as he strode out of the hall.

Their status had never been equal, but for two years, Regulus had only treated him as a brother. Until… The thought slapped him in the face. *Adelaide.* What if Regulus didn't need him now that he had her? Would all his scheming and helping result in him losing his brother? Blaming the woman who had risked her life for Regulus and whose parents had been captured was wrong, but the thought persisted. Dresden was just getting his confidence, accepting that he didn't need the nobles' approval to be proud of himself, and finally had been secure in his friendship with Regulus. Now his confidence was unraveling.

By the time Dresden had donned chainmail, strapped his scimitars to his back, and headed to the stables, his distress had faded into understanding and shame. He knew Regulus didn't see him as a mere vassal. And regardless of status, a friend would express his concern in private, not throw accusations in public.

Besides, Regulus had to be stressed. Taking Belanger castle was a bold move, one that declared Carrick thought he had already won, and no action was off limits. Regulus was thoughtless with his words, but he had a lot on his mind. And Dresden was frightened and angry, but it had been wrong to take out that anger on a friend in distress. They had both behaved poorly.

Dresden waited while a stable boy saddled Horse, turning the conversation over in his mind, thinking about ways he could have handled his shock better.

Regulus walked in and spoke to another stable boy. Dresden mustered his humility and approached him. "Can I speak with you?"

"Actually, I was going to ask you the same," Regulus said quietly.

They moved out of the stables, but Regulus spoke first.

"They told me what Carrick did." His brows furrowed and his voice wavered.

Heat flared over Dresden's face.

"I'm sorry…" Anguish twisted Regulus' expression, and Dresden's fear of losing his friend crumbled.

"I told you I'd take a beating for you someday." Dresden tried for a half-hearted smile and wink to diffuse the awkward conversation. "I'd say we're even, except a belt doesn't leave the scars a whip does."

"You never owed me."

"And you never owed me, but you don't listen," Dresden countered.

Regulus mussed his hair and rubbed his sword hilt. "Are you—"

"I'm fine now, Reg." He didn't want to talk about it, and he needed to explain his outburst. "Worse was not knowing if you were alive for the last week. Not knowing if you'd ever come back." He recalled his crushing worry with a stab of indignation. "Why didn't you send word?"

"We were… I… There was a lot…" Regulus' head drooped. "I should have thought to. I'm sorry."

Dresden sighed, unable to hold on to his anger with the sincerity in Regulus' words. "Now you show up, tell me the man who tried to have you killed and beat me is immortal and teamed up with the sorcerer while you're normal again, and you want to face him? I panicked." He crossed his arms. "But I apologize. I shouldn't have publicly challenged you."

"But I shouldn't—"

"No. I was wrong, and I deserved that." He gritted out the words.

Regulus shook his head. "You're my friend first, Drez."

The reassurance was a balm to Dresden's aching heart. "And you're my friend. My brother. Always." He scratched his beard. "But you're my captain and my liege, too." He forced the truth out. "We can't be equals. No matter how much I wish otherwise."

Regulus' shoulders crept upward the way they did when he was embarrassed or guilty, confirming what Dresden already knew—Regulus wasn't leaving him behind, and he didn't like being Dresden's superior. Now that they were alone, they were brothers again, equals in all but title.

"But between us, I'm concerned," Dresden said. "I don't say this to blame you, so don't hear that. Carrick hates you. Enough he took it out on me with his fists and a belt. He'd have used a whip if he had one. He thinks he's untouchable now he's in league with the sorcerer. If Carrick captures the men, what do you think he'll do to them? And you? He'll tear you apart." He hoped Regulus read his fear and understood it wasn't doubt or insubordination.

Regulus fiddled with his gauntlet. "Which is why we won't act until we've scouted out the situation and agreed on a plan." He looked up. "I won't risk you all. The Belangers will have to wait until we have a plan that has a strong chance of success. But I have to try. I promised."

Of course the selfless fool did. Regulus rarely made promises, but never had he broken one, either. "A Hargreaves promise is a powerful thing."

The stable boys led their horses over. Regulus stroked Sieger's neck. "I hope you know, Drez, you're so much more than my knight or lieutenant. I'm sorry if I made you feel otherwise."

"As if I need your affirmation to know how spectacular I am." Dresden grinned and rubbed Horse's nose. Regulus rolled his eyes with a laugh. "Come on. Let's go save your future in-laws."

THE WAY THE rest of the men laughed and sang on the way to Belanger castle, it was easy to forget they were riding to infiltrate a castle held by a sorcery-enhanced Nolan Carrick. Dresden didn't know if they kept the mood light on purpose, or if Estevan and Caleb were really that bad at maintaining a somber mood, but he was glad of the frivolity. Regulus didn't seem to mind, although he wasn't contributing much other than the occasional snicker.

Harold, however, remained at Arrano. He had watched them leave with a spectacular pout while standing next to a moping, whining Magnus. It had taken all of Dresden's self-control not to laugh at the pair. But Regulus was insistent, and Dresden was more than happy to back him up—Harold wasn't going anywhere near Carrick. At least one of them had to live, and sixteen was too young to die needlessly.

"You've lost your mind," Perceval said. "We were in Bhitra."

"No, because Jerrick hadn't joined us yet," Caleb insisted.

"Surely he had. Jerrick!" Perceval moved his muscular gray destrier closer to Jerrick's bay stallion. "The time that Lawrence caught his apron on fire and panicked and dropped the ladle into the fire and stood there screaming while trying to decide if he saved the ladle or himself until Ivan tackled him and put out the flames, you were there, weren't you?"

Jerrick shook his head. "I think I would remember Lawrence catching himself on fire."

"Ha!" Caleb slapped his thigh and his horse snorted. "Told you! It must have been in Khastalland."

"It was Khastalland," Regulus confirmed. "I remember because that was also the night Lawrence decided to try every spice the merchants had cajoled him into buying at once, and the stew nearly melted my face off."

Dresden burst out laughing, recalling a red-faced Regulus spewing stew and yelling between guzzling water, demanding to know if Lawrence was trying to kill him. The stew had made even Dresden sweat, and his lips had tingled for half an hour. Lawrence hadn't experimented with spices after that.

Jerrick chuckled. "Well, respectfully, Regulus, you and spices don't get along."

"No, it was intense," Dresden confirmed.

Caleb and Perceval added their consent, although they weren't much more tolerant of spiciness than Regulus.

"And I thought the only interesting thing I missed joining the troop so late was the time a princess tried to seduce Regulus," Estevan said.

Poorly suppressed laughter moved through the group as Regulus groaned.

"I swear"—Regulus twisted in his saddle to point accusingly at the group—"if anyone so much as *breathes* a word of that nightmare fiasco to Adelaide, I will challenge you to a duel."

"Aw, I think Adelaide would probably find it amusing." Dresden grinned, his smile only getting wider when Regulus scowled. "Not like she can be jealous or hurt, since it was years ago and nothing happened and Adelaide has you now, anyway."

"Who do you think is getting the better end of that, by the way?" Estevan asked. "Regulus or Adelaide?"

Perceval hummed while Jerrick tilted his head to the side and Caleb tapped his chin. Regulus rolled his eyes.

"I did, obviously. Now go back to telling mercenary stories; it was more distracting."

For a moment, the mood grew somber, until Estevan said, "Did I ever tell you about the time I confused a constable into putting out a warrant of arrest for a chicken?"

Ignoring Estevan's new tale, Dresden guided Horse next to Sieger. "How is the plan coming?"

Regulus' lips pinched downward. "Not as complete as I would like. I'm hoping Carrick hasn't closed off the castle and I can send Caleb in. There's a side door we might be able to get in through, but it would be best if someone let us in. Hopefully Caleb can determine if there is anyone still loyal enough to the Belangers to risk helping us. We just need an entry and exit." He bit his lower lip. "But we have to get four additional people out. And I think Adelaide might have mentioned her brother having an infant. I'm trying to decide if we might have to settle for only Alfred and Tamina, and I don't like the idea."

Dresden fiddled with his reins. "We'll figure it out."

"I hope you're right."

"I'm always right."

Not only did Caleb find someone willing to let them in—and who arranged to have the guards near the side entrance drugged—Carrick had left. Where Carrick had gone and if Adelaide was all right made Regulus worry. Dresden shared Regulus' concerns, but he was too relieved with how well things were going and focused on his assignment to worry about a second problem. With Lord Belanger's loyal knights freed, Regulus had sent them to take back the castle.

It had been too long since Dresden had engaged in a real fight, and the rush of battle pounded in his veins. Regulus might have been off fighting monsters for the sorcerer, but his knights had been bored at home for two years. Dresden sidestepped another of Carrick's men and sliced across the man's abdomen. The traitor tumbled over the crenellated walkway above the front gates and fell into the courtyard as two more knights charged at Dresden.

Dresden parried a sword with one blade while blocking the other man's strike with his second scimitar. Keeping the second man's blade engaged, he drew his other scimitar over and cut open the man's thigh. A kick to the wound sent the second man stumbling sideways with a curse. Dresden pivoted and parried the first knight's thrust, then sliced the man's throat. He crouched to avoid the second knight's swing. The man's sword whipped over his head, so close the air displaced by the blade tousled his hair.

Dresden thrust a scimitar into the man's abdomen. The knights fell and Dresden straightened, scanning the moonlit battlements ahead, every inch of his body alert and energized. He didn't get any joy out of killing, but he did out of surviving, and there was only one way to survive a battle—let the blades dance, embrace the fight, claim every victory, and leave all other thoughts or emotion or penance until after the battle was won.

"Why are we even here?" one of Belanger's knights muttered behind him.

"I'm just glad to know Lady Belanger will be well-defended once she marries Lord Hargreaves," the other knight said. "Not that she needs much protection."

The first knight snorted as they continued toward the guard tower on the other side of the gate. "Charing, if I hear that story about the Belanger ladies fighting those bandits one more time, I swear to—"

The door to the guard tower banged open and a man burst out with his sword drawn. Dresden stepped aside and motioned with a scimitar to the charging man. "You were complaining I was taking all the fun?"

The knights made short work of Carrick's guard, and together they verified the rest of the tower was clear. Dresden headed back to the residence to look for Regulus. Shouting greeted him as he entered the castle's foyer.

"You don't even know where you're going!" Lord Belanger grabbed Regulus' shoulder and yanked him around. "We should see if any of the servants overheard anything more that would help us—"

"We? Us?" Regulus shrugged off Belanger's hand. "The whole point was to get you away from Carrick—if you come with me, Adelaide might kill me herself!"

Unease grew in Dresden's stomach. "What's happening?"

Regulus and Belanger turned toward him. Regulus' brows drew low over his eyes, his jaw tight. "The sorcerer found Adelaide and Carrick left to get her! I have to go." He stepped forward and grunted when Lord Belanger grabbed his arm to stop him.

"I'm coming, too," Dresden said. "The men should probably—"

"No." Regulus shook his head. "I'm going alone. I don't know if the sorcerer will be there—"

"All the more reason for help," Belanger said, still gripping Regulus' arm. "Let us plan, get some men—"

"Adelaide doesn't have time for that, and I won't lose any more of my friends!"

Dresden winced, his heart clenching at the memory of Ivan's glazed-over eyes.

Regulus looked away. "Besides, we should leave some men here to keep the castle locked down. No one should come in or out until Carrick and the sorcerer are dead."

Footsteps sounded behind Dresden. "I think the castle is all clear…why does everyone look so grim?" Jerrick walked up on Dresden's side, accompanied by Estevan.

"Good." Regulus looked over at them. "Drez, Jerrick, Estevan, I want you to return to Arrano and keep an eye on things. Keep Harold and Arrano safe until I return."

"I'm coming with you, and you aren't stopping me." Dresden crossed his arms.

Regulus' jaw ticked. "Dresden—"

"Regulus, Alfred!" Lady Belanger ran into the foyer from a door in the back corner, holding a lantern in one hand and dragging along a black-haired maid by the other hand. "Claire overheard! She knows where Carrick was headed!"

The maid gulped. "I… I was tidying—"

"All that matters is the location, Claire," Lady Belanger said with an impatient smile.

"Right…" The maid looked off toward the ceiling and spoke slowly. "The voice Carrick was talking to…he said something like, 'A mile or so north and a little east of Selcairn, in Flitlor Forest, near one of the streams coming off the Old Cairn River. You'll find her inside a shed near a burned-down house.'" The girl fidgeted with the skirt of her dress. "He told Carrick to do whatever he wanted with her."

All color drained from Regulus' cheeks, and Lord Belanger's face took on a green hue. Regulus wrenched his arm out of Lord Belanger's grip. "I have to go *now*."

"She's *my* daughter, Hargreaves, and you aren't leaving without me."

"Or me!" Dresden marched over and pointed in Regulus' face. "You disappeared on me for a week, and I thought you were dead! I'm not letting that happen again."

Regulus groaned. "Fine! You two can come, but only because we're wasting time arguing!"

"Claire." Lord Belanger turned to the servant girl. "Tell the stable master to ready my horse. Sir…" He looked to Dresden quizzically.

"Jakobs."

"Sir Jakobs, don't let your lord leave without me. I need to change and grab some supplies."

Regulus grunted. "There's no time—"

"My. Daughter." Lord Belanger started for the door in the back of the foyer. "She was my little girl long before she was your love, Regulus; don't you dare claim you care about her more than I do."

Dresden looked to Regulus. "You wait here, find Perce and Cal while I go fetch the horses."

Regulus nodded with a discontented scowl.

They departed in short order. Regulus instructed Jerrick and Estevan to return to Arrano, and Perceval and Caleb to help Lord Belanger's remaining knights keep Belanger castle secure. They rode hard and without stopping the rest of the night and the next day, barely speaking. Dresden hoped Adelaide was okay. Besides liking her as a person, he feared what both Lord Belanger and Regulus would do if they didn't find Adelaide unharmed.

THE FIGHT and aftermath once they found Carrick and Adelaide was something Dresden wished he could forget, but he knew would haunt his dreams forever. Sleep eluded him the night of the fight, despite his exhaustion.

Every time he closed his eyes, he saw one horror or another. Carrick burying his sword in Regulus' abdomen or walking away after Dresden ran him through with both scimitars—twice. Carrick's sneering face as he squeezed Dresden's neck and tossed him aside. Adelaide, gold burning in her glowing eyes, the blue light of the magical sword in her hands casting her face in sharp edges, and hungry wings of flame at her back. Regulus, still and pale as death, with a pulse so weak Dresden hadn't been able to feel it. Adelaide's eyes shining with golden fire as she marked Regulus' arm.

He rolled over again. Regulus slept nearby, his chest rising and falling with slow, deep breaths. The sight reassured Dresden, but he had been too close to losing Regulus, and it had shaken him.

Further away, Lord Belanger sat next to Adelaide's slumbering form, keeping watch. His back was to Dresden, and one hand absently stroked his daughter's hair. Neither Belanger nor Regulus seemed frightened by Adelaide's power—or her mark on Regulus' arm. But a mark in the same location as the sorcerer's, with the same power to save Regulus when he should have died, unnerved Dresden.

When the sun shining over the trees forced Dresden to abandon attempting to sleep, he sat up with a groan. His whole body ached. Two fights, a long ride, getting tossed around by the neck, and a restless night on the ground had taken their toll. Whatever wasn't bruised was stiff.

"Morning, sleepy head." Regulus' shadow fell over him.

Dresden grunted and rubbed his dry eyes.

"Here." Regulus held out a water skin, which Dresden gratefully took.

He wiped his mouth and handed back the skin, squinting up at Regulus. Regulus had removed the chainmail, and Dresden's gaze caught on the hole in Regulus' shirt where Carrick had impaled him. "How do you feel?"

Regulus sat down. "Physically, fine. A bit tired. But..." He sighed and looked over. Dresden followed his gaze to where Adelaide still lay in the grass.

Belanger had disappeared.

"She's still sleeping?"

Regulus nodded. "She's hardly moved." He slumped and touched the sleeve over his right forearm. "I'm trying not to worry. The fairies warned binding takes a lot of energy."

Dresden started. "The what now?"

"Oh. Right." Regulus lifted a shoulder. "The sorcerer drained Adelaide's magic. After going to the Belanger estate, where we learned that Carrick had joined the sorcerer, we went to the neumenet tree in Holgren to see if it could help her magic return. It did, but only after Adelaide passed some twisted test from the fairies guarding the tree. They gave her some tips and warnings and things to practice, and briefly mentioned bindings—"

"Wait, what did they look like? What kind of test? You didn't think to tell me you met fairies?" Sure, they had been busy and short on time, and Regulus had a lot on his mind, but…a run-in with creatures some claimed to be mere myth was no small matter. Besides his genuine curiosity, it hurt that Regulus hadn't told him.

Regulus leaned back on his hands. "Um, well." He cleared his throat and looked away. "They…they look like tiny people. I mean tiny, no taller than your hand is long. Except that they have wings. Small, shimmering wings that move like a hummingbird's. But anyway, after the tree gave Adelaide her magic back—"

"Okay, it's not suspicious at all that you skipped the test thing." Dresden crossed his arms. "Explain."

Regulus reddened and muttered something under his breath.

"What was that?"

He spoke too quickly for Dresden to understand.

"Regulus Daveth—"

"The fairies captured me and threatened to take me to their realm as their slave if Adelaide didn't steal magic from the tree the way the sorcerer does and fight them, but Adelaide refused to do sorcery, so she passed the test and they released me and the tree gave her power. Happy now?" Regulus didn't look at him, but his ears were scarlet.

"Happy?" Dresden shot to his feet. "You were *nearly enslaved in the fairy realm?* By all the…" He cursed, shaking his head. "Being your friend is a never-ending cycle of worry, you know that! Always endangering yourself to help others, getting yourself enslaved to sorcerers and captured by fairies—" He cut off abruptly. "By tiny fairies." He chuckled. "No bigger than my hand. You." His laughter built. "The great, feared mercenary Regulus Hargreaves was captured by fairies you could catch in your hand!"

"Yeah, yeah." Regulus glowered up at him. "If you're done lecturing *and* laughing at me, we have a more pressing problem." He gestured toward Adelaide. "She won't wake up. You just shouted to raise the dead, and she didn't stir."

Dresden sobered and sat down across from him.

Regulus rubbed the back of his neck. "I don't know anything about magic, Drez. I don't know if this is normal. The fairies warned her to do a binding only if she knew she had time to recover, but…I wouldn't have thought that meant…this."

"That's all they said about it?"

"Basically." Regulus shrugged. "They told her she'd felt a bond before when she had the sorcerer's mark—"

"Wait." Dresden held up a hand. "I really need you to tell me the whole story. The sorcerer put the mark on Adelaide? He can do that to a mage?"

Regulus' expression pinched as he nodded. "He stole her magic when he removed the mark. Anyway, they said that was the corrupted version. They'd told her how to imbue magic into objects, like the Staff, and said it's like that, but putting the magic into a person with a specific intent." He flopped back on the grass. "Not that I really understand what any of that means."

Dresden was struggling to keep up with all this information, especially half asleep and on an empty stomach. A horrifying thought occurred to him, resurrecting his fear about Adelaide's mark.

"She knew how to do it because she felt the sorcerer do it? You're…enslaved to her now?"

"What? No!" Regulus bolted upright. "How could you say that?"

Dresden held up his hands. "All I'm saying is she learned how to do it from a sorcerer and a bunch of trickster fairies, and put it on you after… Oh, Etiros." He scrambled to his feet and ran to Adelaide.

"What are you doing? Drez!"

But Dresden ignored Regulus running up behind him as he grabbed Adelaide's bare arm and inspected it. He breathed a relieved sigh. "She doesn't have his mark." He stood and turned to Regulus. "Doesn't mean he didn't somehow make her a sorcerer."

"That's not how magic works, fool." Lord Belanger walked toward them out of the nearby trees, his thin lips curved down. "Magic is corrupted by using it to better yourself at the expense of others. Does that look like what Adelaide did to you?" He motioned between his daughter, still asleep at Dresden's feet, and Regulus.

"Look." Regulus pushed up his sleeve. Dresden squinted at the design, the unbroken line like an intricate knot forming something like a diamond between two heart shapes. "It doesn't look at all like the sorcerer's," Regulus continued. "Or feel like it. I can't explain, it just…doesn't."

"I suppose," Dresden hedged.

"The fairies tempted her to use sorcery, and her refusal is why she has her magic at all." Regulus pulled his sleeve down. "She volunteered to be taken as a slave to the fairies' realm rather than become a sorcerer. Do you really think she would give into sorcery now?"

"She *what?*" Lord Belanger took a menacing step closer. "And why would she need to make such an offer? Where were *you?*"

"Being held captive by tiny fairies, apparently." Dresden was too on edge and annoyed with Regulus to come to his defense.

"I tried to tell her to run," Regulus said weakly. "As well as I could while gagged."

Dresden threw up his hands and paced away. Unbelievable. The stress was going to send him to an early grave.

"Listen," Regulus said, "Adelaide and I survived the fairies' test, she got her magic back, we're with her now so she's safe, and there is *no way* she is a sorceress."

Belanger grunted. "She's not safe as long as Kirven and Carrick are alive."

"I know," Regulus murmured.

"What about the wings?" Dresden asked. "The whole flaming wings, massive magic sword, eyes all glowing? Is that *normal* for her? And if so, how was she caught, anyway?"

Belanger's gaze dropped. "We tried to make her not use her power. We thought it would keep her safe." He rubbed the back of his neck. "Maybe if we hadn't, if we had given her the books and encouraged her to practice, maybe she would have been stronger…maybe she wouldn't have been captured. But because of that choice…I don't know what's normal for her. From knowing mages previously… Not unusual, no. And her sword was blue. Every mage I've ever met had magic in a shade of blue."

That aligned with the few mages Dresden had seen in their travels.

"And the sorcerer's magic is green," Regulus chimed in. "But..." He whistled. "I thought I had imagined the wings. A hysteria-induced vision as I was dying."

Belanger chuckled. "No, it was real. And breathtaking."

"Or terrifying," Dresden muttered. "But okay. You've convinced me." He looked down at Adelaide. Only the tiniest movement indicated her slow breaths. "At least for now, I'll believe Adelaide isn't dangerous."

Belanger laughed. "Oh, she's definitely that."

Regulus' scar pulled at his lips as he smiled. "Don't get me wrong, she's not a threat—to us. But my tigress has claws and a mean bite. Took down a mountain troll." He broke into a full-fledged grin as he looked down at Adelaide with admiration and tenderness.

"Troll?" Dresden rolled his eyes. "Part of me does *not* want to know any more about your adventures. The other part needs you to tell me everything, *now*."

"I'll get the food from my saddlebags," Belanger said as he headed toward their horses, tied to some trees nearby. "You can fill your friend in on what he doesn't know—and me on exactly what happened when you two snuck out."

"You...snuck out?" Dresden cocked an eyebrow. Adelaide really did bring out Regulus' reckless and rebellious side. "I'm definitely ready to hear this story."

Regulus explained everything in detail. Dresden made sure of it, stopping him to ask for clarification whenever necessary, and sometimes just to comment or laugh. As Regulus talked, his love for Adelaide radiated from him. From the way he kept glancing toward her, the way he sometimes said her name like a caress, how he described her fighting or her spunk with an awed gleam in his eye. She was a better match for Regulus than Dresden ever could have hoped. It made him look forward to her marrying Regulus, so he could get to know her better. She sounded like she would make a good sister...assuming she didn't steal Regulus from him.

The fear that she might hurt Regulus, the discomfort Dresden felt at how similar Adelaide's powers were to the sorcerer's, lingered in the back of his mind. Worse, his fear resurfaced: Regulus wouldn't need Dresden now that he had Adelaide.

"She argued at first," Regulus was saying, "but agreed to split up. Reminded me of you, Drez, how stubborn she was. You two will probably team up to lecture me when this is all over and we go home." He laughed.

Dresden relaxed, accepting the reassurance Regulus didn't even know he had given.

"Still, though, I wish I had listened." Regulus plucked at blades of grass. "Insisted we stayed together and warned the king. Maybe then she would never have been caught. Never would have been collared, and Carrick wouldn't have been able to touch her. She wouldn't be unconscious now. I was so stupid."

Dresden didn't know what to say.

Belanger cleared his throat. "And I may have made her vulnerable by the very steps I took to keep her safe. We all make choices, and sometimes we make the wrong one." He dragged his hand down the side of his face. "You did the best you could in a bad situation. Both of you did. You tried, and you thought you were doing the right thing. You couldn't know the outcome. More importantly, we can't change the past, son."

Regulus jerked. Dresden guessed Belanger had no idea the weight of his choice of word.

"Mental self-flagellation helps no one, including Adelaide. You have to let your mistakes go and focus on doing the next right thing. It's the only way to keep living." Belanger reached over and brushed a wisp of hair out of Adelaide's face. "And keep doing right by my daughter."

Dresden strummed his fingers on the ground. "So how long do we wait for her to wake up before we move? What if Carrick or the sorcerer come back here?"

Belanger shook his head. "I don't think they will. Carrick ran like a beat dog and neither of them will know that Adelaide is unconscious. I doubt they would expect us to stay here. And I suspect the sorcerer is more concerned about getting to the king."

That allayed some of Dresden's fears. As sore and exhausted as he was, he was in no condition to fight anyone, let alone Carrick or the sorcerer.

Belanger's expression darkened. "I want to warn the king. But I can't leave, at least not until I know my daughter is all right."

"I'm not leaving Adelaide again." Regulus met Belanger's gaze, as if challenging him.

"I wouldn't expect you to." Belanger sighed. "And they'll never let Sir Jakobs have an audience with the king on his own."

Dresden wouldn't have even tried, between not wanting to leave Regulus and not really caring a bit about the king, but he was glad he wouldn't have to refuse.

"We'll just have to hope she wakes soon," Belanger said.

❧⚭☙

When Adelaide finally awoke two days later, she was skittish and closed off. Dresden's suspicions about her mark lingered—until he understood the full weight of what she had suffered. The pain she had endured because she refused to work with or for the sorcerer.

More, Dresden came to understand just how much she loved Regulus. He knew Regulus loved her, but watching Adelaide interact with Regulus over the next couple days as they rode to the royal palace…any remaining fears of Regulus getting his heart broken were buried.

The mark should have been a sure sign, but Dresden had been too anxious to believe it at first. He changed his mind after Adelaide refused to remove the protective mark, even though Regulus' wounds caused her pain, because she refused to leave him vulnerable. She trusted Regulus. She visibly relaxed around him, and all her brightest smiles, when she looked the least overshadowed by her capture, were reserved for Regulus.

Dresden regretted ever doubting her, and he especially regretted doing so to her face.

In addition, Adelaide was good-natured, accepting Dresden's apology readily. She laughed at his jokes and stories as they rode. Some fear that Regulus wouldn't need Dresden now that he had Adelaide still hid in the shadows of his mind, but Adelaide's ready inclusion bolstered his hope. And Regulus seemed to be slowly finding more confidence in who he was, which made Dresden believe he could leave his insecurities about his past behind, too.

Adelaide and Regulus' devotion was Dresden's only consolation when the arrogant king conscripted the pair into his damned guard and forced them to live in the castle like servants. Meanwhile, Dresden and Lord Belanger stayed at an inn in the royal city of Crelburgh. Dresden hated that he couldn't help Regulus and Adelaide, but at least they weren't alone. Adelaide was fierce and powerful. Regulus was still a survivor and the best swordsman Dresden knew, and seemed to be immortal again. Whatever happened when the sorcerer inevitably attacked, Dresden took comfort in knowing that Regulus and Adelaide would have each other's backs.

THE TAVERN on the ground floor of the inn smelled of ale, rum, and boiled vegetables. Smoke hung in the air, wafting from candles and the small fire in the fireplace and from a handful of patrons scattered around the tavern, puffing on pipes. Low conversations, punctuated now and then by a drunken laugh, hummed in the air.

"To this day, I cannot get over how ludicrous the whole situation was." Dresden laughed between sips of rich dark ale.

Alfred wiped foam from his mouth. "Can't blame the woman when she was worried about her daughter." They sat in a corner of the inn's tavern, drinking their third ales, their supper plates long cleared away. It had only taken a few days of sharing a room for Alfred to insist Dresden stop calling him Lord Belanger.

"Definitely the most hilarious misunderstanding I've ever seen," Dresden continued. "Regulus helps a girl get home safely and gets hit with a frying pan and a nasty bruise for his chivalry. She wouldn't have worried if she'd known anything about Regulus other than 'big, intimidating mercenary.'" He propped his feet up on the table, then quickly removed them when Alfred frowned at his boots.

"All the mercenaries said he was a straight-laced stick-in-the-mud. Never did anything wrong or wild. I'd try to get him to go out with me, but he didn't usually enjoy it. Kissed a few girls, always felt guilty afterward."

"Why?"

Dresden scratched his beard. "He felt his father used his mother and Lady Arrano. He didn't want to be like that. And he didn't want to go too far with a girl, make a mistake. He didn't want to father a child who would never know him." He tapped his thumb against his tankard. "His cousin used to refer to him as Arrano's mistake. Never his son. Regulus didn't want to be the reason another child was told they weren't supposed to be born."

Alfred nodded and took a slow sip. "And you?"

"Me?" Dresden grinned. "I'm afraid I'm not so valorous. I never went far enough to get a girl pregnant—pretty sure Regulus would have had my head—

but I'm not one to avoid dark corners if the girl is willing to lock lips for a while."

Alfred snorted and his mouth curved down, but amusement twinkled in his eyes.

Dresden held up his hands. "Hey, I'm not half so bad as some of the other mercenaries. Regulus had no tolerance for assault and tried to discourage any behavior that could cause friction with the locals, but if everyone was willing and no one was hurt, he didn't interfere in his men's business. He became a bit of an expert in diffusing tension between his men and outraged fathers and suitors, actually." He laughed. "Made it all the more hilarious to see him on the receiving end of your outrage."

"You're a bit of a strange one, Jakobs."

"I really did mean it when I said I prefer Dresden," he said, working to keep his tone careless.

Alfred raised a brow. "Does this have something to do with why you haven't ever mentioned your family?"

"No…well, not exactly." For a moment, Dresden considered a lie. But maybe Alfred wouldn't care. If he told the truth…he could ask for advice. Still, he averted his gaze as he quietly spoke his admission. "Jakobs is what I was called when I was a servant."

Silence.

He finally looked up. Alfred had settled back in his chair and watched him thoughtfully.

"You're not going to ask?"

Alfred shrugged. "If you want me to know, you'll tell me. If not, I'm not going to pry. Your past makes no difference to me."

He released the tension that had crept into his shoulders. "Adelaide definitely gets a lot of her acceptance and respect from you."

Alfred smiled. "I'm humbled you think so. She's grown into a kinder woman than I could ever take credit for."

After a moment of inviting yet not pressuring silence, Dresden caved. "I met Regulus because I signed a ten-year contract of indenture to him when I was ten. It wasn't his idea, and he released me early, then I went with him to become a mercenary. He was my family by then, and he had no one else."

"Impressive loyalty."

"Regulus has that effect on people." He took a long drink. "You…don't exactly seem surprised."

The corner of Alfred's mouth twitched upward before settling into a neutral expression. "You mentioned you've known Regulus since you were children. You're a Carasian. Regulus admitted most of his knights weren't born noble. The most logical way for you to have met as children was if you were serving where Regulus grew up. I'd guessed a stable or kitchen boy, maybe personal servant due to how close you two are." He lifted a shoulder. "The indenture part was a surprise."

Dresden watched a candle flicker on a nearby table. "You're close with your children."

"Yes."

"Can I ask your advice?"

Alfred lowered his tankard and nodded.

"If one of them…left you." He looked away from Alfred's steady gaze and traced a knot on the table with his finger. "If he showed up over fifteen years later…would you be happy to see him?"

"Your parents didn't know about the indenture?"

"Oh, no, they did." He laughed uncomfortably. "My father had to sign, too. He didn't want to, but my family desperately needed the money, and I was insistent…didn't really know what I was getting myself into." Another nervous chuckle as he dared a look at Alfred. His expression remained the same; sincere, kind, and engaged. "I left with Regulus without telling them."

Alfred's brows knit. "Why?"

"Brashness. Pettiness. I was young and foolish." He shrugged, but the movement was stiff. "They didn't visit me. I hadn't seen them in seven years, and honestly—I was bitter. Regulus was in a hurry to join the mercenary troop and had a lot on his mind, so things happened quickly. He gave me my freedom and was leaving, and I made the rapid decision to go travel the world with my best friend. Besides, I didn't even know for certain if they would be in the same house. So, I just…left. Sometimes I wonder about trying to find them…but I don't know which would be worse. If I can't find them, or if I do find them."

After a moment, he sighed. "If you were my father…would you want to see me? After all of that?"

"Absolutely." Alfred leaned forward. "I'd want to know my son was all right. Even if I was hurt by the truth, I'd want to know what happened, why my child never came home."

"We'd be strangers now. They might not even recognize me."

"Did your parents love you?"

Did they? His father had let him indenture himself. Even if Da had fought it, he hadn't refused. And he'd visited *once* in seven years. Either his parents were dead, or they hadn't cared enough to try to see him. That thought weighed too heavily, so he ignored it. After all, he had never felt his parents didn't love him before he went to serve Regulus. He wanted to say he didn't know, but the words stuck in his throat.

"I think so," he said instead.

He hoped so.

Alfred shook his head with a chuckle. "A loving parent never forgets their child and will always care about them."

Dresden nodded. He had doubts, but this conversation had gone long enough. He shifted in his chair. "So… Tell me, was young Alfred Belanger a staid gentleman or a ladies' man?"

Alfred lifted a brow. "Do you always deflect with humor?"

Heat rushed to Dresden's ears. "Are you always so blunt?"

"Only on my third ale." Alfred raised his tankard with a laugh.

A shadow fell across their table, and they both looked up at a young man in neat red livery, the royal crest of a crowned dragon emblazoned on his chest. "Lord Belanger?"

Alfred nodded. "I'm Alfred Belanger." He held up his right hand, and the messenger peered at the signet ring on his finger before holding forth a sealed letter.

"A message from His Excellency the king." The messenger bowed.

Dresden took a drink to hide his scowl. He had hoped that perhaps Regulus had sent word. *As if the king would let his new pets off their leash.* He tried and failed to tamp down his resentment. The king of Monparth had only confirmed what Dresden already knew. Kings were like every other noble, using their unquestioned power to help themselves at the expense of those below them. Never even considering using their power to help others.

Well, except for Regulus. And Gaius.

The moment Alfred took the letter, the messenger left.

Alfred shoved aside his tankard and sat up straighter before he broke the seal and read the message. "My request has been granted. We've been given permission to carry swords at the masque to aid in the defense of the king."

Dresden sputtered on his ale and wiped his mouth, coughing. "We?"

"I took the liberty of asking on your behalf when I asked for myself." Alfred refolded the letter and slipped it into his belt before leaning back. "Was I incorrect in assuming you wouldn't want to remain here, useless, wondering what we were doing? I understand you seem to hold little regard for our sovereign, but Regulus has been tasked with protecting him, and I assumed you would like to help him achieve that goal."

"Well, I—yes." He frowned. "I never thought I'd be allowed in. You…got *me* invited to the king's birthday masque?"

Alfred smirked. "Between us…" He leaned across the table and whispered, "I was Gawain's hero when he was younger. There are not many reasonable requests he won't grant me." He leaned back. "Why do you have such a weak sense of duty and respect toward our king, anyway?"

"Why do you care about the king?" Dresden countered.

"He is my king." Alfred's forehead wrinkled, affront in his eyes. "I have sworn my allegiance to him, my fealty. He rules the land, heads the armies, oversees treaties, sets standards and laws, sees to the interests of his lords and listens to our demands, and is enthroned at Etiros' permitting. I owe him my loyalty. It is my sacred duty as a lord of Monparth to serve my king when he calls."

"Hm." Dresden took a long swig of ale. "I'm no lord."

"No"—Alfred's lips pursed—"but you're a knight of Monparth. You still owe him fealty."

"And my fealty he has. I won't disobey. I won't go out of my way to serve, either."

"Why?"

Frustration grew in his chest, and he slammed the tankard down on the table. "I was a servant, Lord Belanger, do you understand? I spent my adolescence obeying the orders of cruel men and fickle women. I could not stand up for myself, could not step out of line, was meant to be quiet, submissive, to anticipate orders, stay out of the way, keep my eyes down. And what separated those lords and ladies from me? Their manners? They were mocking and cruel. Their chivalry? I watched a grown man beat a fourteen-year-old boy, his own cousin, sneering at his pain. What made them special? The biggest difference was the circumstances of their birth, the blood that flowed through their veins, things neither of us had control over. And yet they used it as an excuse to treat us like dogs."

Alfred's expression turned from one of judgment to pity, but that only made the fire burning inside worse.

"Do you know how often indentures don't end, Lord Belanger?" He flexed his fingers. "Any debt the master decides the servant has accrued can be added. A torn shirt? Another month. A broken vase? Another year. A coin went missing? Servant must have stolen it; add it to the debt. Until it adds and adds and indenture isn't a contract, it's a bond, it's slavery. You know how I know?" He met Alfred's eyes, his temper barely controlled. "Because Lord Kimberly told Regulus if he kept track well enough, I could be his servant for life. He encouraged it. Because all the Carasian boy was good for was serving. Regulus didn't, but he could have. And what does the *king* do? Does he make indenture illegal? No. The king does not listen to me or see to my interests, and I don't see why his blood should make him of greater worth than me."

"It is not his blood you respect, but his title—"

"A title he has because of his blood." Dresden snatched his tankard back up. "I will go. I will protect the king. To help Regulus, and to fulfill my oath as a knight. But not because I owe the king anything."

Alfred tapped his finger on the side of his tankard for several moments. "A king is never merely a king. He is a figurehead. He represents Monparth. Without the king, the kingdom cannot stand. I respect my king as my liege and ruler, I have affection for him as my friend—a flawed friend, I will grant, but it is not my place to correct him. But I love him as a representation of the kingdom and people I love. When I serve my king, I serve all of Monparth. I serve my wife and my children and my friends."

Dresden paused with his tankard against his lips. "I suppose I can see that, a bit." He drained the tankard and set it back down.

After a moment, Alfred spoke again. "You said 'us.' Treated 'us' like dogs." His mouth turned down. "And you mentioned a beating. Are you saying Regulus' cousin beat him?"

Dresden ducked his head. "Only once. It was my fault." He cleared his throat. "But Kimberly struck Regulus. Too many times because he was aiming for me and Regulus got in the way, but often aimed at Regulus. Mocked and insulted him constantly. All because Regulus' blood wasn't pure nobility, because his mother was a servant. Kimberly's son called Regulus bastard, never his name. Visiting nobles never spoke up in his defense and sometimes engaged in the mockery. Regulus bore it all without fighting back and rarely complained, even in private."

"No wonder you have a poor view of the nobility," Alfred muttered.

"Well, you're not so bad." Dresden gave him a crooked smile. "I'd toast to you and that son-in-law of yours, but my ale is gone."

"Which son—Gaius?"

"A good man if ever I met one, I think." Dresden nodded. "Gentle but strong, loves his wife, protects his sister-in-law, slow to cast judgment, doesn't look down on common-born knights. And he put himself between me and Nolan Carrick, which took stones."

Alfred grinned. "Sounds like Gaius. I'm pleased to hear it. You know I told him there would be no dowry to test him and he said he didn't care, he loved Minerva, not my wealth? I increased her dowry, just for that. So…can I count on you? At the masque?"

"For you and Regulus and Monparth?" He nodded. "I won't let you down."

He meant it, too. Maybe nobles worth following and respecting weren't quite as unusual as he had thought.

Masque

A couple days later

Location: The Royal Palace, Royal Province of Rinaya

THE WORST part about the exploding glass crashing all around was the timing.

One minute later, and Dresden would have gotten in at least one kiss. Instead, he was using his body as a shield while he shoved the beautiful brunette under the nearest table and screams filled the great hall of the royal palace. He pulled a few shards of glass out of his sleeves and then a larger one out of his shoulder with a wince. At least none of them had done much damage; nothing but a few scratches through his shirt and doublet.

"Are you okay?" Dresden shouted over the shrieks around them. The girl nodded, and he peered out from under the table.

The sorcerer hovered over the tumultuous crowd trying to leave the hall. Up on the dais, guards shielded the royal family and herded them toward one of the two back doors. Green-tinged barriers of light flickered into place in the doorways. The king couldn't escape. The guards pressed close around the king, a couple holding shields over his head.

Green lightning flickered from the gem in the Staff of Nightfall and speared into the crowd, inciting a new wave of panicked screaming and jostling. Someone broke out of the guests and ran toward the dais.

Alfred.

Dresden cursed. He had promised that Alfred could count on him, and here he was, hiding under a table. He ducked out on the side by the wall with the empty window frames as a man nearby was hit by a finger of lightning. The smoking body fell, and Dresden gagged on the scent of burnt flesh. He ran for the dais. One of the guards moved to intercept him, but Alfred spoke.

"Sir Jakobs, glad you're still with us."

The guard nodded in acknowledgment, and Dresden joined them. He drew his scimitars from a single sheath on his left hip—a compromise, as Alfred had insisted the swords on his back would draw too much attention, but Dresden had refused to use a broadsword. He and Alfred stood shoulder to shoulder, tense. Dresden's heart pounded. The lightning stopped, but it afforded him no comfort. The sorcerer could send more at any second, and what would they do if he turned it on them, as he surely would? His scimitars would do nothing against sorcery. But he had made a promise.

"Hello, brother." The sorcerer's voice echoed over the hall, and the crowd quieted.

Green light blocked the entrance, too, and the guests stood still, as if they were trapped. *The windows, you absolute morons, the windows!* Dresden tightened his grip on his swords. Where were Regulus and Adelaide?

"I have no brother." The king's voice was loud behind Dresden.

"Now that's just cruel." The sorcerer smiled like a hyena about to feast. "But then, I *am* here to claim my throne and kill you and your family, so fair." The opal in the staff emitted an emerald glow.

Etiros, have mercy.

Blue light slammed up in a shimmering wall in front of the dais, absorbing the fire blast the sorcerer threw at them. Alfred's relieved gasp matched the spasming of Dresden's heart. *Adelaide.* The barrier grew until it cut the room into two parts—the dais with the royals, Alfred, Dresden, and the guards, and the rest of the hall with…everyone else. The sorcerer cursed as people screamed.

"The windows!" Guests and servants fought each other to pour out the shattered windows.

"About time," Alfred muttered. For some absurd reason, given the dire circumstances, that made Dresden smile.

The sorcerer sent wave after wave of attack against Adelaide's barrier, but it held. Some of the guards battered the sorcerous barriers over the doors, but they, too, held. The sorcerer's assault stopped.

"Belanger!" He threw a fireball into the fleeing crowd. "Where are you?"

Dresden gulped. *Where is Reg? And be careful, Adelaide.*

The sorcerer turned back toward the dais. "You're wearing my crown, brother." He directed a stream of green light into Adelaide's barrier.

"What do we do if her barrier fails?" Dresden whispered.

"It won't," Alfred said without a hint of uncertainty.

"Kirven!" Adelaide's voice. "I'm ready to try again."

But Dresden's attention had been pulled elsewhere. As the hall emptied of guests, two individuals didn't flee, locked in combat. Regulus and Carrick. On the other side of the barrier where Dresden couldn't get to them, couldn't help his brother.

He has Adelaide's bond, Dresden reminded himself. Regulus was immortal;

he would be fine. He needed to worry about himself and Alfred.

Flashes of light and explosions of flame volleyed between the two magic-wielders, but Dresden kept his eyes locked on what he could see of Regulus' fight through the blue glow of Adelaide's wall.

"It's down, the doorway is clear!"

Dresden looked behind him. Sure enough, the barrier on the left had vanished.

"Get the king through!" A royal guard officer with a red sash across his chest pointed at the door, his sword in his other hand. "We go to the tunnels and escape. Some men will remain to guard the way." The officer motioned the royal family and the guards through. Dresden glanced back to see Regulus land a blow on Carrick and stumble back as if he had been hit.

Alfred paused in the doorway. "Dresden?"

He couldn't get to Regulus, anyway, and he had given Alfred his word. "I'm with you." Dresden turned his back on Regulus and Adelaide and ran after the others.

The officer kept yelling at various guards to stay every so often as they raced through a hall, out across a rampart, down a tower, across a small room, and to a wood door. The king pulled a key from a chain around his neck and unlocked the door.

"The door will be locked, bolted, and barred from the inside," the officer said as the royal family entered. "But someone needs to remain out here to slow down anyone who follows—"

"I will stay." Alfred looked to Dresden.

"And I'm with him."

"Good." The officer nodded. "Rogerson, Helvar, and Benham, you're here, too."

The officer and half of the remaining guards went through and closed the door, leaving three guards behind with Dresden and Alfred. The key clicked in the lock. A bolt rasped into place, and a scrape and thunk indicated a crossbeam had been positioned.

Now to wait. And hope that Regulus and Adelaide succeeded.

Alfred paced back and forth in front of the door, his lips moving silently. Praying, it looked like. Dresden gulped. He wasn't sure if he believed in Etiros, truly. But right now? Praying seemed like a good idea.

A guard muttered something about it being too cramped and then headed up the steps they had just come down. Moments later, a shout echoed down the stairs, followed by a moan and a crash. Dresden, Alfred, and the two remaining guards stilled, bringing their weapons up as footsteps approached.

One guard positioned himself just to the side of the archway to the stairs, directly across from the escape door. The other guard cursed and charged into the stairwell.

"Wait!" Dresden stepped forward as the guard disappeared up the steps.

Someone shouted in pain, followed by a groan.

"How many of you do I have to kill?" Carrick's voice.

"That's not possible," the guard said. "You—" A strangled noise cut him off.

The guard's body sailed backward and crashed into the stone wall at the stairwell landing. The body fell into a heap, unmoving, with the neck at an odd angle. Sweat beaded on Dresden's forehead, and he tightened his grip on his scimitars.

More footsteps, and then Carrick walked into the landing. Blood stained his trousers, the long sleeves of his shirt, and his cut and torn doublet. How much of it was his, Dresden couldn't guess. The last guard raised his sword.

Somehow, Carrick got his sword up in time to block the guard's swing at his neck. He moved his blood-stained blade around and forced the guard's sword down, bringing the hilt up with blinding speed to slam into the man's temple. The guard dropped like a stone and sprawled across the floor.

Carrick looked across the room and smiled, his eyes flashing. "Ah. If it isn't my favorite Carasian servant and my betrothed's father." He stepped over the guard's feet. "Move. I have a king to kill."

Alfred took up a defensive stance. "You won't get through this door while I breathe."

"That goes for me, too." Dresden swung his scimitars.

Carrick scowled. "I don't have time for this."

"Too bad." Dresden stepped forward and swung, anticipating Carrick's block but already coming in with his second scimitar. His blade sliced across Carrick's leg, and Carrick cursed.

"Oh, by the way, Hargreaves is dead. Thought you'd want to know."

Dresden missed his next swing and lost his grounded stance. *But Adelaide's bond*—he came to himself just in time to block Carrick's cut, but he had lost his rhythm. Carrick thrust. Dresden parried but wasn't anticipating Carrick's strength.

The blade sliced across his side, leaving a long gash and burning pain.

Carrick laughed as Dresden stumbled back and dropped one scimitar to press a hand to his bleeding side. "Predictable fool."

Regulus wasn't even dead. A trick to distract him, and he had let it work. He blocked another blow, but Carrick kicked his leg and Dresden fell back. His head cracked against the wall, and his sword slipped out of his fingers. Carrick drew back his sword. Reflexively, Dresden lifted his hand to block the blow and squeezed his eyes shut. *This isn't how I wanted to go. Not cowering in front of a man like Carrick.* He forced his shaking hand to the ground and looked up as Carrick's sword swung down.

The ring of metal on metal echoed in the small room as the edge of Carrick's sword crashed into the flat of Alfred's blade. Carrick's glare moved from Dresden to Alfred.

"You're going to pay for what you did to my daughter," Alfred growled. He pushed Carrick's sword up and back and seamlessly transitioned into an attack.

Dresden tried to get up, but his head spun, and his vision blacked out as pain speared through his side. With a groan, he settled back against the wall.

"Come now," Carrick said, on the defensive against Alfred's flurry of cuts, swings, and thrusts. "You—"

"Don't speak, knave." Alfred landed a cut across Carrick's thigh, then a jab that Carrick parried so it grazed his shoulder instead of penetrating his chest.

Alfred was…amazing. He fought like a much younger man, rage across his face.

Carrick parried another thrust with a snarl. "We're going to be family—"

"Over my dead body!"

"So be it, then!" Carrick blocked another swing and stepped closer. Dresden winced at the shrill grating of Carrick's blade as it scraped down the length of Alfred's. Carrick hammered his knee into Alfred's gut.

Alfred moved a step back with a grunt, and that was all the opening Carrick needed. He moved to the offensive, moving like Regulus had when he was the Black Knight—faster than seemed possible, his unrestrained blows carrying the force of a battering ram. Even as fast as he was, Alfred couldn't keep up.

No, no, no. Dresden reached for his scimitar, biting back a curse at the pain in his side. His fingers closed around the hilt as he grabbed the rough stone of the wall to pull himself up.

Carrick knocked Alfred's sword out of his hands and stabbed as Alfred's weapon crashed against the wall with a clatter. His sword buried into Alfred's heart and emerged out of his back.

"No!" Dresden's legs locked as he stared at the blood turning Alfred's pale blue tunic crimson around the blade.

Alfred gasped, a ragged, stuttering sound as his face went bone white.

"You shouldn't have fought me!" Carrick's voice shook. "Stupid old man!" He withdrew the sword and shoved Alfred aside.

Alfred slammed to the floor and turned his head to look at Dresden. Ferocity and desperation warred in his pained expression. "Tell…Ad…" With a final breath, he went still. His eyes stared across the room at Dresden, lifeless.

Tell her what? Dresden's jaw trembled as tears blurred his vision and his chest constricted. He let his scimitar fall and slid down the wall, clutching his side in an effort to slow the bleeding. Carrick pounded and kicked and slammed against the door, cursing non-stop under his breath.

A layer of heavy fog settled over Dresden's mind. Alfred's unseeing eyes bored into him, as if begging him to fight Carrick, but he couldn't. He shouldn't have attacked so quickly. He and Alfred should have attacked together. He shouldn't have lost focus at Carrick's taunting and gotten injured. Alfred should still be alive. He was a good man, a nobleman who deserved his title, a loving husband and father—he shouldn't be dead.

Carrick broke a small hole in the door, reached through, tossed aside the crossbeam, and removed the bolt. The lock wouldn't budge. Carrick pulled on the door, leveraging the hole as a handhold, and ripped the door out of the frame as small pieces of metal plinked to the stone. He dropped the door and ran down the stairs.

Dresden rested his head back against the wall and closed his eyes. Where was Regulus? Why hadn't he gone after Carrick? Was Adelaide okay? What would happen to Regulus if Adelaide died? What would happen to Adelaide if the sorcerer cut off Regulus' head? Carrick seemed to have lied about Regulus being dead, but…what if he had told the truth? Dresden pounded his already aching head back against the stone.

Too many thoughts. Alfred. Carrick. Regulus. The king. Adelaide. The fiery pain in his side. The sorcerer. Regulus. Alfred. Adelaide. The king. *No!* He needed to stop thinking, he needed to—needed to—he needed help. Someone to stitch up his side. He needed to find Regulus. He needed to stop Carrick.

And he couldn't do any of it.

Footsteps came back up the escape tunnel stairs. He opened his right eye a slit and closed it again as Carrick emerged. But Carrick didn't slow, just ran past and back up the tower stairs.

What did that mean? Was the king dead? Had they failed? After everything, after Alfred's sacrifice, they *couldn't* have failed.

Minutes passed. Or maybe hours. He couldn't tell the difference. Multiple sets of footfalls approached down the tower stairs. Dresden sighed and looked to the archway. Whether it was good news or bad news, he would face it.

A man in a royal guard uniform knelt in the landing and checked the fallen guard. His head drooped as he released a heavy sigh before standing and entering the room. The guard made eye contact with Dresden, and something like relief crossed his face. "We have a live one!"

The man checked the guard by the entrance for a pulse, and sadly shook his head before crossing to Alfred. Two more men followed him, another guard and an older man carrying a bag and a lantern. The older man rushed straight to Dresden.

"I'm a physician." He knelt in front of Dresden, his wild, wiry gray eyebrows drawing together as he set down his bag and lantern. "Your side?"

"Yes…" Dresden lowered his hand from the wound.

The man hummed as he pulled a pair of shears out of the bag and cut open the side of Dresden's tunic. "Hmmm." He poked at the wound and Dresden hissed. "Sorry."

Dresden winced as the man felt along the cut. The two guards picked up the body of the guard in the landing and carried him up the tower stairs.

"Here." The physician held out a thick strap of leather. "Bite—"

But Dresden had already clamped his teeth around the leather. He leaned back, closed his eyes, and tried not to think about his injury.

"I take it you've done this before?"

Dresden nodded without opening his eyes. Something splashed over the wound, searing and tingling, and he screamed against the leather. A pinch and prick combined with the burning as the physician stitched his side closed. Dresden clenched the leather between his teeth, focusing on not moving while the man worked.

"Done."

He opened his eyes and let the man take the leather piece back. The physician wrapped a bandage around his middle, over his tunic.

"The king?" Dresden asked, afraid of the answer. "Is he…?"

The physician glanced up with a faint smile. "His Excellency lives and has escaped, and the sorcerer and his accomplice ran. You did well, lad." He tied off the bandage. "You should live. You lost a decent amount of blood, so you'll be weakened. And don't exert yourself or you'll tear the stitches." He stood, took his bag and lantern, and headed down the stairs.

Dresden managed to stand and sheath his scimitars. The guards from before reappeared and moved to Alfred.

"He's a lord. Lord Belanger." Dresden didn't know why he said it. It didn't make any difference—dead was dead. But Alfred deserved to be respected. For the life he had lived, and the honorable death he had died.

The guards just nodded and picked him up. Dresden made his way back to the great hall. Too many bloodstains marred the stone and carpet on his way. *Carrick.* He hurried on, as fast as his aching side would allow, but had to slow as darkness set in and he could no longer see. A couple of torches bobbed toward him.

Guardsmen. "Who goes there?"

"Sir Dresden Jakobs, friend of Lord Alfred Belanger." *Former friend.* His chest tightened. "I'm looking for my friends, Lord Regulus Hargreaves and Lady Adelaide—"

"Haven't seen the mage or her lover." The guard frowned. "She should have stopped this."

Dresden swallowed down his fears of why she hadn't. "Could I have a torch?"

The other guard shrugged and handed over his torch before they continued back the way Dresden had come.

The hall was dark, the candles and torches all extinguished. A few guards' bodies were laid out on the dais. Dresden held up the torch. "Anyone here? Regulus? Adelaide?"

They had to be here. Somewhere. Maybe injured, but alive. They *had* to be.

He moved off the dais into the hall, careful of the glass crunching beneath his boots. His heart leapt at the dark outline of a figure standing in the middle of the hall. A woman with dark hair…

"Adelaide?" He rushed forward, but she didn't answer. "Adelaide?" He looked around, his panic returning. "Where's Regulus?"

She shook her head. Dresden felt the blood drain from his face. "D-dead?"

Again, she only shook her head. He clenched his teeth against his mounting frustration. Had she been struck mute? "I don't under… Captured?" She nodded, and he stumbled backward, everything in him screaming in disbelief and horror. "No… Reg…"

The surrounding darkness seemed to press in on the edges of the torch-light.

"I tried…" Adelaide's voice trailed off, heartbreak in her unfocused gaze.

He cursed and kicked at shards of glass. He should have been there; should have protected his brother. *Like I protected Alfred?*

Alfred.

Dresden's stomach flipped. He looked back at Adelaide's hollow eyes. He'd have to tell her, but he didn't know how, and Regulus needed to be rescued, too.

He breathed in and out slowly, calming himself. Helping Regulus would have to wait. Right now, he needed to tell Adelaide. Regulus wasn't there for her, so Dresden would have to be. The death of her father would not be easy to bear, especially right after losing Regulus.

"I'm sorry, Adelaide. I need to tell you something." This wasn't going to be an easy conversation. He'd had it before, with mercenaries who had lost friends, with family members who turned up in towns they passed through— although Regulus took the brunt of those conversations. It always hurt. She would need support, and he was no Regulus, but he would do his best. "There's not an easy way to say this. It's…your father."

DRESDEN DUCKED into an alleyway and slid to the ground behind a pile of empty crates. He clutched the Staff of Nightfall to his chest. The entire time he'd run back to Crelburgh, he had argued with himself.

Regulus' words echoed in his mind. *"This is magic and immortals. They could kill you."* He hated that Regulus was right. Last time he had faced Carrick, he had failed, and Alfred had died. Could he watch another good person die while he sat by wounded, useless, and helpless? He didn't know which would be worse—if Regulus died and he was there, watching and powerless, or if Regulus died and he didn't even know.

No, he couldn't think like that. Regulus and Adelaide would win, and they would both come back alive. *They lost last time.* He squeezed the Staff. But they had taken away the sorcerer's advantage. Surely that would count for something.

He spent what felt like hours slinking around the alleyways of Crelburgh, keeping the Staff hidden and eavesdropping on conversations—much of which centered on inaccurate rumors about what had happened at the masque. His energy focused around forcing himself not to worry and the occasional desperate prayer to a god he was hoping more and more existed.

Dresden crept as close to the castle as he dared for the second time. Hope and despair fought within him as he dared to approach the end of the alleyway closest to the main gates. A crowd had gathered in front of the closed gates. Dresden frowned, stuck the Staff of Nightfall behind a couple of barrels, and joined the crowd.

"I saw it," a guard declared. "They only just arrived. The lady mage and her lover came in with the heads of the sorcerer and his accomplice! Had the bloody things in a bag; emptied them onto the ground." He nudged the elbow of another guard. "You should have seen the lieutenants' faces at the carnage!"

Dresden could have shouted and leapt with joy, but he stood frozen. Regulus and Adelaide had made it back. They'd done it—the sorcerer and Carrick were dead. And their heads had rolled across the dirt. He smirked.

"So the kingdom is saved?" a woman demanded from the crowd.

The guard nodded. "Aye, looks like."

Dresden came back to his senses and shoved through the crowd to run back to the alleyway. Once he had the Staff, he raced back to the gates, cursing at people who didn't move out of his way fast enough.

"You there!" He pointed at the guards, then indicated himself. "Sir Dresden Jakobs, knight of Arrano, sworn to Lord Regulus Hargreaves, the man who helped kill the sorcerer." Behind him, townspeople gasped. "I need to deliver this"—he held out the Staff—"to Lady Adelaide Belanger, the mage, at once."

The guards glanced at each other.

"Look, I helped protect the king and got a cut in my side, I was there when Lord Alfred Belanger died protecting the king, and I stole this staff from the sorcerer at Lady Belanger's request, so if you don't let me in *right now*, I swear—"

"All right!" The guard who had seen Regulus and Adelaide return held up his hands. "Come on."

The guard led him inside and behind the castle to the enclosed courtyard in the guards' barracks. They entered the building on the right, and the guard approached the officer who had tried to arrest Adelaide. The lieutenant sat at a table in the back room, the quill in his hand flying across a piece of parchment.

"Sir." The guard gave a perfunctory bow. "This man—"

"You!" Lieutenant—Dresden couldn't remember his name, something like Ball—shot to his feet, nearly upsetting the inkpot on the table. He jabbed the tip of the quill toward Dresden, then lowered his hand as his gaze fixed on the Staff.

"Is that the sorcerer's staff? How did you get that? Where have you been?"

"I went with Adelaide to find Regulus and the sorcerer, which we did." He shook the Staff. "They entrusted me with taking the Staff so the sorcerer couldn't use it when they fought."

"And what, he'd left it just lying around?"

"Actually, yes." Dresden jutted out his chin. "Now where is Adelaide? I need to give this to—"

"I'll take it." The lieutenant reached for the Staff, but Dresden drew it back. "I don't think so, Lieutenant Ball—"

"*Beale*." Beale glowered. "I am the current highest-ranking officer in the castle, and that staff must be locked up somewhere safe until the king decides what is to be done with it. Now hand it over, or I will have you arrested."

Dresden frowned. "Fine, but where are Adelaide and Regulus? Not handing this over until I know where they are."

Beale stiffened. "Hardly your concern—"

"Lord Hargreaves is my liege; that makes it very much my concern!"

"Right." Beale pinched the bridge of his nose. "Check his room. You know where it is from staying with the mage. If your liege isn't there, I don't know where he is, and frankly, I don't care. Now hand over the Staff before I throw you in the dungeon!"

"Okay, calm down." Dresden handed over the Staff and hoped one had to be a mage or sorcerer to use it, and it wouldn't be a danger in the hands of a normal person. He rushed out and made his way to Adelaide and Regulus' room.

The door was closed, and no light showed from under the door. He held up his hand to knock, then hesitated. He'd hate to interrupt anything…but they were probably just resting after their battle, and he couldn't wait to talk to them and make sure they were okay. Maybe give Regulus a piece of his mind for ordering him to leave. He knocked. Nothing—maybe a muffled noise? He knocked again, growing impatient. Forget yelling at Regulus, he just needed to see his friend alive with his own eyes.

"You in there, Reg? Adelaide?"

The door flew open and slammed into the wall. Regulus grinned so widely he looked ready to explode. "Drez!"

"Oh, good." Dresden nearly choked on the words, but tried to pull it off as nonchalant. Regulus was fine, the sorcerer was dead, everything was…wait. "Where's Adelaide?"

"In the dungeons." Regulus' grin vanished as he stepped back, allowing Dresden entry.

Dresden stiffened. "What?" He had hoped for a celebration, not this. "They're not still charging her with desertion, are they?"

"Wait, you *knew*?" Regulus lit the lamp on the little table to the side of the room. The orange-red light wasn't nearly as calming as Adelaide's. "Drez, I swear—"

"Hey, you ever tried stopping her from doing something?" Dresden shook off his astonishment and entered the room. "She was throwing magic and fire and telling people off. Besides which, I was on her side. If she was doubling over in pain at what they were doing to you, I can't imagine…" He pushed aside the nausea that resurfaced at the memory of the state in which they had found Regulus. "I was worried."

Dresden sat in the chair where he had kept watch over Adelaide the night before. After everything Regulus had gone through, the torture, whatever the fight had been like, Adelaide being arrested… He decided to go with cavalier and normal to put Regulus at ease. "I like Adelaide's light better. Makes the corners less shadowy."

Regulus cocked his head. "What? How would you know that?"

"Come on, Reg." He leaned back, suddenly aware of how bone-deep exhausted he was. "She lost you; then her father died, and she couldn't save him. And she tried, Reg. It…was rough." He rubbed his beard as he tried to forget her screams echoing in the hall, her tears soaking into his shirt as she cried herself to sleep in his arms. "I wasn't about to leave her alone."

Regulus sat on the bed and whispered, "Thank you."

"What are friends for if not to sleep on uncomfortable chairs and take care of your girl because you're too busy being captured?" He laughed, although it felt weak and stupid. He grasped for a change of subject. "Oh, also, if we ever run away to become mercenaries again, please take her with us. That mage healing is excellent."

"Wait, you were hurt?" Regulus' panicked gaze searched him for evidence of a wound, but Dresden had begged a clean shirt off a servant. "How bad—"

Dresden snorted. The man had been tortured and was worried about him. He shouldn't have expected otherwise from Regulus. "Compared to you? A scratch."

"Is that what Adelaide will tell me if I ask her?" Chastisement crept into Regulus' tone, and Dresden couldn't help but be amused.

"I'm alive, you muscular nursemaid, relax. It was definitely nothing compared to Antar's leg." Dresden hadn't seen the extent of the damage to the lieutenant's leg, but healing it had seemed to strain Adelaide. He sat up straighter. "Which reminds me. As soon as I heard that you two had shown up at the palace with a couple of severed heads—nicely done, by the way, I heard you dumped them out and disgusted the guards, excellent style—I came straight to the palace with the aim of giving the Staff to Adelaide. A pretentious Lieutenant Beale who's very concerned with protocol confiscated it."

Regulus rolled his eyes. "Sounds about right. He insisted on locking up Adelaide until the king can decide if she should be charged with desertion."

"This is why I was on board when you decided to become a mercenary," Dresden said with a shake of his head. "No tradition and nonsense, just whoever fights best and whoever comes through when they need to. Justice is simple, effective, and fair."

Regulus laughed, and the sound was a balm to Dresden's soul. "No nonsense, says the man who is still sore he lost his collection of lucky rabbit feet."

"And look where we are now." He spread his hands as if encompassing their entire situation. "Bet you we never would have met that sorcerer if I'd still had them."

Regulus' lips fought a smile. "That is the definition of circumstantial and you know it."

"We both know I'm never wrong." Dresden placed his hands behind his head and leaned back, basking in nostalgia of the good times as mercenaries. "And I bought those as a laugh, but we had the best luck for the month I had them."

"I'm glad you're here." Regulus collapsed back on the bed. "I just wish Adelaide was, too."

"After everything you two have been through, you're clearly destined to be together. So you can wait another day or two until the king returns from wherever he ran off to and pardons her, as I'm certain he will, because, like I said." Dresden grinned. "Destined for each other. As I knew from the beginning."

"Don't you start; you knew no such thing."

"I'm not sure you've ever thanked me, by the way…"

Regulus laughed. "Okay, once Adelaide is safely with me and in no danger of execution, then maybe I'll consider thanking you for all your interference and nagging."

"You're lucky the only thing within reach for me to throw at you is a lamp."

Regulus laughed again, then quieted. "Thank you, Drez. For everything. And…I'm sorry for ordering you to go." He rolled onto his side and looked at Dresden. "But thank you for leaving." His throat bobbed. "We…we almost lost, Drez. I don't even have the bond anymore. Breaking it is what it took to win."

Dresden's jaw went slack. "What?"

"I don't have the energy to explain it all right now, but…I'm glad you weren't there. I'm glad you didn't see…" He dropped his gaze for a moment with a sigh. "I know it wasn't easy to run away, but I have no doubt Carrick would have gone after you just to torment me. It feels selfish to be glad you survived when Alfred is gone, but…I'm glad I didn't lose you." His breath shuddered, and he wiped away a tear.

"Damn it, Regulus." Dresden looked up at the ceiling and breathed out slowly to stem his own emotions. "Just don't ever do that again, okay?"

Regulus chuckled weakly. "I don't plan on ever facing a crazed sorcerer and his bloodthirsty immortal lackey again, so I hope I won't have occasion to."

"Yeah, well, name your first child after me and we'll call it even."

"And if my first child is a girl?" Regulus' mouth twisted around a poorly suppressed smile.

"Dresdina, obviously."

"That is absolutely terrible."

"Fine, first son, then."

"No promises; pretty sure that's something I need Adelaide's approval for."

Dresden clutched his hand over his heart. "Some brother you are."

œ∞œ

It took a few days for the king to return and summon Regulus and Adelaide. While they had Adelaide's hearing, Dresden walked around the castle grounds, mostly circling around the rear courtyard. He was looking forward to getting out of this palace and back home to Arrano. Just as soon as Adelaide was pardoned. Which she would be. She *had* to be. If she wasn't…well, he might have to help Regulus tear the palace to the ground. Not an ideal way to die. No, she would be pardoned.

Dresden jogged to the castle wall. What was taking so long? He turned and tripped over his own feet, narrowly avoiding falling on his face. Adelaide and Regulus had emerged out of a different door into the castle, led by a servant who left them behind like she wanted nothing more than to get as far away from them as possible.

Dresden didn't have time to consider the servant's strange behavior. He ran toward them, noting with elation that Adelaide's manacles were gone. Regulus and Adelaide clung to each other like they were tied together, all smiles and lovesick eye contact.

He skidded to a stop in front of them, blocking the door to the servants' quarters. Adelaide blushed as they stopped and the two separated a little. "What did the king say? No shackles, so is everything…" A ribbon looped around Regulus' arm drew Dresden's attention. He pointed at it, his mind racing. "What—wait. Is that…" *Oh, they did* not. "A unity cord?" The symbol of a marriage seemed to mock him. He took a couple steps back, shocked at the affront. "Regulus Daveth Hargreaves, did you get married without me?"

"Ah… We, I mean…" Regulus cleared his throat. "The king released us from the guard and then he…we were…Drez—"

"Oh, I see." Dresden waved his hands, torn between genuine hurt and smug giddiness. "I get you two together, and I'm not invited to the wedding! It's fine. I'm just waiting, mad with worry, while you're getting married without me, not even thinking about me, headed to your room clinging to each other like a couple of…"

They had just gotten married. The loving looks, the clinging…he was an idiot. "Oh great Etiros above and all the world below. I—I should go…" Dresden moved into the courtyard, groping for some excuse for his sudden departure that would allow Regulus to enjoy his wife without outright saying, *Have fun, you scoundrel.* "Totally forgot, I need to…uh, see a man about, um…a goat?" It was a terrible excuse. He winked at Regulus and headed into town to give the newlyweds their space. He could get details on their hearing with the king later.

❧❦

A couple days later, the palace was behind them. It felt good to be on the road, blue sky above them, a cool late summer breeze around them, and home ahead. No worries or threats to weigh him down.

Well, they did need to stop at the Belanger castle to deliver the news of Alfred's death to Tamina and Alfred's son. Dresden was glad that task wouldn't fall to him. Adelaide seemed worried about telling them, and he knew it would be difficult. She sometimes got a sad, distant look in her eyes. Dresden had seen enough loss and witnessed enough pain to know that might never go away.

But right now, she was happy, as was Regulus. They rode Sieger together. Adelaide said her lost horse had been a gift from her father, so she didn't want to ride the horse the king had gifted her. Dresden had his suspicions about how much of it was mourning, and how much was an excuse to ride with Regulus. The two couldn't keep their hands off each other. Sure, mostly innocent touches, and if he was honest, it was adorable, but it was also ridiculous. His repeated complaints were met with laughter, but truthfully, he didn't mind. He was happy to see Regulus happy.

But…it did hurt, a little. Ever since they were children, he had been Regulus' person, his closest friend, his confidant. That would be Adelaide now. He didn't begrudge her that and hoped she and Regulus only grew closer. But their little family was shifting, changing, and as much as the change excited Dresden, as much as he loved Adelaide, he also wasn't sure where that left him.

Especially since now his only excuse for not seeking out his family was gone, and he wasn't sure he was ready to face that dragon yet.

"Dresden? Drez!"

He snapped out of his reverie and looked over at Adelaide. "Yes?"

Adelaide laughed. "I was trying to ask you how you think the other knights will react to our marriage. Regulus seems torn on if they'll be more happy or disappointed they missed it." She gave an apologetic smile. "Sorry again you weren't there."

Dresden waved his hand. "The men will be fine. Caleb might bellyache until he learns there was no party, and then he won't care. And damn right you're sorry, *Regulus,* not thinking to send for your brother and matchmaker." Dresden laughed, enjoying Regulus' ashamed grimace.

"Oh!" Adelaide grinned. "I hadn't thought of that. That makes you my brother-in-law. For once in my life, I'm actually happy to have a brother."

Dresden half bowed from the saddle. "I admit I'm a little intimidated that I have to make up for your apparently awful brother—"

"Brothers," Adelaide corrected.

"Ah, so even more pressure."

She laughed. "You're already a great brother, Dresden." Her smile softened. "I never really thanked you. For being there after my father…died. I don't know how I would have functioned without you."

Regulus met Dresden's eyes, and there was silent gratitude in the look.

Dresden shrugged, feeling self-conscious. "Actually, you know, you get *two* brothers."

"Oh?" Adelaide frowned.

Regulus laughed. "You're right, you know who *will* be deeply hurt? Harold.

That boy is going to be so upset with me for getting married without him." He groaned. "It will be a week of pitiful, hurt looks every time I see him."

"Two weeks," Dresden guessed. "He didn't get the honor of picking your wardrobe and doing all the squire services to help you prepare, and he's going to feel cheated as a brother and a squire."

Adelaide grinned. "It sounds like I really did get a whole new family." She leaned back against Regulus' chest. Regulus rested his cheek against her head.

"You two are disgustingly adorable, you know that, right?"

Their laughter filled the empty road. Dresden smiled to himself. He had no reason to worry. If an indenture, a captainship, a lordship, and a sorcerer couldn't break his friendship with Regulus, Adelaide certainly wouldn't. He wasn't losing a brother, just gaining a sister.

PART III
A New Family

SUNLIGHT GLARED over the crenellated wall surrounding Belanger castle. Dresden reined in Horse next to Regulus and Adelaide on Sieger. No one moved on the wall.

"Is anyone there?" Regulus called.

A head popped up between crenellations, shadowed by the blinding sunlight. "Regulus?" Caleb's voice. "Ay, Regulus! And Dresden! Lady Belanger!"

"Actually, it's Lady Hargreaves," Regulus called back. Adelaide giggled.

Caleb hooted. "And I thought no longer being under lockdown would be the best news we could get. Just a moment, and we'll let you in!"

A few minutes later, one of the massive double doors barring the gate swung out, and Caleb and Perceval greeted them—Caleb with a cheek-splitting grin, Perceval with a small, closed-lipped but somehow equally pleased smile.

"What exactly were you two doing?" Regulus asked as they rode forward.

"Nothing!" Caleb said.

Perceval crossed his arms. "Passing time."

"Gambling with the guards?" Dresden guessed.

"Maybe." Caleb winked. "So, all married, back here, does that mean you won? Long live the king and all that?"

Adelaide dismounted. "The king lives. The sorcerer and Nolan Carrick are dead." She said it levelly, but he knew the weight those words carried.

Regulus and Dresden dismounted, and Perceval took Sieger's reins. Dresden motioned toward the castle. "I'll help with the horses and fill Perce and Cal in while you talk to Lady Belanger."

Regulus nodded his appreciation, and Adelaide offered him a weak smile. Her shoulders rose and fell with a deep breath. Regulus took her hand, and they walked across the courtyard together.

"So they couldn't wait, huh?" Caleb heaved a sigh with a shake of his head. "Went and got married without us."

Dresden snorted. "They didn't even wait for me! I was within the castle grounds, but did they send for me first, or even tell me the king had pardoned Adelaide before taking their vows and heading straight to their room? No, no thought for the *entire reason they met at all.*" He crossed his arms and scowled at Regulus and Adelaide as they disappeared through the castle doors.

"I have many questions." Perceval held up a hand. "But first—what about a pardon? Also, why isn't Lord Belanger with you?"

"Ah." Dresden slouched as sorrow pierced him. "Lord Belanger died protecting the king."

Perceval and Caleb gaped. Dresden tugged on Horse's reins, and they moved to the stables, Dresden explaining the major details—with frequent interruptions. They brushed down the horses while he talked, then moved back to the courtyard. Dresden and Caleb sat on a bench in the shade of an oak growing near the entrance to the castle residence. Perceval leaned against the oak's trunk.

Dresden had just finished his story when the double doors of the castle flew open with a bang that made Dresden's heart leap into his throat. Adelaide charged out, her eyes glowing gold. She screamed and threw a fireball larger than Regulus was tall at the stone of the castle, leaving a massive black scorch mark. Dresden and Caleb jumped to their feet while Perceval shoved away from the oak trunk.

Regulus ran out of the castle and in an instant had Adelaide pressed against his chest, stroking her hair as she buried her face in his shoulder. His lips moved close to her ear while her entire frame shook. Lady Tamina Belanger appeared in the doorway next, her flushed face pinched with worry.

Dresden drifted closer, his stomach twisting. Adelaide had expressed concern about how her mother and half-brother would handle the news, but what under the sun had happened in there?

"And you're out of your mind if you even *think* of asking for a dowry, Hargreaves!" A man around Dresden's age strode past Tamina out of the castle, a snarl on his mouth and a red mark around his left eye. Dresden recognized him as Alfred's son.

"Oh, excellent," Tamina drawled, venom dripping from her words. "Withholding a legal dowry gives them a legitimate reason to complain to His Excellency the king about you."

Sir Belanger glared at her. "She married him *after* my father died, making me—"

"*Our* father!" Adelaide pulled out of Regulus' arms. "He was *my father*, too!"

"I agreed to nothing, no marriage, no dowry." Sir Belanger crossed his arms. "And I am giving you nothing after you got Father killed and then your *husband* attacked me in my own home."

"Keep talking," Regulus growled as his hand went to his sword. "I am moments away from challenging you to a duel."

Sir Belanger—or, Dresden supposed with distaste, Lord Belanger now—blanched. At least the heartless cad had the sense to realize a duel with Regulus wasn't a fight he wanted.

"As Alfred had already given Regulus his blessing and permission," Tamina said, one hand planted on her hip, "his agreement with Regulus stands. This would be the case regardless, but I would *love* to see you argue before our king that you have decided not to uphold the wishes of your father, the man who died protecting our king, and provide a legal dowry to your sister and her husband, the woman and man who saved the kingdom. Nothing would give me greater joy than to see you humiliated before our king."

Dresden's mouth twisted as he tried not to smirk.

Belanger turned red to the roots of his hair. "Very well. I don't suppose there is any documentation of the agreed-upon amount?"

"Two hundred gold," Tamina said without hesitation. Regulus jerked, and Dresden's mouth fell open.

"You're lying."

"Prove it." Tamina lifted her chin.

Belanger's nostrils flared. "As you say, Lady Belanger." He cut a glance at Adelaide and Regulus. "I will be right back, so you can be on your way."

Whatever he had said that precipitated Regulus punching him, Dresden imagined it was more than well deserved. What a living pile of dung.

"Good," Adelaide bit out at her brother's retreating back. "I won't stay here a moment longer than I have to."

Regulus cleared his throat. "Lady Belanger, will you accompany us? Arrano is open to you, as your home, if that is desirable to you."

"Thank you for not making me ask." Tamina sagged against the doorframe, the fire leaving her expression and turning into broken sorrow. "I'll have my maid pack a case and stay to oversee packing the rest. Landon will have to send my things, or I *will* drag him to court."

"I..." Regulus rubbed the back of his neck. "Alfred and I never discussed a dowry. And I don't require one."

Tamina smiled sadly. "I know. We did, though. It's more than we had discussed, but Alfred would be on my side if he heard…" She dragged a hand down the side of her face. "I can't believe he's gone."

Adelaide went to her mother and embraced her. After a brief whispered conversation, they turned and went inside, still leaning against each other. Dresden approached Regulus, trailed by Perceval and Caleb.

"What happened?"

"Basically what you saw." Regulus' scar tugged at his deep frown. "We had already told of Alfred's death to Tamina, and she had mostly recovered when Landon arrived. The news shocked Landon. By the time we recounted everything, he had regained his ability to speak, and put it to immediate use accusing Adelaide of causing her father's death and Tamina and Adelaide of bringing nothing but danger and ruin to their family. Said that at least he finally understood Adelaide was only their father's favorite because she was a mage, and all her being a mage had done was kill him and that he wished Adelaide had died instead."

Dresden's fists clenched. "I take it that's when you punched him?"

Regulus' expression darkened further, and his jaw tensed. "No, I punched him after he said at least Adelaide being married meant he only has to be around one Khastallander harlot."

Dresden and Perceval cursed at the same time.

"I'd have killed him," Perceval muttered.

"Going after Adelaide was probably the only thing that stopped me from doing more." Regulus' shoulders hunched as he lowered his head. "She had better self-control."

"Well," Perceval said after a moment, "we're getting not one but two more ladies at Arrano. I think Leonora and Sarah will be pleased."

"And maybe we can actually have a garden instead of whatever overgrown jungle of weeds we have now," Dresden said.

Regulus chuckled, some of the tension easing from his bearing. "Yes, I suspect Arrano will receive quite the renovations."

Footsteps preceded Landon Belanger emerging from the castle. He shoved a bulging sack of coin at Regulus. "Take it and go."

"As soon as Tamina has her things together." Regulus took the coins with a dour expression.

"Her…" Landon nodded. "Good. She should go with her family." He worked his jaw. "You shouldn't have let my father go with you. You should have sent him home."

Dresden scoffed. "Because Alfred Belanger would have listened to him? Would have turned his back on his king? Your father died a hero, protecting the kingdom he loved. Where were *you*? He died proud of his daughter, who was fighting for her family and her king. If Alfred could see you now, would he be proud of you?"

"You…" Landon reddened and stared at his feet. "He was my father first," he muttered. "And he should *still* be my father." He slumped as he went back inside without another word, his feet dragging over the stone.

Facing the Past
A few weeks later
Location: Arrano Castle

DRESDEN STARED across the courtyard at Regulus and Harold practicing swordplay. Regulus lowered his sword and instructed the lad on adjustments to his stance and the angle of his sword. He was busy. Dresden rocked back and forth on his feet. That was just an excuse. An excuse he'd been making for weeks. *Regulus is busy. Regulus looks too happy or too tired to bring it up now.* Always an excuse.

He forced his feet forward. One step. Two steps. He couldn't do this. He turned around. *Coward.*

"Drez!"

He schooled his expression into a lazy smile as he turned back around. "Reg, Harold."

Regulus walked over, trailed by Harold. "I'm not stepping on your toes, am I?"

"Hm?" Dresden frowned.

Regulus motioned to Harold. "Training." His shoulders hitched upward. "I haven't really…he's my squire, I should…but I know you've been training him, I didn't mean to take over or anything—"

"Oh!" Dresden laughed. "No, no. I'm glad you're feeling up to it." He meant it, too. Just another sign Regulus was doing better. Another sign it was time. He gulped. *Say you want to talk to him. Ask. Now, you ridiculous—*

"Something the matter?" Regulus cocked his head. "You seem on edge. If it's not training, what is it?"

He wet his lips. "Actually…I would like to talk to you. Ask you something."

Regulus nodded and handed Harold his sword. "Put these away, would you, Harold?"

"Yes, my lord." Harold bobbed a quick bow and hurried off. Regulus stood still, waiting.

Dresden rubbed the back of his neck. "I'd like…" This was hard. "Would it be okay…" He cleared his throat. Concern filled Regulus' gray eyes. Dresden couldn't do it. Not looking at him. He looked over at a tree covered in bright red leaves. "Can I…" Words vanished from his mind. This shouldn't be that difficult. Maybe it was a sign he shouldn't go.

"Can you what?" Regulus touched his shoulder. "Something wrong, Drez?"

He started to nod, then shook his head. The words rushed out. "I want to go to Lanure. See if I can find my family."

Silence. He couldn't make himself look at Regulus.

"I see." Heaviness weighed down Regulus' words. Out of the corner of his eye, he saw Regulus shift his weight back and forth.

Dresden had been afraid to ask—afraid of offending Regulus, but mostly afraid of going. He hadn't even considered Regulus might say no. It was part of why he had been scared. Because once Regulus agreed, he'd have to go. But if Regulus didn't agree…

"Of course," Regulus said, voice strained.

Relief and panic melded as Dresden forced himself to look at his friend. "Thank you."

Regulus nodded but stared at the ground, his expression tense. *I offended him*. Dresden's heart sank.

"And…" Regulus' chest rose and fell with a slow, deep breath. "If you find them?"

"I thought…" Shame heated his face as he realized how foolish he was being. "I might see…if they would move here. To Arrano. If you approve." He bit his tongue. *Idiot. Making assumptions about what Regulus would allow.*

Regulus' head jerked up, something flickering in his eyes. "Here? I mean, yes. If…" Whatever brightness had shone on his face for a moment faded to guarded shadows. He looked down. "What if they can't or don't want to? I… You know I'm just adding to my family, right? You were my family when I had no one. If you pick them over me, I can't blame you. I just want you to know I'll always think of you as my brother."

Dresden blinked. "You daft—" He blew out an exasperated breath. "I'm coming back, idiot. I just want to know if they're all right and let them know I'm well. I'd like them closer. But I don't want to leave you or stop being your knight." He nudged Regulus with his elbow. "You can't get rid of me that easily."

Regulus chuckled, but it practically sounded like a sob as he continued to stare at the dirt. "Good. Good. I feared you thought I didn't need you anymore."

If only Regulus knew. But Dresden just laughed. "As if." He stroked his beard. "Who would you go to for advice, hm? Cal and Estevan are automatically out. Only fools go to Perceval for advice. And Jerrick I'm convinced throws bread at problems until they go away."

Regulus looked up, a brow lifted in amusement. "Has anyone ever told you that you think too highly of yourself?"

Dresden pretended to think for a moment. "No, never."

"Good. Would hate to think you're undervaluing yourself." Regulus lightly punched his shoulder. "So…when are you leaving?"

He shrugged. "Tomorrow?" He glanced toward the castle, then looked back to Regulus. "I know you're settling in and still in that honeymoon phase, but…any chance you'd come with me?"

"Come…with you?" Regulus gaped. "Me?"

"I just…" He scuffed the toe of his boot against the dirt. "I don't know how it will go if I do find them. Be nice not to be alone. And if I can't find them…really be nice not to be alone."

After a pause, Regulus nodded. "Yes, of course."

"You sure?" Dresden forced a smile. "You seem hesitant to leave your bride."

"Oh, not that." Regulus blushed. "I mean, sure, also that, but more… I have a feeling your parents might not like me. Since I took you away and all that." He cleared his throat. "But yes. You were there for me when I came back here. You need me, I'm there. Brothers."

This time, Dresden's smile was genuine. "Brothers."

A FEW TOWNSFOLK cast curious glances their way as they rode into Wiltsley, but most people paid them only enough attention to stay out of the way of the massive warhorses' path. Dresden's stomach tightened with every hoof fall along the town's dusty road to the tavern and inn. They drew up their horses near the small, ragged stables along the side. Regulus dismounted without hesitation, but Dresden found he had to force his taut muscles to obey.

He didn't know if Regulus had ever been to Wiltsley, but Dresden hadn't been back since he signed the contract of indenture. His stomach writhed. Regulus was already talking to a stable hand. He handed the man a couple of coins, then patted Sieger's neck and whispered to the horse before handing over the reins. The sight made Dresden roll his eyes and eased some of his tension. He'd never known anyone who grew so attached to their animals.

Dresden was more than content to let Regulus take the lead into the inn and secure their room. He smiled when the innkeeper confirmed his parents were still living in the same house. That was all he could manage as his legs threatened to give out. *They're still alive.* The thought should have brought only joy, but dread followed close on its heels. He tried not to think about meeting them—what he would say, what they would do. But he couldn't push his parents out of his mind, not here.

Memories, many no more than murky scraps of faded recollections, assaulted him as the innkeeper led them to a room. None so strong as the memory of the last time he had walked up these creaking wooden steps. He grinned when Regulus glanced back at him, hiding the aching mixture of anger, fear, and sorrow that being back in this building dredged up. Which room had it been? With the worn, round table where he had signed his name and his life had changed forever? He couldn't remember. For all he knew, it was the room that the innkeeper led them into. It might have been the table where Regulus dropped his bag. Or it might not have been. He was going to make himself crazy.

"Hey."

Dresden looked over at Regulus so quickly his neck popped.

"Are you okay?"

He put on his most cavalier smile. "Yes, of course! A bit tired from the day of riding." He stretched as if to prove his point, but Regulus watched him like he didn't believe him. "Think I might walk around town for a bit. Stretch my legs. Want to come?" If he acted casual, Regulus wouldn't worry.

Regulus shrugged. They locked their room and headed back out into the town. After all the places Dresden had been, it seemed humorous he had ever thought Wiltsley big. The town consisted of a handful of slipshod wood buildings sprawled around a central market that was only a livestock pen and space for some carts near the town's tiny chapel.

"Can you get three hundred silver for the animals?"

"No."

The memory Dresden had suppressed for so long slammed into him with the force of a charging destrier.

"You don't understand what you're saying."

He hadn't. His temple throbbed. *Stop, stop.* He didn't want to think about it, didn't want to consider every question that always accompanied the memory. What would have happened if he hadn't volunteered, why his father had agreed, why his father had only visited once, if it was wrong he was glad he had chosen Regulus—*stop.* He had to get away from the questions. He stepped into the thoroughfare in a daze, intent on getting away from the inn, from the marketplace—

"Drez!" Regulus grabbed the back of his collar and yanked him back.

He choked as his tunic bunched against his neck, then relaxed when Regulus released him. Shaken out of his stupor, he noticed the three men on destriers trotting down the road, just a few moments from reaching them. He had nearly wandered right into their path.

But instead of passing, the men reined in their horses and slowed to a stop directly in front of them. A stocky man in brightly colored fine clothing that marked him as a nobleman peered down at them from the lead horse. His brown hair was tied back at the nape of his neck, and something about his square, sharp features looked familiar.

"Lucky your friend pulled you out of the way, foreigner." The nobleman looked down his nose at Dresden, then turned his attention to Regulus with a snicker. "That's quite the..." He blinked once, hard. "Hargreaves?"

"Hendrick."

Dresden's mouth went dry. Of *course* he looked familiar. Idiot. Granted, it had been over ten years.

Hendrick gave a low whistle. "Geneva did *not* do that scar justice." He glanced behind them at the tavern. "Staying at an inn? I can't imagine what brings you to my father's fief, but a fellow lord and the savior of Monparth is certainly welcome—"

Regulus laughed, a cold, mirthless sound. "Only the king's order could compel me to ever set foot in Kimberly castle."

Hendrick's face flushed. "Rather ungrateful attitude toward the man who raised you."

"The man who kept me," Regulus said in a low voice. "The man who mocked me and beat me. I'm not here for you or your worthless excuse of a father. Good day."

Hendrick scowled. "I see you still have the manners of a bastard son of a servant wench. I shouldn't be surprised, considering you still have your loyal dog." His glance cut toward Dresden.

Dresden reached for his scimitars as Regulus stepped forward, gripping his own sword. But then Regulus let out a slow breath and held up his hand. Dresden eased the scimitars back down into their scabbards on his back and glowered at Hendrick.

"If I have no manners, you'll have to blame the man you claim raised me." Regulus' smile was like the snarl of a wolf. "Now go, before I challenge you to a duel for grievances past and present. I was your better at the sword then, and after a decade of being a mercenary and you living a comfortable life in your castle, I imagine that gap has only widened."

Hendrick paled, his eyes wide. "Very well, I won't bother you further." He gave a curt nod, recovering his composure. "Oh…but before I go, did you receive my gift? I sent it after Lady Geneva brought word of your unexpected ennobling. I hope it reminded you what you are. Even now, you might be a hero—but we both know the truth. You're nothing more than the unwanted son of a servant, and there's no sweeping away the dirt in your blood." He spurred his horse forward and he and the knights accompanying him took off at a canter down the road, leaving swirls of dust in their wake.

"What in Monparth was that supposed to mean?" Dresden flexed his fingers, his pulse racing as he ached for a fight. "What gift?"

Stone slid over Regulus' expression. "Nothing."

Dresden cocked an eyebrow. "Oh, so we're back to hiding things, good to know."

Fire burned in Regulus' eyes as he met Dresden's gaze. "Are you sure you want to go there when you're hiding something from me?"

Dresden scrambled to cover his surprise with a light laugh. "Me? What would I be hiding?"

"I don't know, but you're on edge and trying to pretend you're not." He stepped out into the street, and Dresden followed.

"You're just trying to change the subject from whatever it was Hendrick meant."

"If I tell you…" Regulus sighed. "Will you tell me what's bothering you?"

Dresden massaged the side of his neck. "Okay."

Regulus slowed and glanced at him, like he hadn't expected that answer. "I wasn't sure what he meant, either, until he mentioned sweeping away dirt. A couple of months after arriving at Arrano, I received a box. Addressed to me, no indication who it was from. Inside was a note that said 'lest you forget your roots' and…a broom. I never told anyone, just stuck it in the kitchen and forgot about it."

Dresden's heart panged.

"I didn't think we would have the misfortune of coming across any of the Kimberlys," Regulus continued. "I certainly hadn't expected the initial civility…even though some ridiculous part of me thought maybe, after everything, they would apologize. Clearly nothing I do will change their opinion of me." He rolled his shoulders. "Still, I will cherish the look of terror on his face at the prospect of being challenged to a duel." He chuckled.

"I wish you'd done it instead of threatening." Dresden elbowed him. "I imagine he might have wet himself. Would have been something to see you knock him down, too."

Regulus squared his shoulders. "I don't need to prove myself to them. He can think of me what he likes. I have you and Adelaide and the men, and you all know who I am. Besides, no one's opinion changes my worth."

"Hmmm, deep, wise truths there—"

"Yes, yes, you're brilliant and the greatest friend a man could ask for." Regulus knocked his shoulder against Dresden's, making him stagger. Dresden laughed and shoved him sideways.

"So," Regulus said, straightening his shirt, "are you going to be honest with me now?"

Dresden kicked a pebble in the road and watched it skitter over the packed dirt. "It's…hard to be back here."

"Did you come to Wiltsley often?"

"I sometimes accompanied my father to the market." He scratched his beard. "I signed the contract in that inn." The moment he blurted the words, he wished he could snatch them back. Especially when Regulus stopped walking.

"I didn't—"

"No, it's fine." He smiled reassuringly. "Just…a lot of tangled memories and emotions. Thoughts I haven't been dealing with for years." He shrugged, unsure why he was admitting any of this. It was stupid, he should stop—

"Dresden." Regulus laid a hand on his shoulder and turned him so they faced each other. "I'm sorry."

He blinked. "What?"

"I'm sorry I ever accepted your contract—even if I'm unsure I really had a choice." Regulus looked down at the dirt between them. "But mostly I'm sorry that after everything we've been through, everything you've done for me…you don't trust me enough to tell me when you're not okay."

Dresden stammered a moment before he found his voice. "That's not it at all! You've just had a lot going on, so I don't want to burden you more. And I know you'll blame yourself if I'm unhappy, even if it's not your fault. I mean, you're doing it right now! As if the fact I don't know how to be honest that I'm scared, and I'm panicking, and yeah, a little angry and sad, is somehow your fault or a sign you've been a bad friend, and you're *not*. It's this place, it's men like Hendrick and Kimberly and those usurers my father borrowed from; it's the fact my parents are alive, yet they never visited!" He turned away, furiously blinking away tears.

They walked for a few minutes in silence, nothing but the sounds of their footsteps on the road as they wandered further from Wiltsley.

"I don't know what I'm feeling or thinking," Dresden said. "Just that I'm nervous about seeing my parents."

"That's understandable. I would be, too. But whatever you need—to talk, to rant, to go hit something, for me to stand by you—I'm here."

More of Dresden's discomfort and tension faded. "Thank you for always being there for me."

The corner of Regulus' mouth turned up. "You're always there for me. That's what brothers do, right?"

"Right." He nudged Regulus. "And you're getting better at taking my compliments instead of trying to explain why you're not actually that great. Makes me proud. My little Regulus, all grown—"

"Is there a river nearby? I might need to throw you in it." Regulus mussed Dresden's hair, and Dresden ducked away, trying to smooth out the mess.

"Hey!" He scowled at Regulus, who only laughed. "I take it back. At least moody, insecure Regulus teased me less."

"I'm confident your ego can handle it."

Yes, the circumstances of meeting Regulus hadn't been great. The circumstances of being Regulus' friend hadn't always been good and came with plenty of dangers and ups and downs. But maybe the most valuable relationships were the ones that weren't easy or uncomplicated. He wouldn't trade being Regulus' friend for anything.

DRESDEN AND Regulus reined in their horses. The little house didn't look much altered from his hazy memories. Gray light from the overcast sky bathed sturdy wattle and daub walls, although he thought he remembered it being one room, not two. The thatched roof looked in excellent condition, and the front door was worn but solid. At least they had done well with that indenture money. The thought brought some comfort.

Chickens wandered around a large enclosure to one side of the house. Somewhere, a cow lowed. A garden, most of its plants past their prime as winter crept closer, surrounded the side of the house opposite the chickens.

"Are you ready?" Regulus asked. "Or do you want to come back later?"

He had thought he was ready. But he didn't even know what he felt as he looked at his old home. Some confusing mixture of shame, fear, excitement, love, and distance. Eighteen years had passed. Maybe he shouldn't have come back. Guilt filled him. No, he should have come back a long time ago. So maybe a few more hours wouldn't make much difference…

"Yeah," Dresden whispered. "I think…later." He wheeled his horse around, ignoring the accusation of *coward* his mind threw at him.

Something creaked behind him. "Oh!" A woman's voice. "Um." Another creak. "Can…can I help you, sir? Sirs?" Her voice still held a Carasian accent. "My husband is out back."

"Um…" Regulus faltered.

Dresden's chin dropped toward his chest. No more running. He turned his horse back around and his heart spasmed.

A part of him had feared he wouldn't recognize her, but there could be no doubt she was his mother. Wisps of gray-streaked dark hair had fallen free of her bun and curled around her sun-darkened face. Age lined her eyes and mouth. Her rough brown dress of spun wool hung on her lanky frame, but she still stood tall. She looked at Dresden and her lips parted. The basket in her hand tumbled to the ground. She snatched it back up and her expression shuttered, the glimmer of hopeful recognition locked behind dark eyes.

"What is your business here, sirs?"

"Ma." His voice came out in a croak.

She clutched the basket to her chest as her lower lip trembled. "What?"

Dresden dismounted and took a hesitant step forward. His mother inched back into the doorway, clearly ready to shut herself inside. He held his hands out to the sides in a placating gesture. "Ma. It's—it's me. Dresden."

"No." She shook her head, her jaw quivering. "You—you're a hallucination. Or, or a trick, or—"

Dresden took a step forward but stopped when she backed further into the doorway. "Ma…please. It's Dresden. Look." He pointed to his scimitars on his back. "The scimitars Da gave me. I'm here. I'm sorry—"

"Dresden?"

Wetness pricked at his eyes. "Yes, Ma."

Hesitation marked her steps as she crept toward him. He stood still, afraid of frightening her. She squinted up at him. "Dresden?" One trembling hand reached toward his face. "My son?"

He nodded, not trusting his voice.

"Where have you been?" She threw the basket aside and grabbed his shirt. "What happened to you? You disappeared! We didn't even know! Your da went to that awful lord's castle after you didn't come home when your ten years were up, and they told him your master had left and taken you with him three years before that!"

Shame that his parents had found out from Kimberly warred with annoyance. Three years. They didn't even notice he was gone for three years. "I know, Ma, I'm sorry—"

"Sorry! Sorry!" She shook him. "For all we knew, you were dead! Where did you go? Why didn't you come home! Why are you here now! Where have you been? You—you—you…" She wailed and released his shirt to throw her arms around him. She squeezed so tight he could hardly breathe.

"Hana!" A man ran through the garden, a hoe in his hands like a weapon as he charged toward them. "Get away from her, you leave her—" His father stumbled and pulled up short, eyes wide. His tan skin turned ashen.

"Hey, Da," Dresden said weakly.

Ma pulled away, pried the hoe out of his father's hands, and led him over. "It's Dresden." A tear slipped down her cheek. "Our son came home."

For a long moment, his father stared, his expression unreadable. Gray streaked his short black beard and thinning hair. Dresden forced himself to stop wondering what that boded for his own hairline. More wrinkles were etched into his father's face than his mother's, and his father's back had bowed slightly. Da's throat bobbed. "Dresden?"

"Yes."

Da nodded, then fell to his knees. "Forgive me, my son, forgive me; I'm sorry—"

"Da!" Dresden rushed forward and pulled his father to his feet. "What are you apologizing—"

"I shouldn't have let you go, I'm sorry; I shouldn't have let you…" Tears squeezed from Da's eyes. "And I should have visited, but I was too ashamed, and I lost my chance, and I'm so sorry; not a day goes by I don't regret letting you go, don't regret not visiting—"

Dresden shook his head and pulled Da close. He was surprised to find himself several inches taller than his father. "*I'm* sorry, Da…" His throat closed up, swallowing any other words.

After a moment, Da pulled back. He looked over Dresden, studying every inch. Dresden fought the urge to flinch under his scrutiny.

"He looks good, doesn't he?" Ma said, her warm voice full of emotion. "Looks so much like you at his age."

"You still have them." Da pointed to the scimitars. His gaze slid to Dresden's right. "Who's that?"

"Oh!" Dresden blushed at his forgetfulness and looked over at Regulus, still seated on his horse and looking uncomfortable. "Ma, Da, this is Regulus Hargreaves, my—"

Ma made a sound like a hiss through her teeth and drew back against Da's side. Anger flashed over Da's face, followed by horror.

"You…" Da's expression contorted. "You're still…he still… It was supposed to be ten years," he said feebly, pain reflected in his eyes.

Realization hit, and Dresden shook his head. "No! No, it's not like that! He's not my master anymore; he released me a long time ago. Reg, come here."

Da's eyes widened as Dresden motioned Regulus to join them. Regulus' boots hit the ground with a thud, and he strode over. Dresden gripped his shoulder.

"Regulus is my friend. More like my brother, really." Ma's eyes narrowed and her nose wrinkled, so Dresden hurried on. "We've been through a lot together, and he's always had my back. Saved my life more times than I can count,

although I'm sure he can. He's actually a lord now, Lord of Arrano. And I'm…"
He puffed out his chest a little. "One of his knights. Sir Dresden Jakobs."

Da's mouth fell open as Ma gasped.

"It's a pleasure to meet you." Regulus gave a small bow, and Da's eyebrows reached for his shrinking hairline.

"You're a knight?" Ma smiled. "My son, a knight of Monparth?"

Dresden grinned. "Yes."

"Hm." Da eyed Regulus, then looked back to Dresden. "For how long?"

All his pride and happiness vanished. He cleared his throat. "A couple of years."

Da opened his mouth, but whatever he was about to say was cut off by a new voice. "Ma, Da, who's here?"

Dresden turned slowly and looked around Regulus. A young woman with a dark olive Carasian complexion and dark braids wrapped around her head approached them, a baby strapped to her chest and a little girl who looked to be around four years old clinging to her skirts. She glanced at Dresden with inquisitiveness but no recognition, then shifted her attention to Regulus. Her gaze lingered on his scar before she turned her worried expression to Dresden's parents—their parents.

"Is everything all right?" She placed her hand on the little girl's shoulder and drew her in closer. Like Dresden, she had no Carasian accent.

"Tatya?" Dresden's mouth went dry. His sister was grown…with children.

Her expression grew more wary. "I'm sorry, I don't recall meeting—"

"It's your brother," Ma exclaimed with joy. "Dresden came home."

Tatya cocked her head, her lips pursed. "Did he now? You're not dead, then."

Dresden stuttered. "Uh… No. I… It's good to see you, Tatya. All…grown up. With…children." He had known she might not remember him. He thought he'd been prepared for her not to care. But her coldness cut deep.

Her lips quirked to the side, halfway between a smirk and a frown. "Do you not have children?"

He laughed. "Um, no. Not married."

Tatya looked to Regulus. "Who's the Monparthian?"

"Heh…ah… I'm Regulus." He waved, then crossed his arms. Dresden rolled his eyes. At least Regulus' dependable awkwardness distracted from his own.

Tatya's jaw tightened. "Why are you here, Dresden?" Her sharp gaze stayed locked on Regulus.

"I think I should clarify that Regulus isn't my master anymore—"

"Excellent." Tatya pointed at Regulus. "You selfish, vile, heartless monster! Yes, I know who you are. I've heard your name cursed for years, ever since you took my brother and disappeared. I don't know why you're here, but you aren't taking anything or anyone else from my family." She gripped her daughter's shoulder tighter.

Regulus shrank into himself, but Tatya wasn't done.

"Haven't you hurt us enough without coming here—"

"No!" Dresden held up his hands to stop her rant. "I asked him to come! He's my friend!" Regulus hunched his shoulders and stared at the ground. "And my lord, although he's acting like a scolded child right now—Reg, stand up straight!"

Regulus only shrank back more. "Maybe I should go for a bit…"

"No." Dresden sighed. "I know I have a lot of explaining to do. But don't blame Regulus. It's not his fault. The indenture wasn't his idea; he was eleven! When he left Lord Kimberly, he released me from the contract. He asked me to go with him *as his friend*, and I did, all right? He's been my friend, my captain, my lord, and my brother. You want to yell at someone, yell at me. I chose not to come back. Regulus has never forced me into anything." He sighed. "Look…can we go inside to talk?"

"Good idea." Da turned toward the house, pulling Ma with him. "Tatya, come on. Rachel and Warren can meet their uncle."

Regulus looked to Dresden. "Do you want me in there or out here?"

Dresden rubbed his beard. It would be nice not to face them alone, but none of his family seemed happy with Regulus. "Frankly, I want you in there, but…" He sighed. "Maybe wait out here." He patted Regulus' shoulder and walked toward the house.

Tatya followed, casting a glance back at Regulus. "So…you tell your lord what to do? And what does that mean, exactly? You're a regular servant now?"

"No, I'm a knight." He smiled at Tatya's startled expression. "I don't tell my lord what to do, but I do tell my friend what to do. And he's here as my friend."

"Hmm." Tatya led her little girl into the house.

They sat around a worn wood table, and Tatya introduced her children at Ma's prodding. Tatya's oldest, Rachel, climbed onto Dresden's lap and grabbed at his beard, saying, "Uncle Dwesdon?" He wasn't sure what to make of that.

Based on the thin line of Tatya's mouth, she wasn't sure, either. Dresden couldn't blame her. Tatya didn't appear to remember him.

They spent the next couple hours with Dresden relaying everything that had happened in eighteen years. He made sure his family knew everything—all the times Regulus had protected him, all the times he had been there for Regulus, and how Regulus and Adelaide had saved Monparth. He played up his own contribution, of course. After all, he had taken on an immortal, bought the king precious time in escaping, and stolen the legendary Staff of Nightfall. The king had given him a small bag of gold for his help. Regulus and Adelaide had gotten much more and an entire banquet, but they *had* killed the sorcerer and said immortal. Dresden had just nearly gotten himself killed.

Rachel fell asleep in his arms shortly into his story, but when Tatya suggested moving her to their parents' bed, he declined. He hadn't been around children in a long time, but he found he enjoyed cradling his sister's daughter. It made him feel connected to his family. Besides, he was afraid he'd wake her if he moved too much.

"So now that everything is calmed down, and Regulus is doing all right, I wanted to find you," Dresden finished. "I'm sorry I didn't come sooner. Or visit before we left. I was…a coward. And selfish. I didn't know how to say goodbye. I was angry you never visited and worried you'd try to talk me out of leaving with Regulus. Regulus needed me, and I didn't want to be a farmer. I wanted to go on adventures and see the world, maybe make a name for myself as a mercenary. Which I kind of did," he added with a wink that made Ma frown.

Regulus had really been the one to make a name for himself as the captain, but twice another mercenary troop had tried to convince Dresden to leave Regulus and join them. There was never a chance of it happening, but it had boosted his ego both times.

"Honestly, I'm glad I went with him," Dresden said. "But I was young and foolish and didn't realize how long it would be before I could come back. I'm sorry I didn't say goodbye. I'm sorry I didn't send word when I came back, but I didn't know if it would reach you…or what to say." He stroked his niece's hair. His *niece*. It felt surreal. Did he want to have children of his own? A thought for another time. "Forgive me."

"Do you have any idea what you put them through?" Tatya hissed, keeping her voice low so as not to wake her sleeping children. "Da did nothing but get drunk and sleep for two weeks after he found out you were gone."

"Tatya!" Ma snapped.

Da stared down at the table. "I knew it was my fault," he whispered. "I was ashamed. Your ma told me to visit you, tried to get me to take her or Tatya to see you, and I made excuses to avoid it. I didn't want to think about what you were doing, didn't want to know how badly my mistakes had ruined your life, didn't want to know if you were angry with me. Then I was afraid that after so long without visiting, you wouldn't want to see me. And I was right." He held his head in his hands. "I shouldn't have signed that contract."

"Didn't you listen?" Dresden frowned and shifted Rachel so his arm wouldn't fall asleep. "I don't blame you. And good came of it. I'm a knight. And I wouldn't have made a good farmer, I don't think. I liked being a mercenary, and I like being a knight. Not to brag, but Regulus probably would have been a different man without me, a man who wouldn't have been able to defeat that sorcerer." Tatya rolled her eyes, but Dresden ignored her. "And would you still be here if I hadn't taken the indenture? Would you have been able to add that second room? Would there be a cow out back?"

"Two cows," Da mumbled. "No, most likely not."

"So why are you really here? What's the point of finding us now?" Tatya asked, her arms folded across her stomach. She had placed her infant in a small crib in the corner some time before.

Dresden glared at her. "You're angry with me for not coming back, and you're angry with me *for* coming back; what do you want from me, Tatya?" Rachel grunted, and he realized he'd raised his voice. He sighed. "I just…wanted to see you all. Make sure you were okay. Let you know what happened to me." He licked his lips. He could guess their answer, but he needed to know. "See if you wanted…to move to Arrano."

Tatya's face pinched. Da dropped his hands and looked up.

"Leave…our home?" Ma blinked at him. "We've been here so long. We have a life here."

"My husband won't move," Tatya said sullenly. "And I don't want to. I don't know you."

Dresden flinched. He wanted to argue that it was only half his fault, but regardless of fault, it was true. He barely remembered her, too…and he remembered a tiny little girl with missing teeth. Not a young woman with a daughter the same age Tatya had been last time Dresden saw her.

"Tatya…" Da sighed.

"No." Tatya shook her head. "I have a comfortable house and a good life here. My daughter has friends here." That both lightened Dresden's spirits and pricked at his heart. Friends had not been easy for him to find as the son of Carasians, and it pleased him Tatya's daughter wasn't having the same problem. "My husband's parents are here. I'm not moving halfway across the kingdom for a brother who didn't bother to say goodbye just to live as a peasant under the man who owned my brother for seven years."

Dresden's shoulders slumped, but he nodded. He couldn't argue with anything she said.

Ma shook her head. "I'm sorry, Dresden… I can't leave my grandchildren."

"All my hard work and dreams for my family are on this land, in these walls," Da said, then winced. "Other than you. I'm proud of what you've made of yourself, Dresden. I'm relieved to see you again, to know you're all right, that I didn't completely fail you. But we're staying here."

A knock sounded at the door. Da frowned and went to answer, while Dresden tried to twist around in his chair to see without disturbing Rachel.

Regulus stood in front of the door, the top of his head obstructed by the doorframe. Rain fell around him, and water dripped from the ends of his loose curls. "Sorry…it's just… It's been raining for a while; do you mind if I step inside?"

Dresden's eyebrows raised in alarm. Somewhere in the back of his mind he had noticed the muffled patter of rain on the thatch, but he hadn't consciously thought about it—or the fact he had left Regulus outside.

"Of course, my lord." Da stepped aside with a bow. Regulus ducked under the door to enter.

"He shouldn't be in here," Tatya muttered.

Regulus must have heard her, because his face reddened. He looked around at everyone, his expression softening when he saw Rachel in Dresden's arms. "I'm honored to meet you all. Dresden loves you a great deal."

"He has an odd way of showing it," Tatya muttered again.

A frown tugged at Regulus' scar. "I suppose agreeing to ten years of servitude at the age of ten because you wanted your sister to be able to get a new dress that fits her and continue to live in a house is an unusual way of showing affection."

This time Tatya flushed and looked away. Dresden didn't know whether to scold Regulus or thank him.

Water dripped off Regulus and pooled on the wood paneled floor. Dresden started. Wood paneled. It had been dirt the last time he was here. His family had flourished without him. He darted a glance at his father, recalling Tatya's admission. Maybe his absence hadn't entirely been a blessing. The thought both dredged his guilt back up and consoled him. They had missed him. Even all those years when his family never visited him at the Kimberly estate, while he felt forgotten, abandoned, he had been missed.

"I don't suppose there is any chance you would stay here?" Ma asked, but there was no hope in her voice.

Dresden wet his mouth. "Your life is here, but mine is at Arrano. And I swore an oath of fealty."

"An oath I can release you from if you ask," Regulus said quietly. Before Dresden could protest, Da cut him off.

"You would do that?" Da asked. "You would let him go?"

"Dresden has been free to go since he was seventeen. Should have been sooner." Regulus stared at the floor, his hair still dripping. "I'm sorry I separated you, intentionally or not. Until I got married, Dresden was the only family I've had since I was six. I want what's best for him."

A heavy sigh came from Ma. "I think it's pretty clear where Sir Jakobs should be and where he wants to be. And it's not here."

Dresden met her eyes and understanding passed between them. She wasn't angry with him and wouldn't resent him leaving. He looked to Da, who nodded and turned to Regulus.

"Thank you for taking care of my son, my lord."

"I think he's taken care of me more often, Jakobs." Regulus smiled.

"I suppose he isn't so bad," Tatya conceded. Dresden rolled his eyes.

"Will you stay here tonight?" Ma asked.

Dresden shook his head. "We have a room in town." He shifted Rachel again, but this time she woke up. She looked at him in confusion and started to cry.

"Hey, hey, it's okay, Rachel," he soothed. "It's Uncle Dresden."

Tatya pulled her from his arms. The little girl sniffed and looked from her mother to Dresden, then nodded. "Uncle Dwesdin."

"Yeah." He looked to Tatya. "I don't know that I will be able to often, but...if I ever visit...would that be okay?"

Tatya's brow pinched before she nodded. "Of course. And…thank you. For what you did for us."

He nodded as Rachel clambered out of Tatya's lap and went over to stare up at Regulus.

"Did you get hurted?"

Ma gasped. "Rachel!"

Regulus just laughed. "A long time ago. Your Uncle Dresden took care of me."

Dresden's parents talked them into staying for supper. Ma and Tatya made old Carasian recipes that tasted like heaven to Dresden, but the spiciness had Regulus gulping water. Tatya's husband Evan, a stout, boisterous Monparthian butcher, laughed and told Regulus, "You get used to it after a while." They explained that Tatya and Evan lived a short walk away, and they often dined at each other's homes.

After supper, Dresden hid a small pouch of gold he knew his parents would refuse otherwise in a basket near the door, and he and Regulus returned to town for the night, and then headed back to Arrano.

Dresden's heart felt light. He had faced his regret and guilt and fear, and even if it hadn't fixed his past mistakes, it removed a greater weight from his shoulders than he'd even acknowledged he had been carrying. He had put things right with his parents and sister. He was heading home with his brother, to his family—Regulus, Harold, the men, Adelaide, even Tamina now. Even Gaius and Minerva and their newborn, who visited whenever they could. An odd, jumbled family of mercenaries, misfits, orphans, nobles, and heroes, but his all the same.

Maybe that family would grow to include a wife. Perhaps he could seek out Katherine at the next party, ask if she was still single and interested in more. Dresden smiled to himself at the thought.

They rode through the gate into Arrano. Perceval nodded at them from where he leaned against a tree nearly devoid of leaves, watching Jerrick, Leonora, and Tamina argue over shrubbery. The three paused long enough to wave and smile before returning to pointing at various parts of the garden and talking over each other. Adelaide and Magnus ran out of the castle, and Adelaide had her arms around Regulus the moment he dismounted. Magnus shoved between them, whining for attention. Harold jogged over with a huge grin as he welcomed them back.

Whatever the future might hold, Dresden knew one thing.

Every choice, every failure and success, everything good and bad and in between, had led him here. Right where he belonged.

Home.

BELLS
OF
WINTER

A MERCENARY AND THE MAGE
STORY

HAROLD WAS BEGINNING to think he didn't care for winter.

It had taken hours for the fire to warm the small square room attached to the armory so he could work on routine maintenance of Regulus' armor. Even with the blazing fire, he needed his thick wool stockings and long-sleeved wool tunic. A stubborn, piercing chill always seemed to settle deep into the stone of Arrano castle in the winter. The room had one small window with soot-stained panes opposite the fireplace, through which he could make out some falling snow. In the warmer months, he could open that window to keep the stench of the vinegar-soaked rough cloth he used to remove rust from becoming over-powering. But in the winter, the ice-frosted pane stayed firmly shut against the blowing snow.

A set of Regulus' plate armor covered the large table. Harold sat in one of the two chairs, close enough to the fire to feel its warmth without heating the steel. As he scrubbed at a tiny spot of rust along the edge of a gauntlet, he hummed to distract himself from the cold seeping into his fingers. He couldn't relate to the lyrics of the song that came to mind—or what he could recall of them, anyway. Something about staying warm in the winter by kissing under a blanket while snow fell soft in the moonlight. He had vague memories of his father singing it to his mother whenever the first snow came around.

That was the other problem with winter. It always reminded him of his parents.

Harold wasn't certain why. He had memories of his parents from every season, but it seemed like the ones from winter were the strongest. As if those little pockets of memory were all the warmer because of the cold around them. Except he never knew if he was grateful for the memories or not. There was a certain bittersweet blend of love and pain to them, because even a sweet memory of his father planting a messy kiss on his mother's cheek was marred by the memory of blood and screams and troll stench.

He squinted at the gauntlet and gave a sharp nod when he couldn't find any more rust. Cleaning and polishing armor wasn't his favorite chore. It was mostly mindless, scrubbing any spots that had developed rust with vinegar or letting the armor soak if needed, then giving it a thorough polish. He reached for the jar of linseed oil and beeswax mixture to polish the gauntlet and wished for something to occupy his thoughts other than the song and the hollow ache of remembering his parents.

The door to his left groaned open, and he looked up, ceasing his humming. Caleb and Estevan ambled in. That was not the kind of distraction he wanted, and he watched them enter with narrowed eyes. There weren't many reasons for any of the knights to come looking for him here, but those two specifically, and together…trouble would follow, and he had no time for trouble. Not with polishing to finish and other chores to complete before supper and an evening of checkers with Dresden.

"Hey, Harold." Caleb grinned—that overwide, too-friendly grin that said he was up to something.

Estevan rested his hip against the table. "How are you doing?"

"Oh, no." Harold shook his head and polished faster. "I know that face and that tone. You two are plotting trouble, and I won't be part of it—"

"Trouble?" Estevan put his hand to his chest. "Us?"

"Yes, obviously." Harold frowned at the gauntlet as he checked if he had applied an even layer of the protective wax. "You want something, and the answer is no."

"You don't even know what it is yet!" Caleb snatched the gauntlet out of his hands and looked at Harold with the most ridiculous attempt at doe eyes. "It's a great idea—"

"When have you ever had a great idea?" Harold tried to take the gauntlet back, but Caleb clutched it to his chest. With a huff, Harold grabbed a pauldron from the pile.

"We have plenty of great ideas." Estevan took the pauldron from Harold's hands and pulled his chair away from the table, so the armor was out of reach.

Harold crossed his arms and scowled, even though he knew he was too scrawny for the look to be particularly intimidating. Not like when Perceval did it. "What do you want, so I can say no and get back to work?"

"Work, work, work, so boring." Caleb tossed the gauntlet onto the table with a clang that made Harold grimace, then rubbed his hands together. "Sometimes it's a time for fun! Frivolity! Feasting! Festivities!"

Harold lifted a brow. "If you say fornication next, I swear—"

"I mean, sometimes, but not this time."

Estevan shrugged. "Well, maybe—"

"We're trying to talk him into it, man!" Caleb slapped Harold's shoulder.

"Picture it: a party. The great hall all decorated. Us in all our best finery. Music! Dancing! Games!"

"So much food!" Estevan chimed in.

"Hold on." Harold held up a hand. "A party? At Arrano? Have you lost your—"

"Not *just* a party," Caleb said. "A Bells of Winter festival!"

"An all-day event." Estevan moved his hand, palm out, in an arc in front of his body. "Festivities from dawn until night."

"At Arrano?" Harold slumped back in the chair with a sigh. "You *have* lost your minds."

"But doesn't it sound wonderful?" Caleb put a hand on the back of Harold's chair and leaned over him. "We'll do all the traditions. The bells, the candles—"

"The food!" Estevan clasped his hands and looked heavenward. "Sarah has already agreed to help, and she described some of the most delicious-sounding pastries and pies. Monparth may struggle with spices, but they can do pastries and pies."

Harold *did* love pastries and pies...

"The music"—Caleb indicated himself—"headed by me, of course. The traditional decorations, the gifts—"

"A gift exchange sounds particularly fun," Estevan added.

Caleb shot him an annoyed glance. "Yes. All of it. Don't you think it's time this sad old castle saw a party, Harold? And shouldn't Lady Adelaide and Lady Tamina's first winter at Arrano be special?" He knelt and looked into Harold's eyes. "After everything everyone has been through and after defeating a terrible sorcerer, isn't a big Bells of Winter celebration in order? What better way to celebrate all we have overcome? After all, Bells of Winter is a celebration of life."

Harold bit his lip. It sounded fun... And he had never been to a proper Bells of Winter feast. He vaguely recalled some small celebrations with his parents, but nothing so grand as a lordly Bells of Winter party in a castle. And when winter kept reminding him of death—his least favorite subject—a celebration of life sounded appealing.

"I can see you're considering it." Estevan nodded with a smug smile. "Come on. Let's throw a party."

Harold tapped his foot, looking between the knights' eager expressions. They had convinced him, but there was one great big problem they seemed to have forgotten. "Regulus won't let you throw a party."

"Ah." Caleb snapped his fingers. "That's where you come in!"

Oh, the conniving troublemakers. He should have known.

"See, Regulus would tell us no," Estevan said.

"But *you*..." Caleb stood and thrust his hands toward Harold. "You go up to him, give him some kind of sad story about how Bells of Winter makes you miss your family or how you never could afford a proper celebration as a child, make some mention of wanting to celebrate with your *current* family; will melt the big man's heart right into a puddle."

"And then"—Estevan leaned down enough to throw his arm across the back of Harold's chair—"you give him the idea of throwing a party."

"Maybe keep it small to start," Caleb advised. "What if we had a feast? And decorations? And just made it a big event?"

Harold still didn't think it was a wise idea, but their excitement was contagious. But then, that was what they always did. Broke down his hesitation with eagerness and making it sound like a good idea, and then he ended up with fifteen wasp stings, or a twisted ankle, or got chased by a terrifying woodsman with an ax. Still, there couldn't be any harm in asking.

"Well...I suppose I can ask—"

"Ha!" Estevan leapt and thrust his fist into the air.

"I believe he's still in the west parlor." Caleb grabbed Harold's arm and tugged him to his feet.

"What, right now?"

"Yes!" Caleb shoved him toward the door. "Such parties take planning, so time is of the essence!"

"But the armor—"

"Can wait for a few minutes while you attend to this very important matter," Estevan said.

"Important to who?" Harold asked as Caleb pushed him through the armory.

Caleb steered him into the hall. "Parties are very important, trust me."

The knights ushered him downstairs to the great hall and down another corridor to the west parlor. The door was slightly ajar, and light from a fire shone through the narrow opening. At least Regulus would be relaxed and probably alone.

Regulus only used the west parlor for one reason: warming up and drying off after playing in the rain or snow with Magnus. Adelaide had insisted after a soaked, muddy Magnus had jumped on top of her on the bed. Now Magnus was only allowed in Regulus' room when he was dry and during the day. According to Regulus, the huge dog kept jumping on the bed at awkward times or waking Adelaide in the middle of the night because he had laid across her feet, pinning them in place.

Magnus slept in Harold's room now, on a cushion that was nearly as large as Harold's bed—but at least Magnus liked the cushion, because Harold's small bed would never fit them both. Harold had spent the first few nights worried the dog would jump on top of him and suffocate him. A fear he had never mentioned to anyone, of course. It had also taken several nights to get used to Magnus' breathing, but he hardly noticed it anymore.

A gentle push on his back nearly caused Harold to bump into the door. He frowned at Estevan, then knocked.

"Come in," Regulus called.

With a glance back at the knights, Harold pushed open the door and walked in. The crackling fire had made the room comfortably toasty. Regulus sat in an armchair with its back to the door, facing the large window that overlooked the orchard. The curtains were tied back to allow a full view of the large snowflakes drifting through the air and tree branches sagging under a layer of snow that looked like thick icing. A mostly dry Magnus sprawled on his side in front of the fireplace, eyes closed and large pink tongue lolling out of his mouth as he panted.

"Oh, hello, Harold." Regulus looked up with a relaxed smile. He smiled so much more now than he had for the last two years.

"Afternoon, my lord." Harold bowed, even though Regulus had told him he didn't have to. He was going to be a knight one day, and he wanted to do it right. "I just…I was thinking, while I was polishing your armor. The snow…" He glanced toward the door.

Caleb and Estevan stood in the doorway. They nodded encouragingly.

"The snow reminded me of my parents." That wasn't a lie. "Of a song that my father used to sing to my mother. I think it might be a song sometimes sung at Bells of Winter celebrations, and it just made me realize…" He scuffed the toe of his boot on the carpet. "I've never been to a proper Bells of Winter feast. Maybe…maybe we could have a feast this year?"

Regulus' brow lowered. "Hm. I can talk to the cook and Sarah about making something special for supper on Bells."

Out of the corner of his eye, Harold saw Caleb motioning for him to keep going.

"That would be nice," Harold said slowly. "Maybe we could even…do some more? My parents liked to sing, or play some games…"

Estevan mouthed something, but he had no idea what.

"I never really enjoyed Bells of Winter celebrations as a child." Regulus looked out the window for a moment. "It would be nice to reclaim that. And Adelaide mentioned that her mother loves Bells of Winter. Some traditional celebrations would probably bring her joy." Regulus nodded, but Harold was distracted by whatever Caleb and Estevan were trying to signal him with their hands and exaggerated mouthing.

"Un-bite ah?" That clearly wasn't it.

Caleb walked two fingers across his palm, and Harold caught himself frowning. He had no idea what Caleb was trying to say, so he focused on Regulus.

"Um, perhaps…it could be an all-day party?"

Regulus shrugged. "You're certainly free to spend the day however you like. Perhaps some of the men would like to get up to some revelry."

Estevan gave an exaggerated, silent groan.

"Something wrong?" Regulus tilted his head and squinted at Harold.

Harold's cheeks heated. "Oh, uh, no, I just, that is, I thought…" Caleb waved his hands and Estevan dragged his hands down his cheeks, pulling down his lower eyelids.

"What are you looking at?" Regulus turned in his chair.

"Nothing—"

But Regulus had already looked behind him. Caleb and Estevan froze, then quickly straightened and smiled.

"Oh, hello there, Regulus." Caleb scratched the side of his head. "Fancy…running into you…"

"Get in here," Regulus said, his tone unamused.

Estevan and Caleb sulked in, looking rather like children caught with their hands in the sweets. Regulus tapped his boot against the carpeted floor.

"Would I be correct to assume you two put him up to this?"

"Oh, there was no coercion," Estevan said. "See, Harold here, well, we found him all dejected and sad, cleaning your armor practically with his tears because he was missing his parents so badly—"

"I was not!" Harold felt his face go red. "I mean, it is true that I was think-ing about my parents when you two barged in—"

"Aw, come on, Regulus!" Caleb threw his arms out wide. "It's going to be your first Bells of Winter as a married man! First one since becoming a free man again! You have more to celebrate this year than most anyone. We should do it right—ringing of the bells at dawn, decorations, games, singing and danc-ing, a spectacular feast—"

"All right."

Harold blinked. He must have misheard Regulus. Caleb stood with his arms still flung awkwardly out to the sides for a moment before they drifted down.

Estevan broke the silence. "What?"

"I said all right." Regulus pushed off the arms of the chair and stood. "You can throw your party. Do whatever you like. But there are two rules." He held up one finger. "One, it's all at your expense except for food, which I will pay for, and you have to do all the organizing and coordinating and can't look to me for help if it all goes awry." A second finger joined the first as Regulus' expression turned deadly serious. "And two, and this is important: you are to invite no one who doesn't live on Arrano lands or isn't a blood relative of someone who does. Servants and vassals of Arrano and immediate family I will allow, no one else."

"Aw!" Caleb slouched. "But, Reg—"

"I'm just…I'm not ready." Regulus looked toward the fire. "To let the no-bles into my sanctuary. Not yet." His throat bobbed.

Harold lowered his gaze. He'd known that Regulus wouldn't want to invite other nobles. Regulus and Adelaide turned down more invitations than they accepted. Dresden said it was because they were tired of the questions about experiences that still hurt, and of people who never cared about them before suddenly being interested in befriending the famous couple. Harold thought he wouldn't like it, either, if he was Regulus.

Regulus looked back to Estevan and Caleb. "Do we have an agreement?"

Estevan's lower lip stuck out in a pout. "Only food on your bill, and no outsiders invited," he mumbled.

"All right, go on." Regulus nodded toward the door. Harold started to fol-low Caleb and Estevan, but Regulus stopped him with a hand on his shoulder. "Harold."

"Yes?" He looked up and, not for the first time, was jealous of Regulus' imposing height.

"Are you…" Regulus cleared his throat. "Do you need to talk? About…your parents? Sometimes, I think, it can help. To talk."

"I have a little, actually. With Dresden."

"Oh." Regulus' expression fell, and something like hurt shone in his eyes for a moment. "Good. Good." He patted Harold's shoulder and took a step back. "I just…I want you to feel at home here. Like we're your family. All of us."

"You are my family, my lord."

Regulus collapsed back into the chair and sighed with a sad expression. Harold didn't like that he seemed to be the cause of Regulus' sorrow, but he didn't know what he'd done to cause it. Perhaps it would be best to go.

"I…actually haven't quite finished your armor, my lord, so I'm going…to…" Harold pointed toward the door, but Regulus wasn't looking at him, so he snuck away. He paused in the doorway, wondering if Regulus was okay or if he should be worried. Maybe he would ask Dresden about it. He eased the door almost closed, like he had found it. Just before he left, he heard Regulus speak.

"Sometimes," Regulus said quietly, "I don't think I know what I'm doing, Magnus. I just…maybe I shouldn't have made Harold my squire."

Tears pricked at Harold's eyes as he rushed away. He tried so hard…studying and practicing his reading and writing between chores, training with Regulus and the knights, and he did his duties as a squire as best he knew how. He asked Perceval and Caleb and Dresden what squires were expected to do and did it all whenever he could. He wanted to prove Regulus hadn't made the wrong choice, to show how grateful he was that Regulus had saved him after that awful year serving that horrible Segiledan farmer.

Harold knew he wasn't a perfect squire. He was a peasant orphan who was still trying to understand the nobility and their different and confusing world and to act and talk the way they did. But he thought Regulus was pleased with him. Regulus wouldn't send him away for being a poor squire, would he? No, surely not… Besides, why would Regulus say he wanted Harold to feel at home and like this was his family if he thought Harold was a bad squire?

It didn't make sense, and that made Harold nervous. He had to find some way to show Regulus he was trying.

"HAROLD! THERE YOU are!" Caleb grabbed Harold's shoulders and dragged him down the stairs—the opposite of the way Harold needed to go.

"Cal!" Harold tried to push Caleb away, but the knight wasn't having it. "I'm busy!"

"So you are," Caleb said. "We are making decorations, and we require your help."

Panic spiked through Harold. Who knew how long this could take, and he didn't have time for distractions. Not when he was on a mission to prove his usefulness to Regulus. "No, Caleb, I have chores—"

"Chores that can wait. I'm sure Regulus won't mind." Caleb pushed Harold through the door at the bottom of the stairs and into the great hall.

Harold stopped short. All the knights except for Dresden sat around the big table, which was hidden under a mess of pine boughs, crimson ribbons, and bulging sacks. Sarah, Jerrick's wife, sat next to him, and Perceval's wife Leonora sat between Perceval and Sarah. A fire roared in the enormous fireplace at the head of the hall, and the sconces around the hall had all been lit to aid the feeble sunlight coming in through the high, small windows on the long back wall.

"See?" Caleb motioned at the gathering. "Your assistance is required!" He slapped Harold's shoulder and headed to the table, taking a seat next to Estevan and across from Perceval.

Across from Harold, the main door to the hall opened. Dresden strode in, bundled in a thick wool coat and leaving wet boot prints on the stone. He held aloft a large sack. "See? I told you someone would be selling them in town. Crisis averted."

"There was never a crisis," Perceval muttered.

"The dried citrus is a requirement, Perce!" Caleb clutched his hand over his heart. "Where is your festive spirit? Harold knows, don't you?"

Harold blinked, completely lost. "Know what?"

"Using dried citrus for decorations," Dresden said as he plopped the bag on the table and sat on Caleb's other side. "Caleb insists it's not a Bells of Winter celebration without dried citrus."

"Oh." Harold shook his head. "My parents could never afford to use food as decorations."

"All the more reason I'm glad you found them, Drez!" Caleb pulled a length of twine out of somewhere in the chaos on the table, grabbed the bag Dresden had brought, and began threading dried slices of citrus onto the twine.

Dresden shrugged out of his coat and looked at Harold. "Are you going to stand there or come help?"

"I…" Harold backed toward the stairway door. "I have chores—"

"This is your chores now." Dresden beckoned him over. "Come on."

Jerrick turned in his seat to see Harold and held up a small pine bough. "Come help me tie these into some semblance of a garland."

Harold slunk over to the seat to Jerrick's left. Jerrick showed him how he was taking the pieces of pine and tying them together with twine. On his other side, Sarah and Leonora worked on tying big crimson bows.

Harold worked in silence. The ladies chatted about dresses they were making for the celebration. Perceval and Caleb kept arguing over whether Caleb was doing the citrus garland right and whether Perceval's wreaths were lopsided. Estevan and Dresden strung what looked like dried cranberries onto string. Every time the other one poked themselves, they would make fun of each other for their clumsiness, as if they hadn't just poked themselves one minute prior.

It was fun, really, but it wasn't what Harold needed to be doing. Regulus and Adelaide had gone to visit the Drummonds for the day, so Harold had planned to clean their room. It wasn't strictly something he needed to do. Now that Regulus wasn't hiding anything, he let the servants into his room for cleaning. But it was part of his plan to prove his dedication to Regulus.

"Harold?"

Harold startled at his name and looked up. Jerrick leaned toward him, his brow furrowed.

"Is something troubling you, lad?" Jerrick asked quietly.

Harold ducked his head, focused on the pine needles scratching his hands as he wrestled with the twine. "No."

"Well, if you change your mind…" Jerrick shrugged, and returned to focusing on his own garland.

Harold squirmed in his seat. If he could get another perspective, maybe he could make some sense of what he had overheard. But then he would have to admit he had been eavesdropping. Not on purpose, but still. He leaned toward Jerrick and hoped no one else would hear him over the chatter.

"Am I a bad squire?"

Jerrick snorted. "Why, because you're helping us? Of course not."

"No, just…in general."

Jerrick set down the pine garland and turned toward Harold. "Why would you be worried about that?"

Heat crept into Harold's ears. "It's just…I heard Regulus say he shouldn't have made me his squire."

"Heard?" Jerrick narrowed his eyes. "Where? To who?"

Harold shrugged. "I…overheard, on accident. He was talking to Magnus."

"Hm." Jerrick nodded slowly, then turned toward Dresden. "Hey, Drez."

Harold's heart leapt into his throat. "Wait, no—"

Dresden looked up. "Ye—ah!" He cursed and sucked on his thumb as Estevan broke down in laughter. Dresden shot him a glare, then inspected his thumb before turning his attention back to Jerrick. "Yes?"

"Harold—"

"It's nothing!" Harold bent over the table to hide his burning face.

"He's worried he's a bad squire because Regulus told his dog he shouldn't have made Harold his squire."

"Regulus said *what!*" Caleb looked up from his third citrus garland. "You're an exemplary squire. Put me to shame." He grinned. "I took any opportunity to get out of chores."

Dresden rolled his eyes. "Reg and his animals. What else did he say?"

Harold shrugged as he bunched and un-bunched a length of twine. "That he isn't sure he knows what he's doing. But I don't understand, because just before that, he told me he hoped I saw him and all of you as family…but then he said that to Magnus because he must have thought I was gone, and I don't know what I did wrong." He crossed his arms on the empty bit of table in front of him and rested his head on his arms, immediately regretting the action when pine needles poked into his scalp.

Dresden laughed, and Harold raised his head, his face burning.

"Did you respond when he said you're part of the family?"

Harold frowned. "Yes…"

"What did you say, exactly?" Dresden grinned like this was all a big joke.

"I don't know!" He considered for a moment, trying to remember past his current annoyance and embarrassment. "I think something like, 'You are family, my lord.'"

Dresden snapped his fingers and laughed again. "My lord? You're sure you said, *you are family, my lord?*" He laughed again when Harold nodded.

"What's so funny?" Harold demanded. He crossed his arms over his chest and scowled. "What?"

Jerrick shook his head with a soft chuckle. "What do we call Regulus, Harold?"

Harold blinked. "But…he told me to call him my lord…or Regulus, but a squire is supposed to—"

"And that's why he wonders if he shouldn't have made you his squire." Dresden tied off his cranberry string and tossed it around Estevan's shoulders. "I'll bet you anything he's just feeling guilty, because he cares about you and worries you don't realize it. Or, because you always call him 'my lord' and serve him, he fears you see him only as your liege, when he sees you as his brother."

Harold froze. His pulse sped up as his chest constricted. "He what?"

"Obviously," Caleb said. He waved a slice of citrus. "He cares about all of us, of course, but he's extra protective of you."

"No chance Regulus thinks you're a bad squire," Perceval said. "Trust me."

"Oh." Harold hunkered lower in his chair. Often, he caught himself thinking of Regulus as his brother. Sometimes almost even as a father, even though Regulus was too young for that. But that Regulus saw him the same way hadn't occurred to him. In truth, he had noticed that Regulus seemed extra protective of him. He had thought it was either that Regulus still saw him as that battered kid in Segiledus, or because of Regulus' guilt over the time the sorcerer had forced him to attack Harold and Dresden. "So…what do I do?"

"What is there to do?" Jerrick asked as he held up a finished garland and inspected it. He nodded and set it on the floor next to his chair.

"But…he seemed sad." Harold searched for the end of his garland, lost in the mess of pine needles. "I just want him to know I appreciate him and am grateful for everything he's done, and I want to be like him…"

"I've got it!" Caleb jabbed his finger in the air.

Perceval groaned. "This should be good."

"Shush, you." Caleb wagged a finger at Perceval before turning back toward Harold with a grin. "A Bells of Winter gift! You just need to find him the perfect gift!"

"Yeah, no pressure there." Estevan lifted a brow and smirked at Caleb.

Harold fidgeted. "I was trying to do extra chores and tasks for him—"

Dresden shook his head. "Oh, no, if Regulus is feeling guilty about not being closer to you, that will only make him feel worse."

"But I don't know what to get him." Harold looked around the table help-lessly. "I'd need a gift that says that I do see him as family *and* how glad I am to be his squire. And…and his brother." He was still having some trouble be-lieving Regulus really cared that much about *him*. Some poor, scrawny peasant boy Regulus had rescued.

"Sing him a song!" Caleb said.

"Don't be ridiculous," Perceval snapped. "Give him a new sword."

"I can't afford that." Harold shrank back into his chair.

Estevan waved his hand. "Regulus has enough swords, anyway. Give him a fancy doublet. A fur-lined cloak. A fancy, silky tunic that Adelaide will want to touch all the time."

Harold scrunched his nose. That was something he'd rather not think about.

"Do you have any idea how long I have been trying to get Regulus to dress nicer?" Dresden asked. "It's a waste of time."

"Well, what do you suggest, then, oh expert one?" Estevan pointed his cranberry-stringing needle at Dresden, and Dresden leaned away from him.

"Hm." Dresden stroked his beard. "A pet?"

"That I'll end up taking care of?" Harold shook his head.

"Fancy new tack for Sieger?" Leonora suggested. "I don't actually know where one gets silver-gilded reins or engraved chanfrons, though."

"I know." Jerrick sat up straighter. "Food! Perhaps nalotavi—"

"I'm already baking nalotavi for the feast, honey." Sarah patted Jerrick's hand.

"Right." Jerrick hummed to himself. "Oh, a nice, rich mead. Or wine. En-joyable, and he can have some with Adelaide before—"

"There is an innocent present!" Dresden thrust his hands toward Harold.

Harold snorted. He'd never admit he was grateful for Dresden's interrup-tion. Not that physical intimacy was a disagreeable subject, but…it was some-what gross to think about in terms of Regulus and Adelaide.

Leonora straightened a stack of red bows. "Perhaps you should ask Adelaide for ideas."

"I think it should be something personalized," Sarah said. "Something unique. Something you can't just buy in town and he wouldn't think to get for himself."

"So…an engraved knife." Perceval nodded. "Less expensive than a sword."

"What is it with you and the weapons?" Caleb huffed. "Nothing says 'you're like family to me' more than 'here, go kill something.'"

"He doesn't have to use them to kill something, numbskull." Perceval waved a small pine bough at Caleb. "It's better than singing a song. What kind of stupid gift is that?"

"Ladies love when I sing to them."

"What does that have to do with Harold and Regulus?"

"Calm down, you two." Leonora kissed Perceval's cheek, and his expression immediately softened as his posture relaxed.

Harold scratched his beard. It wasn't nearly so thick and manly as Dresden's, but he was working on it. "There's less than a fortnight until Bells of Winter. What can I have made special for him in such a short time?"

"Don't worry," Dresden said as he looped another strand of cranberries around Estevan's shoulders. "You have some time to think about it. I'll think on it, too."

"Now!" Caleb clapped his hands. "Time to combine everything! Bows and cranberries attached to pine garlands and citrus wrapped around the wreaths. Perce! Where are all my wreaths?"

"*Your* wreaths?" Perceval picked up a stack of wreaths; how many, Harold couldn't tell amid the chaos of pine. "Why don't you make them if they're all yours?"

Harold blocked out their routine bickering as he checked the length of his garland. It was a bit shorter than the others, so he reached for more pine only to find it all connecting to other garlands. It would have to do.

FOR THE NEXT two days, the question of what to get Regulus plagued Harold. While he did his chores or practiced horse mastery with Jerrick or knife work with Estevan and Adelaide or fist fighting with Perceval, in the back of his mind, he was searching for an idea. He was practicing his handwriting by candlelight in his room and despairing over finding a gift when someone knocked on his door.

"Come in?"

The door groaned open, and Regulus poked his head in. "Hey, Harold—"

Harold jolted to his feet, nearly spilling his pot of ink. "My lord! Sorry, was I—"

"No, no!" Regulus moved his hands in a settling motion. "You're fine. I was wondering if you'd like to spar with me." He shrugged. "If you're not busy. More as…well, as friends, than necessarily as, you know, lord and squire." He tugged on his tunic collar.

Harold stared at him until his mind caught up. This was a perfect opportunity to show Regulus that he didn't see him only as a lord. "Yes!" That sounded over-eager. "I mean, yes, that sounds great." It felt odd to leave off *my lord*, but calling Regulus by his name to his face was too strange to even attempt.

Regulus smiled, one of his big, genuine smiles that stretched his scar. "It's windy and blowing snow everywhere, so let's meet in the hall. I'll grab my practice sword."

Harold always enjoyed sparring with Regulus. He enjoyed spending time with Regulus at all, but Regulus was the best knight to practice swordplay with. Regulus was patient, never laughed when Harold made a mistake, and gave good tips, but also didn't go easy. It made Harold feel respected and capable.

They took a break to get a drink of water from a pitcher Harold had brought in. Regulus hooked a chair with his foot and sat down, and Harold set next to him.

Regulus set his pewter cup on the table. "You're going to make a fine knight, Harold."

Harold ducked his head to hide his grin, even as he sat up a little straighter. "Thank you."

Regulus tapped his forefinger against his cup. His gaze darted around, and he shifted in his seat. Harold braced himself. Those were all classic signs that Regulus was trying to say something that made him uncomfortable. Would he tell Harold he didn't want him as a squire anymore?

"Harold…" Regulus rubbed the back of his neck. "There's something I should tell you. Something Perceval has been telling me I should tell you for several months, but the thing is…it could change. And I didn't want to worry you."

"Worry me?" Harold's eyebrows lowered. His leg bounced as his nervousness rose.

"I didn't want you to think…after everything, with losing your parents, and the mercenaries, and everything that happened with the sorcerer, and—well, everything. And I know you don't want to be left alone, so I didn't want to bring up the subject when it might not matter, but I was talking to Dresden and he mentioned you might not understand that you're much more to me than just my squire, and Perceval thinks it would be wrong to spring it on you should anything happen, so then I thought I should tell you just in case, but then is it awkward if Adelaide and I have children?"

Harold gaped. He wasn't sure if it was only how quickly Regulus had spoken that made his ramble unintelligible, or that what he'd said just didn't make any sense. "I'm sorry?" He wasn't quite certain if he was apologizing for not understanding Regulus or for causing whatever was bothering Regulus.

"No, I'm sorry, that was…" Regulus massaged his forehead. "Okay. Harold." He met Harold's eyes, his own grave.

Harold swallowed. This was it. Regulus was going to tell him he didn't want him as a squire anymore.

"I made my will," Regulus said.

That wasn't what Harold had expected at all. What did Regulus' will have to do with him?

"One of the first things I did after I arrived was draft a will naming Dresden as my successor. He was a bit angry with me when he found out." Regulus smiled faintly. "Apparently he doesn't want to deal with the headache of trying to maintain the claim if Baron Carrick challenges my leaving my estate and title to a foreign commoner with no blood ties."

Harold slumped back in his chair. Despite the heat of the fire and the exertion, his hands felt cold. Regulus was right. He *didn't* want to think about Regulus dying. It made him want to bury his head under a pillow, or talk about anything else, anything at all. And what did this have to do with him?

"Anyway." Regulus took a sip of water. "About…I suppose about a year ago, now, I amended the will. If I die childless, everything goes to Dresden. But if Dresden dies as well, or is missing or something…"

Harold's toes tapped inside his boots as he stifled the urge to leave to make this conversation end. If Regulus and Dresden died, he would be alone again. Abandoned.

"If Dresden can't inherit"—Regulus met Harold's eyes again—"everything goes to you."

Harold's chest constricted. Regulus' voice sounded muffled as he continued to speak.

"My title as lord, the Arrano castle and holdings, everything would be yours."

Harold blinked as the room tilted and Regulus' face went out of focus.

"Of course," Regulus said, sounding far away, "if Adelaide and I have children, that would change, as the law requires that blood offspring are given precedence. Adelaide knows and is fine with it, of course… Harold?"

Harold tried to nod, but somehow instead tilted off the chair. Regulus caught him and pushed him back upright.

"Hey, easy." Regulus poured more water and made Harold drink it.

Slowly, Harold's mind pulled out of its daze. He sipped his water, staring at the stone wall behind Regulus. This couldn't be right. Regulus couldn't…why would he… Harold finally forced himself to look at Regulus. "Why?"

Regulus sighed. "You're a good young man, Harold. Honest and loyal, even when I don't deserve it. Kind-hearted and hard-working and earnest. You stayed when I wouldn't have blamed you for leaving. And…" His throat bobbed. "I know you see and understand more than you let on. I've seen it in your eyes."

Regulus glanced away, and Harold thought of the blood stain hidden under the rug in Regulus' room, the scars covering Regulus' body as evidence of all he had been through in his life, the days Regulus had spent trying to shut himself away. But those were never the things that Harold felt defined Regulus.

"You deserve so much better than the things you've been through, Harold," Regulus said softly. "In truth, you deserve so much better than me. And I know you could be a great lord if things came to that. It just…made sense. Perceval witnessed the will, and he told me to tell you before we left for Belanger castle, but—"

"That's why you made me stay." Harold leaned back as realization hit. "In case something happened to both you and Drez, you wanted me here."

"I would have left you here either way," Regulus said. "But it was a factor, yes."

Harold nodded, still feeling rather numb.

"I hope you're not offended," Regulus said.

"Offended?" Harold shook his head. "Why would I be offended? Because you didn't tell me? Because you didn't think I would want to talk about… About…you dying?"

Just getting the words out was difficult. He wanted to be strong in front of Regulus, but it was hard, so hard, when the memories were trying to resurface and fears were clawing at his mind.

"I remembered how you looked," Regulus murmured, his voice strained. "After…after the sorcerer massacred most of my men. I've noticed you avoid talking about death."

Harold closed his eyes, trying to block out the memory—his parents' screams, the stench, the sight of the troll… Wandering the Segiledan countryside, starving, his clothes stained with his parents' blood. Completely and utterly alone. The faces of the dead mercenaries haunted him, too. He shuddered. This was exactly why he avoided the subject. A hand gripped his shoulder, and he opened his eyes to Regulus' face close to his own. Candlelight glimmered in the wetness at the corner of Regulus' intent, gray eyes.

"I'm sorry, Harold." Regulus leaned back.

"It's okay." His voice came out small. He took a deep breath to steady himself. "I just don't like to remember them…like that."

"I understand." Sorrow weighed down Regulus' features. "I know you had good parents. I know you miss them, and I know I'm not family. You're like another brother to me, but I understand it might be impossible for you to ever really see me that way after everything I've done. So I didn't want you to think this was me trying to replace your family or something, or maybe trying to bribe you into liking me after I attacked you."

Harold shook his head, hard. "You didn't attack me."

"At least one of us doesn't blame me," Regulus said with a little chuckle. "I can see you're overwhelmed. I'll give you some time to think." He mussed Harold's hair and stood. "I'll take care of this." He piled the pewter cups and pitcher back on the tray. "Take the rest of the day off. If you need to talk to me more, or if you have questions, you can tell me anytime."

Harold nodded. As he mulled over what Regulus had said, an idea solidified in his mind.

He knew what to give Regulus for Bells of Winter.

First, he needed to check with Adelaide and Dresden to make sure. And then figure out how to even do it.

THE DAY OF THE winter solstice saw more activity than the last two years at Arrano castle combined, Harold was certain. While he understood that Bells of Winter always took place the day after the solstice to celebrate surviving the longest night of the year, it seemed poor timing to have preparations for the holiday on the shortest day of the year.

Everyone helped prepare. Regulus had kept a minimal retinue for the two years he had served the sorcerer to help protect his secret and had only slowly been hiring new servants at Tamina's prompting in the last couple of months. Accordingly, the knights were spending the day scattered around the castle, helping with everything from baking to washing table linens.

Someone yelled Harold's name—for what must have been at least the fifteenth time—as he walked down the hall toward the kitchen carrying a stack of pewter serving trays.

"Thank Etiros; I found you!" Caleb jogged after him with a relieved grin.

"Busy." Harold held the pile of trays a little higher to emphasize his point before he kicked open the door to the sweltering, crowded kitchen.

The cook, Jeremy, stirred something in a massive pot. Whatever it was might have smelled savory, but there were too many scents to be certain. Sweat glistened on his brow as he told another servant to cut more carrots.

Sarah had her flour-coated hands planted on her hips. "Jerrick Faras, you put that nalotavi roll down right now!" She blew a strand of blonde hair that had come free of her bun out of her face with a huff.

"Mm, come take it from me." Jerrick waved the flaky chocolate and spice filled roll in front of his nose and moved it toward his mouth.

"Don't you dare—oh, the pies!" Sarah clapped her cheeks, leaving behind flour handprints. "Harold, good!" She pointed at the stone oven in the far corner. "Quick, set those down and pull out the pies—"

"But I need his help in the hall!" Caleb protested.

Harold set down the trays on a flour-dusted but otherwise clear corner of a table. "Dresden needs me to—"

"The decorations!" Caleb wailed.

"The sandglass timer for the pies is done and I don't know how long ago because my *husband* won't stop distracting me!" Sarah glared as she returned to kneading a lump of dough.

"I'll get the pies." Jerrick winked at Harold as he set down the nalotavi roll, uneaten. "Go help Drez."

Harold nodded his thanks and pushed past Caleb before Sarah could think of some other task for him. He'd spent most of the morning running errands for her, taking rolls of bread back and forth from the larger oven outside, cutting up fruit, or fetching things. The rest of the morning he had spent polishing

Regulus' fanciest sword, an opal-studded beauty Regulus had inherited from his father. Most of the early afternoon he'd spent helping Regulus move pedestals, vases full of pine boughs, decorative armor, and long carpets around the foyer until Tamina and Adelaide were satisfied. At least Estevan had volunteered to groom Sieger, as at this rate Harold would be too exhausted to see to Regulus' horse. Although, he suspected Estevan and a couple of the other knights were up to something in the stables the way they kept volunteering recently. That, or they wanted to avoid helping with Bells preparations.

Caleb dashed around Harold and walked backward in front of him. "Whatever Dresden needs help with, it's not as important as the great hall." His lips turned down in a pout.

"Dresden and some servants are clearing snow from the courtyard, so the Drummond ladies don't have to walk through snow." Harold tried to pass Caleb, but the knight kept moving into his path.

"Bah, the servants can handle that! I need you! Perceval quit on me. The hall is only half decorated!"

Harold stifled a grin and rolled his eyes. "Well, if you didn't argue with him so much, maybe he would be more inclined to help you."

"I merely suggested that the wreath was off center, and he huffed off."

"Mm-hmm. Have you tried apologizing?"

Caleb wrinkled his nose. "Not when I'm right."

"Just…do it in the spirit of Bells of Winter. Bye!" Harold ducked under Caleb's arm and took off at a run down the hallway. Shoveling snow sounded more appealing than listening to Caleb chatter while pine needles poked him.

He was reaching for the front door when several voices called his name. He managed to suppress his groan and turned around.

Adelaide, Jerrick, Caleb, and Dresden all stood on the balcony at the top of the stairs, in front of the doors leading to the great hall, looking at each other in confusion.

Dresden pointed at Harold, his brow furrowed. "I was just looking for him to help me with the snow—"

"Sarah needs help with the ginger biscuits, but the molasses makes my hands itch—"

"Did you notice the state of the hall? The decorations? I need—"

"He's my husband's squire, and we can't find—"

"We're running out of daylight to finish the snow—"

Harold gripped the sides of his head. "Enough!" He sighed. "Jerrick, can you switch tasks with Jeremy?"

Jerrick nodded. "I suppose that could work." He turned and left through a small servants' door tucked in the far-left corner of the balcony.

"My lady." Harold inclined his head. "What are you looking for?"

"Regulus' sword belt. He says he had one with silver and green stitching?"

Harold chewed on his lower lip while he thought. "Did you check the wardrobe in the north-east guest room? I put some of the things he never wears in there for storage."

Adelaide brightened. "I'll check; thank you!" She left through the small right-hand side door that led up to the bedrooms.

"Cal, just go talk to Perce," Harold said with a sigh. "If you get him to help you again, I'll help you with anything that's not finished after I help Dresden."

Caleb pushed away from the railing with a groan. "Fine. Only because it's Bells."

Dresden crossed his arms and smirked down at Harold.

"What?" Harold leaned back against the door, unsure if he was more cross or relieved.

"Nicely done. Reminded me of Regulus."

Harold grinned and stood taller. "Really?"

"You'd make a better lord than I would, that's for certain." Dresden headed down the stairs. "You have your speech prepared for tomorrow?"

If he were honest, Harold didn't want to think about his speech. Dresden had concocted an elaborate way for Harold to give Regulus his gift, but it necessitated giving a brief speech, which made him nervous. Not least because despite Adelaide's approval and both Adelaide and Dresden's assurances that Regulus would love the idea, part of him was terrified that Regulus would be offended.

Harold shrugged. "I think so. Don't want to overthink it and it feel too rehearsed, right?"

"Makes sense." Dresden pulled open the front door, and a blast of cold air slapped Harold in the face. "Let's go clear away some snow."

RINGING BELLS awoke Harold at dawn. He laid in the dark, snuggled under his pile of blankets, listening to the ringing. The longest night of winter was behind them. Today was a time to celebrate life and all the highs and lows of the past year. To look forward to what the new year would bring, thank Etiros for His protection, and pray for continued blessings. And of course, to give gifts, as thankfulness should spur on generosity.

He needed to get up. They were having breakfast in the great hall, and Caleb had planned activities for most of the day. But he was content to just lie there, thinking about how much he loved living in Arrano with Regulus and Dresden and the others, basking in the comfort of knowing he was safe and wanted and not at risk of losing his new family any time soon.

Hot breath warmed his cheek, and a large, wet nose bumped his temple.

Harold sighed. "Mag—"

The dog licked his face, leaving behind a bit of slobber uncomfortably close to his mouth.

"Aw, Magnus!" Harold turned his face away and pushed against the soft, furry mass that was Magnus' body.

Magnus whined and put his front paws on the side of the bed.

"No. Get down."

Magnus made a pathetic yowling sound and backed down as Harold sat up and fumbled over his nightstand for the flint and candle.

"You're as bad as having a rooster in the room," Harold muttered. He lit the candle and looked over to see Magnus sitting patiently, his bushy tail wagging ferociously and his tongue hanging out of the side of what Harold would swear was a smile. "Okay, okay; I'm getting up and we'll go to breakfast."

Magnus gave a small, triumphant bark. Harold shook his head and laughed.

The hall was bursting when Harold and Magnus walked in. Servants, vassals, and their families sat at the great table and two extra tables. Conversation and laughter mingled with the crackling of the fire and the bustle of servants bringing out food before sitting down to join their friends and family—Regulus had insisted that no servant would miss out.

Magnus bolted for Regulus, his entire body wagging as he said hello. After he had received a sufficient amount of ear scratches from Regulus and belly rubs from Adelaide, the dog darted over to the corner of the room and his dish full of food. Estevan waved Harold over to an empty seat next to him, by all the other knights seated near Regulus and Adelaide at the head of the great table.

By the time breakfast was over and the sausages and eggs and fresh bread all consumed, Harold didn't think he could move. But Caleb wouldn't hear Harold's—or anyone else's—protestations and forced the knights, Regulus, Adelaide, and Tamina outside into the cold. He led them along a path through the knee-deep snow outside the castle walls to a pile of small wooden sleds.

"Here we go!" Caleb motioned ahead of them with both hands, a grin on his face like he had just given them a fortune.

Harold hadn't seen a play sled since he was seven years old. His father had made him one for Bells of Winter. It was rough and uneven and always curved to the left, but it hadn't mattered. He'd loved that sled until he crashed it into a tree. A lump formed in his throat, even as he fought the urge to run to the nearest sled and dive down the hill. No one else made a move toward the sleds, and he wasn't about to embarrass himself.

Dresden tilted his head. "Where did you get all these?"

"The carpenter in town." Caleb planted his hands on his sides like a man surveying his land. "Rushed production was horribly over-priced, and if you make me use these by myself, I'll sing nothing but sad songs tonight."

"I love sledding, actually, although I haven't gone in years," Adelaide said. She stepped forward, her hand in Regulus', but stopped when Regulus didn't move forward with her.

"I forgot," Regulus whispered. "I forgot that my father took me sledding, right here, when I was six. The winter before he sent me away." He blinked rapidly. "He spent the entire day helping me pull the sled back up and then racing me down."

The mood turned somber. Adelaide looked up at Regulus, her eyes pinched with sorrow. Caleb shuffled his feet, his shoulders hunching.

Harold stepped forward. "I'll race you down, Regulus."

Regulus' head snapped toward Harold. "That…sounds fun."

It didn't take long for everyone to get involved after that. Even Tamina went down once, then declared the trek back up wasn't worth it. She watched for a while, laughing and making playful mock bets with the knights about who would win in races before she headed back inside to warm up.

A while later, Adelaide crashed her sled into Regulus'. They ended up tangled together in the snow, which quickly turned into kissing. Jerrick grabbed Sarah and the two of them went tumbling down the hill together, and Leonora pulled Perceval into a kiss.

"Well, this is just unfair," Estevan complained. He elbowed Harold. "Do you think they'll stop if we throw snow at them?"

Caleb shrugged. "I'd be annoyed, but I'd just join them if I had a lady with me, so I can't blame them." All the same, Caleb declared it was high time they dried off and ushered them back inside.

By the time everyone had dried or changed clothes entirely, it was nearly time for dinner. After dinner, they played games in the great hall—checkers, dice, and cards. Harold lost a game of cards to Jerrick, but then beat him at checkers.

The Drummonds arrived shortly before supper. Gaius' parents accompanied Gaius and Minerva and their infant son, Leon. After saying hello—and laughing over the little sword-shaped wood rattle that Leon was playing with—Harold snuck up to his room and belted on his sword. It was an important part of his plan to give Regulus his gift.

Sound filled the great hall during supper, a racket of voices, laughter, and utensils. The garlands and wreaths and bows hung around the hall or tied onto the iron sconces made the stone feel somehow warmer, cozier. Arrano felt alive in a way it hadn't in two and half years. The air held a festive energy that filled Harold with comfort and contentment. And he didn't think he was the only one. Regulus spent all of supper smiling and laughing, and Caleb and Perceval didn't bicker once.

After eating entirely too much food, including smoked fish, lamb stew, a variety of sweet and savory pies, and pastries that melted in his mouth, Harold helped clear the tables. Regulus' vassals and servants left so they could get home before it got any colder and darker, but only after presenting Regulus with traditional Bells of Winter gifts for a liege—small trinkets or, more commonly, food. Jeremy wouldn't need to cook for days between the leftovers and the gifts.

Then Caleb pulled out his lute and they all sang. Songs about winter, family and friends, survival, and songs of praise and gratitude to Etiros. Jerrick sang a Bhitran song to Hallilek. Harold didn't speak any Bhitran, so he had no idea what the song was about, but it was slow and haunting and Jerrick's rich baritone served it well. Whatever the lyrics were, they must have been emotional, because Jerrick had tears in his eyes when he finished.

After a few more songs led by Caleb—including a scandalous tavern song that made Lady Drummond turn red, had Minerva and Adelaide in fits of laughter, and prompted Regulus to throw his empty goblet at Caleb—they moved on to gift giving.

Harold waited impatiently for his turn. As the lowest ranking member of the party, he had to give any gifts last. He didn't notice what gifts the lords and ladies gave each other as his nervous excitement mounted. What if he forgot everything he wanted to say? What if he and Dresden and Adelaide were all wrong, and it offended Regulus? His leg bounced under the table while the knights exchanged gifts in a chaos of shouting and laughter and opening their gifts all at once.

"It's a beauty, Caleb!" Perceval stood and swung a shiny new sword.

"Good." Caleb waved a hand dismissively. "Apparently weapons are the way you show affection, you big brute."

"Harold."

Harold nearly jumped out of his skin at Regulus' voice. He leapt up, catching his boot on the table leg, and tripped forward before righting himself. He bowed to hide his embarrassment. "Yes, my lord?"

"We all got this together." Regulus nodded to Dresden, who pulled out a lumpy package wrapped in rough linen and tied with a neat green bow.

Dresden walked over to Harold, handed him the package, and sat on the edge of the table. Harold eyed the gift with a frown. What could possibly fit in a light package barely the length of his forearm that would require all the knights to donate toward it?

He pulled off the ribbon and linen, and his frown deepened. He ran his thumb over the iron studs and silver stitching on a beautiful black leather bridle that looked large enough for Sieger.

"Adelaide said I couldn't bring a destrier into the hall," Regulus said with a grin.

Harold's mouth fell open. "A…"

Estevan hooted. "Didn't think I suddenly developed a keen interest in the care of horses and kept stealing your job for fun the last few days, did you?"

"That's why none of you would let me in the stables?" Harold plopped back into his chair, dazed. "I knew something was going on!"

Everyone laughed.

"You'll be eighteen next year," Regulus said. "A knight should have his own horse."

Emotion tied Harold's throat in knots.

"He's a spirited young gelding," Adelaide said. "I think you're going to like him."

Harold wished he could run out to the stables and see the horse right then, but abandoning the party seemed rude. Besides, he still had his own gift to give—

Dresden cleared his throat. "Did you have a gift for anyone, Harold?"

Harold took a deep breath and set aside the bridle, giving it one last yearning look. He stood back up and approached Regulus, who, along with most of the others, had dragged a chair nearer to the fireplace. Sweat slicked his hands, and he wasn't sure if it was from the fire's heat or his nerves.

"I was…" Harold's voice cracked. "I was going to get you something, my lord…Regulus." He hurried on so he wouldn't lose his nerve. "I wanted to get something perfect. Something so you would know I'm so happy and grateful to be your squire, and I wouldn't want to be anyone else's squire."

"Not even mine?" Dresden called.

Harold laughed, although it sounded nervous and awkward. "You're my second choice."

"Figures." Drez winked, and quiet laughter rippled around the group.

"There isn't a gift in the world that equals what you've done for me," Harold said. He stared at Regulus' forehead, too nervous and emotional to meet Regulus' intense gray eyes. "When you took me from that Segiledan farmer, I knew I wanted to be like you. I want to help people and see people the way you do. To put others first and be a hero, like you. Being your squire is everything I want and more, and I just hope I make you proud."

"Of course you do, Harold," Regulus said quietly.

Harold smiled and took another deep breath. "I don't know what gift could say everything I want to say. So I decided not to buy you anything."

Now for the awkward part. The method of presentation was Dresden's idea, and Adelaide and Dresden had helped him pay the blacksmith enough to get it done in time for Bells. Harold feared it would be awkward, but he couldn't think of a better way.

"Instead, I got a new inscription on my sword." He drew his sword, bowed on one knee, and presented it to Regulus on the palms of his hands. "Do you want to read it?"

Regulus' eyes pinched, but he took the sword. "Sure…"

"Why don't you read it aloud?" Adelaide shot a conspiratorial smile at Harold and leaned closer to Regulus. "I'm curious now."

Regulus looked to Harold, as if asking permission, and Harold nodded. His heart thudded against his ribs as Regulus tilted the sword so he could read the inscription etched down the length of the blade.

"Etiros make this sword a tool of justice in the hands of Harold Har—" Regulus choked. His gaze snapped from the blade to Harold and back to the blade as he opened and closed his mouth. "Harold Hargreaves," Regulus murmured.

"I love my parents." Harold pushed the words past his tight throat as he blinked away an annoying wetness in his eyes. "I'll always love and miss and remember them. But you're my brother as certainly as they were my parents, and—"

He stopped as Regulus dropped the sword with a clatter and lunged forward, tugging him into a crushing embrace. Harold froze as Regulus' arms squeezed him, then slowly wrapped his arms around Regulus.

"Are you certain?" Regulus whispered.

"Russell is a fine last name and all." Harold licked his lips. "But I want people to know who my current family is…if that's all right with you?"

Regulus pulled back and wiped a tear from his eye. "Yeah. Yeah, it's more than all right."

"Good." Harold smiled, glad he was already on his knees or he might have fallen over, he felt so wobbly. "Because I kind of already had it engraved into my sword."

Regulus laughed and mussed Harold's hair. "It's the perfect gift, Harold. Little brother." He stood and pulled Harold up. "Where did my goblet go?"

"Here it is." Caleb tossed it back at Regulus.

"Oh, right." Regulus frowned into the empty cup.

"Wine, Captain?" Perceval held up a flagon full of spiced wine.

Harold hurried over and took the wine. He refilled Regulus' goblet and filled or topped off everyone else's, including his own, then turned back to Regulus.

"A toast." Regulus held up his goblet. "To life. Including new life." He looked to baby Leon. "To friends old"—he looked around the knights—"and new." He looked to Lord and Lady Drummond. "To family." He looked to Dresden, and when he made eye contact with Harold, it warmed Harold right to his toes. Regulus smiled at Tamina, then took Adelaide's hand. "To loyalty. To the warmth of home and fellowship in the middle of winter's chill, and the light of Etiros even in the darkest nights. And to a new year surrounded by the people I love." He drew up Adelaide's hand and kissed her fingers.

A smile twitched at the corner of Harold's mouth. He wouldn't be surprised in the least if there was more new life in Arrano by next Bells of Winter.

"Cheers." Regulus took a drink, and everyone followed suit.

The spiced wine was sharp and sweet and added to Harold's contented feeling.

There might have been some chaos, insanity, and plenty of uncertainty on Harold's part in the preparations for the holiday, but the day itself? Harold settled against the back of his chair with a soft smile.

The best Bells of Winter celebration in Monparth had happened at Arrano.

Need more of The Mercenary and the Mage? Check out selinargonzalez.com/bonuses for a cut scene from *Prince of Shadow and Ash*, an alternate Regulus POV scene from SMB Vol. I, a short story about married Regulus and Adelaide, and playlists inspired by the characters.

Enjoyed these stories? I'd appreciate it if you took a moment to write a review, however brief—they're so helpful for aiding other readers in finding books they might enjoy. Thank you for reading, dear book dragon!

Many of the struggles Regulus, Adelaide, Dresden, and Harold face in these books—low self-worth and longing for acceptance, guilt, shame, depression, fear, self-doubt, assault, abuse, loss, complicated family dynamics—are topics that are near and dear to my heart, all because I or people I know have experienced them.

Regulus and Adelaide spend a lot of their story learning to trust and draw strength from each other. While a relationship cannot magically heal anyone—and indeed, Regulus, Adelaide, Dresden, and Harold are all still healing and learning—I do believe in the importance of love and relationships of all kinds (familial, platonic, and romantic) for our lives and mental, emotional, and spiritual health. I personally am so grateful to the people in my life who have supported me. And I am constantly striving to be a better friend to those close to me. I also find comfort in my Lord and Savior, even in the midst of brokenness.

I strive to write healthy relationships between people who make mistakes, are unsure of themselves, and sometimes do the wrong thing, but keep trying, keep listening and supporting and loving each other. My hope and prayer is that Regulus, Adelaide, Dresden, Alfred, Tamina, Harold, and the others encourage you to turn to loving friends and family if you are hurting, and to be that source of love and support for the people in your life. (And to know that you deserve friends who believe and encourage you, not who make you feel worse. ♥) I hope they remind you that whatever hurt you are facing—it will not last forever.

Thank you for following Adelaide and Regulus and company on their journey.

Love,

Selina R. Gonzalez

ABOUT THE AUTHOR

Selina R. Gonzalez is a Colorado native with mountains in her blood and dreams that top 14,000 feet. She loves chocolate, fantasy, costumes, bread, history, superheroes, faux leather, things that sparkle, medieval Britain, snark, dogs, and Jesus—not in that order.

She loves to travel and has driven coast-to-coast in the US, visited Britain three times (once for a semester at Oxford), and moved to Maine for four and half months. She has a list of places to go as long as Pikes Peak is tall, but always comes back home to Colorado.

You can find Selina raving about books she's enjoying (or adding to her bottomless pit of a to-be-read pile) on Facebook and Instagram at @NighTooIsBeautiful and being generally goofy and snarky as well as talking about writing, life, and the antics of her siblings' dogs in her IG stories. Make sure you don't miss any of Selina's future books by subscribing to her newsletter.

Also by Selina R. Gonzalez:

A Thieving Curse (The Miraveld Chronicles book 1)
She must marry the crown prince for the sake of her kingdom. The problem is the cursed dragon-man who saved her life now won't let her leave the mountains, and while he's not the beast she thought him to be…he's the wrong crown prince. A *Beauty and the Beast* reimagining with banter, found family, and goats, about a princess torn between duty and unexpected love.

FREE BOOK

Subscribe to Selina's newsletter at SelinaRGonzalez.com/newsletter-subscription and get *The Dragon Prince's Heart*, a companion novella to *A Thieving Curse*, for FREE, as well as insights into Selina's progress, life, recent and recommended reads, announcements, and more.